SORCERY AND SUBTERFUGE

BOOK TWO

SORCERY AND STARDUST

SAMANTHA STORMFURY

SORCERY AND STARDUST - BOOK TWO
SORCERY
AND
SUBTERFUGE
A second chance.
An old friend.
A traitor.
SAMANTHA STORMFURY
|| BESTSELLING AUTHOR ||

Table of Contents

GLOSSARY OF TERMS

Want to know more about a specific character? You've come to the right place!

I keep a working Character Glossary for each of my worlds on my website.

Check it out here:

www.sliceofsammy.com/character-glossary/

For all those who've ever had to wear a disguise.

CHAPTER
ONE

THE KITCHEN DOOR SWISHED OPEN BUT ARCANA DIDN'T BOTHER LOOKING UP, too deeply enmeshed in the final claws of sleep to muster the energy. The scent of evergreen and cinnamon wrapped tight around her senses as she stared into the depths of her tea, picking out the subtle swirls painted on the bottom of the mug.

"Good morning." Fenris lowered himself into the chair opposite, his voice quiet. He set a mug of his own on the table and leant forward in an attempt to catch her eye. "How are you feeling?"

"Like I got run over by a herd of horses." Arcana grimaced, clenching her fingers around the warm porcelain of her mug. "Fat horses."

"Even after sleeping for two days?"

Her eyes widened, tracking away from the rim of her cup at last. "I held up a *Tower*. Do you have any idea how heavy it was?"

"No," Fenris admitted, leaning back in his chair. Arcana watched as he tousled his own hair, gaze distant. "The more I think about that Tower, what you did, the more I realise it should have been impossible."

"Hmmmm." Arcana swirled her tea, took a tentative sip. "I'm used to being told I'm impossible. That revelation won't get you far."

Fenris exhaled long and slow. "Are you really so determined to be angry with me?"

"I'm not angry," she whispered, flicking a gaze up from beneath her lashes. "Just disappointed."

Silence grew between them, a silence in which Fenris' face was smooth but his eyes filled with chaos. At last, he said; "I'd have been a fool to tell you everything right from the start."

Arcana raised an eyebrow. "It wasn't the start and we both know it."

"Indeed." Those brilliant jade eyes closed. "Have you decided, then, that I am not to have a chance at redemption?"

"I didn't say that," Arcana returned, studying the face he clearly had years of experience in keeping carefully blank. "Just that I'm hurting. The moment you read those books - or whatever it was Flare gave you - surely you realised what a deception would do to me. And yet, even facing an interminable amount of time with only Caelum as a buffer, you still chose to lie by omission."

Fenris' fingers tightened around his mug until his knuckles whitened. "I swore a blood oath to the Weaver when I became a Guardian. I cannot let anything - or anyone - become more important than that, no matter my personal feelings. That said, I would have shared the information with you when we were in space; it would have been senseless not to. I simply did not anticipate Taelon would be able to track me so quickly."

Arcana sighed. He was right, she knew he was right, Caelum had said as much - and yet, her heart ached. That in itself was a bad enough sign that she said; "The Healing Tower was the heaviest thing I've ever attempted to lift in my life. I might be a living magical conduit but even my body has limits - Gravella's death is testament to that."

"Don't blame yourself for her demise," he said gently. "Any weapon becomes slippery when the body is tired."

"Spoken like someone with experience."

"Yes. I have been in such situations before myself." Fenris nodded, then; "Is the magic really like a flowing river?"

"More like riding lightning." Arcana's mouth twitched wryly. "Perhaps we're not so different after all."

"No. I, however, cannot buy myself time with an overabundance of firewhiskey," Fenris' eyes twinkled with mischief, his posture more relaxed than Arcana had ever seen it. A glimpse of the man underneath the warrior – penance, perhaps, for his previous mistake?

Deciding to accept the peace offering at face value, Arcana relaxed enough to offer an inelegant snort. "I didn't buy time, I borrowed it. A dangerous, stupid game to play. Just be glad Flare had that firewhiskey in the first place."

"Glad? I'm not sure about that." Fenris' smile was rueful as he extended a long, elegant finger. "You bit me."

Arcana's answering blush was slow, warm – and fascinating, apparently, for Fenris' gaze went straight to her throat, watching the colour bloom. The rest of his body maintained the illusion of relaxation and he even went so far as to lace his fingers behind his head, but those jade eyes did not lie. Arcana's lip twitched, amusement taking the keen edge off her embarrassment. "You keep forgetting that I can see where you're looking."

He blinked. "What?"

"Your eyes," she gestured with her teaspoon. "I can read them - and you - like an open book."

"I..." and now it was Fenris' turn to blush, an interesting dusky pink which rode high on his teal cheeks. Arcana's grin widened, became wicked - the first real smile she'd cracked since she awoke. Fenris rested both elbows on the table and buried his face in his hands. "Weaver save me."

Arcana gave him the grace of a full minute before she stirred her tea noisily. "So where are we going?"

"I don't know," Fenris answered, voice muffled behind his palms.

"You don't know?" Disbelief crept into her tone.

Fenris' fingers cracked slightly, the glow of his eyes leaking out across the back of one hand. "After I recovered from the initial shock of Caelum flying the ship, I stopped asking questions. He was..."

"Pissy?"

Fenris sat up slowly, dropping both hands to the table. "Pissy." He tested the word and snorted. "I suppose that is an accurate enough description."

"Caelum doesn't like anyone staring when he flies. I used to pilot the ship, but he's the one with the internal compass, so we found someone to modify the ship's systems for us." Arcana offered a lopsided smile. "Now he's a certified space deer."

"Somehow I doubt there is true certification for such a thing." Fenris' answering smile was soft but somehow more real than anything he'd yet shown. He examined his knuckles for a moment then looked up, meeting her eyes. The glamour rose around them, tugging at Arcana's soul. "I am glad you have begun to recover. I was worried."

"Stop that," she murmured.

"You already know I can't."

"Why? And don't tell me it's because of your rogue fey blood - most halfbreeds get diluted powers at best." Arcana wanted to snap at him but the words came out dreamy. His glamour was like a warm, fluffy blanket; for a long moment she wondered why anyone would find it threatening.

Fenris sighed, breaking the eye contact. "My father's people - Taelon's people - are vampiric."

"I *knew* you were related to him." Arcana snapped her fingers.

Fenris' voice turned stiff. "Taelon is of no biological relation to me at all."

Arcana rolled her eyes, reaching across the table to tap him on the wrist with her teaspoon. "I didn't mean it like that - I meant that I could see enough visual similarities for shared genetics." His eyes narrowed suspiciously and she snorted a laugh. "Oh come on. You're both tall, with glowing eyes and fangs - it was enough. I can see why they hated you, though."

"I beg your pardon?" Impeccable manners, but an expression Arcana could only describe as 'beautiful death' set his face like plascrete.

"They were jealous." She kept her voice soft, wondering for the first time if Fenris' flawless steel facade hid something far more vulnerable than at first appeared. "Think about it. Taelon is *terrifying* to look at; he's broad and veiny and he's got muscles on his muscles. It's a wonder he can even walk." Arcana shuddered in distaste. "But it's not all about who can crush an egg between their pectorals, or who has the thickest neck. You got all Taelon's positives - speed, strength, night vision and so on - but none of the downsides. Your mother's fey genetics blessed you with the elegant bone structure and flawless grace that fairies wear so easily. I've dealt with enough of them over the years - even the truly awful ones are possessed of that ethereal beauty." Arcana waved a hand at his now-thawed face. "I'm sure you own a mirror. You know what I mean."

"I might - but I confess a particular pleasure in having you explain it to me." Fenris' smile was slow in coming, a wicked thing that was better suited to a bedroom than the kitchen of a spaceship. Arcana felt her breath catch as he let his facade slip, the sensual and quintessentially male expression transforming his face from beautiful to devastating. "In light of our recent misunderstanding, I'm relieved that you find me attractive on any level at all."

Arcana narrowed her eyes, refusing to allow him to see how much the real Fenris shook her. "I could still turn you to stone, you know."

"I have no doubt." His grin widened and he splayed his hands on the table, deliberately drawing her attention to his fingers. "The question is, would you want to? I wouldn't be nearly so delicious then."

"I was drunk," she snapped, crossing both arms over her chest. "Consider it penance for being a jerk."

His amusement faded but the cool court-calm which she'd become used to didn't entirely reappear. "Done."

Arcana shook her head, trying to divert her consciousness from the mystery of his personality. "So, part vampiric, huh? Are we talking bats and coffins here? Do you melt if I feed you garlic?"

"No. Just the drinking blood part." Fenris leant back, baring teeth to show off his fangs. "My father's people are warriors and hunters. They use a glamour to calm their prey before drinking."

"Why?" Arcana frowned. "Surely if they're all built like Taelon, it'd be a small matter to overpower someone."

Fenris shrugged. "The blood is better if the prey doesn't struggle."

"So you got a double dose of glamour DNA?"

He nodded. "That is my mother's theory, in any case."

"She's as good an authority as any." Arcana drummed her fingernails rhythmically on the table top. "If you're vampiric, how come I've seen you eat?"

"Halfbreed," Fenris shrugged again. "I don't have to drink blood - I can also eat. I certainly prefer it."

Arcana studied the way his nose crinkled delicately. "You've done it, though."

"Yes. There have been occasions." Fenris nodded, his face stark. "My father taught me to hunt as a child but it quickly became apparent that I didn't enjoy it. Blood is... If my life depends on it, I can drink it. And I have. But out of preference? Food is infinitely better."

"I'll bet." Knowing what little she did of his youth, Arcana surmised Fenris' dietary preferences would have been yet another opening for ridicule. She stared into the bottom of her cold tea, swirling the amber liquid with the same care Flare did his firewhiskey.

"You..." Fenris' voice was hesitant enough that Arcana looked up. He swallowed. "You don't smell afraid."

Arcana raised an eyebrow. "Of what? Your fangs?" He didn't answer, so she snorted and shook her head. "Don't be ridiculous. If I freaked out over everything that had teeth, I'd never get out of bed in the morning. Besides, I already bit you, remember? Clearly not an issue. In fact, if it makes you feel better, you're welcome to bite me right back."

Fenris slid back his chair and padded the few steps into the kitchen, muttering under his breath in a language she didn't recognise. Arcana watched him out of the corner of her eye, his shredded clothes hanging loose from that lithely muscled frame. They'd never been intended as outer wear - basic linen pants and an undershirt, loose enough to be tugged on and off over his head. Almost, but not quite, pyjamas; an ensemble to provide basic comfort beneath that suit of plate armour she'd peeled off him... how long ago? Weeks? A month? Maybe longer. The pants were ragged, Fenris' own exertion and likely more than one warg rending enough holes that she could piece together a rather excellent view of his muscular thighs. Which, of course, she would never do. Arcana drew her eyes upwards, determinedly uninterested. Fenris was rummaging in the chiller unit, still muttering to himself - though it sounded more like a prayer than a string of curses. A long slash down the back of his shirt revealed most of one teal shoulder blade and the sleeves were ribbons from the elbow down. Arcana already knew that Lesce had hastily stitched the slashed front closed - but as Fenris straightened, Arcana caught several snatches of light through smaller, somehow more vicious gashes on the front. Revealing glimpses of chest and abdomen she was most certainly not ogling. At all.

"Hungry?" Fenris' words were soft but she jumped as though bitten, fingers tightening around her mug. He looked like a vagabond rather than a warrior and for a moment Arcana wondered why he hadn't changed - until she realised he had nothing else to wear. Even the remnants of his armour had been left behind on Sorcen.

"Hard to tell if it's hunger or nausea," Arcana answered, forcing a watery smile onto her face. She could offer him some of her own clothing, perhaps? A critical, sweeping eye had her dismissing the notion immediately. There was nothing in her wardrobe that would fit him.

"There's not much here, but..." Fenris returned to the table with several thick slices of buttered bread and a wedge of cheese. "I think you should eat. You look decidedly sallow."

Arcana blinked up at him, one hand splayed across her sternum. "Sallow? What does that even mean?"

A singular brow winged upwards. "Sallow. Unwell. Off colour. Jaundiced -"

"Right, yes, thank you," she waved a dismissive hand, pressing the other to her temple and massaging. "You really know how to compliment a lady, telling her she's gone yellow. I'm not even sure I *can* change colour."

"You can," Fenris plunked a slab of bread on the table in front of her, followed by half the cheese. "Soft as new fallen snow indoors, glittering like ice in the sunlight. A shimmering star in the darkness... and a delightful tint of rose when you blush."

Arcana pressed both palms to the heat that was indeed warming her cheeks. "I'm not sure if I like this newfound honesty of yours or not."

Fenris slid into his chair, examining his cheese as though they were discussing something as trivial as the weather. "I broke your trust and I am trying to repair it."

"With cheap flattery?" Her temper flickered.

He gave her a flat look. "With the truth."

Arcana shivered and took a bite of her bread to avoid meeting his eyes. "Your eyes must be broken, then."

"I beg to differ - it is your perception of yourself that has been damaged." He muttered under his breath in that same, strange language and then said; "I am sorry for breaching your trust, Arcana. I was afraid."

"Afraid?" Arcana looked up, surprised - to find Fenris mindlessly crumbling his cheese into tiny pieces. She reached across the table and slid a slice of bread underneath, where the crumbs rained down and stuck to the thick layer of butter. "Why would you be afraid?"

"Taelon attacked the Timeless Kingdom. He slaughtered a great many Guardians and Wardens, recruited just as many and is now hunting the rest. I do not know where they are. I do not know where the Weaver is. I do not know who to trust. I don't know what to *do*." Fenris ran out of cheese and blinked sightlessly down at his empty fingers. "When I woke up in the ship, I assumed you were one of Taelon's operatives. After you saved me from the warg my instinct was to trust you - but I had also trusted Taelon and been proven wrong."

"So you began to question everything you knew."

"Yes. I wanted to trust you but I no longer trusted myself. I still don't." He grimaced. "I fed you titbits of information, watching your reactions in the hope that they would give me a clue as to your intentions."

"And?" Arcana bit into the hard wedge of cheese, savouring the sharp tang as she chewed mechanically.

"They are good." Fenris hung his head. "I am indebted to you and to the people of Sorcen, who bought my life with their own."

"Ugh," Arcana slapped one hand on the table, glaring at Fenris over her second slice of bread. "Stop being so nice. Defend yourself, at the very least!"

"No. I was wrong. Why argue?" He lifted his head, expression suddenly suffused with predatory intensity. "Tell me you would have done it differently."

"I can't," she ground out. "I didn't trust you either. Until Taelon showed up in person, I still wasn't sure the whole Weaver story wasn't completely made up. Everyone seemed to like you but I couldn't shake the feeling something was off."

"You were right," he nodded his head in acknowledgement.

"That doesn't make me feel better!" Arcana bit viciously into her bread, forcing her breathing to slow and calm. When at last she swallowed, her voice came out far more even. "All those things that happened - the people that died - they're partially my responsibility. I took you to Sorcen, after all. But if I follow that line of thought, who am I really angry at? You? Myself? Caelum, for finding you in that frozen ruin? Taelon, for attacking you? The Weaver, for choosing to make you a Guardian? Your mother, for giving birth to you?"

Fenris' lip twitched in amusement but he had the good sense to smother it and simply said; "Algae was the one who betrayed your people."

"Algae?" Arcana snorted and shook her head. "That piece of trash was just a tool. Taelon would have invaded with or without him, we both know that."

"Are you mad at Flare for killing him?"

"What? No." she swallowed, the last of the bread like ash in her mouth. If honesty was the theme of the morning, so be it. "I almost didn't believe it was real. So much so that I tried to call Flare as soon as I woke, but we were out of range. I feel... free. Relieved."

Fenris gave her a too-knowing look, then very carefully picked up his cheese covered bread and began to eat. "There is absolutely no shame in feeling that way."

"Perhaps." Arcana sucked on the inside of her teeth, watching him from across the table. "So what now?"

"I might ask you the same," he rolled one shoulder in a shrug. "I have spent the last few days worrying you may never wake, for all Flare's assurances otherwise. Now that you *are* awake, I am forced to confess I have not thought beyond these moments."

"You've spoken to Flare?" She gripped the edge of the table in white knuckled fingers. "How is he?"

Fenris shook his head slowly. "Not good. He has taken on the duties of Fire Elder, but is not pleased about it. He also said he sent you a message in the usual way."

"Hah!" Arcana noted his curious glance and grinned. "Not as mysterious as it sounds - Flare records messages and then sends them to me with a riddle to crack the encryption."

"And you return them in kind?"

"Yup." She nodded. "It's helped a lot over the years, knowing he's still listening." It sounded silly out loud but Fenris inclined his head as though they were the most sensible words Arcana had ever uttered.

"Flare is a good man."

Arcana blinked at the hitch in his voice. "What went on between you two?"

"Ah." His lips flattened into a line. "Flare took it upon himself to... initiate a discussion."

"A discussion?" Arcana repeated.

Fenris shoved his chair back, sweeping crumbs into his open hand and emptying them in the sink. For a moment, Arcana didn't think he was going to answer, as he returned to collect her mug and set it upside down in the wash drawer. But his nose crinkled as though losing an inner debate and he said: "Flare kissed me."

"He *what*?" Arcana shot upright, her own chair clattering across the floor behind her.

"I believe your brother was trying to prove a point, but I also believe that if I'd welcomed his advances, he would have followed through." Fenris' face was flustered, a mixture of embarrassment and relief at having shared something that obviously troubled him.

How to approach it, though? Arcana cleared her throat, and then again. "Flare's pansexual; he's drawn to anyone who fascinates him, regardless of gender or even species," she said at last, her tone careful. "You could've had your way with him all over the place and nobody would have blinked."

Fenris blinked, absorbing that information with the barest hint of a blush. "I prefer women."

Arcana opened her mouth and hesitated. Many a male - and some females - had said those exact words before they'd slept with Flare, but now didn't seem the right moment to share that particular gem. She focussed on the subtle undercurrents that had carried through Fenris' voice, tried to unpack the layers. "You... don't know how?"

He gave her a long, dryly amused look. "I know how."

"Then what exactly bothered you about it?" Because there was something, an indefinable something, tugging at the back of Arcana's mind.

"The whole scenario took me by surprise. Flare attacked me and I thought I had him down. Then -" Fenris shook his head, body stiff with disbelief. "He transformed into an entirely different creature and kissed me."

"You sound more upset about the losing than the kissing," Arcana said at last.

Fenris tilted his head, tousled curls rippling with the movement. It reminded Arcana of a deep, dark sea - not blue, not green, but some elemental blend of both. "Perhaps that *is* the problem. I did not anticipate the... full breadth of his skills."

"Because he's a sorcerer?" Arcana bent to retrieve her fallen chair, leaning across the back of it. "That's a common one. People see the magic and think it's all we've got."

"I suppose you have the lingering mythology of Old Terra to thank for that."

Arcana paused for a moment, considering the ancient Terrans who had long since faded from existence; their planet gone, their genes spread and blended throughout the galaxy until little more than memory and stardust remained. "Perhaps. In some cases it's true - a stereotype has to come from somewhere. But Flare is obsessive about eliminating his own weaknesses."

"It shows." Fenris leant one hip against the bench. "I told him he was a dangerous man and I meant it. I will have to work extensively to reverse my prejudice, for even now my heart insists that you shouldn't be able to best me in a fight."

Arcana narrowed her eyes. "Flare? Or me?"

"I'm not sure I want to test your temper by answering that question honestly." Fenris' lips stretched into a slow, wide smile. "You might drop a building on my head."

Arcana wasn't so easily distracted. "Is it really so impossible to imagine I might beat you in a fight?"

"I have seen you do incredible things, and yet..." Fenris hesitated, sizing her up in a way that made Arcana's skin itch. As though he could peel her apart and make jewellery from her bones. "I don't know," he said at last.

"Huh." Arcana drummed her fingers on the back of the chair, then leant over to palm the ship's communication interface. "Caelum?"

"Here," the deerken's face flickered into view. "You're looking better. Less yellow."

"Thanks," Arcana rolled her eyes. "Are you busy?"

"Just flying the ship," he responded, eyes fixed on something off to the left. "But if you need something, I can set us in mindless motion - it's basically what we've been doing anyway."

"Good." Arcana tapped a finger against her lip in thought. "Fire up the training room and meet me there in five minutes."

"Sure." Caelum nodded and the screen flicked off.

"The training room?" Fenris followed her to the door, his face a symphony of disbelief. "You intend for us to fight?"

"You bet I do. I'm not traipsing across the galaxy with a man whose opinion of himself is taller than he is." Arcana palmed the doorplate and strode towards the elevator. "Caelum will mediate, so you can't say I cheated."

"A man whose - Arcana, I meant no personal offence," Fenris choked, eyes wide.

"Oh, I know that. But I also need to know that if shit gets real, you're behind me-"

"Of course I am-"

"Not as a protector," she cut him off, holding up a hand to forestall his reply. "As an equal. An ally. Relying on me to do my part in the same way I would expect you to fulfil yours."

Fenris growled, a feline sound of pure frustration. "I do not disagree, but think for a moment. You've been awake for only a few hours, and barely eaten."

"I slept for two days. I feel fine," Arcana snapped, breezing into the elevator and jabbing at the controls. "Exercise will do my *sallow complexion* the world of good."

Fenris fell silent at that, drumming his fingers on one thigh. The elevator hummed through the ship and Arcana wrapped her irritation closely about her shoulders lest she think too much about the heat leaking from his body. She all but fled when the elevator door swished open, booted feet clattering across the metal floor. Fenris followed slowly, whistling between his teeth in admiration as he stared out at the cavernous space before them.

"You like it?" Arcana asked.

"It's incredible," he answered, moving to the guard rail for a better view. "Where are we?"

"The cargo bay. The ship originally had both a cargo bay and a fighter hangar, but I certainly don't need both. So I combined them and had the leftover space turned into this." She waved a hand at the variety of plat-forms, pits, pools and protrudances that marked the training room's various terrains. "I'm surprised you didn't explore this far down."

Fenris shook his head. "There was no need."

"He was too busy hovering near your bedroom door," Caelum corrected, appearing on the opposite side of the room. "That, or hanging over my shoulder."

"I do not hover," Fenris spluttered, colour staining his high cheek-bones for the third time that morning. Arcana decided, in that instant, that she enjoyed seeing him without his usual mask of court calm and would endeavour to keep it removed. Oblivious to her thoughts, Fenris crossed his arms and said; "I was merely concerned for Arcana's welfare."

"Sure." Caelum climbed a shallow ramp, sauntering over to the control panel set into the back wall. A few delicate touches from Caelum's nose bought it flickering and beeping to life, long lines of text flowing over the screen. He flicked a glance back at Arcana. "You sure you're ready for this?"

"Oh for Sorcen's sake, you two are worse than Lesce!" Arcana growled, fisting her hands on her hips. "You can feel me out, can't you? Answer your own gods-damned question."

Caelum paused with his nose hovering over the panel, eyes whirling. "Okay, I believe you. How far? And don't say-"

"All the way." Arcana rolled her eyes at his long look. "I'm not half-assing this, Caelum."

"Your funeral." The deerken prodded the control panel with swift precision. The lights in the room shifted and brightened, revealing several tall, robust looking trees spaced evenly through the training arena. The computer began a series of start-up checks, thrusting fire and water from the roof and walls in a complicated set of sprays and spurts.

"Incredible," Fenris said again, his face wreathed in delight. "I've never seen such a thing."

"I designed it myself." Arcana toed off both boots and shucked her outer robe, revealing comfortable leggings and a tank top beneath. "Once the computer has finished the safety checks, we can start."

"What are the rules?" Fenris tugged his tattered shirt off over his head, giving Arcana a clear view of his sculpted chest and stomach, the landscape somehow enriched by that long, thin scar running diagonally downwards. Her eyes tracked the scar tissue of their own accord, breaking off as it disappeared beneath the waistband of his pants, along with a host of other interesting lines and curves. She looked hastily away as he dropped his shirt on the floor and turned to face her. What in the name of Sorcen's seven gods was wrong with her?

"Rules?" Arcana paused, reining her treacherous thoughts back in. "Caelum has the last word and if he calls stop, we stop. If someone yields, we stop. The room is equipped with traps which rotate and trigger at random so even I don't know what and where they'll be." She pointed to a rack against one wall. "I usually go in unarmed but there are some practice weapons over there if you prefer."

"Thank you," Fenris nodded.

The computer beeped an affirmative tone and Caelum announced; "All clear."

Fenris smiled. "Well then, shall we begin?"

"Of course. Good luck," Arcana gave him a lazy salute and vaulted the barrier, dropping like a stone. Freefall flipped her stomach over but she landed on a sprung section of the floor and vaulted upwards again, landing neatly on a series of wooden platforms that crisscrossed the chamber.

A quick glance over one shoulder confirmed that Fenris had disappeared. If the battle with Algae was anything to go by, Arcana had no doubt that Fenris would try to end the bout simply and swiftly. If she hid, his nose would easily find her - which meant the best option was to stay in the open to try and draw him out. Arcana padded across the wooden platform to stare out into the arena. Fenris was faster and stronger, so the only chance at victory lay in keeping her wits about her. And trusting her magic, which was spread around her feet like a net.

The wood behind Arcana creaked and she ducked, swinging under Fenris' arm as his training sword swished through the air above her head. She leapt from the platform and into space, flinging an arm out as she went. A nearby rope curled around her extended wrist and Arcana swung away, making a chopping motion with her free hand. The wooden platform beneath Fenris cleft in two.

He fell, hit the ground and sprang upwards, thrusting the sword through his belt as he arced towards her. Arcana released the rope at the apex of her swing, catching onto a rung hanging from the roof. She twisted her fingers and the rope snaked away, binding Fenris' ankle and yanking him out of the air.

Arcana dropped down onto a ledge, rolled and dove into the narrow pool of water below. She drew in the essence of the pool, filling her lungs with air taken straight from the water. She sank further, swimming through a narrow tunnel and emerging on the other side of the chamber. Raising her head slowly, Arcana crested the lip of the pool and examined the area. The rope lay in pieces on the floor and Fenris was nowhere to be seen. Why wasn't he using his preternatural speed? Had he thought to give her a head start?

The thump of wood on wood caught her attention and Arcana turned in time to see Fenris duck under a flight of projectiles which had launched from the wall nearby. She spread both hands and the pool lifted her up, sending forth a wave of water which hit Fenris squarely in the chest and knocked him backwards. Arcana landed on the floor in a crouch, gathering her energy for a second blast - but Fenris was gone.

"Shit." Arcana whirled and started to run for a ladder on the wall, water sheeting off her. She barely made three steps when Fenris' warm body cannoned into her from behind, sending them both tumbling and bouncing across the wet floor, his superior speed and strength definitely now in play. The Guardian pinned Arcana's arms and flipped her to face him, rolling chest to chest with her until they crashed unceremoniously into the side of the chamber.

Fenris' eyes blazed with jade fire, dark teal hair almost black where the water had plastered it to his face. His arms locked behind Arcana in a vice grip, his body moulded against hers, superior weight preventing her escape. Fenris grinned to expose fangs, nostrils flaring - scenting victory. Arcana shivered, and not from the chill of being so recently dunked in the pool. He was pure male in that moment, the effect on her senses so devastating she was completely diverted from the idea of winning the battle if it meant another few moments in his embrace.

Rather than fighting the sensuality between them, Arcana raised her chin and looked Fenris dead in the eye. He froze as his glamour rose around them, sliding over Arcana with that tickling warmth which had so confounded her at first. What did he feel, locked together this way, their bodies so perilously close, their minds even closer? As though in answer, Fenris shifted above her - ever so slightly loosening that iron grip, his thoughts as derailed as Arcana's had been only moments before.

It was enough. Arcana struck, using the water clinging to their bodies to sluice him straight off her, tumbling that lithe body to one side as she rolled to her feet. Fenris' gasp of surprise became a grunt as he thumped hard against a barrier but Arcana wasted no time on remorse, scrambling blindly into a maze of tall pillars and shadowed nooks.

A low, bestial growl broke out behind her and she grinned. Win or lose, perhaps now Fenris would take her seriously. A flicker above caught Arcana's attention and she gasped to see him leaping from pillar to pillar over her head, accelerating into a blur. It was a beautiful combination of deadly power and grace, so much so that Arcana failed to notice the floor opening beneath her feet. Her stomach twisted but she managed not to shriek as she dropped into a narrow tube, unable to do more than pull her body into a straight line.

Arcana erupted into the air feet first, the room spinning around her. Fenris was waiting two paces ahead, clinging to the side of a metal pillar with what appeared to be will alone. He'd lost his sword but as Arcana watched, Fenris drew a training knife from his belt and clenched it between his teeth. Waiting. As she began to arc back towards the floor, looking for a way to cushion the inevitable fall, a geyser of fire shot out of the wall and enveloped Arcana in flames.

She dumped her water magic, desperately absorbing the fire before she caught alight herself, blending with the heat and sailing out the other side as the geyser cut off her view of Fenris. Arcana hit the floor hard enough to lose her breath but managed to roll to her feet, blackened and shaken. She slid around a corner, leaning her head back against the wall as her addled wits struggled to reassemble. She'd been careless and almost paid the price - not to mention, she now stank of soot and singed hair, an easy target for Fenris' sensitive nose. If she wanted to stand even the slimmest chance of victory, she needed to focus and keep moving.

Arcana staggered out into the open, casting around for a sign of the Guardian. The pillar he'd clung to was vacant but she knew he wouldn't have gone far. She needed to mask her scent before - Arcana pulled up short as Fenris dropped to the floor in front of her, the metal shuddering at the impact. Too late. The Guardian rose from his crouch with deadly intent, training knife gripped in one hand and those brilliant jade eyes locked on her body.

Taking a deep, steadying breath, Arcana slid into a fighting stance. She'd never been good hand to hand. Was laughably terrible, in fact, though Flare had insisted she learn the basics anyway. Arcana clenched both fists and her hands burst into flame, casting flickering shadows over the walls around them. She stood almost no chance this way but she'd be damned if she didn't go down swinging. Fenris' lip twitched but whether it was in amusement or anticipation, Arcana couldn't tell. He was faster. He was stronger. He was a warrior - and he knew it.

Fenris lunged in, easily evading her clumsy attacks and stepping inside her guard. He twisted one arm around hers, bending her flaming hand even as he swung the knife up towards her throat. Arcana pumped magic through her veins, channelling the fire directly into her skin and heating her body into a living brand. Fenris cursed and let go, spinning away. Arcana followed the movement of his body on instinct alone, knowing she would have only one chance for her gamble to work. Her fingers brushed the flat of the knife. It burst into flame and Fenris dropped it, jumping back as ashes sifted to the floor.

Arcana's breathing came ragged as she completed her spin, bringing the heels of both palms together and blasting a fireball the size of her head in Fenris' direction. He ducked beneath it. Arcana strode towards him, blasting another, and another, filling the air with crackling flame. Fenris retreated, gracefully dodging the missiles Arcana lobbed with ever increasing speed. They reached the pillars and he leapt upwards, digging one hand into the metal to cling to the side. She threw a fireball directly at his head, watching as Fenris ducked, momentarily distracted as his fingers scrabbled to retain their purchase on the smooth plasteel.

Arcana dropped to the floor, splaying both hands across the exposed metal and dragging the ship's energy into her own. The pillar above her ruptured instantly, peeling backwards and trapping Fenris in a thin, solid roll of plasteel. The muscles in his neck bulged as he tried to free himself but Arcana could sense the strength in the ship and knew it was to no avail. Their eyes met and held, silence stretching between them. Arcana slowly rose to her feet, magic pulsing in time with the beating of her heart as Fenris struggled - and subsided.

"I yield," Fenris called. At once the chamber deactivated, lights equalising as the hazards powered down. Arcana waved a hand to unroll the metal and set Fenris free. He dropped lightly to the ground a few paces ahead, chest heaving with effort.

"Arcana wins," Caelum's voice rang out across the chamber.

Fenris stalked over to her, extending one trembling finger to point up at the pillar. "What was that?"

"Magic." She gave him the same flat, intense tone, lifting her chin as he crowded her space, his night-time scent overlaid with sweat, soot, and the barest hint of cinnamon.

"Magic?" Fenris' eyes narrowed. "Fire, water, earth - those I have seen you wield. Not... whatever blend of alloy *that* is."

Arcana blinked, refusing to be intimidated. "Moulding metal is a part of earth magic. Not that it matters, where I'm concerned."

"Explain." The voice of a commander.

Arcana grinned. He'd lost and he was not at all pleased - a fact that, in turn, pleased her no end. "I told you once before, I absorb the dominant energy in my surroundings." She shrugged. "If I concentrate, I also have access to things a normal sorcerer shouldn't - the plasteel in the ship, the energy in the star drive." Arcana deliberately looked up from beneath her lashes. "Even tea and coffee."

He frowned. "Tea and coffee?"

"It took some practice, but yes. Whatever I can absorb, I can control." She shrugged. "It's not perfect - I can't absorb everything - but it leaves me with a few tricks up my sleeve."

Fenris was silent for a moment, one hand drifting to the long scar across his ribs. As his palm flattened over the ridged flesh, his eyes flicked down to hers. "I never anticipated magic being used the way you command it. You more than made up for my physical advantages."

"You're faster and stronger in every way." Arcana conceded a step as Fenris pressed in, tilting her head back to keep her eyes on his face. Her shoulders bumped against a pillar - trapped. "It was a close call."

"It was not a close call at all," Fenris' voice had dropped an octave, accent thickening as it slid along her bones like crushed velvet. He reached out a slow, trembling hand and brushed Arcana's hair back from her face. "I anticipated a quick, clean victory every step of the way - but catching you was like trying to hold running water. I am humbled in my defeat."

Butterflies took wing in Arcana's stomach as Fenris bent his head to look into her face. The pillar pressed into her damp shoulders and she bit her lip - until she realised he'd left plenty of room for her to sidestep away if she so chose. Arcana willed her legs to move, to slip her into safer territory, but her traitorous knees remained locked. She cleared her throat. "I trust now you'll stop underestimating my abilities."

"Of course." One long, muscled arm rested on the plasteel beside her head. Still leaving an escape route, as though Fenris knew she'd been cornered in the past. His smile was slow and soft as he murmured; "Will you accept my apology - again?"

Arcana examined his face, beaded with sweat and grime, and tried to weigh instinct against the resistances in her mind. Their eyes met and once again she felt the warm cloak of his glamour. Her heart raced in her chest, their bodies so close she was sure Fenris would feel it. Goose bumps swept her arms as she realised she could feel *his* heartbeat, strong and steady against the swell of her breast - and that their two hearts thundered in unison. Fenris inhaled, sending shocks of awareness through her body, his glamour sliding over her skin with a texture somewhere between feathers and velvet.

"What does it feel like to you?" The words tumbled out before she could stop them. Dangerous, dangerous territory - so much so that her whole body shook. "The glamour."

Jade fire stuttered as Fenris considered, now so close they shared breath. "Like riding lightning."

His voice was rough enough that Arcana believed it, knew he'd deliberately chosen to offer her own words back to her. She swallowed. If she so much as breathed too deeply, their lips would collide. Her heart contracted, shrieking in warning, but she couldn't look away, couldn't bring herself to move from that single, electrifying moment. Fenris' fingers scraped on the plasteel beside her head, flexing as though he were about to close the distance and - a torrent of frigid water drenched them both as the sprinklers in the roof turned on at full power.

Fenris leapt back with a yelp, then shook in silent laughter, his head tipped back towards the ceiling. He closed his eyes, water streaming down his body and dripping from the tips of his fingers. Arcana took advantage of his distraction to gulp down great breaths of fresh air, unsure whether she was relieved or disappointed that they'd been interrupted. Relieved, she told herself firmly. Definitely relieved. And her knees weren't weak from how close they had stood - no, she'd just over-exerted herself too quickly after waking.

Yeah, right.

"Sorry," Caelum's voice sounded anything but as it drifted through the arena. "I thought you were out so I ran the cleaning cycle."

"It's fine." Arcana pushed off the pillar and began picking her way across the slick floor, leaving Fenris to his own thoughts as the sprinkler's freezing water sloughed over her skin. "I needed to wash off all this soot anyway."

Caelum waited at the top of a narrow set of stairs, watching Arcana with swirling night-sky eyes as she climbed towards him. "You okay?"

"Of course. I slept for two days, remember?" It wasn't what he was asking and they both knew it, but Arcana wasn't in the mood to discuss her confused feelings - particularly when Fenris' boots clanged on the stairway behind her. She strode across the platform towards a shelf of towels, tossing over her shoulder; "It felt good to exercise."

"You moved well. It was a good match," Caelum added, bumping Fenris' dripping shoulder with his nose. Arcana snatched two towels from the shelf and threw one at Fenris. His eyes widened a moment before it hit him in the head, wrapping halfway around his neck.

"Thank you." His voice was dry as he tugged the towel free and began rubbing his body briskly, muscles sliding under silken skin.

Arcana blinked and looked away before she could blush, keeping her voice neutral. "Welcome."

"So now that you've both slept, eaten, and beaten each other senseless, I think it's probably time to talk about what we do next." Caelum poked at the arena control panel and the sprinklers shut off. "We can't keep blindly flying through space forever."

"We need food," Fenris said, dropping the towel to snatch up his tattered shirt. He grimaced as he slid it carefully over his head. "And, at the risk of sounding conceited, I need some clothing."

"Not conceited - too much longer and those will fall apart. There are some things I just don't need to see," Caelum announced, shaking himself thoroughly. "I'd like to know why the ship wasn't reloaded before we left but that's probably a moot point now."

"Food... clothes." Arcana sucked on her teeth. "Where are we?"

"Fourth quadrant south of Sorcen," Caelum supplied.

Arcana sighed, seeking momentary solace behind closed eyelids. "Burke, then."

"Don't sound so pleased." Caelum tilted his head at her. "She's supposed to be your friend, remember?"

"When she's not nagging us to work for her." Arcana winced, echoes of their shouting reverberating through her mind. "It didn't end well last time."

"It's her job to be pushy," Caelum flicked his tail indifferently. "Otherwise those vagabonds would overthrow her."

"Who, exactly, is Burke?" Fenris looked carefully from one of them to the other, rubbing damp hair with his towel.

"When I first left Sorcen, I did so without any money and certainly very little understanding of how the galaxy works." Arcana's mouth twisted into a bitter smile. "Flare put me in contact with one of his... trade associates. Nolan hired us as mercenaries for a while and taught us the ways of the wider universe. Burke is his daughter. We became friends and worked closely together until her father died and she took over the space station."

"And then you fought?" Fenris guessed.

"Not immediately. Burke thought that Caelum and I didn't capitalise on our talents properly," Arcana bunched her towel in both hands, jaw set. "There were certain types of missions she wanted us to do that I wasn't interested in."

"Head hunting, mostly," Caelum said, yawning.

Fenris placed his towel carefully in the waiting clothes bin. "I've seen you kill before," he said slowly.

"I'm not an assassin - I don't kill for money, with no questions asked. And I won't," Arcana added, her tone edged. "It's different."

"That's leaving out the part where a great deal of those missions required... how would you put it? A woman's loving touch." Caelum's tongue lolled out of his mouth in amusement.

Arcana snorted. "I'm many things. Seductive is not one of them."

There was a short, loaded silence before Fenris said; "There is honour in standing by your morals."

"Thank you," Arcana inclined her head, scraping her tangled hair back into an elastic. "Burke, however, doesn't agree. I drop in every now and then - for tea, biscuits, and the same old argument."

"Shall I set a course for the station, then?" Caelum asked idly.

Arcana levelled him with a flat look. "You already have."

His tail twitched once, twice. "Maybe."

"How long have we got?" Arcana asked, rolling her eyes.

"Another fifty hours or so, unless you want to overcharge the crystal array," Caelum drifted to her side, his soft nose tickling her arm. "It will do you good to clear the air."

"Yeah, right. I'd prefer not to overcharge the engine unless it's an emergency. If we fracture a crystal, we'll be easy targets for Taelon." Arcana looked to Fenris. "Speaking of, any idea where he is?"

Fenris closed his eyes, breathing slow and steady. "Not close. He... I do not think he is currently seeking me. Us."

"Planning his next move," Caelum guessed.

"That is likely," Fenris agreed, inclining his head.

"So... we should be fine for now. And fourteen hours is enough time for some good sleep and a little more training before we hit Burke's place." Arcana tapped her chin as she spoke.

"You want to do that again?" Fenris asked, gesturing back at the arena.

"Yes. Over and over," Arcana nodded. He blinked at her slowly, then craned his head to look at the training chamber, the light glinting off his smooth teal skin.

"As much as I enjoyed the experience," Fenris' voice dropped an octave as he looked back at her, eyes blazing, "Are you really so keen to teach me a lesson?"

"The opposite," Arcana replied, clearing her throat. "We need to learn to work together. I've only ever fought alongside Caelum before and that's cheating, because we're part of each other already. It will take us a couple of days to make it to Burke, and I suggest we use that time as best we can."

Fenris pursed his lips as he considered her words. "A wise idea. I am not used to functioning as part of a cohesive unit in that way, either."

No, because he was normally in charge, or going it alone. But rather than say those things aloud, Arcana simply nodded. "Well, I'm ready whenever you are."

"I am always ready." That slow, predator's smile curled his lips and Arcana's toes curled along with it. Probably because she wasn't quite dry and the floor was slippery. Obviously. Fenris raked her with a long, hot look and said; "For now, however, I might indulge in a good wash. If you'll excuse me?"

"Of course," Arcana pasted a smile on her face, hoping - probably in vain - that he couldn't hear the traitorous thundering of her heart. Rather than comment further, Fenris bowed and strode to the elevator, damp trousers flapping around his ankles. The door swished open as he approached and sealed the Guardian inside a moment later.

"Well that was interesting," Caelum said as soon as they were alone.

"Shut up," Arcana growled, rubbing at her face.

"I wonder what would have happened if I hadn't turned the sprinklers on?" Caelum's chest rumbled with laughter. "You felt very conflicted."

"Shut up!" She hissed, her cheeks burning.

"Would you have kissed him?" Caelum pressed, tail switching idly. "I couldn't decide if you were terrified of kissing him or of *not* kissing him."

"I'm not going to kiss him."

"Really?" His voice was a mockery of disbelief.

Arcana clenched her hands in her towel, gripping so hard her bones creaked. "Do you exist purely to torment me? Or is this your twisted idea of trying to help?"

"I haven't decided that either," Caelum said, his voice unrelentingly cheerful. "You never look at anyone, so I'm intrigued - I've never seen you this way before."

"I'm not any way," Arcana snapped. "Did Flare put you up to this?"

Caelum snorted, shaking himself thoroughly. "What, making you ogle an excellent example of a half-naked man? How could Flare ask me to make you do that?"

Arcana stared at him for a heartbeat. Two. She shouldn't ask, shouldn't ask - "How in the name of running water would you know what an excellent example of a half-naked man is?"

"Because I can feel your emotions," Caelum returned, his eyes swirling and dipping mischievously. "And apparently I can read them *much* better than you."

"Great Gods of Sorcen. I knew I shouldn't have asked," Arcana groaned, burying her head in the towel and scrubbing wildly at her hair. Anything, really, to avoid meeting Caelum's too-piercing gaze.

"There's nothing to be ashamed of." Caelum ducked as she threw her towel but it tangled in his antlers nonetheless. He looked out from underneath, completely unperturbed. "It's perfectly natural to look, you know. It might even do you good."

"*What* might do me good?" Arcana put every ounce of threat she could muster into that one sentence.

Caelum's mouth dropped open in a grin. "You know."

"I am *not* having this conversation with you," Arcana snapped, moving to the control panel and sliding the keyboard out. "In fact, I also need a shower."

"Then what are you doing?" Caelum asked. His voice still echoed with amusement but he made no move to pursue the topic further, for which Arcana was eternally glad. It would have been messy to skin him alive.

"I'm sending Burke a little note," Arcana answered, her fingers flying over the keys. "So she knows to expect us. And I'm attaching a shopping list for good measure. Who knows how long before Taelon decides to chase us? I'd rather be in and out as quickly as possible."

"She'll expect us to stay at least one night," Caelum warned.

"One, perhaps. But no more," Arcana allowed, tapping away at her list.

"Well, I don't need a shower so I'll head back to the bridge and keep an eye on things. I'll check in later," Caelum said, snuffling at her cheek in the deerken equivalent of a kiss. He paused, and then: "You've been alone for an awfully long time. Would it really be such a terrible thing?"

Arcana turned her head to plant a kiss on his nose without taking her eyes off the message she was composing. "You know how I feel about this topic, Caelum."

He moved to the service elevator and then paused. "Algae's dead, you know. Don't give in to his ghost." Before Arcana could find something else to throw at him, the doors swished shut and he disappeared.

Arcana growled low in her throat, tapping the display panel for a log of the ship's inventory. She screwed up her nose at the low level of their provisions and set to work writing a lengthy list of items for Burke to accumulate on their behalf.

What should she do about Fenris? Arcana's fingers faltered on the keys and she bit her lip. If she was smart, she'd stay away from him and not look. By all the stars in the universe, just leave him alone. Save herself the embarrassment, the pain; the wounds she'd have to crack open and address in the process. *But you've already looked*, a little voice whispered. An image of Fenris rose in her mind, his shirtless body cloaked in lean muscle and fuelled by the jade fire in his eyes. Arcana growled again and slammed a clenched fist down onto the metal border of the control panel. Sparks flew from the tops of her knuckles, a rainbow of shimmering lights that popped and fizzed in time with her thoughts.

"Get a grip," she told herself, giving her hand a shake. Breathe. In, out.

Push it aside. Concentrate. Lips pressed into a thin line, Arcana finished the last of her missive and sent the message.

Time to shower and rest - except that a terrible restlessness had come over her, the feeling that her skin didn't quite fit her bones. If she lay down, she would surely sleep - but Arcana was just as sure she would find her dreams haunted by an endless replay of her bout with Fenris in the arena, or worse; that conversation with Caelum. An errant trickle of water leaked from her hair, rolling off the edge of one eyebrow to plop on the floor. No shower. No sleep. She needed to *do* something.

So Arcana pushed the control lever for the training arena up to full then turned and sprinted for the railing, diving blindly into space as the room whirred to life.

CHAPTER
TWO

"Sorry I'm late." Arcana hurried out of the elevator and onto the bridge.

Caelum was kneeling on a low couch in front of the windscreen but he glanced over his shoulder as the elevator swept shut. "Not late - just in the nick of time."

"Good." Arcana nodded a greeting to Fenris, who was propped against a bulkhead, and slid into the co-pilot's chair. She wrapped both hands around the steering mechanism and gave an experimental tug. "I'm active."

"I can see that," Caelum returned, smoothing the ship back onto their prior trajectory. "Now keep your hands to yourself."

Arcana held her hands up in surrender. "She's all yours."

"When you spoke of Burke earlier... I did not realise she owned Corrin's Run," Fenris said, his eyes trained on the spacescape before them.

Arcana followed his gaze, taking in the swirling mass of asteroids and beyond, the blinking lights of a space station. "You know of Corrin's Run?"

"Only by reputation." Fenris waved a slender hand out the window. "Corrin's Run is one of the most famously independent trade stops in the galaxy - a claptrap organisation of spacedust, old ship parts, mostly honest smugglers and hardened criminals."

"Among other things," Arcana smirked. "I'm glad you read the tourism brochure. We wouldn't want you to go in unprepared."

Fenris simply shook his head, as though no amount of preparation could possibly make him ready for such a place. "If this is where you learnt the ways of the universe, it's no wonder you're filled with such distrust."

Arcana opened her mouth to answer when an unfamiliar voice crackled through the cruiser's speakers. "Unidentified vessel, you have entered Corrin's Run space, please identify yourself."

Clearing her throat, Arcana reached out and flipped a blinking green switch on the console in front of her. "Good afternoon, Corrin control. This is the *Wandering Sorceress*, requesting permission to dock and come aboard. Clearance code twenty two, forty seven major."

"Acknowledged, *Wandering Sorceress*, you are cleared for docking at Gate Four." The comm unit's display blinked with a quick visual of the docking gate in question.

"Thank you, Corrin control. We are inbound."

"The Curator eagerly awaits your arrival, Arcana. Control out," said the voice.

Arcana flipped the communicator off and tapped at the shield display, diverting control to the panel on her steering column. "Okay, let's do this. I've got the shields."

"Going in." Caelum nosed the ship into the asteroid storm. "Let's see if we can set a new personal best."

"Timer's on," Arcana grinned, flicking the appropriate switch.

Fenris swore and flinched from the windscreen as Caelum kicked the ship forward, swerving around a sharp-edged projectile the size of a house. "Is there a permanent route through?"

"No. The asteroids are in a constant state of flux which makes their paths impossible to predict." Arcana flared power to the forward shields as an asteroid sheered in half, peppering the cruiser with debris. "Caelum thinks it's a hoot."

"It certainly makes for an excellent defence mechanism," Fenris noted.

Arcana nodded. "I'm pretty sure that's what the original Curator had in mind."

Caelum pulled the cruiser upwards, slipping over the top of a slowly spinning, disc shaped rock and then shunting sideways to avoid several long shards that appeared from beneath. Arcana surged power to the lower shields and the cruiser bucked as one of the sharp rocks collided with the shield's edge. Fenris stumbled, clutching with white knuckled fingers at the back of Arcana's chair.

"Shields at seventy five per cent." Arcana eyed the display in front of her, evening out the remaining energy. "That was bigger than it looked."

"We'll be fine. Almost there," Caelum said. The ship dove suddenly, sweeping around a cluster of smaller asteroids, then banked left beneath a larger projectile before breaking out into clean space. "Done! How did we do?"

Arcana poked the timer critically. "Two seconds short of a new PB."

"Ugh!" Caelum shook his head in annoyance. "It's been a while, I suppose. Oh well. Gate four, here we come."

Corrin's Run loomed ahead; a nebulous collection of spheres, domes and haphazard wreckage that had been joined into a single unit. The ungainly mess of cables and welding was crowned by a series of platforms that seemed to jut out at random. Large yellow characters splashed across the mismatched grey shell in a variety of languages, reflected by the station's running lights until they glowed like living things.

Fenris craned his head to get a better view. "Those are not very welcoming messages."

"You can read all that?" Arcana asked.

He shrugged. "Most. I'm assuming they are all a variety of the same warning."

"So I'm told - and they're paired with an equally unwelcoming arsenal of heavy laser batteries and fighter squadrons." Arcana pointed to a cluster of hangar doors, inside of which she knew the ragtag collection of combat craft resided. "Nobody lands without the Curator's permission."

"I've heard many things about this facility but never had the occasion to visit." Fenris twisted his head back and forth as Caelum closed in on the docking gate. "How do the larger ships trade here? We're barely going to fit inside the hangar."

"Bigger ships wait outside the storm and smaller transports come and go on the Curator's word. Anyone who argues does so with the laser batteries," Arcana chuckled.

"There haven't been many." Caelum answered Fenris' unspoken question. "But the wreckage of the ships makes the storm more interesting."

A giant hole appeared in the side of the station as large doors retracted, allowing enough space for the cruiser to sweep inside. A thrumming energy field passed over the ship as it entered, containing the station's atmospheric pressure within the large cargo bay. Caelum guided the cruiser gently onto the landing pad and Arcana reached over to the main control panel, flipping the required switches to power down the crystal engines.

"Welcoming party incoming," Caelum announced, ducking out of his headset and climbing off the low couch. "I'd say about five minutes."

"Really? They're eager." Arcana swung out from under the steering yoke and pushed upright, grabbing her leather satchel from where it hung on the bulkhead.

Caelum crossed to the elevator and nudged the panel with his nose. "Burke's probably got a job she needs you to do."

"She's always got a job for me to do." Arcana settled the satchel across her chest as the elevator doors swished open, adjusting her clothes to accommodate. There was no place at Corrin's Run for the softness of dresses and leggings, so she'd opted instead for a snug pair of dark jeans and calf high black boots. An armoured corset cinched her waist, black silk and lace disguising the defensive nature of the garment. She'd chosen a tight fitting black knit sweater to go over the top, hugging dips and curves and boasting a low enough neckline that Arcana's corset-amplified bosom was all but on display. The layers of black were complemented by a thick, silver chain around her neck and a matching bracelet at one wrist. The jewellery clinked as Arcana walked, the links on the chain almost big enough to fit her fingers through and faceted to catch the light so that the silver sparkled like diamonds. She'd chosen dark clothes to highlight her salt-white skin, and silver pins adorned partially upswept hair, glittering like stars in the light. Stray stands framed Arcana's face, making her flat, black eyes all the more unusual - and terrifying. She caught Fenris glancing at her for the third time in a minute and raised a questioning brow. "What?"

"You look..." he trailed off. "I have never seen you dressed like that before."

"Corrin's Run is a dangerous place." Arcana shrugged. "We have to wear masks here and this is a key part of it. It's easier to look terrifying and have people imagining the dark side of my magical abilities than it is to actually demonstrate them."

"There's a dark side?" Fenris asked.

"Don't look so surprised." Arcana offered a half smile which didn't reach her eyes. "There's always a dark side. I just choose not to embrace it."

"I see." After a moment's hesitation, Fenris frowned down at his tattered rags. "Should I be... making adjustments?"

"Depends." Caelum tilted his head as the elevator swooshed down-wards. "Do you want to look like an escaped hospital patient, or a warrior?"

Fenris blinked once, long and slow, then turned to Arcana. "Fix me, please."

Arcana choked on a laugh, running a swift glance over his body. What could they do? The image presented by a change of clothes could be everything in a place like Corrin's Run, but Fenris was too much the warrior to be portrayed as anything else. Which meant working with his natural qualities, enhancing, twisting a little... she snapped her fingers as an idea blossomed in her mind.

"Okay. Shirt off." Arcana flipped her satchel open and began rummaging inside as Fenris complied with her instruction, ragged linen now bunched in his fists. "You won't need that – stash it. Then put the greatsword back on."

Fenris slid the shirt into his leather pouch and resettled the scabbard across his bare chest. The strap ran the opposite direction of his long scar, giving the Guardian a savage, almost barbaric appeal. While striking, it made him look like an escaped prisoner; a mask which would be far too troublesome to maintain given the cool arrogance Fenris wore like a second skin when out in public. No, their best bet would be to play on that arrogance, to twist Fenris into something not so easily recognised by any eyes or ears Taelon might send drifting through the trade stop after they had moved on.

With that in mind, Arcana drew a red scarf from her satchel, unfolding it to reveal a large rectangle of scarlet cotton with an elegant red and gold trim. Before Fenris could question, she looped it over one shoulder and around his neck, folding and arranging until he looked like a foreign prince, chest almost completely covered in soft folds of red. Another quick rummage in the bag produced a gold hairpin with a sharp point. Arcana twisted the scarf together at Fenris' opposite shoulder, just in front of the greatsword's hilt, and used the pin to secure the scarlet fabric in place.

"Not bad," Caelum approved. "Pants, though."

"Give me a minute," Arcana muttered, crouching to tug at the frayed hems of the trousers in question. Fenris stood still as a statue whilst she rucked up the legs, tucking the bottom edge into his boots and arranging the remains so that they billowed out over the top. She flicked a glance upward, eyes skating over the sculpted planes of his abdomen and across the soft scarf to where his jade eyes flared bright. One hand wandered back into her satchel, the other Arcana extended, palm up, as she met his gaze. "Belt."

He hesitated. "But-"

"*Belt.*"

Fenris stared down at her, expression somewhat forlorn as he undid his belt with those pianist's fingers. He fisted one hand in his now dangerously loose trousers and drew the long strip of leather free, coiling it into Arcana's outstretched hand. "I like that belt."

"You'll get it back." Arcana dragged a long, thin silver chain out of her bag - a necklace Lesce had once given her which was strung with fine, burgundy glass beads. She twisted the chain around the leather belt, followed by a short length of tassled black cord, then offered it back to Fenris.

"You will need to close your eyes." He glanced between his hands - holding those trousers in place - and the belt. "Even I am not that talented."

"Oh for Sorcen's sake," Arcana snorted; then rose up on both knees and began threading the belt back through his trousers herself. "It's not like they're waiting on us or anything." As though on cue, the elevator door swished open, revealing the combined cargo and fighter hangar and the exterior airlock.

"Another minute won't kill them," Caelum declared, blocking the elevator's attempts to close with his hindquarters. "Besides, I'm interested to see how this turns out. You're actually getting somewhere."

"I'll take that as a compliment." Arcana steadied Fenris with one hand on his hip while she navigated the belt past his clenched fingers. The Guardian's skin was smooth and warm, the curve of his hipbone fitting snugly into the palm of her hand. He fidgeted and she dug her fingertips in, flicking him a glare. "You could *try* to be helpful, you know."

"Ticklish," he managed - and his face had indeed blanched a strange shade of pale. The chain on the belt snagged and Arcana altered position, leaning her cheek against his ribs as she sought to get a better view of the tangle. Fenris hissed as her hair slid over his skin, voice strangled as he said; "That's not helping."

"Don't be such a baby." Arcana leant backwards, buckling the belt tight and arranging loops and lengths of chain so that they hung down from one hip, the burgundy beading glinting like drops of blood. She stood and Fenris watched with trepidation as Arcana pulled a black kohl pencil from her satchel. "Now hold still. If you're too ticklish for this, you'll ruin it."

Fenris' throat bobbed as she stalked closer. "What are you-"

"Just do as you're told for once and hold still." Arcana took Fenris' exposed bicep in one hand, ignoring Caelum's snigger. She lifted the kohl pencil and slashed a set of quick characters from shoulder to elbow, returning to each to add decorative accents. Fenris, as instructed, remained still as a statue - until Arcana tugged imperiously on the scarf. He bent at the waist, nostrils flaring as she clenched his jaw in firm fingers and began adding dark smudges around both eyes. Arcana tilted his head this way and that, admiring her handiwork with a little nod. Fenris' hair hung longer than when they had first met, partially obscuring his face and enhancing the green glow of his eyes. With the addition of the kohl, he looked positively mysterious. Arcana's heart skipped a beat but she ignored it, reaching out to tussle those soft curls - silk between her fingers - and resettle them to her satisfaction.

"I like it." Caelum's mouth was open in a wide grin as Arcana stepped back. "You should've gone into theatre."

Arcana grunted, fists on her hips as she admired her handiwork. Fenris *did* look good - like a war-god stepped right out of some ancient, desert climate; tall and brooding. "It'll do."

"What is this language?" Fenris' eyes dropped to the long line of runes on his arm. "I do not know it and yet it seems familiar."

"Ancient Sorcen - you saw it on the blood sorcerer's tomb. I chose it because it's fancy looking and not many other people can read it; certainly no-one who's offplanet aside from me."

Fenris twisted his arm to try and get a better look. "I hope it's nothing inflammatory."

"No, just a random collection of characters that I picked because they're more ornate. That one means 'lunch'," Arcana pointed to the rune in question. Fenris blinked, then huffed a laugh. "Oh, and it's waterproof, so you don't have to worry about accidentally sweating it off."

"And you think this will... provide the desired effect?" Fenris twisted, trying to assess himself.

Arcana grinned, slipping past Caelum and into the hangar. "Definitely. Just act like some sort of sexy, arrogant warrior prince and you'll be fine."

Fenris blinked. "I'm not entirely certain I can manage sexy."

He already had but there was no way in any lifetime Arcana was willing to say that out loud. So she shrugged and said; "I know for a fact that you can do arrogant just fine. Stick with that if you're worried."

Fenris looked as though he would respond but Arcana poked a nearby control panel and the airlock recessed, lowering a ramp into the docking bay. Caelum stepped through first, the artificial lights glittering off bladed antlers. His hackles were up as he descended, ears pricked forward. Arcana gave Fenris a final, challenging look, watched as he straightened his spine, and then swept past him to follow Caelum down the gangplank.

"Arcana." A stocky, grey-skinned woman wrapped and draped in layers of cream gauze stepped forward, extending all four of her arms in welcome. The docking bay was a mess of half opened crates and containers, with straw strewn over a great deal of the buckled metal flooring. Two guards wearing blasters and solemn expressions flanked the woman, while several workers toiled in the background and tried not to look like they were eavesdropping.

"Burke." Arcana stepped into the other woman's embrace and squeezed tight. Burke squeezed back, drawing away just long enough to bump her forehead against Arcana's. "Always a pleasure."

"It's been too long," Burke tutted. Sharp blue eyes flitted over Arcana's shoulder and widened, long lashes sweeping up in surprise. "Who is *that?*"

Arcana smiled. "Allow me to introduce my hire, Fenris. This is Burke, the Curator of Corrin's Run."

"Pleased to make your acquaintance, my lady," Fenris' accent was thick and rolling as he took one of Burke's outstretched hands and bowed over it.

"Oh my." Burke fanned herself with her reclaimed hand, pale blue eyes travelling the length of Fenris' body. "Welcome, indeed."

"Your establishment is most impressive." Fenris tilted his head back to appreciate the full height of the space station. "Truly a feat of engineering."

"I'd be delighted to give you a tour," Burke returned, reaching up to shuck her gauze hood. Beneath the wrappings her skull fanned out into a boned frill, topped with an array of small horns much like a crown. Her eyes were trained on the Guardian, the slits of her nostrils flared wide to take in his scent. She reached out with one grey hand to grip Arcana's wrist and tugged. "Assuming, of course, you'll be staying? I've had a room prepared."

"Perhaps one night," Arcana allowed. "We're on a schedule."

Burke's eyes drank down Fenris like a fine wine. "Four nights."

"One."

"Three."

"*One.*"

"It'll be nightfall aboard the station in less than an hour; one night will leave us too short on time to load the provisions aboard your ship." Burke at last turned towards Arcana, fingers tightening on her wrist. "And we have so much to discuss."

Arcana sighed, ignoring Caelum's laugh-turned-cough. "Fine. Two nights - but that's it, Burke."

"Excellent," Burke purred, releasing Arcana's arm at last. She looked up at Fenris from beneath impossibly long lashes. "I look forward to becoming better acquainted."

Arcana stepped swiftly in front of Fenris, crossing both arms over her chest. "You're in heat."

"Is it that obvious?" Burke pursed her lips, sweeping Arcana with an assessing gaze.

"Yes. Where's your mate?"

Burke waved a lazy hand. "Phase will be joining us for dinner, don't you worry. In the meantime..." she winked at Fenris. "You'll have to make do with me."

"Keep it in your wrappings," Arcana snapped, eyes narrowed.

"Why?" Burke's head tilted; a raptor's predatory movement. "He yours?"

"I-" Arcana paused. Illithai in a heat frenzy coupled often - mostly with their mates, if they had them, but with whoever they could find if there was no other alternative available. If she laid claim to Fenris, Burke would leave him alone - provided Arcana prove they were together, of course. Much as something deep inside her smouldered when she ran her eyes over his body, Arcana was in no position to be thinking along those lines. No, she would not make the mistake of opening herself up to such vulner-ability; in that, Algae had done his work too well. Never again would she allow herself to be whittled away, forced into a strange shape to accommo-date another. Not to mention, a quiet, cruel voice inside her whispered, only someone as sick and perverted as Algae would be interested in a woman who looked like a cross between a demon and a walking corpse.

So she crushed the part of her that wanted to ogle Fenris, buried it deep, and straightened her shoulders. She was not a pity case, she was a grown woman. Broken, perhaps, without the true depth of emotion that her younger self had once felt - but it was those very feelings which had allowed that same younger self to be ensnared by a slimy serpent with a charming smile. Better to keep Fenris at arm's distance than to try and explain that she was empty deep inside, numb and hollow and echoing where her heart should have been. Better to behave as she had promised; a warrior helping him return home, to his people, his kingdom, his queen. And perhaps... she swallowed heavily, not daring to glance over her shoulder at the Guardian. He'd turned Flare down because of his gender but Burke was female. Short, curvaceous and beautiful. Perhaps he wouldn't mind all four of her hands on his body - perhaps it would help to put that much needed distance between them. Arcana looked at Burke, eyes and voice cool as she said; "I was hired as Fenris' bodyguard; no more and no less. See to it that you give him back in one piece - provided you can get Phase on side, of course."

Burke snorted. "He *is* notoriously jealous."

"He wasn't raised Illithai. We've been over this." Arcana shook her head, already tired of the familiar argument. "Now are we going to stand out here all day, or have your hormones addled your senses so completely that you'd like to drool over Caelum next?"

It had the desired effect; Burke threw a startled glance at the deerken and then laughed out loud. "I prefer my men with hands and lips at the very least, and well you know it. Come along then; I'll show you to your rooms. You'll join us for dinner, of course?"

Arcana opened her mouth but Fenris stepped past, offering one arm to Burke as he replied smoothly; "Of course. It would be our pleasure." He threw a sultry glance over his shoulder at Arcana. "You did not tell me our host would be so charming."

Arcana rolled her eyes and fell into step behind him. "You never asked." Fenris offered her a smirk and then turned forwards, leaning attentively towards Burke as she began describing the various assets of the station. They made an impressive pair; Burke's gauze wrappings trailing as she strode for the access doorway in the opposite wall and Fenris' red scarf gleaming the colour of blood. Arcana eyed him from behind as they walked. She'd done a good job - even the tears in those tatty linen pants only added to his unearthly appeal.

Burke's airy chatter was a welcome interlude to the greasy looks of the station crew who passed them by, many of whom worked to pay off debts or support filthy personal habits. Those few who recognised Arcana wore slightly less surly expressions but were no more sturdy of character than their temporary counterparts. Arcana bared her teeth on more than one occasion as they stalked through the maze of grated walkways and narrow corridors that made up the framework of the lower parts of the station. It took little more than that, or a glance at Caelum's bladed antlers, for most to avert their eyes - though Arcana felt a constant itching between her shoulder blades and was on alert all the way to the elevator.

"This way." Burke poked at the elevator's controls, waiting as the ancient cables groaned into action. The travel car that appeared was little more than a rusted cage and Burke gripped the warped doors with all four arms to pry them open. She gave Arcana a smirk as she gestured them inside, trailing one of her arms down Fenris' bicep as he passed. Arcana stiffened, biting down on her waspish comment. There was no reason to stop Burke touching the Guardian - though Arcana's stomach twisted at the idea that for all her resolve, *she* might not enjoy watching it. As though sensing Arcana's internal conflict, Burke's self-satisfied smirk widened to a toothy grin as she dragged the elevator doors closed behind them. Safe inside - for now - from prying eyes, the Curator's elegant facade crumbled and she looked Arcana up and down with a familiar, well-practised eye. "You look good. I trust your family is well?"

"Very." Arcana, too, allowed her facade to loosen a little, though not so much that Burke might see beyond it to the turmoil within. "Lesce is a grandmother now."

"And Flare?" The Curator asked. "I hear he's recently become the Fire Elder."

Arcana raised an eyebrow. "Word travels fast."

"Nothing official's been said yet, but I have my channels." Burke winked, pressing a finger to the side of her nose.

"I wish the circumstances of Flare's ascension had been better." Arcana grimaced. "He's reluctant to take on the position."

"If anyone can help stabilise your people after the deaths they suffered, it'll be Flare." Burke tilted her head, the fine string of beads hanging from her boned frill clicking softly. "I always thought he was wasted on the front lines."

"It's been a long time since Flare's been anywhere near the front lines," Arcana replied. "The Council haven't let him out of their sight for almost a decade."

Burke frowned at that. "Was he leashed to one of them?"

"No more than he's ever chosen to leash himself to anyone else," Arcana answered, her tone carefully neutral.

"Hah! I was hoping you'd bring him to visit me, honestly. Thirty years on and I still remember it so clearly." Burke shook her head, wrapping all four arms around her body. "What a man."

"So I'm told," Arcana chuckled, allowing her eternal amusement at Flare's antics to colour the carefully crafted personality she'd developed for this place and this place alone. "I'm sorry to say that my brother doesn't appeal to me where the bedroom's concerned."

"Oh yes, I forget your race frowns on inter-breeding." Burke pursed her full lips. "Shame, really - you're missing out! Few men in the universe can compare but don't tell Phase I said that." The elevator ground to a halt and Burke pried the cage open, revealing a short corridor with a trio of doors at the end. She led them to the centre door, which opened onto a wide, well-appointed hallway. Though the station's metal skeleton was still visible, a long, pale blue carpet cleft the centre of the floor and the walls had been painted in creams and golds. Paler blue hangings and slender, elegant hall tables dotted the landscape, providing a much needed break from the functional nature of the space station.

"Rito!" Arcana clapped her hands in delight as a heavily tattooed man stood from where he'd been perched on a low footstool. He was short, the top of his bald head barely passing Arcana's elbow. One heavily ringed ear tapered to a point, the other a ragged mess of flesh scarred with tiny puncture marks down one side. Four sharp lines of teeth glistened inside his mouth, topped with a strong nose and eyes like molten honey. Vines and swirls were tattooed over every inch of visible skin and Rito wore only a bandolier full of knives, a pair of black leather shorts and a gold chain that stretched from left nostril to ear. He looked every inch the pirate he was - and his grin was as wide as his open arms as Arcana threw herself into them. "I thought you left."

"I did, lass." Rito's rolling baritone was at odds with his stature, as was the strength with which he hefted Arcana in his arms and swung her around. "The mistress lured me back with tales of treasure as far as the eye can see."

"That, and you lost everything you own to Phase in cards." Burke's voice was dry with amusement. "I trust you can find your way from here, Arcana? If you'll excuse me, I need to make our dinner arrangements." She raked a long, hot look over Fenris and purred; "I'll see you there."

It was more than an invitation to dine, Burke's expression so scandalous that Rito gave a loud guffaw. Fenris took one of Burke's calloused hands in his own and flourished a bow over the top of it. "I shall count down the minutes," he promised, and Arcana had to bite her tongue to keep her jaw from dropping at the timbre of his voice; as indecent - if not more - than the one Burke had just used. Fenris straightened, jade eyes burning as he brushed a kiss into the centre of Burke's palm and then pressed it to his heart. "Until then, Curator."

"Indeed." Burke retrieved her hand and swept away in a flurry of gauze, disappearing back into the elevator with a sinful smile.

"Well now." Rito's voice was full of humour as the elevator rattled out of sight. "Your hire sure knows how to make an entrance."

"Yes," Arcana drawled, refusing to look at Fenris. "He certainly does."

Rito set her down on the floor and swaggered up the hall, calling over one shoulder; "We didn't know you'd be bringing company, lass, so I only sorted one room. Want me to whip up another for your friend?"

"That won't be necessary," said Fenris smoothly.

"No?" Rito accorded Arcana a large wink as he pushed one of the doors open and said; "Better enjoy him while you can, sorceress. Once Burke gets her claws in, he'll be gone the rest of your stay."

"You filthy vagabond!" Arcana flicked him on the shoulder. He only grinned back at her. "I'm his bodyguard. Nothing else. I'll see you at dinner?"

"I'll be serving it," Rito agreed, then turned and sauntered away.

Arcana spun on her heel and moved into the suite, restless legs taking her across the private lounge area to a long window that looked directly out into space. The door snicked shut behind her and a moment later, the bedroom door whirred open and closed again. She loosed a long breath, clenching her hands to hide their shaking. No doubt Fenris had gone to rest before his *encounter* with Burke in a few hours. Arcana glanced at the silver clock on the wall. Make that half an hour, at most. Not that it bothered her what Fenris did with his time - or his hands, or his lips, or anything else. Not one little bit.

"What a fabulous view." Fenris moved to the window, eyes trained on the asteroid storm before them. He was close enough that warmth seeped from his body to hers, sending an involuntary shiver up her spine.

Arcana startled a half step away from him. "What are you doing here?"

"Would you prefer I was somewhere else?" One eyebrow slithered upwards, the hint of a smile tugging his mouth.

"I thought-" she threw a glance over her shoulder. They were alone.

"Caelum said he had a headache," Fenris supplied. "Weren't you listening?"

Arcana turned resolutely back to the window. "I was thinking of other things."

"Like how to be my bodyguard?" His voice trembled with laughter.

She frowned. "I don't see why that's funny - lots of rich people hire them. It was the best I could do on short notice."

"I wasn't laughing at the idea, merely... never mind."

"I won't," Arcana said loftily, tracing the path of what had once been the barrel of a blaster cannon as it swept through the asteroid storm.

Fenris thrummed beside her, his body so taut she knew he was searching for the right words, the right question. "You seem displeased," he said at last.

Not now. Under absolutely no circumstances was she admitting what lurked in the back of her throat. "I didn't want to stay two nights," Arcana replied.

"We seem to have little choice." Fenris shrugged. "If the ship truly cannot be loaded in time, then we will have to wait."

"I know; that's the only reason I agreed. Burke enforces strict hours and pushes her people hard but when the sun goes down she lets them off their leashes - nothing short of the station's complete and utter destruction would change that." Arcana forced a smile on her face, turning away from the window. "Trust me, in about twenty minutes there'll be a knock at the door to escort us to dinner."

Fenris looked down at himself, tugging the edge of the red scarf. "I can't believe this actually worked."

"Haven't you looked in a mirror yet?" Without waiting for an answer, Arcana tapped two fingers on the window pane in a series of quick beats. The plexiglass shimmered, the spacescape disappearing as it became reflective.

Fenris retreated a few steps from his own reflection and Arcana didn't bother to mask the giggle which slipped between her lips. "I look..." he trailed off and shook his head. "Not like myself at all."

Arcana grinned. "That was the whole point, as I recall."

"Am I truly so terrible a sight in my own skin?" Fenris' tone was light and teasing as he fisted one hand on his hip, twisting to get a better view of his reflection.

"The pyjamas were getting a little worn," Arcana said dryly.

"Pyjamas!" He spluttered indignantly. "I'll have you know that not wearing anything under a suit of plate armour is tantamount to suicide. The chafing is horrific."

Arcana barked a sharp, short laugh. "The hidden dangers of body armour? I'll take your word for it." She sobered and tilted her head. "I think we're just lucky that with less than half an hour until dinner, Burke won't be expecting us to change outfits."

"Is dinner normally a formal occasion?" Fenris asked.

"No, but she likes to make an impression. Particularly during heat fever." Arcana tapped on the window again and the reflective surface subsided, revealing the stars beyond. "I wish I'd known about *that* before we got here."

"It's nothing she can help." Fenris strode to the slim bar set along one wall and began sniffing decanters. Arcana watched in silence as he selected one full of clear, amber liquid and poured a finger's worth into a squat glass. "Accarat?"

"No thanks. Have you forgotten what happened with the firewhiskey already?" Arcana frowned. "I try not to drink unless my life depends on it."

Fenris shrugged, downed the liquor in one smooth motion, then poured himself a second. "I'd say the same but it would be a lie."

"I've seen you giggly already, remember?" Arcana watched the muscles in his throat work as he downed the second round, then set the glass gently back on the sideboard. "I never really understood the idea of getting blind drunk, to be honest."

"Sometimes it helps to settle nerves," Fenris said, replacing the stopper in the decanter. "One or two drinks, that is - not drinking yourself into oblivion."

Arcana raised a slim brow. "And what would the Overlord of the Timeless Kingdom possibly have to be nervous about?"

"Overlord," Fenris repeated, then shook his head. "Weaver save me but I hate that title."

"I noticed you don't use it often."

"Not unless I have to. It carries little weight anywhere but the Timeless Kingdom and tends to annoy figures of authority." His grin was a quick, vicious sliding of lips. "Sounds too much like conqueror."

"And the nerves?"

"What nerves?"

Arcana flicked a finger towards the now empty glass. "You said it helps to settle nerves."

"So I did," Fenris agreed, planting one hand on his hip. Then; "I am not normally in the habit of explaining myself."

"Well, there's a first time for everything, isn't there?" Arcana challenged, grinning as he shifted on his feet.

Fenris frowned, drumming long fingers against his own hip bone. "There is a lot at stake here. The pressure of politics is not something I enjoy at the best of times - here, in an unknown environment, I find myself uncomfortable. This role is easier with Burke's current emotional situation," A quick, bitter smile, "But is not one I would usually play. To say I feel off-kilter would be a gross understatement."

"Fair enough." Arcana sagged onto a chaise lounge that had seen better days; it creaked under her weight. She ignored the sound, propping booted feet on the scarred coffee table, then leant her head back and closed her eyes. "I'm not looking forward to this, either."

"I saw the way the workers flinched from you." The squeak of loose springs across from her was the only indication he'd sat. "It must have taken a lot of work to build such a reputation."

"Hah! Not at all. The flinching happens almost everywhere I go - it's the eyes." Arcana tried to sound flippant, but wasn't sure if she quite made it.

"What's wrong with your eyes?" Fenris sounded so genuinely mystified that Arcana managed a chuckle.

"Haven't you looked at them? Flat, black, expressionless - like a dead thing." She shrugged, her body undulating on the chaise. "At least, that's how most people describe it."

Fenris growled low in his throat. "I like your eyes."

Arcana cracked an eyelid, rolling her head along the back of the chaise to pin him with a long look. "You'd be the only one. Even my mother screamed the first time she saw me like this. What Flare once termed 'classic revenant'."

"I never thought I was particularly stifled in the vocabulary department until I met you and Flare," Fenris mused, propping his head on one hand. The shadowing around his eyes made their inner fire all the brighter and Arcana struggled not to stare as he looked up at the ceiling, repeating; "Classic revenant. It is as though I never learnt to speak."

"Glad to contribute to your education." For a moment Arcana was worried a too-old, too-familiar bitterness had crept into her voice but the Guardian chuckled in response to her comment, his posture remaining relaxed.

"I also feel compelled to point out that 'classic revenant' is rather inaccurate." Fenris clicked his tongue, gaze suddenly intent as he searched her face. "I think 'aggressive ebony' or perhaps even 'beyond midnight' would be a far more poetic description for the windows to your soul."

Arcana shifted uncomfortably in the chair, dipping her head to hide her blush. "I can honestly say that whilst Flare has a great many skills, poetry is not one of them."

"Really?" He looked surprised. "I thought all great lovers were poets."

"Flare once told me that anyone who needed poetry to entice their partner to bed was in sore need of a better imagination." Arcana tapped one finger to her temple.

Fenris laughed. "That does sound like Flare. So tell me, while we are on the topic of imagination: what is this strange rivalry you have with Burke?" He flicked a long finger towards the clock. "Someone will arrive to collect us any minute, if your judgement of time is correct, and I would not wish to give the wrong impression by acting inappropriately."

"You already know the basics; she wanted me as her personal whore and assassin. I didn't want to be." Arcana waved a hand dismissively, refusing to think too closely over the old, festering argument between them.

"The Illithai are far more openly sensual creatures. She may not see it as whoring," Fenris said quietly.

"I know - but while Burke is a fully initiated Illitani clanswoman, she's also spent most of her life here, on the station. She knows how the universe works." Arcana paused, shook her head. "Once, I thought she knew how I worked, too."

"You were friends. That's why she asked after your family."

"We were good friends," Arcana agreed, "But she wouldn't let it go. Couldn't see me as a person anymore, only a potential avenue for more coin. Last time I was here, she tried to blackmail me into taking a mission that would have put me in a situation I didn't like."

Fenris raised a brow. "What sort of information could she possibly have on you?"

"It doesn't matter; it was all fabricated anyway." Arcana blew out softly between her teeth. "Burke thought if she could get me to do it just once, I'd see it wasn't so bad and come back for more." The betrayal still smarted, even now, enough that her voice was hoarse as she admitted; "I used my magic to destroy her office, chained her to her chair and told her I'd kill her if she ever tried to manipulate me like that again."

Fenris was quiet a long moment. "You wouldn't have done it."

"No," Arcana agreed, then favoured him with a chill smile. "They don't know that, though. The face I wear here is not my own."

"I've noticed," Fenris inclined his head solemnly. "I've employed such a defence mechanism myself on many occasions. Sometimes it is an unavoidable necessity."

Arcana considered that statement a long moment, unable to shake the feeling that the cool, implacable face of the Guardian that most people saw was, in fact, merely another mask. The Fenris she had glimpsed in their rare moments of privacy seemed rusted somehow, as though his gentler nature was stiff from disuse, though no less warm. What had happened to force the man inside to bury himself beneath so many layers of armour? Duty, honour, chivalry - all admirable traits but also things that, when bound together with that implacable, almost infuriating calm, became a shell more impenetrable than the full suit of plate Fenris had been wearing when they first met.

Intrigued in spite of herself, Arcana said; "I suppose the true question is: at what point do you wear a mask so long that it becomes impossible to remember your true self?"

"I cannot answer that." His face was smooth but Arcana caught the flicker deep in his eyes which she had come to associate with, if not an outright lie, a misdirection of attention. "Can you?"

"Perhaps." She smiled sadly. "I left the Run when I realised the lines between the woman I wanted to be, the woman I had been and the woman my mask demanded me to be were blurring. Caelum and I took a fake hire, jumped in our ship and whisked off into the proverbial sunset the very next chance we got."

"And nobody thought to ask questions?"

"Nobody ever knew - one of the main rules is that a hire is a confidential arrangement," she returned. "With that in mind, if anyone asks questions, play things down. The less specific information you give, the better. I'd say try to be charming but I think in her heat fever you could call Burke any number of curse words and she'd still smile." Arcana stretched languorously, shoulder joints popping. "Whatever you do, keep an eye on Phase. He... doesn't handle heat fever well."

"You said before he wasn't raised Illithai," Fenris said, the question implicit in his statement.

"Phase was abducted from Illitani as a broodling and sold into slavery. By the time the Matriarch staged a rebellion and the people were freed, he was already an adult." Arcana sighed. "Being offworld, Phase never completed his Temple Rites at the appropriate ages, so he had to either choose a life in exile or return, be castrated and put to work as a labourer."

"He never returned."

"No. Phase worked for a smuggler for a while, which is how he ended up stopping in here." Arcana jerked her chin at the station wall. "Once he met Burke, it was a done deal almost instantly."

"An Illithai with a common upbringing - no wonder the customs of his people are hard to swallow." Fenris nodded sagely. "I will tread carefully. I should not wish to invoke a jealous rage in Phase that would drive a further wedge between you and Burke."

"I appreciate the sentiment, but it's unlikely to happen. Phase is notoriously jealous but he'd never attack you in front of Burke - she's the dominant personality and would never allow it. She might slobber on every male who's foolish enough to come close but it's been a long time since I've seen anything more than that. Burke would never bed another man without Phase's consent." Arcana hesitated, her next words turning to ash inside her mouth. "You'd be more likely to offend Burke if you spurned her entirely."

"Thank you. I will keep that in mind." A pause, and then: "If you dislike the role of hard-edged mercenary, why do you keep playing it?"

"There isn't much other choice - nothing palatable, anyway." Arcana smiled, twisting her lips to bare teeth. "This place runs on, and respects, only strength. It's cruel and cunning and everything is a game. Emotions exist but they're secondary to power, lust, money and greed. Any other face but this one would involve displaying a weakness or becoming something even further from myself."

"I suppose that makes sense." Fenris nodded. "And Caelum? What does he do?"

"I pretend to be a dumb animal and keep my mouth shut to back that image up. You'd be amazed what people say when they think you don't have the capacity to understand or respond," Caelum said, yawning as he wandered out into the main room. "It's annoying, though. I grind my teeth a lot - hence the headache."

Fenris looked amused. "Better than goring the rabble, I suppose."

"Exactly."

"But what of Burke and Phase?" The Guardian's head titled in question. "Have they not become suspicious, over the years?"

"Oh, they know I can talk," Caelum rolled his shoulders in a shrug. "But Arcana managed to extract an oath from both of them to keep their traps shut about it. Say what you will about those two, but when they give their word, they keep it."

"That makes sense," Fenris nodded. "Often a mercenary has little of true value above their word - to break an oath is to permanently sully your reputation."

"Exactly." Caelum shot a star-filled look in Arcana's direction. "We're all clear, by the way."

"I should hope so." Arcana dragged both knees to her chest and propped her chin on top. "I only gave you five minutes before I started talking out of turn."

Caelum snorted. "Five? It took me less than a minute to jam the signals. It's almost like Burke *wants* us to do it."

Arcana frowned. "So what've you been doing in there for twenty minutes?"

"Well, first of all, I actually did have a headache. Second, seeing as we're going to be here two nights, I rerouted the audio and visual output from our room and then spliced it into that of the crew's quarters so that it won't be as immediately obvious that the transmissions are not ours."

Caelum rolled his shoulders in a shrug. "Should last until they do a drive dump in a week or so."

Arcana grinned at the incredulous look on Fenris' face. "This place has eyes and ears everywhere. Caelum's got a knack for taking care of it."

"But..." Fenris frowned and shook his head. "I do not wish to cause offence with my skepticism, but he doesn't have any hands."

"I'm very good with my tongue," Caelum replied, his expression completely deadpan. "You'd be surprised what you can achieve with enough length - and excellent muscle control, of course."

Fenris made a choking sound, eyes wide. "Certified space deer indeed," he managed.

Caelum's aforementioned tongue lolled out in a grin. "You know it. I stay silent here so that nobody works out I'm really the brains of the operation."

"Right," Arcana rolled her eyes.

A knock at the door interrupted Caelum's retort. Arcana rose to her feet, straightening her jumper beneath the strap of the leather satchel. Fenris stayed lazing on the couch, watching through half-lowered lids as Arcana - trailed half a pace behind by Caelum and his bladed antlers - palmed the control for the door. Rito stood on the other side, wearing a polished black bandolier and matching tailored shorts. His skin had been oiled to a gleam, the swirling designs on the top of his head a deep blue-black in the artificial lighting.

"I've come to collect you for dinner," he announced, baring all his teeth in a dazzling smile.

Arcana leant casually against the door jamb, running a sweeping glance over his short, stocky figure. "You're dressed up."

"Burke doesn't like grease stains at the dinner table." The pirate twisted to look past her at the interior of the room. "Is his highness deigning to join us?"

"Of course." Fenris rolled smoothly to his feet, sauntering to Arcana's side. "I would hate to disappoint the Curator."

"In her current state? Yes, you would." Rito's grin took on a vicious edge but he stepped back from the door and waved a hand. "Come on. I'll take you up."

Arcana stepped into the corridor, making a show of glancing up and down before she jerked her chin for Fenris to follow. He stepped to her side, flanked by Caelum while Arcana elbowed the controls and the door swished shut, the light blinking red to indicate it was now locked. Rito slid his hands in his pockets and sauntered away, whistling cheerfully.

"So how long have you been back?" Arcana fell into step beside the pirate, leaving Caelum and Fenris to trail along behind. Rito's bandolier was polished until it glistened and she frowned as she ran a finger across the top of it, the essence of the leather whispering through her senses. "I thought you lost everything you owned in cards? This is new."

The pirate glanced up at her, light glinting off the gold chain linking nostril and earlobe. "It's new," he allowed. "I crawled back a couple months ago. Things were in pretty bad shape, so Burke outfitted me with a couple new bits and pieces. And took it out of my pay, of course."

"Of course." Harsh, that reality, but true for many of the unsavouries who came to Corrin's Run - held to Burke because they owed her, one way or another. "Must have been a pretty bad blunder, considering you were paid up before you left."

Rito said nothing, leading them through a door that looked the same as any other, then down a shorter hall and into a far more sophisticated elevator than the previous one. Still the same cage format, but the brass doors were straight and polished until they shone, the floor lacking any suspicious stains. The control panel didn't even spark when Rito touched it. He grinned at Arcana's raised eyebrow. "She's been making some improvements. Here and there, when there's coin for it."

"About time. I'm surprised this place didn't fall apart years ago." Arcana leant against the guard rail and crossed her arms over her chest.

"You know Nolan ran it down. Recovery is a slow process," Rito replied.

"Indeed," Arcana gave a sharp nod. "You, however, seem exactly the same. Still following me around like a bad smell."

The pirate bleated a loud, rolling laugh. "Just following orders and you know it. Someone has to look after our vagabond princess."

"Look after or watch over?" Arcana let her voice take on a silken edge. "Burke has to have told you about our little altercation by now."

"Whichever helps you sleep at night - besides a blaster underneath your pillow, of course," Rito purred back. "Burke told me what she needed to but it's nothing new. You were always difficult."

Arcana cocked her head. "I hardly see how refusing to become a whore for Burke to pimp out at will is 'difficult'."

"She stood to earn a lot of gold - and so did you. And still would, if you ever changed your mind," Rito added, fiddling with some of the filigree on the cage.

"My body is not a form of currency," Arcana snapped. Making a concerted effort to forge her temper into something more useful, she uncrossed her arms and leant forward. "Did Burke tell you about the conversation we had *after* she sought to change my mind?"

"Naturally, lass. You two always enjoyed idle threats but I think you got under her skin this time." Rito's teeth flashed in a humourless smile. "Suffice it to say that I'll be close by - very close by - for the duration of your stay."

Arcana nodded and lapsed into silence. She'd expected little else; Burke would be a fool to trust her so swiftly after the fight they'd had. If she truly owned Rito as completely as the pirate made out, he'd have no qualms about following Burke's orders regardless of the tentative friendship he and Arcana shared. That was the way places like Corrin's Run operated; loyalty bought by coin and friends who would probably miss you after they'd shot you in the head to collect the reward.

The elevator slid to a stop and the doors whooshed open. Rito gestured them into a round foyer, the walls clad in smooth, dark wood and the floor carpeted in cream and gold. Rito crossed to a door set in the far wall - a proper door, with a round brass handle - and swung it open with a mocking bow.

Arcana slid through first, Fenris and Caelum following. The room was long and narrow, most of the available space dominated by a rectangular dining table large enough to seat twenty people. The matching chairs still smelled new, even to Arcana's untrained nose. The wall on one long side of the room was all plexiglass, revealing an intimidating view of the asteroid storm. Rocks and debris passed so close to the exterior that Arcana guessed they were in one of the many protuberances that jutted from the side of the station. The two narrow walls ahead and behind were clad in the same dark wood as the foyer; a door set in one and a small bar standing against the other. The second long wall was also plexiglass, looking down onto a cavernous room below. The glass was vaguely tinted, enough so that Arcana guessed it to be a mirror on the other side and that the people dancing and drinking in the pleasure hall beneath had no idea they were being watched. Lights whirled and flashed, making it almost impossible to pick out an individual person on the dance floor - particularly as bodies were already pressed so closely together it was a wonder anyone could breathe. They swayed to the music as a single unit but the plexiglass must also have been soundproofed, for Arcana had to strain her ears to hear so much as the persistent rumble of the bass from the speakers below.

"A club?" Fenris drifted to the window, eyes trained on the revelry.

Directly beneath them, Arcana noted the leading edge of a long bar, staffed by creatures who resembled enormous, bipedal stick insects.

"I told you they party in style," she replied. They were alone in the room but Arcana knew better than to assume that meant privacy, so rather than say more, she drifted towards the far end of the table. Four places had been set with silver plates and cutlery, cut crystal glasses shimmering atop the small bar. "Looks like it will indeed be a private dinner."

"Would you rather a larger function?" The door at the opposite end of the room opened to admit Burke, who swept towards them in a trail of pastel blue and cream gauzes. She'd accented her large grey eyes with thick kohl to mimic Fenris', the smudges making her eyelashes seem even more enormous than they actually were. A silver chain hung about her throat, more functional than decorative for all it was polished to a fine sheen. It disappeared into Burke's wrappings, concealing whatever hung from it in the safety of the multi-layered gauze.

"A larger function?" Arcana repeated, twisting her lips into a thin smile. "I'm surprised you even have a room like this; usually you prefer to be downstairs."

Burke waved a dismissive hand, her eyes on Fenris, who had turned from the window and offered a flourishing bow. "We can dance later. I wanted a more... intimate setting for now."

"An excellent suggestion." Fenris took the hand Burke offered and pressed his lips to her knuckles, blazing eyes steady on her face - somewhere in the vicinity of her chin. Arcana wondered, for a flash of a moment, why he didn't just snare everyone in his glamour and perpetually get whatever he wanted. Surely any number of situations would be infinitely easier if he could just make things go his own way all the time? Providing, of course, that he could actually control someone completely. Arcana blinked as she realised she knew very little at all about Fenris' glamour - aside from being immune to it herself - and made a note to remedy that as soon as possible. It clearly wasn't as simple as it seemed in her mind, or he wouldn't have bothered going to the trouble of attempting to appear civilised, to fit in with the surroundings in which he found himself. Arcana swept her eyes up his body, noting the casual way Fenris curved towards Burke's flushed face, speaking softly with his lips still pressed to the Curator's grey skin. He'd denied knowing how to be sexy but he either had absolutely no idea how wrong he was or had been deliberately lying, because the male in front of Burke at that moment was nothing if not a decadent, sensual temptation. Long lines and smooth curves, shadowed eyes and a wicked, bedroom smile which Arcana could more than appreciate even if she had no wish to touch. Which, she told herself firmly, she definitely did not; it was simply a matter of one professional actor admiring the talents of another and nothing more.

A low growl cut the room and they turned as one towards the sound. The door through which Burke had entered remained open and a burly, grey-skinned male stood in the doorway, his blue eyes pinned on Fenris and Burke.

"Ah, Phase, darling. There you are." Burke didn't bother to free her hand from Fenris' grip, merely extended one of her others as Phase stalked closer. He had a long face with slashes for nostrils and an elaborate bone headplate very similar to Burke's, though on a smaller scale. He only sported two arms but his torso curved backwards into an almost feline body covered in grey hide and four legs that ended in clawed feet. Burke smiled up at him, smoothing two of her hands across his tattooed chest. "This is Fenris, my love. And surely you remember Arcana?" Swift fingers curled beneath Phase's jaw and twisted his head in Arcana's direction.

"Hello, Phase," Arcana flicked him a lazy salute. "I see you haven't killed her yet."

Phase grunted in acknowledgment, prying his chin free of Burke's grip and turning back to Fenris. "No," the Illithai male said, his jaw clenched. Arcana swallowed her laugh; jealous, as always. It was a very rare thing for Phase to agree to share his mate with another - in fact, in all the years Arcana had known them, she could only count two occasions in the past when the Illithai male had relented. Both of them, predictably, had been for Flare.

Burke, however, seemed undaunted by the prospect as she waved a dismissive hand. "Always so dramatic. You haven't even met the man."

"It is an honour," Fenris released his grip on Burke's fingers, straightened and offered his forearm to Phase. "Burke speaks highly of you."

The Illithai male sneered down at Fenris' teal skin as though he might spit on it and said nothing.

"You'll have to excuse my mate's manners," Burke's voice was sharp with reprimand. "His Universal Galactic leaves something to be desired."

"Of course," Fenris said smoothly. His hand still extended, he smiled at Phase and spoke in a lengthy procession of clicks and squeaks. Both Phase and Burke's jaws dropped open. In fact, it was all Arcana could do to keep her own astonishment off her face as Phase grudgingly answered, then reached out to clasp Fenris' forearm after all.

"You speak Illitani." Burke's eyes were lit with curiosity, the heat fever fading for the first time since their arrival.

Fenris smiled, charm oozing from his pores. "I have a basic under-standing, though it has been many years since I laid eyes on the temples of Bel-Itan."

"Outsiders do not get to lay eyes upon our sacred temples," Burke parried swiftly.

Fenris' smile only widened, becoming equally more mysterious and seductive. "No," he agreed. "They do not."

Phase titled his head in obvious question and Fenris began speaking, weaving his hands in time with his story, the strange language of clicks and squeaks a velvet rumble on his tongue. Phase stiffened at first and then slowly relaxed the more Fenris talked.

"Arcana!" Burke turned an accusing look in Arcana's direction. "You didn't tell me your charge was involved in the coup that installed Matri-arch Shirgul and freed my people from slavery."

Arcana hid her surprise by leaning against the back of a chair and hooking her thumbs into the waistband of her jeans. "I'm his bodyguard, not his nursemaid. I know only what he's chosen to share the last few weeks - and I've not asked more than that."

Phase made a guttural, demanding sound. After a moment's hesitation, Fenris caught at his belt and pulled the waist of his pants lower down on his hips. On the left edge of his pubic bone, perilously close to the seam of hip and leg, a tiny black swirl had been tattooed. It was small enough to be a birthmark, perhaps a collection of dark freckles; but Arcana had seen enough Illithai writings during her time with Burke to recognise the insignia of Matriarch Shirgul. The insignia of the rebellion. She sucked in a quiet breath as Fenris, his face serene, allowed Phase to bend so close he could have licked that tattoo if he wanted. It was proof - irrevocable, unde-niable proof that Fenris had been part of that rebellion, and had walked out the other side with the Matriarch's highest honours.

"Interesting." Burke's eyes were glued to that extra scrap of teal skin but Arcana knew the other woman wasn't interested in the tattoo, nor the reason Fenris had it - more the tantalising glimpse of his flesh. Indeed, Burke blinked in disappointment as Fenris settled his trousers back into place, covering the marking. Arcana stared blindly at the carpet, trying to gather her thoughts. If Fenris had been part of rebellion - at the behest of the Weaver, no doubt - that was what, ten years ago? Fifteen? The war itself had raged for three. How many other battles had the Weaver silently intervened in? How *old* was Fenris? Arcana shelved her thoughts as Burke sidled up to her and breathed; "Tell me you've slept with him."

"What?" Arcana choked. "No!"

"Whyever not? Are you *blind*? You don't even have the excuse of being related to this one." Burke tutted a swift reprimand, her eyes riveted on Fenris' body. "A shame. I was hoping you'd taken the opportunity to strap yourself aboard; I want to know what he likes."

"I... we... he's not a carnival ride, Burke," Arcana managed, pressing her lips into a thin line. Fenris, deep as he was in animated discussion with Phase, blinked rapidly as though he'd heard every word. Which, with his exceptional hearing, he likely had.

"You don't think so? Because I could list his attractions all day." Burke whistled softly between her white, even teeth. "You are female, right? At least acknowledge those paradise lines are divine."

Arcana's traitorous gaze indeed dropped to Fenris' hips, where the lines that formed the seam between his leg and pelvis arrowed temptingly into his trousers. Well aware that Burke was watching her like a cat ready to pounce - and that Fenris was probably still listening - she shrugged one shoulder and said; "Nothing special."

"Matriarch save me, if you can't even agree to *that*, there's no saving you." Burke threw up her topmost set of hands in disgust. "Honestly, one might think you protest too much."

"Save it for the suitors, Burke." Arcana rolled her eyes. "Or have you slept with every other male on the station?"

"Ugh, of course not." Burke sighed gustily. "It's lucky Phase has such stamina, or I'd be forced to argue with him far more often than I do. This one, though... I might win this one. Phase likes him."

It certainly seemed that way - the Illithai male had taken Fenris to his seat and was in the process of pouring him a drink, still twittering and clicking in his native language. Fenris listened attentively, adding a comment here and there, accepting his glass gracefully and sniffing once in appreciation before he sipped.

Arcana swallowed heavily. What if Phase lifted that jealous ban on outside lovers? What if Fenris chose to accept the offer to sate Burke's almost insatiable lust? It didn't matter, she told herself, following Burke to her own seat at the table - across from Fenris, and next to Phase. As far away from Fenris as Burke could possibly seat her. Arcana forced herself to take a deep breath, smoothing salt-white hands over an equally white table cloth in an effort to maintain her cool facade. If she dropped her mask now, she would never regain it, would lose perhaps the only advantage she had against a personality as forceful as Burke's. Focussing on the crisp linen beneath her fingertips, she forced oxygen in and out of her lungs in long, measured motions. It didn't matter if Fenris slept with

Burke. They were both adults and it was not for Arcana to dictate how they spent their time; after all, she'd agreed to help Fenris return to the Timeless Kingdom and nothing more. Taking out Taelon and rescuing the Weaver meant Caelum would finally be able to answer the questions which had plagued him since the moment of his chaotic birth. In doing so, his mother's spirit could finally be honoured and he would gain much needed closure. Arcana toyed with the hem of the table cloth and nodded to herself. Yes, that was all that mattered; solving the mysteries which bound herself and Caelum together. If that journey demanded Arcana herself witness something unpalatable - like the way Burke was fluttering her extraordinarily long eyelashes at Fenris - it was a small price to pay for Caelum's peace.

Satisfied her calm was restored, Arcana watched as Burke slid into place between Phase and Fenris, laying a casual hand on each of their wrists. The Curator flashed Arcana a smile that was pure feminine challenge but Arcana, safe behind the walls of her mercenary mask, simply rolled her eyes and lounged deliberately in her chair.

"I hope you're all hungry." Burke raised her upper set of arms and clapped once, sharply. The door swung open and Rito swaggered in, a selection of plates and dishes balanced precariously atop his swarthy arms. "Dinner is served."

As Rito began depositing covered dishes and bowls on the table, Phase jerked his chin and squeaked at Fenris. The Guardian blinked. "Arcana?"

She looked up from spooning greens onto her plate. "What?"

"Phase is asking how we met."

Arcana gave Phase the most brilliant smile her fakery could muster. "Oh, that. I found him broken and bleeding on some backwater planet, up to his eyeballs in trouble. You know the type." Fenris' jaw dropped in astonishment but Phase simply nodded. Arcana waved her fork lazily. "Once Fenris saw the value of my particular skill set, it was only a matter of time before he offered a contract."

"And what, exactly, does Arcana do for you?" Burke asked, batting her lashes slowly. One of her hands slithered up the length of Fenris' arm, caressing the ancient Sorcen characters before sliding over the curve of his shoulder and under the leading edge of the red scarf.

Fenris turned his head towards Burke, resting his chin on her outstretched wrist. He smiled to show fangs, brilliant white against the smooth teal of his face. "She protects me, of course."

"From what?" Burke tilted her head, the movement suggesting there could not possibly be anything from which Fenris couldn't protect himself.

"Forgive me, Curator, but the plight of my people - and myself - remains my business alone." Fenris gently scraped his teeth over the back of Burke's wrist and her eyes immediately glazed. "I'm sure you understand."

"Of course," Burke purred. "I meant no offence."

"None taken." Fenris tilted his head, motioning towards the table. "May I?"

"It's not necessary," Burke began.

"I insist," Fenris said, and began to swiftly serve her from the multitude of covered dishes on the table. Burke and Phase watched his movements closely, the former all but panting over her rapidly filling plate and the latter with a careful, considering smile on his face. He *was* going to say yes, Arcana realised. It was evident in his soft voice, the warmer set of his shoulders, the way he refilled Fenris' wine glass.

Arcana ate mechanically, unsure of what it was she actually consumed - she was surprised she could swallow around the choking sensation in her throat. Years of practice kept her body moving, her face calm but no amount of determination could halt the dismay twisting her heart. Caelum's nose bumped her shoulder and she paused to bury her hands in his fur, murmuring comforting nonsense whilst her heart thumped a ragged, desperate rhythm in her chest. It didn't *matter* if Fenris slept with Burke - but no matter how many times she repeated that phrase over and over in her mind, her composure was shattered and would not be repaired. Arcana closed her eyes and was immediately presented with an image of Fenris and Burke together between the sheets; she snapped her eyelids up again with a speed even the Guardian would have envied, had he been looking. Which he wasn't, because he only had eyes for Burke. Arcana dug her nails into her palms. It didn't matter. It *couldn't* matter, because she was numb inside. Dead. Empty.

"You were hungry," Rito appeared so suddenly at her elbow that Arcana jumped.

"What?" She managed.

"Your plate. You cleaned it - and you *hate* meatloaf." Rito cast a meaningful glance at the empty plate now in his hand. Arcana blinked owlishly down at it. Meatloaf? No doubt Burke had chosen it especially to goad her but Arcana had been too busy trying not to vomit to even realise. She choked on a bitter laugh, turned it into a cough. Rito grasped Arcana's shoulder, leaning over until his tattooed face filled her vision. "Too much wine? You look unwell."

Arcana's eyes strayed pointedly to her dry, clean glass and she lifted her chin, making them eye height - though she remained sitting down. "I'm the same shade of white as usual, thank you very much."

"Well then, lass, maybe you *should* have something to drink, because you look right awful," Rito snorted.

"I was lost in thought, contemplating my next step." Arcana clutched on a grain of truth, warped it, and offered it up. "As for feeling unwell - I have no need to witness *that*." She waved a hand at the couple across from them, where Fenris was now leaning over Burke to hear what she murmured in her native Illithai. How convenient that they all spoke that clicking, squeaking language and Arcana did not - so much the easier to remove her from the conversation.

Rito snorted a quiet agreement. "Nobody needs to witness that. But Burke... you know she can't help it."

Arcana raised a single brow. Was he defending Burke? "I know how it works. I've seen it before."

"I know, lass, I just mean that perhaps you should cut her some slack." Rito's nose twitched, setting his chain tinkling. "Another week or so and she should be out of it. Then it's back to business as usual."

"For another six months," Arcana offered him a lopsided grin.

Rito smiled. "It could be worse."

It was about to be, Arcana realised, for Burke and Phase stood in one smooth movement and beckoned Fenris to join them. He rose slowly, one hand splayed on the tabletop while the other tossed back the last of his wine.

"We're going to dance," Burke announced, smirking down at Arcana. "Care to join us?"

"What about dessert?" Rito protested indignantly.

The Curator shrugged, raking eyes like hot coals over the planes of Fenris' chest, as though she could see right through the scarlet scarf. "I'll have my dessert later."

The pirate slid a wounded glance towards Arcana. "What about you? I won't tell you how hard it is to source nightfruit out of season, and it's already prepared. If someone doesn't eat some, it will go to waste."

"I should stay with my hire-" Arcana began.

"He looks like he can take care of himself," Burke purred, placing the palm of one hand on Fenris' sternum. "Besides, nobody will harm him while Phase and I are with him. You have my word."

And Burke was nothing if not true to her word. Arcana's eyes slid to Fenris but that blazing gaze was focussed on Burke's grey bone frill with devastating intensity. He knew Arcana was looking, too, because he waved a dismissive hand and said; "I will go. Consider yourself dismissed for now."

Dismissed. The word rang in Arcana's head and she clenched her spoon in a white knuckled grip. It was all part of the act, an employer releasing her from duty for the night but it smarted in a way she knew wasn't normal. Arcana forced herself to wave nonchalantly in acknowledgement as Fenris followed the two Illithai out of the room, the door snicking shut behind them.

"You'll still have dessert, lass?" Rito's voice, soft and insistent at her shoulder.

Arcana grunted noncommittally, wanting nothing more than to return to her quarters and seethe. It wouldn't be wise, however, wouldn't fit her mercenary image - and instinct told her the pirate would only follow her home in case she decided to carry through with her threat to the Curator. So she turned a brittle smile to Rito and said; "I love nightfruit."

"Thank the stars for that." The pirate disappeared out the serving door, leaving Arcana alone with Caelum. She longed to speak with him but didn't dare, instead drumming her fingers on the tabletop in feigned impatience. Rito returned quickly enough that Arcana believed his story about the fruit already being prepared. He set two bowls down, one in front of her, then one at the empty place to her right.

Arcana's temper faltered as Rito settled onto the chair beside hers and began spooning pink nightfruit into his mouth with ill-concealed delight. Using the silence to regroup, she pasted a smile on her face and said; "Looks like you love nightfruit too."

"My favourite, lass." Rito nodded around cheeks full to bursting and Arcana snorted a laugh. After a long moment, the pirate frowned and said; "So you're really not sleeping with him."

Arcana's spoon clattered to the tabletop. "*Why* does everyone keep asking that?"

"Professional curiosity." Rito shrugged, turning away from her clenched jaw and heaping his spoon with more nightfruit. "That, and I probably spend too much time around Burke."

"He's paying me." Arcana enunciated each word clearly, as though speaking to an errant child. "It's a contract."

Rito cracked a grin, pink juice dribbling down his chin. "There's more'n one type of payment, lass."

"Don't start," Arcana growled. "You know how I feel about that particular sort of *payment.*"

"You must have someone real special at home, then." Rito titled his head to the side. "Most mercs aren't that fussy when it comes to scratching itches."

Arcana gave him a long, flat look, the sort of look which would have strangers bolting. Rito, however, bared all four rows of teeth in silent laughter, shovelling yet more nightfruit in on top of what was already in his mouth. Arcana sighed, reaching up to feed Caelum a piece of her own nightfruit. "You should know by now that I'm not 'most mercs'. No, I'm quite happy on my own, thank you." Rito quirked his brows suggestively and she thwacked him with the back of her spoon. "Not like that! Honestly, it's as though you people have only one thing on your mind."

"There's not a lot to do here, you know," Rito mumbled, unashamedly drinking the juice out of his bowl. "Work during the day, drink and dance and screw at night."

"And gossip over cards, no doubt." Arcana smiled in spite of herself, turning to look out the plexiglass window at the dance floor below. She couldn't see anyone familiar through the gyrating press of bodies, artificial smoke and flashing, coloured lights. Probably a good thing - dinner had been difficult enough.

"Information is currency." Rito nodded, then wiped his face on a napkin. He pushed out of the chair and clapped Arcana soundly on the shoulder. "Come on. You're off duty; I'll buy you a drink." She flicked a pointed look at the bar beside him and Rito sneered. "Toffee crap. Downstairs, that's where the real drinks are, lass. Come on."

Arcana let her eyes rove over the empty room, echoing with her summary dismissal. For all Fenris was supposed to be playing a part, the words had stung - and perhaps because of that sting, Arcana gave herself over to the fierce restlessness rising within her. She pushed back her chair and gave Rito a glittering smile. "Sure. Lead the way."

Rito swaggered off and Arcana followed after a cursory glance over her shoulder at Caelum. The deerken flickered his ears; a normal enough movement if picked up on surveillance but a clear signal to Arcana that he had her back. She felt a surge of love and Caelum's eyes softened, their swirling stars smooth with returned affection as he trailed her through a service door.

Unaware of the silent exchange, Rito led the way down a narrow flight of stairs, their boots clanging against the metal grating, and through another service door into the club. Walking into that music was like walking into a wall; a living, breathing, writhing wall. Arcana paused a moment to let her eyes adjust to the semi-dark, artificial smoke curling into her lungs, through her veins. It was hot, way too hot to be wearing both jeans and a jumper; in fact, most of the dancers barely wore anything. Even Rito, in his shorts and bandolier, appeared overdressed. Arcana peeled her jumper off, jammed it in her satchel and then looped the leather strap over Caelum's head, settling the bag against his chest. It would be safer there, where thieving hands would think twice before braving the deerken's bladed antlers.

Rito let out a low whistle. "Mother of stars, lass, do you normally kick about in that?"

"In what?" She glanced down at her black corset, overlaid with lace and set with silver accents. Her breasts swelled over the top, giving Arcana a far more generous décolletage than she would otherwise claim, and left a good two inches of abdomen exposed before the waistband of her jeans scraped across her hipbones. The corset was sleek, distracting and above all, boned and lined with a thin layer of armour - but Rito didn't need to know that. She glanced back at the pirate and raised a brow in challenge. "What's wrong with it?"

"Nothing." His gaze travelled slowly from shoulder to hip. "Nothing at all - you'll fit right in." Rito grinned and jerked his chin towards the bar. "This way."

Arcana frowned, certain she'd missed some sort of inside joke, but followed the shorter man as he skirted the room, deftly avoiding the worst of the crowd on his way to the long bar. Arcana looked up to where she knew the dining room was but as she'd expected, only a long, dark-tinted mirror gleamed back at her. Rito was already ordering when she slipped behind two grease-stained men jabbering in their own language. The men took one look at her and slunk away, forked tongues hissing between broad, flat teeth.

"Mechanics," Rito grunted from beside her elbow. "Flighty lot."

"How can you tell they're mechanics?" Arcana narrowed her eyes at the men, whose oil-slicked muscles and tattered headcloths did nothing to impart their profession.

"They have to file down their tusks so they don't get their heads stuck." Rito tapped the corner of his mouth and Arcana blinked, recalling the blunt incisors she'd mistaken for wide, stumpy teeth. The pirate grinned, his nose-chain glittering with blue and green light. "Good to see there's some things about the Run you don't know, lass. Here."

"Bleeding virgin?" Arcana raised an eyebrow at the drink he'd pressed into her hand; a combination of swirling blue and red. She nodded her thanks to the insectile creature behind the bar and received a chittered response all but drowned out by the beating heart of the music. "I haven't had one of these in years."

Rito huffed in approval. "I made a good choice then. Shall we?"

"Yeah, sure. After you." Gripping her drink in tight fingers, Arcana slithered after Rito as he continued skirting the crowd, finally coming to rest in the shade of a large potted plant. They were almost directly underneath one of the enormous speakers and the sound of the music vibrated in Arcana's sternum - the effect only increasing when Rito tugged her down to sit beside him on the thick rim of the plant pot.

"It's a wonder any greenery survives here," Arcana said, sipping her drink. The hard liquor burnt all the way down her throat. Not as potent as firewhiskey but significantly rougher, with a sweet edge that made her breath chill in her throat when she inhaled. Rito tapped one ear and then pointed up at the speaker. Wondering why he'd chosen such an unusual place, Arcana put her lips against his lobe and repeated her earlier observation.

"It's fake," the pirate laughed, his voice almost a shout. Beside them, Caelum reversed carefully down the side of the plant, almost entirely hidden from view by the leafy fronds. As Arcana made to pull away, Rito hooked his free hand in the thick chain around her neck, preventing her escape. "Two o'clock. Look."

With little other option, Arcana tilted her head and followed his instruction. Smoke clung to everything, pouring out of a machine nearby. Silhouettes ground and writhed against one another, and Arcana blinked and turned away from a couple who were doing a very different kind of dancing up against the wall. Surely that wasn't what Rito was intending her to see, pirate or otherwise. She tracked her gaze left and paused as the smoke cleared enough to reveal a very familiar profile.

Fenris moved like oil on water, his body boneless as Burke twisted him around her. Phase stalked nearby, watching more than participating, as his mate swept all four hands up the side of Fenris' hips, his torso, the topmost set winding around his neck. For all Burke's gyration was horrifically sexual, it was Fenris whom Arcana could not look away from. He slipped and slid in the other woman's grasp as though she were no more than air, his movements as sultry as they were effortless.

"Why did you want me to look at that?" Arcana barked - louder than she intended, but the music was such a cacophony that her words were snatched away.

Rito leant closer, his short, thick fingers tugging at her necklace until the curve of her breasts brushed his bicep. "Don't look *at* them, lass. Look past them. Tell me what you see."

Arcana wet her lips with a trembling tongue. She didn't want to look back, didn't want to see Burke painted all over Fenris like a cat marking territory. But it seemed Rito would not be satisfied otherwise, so she again twisted her head, squinting past the trio and into the smog beyond. Lights. Music. People dancing, swaying... stalking. There, with a pair of goggles that glowed a similar shade of pink to the flickering strobe lights above. Dancers moved around the figure as though it were invisible. The fog closed in, a thick, roiling cloud, then parted again - and the figure was gone.

"What was that?" Arcana strained against Rito's grip but the pirate was unforgiving, the muscles in his forearm tensing to prevent her movement.

"Stop it or you'll give us away," he hissed, lips moving against the shell of her ear. Arcana turned back to protest and found Rito had shifted his position on the pot so that whilst they were still technically beside each other, he was now facing her, his head bent so close that she could see little other than the tattooed join of his neck and shoulder, and the sweeping, glistening planes of his back. "Have a drink and pretend like you're into this, lass. Please."

Arcana took a hasty swig of her bleeding virgin, forcing her thoughts into neat, clean lines as the liquor burnt and cooled her throat simultaneously. When the glass was empty, she threw it into the plant pot and deliberately placed her lips against the smooth skin of Rito's cheek. "What was that?"

"There are eyes and ears everywhere." Rito shuddered, arms flexing as he dragged her against him. Arcana forced herself to go pliant, allowing the pirate to twist her until she was cradled down the length of one arm, half sitting in his lap. Rito bent over her, free hand clenching on her bicep. Warm lips brushed her forehead, the corner of one eye. "Whatever you're mixed up in - I hope it's worth it."

"Worth what?" Arcana arched into his touch, breathing the words against his jawbone. She understood now, why he'd chosen this spot underneath the speaker, why Rito pressed them together as though their skins might blend - to drown out whatever other ears might be listening in.

The pirate growled something inarticulate, hands bracing her waist, her ribs, his lips trailing a blazing path along her collarbone. Arcana gasped at the scrape of sharp teeth as Rito dragged his way up the column of her neck, rasping against her skin; "Worth this."

Worth touching her. Worth bridging the gap between his revulsion and her body. Rito had shuddered as he pulled her close, not from fear of their discovery by whatever nameless threat loomed overhead but because of Arcana. The pirate crushed her against him, his fingers tracing the top edge of her corset, brushing the flesh of her breast - and slipped something cold down her cleavage.

"What-"

"Don't," Rito growled in her ear, his whole body shaking as he nipped at Arcana's chin. "Look later. Make it count." The pirate rolled to his feet, sliding her through his arms so that she hit the floor standing.

Arcana made to pull away but Rito's hand was again bunched in the thick chain of her necklace. Her blood ran cold, magic surging. It was done, whatever message he sought to deliver now tucked safely within her corset - and she wanted to wash him off, to wash off the shame of how even a man she'd thought a friend couldn't bear to touch her. Business here - it was all business and plotting, and this was just another tool to communicate. Precisely the reason Arcana had tried to distance herself from the station in the first place. Temper sparked and she laid a warning hand over the fingers Rito had twined in her necklace. "Enough."

"Wait." Rito laid his forehead against hers for a long moment. "You need to get your hire out. He's in danger down here - you both are. Get him out. Now."

Rito pressed a kiss to the hollow of Arcana's throat and released her. Caelum stood quietly to one side but his eyes were lined with silver; whether from the club's unusual lighting or Arcana's own leaked emotion it was impossible to tell. She stared down at the diminutive pirate as he swiped his drink from inside the plant and slugged the last of it in one go. As though it would wash away the taste of her skin from his lips.

Arcana turned and disappeared into the crowd without a second glance. Whatever had just happened, she'd sort it out later. For now, she had no doubt Rito's warning was sincere, and shivered at the remembered malice in those pair of glowing goggles. Fenris. She had to find Fenris.

The crowd shoved and grunted around her, the music a living thing. For a moment Arcana despaired of ever finding the Guardian in the press of people, particularly now he had vanished from where she'd last seen him. Bodies stretched in all directions, a tangled forest of arms and legs coated in glittering sweat. Thick, clinging smoke blurred faces and softened features, the coloured lights turning skin and hide and strappy leather into a blend of blues and greens with blushing pink highlights. Arcana stumbled as dancers bumped and ground against her, oblivious to her personal space and ignorant of the physical features that usually set her apart.

Magic rose around her but Arcana only had the smoke, coating the inside of her lungs and stinging her eyes. It would cloak her but that would make it even more difficult to find Fenris among the crushing mass of creatures thronging inside the club. For the first time in half a century she was completely invisible and whilst that might have been a boon on other days, today it was infuriating. If she couldn't see Fenris, if he couldn't see *her*, how would either of them see their phantom stalker?

Arcana swirled the smoke closer to the ceiling, looking for a change in air current that might point to a hiding place or even hint at movement. Nothing. The club's air was thick, still but for the relentless pounding of the music. The nameless threat Rito had gone to such great pains to point out could be anywhere or anyone.

A dancing, grinding body jostled her for what felt like the hundredth time and Arcana cursed under her breath. If only there was a way to part the crowd, to see better - wait. Dredging around inside herself, Arcana put together a blend of emotion, a longing, a need - and did her best to feel it as strongly as possible. At first nothing happened, then the crowd began to subside, melting away like mist in the sun. She saw Caelum's nose first, then the smooth planes of his precious silver-grey face. Coloured lights refracted off his bladed antlers as though he wore a thousand tiny mirrors, his bulk such that even in the crowded club, addled with drinks and the gods knew what else, people stepped back to let him pass.

"You called?" His voice was thready in her ear.

"Thank Breogh." Arcana threw her arms around Caelum's neck, soaking up the comfort of his fur. "I wasn't sure that would work."

"It took me a minute to understand. What is it?" His ears were laid flat, eyes wide. "I don't like this place."

"Me either." She ran soothing hands over his neck and shoulder. "Something's wrong. Rito said we need to find Fenris and get out."

"You mean the two of you were actually talking?" Caelum's snort was so violent she felt it rumble through his body even over the thumping beat of the music. "Could have fooled me."

Arcana paused at that. "You knew it wasn't real, right?"

"Of course I did." Caelum lifted his head for a long moment, eyes taking on a green sheen in the glow of a strobe light. Scanning the crowd.

His chest rose and fell swiftly, discomfort evident in the tense lines of his body. "I assumed you were just trying to piss off Fenris."

The deerken began to push his way through the crowd and Arcana hurried to keep up, snagging the smooth base of an antler in her hand to tilt his head towards her. "What?! Why would - I don't care what Fenris does with his time."

Caelum stopped dead at that, the lack of movement so sudden that Arcana walked right into the side of his face. "Stop lying to yourself. You were in such a mess of anger and despair I had to shut you out almost completely - so yes, I thought Rito was a revenge plan."

Arcana's heart began racing and it had nothing to do with their impending danger. It hadn't been like that - had it? She drew breath to defend herself but didn't know where to begin, mouth working soundlessly while the heavy bass bludgeoned her senses. "Caelum-"

"Forget it. You need to have it out with Fenris, not me. Now come on." Caelum pulled his lips back in a wordless snarl and turned away. Arcana wound her fingers in the fur of his neck and followed, trusting his superior height and weight to lead them in the right direction. Nothing else mattered right now, as long as they found Fenris and got back to the safety of their suite. Caelum's head shook back and forth as though he knew and disapproved of her train of thought but Arcana had no time to dwell on it, because the crowd parted and she spotted Phase. And where Phase was...

Fenris turned as she approached, as though even with the thump and the roar of the music, he could hear her. Burke slithered along one side of him, eyes half slitted, and Arcana assessed anew that gleam in her friend's eye. Heat fever, yes, but also something else. Which she might have noticed earlier, if she'd not been so caught up in the idea of Fenris and Burke tangled together between the sheets. Arcana chewed her lip. Maybe Caelum *was* right - and what sort of person did that make her?

"So, you decided to join us after all." Fenris' expression was purposefully blank as he swept a gaze from her hair to her boots and back again. Where his face was a carefully crafted instrument, honed and hardened through years at court, his eyes were not. Arcana swore there was more heat in that one look than in the entirety of her encounter with Rito. But if Fenris felt that same flicker of fire, he didn't let on, simply allowed a lazy smirk to curl his lips.

Arcana swept right up to him and wrapped both hands in his scarf – a mercenary angry her hire had escaped. As she dragged him down, rising on tiptoe to do it, magic sang in her veins and the artificial smoke swirled in close, blocking the rest of the club from view. Had those goggles just been for the dark, or could they pierce this cloying fog, too? Better to take no chances.

"Time's up," Arcana growled, so close to that she could feel his warmth soaking into her. "Let's go."

Fenris didn't move.

Arcana flicked a look at Burke, barely visible through the haze, but the Illithai's gaze was fixed firmly on Fenris, as it had been all night. It wasn't desire that clogged her face now, but something else - something which had paled her grey skin until it was almost blanched white. Arcana drew back from Fenris to ask him what the matter was when his fingers wrapped her biceps in a bruising grip. She barely had time to register the odd look on his face before he crushed his nose against her neck and inhaled. Right where Rito's teeth had been.

The growl that came out of him was unlike anything Arcana had heard, and it was certainly not the noise a wealthy merchant prince made when ordered to leave the party by his bodyguard. *Where is he?*

"Stop it," Arcana gasped. Death stalked in Fenris' words, a vicious, painful death by rending hands and gnashing teeth. "Let me go." She flattened her palms against Fenris' chest, thickening the smoke around them. He didn't move, didn't answer except to tighten his grip on her arms, his heart thundering against Arcana's hand. Panic flared as he dragged her closer, that growl still reverberating beneath her palms - And then Burke was there, sliding her hands over Fenris' body, neatly separating them as she coaxed him up and away.

"For later," Burke winked and drew out the chain which had been partly concealed in her wrappings. A key dangled from it in place of a pendant. The Curator fastened it around Fenris' neck and stepped into the circle of his still-rigid arms, pressing a kiss to one cheek. He stared down at the key for a long moment, as though he could no longer remember the part he was supposed to play. Then Fenris slid the chain around his neck and dropped the key behind the safety of his red scarf, bending to Burke's ear. She grinned in response to whatever the Guardian said, long lashes dipping, then released him to step away.

Arcana tugged insistently on the end of that red scarf and this time, swaggering and indolent, Fenris followed. Caelum pushed up close and Arcana kept the smoke cloud thick around them as she threaded her way across the floor and shouldered the service door open, ushering first Caelum and then Fenris through. She cast her eyes over the dance floor one last time and could have sworn she saw the flash of pink goggles up in the rafters, but when she looked twice, it was gone. Arcana swallowed heavily and dragged the door shut behind her, sealing them off from the club.

Fenris had his mouth open, lips peeled back as he stared down at her, but Arcana shushed him with an angry prod to the chest. "You hired me to watch your lazy ass, you sure as hell better follow the rules I set. Otherwise I'm calling this off."

"It was just a dance," he purred, straightening. "I wish I could say the same for you."

"If I were you, I'd keep stones in my pockets whilst inside a glass house." Arcana shoved past Caelum and clattered up the narrow stairs, coughing the last of the smoke from her lungs. She dragged one hand down the wall of the corridor, letting her magic settle back into the bones of the space station as they hurried down the hall to the elevator's gilded cage. It slid smoothly open at her touch and Caelum head-butted Fenris inside. The journey back to their room was swift and silent, with Fenris making a show of yawning widely and Arcana casting furtive glances behind them with almost every step. When at last the door to their suite snicked shut behind them, the blinking light turning from green to red, Arcana breathed a sigh of relief.

"What was all that about?" Caelum wasted no time in rubbing his cheek against hers. "You look like you've seen a ghost."

"Not a ghost. It was - I don't know, but I sure as hell intend to find out." Arcana shivered, the memory of those pink goggles raising the hairs on her arms. "We need the datapad."

"I'll get it." Caelum touched his nose to hers and disappeared into the bedroom. Rather than look at Fenris, Arcana strode to the sitting room's window. Less impressive a view than the one from the dining room, but still better than the Guardian's face, or the odd tornado of emotion which clawed at her chest from inside.

"What happened to you?" Fenris, it seemed, did not share her aversion to talk. He appeared by her side, so close that a deep inhalation would brush their arms against each other.

"Nothing," Arcana returned.

"You have *teeth marks* on your neck." His voice echoed a growl and Fenris paused, hands clenching into fists as he sought the same calm Arcana had spent her entire evening seeking. "I can smell him all over you."

Arcana blinked at the memories his comment invited, one hand pressing against the odd, empty feeling in her stomach. Her skin felt oily where Rito had touched it, as though some lingering essence had sunk into her flesh without her permission. But Fenris - he'd spent the better part of the evening all but drooling over Burke, and he thought to question *her*?

"Not that it's any of your business," Arcana said loftily, "But I'm fine."

"Fine? You come back here looking like that and try to tell me you're *fine*?" Fenris snarled. "I can smell your lies."

"Well, good for you. Has it occurred to you that maybe I don't want to talk about it?" Arcana hissed, flattening her palms against the window. The essence of the space station sang in her blood, steel and glass and grease coiling inside her veins.

"A fairly hypocritical position, considering your recent speech on the value of honesty and the uselessness of secrets." Fenris' voice was so tart that Arcana startled, blinking twice as she replayed his words over in her head.

"You want honesty?" She swung around so quickly the rug beneath her feet puckered beneath one booted heel. "I'm trying to get us in and out of this place as smoothly as possible, and all you're thinking about is getting your end wet. Do you have any idea how long we'll be stuck here if Burke gets her claws in you?"

Fenris was silent, mouthing 'getting your end wet' back to himself as though to be certain it meant what he thought it did. His lips thinned. "You set me a role; I merely endeavoured to play it. No self-possessed male would be foolish enough to ignore an Illithai female in the grip of heat fever."

"She's mated," Arcana growled.

"Meaning he only has to approve potential partners before things go ahead, and is likely to join in himself," Fenris returned. "Don't think to lecture me on the Illithai - I know their culture."

"Ah, yes, I forgot you were basically Illithai royalty." Arcana spat the words, miming a crown atop her head. "You want to go down that track? Fine, let's go there - I thought you didn't like the company of men. Sleeping with Burke might get you more than you bargained for where Phase is concerned."

Fenris braced both hands on his hips. "I don't bed males, that is correct, but if Phase was serious about allowing Burke to enjoy my company, then he'd find a way to work around that. I might point also out that *you* were the one who told me it would be offensive to turn her advances down."

"Oh, no. Don't you *dare* blame Burke on me." Arcana crossed her arms over her chest. "You're an adult. You can make your own decisions."

Fenris leant closer, his breath hot against her face. "That I can."

"Good." Arcana lifted her chin. "Screw her senseless for all I care."

Silence. Then, soft and deadly; "Perhaps I will."

No. Magic screamed along Arcana's bones, the torrent so thick and heavy she thought she might come apart. The windows - the entire room - creaked and shuddered, the window sill beside her popping a rivet which Fenris snatched out of thin air without so much as a glance. He was staring at Arcana, breathing uneven and burning eyes wild. "So *that's* what this is about. You don't want me to sleep with her."

"I don't care who you sleep with." The room flexed again and Fenris' eyes flicked outward, following the very real ripple of movement.

"I beg to differ," was all he said. Softly, quietly, as though trying to talk her down - but Arcana could hear the steely edge in his voice and knew he was as furious as she. Fenris threw the rivet to the floor, where it embedded point down in the carpet, and said; "Rito wants you. Did you know that?"

"What?" Arcana's magic arrested and she stumbled back a step in shock. "No. It wasn't like that."

"I could smell it all over him, even before we went down to the club. His story about debts was a lie." Fenris rolled his shoulders, the artificial light glimmering down the gold trim on his scarf. "I'm willing to bet the greatsword that he came back for you."

Arcana's tongue didn't fit in her mouth, but she managed: "Don't be ridiculous. I've known Rito for years and-"

"And he's likely loved you for most of them," Fenris continued ruthlessly. "It's easy to see why. Strong, sassy, beautiful..."

"Stop it. Don't say that."

"Beautiful?" He purred, each syllable coating his tongue like warm honey. "Why do you think Burke has been after you to undertake all those missions, all these years? Hair like a raven's feathers, eyes like onyx, skin like starlight - and those curves - well, surely you own a mirror."

Mocking her. He was mocking her with her *own words.* Arcana's shriek came from someone else; it had to, for she'd never heard such a tortured sound from her own lips, and surely didn't possess the facility to utter it. Fenris' kohl-smudged eyes widened ever so slightly as she threw herself at him, as the floor magically tilted away beneath his feet to throw him off balance. Arcana's slap echoed through the room, pistol-sharp, and she raised both hands to shove him in the chest as hard as she could. Fenris took the blow without so much as a flutter of lashes, teal arms snaking around her waist as he fell - crashing through the coffee table and dragging them both to the floor.

"Fuck you," she sobbed, raising a hand to slap him again. Fenris moved like lightning, fingers curling around her wrist before she'd completed her next breath. The other hand splayed across her spine, pinning her in place against the hard length of his body - hot as a brand and solid as oak. Immovable.

Unlike those wretched lips, which were still talking, still as calm and even as when he had started. "Would you like to?"

"What?"

Fenris' eyes tracked her face, his fingers trembling where they ringed her wrist. "You heard me."

Arcana's magic died; whistling right out and leaving her feeling hollow. "I don't - I don't do -"

Now his lips curled into a smoky, sultry smile. "You don't know how?"

The rage sputtered out next, drowned by a sudden and overwhelming tide of embarrassment. Arcana lowered her forehead onto Fenris' chest and muttered; "You've read the book. You already know the answer to that."

"I'm not interested in the damned book." He released her hand - probably scenting that the violence within her had died - and curled his fingers in her hair. "I'm interested in you."

Safe in the folds of his scarf - *her* scarf, dammit - Arcana fell very, very still. Where she had expected their argument to go, she wasn't sure; but this certainly wasn't it. In the end it was confusion that dragged honesty from her: "I'm not like Flare."

"I know." Something like bitter amusement coloured Fenris' tone. "He said the same thing himself. I still don't see, one way or another, how such a fact is relevant. If I wanted Flare, I'd have accepted his offer back on Sorcen."

Arcana drew a deep breath and let the truth out, cutting though it was. "I've had my fair share of controlling, conniving, bullying relationships and am in no mood to make that mistake again."

Strong arms tensed around her waist and when Fenris spoke again, his voice was flat and cold. "Do *not* presume to lump me in the same category as Algae."

"Oh?" Arcana gritted her teeth against the fabric beneath her, steadfastly refusing to look at him. "Because you were so excellent at listening to me when I was panicked on the dance floor earlier - not because of Algae, but because of *you*."

"That was different," Fenris hissed - but his arms loosened, just a fraction. "You don't understand at all, do you?"

"Not in the slightest." Arcana loosed a sharp, bitter laugh. "Just forget it. I've got enough baggage to weigh down this entire space station and whatever's left over doesn't have the capacity to care. You'd be better off screwing Burke."

"I have no interest in Burke in any capacity, least of all in screwing her," Fenris snapped.

Arcana blinked at the simple honesty in his words. Memories sliced through her bitterness: Fenris' feral expression when he'd scented Rito on her body, how he'd struggled to maintain his composure in the centre of the dance floor, even after Burke had been all but licking his face for most of the night. And slowly, so slowly, she raised her head. "You don't?"

Fenris shook his head ever so slightly, and though the corner of his lip curled, his face was intent. "No more than you want to sleep with that useless pirate."

"But-"

"I gave her what she expected," he said. "No more, no less. I said it before, and I meant it; you gave me a role to play. I am playing it, regardless of the fact that 'arrogant and sexy' is so far beyond the realms of my reality that I needed a stiff drink to try and make it work. You, however..." Fenris drew in a long, deep breath. "Why did you do it?"

"I didn't *do* anything," Arcana growled. Fenris' eyes simply slid down her face to her neck, where they rested with bone-crushing intensity.

"Where I come from, that's a claim. And a challenge," he added.

Arcana raised trembling fingers to the soft graze down the side of her throat. "Don't be a fool. It was a ruse - he could barely stand to touch me."

"If you believe that, you truly are an idiot." The least cultured words Arcana had yet heard out of his mouth. Fenris' eyes narrowed as he searched her face. "You really have not realised how that tiny, tattooed vagabond covets you?"

"That's got to be the most ridiculous thing I've ever heard. He was shaking with disgust," Arcana growled.

"Are you so sure?" A single eyebrow winged skyward. "Is it so impossible to believe he might tremble at an opportunity to get close to you? That, distasteful as it is, his baser instincts might get the better of him when an opportunity presents itself to claim you?"

"I'm not some prize to be stolen and kept," Arcana managed. She should have been furious but the implication of Rito's ulterior motives were too enormous. Her mind turned back to the words Fenris had spat earlier. *He's likely loved you for most of them.* Arcana's stomach clenched, horror creeping through her veins. "That can't be right."

"No? I think at this point you're only lying to yourself." The words were sharp but his voice had gentled, as though Fenris knew - perhaps more so than she - what a betrayal the claim had been.

Arcana's fingers drifted once more to her neck, to the grazed flesh there. "How could he?"

"It's in his nature to take. Some of the more predatory races are like that; claim first, talk later." Unspoken was the understanding that Fenris had grown up amongst just such a race. "It is a thieving of choice, of will, which I will not allow."

"Don't say that." She shook her head. "It's not your place to make that call - I'm perfectly capable of knocking Rito's teeth out myself."

"I know that," Fenris agreed, his hands sliding up to her waist, his fingers hot and firm across the bare flesh of her lower back. "But I also know the painful past from which you come, and can guess how deeply such a wound might cut. Is it so terrible to think I might be enraged on your behalf?"

Long fingers began to move, a soothing massage across the base of her spine. Arcana gasped at the heat in Fenris' touch and opened her mouth to squash him back into place - but it was too late. They were beyond that now, beyond the ability to pretend there was nothing but professional courtesy between them. And his hands felt so *damned good*. With that thought like iced water over her soul, Arcana said; "You can be enraged on my behalf. But I'm still knocking Rito's teeth out myself."

"All right." Fenris' fingers curled around the bottom edge of her corset, his knuckles smooth and solid against her skin. He muttered something under his breath, a rolling, elegant language Arcana guessed was some sort of fey dialect.

"Are you swearing?"

"No. I just-" he broke off and blinked. "Why is there a data chip in your cleavage?"

"Oh!" Arcana followed Fenris' gaze downwards, where the shimmering swell of her bosom was sandwiched rather indecently against his chest, the glint of the data chip clearly visible between her breasts. Arcana cleared her throat. "*That* is what Rito went to such lengths to give me." She ignored his snort, raising her head to glare down her nose. "Never mind that now - what are you doing looking in my cleavage?"

"I caught the shine of the chip in the light." Fenris dragged his eyes up to her face, his breathing ragged. "I'm sorry if you misconstrued my behaviour in the club as threatening. I..." He trailed off and shook his head, hands dropping from her body to thump against the floor. "I'm at a loss, Arcana. I cannot think, cannot focus. Tell me what you need. Please."

Arcana scrambled off him, coming to her feet so quickly she staggered. Her thoughts turned back over the last few minutes, tinted with panic at what now loomed between them. She watched Fenris from beneath her lashes as he slowly pushed upright, smashed wood and shattered glass cascading off his body in a glittering rain. He'd been just as angry - if not more - than she had, and in the process had offered up something of himself. A sacrifice to gain clarity, edging them both towards a reality Arcana wasn't certain she'd ever be ready for.

She licked lips that were suddenly dry and for all Fenris appeared nonchalant, his entire attention locked onto that one small movement. Arcana's voice was hoarse as she said; "I don't know. Some elemental part of me is broken and I don't think it can be fixed."

Fenris' nostrils flared, a delicate movement that she may have missed if not for the time they'd spent together already. "There is an old Terran saying; 'We are all broken. That's how the light gets in.'"

"Earth and her Terrans were destroyed thousands of years ago."

"And yet, hope lives on," he said gently. "The planet may have died but the people resettled. They found a measure of peace in a new place."

"You can't be serious," Arcana muttered. Fenris shrugged, calmly untangling a piece of glass from his – her – scarf. She swallowed. "You'd be better off looking elsewhere."

"No."

Simple, calm. Final.

"Why?" It was little more than a breath.

"*Why?*" The ghost of a smile. Fenris blurred, and before Arcana could blink he was in front of her, crowding her space. "Tell me you don't feel it. Look me in the eye and tell me you don't feel it."

His glamour already rose around them, thick and heady as a rose-kissed breeze. Arcana wanted to wrap it around herself at exactly the same moment she wanted to punch Fenris on the nose. "I can't."

"That's why." Another dangerous truth, the words like shards of glass between them. Arcana wondered how many more she could swallow before they sliced her apart.

CHAPTER
THREE

"Is it over?" Caelum's head poked out of the bedroom, ears laid flat against his skull. "I've got the datapad."

Arcana blinked, swallowed around the razorblades in her throat. "Datapad?"

"Yes, that thing you asked me to go and get right before you started smashing things, remember?" Caelum wrinkled his nose in distaste.

"I..." Arcana shook herself, grasped her frayed thoughts. "It took you long enough."

"There is no way in this life that I'm sticking my nose between the two of you in moods like *that*," Caelum tossed his head. "I might be bound to stay within thirty paces, but there *is* such a thing as privacy and self-respect, you know."

"Arcana and I are still in the middle of our discussion," Fenris said smoothly, crossing both arms over his chest.

Caelum's brows climbed as he took in the smashed coffee table, Arcana's flushed face and Fenris' debris-littered clothing. "Remind me never to discuss anything too serious with you."

Fenris gave the deerken a scathing look and opened his mouth, no doubt to send Caelum away. Arcana was faster. "It's fine. We have more important things happening right now." She reached into the top of her corset, carefully ignoring Fenris as she dug between her breasts and yanked out the data chip. "Here."

"Hah! Give me a second." Caelum twisted out of sight, then reappeared with a slim datapad clenched between his teeth.

"Excellent." Arcana stepped away from the wrecked coffee table, accepting the datapad and inserting the chip into the base. The portable unit flickered to life, displaying several scrolling bars of numbers as it analysed the chip. A small rectangle appeared on the screen, with space for four characters and a single, blinking demand: PASSCODE.

Caelum grunted. "Now what?"

Fenris drifted closer, maintaining a respectful distance as he peered over Arcana's shoulder. "Surely Burke wouldn't have gone to such trouble to deliver that and not provide you with the key."

"The key!" Arcana snapped her fingers and turned to Fenris. "May I?"

He drew the chain over his head and offered it. "Of course."

Arcana turned the key over in her fingers. The head was flat and faintly hexagonal shaped, extending into a long, cylindrical barrel. Digital receptors had been laid over the top of the smooth silver, adapting the traditional style to a very different type of lock - but it was still, no matter how she looked, intended for a door rather than a datapad.

"Wait," Fenris leant closer, grabbing her wrist when she made to put the key aside. "Look at the barrel." Arcana squinted and shook her head; his eyes were far sharper. After a moment's hesitation, Fenris took the key from her with gentle fingers and peeled off one of the digital receptors. "This one isn't real."

Indeed, it was little more than a foiled sticker. And beneath, crudely etched, a string of four numbers. Arcana snorted and shook her head.

"What?" Caelum asked.

"It's Flare's birthday." Arcana turned back to the datapad and swiftly entered 2011 into the blinking box. "Only Burke would find that amusing."

"Using a birthday as a password is a terrible idea." Fenris shook his head as the datapad blinked and bleeped, accessing the depths of the chip.

"Considering only Burke, Phase and I know she's slept with Flare, it's not as terrible as it sounds. Nobody would ever guess." Arcana frowned as the datapad displayed a blueprint of Corrin's Run.

"I'll admit I was shocked when Burke mentioned it back in the elevator," Fenris returned, then huffed a laugh. "Although knowing Flare, even briefly, I am not entirely sure why I was surprised."

"He's got a talent for getting what he wants, and he charmed Burke twice," Arcana said absently, tapping the screen to zoom in on a room that had been highlighted in yellow. "What is that? Caelum?"

"Looks like one of the storage rooms." Caelum leant over, his massive head partially obscuring Arcana's view. "A little behind and below us."

"And I'll wager that's the key to the door." Arcana flicked the key in question, watching it shimmer in the light as it swung back and forth on the chain. "But why the elaborate deception?"

"There is clearly something Burke wishes you to see, something she felt unable to discuss in public," Fenris said, looping the chain back around his neck and slipping the key safely into his - her? Arcana gritted her teeth - *their* scarf.

"In the club, Rito said there was danger," she allowed. Fenris stiffened at mention of the pirate but said nothing, so Arcana explained about the shadowy figure in goggles that she'd glimpsed through the smoke. As she finished, she looked up at Caelum. "And you did say their signals were easy to jam."

"As though Burke wanted us to do it," Caelum repeated his earlier words, now tinted with astonishment. "She *did* want us to do it - so we could discuss this in relative safety. Not from Burke, but from... whatever else is going on here."

Arcana chewed on the inside of her cheek. "We're stuck here for at least another twenty-four hours until the ship is restocked. I say we go and check it out."

"When?" Fenris stretched and winced.

"Now - unless you're looking for an early bedtime?" Arcana raised an eyebrow.

The Guardian's face went carefully blank. "Now is fine."

"Wait," Caelum's nose twitched. "I smell blood."

Fenris looked immediately guilty, so much so it was almost impossible to equate his earlier acting with the same man who now stood in the sitting room. Arcana fisted a hand on her hip. "What have you done?"

"He's bleeding," Caelum announced, having circled soundlessly around behind the Guardian. "Did you smash that furniture with your *back*?"

"Smash the... turn around," Arcana ordered, shoving at Fenris until he obliged. The smooth, teal planes of his back shifted with subtle musculature, the edge of the scarlet scarf rucked up almost around his neck - from the fall into the coffee table, Arcana supposed. The greatsword had taken most of the impact but she gasped to see several long cuts along the lower edge of one shoulder blade, complete with embedded shards of wood and glass. Arcana swallowed. "Fenris, I... I'm sorry."

"I am as much to blame." The Guardian shrugged, then hissed as the movement tugged at his wounds. "It is nice to see your temper."

"Aaaaand that's my cue to get the medical kit," Caelum declared, slipping through the door to the bathing room.

Arcana pressed her lips into a thin line, glaring at the broad, sweeping lines of Fenris' back. She knew he'd laid a carefully baited trap and felt her aforementioned temper spiking as she walked right into it. "I don't see what my temper has to do with anything - and I certainly wouldn't call it 'nice.'"

"Anger is emotion, which in turn is better than that cold emptiness Flare's so terrified of," Fenris answered. Caelum returned with the medical kit and swapped it for the datapad, retreating onto a long, low divan to examine the station blueprint in greater detail.

"I can smile or laugh just like anyone else," Arcana snapped, hoping the smell of Fenris' blood masked the scent of her lie. She flipped open the kit's lid and pulled out a pair of tweezers. "In fact, with the exception of a certain Guardian's influence, I'm fairly even tempered for the most part."

Fenris grunted as she set to work removing the splinters of wood and glass, twitching until she wrapped her free hand around the curve of a rib. The moment her fingers laid across his skin, he went suddenly and totally still, as though afraid of spooking a wild animal - though he growled and muttered with each sliver Arcana prised free of his flesh. "Even tempered is fine," he panted eventually. "Actual temper is better."

"Actual temper is better?" Arcana repeated, dropping the tweezers and rummaging for a disinfectant. She found some foil-wrapped wipes, tore one open and began gently cleaning his wounds. "Why in the name of Sorcen's seven gods would you *want* me to be angry at you?"

"Sorcen has seven gods?"

She frowned at his long, sweeping spine. "Yes. One for each school of magic, one above and one below. And you're avoiding the question."

"Anger means you feel something. Anything is better than nothing," Fenris said. She prodded him in the side and he jumped. "I am not trying to be obtuse. If you are angry with me, it shows…"

"Shows what?"

"Tell me about the Gods."

Arcana sighed at the firm dissuasion in his tone. She should be thankful he was trying to steer her away from such dangerous ground, but it only irritated her further to wonder what he'd been about to say. "Not much to tell. Like I said, one for each school of magic: Firius for Fire,

Zephys for Healing, Gronus for Earth, Florys for Nature and Oceaus for Water."

"Fairly straightforward," Fenris shifted slightly as she dropped the now bloody wipe and popped open a jar of salve. "And... above and below?"

"Craddagh, the Unmaker, lies below. When we die, she breaks down our souls and feeds the pure parts up to Breogh, the Maker, to forge into new souls. The undesirable parts are thrown into Craddagh's cauldron and boiled into nothing. Forgotten." Arcana smeared salve on the cuts, which were shallow and should heal swiftly. Fenris hissed again. "Sorry."

"It's fine. I... ticklish," he managed, his voice oddly strangled. "So Breogh and Craddagh... light and dark?"

"Essentially. They provide balance, twined together in an endless cycle of death and rebirth, embracing and renewing the other five gods - and all magic - with their wisdom. When you fall out of balance and lose the path, either Breogh guides you home, or Craddagh comes to collect you for the cauldron." Arcana frowned, tilting her head to one side. "Or so the story goes."

"That is why Pytch said he hoped Algae disappeared into the depths of Craddagh's cauldron. To be unmade and forgotten."

"Yes." Arcana hesitated, re-sealing the jar on the salve and setting it back into the kit. "Why the sudden interest in a history lesson?"

Fenris turned to face her and for a long moment, Arcana thought he might not answer. He searched her face, skittering away from actual eye contact to examine the dips and swirls of her complexion. "In one of the books Flare gave me," he said at last, "A scholar theorised that you had been unmade by Craddagh and remade by Breogh, gifted back unto Sorcen as something Other."

"Superstitious nonsense," Arcana muttered.

Fenris shrugged as though he hadn't quite decided. "The text said there was something of Breogh's soft starlight in your skin." He trailed a trembling finger down her cheek and Arcana bit her tongue to keep from startling away. "And something of Craddagh's compassionate shadows hidden in the depths of your eyes. The daughter of Sorcen's penultimate Goddesses, a creature of perfect balance and depthless magic."

"There have been plenty of theories on what happened that day, all extrapolated from my account of the experience and embellished by fusty, blustering scholars with nothing better to do than dream." Arcana's voice was breathless as Fenris took her chin in gentle, hesitant fingers, at last tipping her head back to make eye contact. It was as though a very real spark passed between them, the glamour a sweeping tide rather than a soft cloak. "What are you doing?"

"Looking," Fenris replied, searching her depthless eyes with his own blazing ones. "You said before many see undeath. A revenant."

"What do you see?" Dangerous. A stupid, useless question.

"Everything," he breathed.

Arcana thought her heart might stop at the exact same time she made a mental note to thump Flare until he bleated the next time they met. *Why* would he give Fenris those foolish, nonsense books? Some filled with religious zeal and others no better than a cheap town crier's tabloid! She gathered her scattered wits and said; "What in the name of boiling water does *that* mean?"

Fenris blinked and dropped her chin, backing up a step. He ran one hand through his hair and began muttering under his breath in that same, lilting fey language she'd heard before - and this time, he was clearly telling himself off.

She let him.

"Any idea on the best route?" Arcana crossed to Caelum, gladly turning her back on the Guardian. The deerken looked up from the datapad between his knees and swept her with a too-knowing glance, prompting Arcana to lean so close the fur of his ear tickled her upper lip. "Unless you want to become a floor rug, I'd answer the question, rather than say whatever else is on your mind."

"I've studied the blueprints at length," Caelum replied, flicking his ear so that it swatted her nose. "I think we can be there in just a few minutes. Whenever you're ready, of course."

"I'm ready," Arcana told him, bracing both hands on her hips and tapping one foot.

Caelum unfolded his long legs from the couch and appraised her appearance. "With all that weaponry on display?"

"What?" Arcana stared down at her breasts, heaving upwards beneath the merciless push of the corset. In all the struggle, they'd managed to wriggle considerably closer to freedom. Blushing, she turned away and did her best to shove them back where they belonged, wondering all the while how women with legitimately large assets managed it. "I wore it because it's armoured."

"I know," Caelum replied, and she didn't need to turn to know his mouth hung open in laughter.

"It's armoured?" Fenris sounded genuinely surprised and before Arcana realised what he was up to, he produced a knife from somewhere about his person and poked her between the ribs. The point of the blade clinked gently and refused to pass through. "Clever."

Arcana snatched the knife, channelled the steel and glass soul of the space station, and tied the blade in a knot. "What were you thinking? You could have skewered me!"

"Not without your permission," he said, his face carefully innocent. Arcana dropped the knife and snarled but Fenris' grin widened into the rogue's expression she'd become quite fond of - not that she was willing to admit it out loud.

Arcana strode to the door and palmed it open. "We're wasting time. Let's go."

"Satchel?" Caelum glanced down at the leather bag still bumping against his chest.

"You look after it. It's safer there for now." Arcana slid out into the empty hallway, Fenris hard on her heels. His hands twitched as though he wished to draw the greatsword but he tucked them through his belt instead, affecting the indolent arrogance of a merchant prince.

A chill raised across Arcana's skin and she glanced up at the air ducts, barely visible beneath the various struts and crossbars that made up the framework of the roof. Fenris followed her gaze, his body a beacon of warmth beside hers. "What is it?"

"I don't know. It... does it seem colder to you?" Arcana waited for him to snort, or make a snide remark about her lack of clothing - but Fenris simply flexed at the knees and leapt straight upwards, disappearing into the tangle of rods and wires overhead without so much as a backward glance. Arcana blinked in surprise at such a casual display of his preternatural speed and strength, staring for a moment at the place where Fenris had disappeared. When no sign nor sound drifted down, she made her way down the hall to where Caelum waited by the elevator shaft.

Fenris dropped from the ceiling to land a hair's breadth in front of her, close enough - and silent enough - that Arcana instinctively flattened her hands against his chest lest she cannon headlong into his body. Her heart thumped in her throat and their eyes met for a wild, blazing instant before Arcana snatched her hands away and muttered; "Sorry. What did you find?"

"Nothing," the Guardian shook his head. "But I feel you are right. Does Burke usually lower the temperature at sight?"

"No. The station is old and too claptrap - changing the temperature at will isn't easy." Arcana glanced back upwards. "It's probably nothing."

"Perhaps. As long as there are no changes in the atmospheric pressure, we should be fine." Fenris leant over and prodded the elevator controls. "Down?"

"Down," Caelum agreed quietly, gliding inside the gilded cage. "Two floors underneath us."

Arcana backed into the elevator, curling her fingers in Caelum's fur as Fenris selected the appropriate floor. Her eyes flickered incessantly around the travel car's interior, partly avoiding Fenris and partly searching for a shadowy figure in pink goggles who never appeared. The temperature rose as they descended, each cloaked in the silence of their own thoughts. By the time the gilded doors opened into a service corridor, the air was stiflingly humid and Arcana was covered in a sticky layer of sweat.

"The temperature normalisation is definitely not working." Caelum moved ahead of them into the corridor, his fur shortening until it was barely an inch long. The summer coat made the black ruff down his spine jut out like a ridge and emphasised the mottled markings on his hindquarters. Impossibly long legs swept down to cloven hooves that were almost comically narrow, each so small they seemed little more than tapered points - certainly not large or firm enough to support the body above, which appeared gargantuan in comparison.

Fenris stood very still, watching the deerken's graceful progress along the corridor. "I feel I shall never grow tired of watching you float."

"I'm flattered," Caelum snorted, shaking his head. His antler rack was so large and widespread it seemed disproportionate to the rest of his body, for all the breadth of his chest would put most other creatures to shame. "Would you like me to do a quick spin for your entertainment?" When Fenris didn't answer, Caelum looked over his shoulder, the corridor's dim lighting making his bladed antlers appear to glow with their own light. "Now Arcana's staring, too. What? Something on my face?"

Arcana shook her head. "It's the fur. I don't normally see so much of you."

"Yeah, well, I feel as naked as I look," Caelum shook his great head, waspish tone a sharp contrast to the elegant lines of his body. "Now come on. I've got the creeps down here."

"It is particularly atmospheric," Fenris agreed, loosening the scarf with one hand. "And hot."

"You can say that again." Arcana followed Caelum down the hall, booted feet clanking on the metal walkway. This section of the station was dented and warped, a stark reminder of how primitive Corrin's Run had been when it was first lashed and bolted together out of broken ships and salvaged parts. Steam curled beneath the grating and Arcana squinted at several dark, half-faded stains clinging to the plasteel. Oil, most likely.

"Here it is," Caelum stopped so abruptly that Arcana almost walked into his hindquarters. "Storage unit 416b."

The door - one of many mismatched portals along the hall - had been wrenched from the exterior of a battleship. Heavily armoured plating still bore the scorch marks of a laser battery, right beside the half-flaked paint job of whomever the ship had once belonged to. Arcana laid a palm against the solid plating and frowned. "Shut tight; if I wanted this open without the key I'd have to work very, very hard."

"Lucky we have the key, then." Fenris drew the chain over his head and approached the sleek black lock set into the wall. Two lights, one red and one green, perched like eyes above a small, round recess no thicker than a pen. The Guardian slid the key home and Arcana held her breath as the hexagonal head clunked against the outer casing. If they were wrong… but no. The green light blinked and the armoured door irised open with a gentle hiss.

Darkness greeted them and Arcana scented blood and death so thick and cloying that her eyes watered and she put a hand over her mouth. Whatever - whoever - was inside the storage unit had been there for a while. Arcana swallowed bile and managed; "We need a light."

"Leave that to me." Fenris drew the greatsword and strode into the inky black. Arcana stared after him for a long moment before she recalled he could see in the dark - and then he must have palmed the controls, for the chamber was suddenly flooded with too-bright, artificial lighting.

"Great gods of Sorcen," Arcana breathed. She forgot the smell, forgot the heat - even more oppressive inside the chamber - and ushered Caelum through the portal, tugging the key out of the lock as she went. "What happened here?"

Blood splattered the walls and would have pooled on the floor, but for the fact that it had sunk through the grating to drip into the sub-flooring beneath. Great claw marks rent one wall, accompanied by several round punctures that Arcana recognised as coming from Burke's high powered crossbow - or one very like it.

Caelum laid his ears flat to his skull. "Something very, very bad happened here, that's what."

Arcana crossed to the punctures, ignoring the way the blood-coated floor sucked at her feet. The crossbow bolts had been removed, giving her an excellent view of the depth of the holes they had created. "These were shot at close range."

"For good reason." Fenris stood before a tall cupboard, face grim. "Brace yourselves." He swung the cupboard wide, the artificial lighting casting a pale blue haze over the contents. Two - three bodies, piled on top of each other in a tangled mess of bloodied limbs. Arcana saw humanoid frames covered in dark skin and even darker fur. Long, powerful legs, still clothed in stained pants and shorts. Muscular arms that could have been human but for the fur, and the hands ending in claws. Heads warped by canine muzzles, sharp teeth and pointed, lupine ears.

"Warg," Arcana whispered. Staked into the forehead of the topmost corpse was a long, thick crossbow bolt with Burke's striping along the shaft.

Fenris curled his fingers around the bolt and yanked, freeing it with a squelch that turned Arcana's stomach. "There is something else here," he said, offering the bloodied trophy.

"Another key?" Arcana crinkled her nose at the smaller, more traditional scrap of metal which had been taped to the shaft of the crossbow bolt. "This is getting ridiculous."

"Considering the state of the room, I wouldn't want to leave any messages or clues just lying around. There's a lockbox over here." Caelum drifted to the opposite corner, where a small box sat atop a wooden crate. Both crate and box were clean, with enough scuff marks on the floor that Arcana knew they'd been hauled in after the battle.

"Lockbox it is." Arcana took the crossbow bolt and slid the key free, grimacing at the blood smeared across her fingers. The humidity in the room was so fierce that it was still slippery and wet, as though the warg had only been breathing moments before. Arcana suppressed a shudder as she stalked over to the lockbox, spun the key in the lock and flipped back the lid. The interior of the lockbox was lined with black velvet and contained a small, white envelope with Arcana's name scrawled on the front.

"What is it?" Fenris peered over one shoulder.

"One way to find out." Arcana turned the envelope in her hands and tore it open. A photograph fell out, showing a young woman with short cyan hair and sparkling aquamarine eyes. She held a four-armed child in her lap and the two were laughing. They were both covered in flour and the child had a cupcake in each hand, bright pink frosting smeared on her face.

"Oh wow," Caelum murmured.

"It that *you*?" Fenris asked, leaning in for a better look. Despite the carnage, the stench and the heat, Arcana huffed a laugh at his astonishment. "You look even younger than the pictures in those books."

"When I first met Burke, she was a child. Four years old, to be exact." Arcana's voice softened at the memory. "Her father, Nolan, had recently procured Corrin's Run and came to Sorcen to establish a trade agreement."

"Which is how he met Flare," Fenris guessed.

Arcana nodded. "Yes, Flare was well entrenched in higher duties by then. Anyway, it was my job to cater the banquet - well, the dessert portion of it. Burke found her way down to the kitchens and we had so much fun together, icing cakes and mucking around. Flare took this picture. I didn't even know she had it."

"But why leave it here, with the dead warg?" Caelum wondered.

"I don't know." Arcana flipped the picture over with a heavy sigh, intending to slip it back into the envelope, then stopped. A tiny data chip was taped to the back of the plast. "Ah."

"I'm beginning to sense a pattern," Caelum announced, raising his head so that Arcana could rummage in the satchel for the datapad.

"Whatever is on that chip must be very important, if Burke went to such lengths to lead us to it." Fenris plucked the chip from the back of the picture and slipped it into Arcana's palm, taking the plast for himself. "You look different with short hair."

"Not to mention the waves," Arcana tugged on a lock of her black hair. "It went straight after Caelum."

"I always thought the freckles were cute," Caelum chimed in.

"I forgot I used to have freckles." Arcana pulled the datapad free and slid the chip into the bottom. She tilted her head to look at the picture again. "I was so young there, barely eighteen years old. When I next saw Burke, she was grown and I was bonded to Caelum."

"Did she recognise you?" Fenris asked.

"Yeah, though she already knew what had happened. It was Flare who took her attention on that visit, anyway," Arcana snorted, rolling her eyes at the memory. The datapad bleeped and she was immediately greeted with a password request. "I suppose I should've been expecting that."

"It must be something you would be able to work out, or she would have never given it to you," Fenris said. "That's certainly been the pattern so far."

"Hmmm." Arcana frowned over at the picture of her and Burke as a child, still cradled in Fenris' hands. "Something only the two of us would know, or remember. I wonder."

"Don't get it wrong," Caelum warned. "See that symbol in the bottom corner? The chip is set to wipe itself if you enter the incorrect code."

"No pressure, then." Arcana tapped in the six digit code and smiled as the password turned green. "Hah!"

"What was it?" Fenris asked.

"The date we first met, when this picture was taken." Arcana smiled, tapping the image. "Burke set the precedent with Flare's birthday earlier; a pattern, like you said. Nobody else would know the date off the top of their head - in fact, only Flare or I would be likely to know it at all."

The datapad's screen blurred and flickered, and Burke's face appeared. Her expression was sombre, her figure considerably slimmer and younger than the woman they had dined with a couple of hours before. "Arcana, if you're watching this, then something has happened. Hopefully I'm not dead, but if I am, then I'm sorry we didn't get a chance to have one last firewhiskey together. Whatever I've left you on this chip will be important. Thank you for always being my friend." Burke smiled, then blew a kiss. The image faded.

"Interesting," Fenris noted into the silence. A directory of files appeared, each carefully numbered and labelled. "You appear to be her backup plan."

"It looks that way. She must keep the chip close at hand and update the information as it becomes relevant," Arcana murmured, tapping the first file. A different woman's face appeared, long and vaguely serpentine with rust coloured skin and large, slitted yellow eyes. A warg stood on either side of her, their eyes half lidded and lips curled in a perpetual snarl.

"Greetings, Curator. I am Shirimm and I speak on behalf of The Pariah, High Custodian of the East and Executor of the Shimmering Armada." Shirimm inclined her head, hair the colour of dried blood tumbling around her face. "I apologise that we cannot meet in person but I trust you will find this message on the bodies of my messengers. I hope their end was swift, and that not too many of your people fell in the chaos." The woman's face split into a nasty smile, displaying curved, needle-like fangs that further enhanced her resemblance to a snake. Shirimm took a moment to stare down the barrel of the camera, tapping her chin with a short, taloned finger. "I come to you today as the herald of a new era in which the mighty warg will feature prominently. Co-operate, and you will be allowed to continue running your operation under the Pariah's supervision. Your duties, of course, won't be too taxing; I know a savvy business-woman such as yourself has many demands on her time already. With that in mind, my representative will be making contact soon to establish a new set of protocols for your trading programme and to install some extra routes to your current setup. I would advise you to consider your response to these changes carefully." Shirimm's cold smile turned positively arctic, those yellow snake eyes narrowing. "If you refuse to co-operate, I will personally ensure Corrin's Run is destroyed and that every last person on it, their loved ones, their families and their planets, will be devastated post-haste. The Pariah looks forward to hearing your decision, Curator. Until then, I hope your day is a pleasant one."

"Wow," Arcana said as the screen went blank. "What a bitch."

"You have no idea." Fenris' voice was hoarse and Arcana was surprised to find his face blanched.

"What is it? Do you know this Pariah?"

"The Pariah I have never heard of. Shirimm, however..." his throat bobbed. "She used to be a Guardian."

That was pain in his voice, real and raw. Arcana laid her hand against Fenris' arm. "I'm sorry. It does explain the warg, though."

"Yes." Fenris' muscles clenched beneath her fingers. "Taelon has a hand in this - whatever it is. The sooner we find him and free the Weaver, the better for everyone."

"We'll free the Weaver," Arcana promised, "Although I'm curious about how someone so all-powerful got jumped by Taelon, of all people. I mean, the guy oozes crazy."

Fenris raised an eyebrow. "The Weaver is not all powerful. Her power is consumed by and limited to the creation and manipulation of the weave. She is the master of time, the mother of all realities and universes - but she is also a slave to those things. To tear out a section of the weave is to tear out part of herself; and that is before we discuss the effect such an action would have on the rest of the fabric." His long fingers plucked at the cotton scarf. "Imagine there was a pull here. The site of the pull, whilst appearing the most violent problem, is actually only the beginning. The thread which has been tugged out of place has a negative effect over a far larger area, and is infinitely more difficult - sometimes impossible - to repair."

"Right, but can't she just weave everyone into being nice and avoid the conflict in the first place?" Arcana asked.

"Of course not," Fenris wrinkled his nose. "The Weaver makes the fabric - it is Auron who breathes life into the multiverse. And neither he nor the Weaver are responsible for free will."

"So... Taelon's an asshole and there's nothing we can do about it?"

Fenris curled his top lip back from his teeth. "Essentially. As for controlling the Weaver, Taelon came in under the pretence of peace, a lost hero returning home. None could believe it when he declared the Keeper of Life deceased and offered to take Auron's place as the Weaver's consort." The Guardian shook his head, face etched in sorrow. "When she refused, Taelon became aggressive and called the warg to battle. He immobilised the Weaver by the simple expedient of cutting a hole in the weave."

Arcana froze. "Are you saying Taelon cut a hole in *reality*?"

"Indeed," Fenris shuddered. "The Weaver's scream - I have never heard such a thing. All of her energy became focussed on those severed threads and the lives and worlds that depend upon them. The warg attacked. Guardians and Wardens fought and died. Beyond it all, the Weaver spoke into my mind and bade me close the portals to stop the warg overflowing into the rest of the multiverse. Which, insofar as that plea goes, I have failed to do."

"Not entirely your fault - you were vastly outnumbered." Arcana sucked on her teeth for a long moment, brow furrowed. "I was hoping that at some point or another the Weaver might lend us a hand in this mess but if what you're saying is correct, then we're on our own."

"That depends. I have no idea how Taelon is continuing to hold sway over her, but I would imagine that either threatening or further damaging the weave would be enough to keep the majority of her attention occupied. However, if our theory is correct, the Weaver was able to interfere enough to send you across the universe to rescue me." Fenris shrugged, as though being almost murdered by a former ally and then saved by strangers were part of his morning routine. "My personal belief is that she will do what she can but yes, I think any interference from the Weaver directly will be so limited as to be almost non-existent. We are better off acting as though we are alone."

"Which leads us back to Burke," Caelum waved his nose at the data-pad. "I'd wager the 'representative' Shirimm spoke about is whoever Arcana saw in those goggles."

"Keeping an eye on things - literally." Arcana flipped to the next document and discovered images of the room in which they now stood, slaughtered warg pinned to the wall amongst the wreckage of an exploded shipping container. "Looks like the warg managed not to take anyone else out when they arrived."

"Small mercies." Caelum leant in closer. "Is that a map?"

"Detailing the Pariah's new trade routes," Arcana nodded, scrolling further down. "And a list of terms that Burke needs to adhere to."

Caelum grunted. "They're taking a big cut. No wonder Burke's pissed off."

"That and she's no longer in control of her own station," Arcana added. She tapped on a file entitled 'Bugs' and frowned at yet another blueprint of Corrin's Run, marked with a multitude of crosses and circles. She showed Fenris, whose eyes narrowed as he translated the alien writing.

"These are the surveillance taps they've found so far, along with notes on the camera system and the audio system. Looks like everything of note is being watched." He zoomed in on their current location. "Nothing down here."

"Not much point bugging the storage units - or maybe they just haven't gotten around to it yet," Caelum murmured.

"Considering the amount of time it would take to lay specific instruments, I'd say the latter." Fenris tilted his head to the side. "If I were to make a wager, I would bet that the moment Taelon had the Weaver secure, he unleashed his people - this Pariah is obviously some sort of general of his. There will be more warg incoming."

"Agreed." Arcana backed out of the blueprint and began scrolling through a list of inventory, things that were being shipped in and out at the Pariah's request. "We need a plan."

"Yes. The sooner we leave, the better," Fenris said. There was something so strange in his tone that Arcana glanced up at him.

"Tell me you're not suggesting we just leave Burke here?" Arcana asked. He was so quiet that her stomach bottomed out. "How can you even consider that?"

"It is not a notion that sits well with me but I have a great many other things to consider. I swore a blood oath when I became the Overlord; a blood oath that dictates I must set the needs of the Timeless Kingdom above all others, including my own." Fenris shifted uncomfortably from foot to foot. "My role is oft a lonely one, a difficult one. I accepted it because I, like Taelon before me, have very few personal ties and an unwavering loyalty to the Weaver."

"Are you saying," said Arcana quietly, "That this situation calls your oath into question?"

Fenris hesitated. "If Taelon is truly spreading his influence across the galaxy, there will be far more people than just Burke suffering. Corrin's Run is a halfway point for Taelon's ships and his armies but at the end of the day, it is no more and no less than that. If we - if *I* - were to be captured or killed attempting a rescue mission, then nobody will *ever* stand against Taelon." Fenris ground his teeth, his eyes imploring her to understand. "So

far, the risks we have faced together have still pointed us toward my ulti-
mate goal; the Kingdom and my queen. But this, now… I have no choice
but to wonder if the station warrants endangering my life to save it,
regardless of my personal feelings."

Arcana stared. He was actually suggesting it - that they run, and leave.
"People will fight Taelon and the warg; the people of Corrin's Run, particularly, will fight for their home."

"Yes, but without a true understanding of Taelon, without freeing the
Weaver, there will never be victory. Once Taelon breaks the Weaver down -
however he plans to do so - he will be able to control the weave and
simply excise anybody who argues with him. I can assure you that once
entire solar systems start winking out of existence, the remaining peoples
will submit quickly." Fenris swallowed heavily, running one hand through
his hair and streaking it with warg blood. "I am loathe to leave but you
saw Shirimm - she was a Guardian. Sworn to protect the Weaver, to ensure
balance through the universe. Even she has turned towards this madness -
a madness that must be stopped before we are all consumed."

Arcana's stomach turned to lead in her gut and, temper rising like a
cloak, she snapped; "What if it was me in Burke's position? Would you go
to the Timeless Kingdom and leave me here to rot?"

Fenris tapped his foot. "That is a ridiculous question, because it is not
you in this position."

"You didn't answer."

"I don't know!" Fenris shouted, slamming one fist into the wall. The
tortured metal dented under the force of his blow. "I do not know. I swore
a blood oath to protect the Weaver to the exclusion of all else, including the
song of my own heart. It doesn't matter what I want, what I think. I *swore*,
Arcana."

She went cold all over, staring down at the datapad without really
seeing it. When she spoke, her voice seemed to belong to someone else.
"The fact that you're even hesitating is all the answer I need."

"Arcana-"

"Shut up."

"Please, just listen -"

"To what? More pathetic excuses? You have to be the most self-
absorbed, cowardly excuse for a warrior I've ever seen. It's just as well the
Weaver's locked up right now, because if she were here to witness what
you just suggested, she'd be ashamed," Arcana spat. Fenris went white,
jaw dropping open and hands slackening at his sides. Arcana stormed to
the opposite side of the room, heedless of the fact that she was now

standing in front of the pile of dead warg. Caelum drifted after her, the hackles down his spine stiff with anger. Fenris, to his credit, made no attempt to follow.

"What do you want to do?" Caelum asked quietly.

"Aside from murder that no-good excuse for a male on the other side of the room?"

The deerken's ears flickered. "Aside from that."

"I'm not sure. There must be some information in here that can give us some direction. Burke wouldn't have supplied it otherwise." Arcana scrolled further down the inventory and froze. "Caelum... are they what I think they are?"

The description was in the same alien language as before but the picture showed three round crystals, each one large enough to fit in the palm of Arcana's hand. They were a pale, icy blue, veined with white - and though she'd never seen one intact, incredibly familiar. Caelum flicked a glance at Fenris, who was pressing the heels of his palms into his eye sockets and muttering under his breath. "Yes, I think they are," the deerken breathed.

Portal crystals. And if Taelon got his hands on them - Arcana swallowed heavily, expanding the log for further information. The crystals were part of a shipment of valuables currently sitting in one of Corrin's Run's many loading bays ready to be shipped out in the morning. Arcana searched for a record of where the ships were headed; there was none, meaning that if the ship left Corrin's Run, the crystals would be lost. And whilst Arcana was angry enough at Fenris to consider letting them go, there was more than her scalded feelings at stake. Not that she was in a mood to share that with Fenris. Rather than engage him in conversation, Arcana backed out of the file and began searching the rest of the data chip. Barely two files down, she opened an image and froze.

"Oh," said Caelum.

It was a picture of Fenris, his face set in a serious expression as he watched something to the left of the frame. He wore the plate armour she'd first seen him in, though polished to a high sheen and lacking the enormous slice through the middle. His dark hair was cut shorter and he was much younger but there was no mistaking the jade fire burning in those eyes, nor the high cheekbones or the set of his long, clean jaw. Fenris had the greatsword clasped in one hand, point down against the ground in a position Arcana had seen often during their stay on Sorcen. The reward for his capture - alive - was enough to build Corrin's Run from scratch twice over. Arcana raised a hand to her lips, heart thumping. Burke had known from the start, and chosen to protect him anyway. Asked and asked and asked about a personal connection between Fenris and Arcana; not because she wished to keep him for herself, but to ascertain if keeping him out of Taelon's hands was worth both the personal risk and financial loss.

"You want to know if Burke's worth saving?" Arcana stomped over to Fenris and slapped the datapad against his chest. "Look at this."

Fenris took the datapad gingerly, jaw clenching as he turned it over and saw his own face staring back at him. His hands shook as he read the few notes beneath, as he saw the vulgar amount of gold on offer and made the same connections Arcana had done. "I-"

"Signed and officiated by the very same Pariah you wish to ignore." Arcana's cool voice cut over whatever Fenris had been about to say - she didn't care. Cloaked in the safety of her rage, she gripped his wrist in vicious fingers, tilting the datapad towards her. "You should also see this."

Fenris gasped as she showed him the portal crystals. "Where are they?"

"Down in one of the storage bays. Their ship departs in the morning," Arcana said coldly. "Not that it's any concern to you, seeing as your intention is only to cut and run. What a shame."

He closed his eyes for a long moment, expression pained. "Your point is taken," Fenris said finally. "Perhaps we should liberate the station before we go."

"What an *excellent* idea," Arcana clapped her hands together and flashed a smile that was no more than a baring of teeth. "I'm so glad you thought of it."

"Where do we start?" Caelum very deliberately inserted his head between the two of them, pushing forward until first his antlers and then his broad shoulders forced both Fenris and Arcana to retreat. "Because right now we have little more than a shady figure in unusual eyewear, a bunch of blueprints and a partially stocked ship."

"You forgot the dead warg," said Arcana, brows pinching in thought.

"I felt they weren't worth mentioning, based purely on the fact they've been dead at least a week," Caelum returned. "Unless you're in the market for a fur coat, they're not much use to us."

"Whoever the Pariah has stationed here will be keeping close to Burke. If we can get to her, we find them." Fenris tilted his head in thought. "Once Burke and Phase are safe, we should be able to extend their influence through the station sand reclaim it. Arcana -" he hesitated, a flash of emotion twisting his face before it smoothed. "With the right school of magic at your disposal, could you wipe all the bugs in one sweep?"

Arcana clenched her fists. "That would require electricity. A lot of it."

"Is that bad?" His brow furrowed. "You said you could absorb dominant energy."

"I can, and electricity is no different. I could also absorb the energy of a laser, but that would mean, oh, I don't know - *being shot by a laser*," Arcana threw up her hands. "Maybe electrocution wouldn't be such a bad way to go, you know? It might even tickle."

"It would hurt you." His voice was flat, and Arcana knew Fenris was grappling with the urge to call her on her attitude.

Rather than punch him in the middle of his exquisite mouth, Arcana smiled sweetly and said; "No shit."

Caelum raised his eyes to the ceiling, then shoved Arcana hard with one shoulder. "Stop being an asshole."

"I wouldn't have to be if Mr. Extreme Jerkishness over there wasn't such a-"

"I said enough," Caelum snapped, his neck arching. Arcana's mouth clicked shut. "Yes, Fenris is being a jerk. Yes, you're righteously indignant. But right now we are trying not to be killed, so if you don't mind, I'd prefer if you both put your raging hormones aside for *one minute* and focus." The deerken swung his head menacingly between them.

Arcana crossed her arms over her chest. "I wasn't the one who suggested electrocuting me."

"Gods above, Arcana, I swear I will gore you if you do not shut your mouth," Caelum growled. "First of all: Fenris is still learning about your magic. He has as little understanding about you being electrocuted as you did the day you grabbed hold of the lightning rod on top of the Healing Tower." Arcana held both hands up in defeat and Caelum swung towards Fenris. "Second of all: If we can get to Burke she can give me access to the station's inner systems. I can shut down all the bugs. No magic needed."

Fenris nodded and though his face was still pale, his eyes were steady as they locked on Arcana. "Can you get us to Burke?"

"Yes. If we go quietly, it'll look like I'm escorting you to her bed - which everyone will be expecting by now anyway." As the words left her mouth, Arcana realised how neatly Burke had arranged things, how much trouble she'd gone to so that the situation appeared just so. And in a fit of childish temper, Arcana had overlooked all of it. Her cheeks heated in shame, so much so that she pressed her palms against them. The heart of the station pulsed through her veins and she could have sworn it lurched as she ground her teeth against each other.

A firm grip steadied her elbow; Arcana lowered her hands to slap Fenris away only to stare into sudden, complete darkness. What...? Somewhere in the bowels of the station, the sound of tortured metal and raging energy wrenched at reality. In the vast, cold darkness of space, Corrin's Run coughed.

Arcana's teeth rattled as the impact threw her to the floor, right into that sticky, week-old blood. She heard Fenris go down beside her, then the sound of boots on plasteel as he flipped upright almost immediately. A long moment later the emergency generators kicked in, filling the room with an unearthly red glow.

"Thermal charge," Fenris said grimly.

"We need to get out of here," Caelum warned - still upright, as though the shockwave was of little interest to him. "It won't be long before the generators start shutting down oxygen to the non-essential levels to conserve power. Ten minutes at most."

"Dammit." Arcana got her hands beneath her and heaved, wincing as the grated floor dug mercilessly into her palms. Warg blood had tattooed the fine grid pattern into the skin of her shoulder and chest - and by the feel of it, her cheek. She raised a wrist to wipe it off and froze, eyes on the wooden crate upon which the lockbox had stood. It had fractured in the blast and a few stray strands of packing straw had fallen free, revealing a tantalising glimpse of colour. On her knees in the gore, Arcana crawled to the crate, wrapped bloodied fingers around the wood and heaved. Nothing happened. "Fenris. Help me with this."

He was behind her in an instant, leaning around to grasp the broken edge of the crate. Muscles flexed against Arcana's back and the wood snapped off as though made of peanut brittle. She yanked the straw aside and drew out two wrapped parcels that, according to their packing sticker, had come all the way from the third moon of Rivayek. Fenris grunted as she slapped the navy package against his chest. "What is this?"

"Clothes," Arcana said, shouldering out of the circle of his arms. She stood, laying her own pale blue tissue paper on top of the crate, and wiped her hands on her jeans. "Trust me, we want to take a few minutes for this."

Inside her package were a black pair of pants and a matching jacket; they looked like leather but Arcana knew otherwise. The clothier Burke favoured was an expert with an artificially blended fabric which was light as cotton, looked like leather and was strong enough to withstand most blasters. It cost a small fortune but when it was money or life, well, it wasn't really a choice at all, was it? Arcana set the clothes aside and hauled more straw out of the crate, spreading it over the floor to cover that awful, stinking blood.

"What are you doing?" Fenris' voice hitched as she leant one hip against the crate and peeled off a boot.

"Getting changed - unless you'd prefer to try this rescue while you're almost naked?" Arcana didn't look at him as she yanked off the other boot. "I, for one, am taking any edge I can get." She unhooked her jeans and began to wriggle them down over her hips.

Fenris made a choking sound and Arcana glanced up in time to see him face the other direction, his own armoured clothing - still wrapped - clutched against his chest like a shield. Just as well, because it meant he couldn't see the vindictive twist to her lips as she tugged her jeans off and cast them aside. The new pants were a perfect fit, snug and flexible all at the same time. There was no top, but the jacket slid on easily over her armoured corset. Arcana zipped it up halfway, conscious enough of the oppressive humidity to need some air, even if the fabric was far more breathable than it appeared. She tugged her boots back on and said; "Your turn."

Caelum was waiting by the door, face tense. While Fenris muttered under his breath and rustled about in the straw, Arcana crossed the room to bury her hands in his fur - and realised as she got there that it was still too short.

"You want a look?" Caelum muttered, his eyes fastened over her shoulder where Fenris was undoubtedly in some state of undress. And could hear them clearly, Arcana reminded herself.

"Of course not, you mannerless beast," she chided, her voice low enough that it wouldn't seem like she was intending to be overheard. "Give the poor man some privacy."

Caelum huffed a laugh, lowering his head to rub an ear on a foreleg. The station juddered again and Fenris spat out a muffled curse before he appeared at Arcana's side, buckling the greatsword on over his jacket - which he had left completely open, baring a wide expanse of muscular chest no longer concealed beneath the scarlet scarf. Arcana blinked, wrenching her gaze away from all that perfect teal skin and ignoring the pale line of Fenris' scar that beckoned her to look further.

"I've got your things in my pouch. I'll give them back later," Fenris said. His pants fit so well he didn't need a belt - they were sculpted to his backside and legs like a second skin, the black fabric disappearing into his scuffed combat boots. Arcana closed her eyes, reminding herself firmly that she was angry. It didn't help, the tight curve of Fenris' backside seemingly branded onto the inside of her eyelids. Great Gods of Sorcen, what was *wrong* with her?

"Sure," Arcana's voice was strangled as she turned away and slapped the controls for the door. "Now let's get out of here before we suffocate."

Steam billowed through the open doorway, accompanied by the thick whooshing of a burst pipe. Caelum swept into the hall, his silver-grey fur rapidly fading into the clinging, wet mist. Arcana followed, her hair wilting the moment she was exposed to the moisture. Hot steam became condensation which coated her face and neck and dripped down between her breasts, making the corset instantly torturous. Arcana spread her magic through the walls until she discovered a fractured water pipe and squeezed the jagged edges against one another until they sealed. The humidity immediately lessened and she waved the fog out of her face as they jogged back the way they had come.

"Elevator's busted," Caelum reported. Steam swirled around his antlers and curled beneath his belly but when Arcana touched his fur it was soft and dry. She looked down at herself, moisture clinging to her eyelashes and running in rivulets across her chest, then up at Fenris. His dark curls were glued to his head, his lashes were heavy with glittering droplets and water streamed down his face to drip steadily from his chin. She glared back at Caelum. He shrugged. "Not my fault. Blame genetics."

"Of course," Arcana snorted, shaking her head. "Blame the magically-clean-deer gene. Why didn't I think of that?"

"No need to get catty." Caelum poked her with his nose and then shook the clinging water droplets away. "Ew, it's weirdly warm."

"Try wearing it." Arcana moved to the wall, flattening her palms against the plasteel panelling. "Forget the elevator; it would've been shut down as part of the emergency procedures anyway. What I'm looking for is... here." She reached to the top corner of a panel and pressed the heel of her palm against it. The wall clicked and swung open to reveal a narrow set of stairs.

"A serviceway," Fenris nodded. "Excellent."

Arcana nodded, ducked through the hole and began the long climb upwards. Phosphorescent strips along the roof gave off an eerie green glow that was only marginally better than complete darkness and Arcana ran her fingers along the narrow sides of the stairwell for balance as she went. Caelum and Fenris moved like ghosts in the gloom, so silent she only knew they followed because nerves had her habitually looking over one shoulder.

After six flights of stairs, Arcana pressed one eye to a vent and spied the richly appointed hallway that stretched outside Burke's private rooms. She raised a hand and Fenris appeared beside her, eyes closed and head lowered as he listened. For several heartbeats there was only the sound of Fenris' breathing, then the Guardian raised three long, slender fingers and jerked his chin to the left.

Arcana set both hands to the vent; large enough for them to dive through. Fenris met her eyes and nodded. She pushed against the metal frame, as hard as she could - backing that thrust with magic. The vent shot out into the hall, Fenris following behind in a movement so swift and smooth Arcana lost track of him. By the time she checked the headlong flight of the vent so it didn't crash and clatter to the floor, Fenris was wiping the greatsword on a nearby tapestry. Three headless bodies lay at his feet, their blood soaking the ivory carpet.

Fenris pressed a single finger against his lips as Arcana climbed through the vent, turning back to help Caelum. She guided his antler rack, one side at a time, then watched as he wriggled his considerable bulk through an opening that had never been designed to accommodate him. It was slow, painfully so - but if Arcana were to use her magic to widen the vent, the sound would echo down the corridor and ruin any element of surprise they had. At last Caelum got to his feet, shook himself all over, and moved to join Fenris at the end of the hall.

The door to Burke's room was a solid sheet of plasteel with a DNA lock; one of the most sophisticated that money could buy. Arcana eyed it a long moment, then the bodies on the floor. They wore matching grey leathers emblazoned with an insignia Arcana had never seen before; a bird wearing a broken crown. Each was humanoid and carried a weapons belt but they weren't warg and there was nothing to discern them as enemies. Arcana kept her voice low, knowing Fenris would hear it, and said; "I hope you know what you're doing."

"Not for a long time," he answered grimly, his eyes on the severed heads. "But these traitors have paid their debts."

Arcana winced at the pain in his voice. Whoever these people had been, Fenris had known them - and that alone told her enough about their allegiance. She laid her hands flat against the door, sending her magic into the thick layers of steel. Without Burke or Phase on hand to provide their DNA sample, there was only one way in - something Burke had to have known when she sent Arcana that data chip. She looked up at Fenris, who took a moment to zip his jacket before nodding in readiness. Caelum, as always, stood serene, the only hint of nerves in the soft swishing of his stumpy tail.

Magic surged as Arcana flexed her fingers and the door blew apart. Shards of plasteel blossomed away from her like the petals of a silver flower, revealing a single figure waiting in the foyer. Dressed in thick grey leathers that matched those of the fallen guards outside the door, their opponent held a wickedly curved blade in each hand. Twin points of pink light winked from deep within the goggles which had haunted Arcana since she'd first glimpsed them down in the club.

"I was starting to think you weren't real, you know." Arcana stepped through the remains of the door, tearing sharpened pieces of metal free with her magic and sending them hurtling towards her opponent. The figure spun and slashed, curved swords ringing like bells as they deflected several of the shards. Arcana paused just over the threshold, eyeing the leathers, the posture - male, she decided - and sighed. "I'm not sure if I'd prefer you were a figment of my imagination or not."

Throaty laughter rang out - and then cut off as Fenris stepped to Arcana's side. For a long moment, there was only the thrum of the pink goggles and Fenris' ragged, enraged breathing; then the figure leapt forwards, his sickle swords a blur of motion as he went not for Fenris but Arcana. Metal crashed against metal and the grey-leathered male staggered backwards, fumbling his blades. Fenris appeared not to move but Arcana had seen the flash of silver as the greatsword arced in front of her face, parrying the blow with breathtaking speed.

"There is no mercy for traitors," Fenris said quietly, his knuckles white on the hilt of the greatsword as he watched the goggled figure adjust his sickle blades in hands that trembled. "You know that."

Arcana looked up at Fenris, whose eyes were wild, and laid a gentle hand on his forearm. "Try not to kill this one on sight. He might know something useful."

The Guardian's eyes swivelled to hers, a movement none but the two of them would ever notice. There was pain in their depths, wrenching pain - but determination, too, and a cold, cold rage. "Perhaps," Fenris said quietly, "You might assist me in that."

Because in his current mood, whoever was behind those goggles wouldn't get a word out. Sensing the undercurrent of the conversation, the opposing male leapt backwards, disappearing into the sitting room beyond. Arcana flicked her fingers, lifting shards of plasteel from the floor and swirling them around her like a shield as she swept into the sitting room. A flash of grey to the left was all she needed to aim. Plasteel thunked into wood, accompanied by a definitely masculine yelp and their would-be assassin was quite suddenly pinned to the expensive oakfern wall, sickle blades tumbling from nerveless fingers.

Fenris flowed into the room on silent feet, Caelum a shadow at his heels. He laid the tip of the greatsword over the assassin's heart, face closed as he stared down at the half-moon swords on the floor. "Grayen."

"Arcana?" Burke's voice echoed from nearby. "In here!"

"Will you be all right?" Arcana asked.

"Yes. You get Burke." Fenris pressed the greatsword more firmly against Grayen's chest. "This traitor's going to answer some questions."

There came a metallic cry of pain but Arcana ignored it, crossing to the door she thought Burke's shout had come from. It slid open as she approached, revealing the Curator chained up in the shower unit, blood leaking from a cut above one eye. "The shower?" Arcana waved a hand and the chain links sprang apart, clattering into the ceramic base. "You don't look *that* filthy."

"Very funny, Arcana." Burke stepped over the twisted remains of her bindings, rubbing at the welts on her wrists. "They had Phase in the bedroom. Wanted us separate."

"Smarter than they look, then."

"Yeah. Thanks for coming, by the way." Burke reached out with all four arms and drew Arcana into a strong, back-slapping embrace. "I wasn't sure you would until I heard the door blow apart."

"It took me a while to work out the clues." Arcana squeezed in return and then drew back, running a critical eye over the Curator to make certain there were no other injuries. "You said they *had* Phase in the bedroom. Where is he now?"

Burke pressed a hand to the cut on her head and grimaced. "The office, I think," she said at last. "They wanted the combination to the door - which I changed as soon as Rito gave you the data chip. I'm assuming they've taken Phase there to force him to restore power to the station."

"Then we need to hurry." Arcana made to whirl back to the main room but Burke grabbed her wrist, spinning her back until they were face to face.

"I'm sorry," the other woman said. "I said and did some hateful things when we last met, and you still came for me when it counted. I'm sorry."

"Forget about it." Arcana gave her friend a half smile. "No matter what you spit out of that foolish mouth, I'll always come for you."

"Even when I'm licking your lover's chest?"

"He's not my lover." Arcana rolled her eyes, cooling her blush by thinking about the way Fenris had suggested they leave Corrin's Run to sort things out by itself. Then; "You were licking his chest?"

"I *am* in heat," Burke had the grace to look wounded, even as her eyes sparkled with mischief. "And you have to admit, it's a glorious chest."

"I haven't noticed," Arcana said flatly, pressing her fingers into her eye sockets.

Burke's hands circled Arcana's wrists, dragging her arms down to reveal the other woman was now close enough to share breath. "Liar," Burke whispered, grinning wide. "You almost turned green at the dinner table."

"Watching you drool on your guests has that effect on me," Arcana growled. "Now come on." She wrenched her hands free and strode back into the sitting room, where Fenris was still staring at their goggled assailant - only now Grayen was slumped on the floor, a single, telling wound through the heart of those grey leathers.

Fenris didn't turn as she approached and laid a hand on his bicep. Didn't break his stare. "Grayen was once a Guardian."

"I'm sorry," Arcana said, and meant it. She couldn't begin to imagine having to despatch someone she'd known and possibly cared about - yet Fenris had done it four times in as many minutes.

"He said - he said some follow Taelon for fear, some because they truly believe in his ideal for a universe where they are as gods. Others still fight and run... but most of those are Wardens, trying to keep the deerken safe." Fenris blew out between his teeth, pain flickering in the depths of his burning gaze. "Less than a quarter of the Timeless Kingdom has remained loyal to the Weaver. Less than a *quarter* of my people have chosen to fight for freedom, while the rest -" Recalling where he was, Fenris stopped. He closed his eyes a long moment, rolling uneasy shoulders, then turned to face Burke.

"The clothes of a warrior suit you," was all she said.

"Thank you, Curator. I am glad to see you unharmed." Fenris gave a stiff, half bow, more acknowledgement than anything else, and looked towards Arcana. "Where is Phase?"

"Not here," Caelum stepped out of the bedroom, a shredded sheet tangled in his antlers. "Though he was."

"Did you have to destroy my linen to work that out?" Burke grumped, crossing to help untangle the sheet. With her four arms, she made short work of the job, pressing a soft kiss to Caelum's nose when she was finished. "Thank you."

"For someone whose mate was dragged kicking and screaming down to the office, you seem remarkably calm," Arcana noted.

Burke only grinned. "Rito's waiting in the office. With his musket."

"You gave that pirate his ridiculous blaster back?" Arcana demanded, her eyes wide. "Are you crazy?"

"Desperate," Burke corrected. She flicked a glance at Fenris. "Are you sure you don't want to split his bounty with me?"

"No," Arcana crossed her arms.

Burke huffed a laugh. "I somehow knew you'd say that, regardless of whether you're swapping fluids."

"We're not," Arcana growled. Caelum sniggered, and she levelled a finger at him. "Shut up."

Burke's grin turned wicked but she spread all four hands in a gesture of peace. "All right, all right. Let's not start *that* argument again. Now, if Rito's followed instructions, the thermal charge should've taken out power to half the lower decks, including several docking bays." Her amusement turned vicious. "He will also have disabled all the jams and bugs on the station with an EMP."

Arcana recalled the two different blasts she'd felt in the storage room and nodded. "Are there any warg here?"

"They have some in their ship," Burke nodded, her smile still firmly in place. "Without power, however, they can't get access to the station proper. Unless they want to swim through space, of course."

"How many are aboard Corrin's Run?" Fenris asked.

"No warg, but a great deal of the other crew members came in when the ship first arrived and I wasn't allowed to count them." Burke shrugged. "I did anyway. There are a good thirty or so stationside."

"And the Pariah? What can you tell us of him?"

The Curator's eyes hardened. "I don't know who the Pariah is, or where he's from, but he sure as hell isn't taking over my station without a fight."

"I'm happy to help you get it back but there's one more thing we need to ask about." Arcana motioned to Fenris. "Something he needs."

"The cargo you had logged on the chip. Three blue crystals," Fenris shaped the orbs with his hands. "I need them."

Burke tilted her head. "They were supposed to be loaded in the morning, along with everything else the Pariah demanded. Unless our visitors have moved them, your crystals should be in the cargo hangar closest to the Pariah's transport. Once these cretins are dealt with, you may have them with my thanks."

"No payment needed?" Arcana whistled low and long. "You're awfully gracious today."

"You came for me when I wasn't sure if you would." Burke smiled, a hint of bitterness twisting her lips. "That alone is payment enough."

Fenris sheathed the greatsword with barely contained violence, his jaw clenched so hard that a muscle in his face twitched. His jade eyes were haunted as he bowed to Burke and said; "You do me a service greater than I have earnt, Curator."

"Oh?" Burke seemed to consider that, looking between Fenris - his emotions tightly controlled - and Arcana, who was fairly certain her lingering rage was visible on her face. The Curator raised a brow at Fenris and said, softly; "Then earn it."

Guardian and Curator stared at each other for a long moment and then Fenris clicked his heels together and bowed deeply. "I swear to you it shall be done."

Burke inclined her head in acknowledgment. "Good."

"So what now? We wait for Phase?" Caelum shook his head, the movement echoing down his body - and with it, his fur began to lengthen, finally returning to normal after the horrid humidity of the lower levels. Arcana immediately buried her hands in those precious few inches of silver and grey, earning herself a teasing nudge from Caelum's shoulder.

"We need to wait until Phase has the office secure. Once that's done -" Burke broke off as a beeping noise sounded within her pale blue wrappings, and pulled out a communicator. "Tell me good news."

Phase's voice clicked and squeaked through the tinny speakers and Arcana listened with a furrowed brow, finally looking to Fenris for assistance. "They're safe," he translated. "Rito's weapon... appears to have vaporised whoever was escorting Phase."

"Rito's musket is a custom model. Looks like the old pirate weapon it bears the name of and packs enough firepower to, well, disintegrate people. It's better short range," Arcana added, nose crinkling.

"Phase is going to start restoring power to the station but we'll leave the transport ship in lockdown." Burke flipped the comm shut and slid it back into her wrappings. "I don't want the Pariah getting wind of this before we're ready to-"

"It's a little late for that," hissed a voice, and out of thin air stepped a short, muscular woman with rusty brown skin and hair the colour of dried blood. One taloned hand was already around Burke's throat, the other jabbing a syringe into the Curator's side. "I can assure you, The Pariah will soon be well aware of your betrayal."

"Shirimm." Fenris' voice was cold as the glacial planet upon which Arcana had found him. Up close, the former Guardian was both more and less intimidating than Arcana had expected; her diminutive size made her seem almost doll-like, but for the fact that she was now hefting an unconscious Burke with only one arm. Her other hand brandished a sleek blaster pistol she'd whipped from her belt - where the syringe had disappeared to, Arcana could only guess.

"Fenris?" Shirimm's face registered surprise for a fraction of a moment before her yellow snake eyes slitted. "You're alive."

"Try not to sound so disappointed." Fenris had the greatsword in his hand but before the tip so much as twitched, Shirimm pressed the snout of her blaster against Burke's neck.

"Don't move, *Overlord*," The other woman spat the title so that it became a vulgarity. "Or the Curator dies." Her serpentine face tilted, forked tongue flickering from between sharpened teeth. "I should've guessed - only you would be arrogant enough to take on this entire station single handedly."

Fenris gestured to Arcana. "I am not alone."

"A mercenary?" Shirimm swept a dismissive gaze up and down Arcana's body. "Or a useless Terran pleasure slave?"

"You and I both know there are no full blood Terrans left," Fenris sounded exasperated, as though, in spite of the situation, this was a familiar argument. "She is a mercenary, yes - but after the stunt Taelon pulled, you cannot have expected me to be left with other options."

Shirimm snorted. "And you think a hired blaster will help you protect that deerken? Don't think you can hide him, Overlord. We're slowly collecting them all - and yours will be no exception."

"Collecting them? I thought Taelon's mighty warg were far superior," Fenris mocked, digging the greatsword into the carpet as he bared his teeth.

"Taelon does not need to explain himself to the likes of you," Shirimm hissed.

Fenris barked a sharp, bitter laugh. "Nor would I wish to hear it after those twisted delusions he spat at us in the Weaver's chambers. Have you gained the importance you always desired, Shirimm? I would think not, if Taelon handed you off to this Pariah for patrol duty."

"Patrol duty?" Shirimm sneered, fingers twitching around Burke's throat. "This is no patrol. The Pariah is one of Taelon's three generals, and *I* am his left hand. I didn't come here to visit this snivelling station; I came for these." Quick as lightning, the hand holding Burke shifted and Arcana caught the brief but unmistakable flash of a portal crystal before it once again disappeared. "No simple lackey could be trusted to retrieve something so valuable."

Arcana choked, biting her tongue to keep from saying what was foremost in her mind. Shirimm's chest was so puffed with zealous pride that the wrong word or action would likely end Burke's life so she pasted a bored look on her face, saying to Fenris; "This job gets more irritating with every passing moment, you know. I'm tempted to double my fee."

"Fortunate that you're not paid to feel, but rather shoot when directed," Fenris returned, his voice sharp with reprimand. He took a half step forward, looking down his nose in disdain as Shirimm shoved the blaster more tightly into Burke's throat. "Where did you get those?"

"The crystals? A great many Guardians died defending these, but in the end..." Shirimm grinned. "None can stand forever before the might of the warg."

Fenris tilted his head to the side, leaning against the greatsword in a contemplative manner. "Only Murtagh can get them out of a portal."

Arcana knew that for a lie but Shirimm bounced with barely contained glee. "He did. The useless fool was stupid enough to let them out of his sight."

"So Murtagh lives." Fenris straightened, the muscles in his forearms bunching as he shifted the greatsword - drawing attention to the lethal blade whilst still keeping it point down on the floor. "Interesting."

Shirimm pursed her lips, face blanching as she realised she'd given away information she was probably supposed to keep to herself. "It matters little," she hissed. "You won't be able to do anything about it. Last I saw Murtagh he was fleeing with his tail between his legs."

"If he lives, then there is always something to be done," Fenris returned. His eyes narrowed. "You have betrayed your own people, Shirimm. Betrayed *me*. Why?"

"Perhaps I'm just tired of living in the shadows, protecting a universe that cares little for me in return." Shirimm shrugged, but her shoulders were tense. "And as for *you* - I would've followed Taelon to the burning hells of Ornmar and back for the chance to kill you, no matter what his other promises were."

"Do you truly hate me so much?" There was sadness in Fenris' voice now, a weariness in his handsome face.

Shirimm's lips pulled back in a snarl. "You know what you did. Tell me, Overlord - did you use it on your pretty little mercenary, too? Did you wrap your fist around her mind and squeeze, rather than shell out gold to hire her? You had to - mercs don't follow and shoot for free."

"You know nothing about my relationship with Arcana, least of all how I acquired her services," Fenris said coolly. "I'd have thought you better than this, Shirimm. Have you not tired of spilling lies about my glamour after all these years?"

"Lies?" Shirimm's hissing voice lowered, the sibilant syllables running together. "The only liar here is *you*. Did you walk her right into your bed, Overlord? Did you hold her still while you stripped her off, or did you force her to use her own hands while you watched?"

"Enough!" The roar that broke from Fenris was a terrible, primal thing. In less than the time it took to blink, he'd gathered the greatsword and leapt. Shirimm moved just as fast as Fenris, laughing as she dragged Burke hard against her chest and slapped the activation switch of the teleporter around her neck. When Fenris slammed the greatsword down, it buried hilt deep into the steel and carpet flooring of Corrin's Run - but Shirimm and Burke were gone.

CHAPTER
FOUR

Fenris crouched over the hilt of the greatsword, lips peeled back in an expression so ferocious that Arcana's heart stuttered in her chest. If he heard, the Guardian took no notice - he stared unseeing at the place where the greatsword's blade had plunged through the carpet.

"Fenris?" Arcana laid a gentle hand on one shoulder. He flinched at the touch, as though expecting a slap. She thought over the words Shirimm had thrown at him like weapons - words she had known would provoke Fenris out of his calculated calm. "Those things Shirimm said -"

"Leave it." His knuckles tightened on the leather-wrapped hilt of the sword until bones pushed against skin.

"I don't believe them." Instinct said she should step away; sheer bloody-mindedness demanded otherwise. Fenris had gods-knew how many years of complex history with these people, and clearly something even more so with Shirimm. Arcana was nobody, an outsider - but she knew how it felt to be cosmically alone, lost in a reality not of her own making. Forcing herself forward, she cupped Fenris' face in both hands and wrenched it upward. "I don't believe you did those things, whatever they were. You are more of a person - more of a *Guardian* - than Shirimm could ever hope to be."

"You don't know her," Fenris ground out.

"I don't know her," Arcana agreed, still seeking those eyes. "But I know *you*." She threw everything she could into that word, ignoring, for the moment, how angry she was. This terrifying emptiness was far worse than anything they'd yet fought over - and with sudden clarity, she understood what he'd meant when he said her temper was better than nothing at all.

Fenris blinked, slow and long and lazy, as though he were struggling to swim to the surface of his own thoughts. And then, his predatory swiftness snuffed out, the Guardian leant forward until his forehead bumped against her abdomen. "I do not deserve such empathy."

"You do." Arcana dared to comb her fingers through his silken curls; soft, soothing motions her mother had once offered as comfort when she was a child. Fenris groaned at the touch and slumped wholly against her, his face sinking into the fabric of Arcana's jacket as he wrapped both arms around her legs. Her heart skipped a beat as his warmth and strength bled into her skin, the slide of his hair sweet seduction against her fingers. "We'll get her, Fenris. I'll carve her traitorous heart out myself if I have to." He shuddered against her, muttering something incoherent into her ribs. Smiling her nastiest smile, Arcana said; "You know what? Carving out her heart is too merciful. I think I'll cut out her tongue and stick it where the sun doesn't shine first."

Fenris pressed harder against Arcana, his arms so tight her bones began to creak but his chest rumbled with the unmistakeable sound of laughter. "I think I should like to see that."

Buoyed by the flicker of personality, Arcana gave her most theatrical sigh. "Well now, that depends on if you're a good boy or not, doesn't it?" When he chuckled again, she looked up at Caelum. "Thoughts?"

"Aside from recommending a rusty knife? Shirimm used a personal teleporter. I'll wager she's on board that transport ship," Caelum said quietly. "If the docking bays are still locked down, we might be able to catch her and rescue Burke."

Fenris took a deep, shuddering breath against her ribs before he said; "How far?"

"Far enough." Arcana clicked her tongue against her teeth. "Caelum, get Phase on the comm, and let him know what's happened. Find out which bay holds Shirimm's transport and we can meet him there."

"Rito's with him," Caelum reminded. "I can go audio only but he'll still hear my voice."

Arcana made a guttural sound in the base of her throat. "Send emergency alert code four six six eleven and give him ten seconds before you call through. Phase will know to put a headset on before he answers."

"You got it." The deerken went to the unit on the wall and started jabbing it with his nose.

"Fenris?" Arcana coiled her fingers further into his hair, watching the play of the dark teal curls as they slipped across her salt-white skin. "Are you okay?"

Slowly, reluctantly, Fenris loosened his grip. "No." He reached up with gentle fingers to slide her hand from his hair, rubbing his cheek against her palm for a moment before pushing upright. "But we need to get to Burke before Shirimm does something foolish."

"All right." Arcana squeezed his hand and let go.

Fenris yanked the greatsword from the floor with a singular heave, jaw twitching as he jammed the enormous blade into his scabbard. "I would, you know."

Arcana frowned. "You would what?"

"I would come for you. If this was you." Elegant hands clenched to fists. "I would come for you and I would not stop until you were freed - my oath be damned. I would do it."

Arcana saw vulnerability flash in his eyes and something akin to shame. So she softened her face, reached up to brush a thumb across his cheek, and said; "I know." It didn't excuse the arguments, didn't change the chaos coursing through her blood but for now, it was enough.

Fenris straightened his shoulders and nodded. "I am glad. I -" he broke off, frowned. "The Weaver surely put us together for a reason but she would just as surely be aware that I am used to acting alone. I feel… It is an unexpected development and I am still learning."

Lips twisting, Arcana dropped her hand and turned towards the curled remains of the door. "Trust me, this isn't what I planned to be doing today, either."

She strode away before he could reply, Caelum hurrying across the room to her side. "Phase is on his way. He's restored power across the station, with the exception of docking bay eleven - which is our destination. Shirimm's crew are largely unaccounted for and I'm willing to bet they'll be looking for blood."

"That's to be expected," Arcana said, stepping carefully into the hallway. "I almost feel sorry for anyone stupid enough to get between Phase and his mate."

"As it should be. A mate's needs come before all other things; in that, fey culture agrees with the Illithai." Fenris paused by her side, face grim as he stared down at the bodies of his former comrades. "What is the quickest way to the ship?"

"We need to go down - but we can only get part way from here."

Arcana spun towards the elevator, tapping her chin in thought. "I'm willing to bet Shirimm's people will be waiting for us."

"Likely." Fenris' hands twitched as though he'd reach for the greatsword, then relaxed. "Whilst I have no issues with head-on confrontation, the risks will be high. Do you have another idea?"

"Yeah. I don't think we can avoid a fight entirely, but I've got a couple of tricks up my sleeve." Arcana chewed on her lip a moment. "Get back into the service staircase and I'll catch up."

"Very well." Fenris helped Caelum through the vent and then ducked inside himself. Arcana counted to ten then hit the elevator's call button, racing back to the stairwell and leaping into the gloom. With a flick of her fingers the vent settled back into place, leaving no evidence they'd ever been there.

Taking care not to clatter her boots against the stairs, Arcana hurried to catch the two males who'd gone ahead. The serviceway rumbled as the elevator moved past, carrying the gilded cage - and anyone who might be waiting inside to ambush them - up to the floor above. Arcana followed the stairs downward, breathing a sigh of relief when she caught sight of Caelum's fluffy tail. After countless sharp right turns, the stairs ended abruptly at a flat metal panel.

Arcana squeezed around Caelum as Fenris pressed an ear to the dull surface, one eye shut and the other narrowed. When he straightened, he met her gaze and held up two fingers, jerking his chin to the right. She nodded, waving him aside to set both palms against the metal sheet in front of her. Magic surged and the panel popped soundlessly off the wall. Arcana stepped silently out into the hall, the square of plasteel floating ahead of her, and turned in the direction Fenris had indicated. Two figures in grey leathers crouched at the base of the elevator shaft, hooded faces craned upwards and blasters cocked in their laps. Arcana sent the panel sailing noiselessly down the passage, the leading edge colliding with the back of one head, then the other.

Fenris blurred and then quite suddenly was kneeling beside the figures, confiscating their weapons and peering beneath their hoods. "Unconscious."

"Anyone you know?" Arcana asked.

He shook his head. "No. I'd guess there are no more of my people here besides Shirimm - she's too greedy to share power more than necessary and hired guns are much easier to control."

"I guess that makes sense." Arcana pressed the plasteel panel back against the wall, smoothing it into place with her magic. "It'll make things easier for us, too."

"Speaking of making life easier, we need to keep in mind that there are only three of us and a possible zillion of them." Caelum stared up and down the short hall. "Can you fix things so nobody can get in?"

Arcana chewed her lip in thought. "Maybe. This place is held together by spit, grease and willpower - if I yank the wrong panel, the entire station will come apart." She set both palms against the wall, magic spreading out in search of hinges and locks. The hallway had several doors whose mechanisms were easy to twist, the echoing screech of tortured metal sending shivers down Arcana's spine. She turned her attention to the elevator, curling her senses around what she already knew was an integral part of the station. To damage the elevator was beyond risky so in the end, Arcana settled for twisting the delicate gilded gate which cordoned off the actual shaft. It wasn't much but it would have to do. Stepping away from the wall, she rubbed both palms on her thighs and said; "Okay. Let's go."

Fenris turned unerringly to the one door Arcana had left untouched. He drew the greatsword and palmed it open, the blade angled back down the length of his arm as he gestured for Arcana and Caelum to follow. They emerged onto a landing overlooking an enormous, misshapen room easily six stories tall. The floor was piled high with shipping containers of all shapes and sizes and a latticework of narrow staircases clung to the outer walls. A veritable honeycomb of doors and landings were connected by a series of interconnected bridges, railed with no more than waist high cabling and giving the area an unfinished, empty feel.

Fenris strode to the thin rail along the edge of the landing, his burning gaze fixed on the myriad of choices before them. "Which way?"

"If we cross the second left bridge, we can get to the next elevator. Then we cut down and back -" Arcana broke off as one of the hexagonal doors opposite them swished open, revealing a group of grey figures equipped with the same sleek, silver pistols Shirimm had carried.

"Down!" Fenris exclaimed.

Arcana threw herself into the relative shelter of the door recess as a hail of blaster fire peppered the ground, narrowly missing her legs. Caelum raced to her side but his body didn't fit in the shallow alcove so Arcana jerked one arm up, tearing a panel from the floor with her magic to create an impromptu shield around them both. The panel spat and sizzled as a second round of blaster bolts slammed into the other side but it held, giving Arcana enough time to breathe and check her companion. "You okay?"

"Yeah. That was close." Caelum jerked backwards as a streak of orange sizzled past his nose. "Where's Fenris?"

"I thought he was with you." Arcana peered out into the chamber. Their attackers stood back to back in a small group, blaster fire scorching the walls seemingly at random. Straining her eyes, Arcana tried to follow the pattern of their attacks, the corners of her mouth stretching into an appreciative grin as she saw the greatsword flash. One of the workers yelped in alarm as his blaster fell to the floor, the barrel sheared in half.

"Aren't you going to help him?" Caelum asked as another blaster clattered onto the deck in pieces.

"Who, Fenris? I can't even see him! Besides, he doesn't look like he needs it."

"And when all the lasers are gone? He's trying very hard not to kill these ones," Caelum pointed out. "Look, they're backed against the wall and everything."

"Oh, all *right*." Arcana raised a hand, rolling her wrist in a circular motion. The metal sheeting on the opposite wall peeled and curled in response, bundling the group of would-be assassins in a tight roll of shining plasteel and pinning them against the exposed framework of the station. The warehouse was suddenly silent and Arcana stepped into the open, one hand propped on her hip. "Happy now?"

"Of course." Caelum's ears flickered in amusement as he emerged from behind the plasteel shield. "They look cosy."

Arcana snorted and opened her mouth to reply but gasped instead as Fenris dropped neatly to the floor less than a pace ahead, the greatsword already back in its' sheath. His body crowded hers, shoulders broad and scent everywhere as he bent to peer into her face. "Are you hurt?"

"No." She took a half step back so they didn't bump heads and looked up. "You?"

"I am uninjured. Thank you for your assistance." Fenris glanced at their prisoners and a spark of mischief flickered in the jade fire of his eyes. "Did I look so spectacularly helpless when you did that to me?"

Arcana eyed the pale faced prisoners and pursed her lips. "Oh, yes. Although I don't recall you whimpering quite so much."

Fenris snorted and though his face was still deadly serious, some of the tension bled out of his shoulders as he stalked across the bridge. "Where is the ship going?" he asked the nearest prisoner.

The woman snarled and spat at his feet. "Like I'd tell a green skinned freak!"

"Of course not," Fenris agreed, completely unfazed by the woman's insult. He slipped the sleeve of his jacket over one hand and bent to scoop up the still smoking barrel of a blaster, blowing idly on the hot metal. "But if not me, then perhaps my lovely companion?"

"Are you nuts? She's as creepy as you are!"

"Wow." Arcana crossed her arms over her chest. "I hope you realise my friend could've easily killed the lot of you."

"So you say." The woman lifted her chin defiantly. "You can't intimidate us with flashy moves and parlour tricks."

"Parlour tricks?" Arcana snorted and hooked her thumbs into the waistband of her pants. "Whatever helps you sleep at night, I guess."

Fenris spun the shorn-off blaster barrel, steam curling up from where it lay against his sleeve. "You owe the Pariah no loyalty. It would be in your best interests to help us and live." His expression was cold as he focussed on the trapped woman. "I will only ask this once more. Where is the ship going?"

"Go to hell," The woman spat.

"Very well." Fenris set the tip of the blaster against her neck and she screamed, twisting away from the hiss of her own burning flesh. Arcana swallowed bile as the Guardian lent in, whispering in her ear. The woman shook her head, face pale as Fenris raised the blaster to eye level.

"Stop! Please, stop." A wiry man further down shook lank hair out of his face, eyes wide as he stared at Fenris. "I'll talk."

"Don't tell him anything," the woman growled.

The man shook his head. "No salary is worth losing an eye, Lulle." He looked over at Fenris. "We don't know where the ship is going. That crazy snake bitch has all the co-ordinates on her personal datapad and feeds them into the Nav system while we're prepping to jump. We're crew and hired guns, nothing more. She has all the locations, I swear."

Fenris considered the man's words, the sleeve of his jacket beginning to smoulder beneath the heat of the metal in his hand. At last he nodded, dropping the barrel of the blaster onto the deck with a clatter. "You speak the truth. Thank you, friend."

"Wait," the man called as Fenris turned away. "You're not going to just leave us here, are you?"

"I made no promise to set you free." Fenris shrugged, slipping his hands into his pockets. "The people of Corrin's Run will liberate you eventually."

"What? They'll kill us!" The man protested.

Fenris turned at that, throwing a scathing look over one shoulder. "As you would have killed me and mine. I think you will find, however, that if you are willing to bargain your service to fix the damage your people have caused to the station, then you may yet keep your lives."

The group behind them fell silent, and Arcana didn't dare look back as she hurried to the other side of the bridge and palmed open the door. Only when it was safely closed behind her did she turn to Fenris. "Was that necessary?"

"Yes."

"You *tortured* that woman!" She hissed.

"Perhaps I did." Fenris' eyes shuttered, the jade fire little more than cooling embers as he looked down his nose. "I would have done whatever I needed to get our information. That is my job."

Arcana shook her head. "I don't understand - couldn't you just use your glamour and *make* them talk?"

If she thought Fenris' gaze had been cold before, it was nothing compared to the ice which rolled off him now. "No."

Arcana fought a shiver, clinging to the awful scent of the woman's burning flesh. "Surely looking someone in the eye to make them obey your commands is preferable to branding them with the shorn-off nose of a blaster!"

"It isn't." Fenris turned as though to dismiss her, but Arcana's temper flared and she snatched at his sleeve, swinging around in front of him.

"Why not?" She demanded. "When you tried snaring me on Sorcen, you didn't think twice. How is this different?"

Fenris went deathly still, his eyes achingly empty as they dropped to examine the pale fingers Arcana had fisted in his jacket. "When I looked at you on Sorcen, my intent was only to ascertain whether or not my abilities had returned to full strength. You should have felt the tug of my glamour and no more." He paused, worrying his lower lip in a rare sign of agitation before adding; "That would not be the case here. In order to get the sort of information you're talking about, I would have had to peel that woman's mind open and climb inside."

Arcana flinched from the image his words conjured. "Couldn't you just ask her to talk?"

"My ability doesn't work that way. For simple actions, yes, but not for complex thoughts, particularly something the other party does not wish to share." Fenris shrugged off Arcana's hand to pace back and forth in the small antechamber. "I don't know what you feel when I look at you, but if you were normal... I could break into your mind and make you do anything I wanted you to do, feel anything I wanted you to feel. You'd tell me your deepest, darkest secrets - but in extracting them, I would tear you apart so thoroughly you'd never go back together again. And the worst part is that you would enjoy every sickening second. By the time I was finished, you'd come slavering on my shoes, begging for me to do it again and again and again until there was *nothing left*."

Arcana tilted her head to one side, absorbing both the words and the undercurrents beneath them. "It sounds like you're afraid of your glamour."

"And if I was?" His voice was low, deadly.

"Then I'd say you're sensible, but only to a point. Have you ever learnt how to control it?" Arcana asked. The jumping muscle in Fenris' jaw gave her the answer and she shook her head. "Why not?"

"It cannot be controlled. My mother barricaded the glamour deep inside of me when I was young. The vast majority of it is beyond my reach and the remnants, such as they are, leak from the seal against my will." Fenris pressed both hands to his chest, as though he would extinguish the great beast slumbering inside. "I have tried to control the energy over the years and found the task impossible. The best and only way to keep others safe is to maintain a measured distance from them."

Arcana recalled his lonely words about an Overlord having no personal ties and rubbed at her temples. "Okay, so tell me straight - What would've happened if you'd looked that woman in the eye?"

"If I had looked that woman in the eye, she would have become placid, awaiting my instruction." Fenris paused, blowing air into his cheeks before adding; "I can implant basic suggestions - things like 'walk away' or 'sit down' - but I must maintain eye contact if I wish those actions to be carried out. Once the eye contact is broken, she would have returned to herself, with full memory of my control."

"That doesn't sound so terrible." Arcana frowned. "You said you can turn people into mindless, slavering beasts. If your glamour is locked away, how would you know-"

"My mother locked it away for a reason," Fenris said, his voice flat and empty.

"A magic you fear is twice as dangerous as one you can leash," she said softly. "You should learn to control it."

"How? There is no-one to teach me and I have not the courage nor inclination to learn - even assuming my mother could unleash it." Fenris shook his head, face haunted and shoulders curved inwards. "I do not know the particulars of her binding spell and I have never asked. I am simply grateful that her interference has allowed me to have as normal an existence as could be expected for one such as I."

The self-recrimination in his words made it even more difficult for Arcana to maintain her temper. "But-"

"No." Fenris shook his head. "Crippling someone's mind is not an ability I will ever consciously utilise. If that means I must use physical methods to extract information then so be it. You may add such torture to the long list of my sins." He stalked the length of the corridor and reached for the elevator without a backward glance.

Arcana wrapped both arms around herself and squeezed. She knew how it felt to be dragged along behind the chariot of fate, lost and alone; in that they weren't so different. She watched as Fenris' long, scarred fingers curled around the dented filigree of the elevator's cage and wrenched. The two halves sprang apart with a metallic shriek, showering the Guardian in a thin layer of rust which clung to his sweat-sheened skin like dried blood. The violence of his action was at such odds to the male she'd heretofore known that Arcana winced, knowing she was to blame.

"Would you have done it differently, if you were him?" Caelum breathed into her ear, low enough that even Fenris wouldn't have heard over the shriek of tortured metal.

"No," Arcana sighed. "I wouldn't have." Because whilst she still didn't condone what he'd done, she could understand why he'd done it. She followed Caelum into the elevator, leaning against the warped metalwork as Fenris dragged the cage door closed. Questions piled up in her mind and she pinched the bridge of her nose, trying unsuccessfully to sort through the chaos. She glanced at Fenris and found him watching her, fingers clenched so tightly in the open wirework of the elevator that he'd twisted it even further out of shape. Unable to stand the turmoil in his expression, she murmured; "I am officially tearing up your perceived list of sins."

He blinked. "Why?"

"Because..." Arcana sighed. It was only fair, really, to trade one jagged shard of truth for another. "Because if you have one, then so do I."

A moment's charged silence passed between them and then, astonishingly, the corner of his lip twitched ever so slightly - a movement Arcana knew she'd have missed entirely a few weeks ago. Fenris slowly relinquished his torturous grip on the side of the elevator and crossed his arms. "Very well - we will abolish my list, if only for the absolution of your own."

Arcana felt her own lip twitch in response. "Deal."

"What now?" Fenris asked. Arcana had the distinct feeling he wasn't referring to their current situation but rather the tentative truce - and sudden slipping of shields - between them. She tried to imagine how he must feel, his entire world built on a towering edifice of isolation that had been tipped upside down and spat upon by the people he had once led and loved. The idea of such loneliness, of such incredible self-sacrifice, scoured her to the bone and she sought instinctively for a way to bridge the divide between them.

"How old are you?" The question slipped her lips without thought, and Arcana's blink of surprise was in complete synchronisation with Fenris' own. Why in the name of the Gods had she asked that?

"How old are *you*?" Fenris returned, his court-calm facade dissolving to show the flustered male underneath.

Delighted by how very human he seemed in that moment, Arcana seized the distraction and offered a half smile. "You've read the books. You know how old I am. And, depending what Flare gave you, you know my birthday, my star sign and how many days are in my monthly cycle."

"You don't have a monthly cycle," Fenris said absently, his gaze far off. "It stopped once you bonded with Caelum."

Arcana rolled her eyes to the ceiling. "I'm going to kill Flare when I see him next. And the rest? Come on, indulge me."

"You are seventy two years old, born on the sixth day of the sixth month in Sorcen's fourteen-month calendar, in the early hours of the morning. Your astrological sign aligns with Betelgeuse and the Dog Star, which, if you follow the superstitious trappings of your people, accords you loyalty, a fierce temper, a healthy side of shyness and an unusual affinity for the number eleven." Fenris' voice smoothed out as he spoke and by the time he finished, there was a mischievous twinkle in those jade eyes.

Arcana huffed a laugh, tipping her head back to stare at the roof as the elevator slid along the shaft. "Well now, seeing as you know all there is to know about me, I think it's only fair I learn something about you, isn't it?"

"I suppose." Fenris was quiet for a moment, waiting until Arcana turned her head to catch his eye. "I am one hundred and forty-nine years old. In your Sorcen calendar, my birthday would be..." he fell silent, lips moving in calculation. "My birthday would be the twenty-ninth day of the seventh month."

One hundred and forty nine years. Arcana blinked rapidly, letting that sink in. It wasn't a large number - the average Sorcen life expectancy was a good three centuries - but he was certainly older than she'd expected. Rather than let her astonishment show, Arcana raised an eyebrow and said: "So that aligns you with Callisto, and the Maiden. Hard edged, with a soft touch. Stubborn, persistent and with a calling to water." She flashed him a grin. "You would have made a good healer."

Fenris raised an eyebrow. "A calling to water?"

"Do you like long showers?"

His answering grin was wicked. "You have no idea."

Arcana shivered beneath the heavy velvet of his voice, a blush heating her cheeks. The elevator was abruptly too small, Fenris' shoulders too large, his bearing incalculably masculine. This, she thought, fighting to steady her traitorous breathing - this was the man underneath, the man he covered with copious layers of both emotional and physical armour. Every instinct screamed danger but Arcana couldn't help the half step she took towards him, drawn by the warmth in his face. Fenris blinked, his expression shifting to one of surprise - and the carriage pinged and slowed to a stop.

"Nobody ever asks about *my* birthday," Caelum said tartly, neatly breaking the tension as he stepped past Arcana and rapped a forehoof on the cage door. Fenris obligingly reached over to haul the door open, earning himself a sharp look from Caelum in the process. "I'll have you know my astrology is just as interesting as Arcana's."

Fenris barked a short, sharp laugh and waved the deerken out ahead of him. "Your birthday is the fourteenth day of Sorcen's tenth month. Aligned with Groudus and the Centaur. According to your interesting astrology, that makes you sweet, headstrong and unusually interested in flowers."

"Well." Caelum's ears flickered, his tone clearing. "Flowers *are* rather delicious."

The Guardian grinned, ruffled the fur between Caelum's antlers and glanced back at Arcana. "Where now?"

"The best place to meet Phase will be at the accommodation for visiting crew. It's closest to the bays we need." Arcana ducked under Fenris' arm and stepped into the short, empty hallway. "With any luck, there'll be fewer people trying to kill us this way."

Caelum snorted. "Reassuring."

"If Shirimm has truly raised the alarm, her crew will be spreading through the station to lie in wait for us." Fenris yanked the elevator door closed behind him. "I wish I could put my faith in luck, but somehow I doubt it will be smiling upon us today."

"Well then, keep your sword hand limber, I guess. And maybe your ears?" Arcana pointed to the lone door opposite. Fenris pressed his ear against it for a long moment before swinging the door wide, revealing a large foyer which had, like many areas aboard Corrin's Run, been turned into an impromptu storage room. Bags, baskets and crates lined the walls and crowded the floors, leaving a maze whose wobbly walls stood even taller than Fenris' generous seven feet.

"Ready to be loaded in the morning, you think?" Caelum wandered over to the nearest pile of bags and sniffed. "Smells like grease and body odour."

"They definitely look like personal belongings. Shame we don't know which ship they're for." Arcana threaded between the piles, heading for the door in the opposite wall. She'd barely gone five steps when an enormous explosion rocked the station and for the second time in an hour, Arcana slammed into the grated flooring. The impact knocked the wind from her body and sent her rolling haphazardly into the side of a crate, which promptly tipped a pile of other boxes and bags on top of her legs, pinning her in place. A second impact shuddered through the station and Arcana threw out her magic to soothe the bucking floor but it was no use, the explosion sending a fresh round of luggage raining down around her. Crossing her arms over her face like a shield, Arcana took the brunt of a falling case with a grunt, shoving it aside as the commotion eased.

"That sounded like a laser battery." Fenris heaved a duffel bag out of the way and clambered out of his own pile of luggage. He negotiated toppled crates and upended suitcases to kneel beside Arcana, examining the heavy bags on her legs. "Are you all right?"

"Fine," she managed, pushing up to her elbows. "Caelum?"

"Here." His head, followed slowly by the rest of him, appeared around the edge of a large basket. "We need to-"

The third impact was by far the most violent. Arcana glimpsed Caelum toppling sideways in a bundle of hooves and bags before a shadow fell across her vision. She looked up to see an enormous crate tipping towards her and though she groped at her magic, knew there was no way to stop it. She turned her head to the side and closed her eyes, praying it wasn't as heavy as it looked - but the blow never came.

"Arcana?" Her own name, sent down her ear on a shiver of air. Arcana opened her eyes to see Fenris braced over her, bearing the weight of the wooden crate across his shoulders with the gods knew what else piled on top. Relief painted his features for a fraction of a second before he said; "You need to get out of the way."

"Trapped," Arcana muttered. Boxes and bags hemmed them in from all directions... bar the floor. Arcana drew a deep, steadying breath. "Caelum? Can you hear me?"

"Yeah." Shaky but nearby.

Arcana swallowed. "Brace yourselves."

"This is going to hurt, isn't it?" Caelum grumbled.

"It might." Arcana set her palms against the metal floor, sending her energy between spars and wires and tubing until an empty space signalled the room beneath. With a silent prayer to any listening gods, she flexed her fingers and the floor cleft in two.

For a moment, there was only the stomach-lurching sensation of free fall and a painful tingling in Arcana's legs as, now freed from their imprisonment, blood began to flow anew. Fenris' eyes went wide as they began to plummet, the precarious collection of boxes and bags becoming a dangerous rain. He heaved aside the crate he'd been supporting and dragged Arcana into a fierce embrace, one arm supporting her shoulders and the other beneath her knees, curling his body around hers until she breathed deep of the night-time forest and nothing else. Arcana knit her fingers together as they shot out the other side of the impromptu tunnel, closing the floor - which was now the roof - and sealing in most of the luggage before it could crush them.

"Hold on," Fenris warned. They slammed into the floor with a ringing crash that he absorbed with barely a flex of his knees. Debris rained down around them, a deadly combination of smashed luggage and broken steel that Fenris sidestepped with preternatural speed. They shot around the room so swiftly Arcana closed her eyes and clutched at his chest, concentrating on the steady sound of Fenris' heart and the whipping of the wind created solely by his movement.

It was over as suddenly as it began, the Guardian's motion arresting so abruptly that Arcana's stomach lurched in protest. What had once been a simple suite of rooms was now a mess of splintered furniture and torn baggage. Still cradling Arcana against his chest, Fenris crouched atop a fractured crate, his skin slick with a sheen of sweat and his body thrumming. She looked up to find him already watching her, jade eyes burning feverishly bright. The glamour rose around them like a tide, crashing over Arcana's senses and stealing the breath from her lungs in place of a tingling, electric energy which reflected the half-wild look on Fenris' face.

"Well." Caelum erupted from the remains of a faded divan, kicking aside bits of shattered wood and fuzzy stuffing with such ferocious intent that Arcana jumped, tearing her gaze from Fenris' whilst a blush rode high on her cheeks. Nose wrinkled in disgust, Caelum picked his way out of the wreckage and shook himself all over. "Let's not do that again any time soon."

"Where are we?" Fenris jumped down to the floor, lowered Arcana to her feet - and snatched her against his chest as she staggered and hissed. "You're hurt."

"I'm fine. Just some bruises." She tested her legs a second time and winced as her shins groaned in protest. "We're in the level where visitors are housed, but a little lower than I originally intended. Are you okay?"

"I believe I'll live." Fenris' lips curved in a lopsided smile. He released her more carefully this time, one broad hand splayed across her back until he was certain her legs were steady. "That was quick thinking."

Arcana smiled in return, brushing an errant lock of hair out of her face. "Thanks."

"I'm fine too, thanks for asking." Caelum's acidic tone had Arcana giggling, and she picked her way through the wreckage to throw her arms around his neck. The deerken huffed into her hair and said; "You know, 'brace yourself' isn't really adequate warning for 'I'm going to take the floor away'."

"Sorry. I wanted us out of there as quickly as possible." She kissed Caelum's furry nose to emphasise her apology. "I wonder what happened?"

"Nothing pleasant, that's for sure. Those explosions were all on one side of the station," Caelum replied.

"Maybe Phase will know." Arcana pulled away, moving to the door. The frame was warped and the panel a sparking mess, so she wrenched the steel apart with magic instead. The hall beyond was empty, the walls ruptured in sections so that supports and wiring were exposed, but nothing appeared beyond repair.

"We should - wait." Fenris dragged Arcana back into the room and held a hand in the air for silence. Shaking him off, she frowned and strained her ears. Someone was moaning and grunting, the sounds accompanied by a wet, dragging noise.

"Whoever it is, they're injured," Caelum murmured.

"Wait here." Fenris stepped smoothly into the corridor and leapt upwards, disappearing silently into the ruined roof. After what seemed eternity but was likely no more than a minute, a startled yelp echoed from around the corner and a half-charged blaster whined, the pathetic sound cut short by a metallic swish and thump.

"Did you *have* to?" The indignant voice was deep, rolling, and familiar.

"Yes." Fenris emerged from around the corner, a glaring Rito slung under one arm. The pirate's tattooed skin was smeared with blood in a variety of shades, some of it his own, and he cradled what remained of his musket in both hands.

"Rito!" Arcana helped Fenris settle the pirate against one wall. He had a large gash down the side of his face which looked shallow, but one leg was bent at an unnatural angle. "What happened?"

"Phase and I were coming to meet you, lass - then the station blew apart." Rito's snort turned into a snarl as Fenris prodded at his leg. "Leave it, you ass. It's broken."

"I can see that." Fenris ignored the pirate's string of foul curses as he peered up the leg of Rito's shorts. "It needs to be straightened and set. Unless you wish never to walk again?"

"Fine." Rito's face turned ashen as Fenris began sorting through the debris for a splint. "Wait... not yet. Let me talk a minute first, in case I faint when you - you know."

The Guardian paused with two broken pipes in hand. "Go on."

"It was the ship... the warg ship. They've blown a hole in the side of the docking bay and are out." Rito grimaced, wiping a hand across his bleeding forehead. "They've got Burke on board."

"Gods *dammit*," Arcana seethed, running a hand through her hair. "Where's Phase?"

"He went looking for you. I stayed behind, for obvious reasons." Rito waved a hand towards his leg. "I was trying to find some cover when captain magnificent here showed up and cut my musket in half."

The pirate's indignation was palpable but Fenris merely raised a sculpted brow. "An understandable reaction considering you attempted to shoot me." He extended the two wrinkled pipes toward Arcana. "Can I ask you straighten these? I need to find something to bind Rito's leg."

"Sure." Arcana settled herself more comfortably on the floor, reaching over Rito's legs to accept the slim pieces of metal. She curled her fingers around the piping and sent her magic inside, straightening dents and kinks until both pieces were whole again.

"You look pretty banged up, lass." Rito was watching her through eyes narrowed in pain, his head resting against the side of the station. Arcana looked up from beneath her lashes, recalling Fenris' declaration of the pirate's feelings. It seemed absurd, couldn't possibly be true. And yet, now that Fenris had wandered off... Rito's eyes strayed to the bite mark on her neck.

Arcana raised her fingers to it, wishing her hand didn't tremble, and said quietly; "Why?"

"It was an accident," Rito croaked. "I... got carried away."

"I don't believe you," Arcana whispered, heart frozen in her chest. "Tell me the truth or I swear I'll walk away and leave you here to rot."

Rito flinched. After a long moment, the pirate licked his lips and said; "It truly was an accident. Burke instructed me to pass you the chip once she had captain magnificent out of the way. The plan made sense; invite you down for a drink, talk to you under cover of a little something else and our uninvited guests would never know there was more to it than two mercs letting off steam the way we're known to do. I only ever meant to hold you... but then I saw it."

"Saw what?"

"The way *he* looks at you when he thinks you're not looking." Rito shifted position and hissed at the pain in his leg. "And when I saw his face, I-" he shook his head.

Arcana clenched her hand into a fist, crushing the pipe she'd just straightened. "So you're telling me you made an assumption based on another person's expression - someone I was hired to protect, someone you know nothing about - and decided what? Whoever bites first wins?"

Rito raised an eyebrow. "That's how it works where I come from, lass."

Arcana's breath froze in her throat. Her heart stuttered and for a long moment she thought it would stop. "I am not a *possession*." That voice didn't belong to her, it couldn't - it was too cold and empty. "Where I come from, we take people out to dinner, or buy them flowers. I didn't even know what had happened until Fenris explained it to me. Did you think, for a moment, how that sort of violation might make me *feel*?"

"I have no idea how you feel! I waited half a lifetime for a peep under the hood but you never so much as blinked my way. Can you really blame me for taking a chance when it's presented?" Rito slumped down further against the wall. "I figured you wouldn't really understand, and if you did - well, I hoped you'd come around eventually."

"Then you know nothing about me at all." Arcana straightened the pipe with a snap, then dropped it on the floor, pushing to her feet. "And I have no wish to know anything more about you." She spun away, storming for the far end of the corridor. Fenris stood in the doorway of the suite they'd wrecked, strips of torn clothing dangling from one fist. Arcana extended a hand, setting it over Fenris' heart, and looked up to meet those burning eyes. His glamour immediately cloaked her, warm and ticklish and... comforting. So she did not feel angry, or afraid, or anything but grateful for his presence as she said; "He's all yours."

He lowered his lids once, though not far enough to break their eye contact. Arcana breathed in his night-time forest and cinnamon scent, filling her lungs and pushing away the queasiness her conversation with Rito had created. In a voice like sighing leaves, Fenris said; "Are you all right?"

"I will be." Arcana wanted to take to her own throat and scratch off the fine grazing but settled instead for clenching her fists so tightly the nails dug into her palms. "Bind Rito's leg and leave him. We need to find Phase."

Fenris nodded, holding her gaze a fraction longer before she slid her hand from his chest and kept walking, refusing to look back over her shoulder to see what Rito thought of their interaction. What he thought of the way Fenris 'looked' at her. Arcana swallowed her snarl. She was done with conniving, controlling males; first Algae and now Rito! They could both rot in Craddagh's cauldron for all she cared. Caelum nuzzled at her shoulder as she approached and Arcana twined her fingers in his fur, accepting the comfort as she used her magic to open the warped door at the far end of the hall. The deerken shoved his bulk in front, checking the room beyond carefully before he stepped around the corner and out of sight of the pirate in the hall.

"Pig," Caelum commented as Arcana swept through the door and set her back against the wall on the other side. Behind them, she heard Rito's muffled scream as Fenris set his leg. "He doesn't deserve that wad of cloth he's biting on."

"Forget it." Arcana tilted her head back to examine the twisted wiring in the roof cavity. "He's not my type anyway."

"Doesn't excuse him taking liberties where he shouldn't," Caelum answered.

"Liberties?" Arcana cut him a dry glance. "Have you been reading period romances again?"

Caelum bumped his nose against her. "I'll have you know that Lord Whitehaven is a very sensible man. He would *never* bite an innocent lady."

Try though she might, Arcana couldn't help the giggles which overcame her, pushing and sweeping their way up and out until, by the time Fenris arrived, she was caught between a bought of hiccups and a fit of coughing.

"What in the name of the Weaver?" Fenris turned wide eyes from Arcana to Caelum, who shrugged.

"Don't blame me," said the deerken. "It was Lord Whitehaven's fault."

Arcana snorted and thumped her chest, blinking back the tears which lined her eyes. "Stop it," she managed, waving a warning finger. "We need to keep moving."

Fenris gave her a long look before he crossed the mostly empty foyer and pressed his ear against the door. "What is on the other side of this?"

"A cool room, then the kitchens, which adjoin both a bar and servery. There's a bridge beyond that which connects to the docking bays on this side of the station - we're going to end up back at the *Wandering Sorceress* instead of where we should've been." Arcana swallowed the last of her mirth, moving to join him.

Fenris ran his hands over the door, leaning back just far enough to examine the mechanism. "Can you contact Phase at all?"

"I tried while you two were with Rito." Caelum's tail swished back and forth. "He either isn't answering or his gear got fried."

"If Phase's gear was fried and he was looking for us..." Arcana furrowed her brow. "I wonder if he'd head for the *Sorceress*?"

"A reasonable assumption, particularly if he wishes to pursue Burke." Fenris nodded.

"Okay, so heading back to the ship isn't so bad after all." Arcana sucked on her teeth a moment. "Other than the fact that if Shirimm's mercs have half a brain between them they'll be headed for the *Sorceress*, too."

"Agreed - we must proceed with caution. The room beyond sounds empty, but I cannot hear further than that." Fenris palmed the door and to Arcana's surprise it slid open, albeit with a terrible squealing of metal on metal.

She stalked into the store room beyond, navigating rows of shelving until she reached the door to the kitchens. It was already open, revealing a cooking area beyond that was mostly obscured by great clouds of steam. Fenris drew to a halt beside Arcana, nostrils flaring as he scented the path ahead. He flicked a glance at Caelum and held up two fingers.

The deerken's nose twitched and he nodded. "Chef and assistant. They've been here for years - I know their scents."

For the barest of moments Arcana wondered what it would be like to build pictures of the world with only her nose as guidance. It seemed another language, something far more intricate and perhaps even more intimate than the way her own senses worked. Then the chef's assistant came strolling into the store room with an empty bowl in his hands, whistling tunelessly. He caught sight of them and stopped, whereupon Fenris drew the greatsword in a flourish of shimmering silver. The assistant dropped his bowl with a loud crash and began backing up with both hands raised, his face pale with fear.

"Demmon? What're you -" the chef raised his meat cleaver as Arcana stepped through the steam, holding her own hands up in a placating gesture.

"It's only me," she said, wishing she could remember the man's name. "We're just passing through. Have you seen any of those brutes in grey leathers?"

The chef pursed his lips a moment, glancing pointedly at the greatsword. When Fenris sheathed the blade, he turned to bury the meat cleaver in a nearby wooden block and grunted. "Seen a few about an hour ago. Went through the servery; dunno where from or to. Not that I care! That damned blast upended tomorrow's stew and now I've gotta start fresh."

Caelum stalked toward the archway and peered through. "Servery's empty."

"'Course it is," the chef snorted, bracing his hands on his hips. "It's the middle of the night." Then he blinked, twice, and peered at Caelum. "Did that thing just talk?"

"It's the way the room echoes. Sure can be deceiving sometimes, right?" Arcana smiled her sweetest smile. "Thanks for the help." She snapped her fingers, a summoning sound that bought Caelum trailing blank-eyed to her side. "If it's all the same to you, I'll take my hire and be on my way."

"Sure. Nice seein' you." The chef waved a chubby hand, still frowning at Caelum as they slid past the cooktops, pots and sink.

"Good luck with your stew." Fenris sketched a quick bow and then they palmed the door - this one opening without protest - and hurried through.

"That was close." Caelum sagged as the door swished shut. "I forget, sometimes."

"Don't worry about it. Right now, the chef hearing you speak is the least of our worries," Arcana told him.

Fenris' eyes tracked the length of the long, narrow corridor which was not really a part of the station so much as a giant spoke between sections of a wheel. The roof was made from clear plexiglass and showed space beyond, the vast blackness swirling with stars and the ever-present asteroid storm that ensconced Corrin's Run. "This is not a place we want to linger in."

"No. And it's not that I don't trust the chef, but..." Arcana turned to lay her hands against the door.

Fenris watched the metal twist and pucker, his eyes narrowed. "How long will that hold?"

"Depends. It won't open on command but there are other ways through." Arcana flicked him a glance and got a grim nod in return. She pushed away from the door and started along the tunnel. "Like you said - not a place we want to linger."

"With all the explosions tonight, I'm not sure that anywhere aboard the Run is ideal at the minute." Caelum's nose appeared over Arcana's left shoulder and she reached up to scratch beneath his chin. "At least everything here is in one piece."

"Oh, please. It wouldn't be a proper visit if something didn't get wrecked." Arcana tried to keep her tone light, all the while casting a look over her shoulder. Caelum's bulk blocked the majority of her view but the door behind them remained closed. When Arcana turned back, Fenris stood before the final door, once more placing his ear against it.

"Too much noise on the other side for me to make anything out," he said finally.

"I can't say I'm surprised - the docking bay is through there. Even at this time of night, it'll be noisy." Arcana chewed on the inside of her cheek. "Well... here goes." She leant around Fenris and palmed the door open.

Phase stood on the other side, with an array of armed dock workers around him - most of them in pale grey leathers carefully disguised by grease and tools, or open jackets tied around the waist. Phase spoke in low tones but it was impossible to miss the anger evident in the lines of his body, or his short, sharp gestures. The *Wandering Sorceress* hung in space outside of the docking area, her running lights illuminating the side of the station and the several smaller shuttles parked up the far end of the bay. Every set of eyes swivelled to watch as the door swished open, followed quickly by shouting and a bristling array of weaponry.

"Run!" Phase cried, waving his arms.

Arcana ducked back around the edge of the door frame as several blasters fired in their direction. Fenris slapped the controls on the door and it swished closed, catching the blaster fire with a clanking groan. He drew the greatsword in one fluid motion, wrapped both hands around the hilt and drove the blade into the control panel, destroying it in a shower of sparks.

"Now what?" Caelum asked. "I didn't see a thing."

"Phase is in there, with a bunch of workers - mostly Shirimm's people - who want to shoot us, not help us. And the ship's out in space in a holding pattern," Arcana spat.

"They're really making this difficult, aren't they?" Caelum's ears flickered, then his eyes went wide. "Behind us!"

A muffled explosion sounded from the kitchen and Arcana spun around as the door behind them buckled, one corner melting to admit a rainbow of weapon fire. Fenris leapt overhead, greatsword flashing as he deflected the shots, landing neatly in the centre of the walkway. "Close it!" He shouted. The greatsword's enormous blade shone like a mirror, twisting this way and that with breath-taking speed and precision. Every blaster bolt that hit bounced off with a *ping!* and ricocheted harmlessly into the floor or walls. "Quickly!"

Arcana laced her magic through the ruined door and grimaced. "I can't! The walls are too thin - I'll tear a rift in the side of the station."

Fenris deflected a blaster bolt back through the opening with a snarl. A scream sounded in response and the incoming fire hesitated. "Find another way. I cannot hold this forever."

Part of Arcana doubted that but her thoughts were interrupted by Caelum shoving with his shoulder. "They're cutting through this door, too."

"What? Damn! Okay, new plan." Arcana reached into the leather satchel still slung around Caelum's neck, rummaging through the contents until she found what she wanted. "Fenris, duck!"

The Guardian followed her instruction without question, his green eyes tracking the smoke grenade Arcana sent arcing overhead. Her magic guided the projectile through the hole in the door, where it detonated immediately, smoke billowing out into the walkway. Fenris was on his feet in an instant, swinging the greatsword as he dove into the roiling mess.

An ominous hissing noise called Arcana's attention to the door at her own end of the corridor. She leapt aside as it melted into a puddle of slag, revealing a woman carrying a rocket launcher. The merc aimed upward and fired the rocket straight into the ceiling, shattering the plexiglass with the sheer weight of the warhead alone. Then the rocket detonated and the force of the explosion threw Arcana to the floor, Caelum landing squarely on top of her. A howling noise filled the tunnel and she scrabbled desperately for purchase as the atmosphere began to suck out through the shattered ceiling.

Caelum dug his hooves into the grated flooring and held, the weight of his chest pinning her down. "I've got you. Close the hole and -"

Agony slammed through Arcana, arching her spine and tearing her fingers from their precarious hold. She tried to scream but there was no breath in her lungs; tried to twist and could not move. Caelum jerked against her, his body bowing in pain as he lost his grip and they began to float. Fire worked Arcana's veins a second time, an invisible force flipping her end over end. She glimpsed Caelum tumbling in a similar fashion a few paces away, his body wracked with blue electricity, and realised at last what had happened.

Someone had shot them with a godsdamned *lightning cannon*.

Moments became aeons as Arcana focused on flexing her fingers, on trying to gather her wits, her magic, and close the hole in the side of the space station. Then the lightning cannon hit her again and it was all she could do to stay conscious while electricity arced and snapped across her flesh, pressing her teeth together until they ached. The shockwaves slapped her magic aside so thoroughly Arcana was dizzy from it, tears leaking unbidden down her cheeks. Another shot went past her, a ball of crackling blue that shoved Caelum through the hole in the ceiling and out into space. Arcana stared, helpless, unable even to scream as the merciless vacuum sucked him around the side of the space station and out of sight.

Just like that, the deerken was gone. Arcana's heart cracked, a fissure through which an agony unlike any other began to leech, eclipsing even the consuming burn of the lightning cannon. She stared in horror at the hole in the ceiling, the escaping atmosphere sucking her inexorably towards it. Space would surely claim the deerken before he could float far enough away for the elastic band effect to kick in - and as soon as Caelum's heart stopped, hers would, too. Light refracted off shattered plexiglass and Arcana blinked through a prism of rainbow tears, unable to think past the screaming inside her soul.

A solid arm wrapped Arcana's waist and slammed her down, body to body. The whipping wind caught her clothes, her hair as she looked up - or was it down - into Fenris' burning green gaze. His glamour rose around them, cleaving that awful emptiness, and she took a great, wrenching breath of too-thin air. The Guardian's jaw was set, the warmth of his body a beacon she couldn't ignore no matter how she tried. His fingers curled around Arcana's ribs, pinning her so tightly to his chest her bones creaked. The other hand was clenched around the greatsword, driven into the walkway as an anchor against the awful, impossible sucking of deep space. Blood spattered his face and neck, and Arcana raised a twitching hand to stroke one sweeping cheek bone. Perhaps, if she couldn't see Caelum one last time, Fenris was not such a bad option. Even covered in blood, he was breathtakingly beautiful - and his lips were moving, speaking with that velvety rumble, though she couldn't hear anything over the buzzing inside her head.

Fenris' lips moved again and it was a supreme effort to focus, to hear as he shouted; "The lightning! Do you have the lightning?"

"It doesn't matter," Arcana wheezed, her lungs fluttering. The air was fading fast - and still the relentless vacuum of space sought to tear them free of Corrin's Run. "I've lost Caelum."

"*No.* If you live, so does he." Fenris bared his teeth to show fangs, his voice so sharp that Arcana blinked. His glamour slid along her skin, warm and real and comforting, pushing against the terrible, reaching dark that sparkled at the edges of her vision. "Pull yourself together and let's go get him."

Let's go get him. The words reverberated inside Arcana's skull, setting her heart thumping unnaturally loud in her chest. Behind Fenris, a bloody smear along the wall marked the passing of whoever had used the lightning cannon. And now... The woman with the rocket launcher reappeared in the doorway, her feet heavy in magnetic boots. Time seemed to slow as Arcana stared down the barrel, listening to the click and beep as a rocket was loaded. *Let's go get him.*

Arcana looked at Fenris and smiled a thin, cold smile. "I have the lightning." She raised her arm and blue electricity arced from her palm, striking their opponent square in the chest. The other woman screamed, her body convulsing - and fired the rocket straight into the doorframe beside her.

Blood and body parts flew past Arcana in a crimson storm but she was already moving, turning in Fenris' arms to crawl up his body. She slipped her fingers into the thin grid of the metal grating and swung arm over arm to the door. Fenris appeared beside her, holding tight in a similar fashion, the greatsword now sheathed across his back. Arcana caught the shattered edge of the door in one hand, electricity arcing from her fingertips and bouncing haphazardly through the doorway. She sent out one last, frantic pulse and then pulled herself into the docking bay, ignoring the sharp metal cutting into her palms. Three more members of Shirimm's crew lay on the floor, jerking and twitching as blue lightning crackled across their bodies.

"Are you hurt?" Fenris shouted into her ear, his voice snatched away by the whipping wind - a stark reminder that they were still losing air at an alarming rate.

"No." Arcana trusted his ears to pick up her voice and was rewarded with a squeeze of her fingers in acknowledgment. "But I can't see Caelum anywhere."

"What about the elastic band effect?" Fenris crouched beside her, his words punctuated by great, heaving gasps as his body, so much larger than hers, struggled for air.

"I don't know." Arcana shook her head. The enormous docking bay doors were open, the atmospheric shield that stretched over the giant hole allowing an unprecedented view of the *Wandering Sorceress* floating just outside. She gained her feet and looked past the ship, searching the sparkling darkness. The area was littered with debris from the shattered corridor but none of it took the form of a deerken. "Wherever he is, he must be too close."

"Down!" Fenris threw Arcana to the floor, covering her with his body. Laser fire flashed, the heat of it brushing her nose and leaving behind the faintest whiff of singed hair. Arcana peered out from beneath the curve of Fenris' shoulder in a vain effort to see their attackers, but he pinned her in place with a decisive movement of his hips. "Stop it," the Guardian growled. "We need to think for a moment."

"We're running out of time," she wheezed, elbowing him in the ribs. "I need to find Caelum before his heart stops."

A blaster whined and Fenris rolled them sideways with a muffled curse. Arcana wriggled in his iron grip, trying in vain to get free and upright but Fenris held firm, growling nonsense in her ear. Caelum. She had to find *Caelum*. The area was filled with shipping crates, no doubt the last of the supplies that had been destined for their ship in the morning. The tall, haphazard stacks of boxes made it impossible to see where their enemies were hiding.

"Dammit, Arcana, *stop*," Fenris rasped, rolling them into the relative shelter of an overturned tool cart. He braced his elbows either side of her face, baring his teeth. "If you run out there now, they'll pick you off and I can't keep up with the air so thin. We need to draw them out."

Realising he was right, she stopped struggling. "Create a distraction and I'll use the lightning to clean the bastards up."

"Consider it done - but we will only have one chance. Now run," Fenris commanded. Arcana opened her mouth to remind him that they were lying on the ground when quite suddenly they were upright, the Guardian tugging her across the open space behind him. Three steps, four - and another volley of blaster bolts tracked across the floor towards them. Arcana spotted a trio of silhouettes crouched behind a tall shipping crate, one firing whilst another reloaded. She clenched her fist and lighting sparked but before she had a chance to release it, heavy laser fire cut across the front of her vision. The shipping container shattered in a shower of splinters and half-slagged food cans, the wind from the smashed corridor dragging away the explosion and snatching at the screams which punctuated it. Screams that were abruptly cut off by a second barrage of that same heavy, sizzling laser fire. Arcana swallowed. She knew that hum, knew that particular hue of energy - an icy shade of mauve that came from being focussed through a Sorcen crystal array. Slowly, carefully, Arcana turned her head to the side. The *Wandering Sorceress* had moved from her holding pattern and was now squarely in the entrance of the docking bay, heavy laser batteries trained on the area.

"We'll be out of air in a minute," Fenris wheezed, his face pale. "And we cannot fight the ship."

"Watch me." Arcana's teeth clenched, her eyes tracking over the hull as she began gathering and amplifying the lightning in her blood. She might be about to die, but she'd be damned if she didn't take as many assholes as possible with her. She took a rattling breath and stared through the windscreen onto the bridge, straight into the eyes of - "Caelum!" Arcana shrieked, tears spilling down her cheeks. Sure enough, Caelum stood upon the bridge, his antler rack covered in frost and his starry eyes reaching for hers even across the distance of space.

"Thank the Weaver," Fenris breathed - and then coughed. "Arcana, we need to move." As if in response to his words, the cruiser's cargo ramp lowered and the *Wandering Sorceress* inched closer to the docking platform. Arcana took three steps forward and then stopped, a flicker of grey catching her eye.

"Wait!" She grabbed Fenris' arm as he made to drag her away. Phase's legs stuck out from behind a support pillar, his long, curved swords discarded on the floor nearby. Fenris strode quickly to the Illithai, his fingers a brand around Arcana's wrist - though he released her to crouch beside Phase, placing his ear to the other's chest.

"He lives, but I am flagging. Help me," Fenris grunted as he dragged the unconscious male upright, staggering under the weight. Arcana rushed to Phase's other side, stuffing his swords into their scabbards and sliding under his limp arm so she could help Fenris drag the enormous Illithai towards the ship. Her lungs burned and spots danced at the edges of her vision but she dug nails into her palms in an attempt to focus and pushed onward. One step. Two steps. Up the ramp.

"Here." Caelum appeared beside her, nosing at one shoulder until she slung an arm across his back. "Come on. Almost there."

The deerken dragged them all up the ramp and into the ship, Fenris and Phase now mere shadows in Arcana's peripheral vision. Caelum deposited her on the floor and disappeared - he'd spoken, but she had no energy left to comprehend what had been said. Blood roared in her ears, almost drowning out the hiss of the airlock as it irised shut and the hum of the crystal engines as the ship began to move. Arcana turned her face into one arm, head swimming as Fenris' body thumped down beside hers.

It would be so easy to sleep, to drift away on the cotton of her mind but even as Arcana contemplated doing just that, cold air sliced into her lungs. She coughed and gasped, her eyes flying open. The second breath hurt as much as the first, the air slapping against her teeth and sending a chill to the depths of her soul. Something warm brushed her fingertips and she looked up to see Fenris' fingers curled against her own, a tentative touch which flitted away before returning, those long green digits brushing the length of her smaller, paler hand.

Arcana drew deep, burning breaths into her lungs and tilted her head to stare at the Guardian before her, the movement more difficult than she cared to admit. Fenris remained face down on the floor, ocean-dark curls tumbling across his cheek and brow, eyes closed. Taking advantage of his inattention, Arcana raked her gaze down the sculpted length of his body. It really was unfair, the way Fenris' black clothing clung to every lean inch - enhancing pale scars, contrasting soft teal skin and displaying every tempting ridge and hollow in a way his tatty linens had not. In that moment he wasn't the injured knight she'd rescued, nor the cool warrior who'd followed her to the zombie pit; not even the dangerous warrior prince who had leered at Burke as though born with the expression on his face. No, this was someone else again, someone more rugged, more real.

Battle-hardened, Arcana thought; a force of will forged in fires she was certain had been far worse than he'd yet let on. She shifted her gaze to Fenris' hand, to those scarred, calloused fingers resting against her smoother ones and was seized by an overwhelming urge to curl her body against the length of his, to draw his arm across her chest and tuck their entwined hands beneath her chin. Arcana craved the heat of Fenris' body pressed against hers, their lungs shifting together, the thump of one heart echoing the other. Her breathing sharpened as she battled with herself, eyes still glued on the place where their two fingers touched, mind awhirl with a cacophony of voices. Something inside her tightened, something warm and solid and real -

"Arcana?" Caelum's voice broke the spell and she rolled to one side, head spinning from the sudden movement. Dragging herself to her hands and knees, Arcana reached up as Caelum lowered his head, throwing her arms around his neck with a strangled sob.

"Caelum," she breathed, clinging tight as the deerken raised his head and set her on her feet. Arcana sagged against his body, running her hands over the lines of Caelum's shoulders, his spine, checking for injury. "Great Gods of Sorcen, you're all right. I thought I'd lost you."

"Turns out I'm not so easy to lose." Caelum nuzzled her hair and Arcana let out another sob, squeezing until he grunted a soft protest. His fur smelled of cocoa and burnt sugar, sweet and solid and infinitely comforting - albeit tinged with the frost of space.

"How are you alive?" Arcana managed at last, taking his precious head between her hands and kissing his nose. "When you were sucked outside..."

"I know." A single ear flickered, the only sign Caelum had been bothered by his ordeal. "Two things. One, the angle of the vacuum swept me up against the side of the *Sorceress*, which was awfully handy. Two, and probably most noteworthy, I can breathe in space."

Arcana's jaw slackened and she stared in disbelief. "You *what*?"

"I can breathe in space. Or rather, I can comfortably not breathe in space." Caelum frowned, both ears flickering at the inadequacy of his explanation. "I held my breath at first but I hit the ship so hard the wind was knocked right out of me. I opened my mouth on instinct... and was fine. I felt like I was breathing but it's space. There's nothing there."

"How it that possible?" Arcana breathed, fingers tightening on his jaw.

"It's because he's a deerken." Fenris' voice was hoarse as he pushed up to his knees, face twisted into a grimace.

"Welcome back," Caelum said. "How do you feel?"

"I feel - ugh, my chest." Fenris grabbed at the front of his jacket with one hand, closing his eyes and taking a few deep breaths. "That was distinctly unpleasant."

"Unpleasant," Arcana echoed, glancing down at Phase's unconscious body, "Is not the word I would use."

Fenris gave her an edged smile. "I was trying to be polite. I am most grateful for your help, brother," he added, nodding to Caelum.

"Any time. Sorry I wasn't faster." Caelum's lip twitched in a humourless grin. "You look like shit."

Fenris barked a laugh which quickly became a cough. Arcana reached into one of the nearby supply crates and dragged out a jug of water, tugging it awkwardly across the floor. "Here. I assume you can manage that?"

"Thank you." Fenris smiled up at her, the corners of his eyes creasing. He punctured the seal with a finger, then wrapped one hand around the neck of the jug and hoisted it to his lips for a large swig.

Fascinated by the way his throat muscles worked - and terrified of that same fascination - Arcana turned back to Caelum. "Keep talking."

"Seeing as the *Sorceress* was pulled away from the dock, I guessed that Shirimm had someone stationed aboard. I climbed around the hull, opened an access hatch and came in." Caelum shrugged as though it were no mean feat.

"What happened to the hijacker?" Arcana asked.

Caelum's spine stiffened. "He went out the way I came in."

"Good." Arcana leant forward, resting her forehead against Caelum's. *"Good."*

"Can we go back to the breathing in space part?" Caelum pinned Fenris with his starry eyes. "You said it's because I'm a deerken."

Fenris nodded, sitting back on his heels. "I am hypothesising, of course, but it makes a certain type of sense. Normal deerken blend into their environment; they are never truly anchored to any one singular place, time or existence, save when in the Timeless Kingdom. Your body, however, does not fade; it adapts, changing to suit the environment. We've seen it with your fur, your antlers - so instead of walking between space the way a normal deerken would, you simply became a part of it."

"Huh. Makes sense I guess," Caelum nodded, his gaze speculative. "So if I went and flushed myself out the airlock..."

"Let's not," Arcana held up both hands, her heart skipping a beat as she recalled the sight of Caelum being sucked out of the shattered window.

"Hypothetically," Caelum reassured.

Fenris merely shrugged. "If you flushed yourself out of the airlock, you would be fine."

"Okay, so... what now?" Arcana stared intently at the blood spattering her boots, trying to organise her thoughts. "Burke's gone. Phase is unconscious and Corrin's Run is... I don't know."

"I already contacted the station. Rito's in charge until we get back," Caelum shrugged and yawned, eyes twinkling as he relished the ensuing silence.

"Get back from where?" Fenris said at last.

"Rescuing Burke, of course."

Arcana gasped. "You know where she is!"

Caelum grinned. "Sort of. When Shirimm flashed those portal crystals earlier, I realised I could feel them, just like the portals. Shirimm has both Burke *and* the crystals on board her ship, going... that way." Caelum jerked his head over one shoulder in a vague gesture. "And we're following them."

"You entered jump space without a course plotted?" Fenris' eyes went wide.

"We have a course. I'm the course," Caelum responded. The Guardian stared at him for a long moment, then shook his head and waved a trembling hand, as though to bat away the uncomfortable notion.

Arcana chuckled, her heart warming. "So once we catch them, with Phase in tow, we can rescue Burke and get those stones."

"Yup." Caelum's answering smile was so wide she thought his face might split apart.

Arcana planted a sloppy kiss on his snout. "I love you."

"I know," Caelum said airily. "Feeling's mutual."

Fenris made a choking sound and shook his head. "A blind jump... I need a drink."

Arcana cut a glance at Fenris, who looked decidedly paler than he had moments before. "I think you upset him."

"Looks like it. I have to get Phase sorted out but once that's done, I'll show you where the firewhiskey is," Caelum offered.

"I might just take you up on that," Fenris smiled and pushed to his feet. "If you like, I can carry Phase wherever you wish to settle him."

"Really?" Caelum gave Fenris a quick once over. "You could barely walk a minute ago."

"The more energy I burn, the more oxygen I need. With plenty of it..." Fenris bent, scooped the giant Illithai male up in his arms, and straightened with ease. "My strength has returned."

"So if I want to get on top of you, all I need to do is cut off your air?" Arcana frowned - and then blushed as Fenris' grin turned wicked. "Forget I said that. I'm still mad at you," she added, levelling a trembling finger.

He inclined his head. "I should very much like to discuss that, actually."

"I need to clear my head first." Arcana massaged her temples. "You two do whatever you need to. I'm going to have a shower and a nap. Maybe a meal."

"Shower, sleep, food - Why does every trip off ship always end the same?" Caelum wondered, leading the way to the elevator.

"Apart from being biological creatures who need all of those things on a regular basis? Because people keep trying to kill us," Arcana answered. The two males fell silent as the elevator swished open and they all piled inside, Fenris carefully propping Phase's limp body against the wall.

Arcana tapped the control panel and the door slid shut, whizzing them up to the residential level. She caught Fenris watching her through half-slitted eyes and raised an eyebrow. "What?"

"That lighting cannon..." he began.

Arcana raised her hand and blue electricity arced between her fingers. "It hurt like hell."

"But?"

"Riding lightning always does," she murmured, then shrugged. "It saved our lives, so I guess it was worth it in the end." Arcana bit her lip and decided to take a risk, watching Fenris from beneath her lashes as she added; "I'm not sorry I killed them, either. It wasn't the first time and it probably won't be the last. You may add it to the long list of my sins."

Fenris' answering smile was long and slow, sending that same lightning zipping through Arcana's blood with frenzied intensity. "I thought we abolished the list."

"Someone has to keep track at some stage, lest one of us goes too far."

The jade fire in his eyes leapt. "I will never let that happen."

"No?"

"No."

"I guess I'll have to take your word for it," she managed, beginning to blush under his megawatt stare.

"Indeed." It should have been impossible but Fenris' bedroom smile widened, his glamour wrapping around her like a cloak Arcana made no attempt to avoid. They stood like that until the elevator pinged again and he gathered Phase in his arms, following Caelum down the hall. When Arcana was at last alone in her suite, her empty bed beckoning, she could think only of the soft warmth of Fenris' fingers as they'd brushed against hers, of her unhinged urge to curl into the warmth of his body and let her cares tumble away.

"Idiot," she whispered.

CHAPTER
FIVE

"Hey sis. How's things? Quieter than here, I hope." Flare adjusted his holocam with one hand, then flopped back into a faded velveteen armchair. "It's been four days since you left. I know you're lazy with these recordings, so Firius only knows when you'll actually watch, but I miss you already."

Arcana sighed and onscreen, Flare's image did the same. She sat quietly at her dark-wood desk, forearms braced on the open journal in front of her as she stared up at the holovid. Flare looked pale and drawn, his normally immaculate orange hair unkempt. Dark bruises lurked beneath eyes the colour of light-shot brandy and the golden freckles which garnered him a sense of boyish charm were stark against hollow cheeks.

"We buried Gravella and Blaze yesterday. It was... well, everyone says it was nice but I hate those things. The Fire Tower had me in Elder's robes before Blaze's were even cold, which I'm sure is no surprise for you." Flare ran both hands through his silken hair, tugging on the ends.

"Not in the slightest," Arcana murmured. "They've been chasing you for years."

"The Earth Tower's taking longer to decide on a replacement. They have a few candidates but it's a case of too young, too old, too this or too that. We might have to push them into a tournament." Flare winced, his gaze drifting to something out of frame. "Nobody even blinked at Algae's death. Pytch found holo footage of him meeting with Taelon at some shady bar on the edge of town - no audio, but it was enough to officially convict him of treason and strip all his titles and honours. I'm sure Algae's spitting with rage, even from the other side."

Arcana shivered, snatching up a pencil from a stack nearby. Even mention of Algae's name was enough to make her nauseous. It was hard to believe she was freed from his sneering leer forever - except, of course, in her dreams. As though sensing the effect his words would have, Flare leant forward in his chair and snagged a mostly empty glass from the desk. His formal robes hung open to the waist, revealing a tanned, muscular chest which had a fan club all by itself, and the thick rose-gold chain of the Fire Elder. Flare took a sip of his firewhiskey then braced both elbows on his knees, expression pensive.

"Just remember that no matter what happens, no matter where you go or what you do, you are my sister and I love your stupid face. Okay? Come back to me, Arcana. I mean it. This Taelon shit is some crazy kind of awful. It's bad enough I have to argue with Gravella's ghost every time I close my eyes - don't add yours to it. Peace." He leant towards the switch and then hesitated, flashing her a shadow of his customary grin and a wink. "Oh, say hi to Caelum and lick Fenris for me. Love ya."

"Love you too," Arcana murmured as the holo flickered and shut off. She spun her pencil around and around in her fingers, staring down at her journal without really seeing the pages. It contained a long handed account of her adventures, accented with a sweeping variety of illustrations and personal annotations. Across the desk were scattered a collection of paints, inks and brushes which she employed as her whim dictated, adding colour and dimension to her writing - a useful distraction when her thoughts were too heavy for a pen. Arcana palmed her pencil into a proper grip and began adding flourishes to a half-finished sketch of Burke's face, replaying the words of Flare's short holo over in her mind. His haunted expression tugged at her spirit and she was not surprised to look down at her page fifteen minutes later and find the haphazard beginnings of Flare's face next to Burke's, his head tipped back and eyes closed as though searching for absolution. Enchanted by the image, Arcana set the pencil down and reached for a brush and her watercolour palette when the door to the study swished open.

Fenris ducked inside, palming the door closed behind him. "Caelum said I might find you here."

"Of course he did." Arcana tapped the paintbrush against her chin, then sighed and plunked it back into a jar. "I'll lecture him later."

"He thought you might say that, too, so we decided a peace offering was in order." Fenris set a tray down on an empty corner of her desk and

Arcana's interest piqued at the sight of a cloche and a fresh pot of tea. Slender fingers, almost too long - he really should have been a musician, Arcana thought, or a masseuse - curled around the cloche and lifted, revealing a selection of roasted meats and vegetables beneath, with a side of rice and a hearty looking orange sauce. "Caelum wasn't entirely sure what might soothe a raging goddess, so I went with my gut and made you some dinner."

"I suppose I can deal with that." Arcana smiled up at him, accepting a cup of tea as Fenris set about filling two shallow bowls with food. The tired look had gone from his eyes and with freshly washed and brushed hair, his appearance had drastically softened. He'd dressed in tight black pants and calf high boots with thick silver buckles, his loose grey t-shirt boasting a deep v-neck that showed off a great deal of smooth, teal chest which Arcana found herself endlessly fascinated by.

"For you." Fenris passed a bowl her way, then crossed the room to collect the spare chair nestled in the corner.

"Thank you," Arcana said as he placed the chair opposite her and sank into it. Worried he'd caught her ogling, she added; "Your clothes seem to fit well - Burke outdid herself."

"I will admit they are not all to my taste, but much better than nothing at all." Fenris winked, collecting his bowl and a fork. "I certainly move better like this than inside that dreadful plate armour."

"I assumed you liked that armour," Arcana remarked, sipping her tea and hiding behind the cup lest he see her blushing.

Fenris shrugged. "There is comfort to be had in ceremony and tradition but no, I cannot say I particularly enjoyed wearing it." Silence fell as they ate and Arcana allowed it to stretch out, considering his words and thinking about her brother, the way he'd been shoved into an ill-fitting role in a similar fashion. Fenris rumbled lightly in his chest, a distinctly feline sound, and when Arcana looked up he said; "You look worried."

Arcana poked and prodded at her rice before saying softly; "I am, I guess. I watched Flare's holovid. Something's not right."

"Oh?" Fenris raised an eyebrow. Arcana hesitated, then reached over to turn the projector on, cueing the short message. Fenris' fork moved mechanically, face intent as Flare's message played out a second time. He dropped his eyes back to his meal when the holo shut down, brows furrowed. "He does look tired," he said at last.

"No quips about licking?" Arcana tried for a teasing tone but fell short.

The corner of Fenris' lip twitched. "You may lick me as you see fit, but I'd rather it not be at your brother's instruction." While Arcana choked on her tea, he added; "I thought Flare was only going to fill the Fire Elder position temporarily."

"That's what he wanted," Arcana managed, coughing the last of the tea away and gasping a breath. "When Flare first imprinted into fire, Blaze recognised him as stronger and offered to abdicate but Flare's too wild at heart for a stuffy office - his words, not mine."

"So he went into the military?"

"Any sorcerer class four and above goes into the military."

"Did you?" Fenris tilted his head, taking her measure with a decidedly professional air. "After you ascended, I mean."

"Not so much... not like what you're thinking." Arcana's lips twisted bitterly. "The Council tried, of course, but I'm terrible at hand to hand combat and I ask too many questions. I couldn't pass the basic training, regardless of the scope of my magic."

He frowned, his look still that of a commander appraising a soldier. "All that says to me is that you didn't have the correct instructor."

"I didn't have an instructor; they just threw me into the academy and watched me drown," she muttered.

"What?" Fenris' spine stiffened in outrage. "No wonder. Every student is an individual, every circumstance unique. No singular mould fits everyone - that's the first thing I ever learnt when taking classes. You don't need a squadron, you need someone hands on."

"Volunteering?" Arcana asked, quirking a lip in silent challenge. "Even Flare agreed I was useless."

Jade eyes narrowed slightly. "Not by the time I'm finished with you."

"There's really not much point; I'd rather you focus on Caelum. Add me to the list for a rainy day," She waved a dismissive hand to cover her embarrassment.

The look on Fenris' face said he wasn't fooled, but he nodded none-theless. "I gather your brother, being who and what he is, never shared your awkwardness when it comes to combat."

"Of course not," Arcana snorted. "Flare's the most magically proficient fire sorcerer in almost five centuries, with a mind like a razor and the heart of a dragon. Everyone loves him - it was only a matter of time before the Council put that chain around his neck."

Fenris drummed his fingers on the desk, no doubt replaying the message over in his mind. "It looks like he knew that."

"He did. I think it's Gravella's death that bothers him most." Arcana took a sip of her tea and shook her head. "I've never seen him so... heavy."

"No death is light," Fenris said gently.

"No, but there was a lot of unfinished business between them. I think, if I know Flare, he's more upset about being deceived all these years rather than the actual manner of her passing." Arcana paused a beat, debating her words, and then shrugged. "That said, he also deceived Gravella, in a way."

Fenris considered the tines of his fork. "I recall Flare assuring you that he made it clear to Gravella there was no hope for permanence between them. He knew she was using him for information."

"He did - but he also didn't go out of his way to remind her of that as the years went on and she grew too attached," Arcana returned. "Think about their positions; a breakup between a Councillor and the First Flame? It would've gotten ugly."

"So he took the easy way out?"

"Essentially. Flare's always been a happy go lucky kind of guy, letting life take him where it will. Everyone leaves his bed happy and returns as they or he feels like it. Gravella's the first person who's ever tried to keep him before and I think, on some level, even though he didn't want *her*, the idea of what she offered appealed to him." Arcana sighed, her heart aching. "Only they both went about it all wrong and now Flare will be battling guilt and grief and a whole host of other unsavoury emotions. It's not easy to recover from a betrayal of trust."

Fenris' fingers clenched so tightly around his fork that it bent in half, and he flicked her a laden look from beneath his lashes. "I too have made those mistakes, and after Corrin's Run... I was wrong and I am sorry. I will endeavour never to disappoint you again."

"It's not about that." Arcana sighed, putting her meal on the desk and reaching over to pluck the bent fork out of his hand. "I've been thinking about this on and off since it happened and once my temper cooled, I realised we come from two very different backgrounds. I can't begin to imagine the difficult choices you're faced with on a daily basis, particularly since Taelon's insurgence turned your entire world upside down." Fenris waited in miserable silence as she pooled her magic and the fork straightened with a metallic ping. "I didn't like what happened on Corrin's Run and I won't lie, if you'd been deter-mined to follow through with abandoning Burke then we'd be having a very different conversation right now - but you saw sense in the end. As for redemption, if you can forgive me, then I can forgive you."

"Forgive *you*?" His face slackened in astonishment. "For what?"

Arcana offered the straightened fork. "For doubting you during the merchant prince act. I told you to act that way, after all - then I reacted unfairly when you followed through."

"Oh." Fenris accepted the fork with trembling fingers, biting his lip in an uncharacteristic display of vulnerability that punched Arcana hard in the chest. He turned the silverware over in his hands, then said; "I heard what Rito said to you."

"I know."

Jade eyes brushed over her neck, lingering on the spot where the graze had been. The mark had faded after a good sleep and a little salve but Arcana nevertheless curled her fingers around the edge of her journal to avoid covering the place where it had been. Fenris noted the motion and reached out to smooth her hands flat. "You have nothing to be ashamed of."

"That doesn't change the way it makes me feel." Arcana's voice was breathy and she tore her gaze from the warmth of Fenris' fingers, forcing them up to his face. "I'm tired of being other people's playthings."

Fenris' thumbs began tracing slow, soothing circles over the back of her knuckles. "I know. I am sorry." He cleared his throat and shifted as though nervous but when he spoke, his voice was steady. "That morning outside your family home, when I looked you in the eye… I knew it was wrong but I couldn't help it. I told myself it was to test my recovery but there was something about you, a draw which I could not deny. So I looked. And for the first time in my entire life, someone looked back."

Arcana blinked. "So it's all because I can look at you?"

"No! No," Fenris shook his head vehemently enough that she was forced to believe him. "I intended to walk away. I thought it was a trap. Flare even warned me off you - but I couldn't go. I couldn't walk away, even though I knew I should have."

"Why?"

"Because I *felt* something. Between us." Fenris took a deep breath and looked up, the glamour wrapping Arcana in warmth and light as their eyes met. "So I stayed. And now I am walking a fine line between duty and disaster."

"Excuse me?" She snatched her hands back as though burned, curling them to her chest when her skin tingled in silent protest of his absence. "Did you just call me a *disaster*?"

"No!" Fenris threw both hands up in the air and growled some fey curses which poured over Arcana's skin like so much honey. "I am saying this all wrong. You have tied my tongue in a knot."

Arcana crossed both arms over her chest, hoping he thought the flush on her cheeks was temper. "Uh huh. I remember doing exactly that, with my awful magic powers."

He growled, the sound adorably exasperated, then looked startled. "*This* is what I'm talking about - my complete inability to temper my responses to your proximity. If we are to truly work as a team, you should understand that my thought processes are compromised."

"Wow." In spite of the odd wrenching in her gut, Arcana laughed. "You really know how to lay down the compliments, don't you?"

Fenris had the grace to look abashed, his high cheekbones dusted with deeper colour. "I am trying to tell you that I do not know what I am doing, or how to proceed."

"What? Are you seriously that much of a control freak?" Arcana sat up straight in her chair, jaw dropping open. "Great gods of Sorcen, Fenris - look, if it makes you feel better, I'm flying by the seat of my pants here, too. There's no magic formula for this, you know."

One eyebrow arched. "Are you admitting there's a 'this'?"

She searched his face, the well-practised facade of calm he wore - as much a suit of armour as that dreadful plate had been. To an outsider he would've looked cool and collected but Arcana knew Fenris well enough by now that she could see the fractures. Feeling unaccountably raw, she managed; "I'm broken, not stupid."

To her surprise, Fenris' face relaxed into a gentle smile, his eyes burning unaccountably bright. "Well, now. I never thought I would ever hear an admission like *that* from your mouth."

"I notice you weren't in a hurry to repudiate it."

"I too am broken," Fenris shrugged lightly. "I said as much to your brother when he decided the best way to try and lecture me was fighting, kissing me passionately and then throwing text books on my bed - in that exact order, I might add." He stretched languorously. "As for your intellect, I adore it as much as the rest of you."

The words were so honest she gasped as though struck. "Fenris, I-"

"Stop," he murmured, arms dropping to his sides. "It was a compliment freely given, not a request. You bend to no-one, Arcana. Your body is your own, your decisions your own - nobody has the right to demand otherwise."

Arcana's eyes burned. She blinked rapidly but the tears fell anyway, streaking her cheeks in silver lines. "Nobody's ever said that to me before."

Fenris reached to catch a shining tear on the back of his knuckle, examined the way it glittered against his skin. "Where free will is concerned, you and I have more in common than you may perhaps think." He painted the tear against his cheek, as though the sorrow was his own. "I would never ask for something that was not freely given."

Arcana watched her tear trace a silver line across his skin, her heart a confused bird in her chest. "The Weaver is lucky to have your devotion."

"Do not think, for even a moment, that I am perfect." Fenris leant back in his chair and propped both boots on the desk. "I almost failed at Corrin's Run. When I scented Rito on you, I..." he filled his cheeks with air and shook his head. "To claim someone without their understanding or consent - even amongst the barbaric customs of my father's people, that is a heinous crime. A claim should also be a surrender, an acknowledgement of equals. And after knowing how Algae tried to own you, seeing another male try the same..." he barked a sharp, dry laugh. "It is as well for the pirate that he was not standing there in that moment."

"So you weren't bothered by-"

"I enjoyed the thought of his hands on you about the same as you enjoyed the thought of Burke's upon me." Fenris' tone was clipped; he squeezed his eyes shut and very visibly forced himself to relax. "Every instinct I had cried out for Rito's blood. His blood, not on the greatsword's edge but on my hands."

"You didn't act, though." Arcana wasn't sure why she was defending the vulnerability in him, but the words tumbled out anyway. "You let me sort it out for myself."

"It angers me that you think the ability to make your own decisions is a gift," Fenris growled, "But yes; it was for you to decide how to proceed. I heard what you said to him and it was enough for me. There is a strength inside you that puts many to shame - myself included."

Now it was Arcana's turn to close her eyes, pressing the heels of her palms into the sockets. Her skin felt stretched, her soul rattling around inside her body as though attempting to escape from a prison. Broken, broken, broken - she repeated the words over and over, as though the mantra would rebuild the defences Fenris continued to dismantle.

We are all broken. That's how the light gets in. Even in her memory, that deep, velvet rumble sent a shiver down her spine. She wondered how much light Fenris allowed through his own cracks, guessed it to be precious little. Was that what drew them together, then? A subconscious understanding of the skeletons in each others' closets? And once the Guardian returned to his place at the Weaver's side, her personal blade to be unleashed wherever necessary, would that fascination hold or fade? It was a sobering thought, one Arcana smothered before it could take hold.

Whatever it was they had between them was nothing more or less than a few winks and wicked smiles - to pin any part of her tattered heart upon it would be foolish. Oddly calmed by that train of thought, Arcana flattened her hands on the desk and forced her eyes open.

When she looked up, Fenris had reclaimed his bowl and was slowly finishing his meal, staring into the depths of the rice as though it held the answers to a thousand unasked questions. He caught her watching and smiled but the expression wavered on his face, a mirage that their shared time together allowed Arcana to see right through. "Did you like your meal?"

Grateful for the momentary reprieve, she answered his shaky smile with one of her own. "I did. Peace offerings are welcome any time."

"Good." He nodded, worry stealing the half-hearted smile from his face. "It's one of my mother's favourites."

"I'm sure they're alive," Arcana said quietly.

"Hard to tell. They have been stationary for some time now." Fenris dug his fork in with vicious intent, brow furrowed. "My father is an excellent warrior with a lot of experience. He would be difficult to overcome."

"And your mother?"

"My mother?" Fenris huffed a laugh. "My mother is the last line of defence. I am torn between hoping she has and hoping she has not been dragged into combat."

"We could search for them," Arcana offered.

Fenris grimaced, his gaze focussed off in the middle distance. "I have thought about it."

"But?"

"The Weaver is still of the utmost importance. If my parents learnt I put their safety above hers?" Fenris shrugged, his face tense. "They took the same oath I did. They would not be pleased."

"And so your heart is at war with your head," Arcana said softly.

His voice dropped an octave to become velvet smooth, jade eyes burning bright. "You have no idea."

"Dammit, Fenris -" she cleared her throat and broke off, staring down at the half finished journal page on the desk. "Why do you keep doing that?"

"I appear to be unable to help myself. Be calm," he soothed, leaning across the table to brush his hand across hers. "Your heart is so wild it might come out of your chest. I mean you no offence."

"That's part of the problem!" Arcana snatched her hand away for the second time in ten minutes, tears pricking the corners of her eyes. "It would be easier if you were awful."

"I shall endeavour to take that as a compliment." Fenris' eyes dropped to the page between them, narrowing as he examined Flare's half formed face. "Is this your journal?"

"Uh... yeah. I write and draw in it when I can." Arcana waved at the bookshelves behind her. "I've always kept one. Writing out my thoughts and feelings helps me to relax and stay focussed."

"And have I made an appearance?"

Arcana snorted. "I thought you were letting me off easy by changing the subject."

A delicate brow arched. "I only wish to know you better - unless you find me repulsive?"

"Of course not!" Arcana spluttered, and then slapped both hands over her mouth. The slow, victorious grin that dawned on Fenris' face matched the heat spreading across her cheeks. "You already knew that."

"I did," he admitted. "I can smell it."

"Then why make me say it?"

"Because I overheard a rather interesting conversation with Burke about carnival rides, in which you vehemently protested otherwise," Fenris chuckled, his grin widening even further, "And I rather fancied digging out the truth."

"Ah." Arcana stared at her desk, wishing it would rise up and swallow her - or better yet, Fenris. The dark wood stayed rebelliously still and when she chanced a peek from under her lashes, he was grinning wide enough to split his face open. Teasing, she realised. He was *teasing* her. So Arcana rallied enough to say; "Too bad for you I don't enjoy cheap thrills."

Fenris tipped his head back and howled with laughter. It was wild and clean, a bell pealing deep in Arcana's soul. She felt a weight slipping from her shoulders and smiled as he levelled a long finger at her and said; "So you *do* have a sense of humour."

"Of course." Arcana flipped a lock of hair over one shoulder. "I can't let Caelum and Flare corner the market on wit, can I?" He chuckled again, his face so open and appealing she found herself saying; "One truth for another. Who was Shirimm to you?"

"Hmmm." Fenris subsided into his chair, slinging one leg over the dented armrest. "I have been wondering when you would ask that."

"And?"

"You may be surprised to know that I have always had a reputation for being somewhat serious - aloof, even," he allowed.

Arcana gasped and clapped both hands to her throat. "What? You, being too serious? Who'd have thought?"

Fenris growled, the velvet sound thrumming down Arcana's spine. "Very. Funny." But his eyes twinkled and he waved an idle hand. "Shirimm and I trained together, a long time ago. I thought we were friends."

"Let me guess - she wanted more?"

"Much more," he affirmed. "I tried to explain a great many things to her; I valued her friendship so I even explained the glamour. Shirimm thought the entire story a ruse, a barrier erected by a shy young man who just needed a firm feminine touch to guide him."

Arcana swallowed as his body slowly but surely tensed. "What happened?"

"She sneaked into my room in the middle of the night and leapt upon me. I woke with such a shock that I looked right at her." Fenris closed his eyes briefly and when he opened them, sadness swam in the depths of his gaze. "Shirimm was ensnared, of course. Only a moment, before I recovered and broke the contact, but... It was enough."

"Enough for what?"

"To destroy us both." Fenris' hands opened and closed, as though he wished abruptly for the greatsword. "I was so angry at the betrayal that I literally threw her out of my room. Shirimm was older than I and technically of higher rank; she did not like being humiliated. She told anyone who would listen that I had implanted a suggestion in her mind to coax her into my bedroom and she had barely escaped with her virtue intact."

"That's awful," Arcana whispered.

"The Weaver dispelled the myths, of course -"

"Including the one about Shirimm's virtue, I hope."

"- but had no choice but to remind everyone that I was not to be looked in the eye. It only served to lend a certain credence to Shirimm's stories, particularly since I was so very self-contained." Fenris laughed, but it was a bitter sound. "True or not, the incident certainly put a damper on any romantic notions I may have had for the future. Wearing a blindfold to bed to avoid accidentally enslaving your lovers is about as appealing as it sounds."

"You've had many lovers?" The words slipped out before Arcana could quite stop them.

"A few," Fenris admitted. "Not many. Enough to realise I, too, was afraid of Shirimm's rumours. If they became a reality..."

"You're not like that," Arcana murmured, her heart aching for his younger self.

"No, I am not, but the glamour has the power to rob me of such choices." He sank further into the chair, voice turning contemplative. "When I first became a Warden I was shocked by the breezy, liberal nature of those in the Timeless Kingdom. There are no children for the Timeless, no diseases - not of that sort, at least - meaning that many Wardens and Guardians prefer loose sexual encounters rather than long standing relationships." Fenris ran one hand through his hair and shrugged. "As I got older I realised that particular lifestyle was not for me. I do not - how do you say it? - play my cards lightly."

"Oh." Arcana clutched at her chest, her heart icing over with the sudden intensity of a blizzard. "No, no, *no*."

Fenris leant forward, brows drawing in concern. "What is the matter? What did I say to upset you?"

Fresh tears spilled down her cheeks and she groped blindly for words. "Did you - I - no children for the Timeless?"

"You didn't know," Fenris realised, his face blanching.

Arcana shook her head. "I always thought - I mean, I figured because of Caelum it might be delayed, but I assumed my cycle would come back. I always wanted - I always hoped - If someone could look at me, could see past the power, past what I'd become…"

No children for the Timeless. The words echoed in her head until Arcana was dizzy, her throat closed. She had lost many of the dreams of her youth but had clung stubbornly to this one, buried it deep inside where nobody would see, quietly tending it in the darkest recesses of her soul. Now that, too, was gone - the final tether to a woman who might have been.

"Arcana." Somehow she was cradled in Fenris' lap, her cheek pressed against his chest. Grief welled in her heart and escaped from between her lips, great wracking sobs that shook her to the core. Arcana clenched her fists in the grey fabric of his t-shirt and squeezed her eyes shut. "I am so sorry," Fenris murmured, his lips in her hair. Arcana ached endlessly, a pain only intensified by the awareness of her body pressed tightly against his, of his thumping heart beneath her ear. She moved to pull away but Fenris' arms tightened, hands warm across her back and shoulders. "Weaver save me; I thought you knew."

"No." Arcana spoke through gritted teeth and choking tears. "I don't know *anything* about being Timeless."

Fenris growled something in that lilting fey language he reverted to in times of stress, and perhaps it was only that he truly seemed to share her heartbreak, but Arcana raised a trembling hand and laid it along his cheek. Her fingers traced the sweeping lines of his face, stretching up to his brow, brushing back the lock of hair that was determined to fall over his face. Fenris groaned as her touch lingered across the bow of his lips, turning towards her hand to nip gently at her fingers. Arcana's mouth went dry as he met her gaze over the curve of her knuckles, the glamour whispering across her skin with the intensity of a thousand feathers. Fenris' mouth traced the outer edge of her palm, his breathing turning ragged as he reached the bend in her wrist - and froze.

"What is it?" Arcana whispered.

"I... I want to bite you," Fenris admitted, his lips tickling the flesh inside her wrist. "Very, *very* badly."

"What? I thought you didn't like that?"

"I don't," he whispered - but the hoarse edge to his voice suggested otherwise.

Arcana swallowed heavily. "I don't understand. Are you hungry?"

"No." His breath was hot and sent lightning zinging through Arcana's veins. "But the compulsion is almost overwhelming."

Fenris' hands splayed across her back, fingertips digging in as though he battled the urge to press her against him. Giving her an out, Arcana realised. An opportunity to run. For the first, most reckless moment of her life, Arcana wondered what would happen if she pressed her skin to his teeth instead. Time hung between them, a moment drawn out into infinity, until the door swooshed open with scimitar sharpness and Caelum erupted into the room.

"What's the matter? Is everything okay? What's happened?" He demanded, eyes wild and chest heaving with effort.

"Caelum!" Fenris jerked his head backwards, chest rising as he inhaled sharply. "Your timing is impeccable."

"Normally I'd call sarcasm, but you look serious. What did you do to Arcana?" Caelum tilted his head to one side. "I can feel her heart breaking."

"I didn't do anything," Fenris said, both relief and regret warring in his voice.

"He... Fenris said that the Timeless can't have children." Arcana wiped at a fresh round of tears. "I can't have children, Caelum."

"Oh," Caelum's shoulders dropped, the blush of leaves across his antler rack withering in the space of a heartbeat. Arcana made to move but Fenris' grip tightened, his fingers curling around her ribs - so she opened her arms and Caelum crossed the room to join them, squeezing his bulk around the edge of her desk until he was close enough for Arcana to pull him against her.

"I am truly sorry," Fenris said quietly.

"It's not your fault. We always wondered." Caelum nudged at Fenris with his nose. "I never wanted to believe I had altered Arcana in that way."

"Timelessness is a strange thing. When the Weaver offers someone a place in the Kingdom, she explains the full ramifications of what it will mean. It's why she rarely takes on anyone young," Fenris said.

"You were young," Arcana pointed out.

"Yes. I thought I fully understood my decision but I was only a youth, for all that my body was matured. The Rikju rarely live beyond sixty years of age - the price they pay for their enhanced strength and speed. With the exception of my father, none of the tribe I knew as a child still breathe the air." Fenris paused, and sighed. "Back then, the inability to reproduce seemed a small price to pay for the opportunity to see an entire universe filled with mystery."

Caelum grunted. "We didn't get a choice."

"No. It seems fate had other things in mind," Fenris said, his accent so thick the words were almost unintelligible. "I am sorry, Arcana."

"Stop saying that," she snapped, squeezing his arm to take the sting from her words. "Caelum's right. We always suspected it - Lesce warned me that if my cycle had truly disappeared, there was a risk. We hoped it would return but it's been fifty years, so I suppose it was only my own denial that stood in the way of the truth. You took me by surprise - and before you apologise again, I know that wasn't your intention."

"It was not, but I should have thought before I opened my mouth." Fenris hesitated, rubbing his jaw against Arcana's hair. "Children are a topic I rarely discuss, if I am honest. I cannot change the choices I have made - and I don't like the eternal conundrum it presents. When I think what my life would have been like if I had chosen to stay with a race of people who blatantly loathed me... It feels like there was never a choice at all."

"Wait - wasn't your mother already a Warden when she met your father?" Arcana asked.

"Yes."

"And she got pregnant with you... how?"

"I imagine in the usual way," Fenris replied, and chuckled when she pinched his forearm. "The truthful answer to that question is that I have never asked it."

"What, never?" Arcana stared up at him in surprise.

"Do you often discuss your parents' mating habits with them?" Fenris returned, raising an eyebrow.

"Er. No. Okay, fair point. Do you have any siblings?"

"No," Fenris answered. "There is only me. And before you ask, I am the only child born to either a Warden or Guardian after they became Timeless."

"Hmmmm." Arcana reached for her journal and a pencil, scribbling a few short notes. "One day I'd like to meet your mother and ask her about this."

"I'll be sure to find something else to do with my time on that day," Fenris replied drily. Arcana laughed, the great tension in her heart shifting. She took a deep, shuddering breath, closed her journal and hugged it to her chest, where Caelum lowered his head to lip at the leather cover.

"Where have you been?" Arcana reached up to pluck one of the withered leaves from his sprawling antlers. "There's dirt in your fur."

"The greenhouse." Caelum nudged her with his nose. "Someone has to tend the vegetables."

"I tend the vegetables!"

"You kill them," Caelum corrected.

"Not recently," Arcana muttered. "Am I never going to live down one misplaced fire spell?"

"Not when it turned our entire crop into a charred ruin," Caelum replied.

Arcana leant back against the hard warmth of Fenris' chest, her arms crossed. His body vibrated beneath her and she realised with a start that he was shaking with silent laughter. "What?"

"How many other hapless victims have fallen before your immense power?" Fenris asked, his eyes dancing as they roamed her face.

"Just the vegetables," Arcana said primly, turning to reach for her teacup. Caelum snorted. "Shut up, you flea-bitten mongrel. I forgot I had fire on me that day."

"So you say, but I have pictures of several batches of campfire damper who might like to disagree with you. I think..." Caelum trailed off, ears pricking and head tilting to one side, causing the remaining leaves on his antlers to rustle softly.

"What is that?" Fenris frowned, his body tensing.

"It's the alarm from the med-bay. Phase is awake," Caelum announced. "Or he's waking, anyway. The sedatives should keep him under until I get there."

Arcana rolled off Fenris' lap, straining her ears. "I can't hear anything."

The two males exchanged glances and then shrugged. It was Caelum who said; "To be fair, the alarm *is* going off up the hall."

"But not here?" She fisted one hand on her hip.

Caelum's ears flickered and he looked pointedly to the journal tucked under her arm. "I didn't want to annoy you until I was sure you were feeling better."

Arcana growled low in her throat, slamming the leather-bound book down on the desk. "There is more at stake here than my ability to jot down thoughts, Caelum."

"Yes, there is - but some things are just as important as a meal and a nap." Caelum lifted his chin, refusing to give ground when Arcana shoved at his shoulder. "You're no good to us at half strength. Filling that blasted book is like therapy for you - better than therapy."

"I don't need therapy," Arcana muttered, but she reached out to stroke the deerken's jaw nonetheless.

"I'm not even going to start listing the things that you need." Caelum turned his face into her palm and huffed it full of hot air. "I can feel what's going on inside you and even worse, I can smell the both of you. It's infuriating."

There was a short, loaded silence in which even Fenris looked surprised. Arcana's jaw worked soundlessly, and she managed; "Journal it is, then."

Caelum had the audacity to look smug. "I thought so. Now, if you'll excuse me, I'm heading down to the med-bay. I was going to ask Fenris to translate but something tells me -" he wrinkled his noise pointedly, "- that you two need to finish your discussion."

"*Caelum.*"

Ignoring her completely, the deerken sauntered out the door with a flick of his tail. Arcana leapt after him but as she reached for the panel to palm the door open, Fenris' hands thudded against the walls either side of her shoulders, pinning her neatly in place.

"Why -" she spun in a fit of temper and froze upon finding his face only moments from her own. "Er. Hi."

"Running?" Fenris murmured, his voice a rough glide across her skin.

"No." Drawn in a way she didn't understand, Arcana splayed her fingers across his chest. "I was intending to skin Caelum and turn his hide into a carpet."

"Really?" Fenris attempted to sound casual but Arcana could feel his heart thundering beneath her palm. "I don't think he'd make a very good carpet." His chest expanded beneath her hand as he inhaled again; held it for a long moment. "I still want to bite you."

A test. Arcana flexed her fingers against his shirt, felt him shiver, decided she liked the reaction. "You said you weren't hungry."

Fenris laughed, low and guttural and velvety, the sound vibrating up Arcana's arm. "It's not that sort of hunger."

"Oh." She slid her other hand across his ribs and felt him stiffen in response, air hissing between clenched teeth. "Sorry. I forgot you were ticklish."

"It's not that sort of ticklish," he admitted, and this time his grin was slow, lazy and wide enough to show fang.

Arcana blinked rapidly and blushed. "Am I really that flighty?"

"Yes." Fenris lowered his head, cheek brushing hers as he buried his face in her neck. Arcana felt the satin of his lips against her pulse as he whispered; "Weaver save me, but you smell good."

"So do you." Arcana's voice was as breathy as his. "What happens if you bite me?"

"Apart from the claim?"

"Does it have to be a claim?"

"No - but I'd be lying if I told you it'd be innocent."

"I think it's too late for that now, anyway," she whispered.

His eyes burned bright. "Yes."

Whatever reticence had held Arcana in check seemed to have disappeared with Caelum, leaving behind unmitigated want. She twisted her fingers in the soft grey cotton of his t-shirt but it wasn't enough, so she caught at the hem and slid her hands across the bare skin of his abdomen instead. He was hot, silken steel beneath her fingers, the sensation stealing her breath and turning her knees weak. A husky growl rattled Fenris' throat and he clenched his fists, crumpling the plasteel beside her head. "Dammit, Fenris, I'm not running. Touch me already."

"I don't want you to think-"

"*Do it*," Arcana growled, digging her nails into his hips.

For a man who could move like lightning, Fenris was agonisingly slow as he slid first one hand around her waist, then the other beneath her shoulders. He heaved great gulps of air as he fitted Arcana against him, first her ribs, then her chest, finally tucking her hips against the line of his.

"Is this okay?" So, so still. A light touch, despite the closeness of their bodies. Letting Arcana know she could back out at any moment, though she knew that if she did, it would shatter something between them forever.

"No," she whispered. Fenris froze, but before he could move, she said; "I want you to look at me."

Fenris shivered and for a moment she thought he might refuse but ever so slowly, his head rose. When he would've straightened to full height, Arcana caught at his face, fingers wrapping around the length of that long, sweeping jaw and tugging him down until their foreheads bumped, silken curls caressing her skin.

"And now?" His breath mingled with hers, no more than an exhalation. Fenris' face was tight with worry - no, with *fear* - and his eyes skittered across her cheeks.

"Look. At. Me." Arcana dug her fingers into his jaw. Burning eyes flicked up and she gasped at the intensity flashing in their depths. Fenris' glamour swamped her like a roaring tide, warming her body from the inside out and brushing her skin with the silken insistence of a thousand feathers.

"Arcana?" Fenris' fingers tightened on her spine and she heard the shadow of nightmares echoing in his voice.

"Do you want to know what it's like when you look at me? How the glamour feels?" She smoothed her fingers down the length of his jawbone, emboldened by his shiver. "Liquid heat and light, filling cracks and shoring up weaknesses, putting champagne bubbles in my blood. It's solid and safe and beautiful," Arcana murmured, and meant it. The reality of his touch - both physical and mental - was all around her, stealing every breath.

Fenris let out a sound that might have been a sob, might have been a laugh. "Thank you." Then, "You don't smell afraid."

"I'm not." Arcana swallowed heavily, breathing deep of his scent. "Now… what happens if you bite me?"

"It is often a commitment, a claim, but it can also be a gesture of trust and affection." The words dragged out of him. "A sharing."

Arcana knew without asking that such a tender vulnerability came not from the Rukkha but his mother's unseelie fey heritage. She wet her lips and watched his eyes track the movement. "Do you normally...?"

Fenris shook his head, the movement undulating both of their bodies in a sensual wave that left Arcana gasping. "No," he whispered. "Never."

"Ever?"

"It's not..." he ran his tongue over his teeth, testing those sharpened incisors and it was all she could do not to whimper at the sight. "Weaver save me, Arcana, if you don't push me away -"

"Do it." The words came out on a breath, so soft as to be only a suggestion of sound.

Fenris froze. "I-"

"I want you to do it." She swallowed, succumbing to the recklessness which had settled deep inside her. "I want to share this with you. I trust you."

"I do not," Fenris replied. His hands clenched to fists against Arcana's spine, the fabric of her simple dress bunched in his fingers. His skin slid against hers as he lowered his head a second time, his breathing ragged. Arcana felt the brush of his lips against her throat, followed by the scrape of teeth. "This is a terrible idea."

Her fingers slid into his hair, tangling in the silken curls. "Yes."

Fenris groaned, brushing his lips over her pulse before pulling back a fraction. Arcana tightened her grip on his hair but he reached up to disentangle her fingers. "Not there; that's for-" he broke off on a curse, sliding her left hand down his face until he could turn his head and nuzzle the inside of her wrist. "Here."

"Okay." Arcana's heart roared in her ears, hitching desperately with every movement of his lips against her skin. "There is fine."

"You need to be certain."

"I am."

His breathing quickened. "Do you still have the lightning?"

"Yes."

"If I -"

"You won't." Arcana watched in fascination as Fenris' jaw clenched, fingers tightening where they laced with hers. He drew her hand back, stretching the underside of her wrist, and drew his tongue slowly across the surface of her skin.

A shiver wracked them both but neither pulled away. Fenris opened his mouth and set his teeth against her pulse, his breath hot. Fangs scraped flesh, languorous and sensual. Someone whimpered; a distant part of Arcana realised it was her. Fenris' other arm tightened around her waist and then, with no further warning, he sealed his lips over her skin and bit down hard.

It should have hurt. Surely, *surely* such a thing should have hurt. But it was only searing, white-hot pleasure that stole Arcana's breath, took the strength from her legs. A thousand oceans crashed inside her mind as Fenris took her weight, cradling her body against the hard lines of his. His throat worked - once, twice - and Arcana's eyes rolled back in her head at the exquisite fire flooding her veins, a great sweeping tide that pooled in her core with erotic intent.

In that moment, he was everything; heat, light, air. Surrounded by evergreen and cinnamon, Arcana could do little more than cling to Fenris, her hand locked tight in his hair, an odd, unfurling sensation in her chest. He relaxed against her, an undulation of muscle that made Arcana feel as though her bones were turning to liquid. A third, gentler pull of his mouth against her wrist and then his tongue was sweeping over the puncture wounds, green eyes burning into her own as Fenris raised his head.

They stared at one another in loaded silence, a moment's shared clarity that was both euphoric and tinged with shock. Arcana brushed a finger across Fenris' damp, swollen lips, her breath hitching at the velvet rumble issuing from his chest. In a voice so husky it didn't even sound like her own, she managed; "How was it?"

"I think you should be able to tell," was the strangled response. Arcana swallowed. If he'd felt even a tenth of the sensations he'd given - she'd known she was in over her head but there was a large chance that, at this rate, they'd both drown.

She opened her mouth to say as much when Fenris jerked against her, eyes rounding in shock. He squeezed her fingers and Arcana gasped as lightning - teal tinted *lightning* - crackled across his knuckles. "Fenris?"

"Oh," he said. Fenris' arms went slack and Arcana stumbled, her legs not entirely sure they knew how to keep her upright. She got her feet under her as Fenris crumpled beneath an invisible blow, flying backwards to collide spine-first with the bookshelf on the other side of the room. He crashed to the floor amid a rain of hefty, leather-bound tomes, both hands clutching at his chest.

"Fenris!" Arcana raced to his side, dropping to her knees as more lightning arced across his body. "What happened? What is it?"

"Magic," He managed, the tiny storm forcing his eyes closed and clenching his jaw so tightly the tendons stood out in sharp relief.

Magic. In her blood. Arcana's throat closed as she recalled the way her entire body had burnt up when she'd bonded with Caelum and those enormous waves of power had torn her apart. Why hadn't she thought it would be in her blood? Why? Biting her lip, she tried to think. "Don't fight it. Relax, let it work its way out."

Fenris opened his mouth as if to reply, only to have it shocked closed, fangs punching through his lower lip. Blood, thick and so dark a red as to be almost black, trickled down his chin and across his jaw. Arcana reached to steady his head but Fenris jerked away, the rejection clear. Ignoring the twist of hurt, she spread one hand over his chest and the other over one thigh, bearing down with all her weight in an effort to contain the convulsions. The storm built with every passing moment, drawing a deep groan from the Guardian as his limbs thrashed against the floor. A wayward kick splintered one side of the bookcase, a dangerous testament to the preternatural strength Fenris usually wore with ease. Arcana deflected a fresh wave of tumbling books with her shoulder, leaning closer to Fenris to keep them from hitting his face.

"Run!" His voice was heavy with strain, eyes rolling wildly in his head. "It's… not safe."

"Don't be ridiculous," Arcana snapped, leaning more weight on her palms. Not that it would be much use if Fenris really put his mind to it - he was strong enough to snap her in half with a wayward thought. Blowing out between her teeth in an effort to calm down, Arcana tried to focus. The magic wasn't subsiding; the effects were increasing, the lighting crackling up her arms and across the floor. If she didn't do something soon, it would be more than just Fenris who was in danger. "Okay, listen to me. I'm going to try and absorb it back. Just… hang on."

"No." He swatted at her arms, tried unsuccessfully to push her off. "Too dangerous."

"Shut up; I can't leave you like this, much less risk the ship's electrical systems." Arcana summoned her magic and swept it across his body, sensing the power coursing through his bloodstream. Surely if the lighting was a by-product of her own blood, she should be able to pull it back? She brushed her senses up against it and gasped as a cacophony of voices roared back at her, a power so vast and dark it made her heart stutter. No wonder the magic was getting worse - it was bonding with the unseelie energy trapped inside of Fenris and multiplying. "Shit. Okay, this might hurt. I'm sorry."

"Don't!" Fenris' voice was tinged with panic but Arcana knew there was no other choice. She reached for the lightning, wrenching it backwards into herself. Something shrieked, the awful sound of twisting metal and snapping nightmares. Raw power slapped into Arcana, hard and heavy, magic to magic. Stars filled her vision but she refused to let go, dragging the lightning back into herself even though it was no longer the same, no longer *hers*. There was an explosion deep inside and Arcana felt something snap; when she blinked, her magic was once more her own and she was lying flat on her back halfway across the room.

"Fenris?" Arcana rolled to her side, got her hands and knees underneath her. The bookshelf had toppled and was now smashed half across her desk, the only sign of him a pair of black boots poking out of the small space underneath. *"Fenris!"*

No answer. Too shaky to stand, she crawled through a sea of books and shattered wood, ducking under the now empty shelf to find Fenris limp on the floor. Arcana set shaking hands to his throat, relieved beyond measure to find his pulse beating slow but steady. The lightning had gone but Fenris was well and truly unconscious, his skin unnaturally pale. Dizziness stole Arcana's breath and she coughed, turning her head to the side to spit blood. "Dammit."

Caelum, Arcana thought dazedly; she needed to call for Caelum - but even the thought of trying to back out from under the shelf was too much. As the last of her strength fled and she collapsed across Fenris' chest, Arcana's gaze landed on the twin puncture wounds in her wrist. They'd crossed a line from which there was no going back, the proof on her flesh irrefutable evidence. She should've been afraid but Fenris' chest was warm beneath her cheek, his sluggish heartbeat a sweet lullaby that soothed her jagged edges. Arcana coughed again; a fine spray of brilliant ruby against the soft grey of his t-shirt. Oops.

Unable to keep her eyes open, she relaxed against the tight wrapping of his muscles, allowed the crawling tide of oblivion to creep up her body. Her last conscious thought, as her fingers twisted weakly into the curls of Fenris' hair, was that as long as they were together, she wasn't frightened in the least.

CHAPTER
SIX

The first thing Arcana did, after waking up alone in the ship's
infirmary, was reach for the medscanner Caelum had left on the bedside
table alongside a tall glass of iced water. Her vitals showed an infuriating
mix of not much, alongside a note stating 'possible internal injury due to
magical backlash; symptoms ceased upon full system rework.'

Arcana frowned, worrying her lower lip between her teeth. Caelum's
diagnosis was likely based on what he'd felt through their soulmerge
when she'd drawn her magic - magic that Fenris had unconsciously
absorbed through her blood - back into her own body. 'Full system
rework' meant that Caelum, devoid of other solutions, had flooded her
system with IV fluids to flush out whatever magic had been previously
stored and trick her body into accepting the water's energy instead. It was
a simple but brutal procedure she was glad she'd been unconscious for -
and which, for some reason, always left her desperately thirsty. As though
signalled by that thought, Arcana's mouth was suddenly intolerably dry
and she snagged the glass of water from her bedside table, slugging it back
in one go.

Thirst quenched, she turned her mind to Fenris. There was no doubt
that the strange, dark energy which had wrestled with Arcana for her own
power was the same energy his mother had sealed away as a child - and
having felt only the brushing edge of it, Arcana could understand why the
older woman had taken the action she had. By ingesting the magic in her
blood, Fenris had not only woken that inner beast but given it strength - a

strength she was fairly certain would have smashed those inner protection spells to so much magical dust in a mindless attempt to gain freedom. A freedom which, in the process, would most likely have killed the Guardian and, if Arcana was any judge at all of the deep well of darkness inside him, probably swallowed several star systems when it eventually imploded upon the moment of his death.

Setting the glass aside, Arcana flicked to Fenris' file and found that he'd woken after a couple of hours with a few bumps and a laceration to one arm caused by the fallen bookshelf - but no real damage from the magical overload other than a mild headache. Frowning over that little fact, she input the code for Caelum's quarters and got a recorded message attesting that he was asleep, Fenris was fine, and that she should not, under any circumstances, be getting out of bed until her energy levels were back to normal. Inclined to agree with that statement, Arcana made to recline back against her pillows and ruminate further as Caelum's image kept talking. Two minutes of astonished listening later, she was throwing back the covers with a snarl. Five minutes after that she was in the shower; ten minutes after that she was dressed and fifteen minutes after *that*, she was storming through the ship towards the rooms Fenris had claimed as his own.

"Arcana?" Fenris leapt back in surprise as she palmed his door open and stalked through it. He wore loose cotton trousers and no shirt, his hair tousled and damp from the shower. A towel hung around his neck and Fenris grasped it in white knuckled fingers as she crossed the room. "I thought you were meant to be resting."

"I am meant to be resting. I was, in fact - but then Caelum said you're trying to avoid me." Arcana slouched casually against the far wall and slid both hands into the pockets of her faded jeans, torn from years of love and use. She'd chosen comfort for the visit, pairing the jeans with a loose, light jumper and leaving her hair unbound. It hung long and straight over her shoulders, the black tresses sharp against the dusky rose of her top. Arcana propped a booted foot against the side of the bed and tilted her head. "So? Is that true?"

Fenris drew the towel from around his neck and tossed it onto the mattress. "Partially." He turned away, scrubbing at the back of his neck with one hand. The ship's artificial lighting gave his pale green skin an ethereal sheen, highlighting the lean musculature of his frame as he braced both hands on the back of a chair. "I felt I needed some space."

"Why?" Arcana spoke through gritted teeth. Fenris fully clothed was masculine enough - shirtless was almost more than the rational part of her brain could take. He wore a fresh bandage around his upper arm, no doubt covering the laceration Caelum had mentioned in the medical notes. The most incredible thing was, no matter how many times Arcana swept her gaze up and down his long, lean frame, she couldn't see a single sign Fenris had experienced a vast magical overload. She sighed. "Forget it. I know why you're avoiding me. Look, it was a couple of hours in the infirmary for you, overnight for me - but we're both fine, okay? Nothing to worry about."

The linen bandage strained as Fenris tensed. "I am not ready to talk about this and you should still be resting."

"Bullshit," Arcana snapped. "You don't get to prod and poke and cajole your way into my life only to shut down now." She brandished her wrist, the puncture marks still clearly visible. "We need to talk about this. *You* need to talk about it."

"And how is it that you know exactly what I need?"

"Don't patronise me, Fenris." Arcana bunched her fingers into the denim of her jeans. "You promised no more lies, remember?"

Fenris hung his head, muttering under his breath. At long last he turned, bracing both hands on his hips. His face was colder than she'd ever seen it, carefully composed into a mask of indifference. "Fine. I should never have touched you. I wish I hadn't."

He looked like a stranger, with his set expression and aggressive posture, and Arcana almost bought it - until she looked into his eyes, and saw the way that jade fire guttered. "Bullshit."

"Stop saying that."

"I'll stop saying it when you stop dribbling it," Arcana snapped.

Fenris blinked, his court-calm mask slipping for a fraction of a second. "I have not been in such an intimate situation with you before. It was overwhelming. I should not have done it and I have no excuses."

"Are you saying you're not in control of your own actions? Because I refuse to believe that for even a moment." Arcana snorted and shook her head, noting the way his face hardened. "Oh come on, Fenris. You're the most tightly laced, self-controlled person I've ever met. Even worse than Lesce - and trust me, that's saying something."

Fenris rubbed both hands over his face, the long, thin scar across his chest shifting with the movement. "When I scent you, I doubt my ability to be rational."

"Now you're saying I smell bad?" Arcana wrinkled her nose, even went so far as to lift an arm and sniff. "I showered and everything."

"Stop being ridiculous." His face slipped into a blend of frustration and reluctant amusement. "You smell like chocolate and burnt sugar."

Arcana blinked. "That's what Caelum smells like."

"You're bound to each other, so your scents are mingled." Fenris hesitated, saw her mouth open, and rolled his eyes. "You're the chocolate. He's the sugar."

"Okay, so I don't smell bad. Why are you losing your mind, then?" Arcana tapped her fingers impatiently against one thigh, saw his eyes flick down to the movement. "I know the magic backlash was bad and that was my fault; I should've thought about it beforehand. We're lucky Caelum felt me collapse and came running, too - but before you get all up on your high horse, I don't regret a moment of it. We didn't know what was going to happen. We couldn't have." A sharp thought occurred and her breath hitched. "Unless you… didn't like it?"

"You know that's not true," Fenris snarled. Curling one hand to a fist, he thumped it against his chest and bared his teeth. "I *wanted* to bite you. And I did it, knowing full well I shouldn't have. Now, when I'm supposed to be focussed on rescuing the Weaver, all I can think about is how badly I want to do it again!"

Arcana took in his flushed cheeks and ragged breathing and raised an eyebrow. "Do it, then."

"What?" Fenris blinked in surprise.

"Right here, this second. This moment. Bite me."

"Have you lost your mind?" Dark brows drew into a frown. "It will likely kill us both."

Arcana waved a dismissive hand. "I got caught off guard last time. It won't happen again."

Fenris stared at her in astonishment. "Whatever are you talking about?"

"The power. Magic," she corrected, holding up a finger when he would have spoken. "The magic is in my blood; that's not normal for a sorcerer but I think we're past the point of comparing me to normal sorcerers. So, far as I've worked it out: you drank my blood, you ingested the magic. And it burrowed deep, deep down inside you and met *your* magic."

"My magic?" Fenris repeated, looking aghast. "You mean the glamour?"

"Call it what you will. You're part unseelie fey - it's all magic of a kind." Arcana scrunched up her face. "The overwhelm you experienced was because my magic was foreign and more than you could bear. You tried to convert it, but the process would've likely shattered the protection spells your mother wove all those years ago - which, by my guess, are tied to your life force. To break them would mean your death. So it's just as well, really, that I made the choice to wrench the power back out of you." She raised a challenging brow and offered a smile that was all teeth. "You're welcome."

"Caelum said you were bleeding internally," Fenris murmured. "That's not a simple retrieval of energy, Arcana."

"No. The power had already begun to be accepted by your own and we had a little wrestling match on the higher plane." She shot him a look from under her lashes. "Something that would never have happened if you'd learnt to control it."

Fenris' jaw clenched. "I have told you already, it cannot be controlled."

"Fine, fine," Arcana sighed, unwilling to have that particular argument again so soon. "So, there are two options. You either bite me again and I, more prepared, handle the power merge before it actually happens -"

"No," Fenris interjected, shaking his head vehemently, "I will not risk your life like that."

"-or, you simply keep your fangs to yourself until we work this kink out."

"Which is why I was trying to avoid you," Fenris finished triumphantly. "If we are apart, then you cannot be bitten and nobody dies."

"What a fabulous notion," Arcana snorted, allowing sarcasm to turn her voice into a blade. "Let's all ignore this and pretend it goes away. Don't be a coward, Guardian. I can't believe I'm about to say this - to you, of all people - but get a grip."

His expression turned dark. "I am neither a coward, nor lacking in any kind of grip; merely uncertain of my limits. You are a walking temptation. Do you really not understand?"

"No, I think it's *you* who doesn't understand." Arcana pushed off the desk and stalked towards him, grabbing the hem of her oversized jumper and tugging it off over her head, revealing the form fitting navy tank she wore beneath. Her hair tumbled over her shoulders, caressing salt white skin as it settled back into place. "If we're to truly work together to rescue the Weaver, which we both know by now is going to be paramount, we need to sort this out. So here I am. Come on - bite me."

Fenris swallowed heavily but held his ground. "No."

"I thought you couldn't help yourself?" Arcana placed one hand on Fenris' chest and followed it in, tilting her head back to look at him. "Breathe in, Guardian. Grab yourself a lungful of fang friendly sorceress."

"Stop it," he growled. "You're being unreasonable."

"Really? One of us is frightened of biting and it's not me. Listen - or sniff, or whatever it is that you do." Arcana walked her fingers up his smooth skin until she cupped his jaw. "Am I afraid right now?"

"No," Fenris allowed, his eyes trained on the part in her hair. Arcana waited, waited... and slowly his gaze slid to connect with her own, his glamour wrapping her in warmth.

"You are *not* a monster. What we shared was dangerous, yes, but beautiful nonetheless. I know we shouldn't do it again but I also know that hiding in your room isn't the answer. I don't believe for a second that your self-control is anything but iron." Arcana released his jaw, bracing her hand on her hip. Though Fenris had made eye contact, his expression remained guarded and even the glamour whispering over her skin was a shade of its former self. She frowned. "Wallowing in self-pity doesn't suit you."

"I am not wallowing," Fenris protested, eyes widening in indignation.

"Prove it."

"I-" Fenris broke off as her slap came from nowhere, catching her wrist before it could connect. "Arcana! What are you doing?"

"I said prove it and I meant it." Arcana shoved at his chest with her other hand. "If you're going to wallow, I'm going to do something about it."

"By slapping me?" Fenris' brows beetled.

"By slapping some *sense* into you. Come on, let's see what you've got when there's no training ring." Arcana's grin was wide and feral and Fenris goggled at the sight of it. "Or you don't hit girls?"

He spluttered in shock, releasing her wrist to back up a step. "You want me to *fight* you?"

"Why not?" Arcana shrugged. "Right now you're fighting you, so you may as well have an actual opponent. This will be more fun."

"I'm not in the mood." Fenris' frown deepened, confusion curving his body away from her.

"Bullshit." Arcana summoned her magic and dragged the rug out from under him. Fenris' eyes widened as he fell, thumping unceremoniously onto the floor at her feet. "Fight back."

"Arcana-"

"Don't take that tone with me." Arcana waved a hand and the floor of the ship lurched, sending Fenris rolling like a rag doll into the foot of the bed. "You've leered and lectured and generally thrown *my* entire world into chaos, and now you think you can just close me off when *you're* confused? I don't think so. My feelings are hurt and I'm angry. Now get up and fight, or I swear I'll just beat you senseless instead."

Fenris stared up at her from the floor, slowly gathering his hands beneath him. Muscles rippled across his back as he heaved upright, backing away to lean a hip against the kitchenette's tiny bench. Teal skin twitched as he clenched his teeth, a myriad of emotions chasing their way across his face. He seemed infinitely weary as he said; "I do not want to fight you."

"Oh please." Arcana seized the damp towel from the bed and dragged the moisture from it with her magic. "Where's the alpha male who was all sweaty and sexy in the training arena? He never ran from a fight."

Fenris froze, his face a mask of shock. "You think I'm sexy?"

"You have *no* idea." Arcana opened her hand and the air above Fenris' head shimmered, forming a tiny cloud which abruptly dumped a shower of rain.

"Are you out of your mind?" Fenris yelped, shaking his head so that droplets of water flew across the room. Arcana stared at the water trickling over his broad chest, the lean, clean lines of his body, and felt the fraying tether on her self-control snap. Her heart thumped loudly in her chest and she saw the moment Fenris heard it, saw the way his delicately pointed ears all but pricked up. He turned his head towards her, blinking as if seeing her for the first time.

Arcana made no attempt to disguise the breathless rasp in her voice. "If I am, it's entirely your fault."

"You are infuriating me," Fenris warned, cutting a glance at the cloud.

"Good." Arcana bunched the towel in her fist and threw it at him. "You're even sexier when you're all wet, by the way."

"*What?*" Fenris caught the towel with both hands, jaw dropping open in astonishment.

Arcana leapt forward, the sound of her slap ringing loudly in the small room. "Gotcha," she whispered. The moment hung between them, the echoing sound of Arcana's hand on his wet cheek, the look of absolute disbelief in Fenris' eyes; the impossibly tiny cloud still determined to spill miniature rain drops over his head and shoulders. Arcana leant in, the cool water streaming over her own face, and put her lips as close to his ear as her heeled boots would allow. "Fight me, Fenris. Right. Now."

He moved, then, a soft shifting of air that left Arcana staring only at empty space. "You don't know what you're asking."

"Why don't you show me?" Arcana banished the rain with a flick of one finger and turned around. Fenris crouched on the foot of the bed, wet hair plastered over glowing eyes and water running in rivulets down his back. "I'm not scared of you, Guardian."

"You should be," Fenris growled and abruptly disappeared. Strong arms wrapped around her from behind and his face pressed against her ear. "I am not to be trifled with."

"Neither am I." Arcana twisted her hands into his soaking hair, arching back against the hard length of his body. She felt the moment Fenris stiffened in surprise and called her magic. The water obeyed, slicking down their combined lengths and shucking his arms free of her waist. Arcana stomped sharply on one bare foot with the heel of her boot and spun away. "You're not even trying."

Fenris hissed and gripped his foot in one hand, face contorted with a mixture of pain and indignant fury. "*You*," he growled. Arcana waved, a coy curling of her fingers - and Fenris bared his teeth, exposing fangs as he returned both feet to the ground.

"Better." Arcana winked in the face of all that predatory focus and danced out the door, palming it shut as she went.

"Oh, no." Fenris appeared in front of her, fists slamming into the steel hallway on either side of her head. He lowered his face towards hers, a feral growl thrumming in the base of his throat. "You don't get to walk away now."

Arcana pressed her hands into the wall, dumping the water magic and absorbing the cool essence of the steel. The floor opened beneath her feet and she poked her tongue out at Fenris as she dropped into the corridor below. "Catch me if you can!"

Two steps later he was back in front of her, gnashing his teeth and throwing a punch she had trouble seeing, let alone sidestepping. Arcana laughed; a wild, raw sound, and waved a hand. The floor buckled, throwing Fenris backwards. He hit the ground with a curse and rolled, dodging from side to side as the panels on the walls came to life, slicing through the air in front of him.

Arcana ducked through the nearest door and into a large, formal entertaining room complete with parquetry floor. She grabbed at the nearest piece of furniture - a dining chair cloaked in a faded yellow sheet - and flung it behind her just as Fenris barrelled into the room. He dove over the chair but landed awkwardly, sliding across the polished floor to slam into the far wall, cracking the thin layer of decorative plaster. Arcana backed away as he cursed and snarled, picking himself up with exaggerated menace and shaking plaster dust out of his hair.

"I thought you were faster than that," Arcana taunted, using her magic to drag tiny pieces of parquetry off the floor. His answer was little more than a change in pitch to the growl which had now become continuous, and Arcana twisted her face into a shit-eating grin. "What's wrong, Guardian? I'm right here. Come get me already." She sent the tiny wooden tiles arrowing after him one by one, forcing Fenris to duck and dip away. He moved with a dancer's grace, skin still damp from the tiny thundercloud she'd summoned. Arcana couldn't resist timing her shots to make him bend and sweep, admiring the lean lines of his body as he neatly dodged each of her missiles. Fenris swung an end table up as a shield and Arcana batted it aside with a flick of her finger; her Guardian barely ducked in time as it flew overhead and smashed into a stack of chairs. Fenris rolled away from a fresh wave of parquetry, muscles bunching as he twisted, flipped over another flying chair and landed in a predator's crouch at Arcana's feet. Lips peeled back from fangs as Fenris snarled, preparing to tackle her legs from under her - only to sit down abruptly as a flying piece of wood thunked him firmly between the eyes.

Fenris roared in outrage and Arcana howled with mirth, opening the floor again and dropping into the greenhouse below. This time he was faster, diving through the hole and swatting the final pieces of parquetry aside like gnats, wrapping those long fingers around her shoulders. Arcana wrenched with her magic and the wooden tiles regrouped to form a short, stout scoop. The parquetry cupped his backside, distracting the Guardian enough that his fingers slipped from her skin and with a flick of her wrist, she flung Fenris into the carrot patch. Arcana didn't stay to hear his muffled swearing - she landed amidst a spray of dirt and sprinted for the cover of some nearby fruit trees.

Her chest heaved with effort but Arcana dared not stop, ducking around trunks and underneath low hanging branches. A heavy weight hit her from behind and they tumbled, a mess of arms and legs and rich loamy earth. Arcana's head slammed backwards into the ground and she saw stars, blinking through the haze as Fenris' hands crashed into the earth either side of her face. A trickle of blood leaked between blazing eyes and tendons stood out in his neck as Fenris loomed over her, baring fangs and growling like a beast.

"Do you want to bite me now?" Arcana's voice was a breathless rasp, her heart hammering in her throat. She tilted her head to one side and exposed her neck in blatant invitation.

"*Yes!*" Fenris roared, slamming his fists into the ground. Clouds of earth flew skyward, pattering down around them like gritty rain. "Weaver save me - yes, I want to bite you. Right here, right now, I want to bury my teeth in your throat and forget *everything*."

"And are you going to?" Arcana whispered. She lay prone beneath him, arms stretched out in the dirt. Fenris arched over her, his hips pinning her legs and his chest heaving in rhythm with Arcana's as he gasped down great lungfuls of air.

"No." Fenris' voice dropped to a velvet growl. "No, I am not going to bite you."

And then he was kissing her, his lips a silken slide against her own, his body taut as though Fenris had surprised even himself. Arcana's hands shook as she slid them over his chest, glorying in the heat of Fenris' body as she wrapped her arms around his ribs and tugged him closer, their bodies moulding together like molten glass. She opened her mouth to his and Fenris groaned, his tongue sweeping in to brand her with heat and light. He scrabbled for purchase in the dirt, a last valiant attempt to give her air, but Arcana let out a growl of her own, nipping at Fenris' lower lip when he would have pulled away. Her fingers twisted into the dark curls atop his head and held fast as fire roared through her blood.

"Arcana-"

"Don't stop." She arched her back as Fenris gave in, nibbling his way along her jawbone to lick the pulse beneath her ear. His chest vibrated against hers, whether purring or growling Arcana didn't pause to consider - or care. She was tight and loose all at once, her skin tingling with a delicious heat that only spread as Fenris' hands moulded her hips, her waist, her ribs, the curve of her breasts. His growl turned to a groan and Fenris rolled, shoulders thudding into the dirt as he settled her on top of his body. Long, elegant fingers clamped her hips against his and she squeaked at the impressive length now pressing into her pelvis. His eyes were wild as he looked up at her, disbelief warring with desire and a vulnerability that made Arcana's heart crack open.

"Are you sure-"

"Dammit, Fenris, shut up and kiss me *right now!*"

Fenris blinked, then framed her face with his hands and dragged her down, his kiss deep and desperate and filled with fire. Arcana melted against him, her body flowing and fitting against the harder lines of his musculature as though it had always known the way. She slid her fingers along his collarbone, over that chest she'd been longing to caress since the moment she'd first seen it. The ridge of his scar brushed her palm and Arcana traced it with a featherlight touch. Fenris gasped her name into her mouth, his velvet accent somewhere between a sob and a plea, and Arcana tore her lips from his to kiss the topmost edge of that scar, where his heart thundered so loudly she wondered if it would leap right out.

"Stars above, woman, you are killing me," Fenris' voice descended into a strangled moan as Arcana began nipping and kissing her way across his chest, nuzzling the hollow where neck joined shoulder. Her tongue flicked over the pulse in his neck, once, twice, before she raised herself up just enough to look down into his eyes. The glamour slid over her, a furious blend of heat and light and the stroking fingers of a thousand feathers. A curious, fluttering heat curled low in Arcana's body, bringing her thighs together and pressing her hips harder against the length of him. Fenris gasped at the movement and Arcana was shocked to see silver lining his eyes.

Well, now. She couldn't have *that*. A wicked smile curved the corners of her mouth and Arcana leant in, slowly and deliberately licking the salty tears from first one side, then the other. Fenris barked a short, throaty laugh, tugging on her hair until Arcana relented and let him kiss her again, long and slow and worshipful, his free hand kneading the muscles along her spine.

When at last they separated for air, Arcana reached to brush his soft curls back with gentle fingers. "You don't feel as though you're dying."

"No," Fenris managed, his voice hoarse. "I appear to be very much alive."

Arcana chuckled, nipping his chin. "See, now, that wasn't so bad, was it?"

"I will let you hit me with all the furniture aboard the ship as often as you like if this is how it ends," Fenris said, his voice so fervent that Arcana laughed again.

"All that and not a single fang, either. You outdid yourself, Guardian," she teased. Fenris' eyes narrowed and he pinched the skin just above the waist of her jeans.

"I still want to bite you," he growled. "That has not changed."

"I know." Arcana leant closer and whispered; "Maybe I want to bite you too."

"*What* did you say?"

She chuckled, brushing a kiss along the tip of his nose. "You heard me."

Fenris gave her a long, slow look, as though she'd suddenly grown an extra head and he didn't quite know what to do about it. He worried his lower lip with his teeth and then said; "I suppose it's not so dangerous if you do it instead."

Joy bubbled in her veins and Arcana laughed, leaning forward to nip at his chin. "Fine; biting can be my job."

He sobered then, shaping her ribs with gentle hands. "I did this terribly backward."

"How so?"

"I should have kissed you first," A lopsided smile, "And bitten you second."

Arcana tilted her head, admiring the way his hair was mussed and his iron-clad composure ruined. "Why?"

"Why?" Fenris laughed, the sound a delightful rumble against her chest. "Good manners, if nothing else. If my mother knew I'd run before I crawled, she would skin me alive." His amusement faded, blazing eyes tracing the lines of her face. "You're too important for me to get this wrong and I've spent the entire time since we met doing exactly that."

"And yet, here we are." Arcana raised an eyebrow when he didn't seem appeased. "Stop sulking, you big idiot, or I'll thump you again."

Fenris pressed his lips together and then snorted, rolling his eyes. "Here I am confessing all my deepest, most embarrassing thoughts and that's the honest best you can manage?"

"Someone has to bring you back down to earth now and then." Arcana leant in to kiss the corners of his mouth, nipping her way across Fenris' lips until his arms tightened over her spine and he raised his head to kiss her properly, a hot, wet, clashing of tongues and teeth. She smiled against his mouth and said; "We still haven't covered exactly why my particular scent sends you into some sort of rabid frenzy."

"Rabid frenzy?" Fenris' laughter bubbled up and he rolled them both sideways in the dirt, tucking Arcana into the curves of his body and pillowing her head on his arm. "I have no idea why the scent of your blood affects me so deeply. It's like something inside you is singing to me and it takes everything I have not to give in."

"I trust you," she said simply.

"So I see," Fenris replied, raising his head to look down at her. "I wanted to tear your head off just now."

"That was kind of the point," Arcana admitted. "I was angry too... and I didn't know how else to reach you through the sulking."

"Am I not allowed to have a moment every now and then?" Fenris tugged one of the straps on her tank top, his fingers lingering at the curve of her shoulder. "I certainly hope beating me up during bouts of bad temper is not going to be a precedent going forward."

Arcana arched into his touch, pressing her chest against the delicious weight of his sternum. "I could always set you on fire."

"Weaver save us from *that*," Fenris chuckled, slumping back down beside her. "I hate to admit it but I actually feel considerably better."

"I should hope so," Arcana snorted, and earned herself a wickedly masculine grin in return. She reached out a finger and dabbed at the drying blood on his forehead. "Although I think I'll try not to cut you open next time."

Fenris caught her wrist in long fingers and stared. "I'm bleeding?"

"Sorry. It was the parquetry." Arcana bit her lip, choking back a laugh as his expression turned indignant. "If it helps, you brought it on yourself."

He narrowed his eyes. "With my sulking."

"Exactly." She grinned and patted him sympathetically on the cheek. "I must say, the expression on your face when I dumped that rain on you was fabulous."

Fenris growled but his eyes were twinkling. "Despicable wench."

Arcana giggled, rolling across his arm to stare up at the fruit trees towering above them. "So what now?"

"I don't know." Fenris sighed, tracing circles over her collarbone with an idle finger. "My plan has been: stay alive, get back to the Timeless Kingdom, rescue the Weaver, kill Taelon. In that approximate order." The corner of his lip twitched. "I didn't plan for this - whatever this is."

Arcana raised an eyebrow. "You're admitting there's a this?"

"Unlike some other people in this room, I've never denied it." Fenris leant over to nuzzle her cheek. "I just don't know the appropriate terminology. I've never..."

"Never what? Tackled a girl into the dirt and kissed her stupid?" Arcana poked him firmly in the chest. "I don't believe you."

"That, actually, *was* a first for me." Fenris nipped at her jaw. "But what I meant was, I have never experienced these overwhelming sorts of emotions before."

Arcana closed her eyes, lost in the feel of his breath on her skin. "Me either."

"In that case, I would suggest we simply... see what happens," Fenris murmured, his lips brushing over the suddenly thunderous pulse in her throat. "We are both finding our way. Perhaps we might find it together."

"Together," Arcana agreed breathlessly, "Sounds like an excellent idea."

Fenris drew back and Arcana opened her eyes to find him watching her with a sombre expression. "I am still not certain I can contain my compulsive need to bite you all over again."

Arcana swallowed. "I'm still not certain I'd stop you if you tried."

"You have to," he said, worry slipping sideways into alarm. "I could kill you. I could kill us both."

She shrugged. "Then don't do it." As Fenris gaped down at her, Arcana raised an eyebrow. "Don't place the responsibility squarely on me - we need to work together on this."

"I don't know how," he muttered, jaw tight. "I have always been alone."

Heart aching at the simple truth in that statement, Arcana feathered her fingers along the jumping muscle in his jaw, her heart jerking when he relaxed against her hand. "Together we are strong, Fenris - far stronger than we would be fighting this attraction alone. I truly believe that."

"I do not know how far I can go."

"What do you mean?"

Fenris shifted against her, his erection rubbing against her core and sending shocks of pleasure up and down Arcana's spine. "I do not know how far I can *go* and not bite you. These two desires are inextricably linked; if I can't bite you, I will kiss you. If I cannot kiss you, I will bite you. And if we -" he broke off, cheeks darkening, and cleared his throat. "I can barely breathe just thinking about it. There is no way I can attest to my self-restraint should I have you naked beneath me; biting is inevitable."

"Then we take it slow. Maybe you'll build up a resistance." Fenris looked doubtful and Arcana sighed, resisting the urge to wriggle against him just to feel the length of his erection all over again. "Are you telling me you want to stop?"

"No!"

"Well, get a grip, then. We've already established kissing is fine; the rest we give over to time and see what happens. I'm not a clothes-off-on-the-first-brawl kind of girl anyway." Arcana offered a lopsided smile and saw his lips twitch ever so slightly in response. "And I know you're about to tell me to blast you to smithereens if you go too far; the answer is that I won't. I'm only going to promise to stop you if you're going to promise to try and resist of your own accord."

"I am not trying to absolve myself of responsibility. It is simply that..." Fenris closed his eyes and took a deep, steadying breath. "I trust you. I don't trust myself."

"You *need* to," Arcana breathed. "I need you to. Caelum needs you to.

The Weaver, your shattered people - everyone needs you on board, Fenris. Let this self doubt go; it doesn't suit you."

"I have been trying to do just that but irrational fears are still fears, however foolish."

"Don't I know it." Arcana shivered a little, then forced a smile. "Share them with me. We'll face them together."

"Very well." Fenris cracked one eye, the jade glow peeping out between long lashes. "I suppose the worst is that with Taelon in control of the Weaver, some might think I'm committing treason."

Arcana snorted. "Now that *definitely* qualifies as irrational. Taelon kidnapped the Weaver - and unless I'm mistaken, your job as Overlord is to stand for her, above all else, correct?"

"Ye-ess," Fenris allowed, both eyes sweeping open.

"Right." Arcana smoothed her palm across his chest, hummed when his breath hitched. "So it doesn't matter what Taelon thinks, or what those traitorous sons of bitches think - You stand for the Weaver, not for them. Your decisions are your own, made for the Weaver's safety and the greater good of the universe. Taelon isn't for *anybody's* greater good."

Fenris tilted his head to the side, lips pursed. "An interesting perspective. I suppose you're correct."

"You suppose?" Arcana flexed her fingers and the dirt around them rose and swirled with menacing intent.

"All right, all right! I submit," Fenris laughed, ducking to bury his face in her neck.

"There's something else you haven't considered either." Arcana wrapped lazy arms around his back, playing with his hair while Fenris purred - *purred* - against her throat. "Think of those Guardians and Wardens who did run; the deerken who are biding their time, waiting for someone or something to come along and give them courage. That's you, Fenris."

"Us," he corrected, his voice muffled against her skin. "I have come to the realisation that this will be impossible without you and Caelum - and that the Weaver knew that, somehow." A pause. "Above and beyond that, *I* need you."

"So we fight?" Arcana asked, a slow smile spreading across her face.

"We fight," Fenris agreed, raising his head to press the ghost of a kiss to her lips. "Whatever would I do without you?"

"Probably bleed less," she allowed. Fenris laughed, the sound sharp and clear, and gathered his arms beneath him in preparation to move.

Arcana tightened her grip, preventing his retreat and earning herself a look of surprise.

"Not that I'm complaining, but do you really intend to lay in the dirt for the rest of the day?" Fenris asked.

Arcana considered. "Just a little longer. It's not like we have a more pressing engagement right now - unless you need to go sharpen your sword or something."

"I should think you've noted by this point that my sword is more than sharp enough," Fenris said, grin wicked as he dropped back onto one elbow and curled his body around hers. "This is an interesting pocket of serenity you have hidden in the bowels of the ship, by the way. I feel as though 'greenhouse' is an unfairly inaccurate description."

"It's mostly Caelum's work. Don't ask me how he turned a simple greenhouse into an organic wonderland, but he did," Arcana replied. "This is where he spends most of his free time."

"I can see why." Fenris took a deep, appreciative breath. "It's beautiful, and if I didn't look up I wouldn't think we were inside at all."

Arcana winced at the hole in the ceiling above them. "Caelum will kill me if he sees the roof like that."

Fenris huffed a laugh. "I have no doubt you can fix it. Are we really still within thirty paces of him? It feels like our quarters are another world away."

"The ship is deceiving like that. In reality, the cruiser is forty paces from one end to the other - as long as we don't accidentally end up on opposite sides, we can pretty much wander the *Sorceress* as we please. The ship is set up so that the chances of being that far apart are intentionally rare." Arcana grinned and added; "Although there were a couple of hilarious accidents while we worked that out. We almost crashed into a moon once, because I went hunting in the bowels of the ship for something whilst Caelum was flying. Because he always jumps to me, he ended up snout-first in a pile of canned vegetables instead of sitting in his pilot's chair."

Fenris shook with silent laughter. "I'll bet he adored that experience."

"It's one of many. Once, at my parents' house, he wandered off too far into the forest and then teleported into my bath - while I was still in it." Arcana chuckled at the memory. "Fortunately he was still a fawn and nobody was crushed."

"I'm surprised. I had assumed you spent most of your time pasted onto each other like true symbionts," Fenris mused, adjusting the fit of her ribs against his.

"Oh, gods above us, no," Arcana laughed. "We'd kill each other."

Fenris nuzzled her shoulder. "I am selfish enough to say I'm relieved to hear that." Arcana let her eyes drift closed, savouring the feel of his long, lean body against hers, the lazy play of his breath in her hair. Fenris, too, seemed disinclined to break the moment and the rhythm of his breathing evened out, his movements edging towards drowsy rather than playful. "If I stay like this much longer, I will fall asleep," he murmured.

"Didn't you sleep earlier?"

"Not unless you count my short bout of unconsciousness," Fenris replied, his tone dry. "I was rather distracted. I went to the training room instead."

"Oh yes, Caelum said he found you there and yelled at you for being irresponsible." Arcana sighed, reluctant to move lest it somehow destroy the fragile connection they'd made. But... "I should probably put the ship back together before Caelum wakes up. Did we destroy any of the plants?"

"Not that I can see. Just made a mess in the dirt," Fenris returned, craning his neck back the way they had come.

"Okay good. I could use a cup of tea, so the sooner this is sorted the better." Arcana yawned and arched her back in a stretch, pressing harder against Fenris' chest and groaning as her joints popped. "All right, get off me. I've got work to do."

"As my lady commands." Fenris leant into her instead, burying his face in her hair and filling his lungs. "I really do want to bite you, you know."

"Do you know what it felt like?" Arcana walked her fingers up his chest and traced the shape of his lips. "Champagne in my blood. I could barely breathe for wanting you."

"You really are trying to kill me, aren't you?" Fenris closed his eyes and shook his head. "Slow death by torturous, cruel woman. That's what it will say upon my tombstone."

Arcana chuckled and snapped her teeth at him. "Better run while you can, then."

"Oh, no. I don't think so." Fenris gathered his legs beneath him and pushed upright, shaking one foot to release dirt from his loose trousers. "You don't get rid of me that easily."

"Good." Arcana allowed Fenris to tug her upright and winced as several of her muscles twinged in protest. "Oh wow. I'm going to be sore tomorrow."

"As am I," Fenris said drily. "Now, how do we get out of here? Unless you want me to carry you back through the hole in the roof, of course."

"No, my legs work fine," Arcana chuckled, and pointed beyond the cabbages to a soft green light blinking on the wall. "The elevator's over there."

"Thanks. I think I might clean myself up and then throw some food together." Fenris hesitated, looking strangely nervous as he said; "Will you join me for a meal?"

"Of course." Arcana raised an eyebrow. "What's with the face? We've eaten together before."

"Yes, but you told Rito that it is customary to take a woman to dinner first." He waved a hand at the churned earth. "I've already done this ass-about and I have no desire to make the situation any worse."

"Oh." Arcana blushed, then pressed her hands to her cheeks and smiled. "Did you really just say 'ass-about'?"

"Your peculiar vernacular must be wearing off on me." Another lopsided grin that made him look decidedly boyish. "So?"

"Food sounds wonderful," Arcana said, unable to stop the way her heart fluttered as Fenris' grin widened. "I'll meet you in the kitchen?"

"Excellent. I believe that makes it a date." Fenris threw her a broad wink and then jogged away.

Arcana watched him go, relieved to see his usual humour restored. After so long pretending otherwise, finally being able to indulge in the temptation Fenris had become was not only a weight off her shoulders but a decadent pleasure. There was no use denying it, even to herself - if Fenris kissed her for the rest of eternity, it still might not be enough.

With that alternately exhilarating and distressing thought foremost in her mind, Arcana used her magic to mend the damage to the garden and return the carrots to their patch. She then swapped energies for the cooler, metallic soul of the ship and knitted the ceiling back together, spending a few extra moments repairing a shattered light panel which supplied essential UV rays to the garden.

The formal dining room was by far the worst off, with several pieces of shattered furniture, a cracked wall and more than half of the parquetry completely missing. Arcana coaxed a table and two chairs back together, mended the plaster and set as many tiles back into the floor as she could find before she conceded defeat and left it unfinished. Knowing Caelum would eventually have something pithy to say about it, she arranged the loose tiles into the shape of a winking face and chuckled to herself as she pulled the door shut.

After a cursory stop by her own rooms to wash her face, brush the dirt from her clothes and fix her tangled hair, Arcana made her way to the kitchen. Fenris was hard at work over the stove, his hair damp from a fresh shower and his body clothed in tight black jeans and a loose knit sweater the colour of rust. He had the sleeves pushed partway up both forearms and was humming as he turned to hunt through the spice jars in the cupboard. Enchanted by the man underneath the warrior, Arcana leant against the doorway and watched Fenris season the pot he had on the stove, the motion bunching the muscles in his arms in a glide of silk over steel.

"Enjoying the view?" He asked, flashing a devilish grin over one shoulder.

"Hah!" Arcana made her way to the bench, where the dusky rose jumper she'd left in Fenris' room was neatly folded. She shook it out and tugged it back on. "Whatever that is, it smells delicious."

"I hope it tastes as such. I also made some tea, if you're thirsty." Fenris waved a hand at the table, where a steaming pot and two empty cups awaited.

"Thanks," she poured tea into both cups and gathered some cutlery as Fenris moved to the table, setting down two enormous bowls of soup.

"It's not much, but it tastes good," he said, dropping into the chair opposite.

"It's better than what I'd be making." Arcana took a deep, appreciative breath as she took her own seat. "I get lazy when I'm only cooking for myself."

"Really? I have always found it soothing."

Arcana scooped up a spoonful, savouring the flavours as they slid down her throat. "Well in that case, I'm going to officially bestow the title of ship's chef on you because this is delicious."

"Weren't you a chef before you met Caelum?" Fenris asked, one brow lifted in query. "You said at Corrin's Run you catered a banquet."

"Oh! No, I decorated cakes." Arcana waved a dismissive hand. "It's not the same as cooking a meal. Give me sweets any day."

Fenris frowned down at his empty bowl. "Really? I'd assume someone who was a professional at one type of food would also excel at another."

"You're good with the greatsword. How are you with a bow and arrow?"

"Good enough, but it's not my strength. I much prefer to close the distance and use my sword. Point made." Fenris nodded, then gave her a strange look. "Please don't tell me you eat cake for every meal."

Arcana laughed. "No! Although I do have a weakness for dessert, I can cook if I need to. Just... not my thing."

"I'm glad I can shore up the tiny gaps in your vast array of talents,"

Fenris shook his head in amusement. "Here I had begun to think you were perfect."

"You two seem to be on better terms," Caelum said from the doorway. He regarded them through narrowed eyes, his head on one side. "No major injuries, I hope?"

"No, although in retrospect I deserved more bruises than I got," Fenris mused, standing to collect the dirty dishes.

"She went easy on you?" Caelum looked surprised.

Arcana shrugged. "He broke quicker than I expected."

"Oh?" Fenris bent and pressed a kiss to her temple, his growl good-natured. "I'll remember that."

"Huh," Caelum remarked, watching as Fenris stalked to the bench and began stacking the bowls into the dish drawer. Starry eyes whirled with amusement as they turned back to Arcana, who was pressing her palms to the inevitable blush Fenris had roused with his husky words. "What did you do to the ship, by the way? I found parquetry in the greenhouse."

"You did?" Fenris flicked a look at Arcana. "I thought you were going to repair that."

"I couldn't find all the tiles," Arcana grumbled, her blush deepening as Caelum's astonished gaze passed from her to Fenris and back again.

The deerken cleared his throat delicately. "Is it from the formal dining room?"

"Yeah."

"I never really liked that flooring, but it's probably better there than in the carrot patch." Caelum flickered an ear thoughtfully. "I'll drop it back to you later."

"Just leave it in the dining room and I'll sort it out." Arcana bit her lip to keep from laughing. "Tell me if you think I got the pattern right so far."

Caelum's brow wrinkled, but he nodded. "I'm not a flooring expert, but okay."

"Thanks. How did you sleep?" Arcana pushed her chair back and crossed the room to hand Fenris her empty bowl. "You must've been exhausted after tending all three of us."

"I slept fine once I knew you were stable. I'd appreciate you not attempting to murder each other next time, though."

Fenris had the grace to look abashed. "It was unintentional, I assure you."

"Like the greenhouse?"

"Well, no…" the Guardian coughed and looked over at Arcana. "I think that particular incident had been building for quite some time."

"Maybe," Arcana managed, her voice choked with embarrassment.

Caelum fell silent as the door swished open again and Phase shuffled in, shoulders curved hesitantly. The Illithai paused with both hands on the door frame and clicked at Fenris, who gestured him inside.

"How are you feeling?" Arcana asked, noting the way Phase's hands trembled. His iron grey skin had a decidedly yellow tinge to it, but he'd strapped a crossover harness to his chest and had twin scimitars sheathed behind his back.

"Hungry," Phase replied. He tilted his head a moment, considering. "Sad."

"Hunger, I can help with." Arcana crossed to the low couch Caelum often used when in the kitchen and began dragging it to the table.

"Let me." Fenris appeared beside her and with a swift bump of his hips, shoved Arcana out of the way and lifted the couch in one hand. "Here."

"Smooth," Caelum commented, as Arcana staggered across the room and then growled incoherently at the Guardian. "Now, now, no killing in front of our guests." He hooked his antlers through the open back of a dining chair and swung it aside so that Fenris could deposit the couch in front of the kitchen table. "There, have a seat."

Phase nodded his thanks and slid onto the couch, bracing both forearms on the scarred table and directing a series of squeaks and clicks Fenris' way. The Guardian dropped into a chair beside him, speaking swiftly in Illitani. Phase looked nonplussed and his tone was decidedly dour but Fenris, by contrast, was more animated than Arcana had ever seen him around someone else. He spoke with confidence and his hands gestured expressively, his replies to whatever concerned Phase quick and concise.

Arcana ladled some soup into a fresh bowl while they spoke and set it down in front of Phase during a lull in the conversation. He looked up and she offered what she hoped was a comforting smile. "Here we go, one hunger cure. The sad is going to take a little more work - but we'll get there, I promise."

"Yes." Phase's eyes shimmered with emotion but he pressed his lips together and nodded. "Thank you."

She nodded and made to step away but Fenris' arm shot out and to Arcana's shock, he tugged her into his lap. He pressed a kiss to the side of her jaw, then said to Phase; "See?"

"What's going on?" Arcana managed, her heart thumping in her chest. Quite suddenly the greenhouse seemed another world away and with both Caelum and Phase staring at her in blank astonishment, she wanted to either punch Fenris or run.

"Phase is worried that I might try to... impose on Burke once we rescue her." Fenris began stroking long, soothing circles up and down her forearms, his chest a steady brace against her back. "I am trying to explain it was a ruse, and that I belong to you."

"You *belong* to me?" Arcana flicked him an incredulous glance.

Fenris' lip twitched. "His terminology, not mine. In Illithai culture, males are bonded to females, not the other way around. Phase seems very convinced by the role I played back on Corrin's Run. By the time we get to Burke her heat fever will be pitched mightily high and if you don't lay a claim to me, Phase seems to think we'll be right back where we started - only he's less inclined to share now that she's been kidnapped."

Arcana closed her eyes. Of course it would come to this - and really, it was no different among others than it was alone with Fenris in the greenhouse - but she'd imagined some time to think, some time to talk with Caelum, rather than being pushed so far out of her comfort zone so soon. Fenris must have felt her discomfort, for he carefully removed his hands from her skin and gave her plenty of space to leave if she so chose.

"Fenris is telling the truth," Caelum murmured into her ear, and Arcana jumped, having not realised he was so close. Fenris' chest rumbled against her spine as he continued speaking with Phase in Illitani, as though it were perfectly natural for her to take all the time she needed.

Scratching at Caelum's chin in an affectionate gesture, she whispered, "I know. I just..."

"Phase is used to seeing dominant women. Expects it, even." Fur tickled her cheek as Caelum nudged again. "That said, you don't have to do anything you don't want to... although we need to have some serious words later about exactly *what* went on in that greenhouse."

Arcana heard the teasing lilt in his tone and straightened her spine. What was wrong with her? The role she'd asked Fenris to play on Corrin's Run had gotten them into this situation, the least she could do was act truthfully to explain their way out of it. She opened her eyes, patting Caelum's jaw in reassurance. Fenris was still speaking to Phase, one arm braced on the table, the other on his hip - carefully not touching her. Arcana's gaze fell to the puncture marks on her wrist and she narrowed her eyes. Had her life really become so regimented that she couldn't stand basic intimacy, even after what they had been through? After what they had *shared*?

Fenris must have scented a change in her, because his clicking, squeaking words faltered and he half turned his head in her direction. "What is it? Why are you angry?"

"I'm not angry." Arcana twisted on Fenris' lap, throwing one arm over his shoulder and gripping his chin with the other hand. Heart a thundering drum in her chest, she tilted the Guardian's head up and slanted her lips across his. Fenris made a startled noise and as his mouth opened she deepened the kiss, wrapping herself in his evergreen and cinnamon scent. Startlement turned to an appreciative rumble as Fenris slid one hand over Arcana's thigh and the other around her waist, leaning them both back in the chair so her body draped across his torso. It was a soft, sweet kiss, gentle and exploratory, but Arcana's breathing was harsh when she pulled away, feathering a final kiss across Fenris' forehead before turning towards Phase.

The Illithai's jaw was slack with astonishment and he leant away as Arcana bared her teeth and growled; "*Mine.*"

"Yours," Phase agreed, holding both hands up for peace. He squeaked and clicked in his own tongue and Fenris answered in a halting, hoarse voice. Phase tipped his head back and laughed, a rough, throaty sound which echoed through the kitchen. To Arcana's surprise, the Illithai patted her shoulder in a brotherly way and repeated; "Yours."

"Well, I never," Caelum managed, his eyes like saucers. "Never *ever*. Did I actually wake up, or am I still dreaming?"

Arcana levelled him with her best flat look. "Would you honestly dream this?"

"With the way your emotions have been going, you'd be surprised," Caelum admitted, then grinned at Arcana's grimace. "Oh come on, you have to let me tease you at least a little. Fenris looks like he's seen a ghost."

"I wasn't expecting such a thorough and practical demonstration but Phase is convinced," Fenris managed. His accent was thick and velvety and Arcana fought the urge to rub against him like a cat.

She flicked the tip of his nose instead. "Are you complaining?"

"Never." His answering smile was sly. "Demonstrate as often as the mood takes you."

Arcana laughed and Caelum groaned. "I thought it was going to be better after we had this out in the open, but you know what? I retract that idea. Now instead of hidden temptation, you're both big, sloppy pheromone cakes just waiting to..." He trailed off, eyes glazing.

"What is it?"

"They've dropped jump space," Caelum murmured, half to himself. His tail flicked back and forth, spindly legs already carrying him to the door. "We're here. I'm going to pull back to real space and set down on the surface."

"The surface?" Fenris curled long fingers around the edge of the table. "The surface of where, exactly?"

"Wherever we are," Caelum replied.

"How do you even know there's a surface to land on?" Fenris demanded, his face twisting with alarm.

"I don't." Caelum's words drifted back to them as the bulk of his frame disappeared into the corridor. "But we're about to find out, aren't we?"

Fenris turned towards Arcana, his face pale. "I'm not sure there's enough firewhiskey in the entire galaxy to prepare me for a blind exit from jump space. What if we emerge in the middle of a moon?"

"Then we won't know, because it'll be a swift ending." Arcana chuckled and reached out to ruffle his hair. "Have a little faith."

"Faith or a swift ending - I suppose you think that's comforting," Fenris grunted, swatting good-naturedly at her hand.

"Just relax," Arcana soothed. She rolled off his lap and hoisted her leather satchel from where it had been sitting on the floor. "Do you want to grab the greatsword before we go?"

"Wait a minute." Fenris blinked rapidly, holding up a hand. "Do you honestly intend to wander out into the potentially hostile wilderness without so much as looking out the window?"

"That's usually how we do it," Arcana admitted, rolling her shoulders in a shrug. "It's never been a problem before."

Fenris rubbed a hand across the back of his neck. "It's times like this I actually miss my armour. Yes, I require the greatsword; I'll meet you at the airlock."

"Sure," Arcana said - but Fenris had already gone, his body a streak of shadow as he raced out the door at hypernatural speed. She looked at Phase and raised an eyebrow. "What about you? Need anything?"

"No." Phase shoved his way off the low couch, shaking out his four legs one at a time. He looked up at Arcana and patted the leather harness for his scimitars. "Ready."

"You sure?" Arcana frowned, running an assessing eye over his pale complexion. "You don't look fabulous."

"Am fine," Phase insisted.

"I'm not sure I believe you, but I suppose it's not my mate's life hanging in the balance." Arcana tapped a finger on her chin and then sighed. "If shit goes down, you better be ready."

"Ready." Phase thumped a clenched fist against his heart and nodded. "Promise."

"All right." Arcana returned the gesture and then pointed at the door. "Come on then, I'll show you to the airlock."

CHAPTER
SEVEN

Arcana led Phase into the elevator and keyed in the hangar bay level, leaning against the wall to rub at a knotted muscle in one arm. It felt like another woman who'd woken a few hours earlier, determined to sort out Fenris' bad temper... only to end up kissing him instead. Barely two months ago she'd have been horrified at the thought of locking lips with anyone - but now, here she was fantasising about the feel of his body pressed up against her own and when she might get a chance to repeat the scenario. A delicate shiver tracked up Arcana's spine. What was she doing, letting him into her life? He, a sworn warrior to the Weaver and she... well, what was that old Terran saying? Jack of all trades and master of none?

Now, now, Arcana chided, turning her face away so Phase wouldn't see it twisting with a confusion of emotions. *Let's not go down that road again.* The day she'd walked away from Sorcen, she'd shut the door on the endless streams of elders and scholars and do-gooders who wanted to use her as a tool even as they quietly excised her from the society she'd grown up in. If not for Flare being well liked and holding a position of authority, the Council of Elders would have found a way to bury her, imprison her or oust her completely a long time ago. Probably about the time they realised that, best efforts aside, Arcana could not be controlled - not even after Algae had left her a bleeding, empty husk.

Flare might not agree but Arcana always knew the only way to keep the fragile tether she had with her family and former life was to realise she no longer fit into it, and to walk away. She'd intended to settle elsewhere but after Corrin's Run and her failed attempt at a mercenary career, she'd decided that the *Wandering Sorceress* was home and that was that.

And then… Fenris. With that smile, and those eyes, and that body. The scent of the night-time forest with a little cinnamon thrown in for good measure. His kindness, his ever-present strength. Oh and the murderous army of warg chasing him, of course - but Arcana was smart enough to admit, even to herself, that didn't bother her. No, she'd gladly wade through a thousand warg if a certain Guardian stood waiting for her on the other side. She sighed. *Pathetic.* And where did that leave her? Feeling completely vulnerable and entirely confused with a good fifty years of baggage breathing down her neck, that's what.

The elevator pinged and the door swept open, revealing the hangar bay. Caelum stood by the airlock with Fenris beside him, wearing the armoured pants and jacket Burke had given them and the greatsword strapped on over his chest. Phase sauntered out of the elevator but Arcana lingered, smoothing out her troubled thoughts with sheer, teeth-gritting willpower so that not even Caelum would pick up on her mood.

Fenris looked up as she approached, his wide grin hitting her full in the chest. No man, woman or creature had a right to a smile like that, surely. Arcana waved a hand at his altered wardrobe, forcing her eyes to travel the length of that long, lithe body lest she get stuck staring at his lips. "You really are fast."

"I've learnt when to be fast and when to be slow." His grin turned wicked and Fenris executed a flourishing bow, offering a folded pile of black fabric. "Despite your protests of preparation, I thought you might like your own armoured clothing. It will be better suited to an unknown environment than what you are currently wearing."

"I guess you're right." Arcana accepted the clothes with a smile. "Thanks."

Fenris offered another ridiculous bow, his eyes glittering with mischief. Arcana ignored Caelum's feigned retching and hurried across the hangar to a stack of food crates, slipping behind them to shuck off her jeans and jumper and swap them for the pants and jacket Fenris had collected. Shoving her discarded clothing into a corner, she jogged back to the others.

"Now that we're all here, I should warn you that we've got a bit of a hike ahead." Caelum prodded a small screen set into the wall with the tip of his nose. It immediately displayed a terrain map detailing a rugged, uneven landscape, with smaller cutaways underneath and copious streams of data scrolling down one side of the screen. "Shirimm's ship landed in that wide, shallow valley to the east. There's some sort of settlement there - I saw spires and towers as we came in but it's hard to get specifics because we're in the middle of a jungle." One ear flickered. "A very thick, very large jungle."

Fenris leant towards the map, brows furrowed. "How close did you get us?"

"Back here somewhere." Caelum motioned towards the craggier ground in the west. "I managed to slip between some foliage and an over-hang. It's not overly close but I didn't want to be detected."

"I'm sure we can manage." Fenris drummed his fingers on one thigh. "Can you tell if the Pariah has troops between the ship and the installation?"

"Not really." Caelum sighed. "There are signs of life but it's impossible to tell who or what those heat signatures belong to." That single ear flickered again. "There is, however, a stationary energy signal between us and them which is very similar to that of the portal stones."

"A portal," Fenris muttered, tapping one finger against his chin in thought. "It makes sense - if Taelon can get the portal network functioning, his armies can move between layers of the weave at will." The Guardian paused, then looked over at Arcana. "I think we should stop past the structure on our way through."

"You don't think it's destroyed, like the one on Sorcen?" Arcana asked.

Fenris rolled his shoulders in a shrug. "It's impossible to tell, but Taelon is no fool. If this structure is intact and he breathes life back into the network, I shudder to think how many will die. The warg plague would be near on unstoppable."

"And you're suggesting what exactly?"

"I do not know yet, not without checking the status of the portal."

Arcana rubbed both hands over her face. "Caelum?"

"Our path to Burke takes us right past the energy signature," the deerken replied. "It won't delay us by more than a few minutes."

"All right." Arcana chewed on her lip a moment and then jabbed a finger at Fenris. "But I want it made very clear that rescuing Burke is our first and topmost priority."

"Of course," Fenris nodded. "I would have it no other way."

"Good. Any questions?" Arcana arched a brow at Phase, who bared his teeth in a vicious grin. "I'll take that as a no."

"Let's get this over with, then. The atmosphere is stable but likely humid, so be prepared." Caelum poked at the airlock controls with his nose and the door recessed, revealing total darkness beyond.

"Er... night time," Arcana said, straining her eyes into the inky black. "Can anyone see?"

"I can," Caelum and Fenris replied in unison.

"Right. Well I can't, so you'll need to give me a lift." Arcana wrapped one hand in the fur at the base of Caelum's neck and swung herself onto his back.

"There is a lot of foliage out there." Fenris said, moving to the edge of the airlock. "And trees with trunks thicker than four of Caelum."

"I did say it was a jungle," the deerken grumbled.

"You did," Fenris agreed. "I did not realise you meant a jungle in which we would be as ants. How long until the sun rises?"

"A couple of hours at least." Caelum drifted out the airlock and down the gangplank. He stopped at the bottom, spotlighted by the illumination spilling out of the ship, and raised his head to inhale deeply. "Maybe three hours."

Fenris cursed and Arcana twisted to look back at him. "Why are *you* complaining? You're nocturnal."

"In my experience, most of the unpalatable creatures a planet has to offer are also nocturnal," Fenris returned. "Like you, Phase cannot see in the dark. We will have to proceed carefully."

"Phase, come and hang onto me," Caelum instructed. "I'll walk and Fenris can play point."

"Yes." Phase picked his way down the ramp to twist a hand in the fur at Caelum's shoulder, his wrist bumping Arcana's knee. "Ready. Will follow."

"You know," Caelum said, furry brows drawn into a frown, "For a man with terrible Universal, you sure have a lot to say."

Phase chuckled and let loose a string of Illitani, waving a hand at his throat.

"He has a speech impediment," Fenris translated. "He can understand you perfectly - his tongue just can't make all the right sounds that Universal Galactic requires for comprehensive sentences."

Arcana turned and stared. "Really?"

"Yes," Phase agreed, smiling. The expression faltered slightly. "Secret?"

"To think, all these years I just thought you were a lazy bastard." Arcana shook her head and then patted Phase's hand. "Don't worry; your secret is safe with me."

Phase grinned. "Grateful." He followed that up with more rapid clicks and squeaks in his own language.

Fenris adjusted the greatsword's harness and nodded. "He's asking if we can get on with it now, seeing as his mate's waiting."

"Well, unless anyone else has some deep, dark secrets to reveal - then yeah, sure." Arcana winked at Phase and he chuckled again.

Fenris snorted, stepping off the side of the gangplank and managing the eight-foot drop the way others might negotiate their front doorstep. Long fingers poked the ship's access panel and the airlock swirled closed, plunging them into complete darkness - save for Fenris' eyes, glowing jade in the night. "I will scout ahead, as requested."

"Won't you be kind of obvious?" Caelum's voice floated out of the dark, thick with humour. "Those eyes are brighter now than ever."

In answer, the twin points of jade fire winked suddenly and completely out. As Arcana's only point of reference in the impenetrable black, she felt the loss more deeply than she would've liked to admit - particularly when Fenris' velvet rumble spoke from beside her knee. "The light serves a purpose, Caelum, as does the lack thereof."

"Point made."

"Excellent. Proceed slowly; I shall return." Long fingers brushed her leg and then disappeared as Fenris melted away. Arcana shut her eyes against the strange disconnectedness of such total night and counted slowly to ten, stretching out with her magic and adding another layer to her senses. When she opened her eyes again, faint patches of starry sky were visible above, glimpsed between stretches of inky shadow. Insects buzzed and clicked around them and Arcana's magic fizzed eagerly through her veins, giving her the impression of a jungle both vast and terribly ancient.

"Okay?" Caelum murmured, his voice carrying easily through the night.

Arcana leant forward over his neck, placing her lips by one furry ear. "Yes. Go."

She felt his muscles bunch and though there was no impact to denote a footfall, Caelum began to walk. Fenris flitted in and out of view as they went, his glowing eyes appearing to her left, then disappearing for a time only to blink into being on Arcana's other side, or in front, when he paused to speak in subdued tones into Caelum's other ear, the soft whisper beyond her ability to decipher.

After what seemed an eternity of floating in the thick, humming pool of night, the shadows began to sharpen, gaining the deep purples and greys of early dawn. Arcana examined the mass of twisting shapes and curling hollows around her, sensing more than seeing giant hanging flowers and thick, glistening foliage. The trees were enormous, their trunks so wide and densely clustered that the thick branches interlocked and overlapped. Caelum's hooves glided down a precarious roadway of looping vines and curled wood, with the true ground hidden far beneath them. Fenris moved in a series of leaps and dashes, his body flitting from perch to perch as he raced to scout the areas ahead and then returned to guide them slowly forwards, his speed and skill of such a level that Arcana wondered how she'd ever held her own against him in a fight.

She turned her face into Caelum's neck and whispered; "Where are we?"

One ear flickered and he stopped, twisting his head to look back at her. In the deep shadows his gaze was eerily dark, the shimmering stars within almost entirely engulfed by lingering night. "We're moving in more or less a straight line from the ship but it's slow going. Fenris has seen and scented a couple of things we'd rather avoid." Caelum hesitated, then added; "Big, toothy kinds of things."

"Warg?"

"Not yet."

"Surprising. This sort of environment would suit them," Arcana murmured, dragging hair off her sweat-slicked neck. "Apart from the humidity, of course."

"If the Pariah has any sense at all, he'll be keeping them on a short leash - or in a cage." Caelum shuddered. "Damned crazy beasts will be just as inclined to kill each other as they will us."

"Good point." Arcana frowned into a mass of flickering shadows. "Come to think of it, how does Taelon control them?"

"Now *that* is the magic question, isn't it?" Caelum chuckled. "Not even Fenris knows. I asked earlier - it's driving him nuts."

Arcana snorted softly. "Everything drives Fenris nuts. He's that sort of guy."

"Yes," Phase said suddenly, his deep voice causing Arcana to jump. "Too serious."

"Great gods of Sorcen," Arcana hissed. "You scared the shit out of me."

The Illithai shrugged, gesturing first at his grey skin, and then at the half-light of impending dawn. "Blend in."

"I do the same," Caelum agreed. "It's princess pasty here that stands out like a sore thumb."

"I am not pasty," Arcana objected, thumping Phase in the shoulder when he let out a loud guffaw. "Shh! I have no desire to fight some sort of giant snake in the dark."

"Oh, don't worry; we're alone for the moment." Caelum raised his nose to the morning air, nostrils flaring. "I think it's going to rain in a few hours. Can you see yet?"

"Sort of. Well enough," she amended.

"Good." Caelum paused, glancing back the way they'd come. "I'd say we're about half way to the portal, but if the road were easier to traverse we could be there in a few minutes."

"I can do that." Arcana stretched and rolled her shoulders. "Where's Fenris? I don't want to accidentally crush him between branches."

"Here." Fenris' silken whisper brushed across her cheek and Arcana bit her lip to prevent from crying out. She turned to see him crouched on a branch beside Caelum, his face slightly above her own, close enough for them to share breath.

"You... don't *do* that," Arcana hissed, her heart thumping erratically in protest. "It's like everybody's out to kill me today."

"Sorry." Fenris grinned unrepentantly, then leant in to brush his lips over the side of her face; a ghostly touch which sent shivers down Arcana's spine. Fangs grazed her ear as he whispered; "And, for the record, you are not pasty. Out here, in the night, you are made of shadows and starlight."

Arcana glowered at him for a long moment, during which Fenris only grinned all the wider. "I thought you were supposed to be out there, looking for 'big toothy things'."

"I was." Fenris leant out further, planting one hand on Caelum's rump for support as he nuzzled into her hair, licked the hollow beneath her ear. "The view back here is better."

Phase snorted, loudly, and clicked something in Illithai. Fenris gave a throaty chuckle and responded in kind, his tone so wicked that Arcana narrowed her eyes and wondered exactly what they were talking about.

"If you're done touching my butt," Caelum said tartly, "I was in the process of asking Arcana to speed this up a notch."

Fenris abruptly disappeared, fading into the ever-lightening dawn with such skill that she blinked, twisting in place to look for him. Broad hands framed her waist a moment later and she yelped in surprise as Fenris plucked Arcana from the deerken's back, cradling her against his chest. Jade eyes settled on Caelum with lazy amusement. "Is this more to your satisfaction?"

"Hey!" Arcana struggled on instinct but stopped when Fenris' stare locked with hers, his glamour raising goosebumps over her skin. "You can't just go around snatching people for your own amusement, Guardian."

"Oh?" He murmured, his voice dropping into that deep, velvet rumble that Arcana was sure would be the death of her one day. "Convince me you don't like it and I'll put you down."

Arcana swallowed and blushed, knowing full well his nose already had the answer to that particular statement. She fought for words and failed but Caelum didn't let her down, his glare roving over both Arcana and Fenris as though he had lasers in his eyes. "You're more cheerful than I've ever seen you, Guardian. What gives?"

"It is the dark," Fenris replied, his body undulating in time with his shrug. "Wherever I am, the night is my home. That, and... impending danger often makes me restless."

"So are you cheerful or manic?" Arcana asked. Fenris lowered his head, his body curling in on itself until he could brush another phantom kiss to the corner of her eye in a deliberately ambiguous answer. "I see." Fangs flashed and for moment she thought he would kiss her, then his arms loosened and Fenris slid her down the hard length of his body until she stood on her own two feet. Arcana shook her head, shoving out of the Guardian's embrace and taking three steps away from him for good measure. "Where to?"

"Straight ahead," Caelum answered, his tone somewhere between frustrated and amused. Arcana dropped to her knees and flattened her hands against the enormous branch. Magic leapt to her fingertips, extending outwards through the tree and into the jungle, deeper and deeper until she lost all sense of self and became sighing leaves and swinging vines, deep floral blooms turning drowsy faces up for the sun's first kiss.

The jungle shuddered and began to move, branches creaking and bending, twisting together to form a neatly braided pathway stretching off into the distance. Arcana's senses followed the wave of power outward, ensuring none of the trees were permanently damaged and that the road she wrought was stable. Once satisfied, she bound the trees in place, smiling as their great boughs settled with an almost human sigh. With a silent murmur of thanks, Arcana reeled her magic back into her body and blinked, surfacing with the scent of wild blossoms coating the inside of her throat.

"Woah," Phase whispered.

Arcana flashed him a grin over her shoulder. "Been a while, eh?"

The Illithai nodded; Fenris stared around him in awe. "I will never tire of this. Ever." He poked at one curving branch with the toe of his boot. "Incredible."

"I'm going to release the jungle as we pass, so stay close." Arcana pushed upright and set off, ducking her head to hide her blush. Fenris sped up until he loped alongside, eyes continuously roving the jungle in all directions. Before she had a chance to think it through, Arcana reached out and poked him in the jaw, right where he'd tensed up so much that the muscle had begun to twitch. "You could cut cheese with that frown, you know."

Fenris stared down at her hand, still lingering in the air between them. "I'm afraid it's in my nature to be tense."

"Guess we'll have to find a way to relax you, then," Arcana teased. Fenris blinked, astonished - and then all that tension melted away as he stuck his tongue out. Arcana laughed, delighted, and returned the gesture, earning herself an inelegant snort of amusement and that wicked, bedroom smile she was quickly coming to adore.

"Stop," said Caelum suddenly. Arcana propped to a standstill at once, the foliage around her rustling as it settled. Metal scraped on leather as Fenris drew the greatsword, his spine bumping against hers as they instinctively stood back to back.

"What is it?" Arcana tilted her head, magic building in her fingertips.

"Nothing. Great Gods of Sorcen, you too?" Caelum turned disapproving eyes on Phase, who had both his scimitars in hand, and then shook his head. "You guys need to take a chill pill or there'll be stomach ulcers all round." He moved to the edge of the interlocking branches and peered over, stumpy tail swishing back and forth. "The portal's below us, that's all."

"I swear I'm going to turn you into a rug one of these days," Arcana muttered, narrowing her eyes at the deerken.

Caelum merely raised an eyebrow. "Stomach ulcer, remember?"

Arcana growled in warning but Fenris spun in place to grab her wrist, brows furrowed. "This is not the time to bicker, either of you." His grip tightened. "Arcana."

With a long suffering sigh, she dismissed the vine which had been about to curl around Caelum's hind legs and hoist him into the air. "Fine, fine. But next time, don't freak us out like that."

Caelum raised a furred brow. "I just didn't want to overshoot, seeing as we're on a time limit. I don't suppose you want to take us down?"

"Wait," Fenris interceded again, holding up a finger in emphasis. "Just wait. Let me check the area before we descend."

"All right." Arcana nodded but instead of moving, Fenris simply stared. She sighed. "Don't worry, I won't get into a slapfight with His Furrishness while you're gone."

"Good." Releasing her wrist, Fenris jumped off the edge of the branch, disappearing into the canopy below.

Arcana peered off in the direction he'd gone until Caelum wandered to her side, pushing his nose imperiously into her hand. "I'm sorry."

"Liar."

"Promise," he insisted. "I didn't mean to startle you."

"Shouting 'stop' in the middle of hostile territory? What did you *think* was going to happen?"

He was silent a moment, then gave her a sheepish look. "Okay, well, maybe I meant it a little bit. But you forgive me, right?"

"Forgive you? Unlikely." Arcana glared for a full minute then rolled her eyes, scratching under his chin. "Okay, fine. I forgive you."

"I knew you would." Caelum sighed, ears drooping in bliss as he leant into the caress. "Ohhhhhh yeah. Right there."

"You're pathetic."

"It's the short fur," he answered. "Makes me itchy."

Arcana eyed Caelum's sleek, muscular body, the silver-grey fur barely two inches long and the black markings across his back and haunches standing out in stark relief. "It was shorter at Corrin's Run."

"That's because we were melting," Caelum sniffed, angling his head to direct her fingers. "As opposed to just sweating profusely in this ungodly humidity. I have a bad enough feeling about this mission as it is."

"A bad feeling?" Arcana paused her scritching in surprise, only to begin again when Caelum grunted and shoved at her hand. "About what?"

"Didn't I just say about the mission?" His tail swished with irritation. "Before you ask, I can't give specifics, it's just an overall feeling of foreboding."

"You didn't think to mention it sooner?"

"What good would it have done?" Caelum rolled his shoulders in a shrug. "We've been going from proverbial frying pan to fire our entire lives - I don't see why a little case of the heebie jeebies would stop us from continuing that stellar pattern of life choices, especially now."

Arcana choked back a laugh. "I guess you're right."

"I often am," he said loftily. "Just do me a favour and be on your guard."

"When am I not?"

Furry brows shot up. "When you're busy mooning over a certain sexy Guardian?" Caelum's words became a squeak as she grabbed a handful of skin and twisted. "Hey, that's my wobbly jowls you're mauling!"

"You don't have wobbly jowls," Arcana snapped back - but she loosened her hold and, after a moment, went back to scritching his fur. "And I don't moon. I don't know how to moon."

"Could've fooled me." Caelum's droopy ear flickered slightly, as though he was trying to think but couldn't quite muster the energy. "Honestly, though, you know I like him. Just try and keep at least one of your eyes focussed somewhere other than his fine backside, okay?"

Arcana snorted a laugh at that, leaning over to kiss Caelum on the nose. "Okay."

They both started guiltily as a thump shook the branch and Fenris landed barely two paces in front of them. "There's a river directly below us," he announced. "We need to aim a little further north. The portal's built atop a stone platform in a small clearing. Most of the area is shrouded in leaf litter but it seems otherwise clear." Jade eyes narrowed as he inspected their studiously innocent faces. "What?"

"Nothing," Caelum answered swiftly. "Just chatting. About nothing."

Arcana elbowed him in the shoulder and cleared her throat. "Is the portal intact?"

"It appears to be, but I didn't get close enough to find out for certain. The lowermost branches were too high - If I dropped down, I may not have been able to return." His mouth tightened and Fenris shrugged uneasily. "We will have to risk it."

Arcana turned both palms towards the ground and summoned her magic. "Okay, here we go. You might want to hold on to something."

The branch upon which they stood lurched downwards, swaying precariously as the trees bent more than double. The forest floor rushed into focus, a confused jumble of rocks, leaf litter and enormous tree roots cleft in two by a narrow canyon. The booming echo of rushing water growled out of the crevasse like an angry beast, accompanied by clouds of spume that stood testament to the strength of the river below.

On the far edge of the canyon perched a large, circular stone platform. Thick roots clutched borders and broke through the paving in several locations, giving the entire area an ancient, neglected feel. The tall, circular portal stood intact atop a dais in the centre of the area, draped with vines and rotting leaf matter. Though the stone platform created a clearing of sorts, the jungle grew thick and strong around it, with the azure sky no more than a far off speck barely visible beneath the canopy.

Directing the knotwork of branches to bend until it brushed the stone terrace, Arcana stepped down onto dappled pavement with her eyes trained on the portal. It was at least three times her height, set into a hefty plinth and covered in runes and carvings - familiar and yet incredibly alien, given that this was the first time she'd seen one of the massive gateways intact. A peaceful energy pervaded the entire area and for a moment, the sighing wind sounded like a woman's voice.

Arcana drifted towards the structure but paused when Fenris appeared at her side, the greatsword gripped tightly in both hands. She took in the rigid set of his shoulders, the muscle twitching in his jaw, and raised a brow. "Sense something?"

The Guardian shook his head, ever so slightly. "Simply taking no chances. If Taelon truly intends to use this portal, he would be a fool to leave it without guard or at least surveillance." Fenris readjusted his grip on the greatsword, the movement smacking of habit, and frowned. "We should not linger here - for a number of reasons." Turning to glance over his shoulder, he added; "Keep watch."

Phase answered in Illitani, drawing both scimitars and setting all four of his paws firmly against the cracked cobbles. With a long suffering sigh, Caelum took up a position beside the Illithai and turned his attention outward. "Remember that bad feeling from before? It's getting worse."

"We'll be quick, I promise." Arcana followed Fenris up the shallow steps and together they stood before the sleeping doorway. A soft breeze tickled Arcana's cheeks, causing the hairs on the back of her arms to stand on end. "Do you feel that?"

Fenris whipped his head around to stare at her, eyes wide. "Feel what?"

"That." Arcana closed her eyes as the gentle touch brushed over her forehead, teased her hair, sighed in her ear. "The wind." When no answer was forthcoming, she opened her eyes again to find the Guardian frowning. "You can't feel it?"

"No," he said slowly, "But I can see your hair moving by itself. Do you sense anything else?"

"A voice. It's like... a song. Or the remains of a song." Arcana shook her head, trying to catch the elusive sounds hovering at the edge of her understanding. "I can't quite make it out."

"Hmm." Again that regripping of the sword and, just as abruptly, Fenris slammed it into the scabbard strapped to his back. "Perhaps you sense the Weaver."

"What does that mean?"

"I don't know." He kicked at a pile of leaf litter, filling the air with a cloud of half-rotten leaves. They settled slowly, revealing a stone pedestal to one side of the plinth. "The portals are connected to her energy, so maybe it is no more and no less than that."

"But… should I be feeling it? I mean, it's not exactly magic, is it?"

Fenris took in a deep breath and held it, watching the last of the leaves sigh against the side of his boots. "Do you believe in fate, Arcana?"

"No. I believe in making my own choices."

"Then you don't think the Weaver used Caelum to send you, ill-advised and unprepared, across the vast expanse of the universe specifically to rescue my useless behind from that crumbling ruin?"

"I do - but it was my choice to go through with it or not."

He tipped his head back, staring up at the curving stonework barely visible beneath layers of foliage. "That is true."

"I've always believed that life isn't about what happens to us, but about what we do with what happens to us." Arcana reached for the stone pedestal Fenris had uncovered, tracing her fingers over the large, curling rune etched into the surface. Bordered by a circle of smaller characters that seemed decorative at first glance, the power humming through the slender pillar said otherwise. "We all have choices to make, Fenris. Good ones, bad ones. They shape us. But tools of fate? No. I refuse to believe I am anything other than who I've decided to become. Why?"

"I think…" Fenris hesitated, then laid his hand over the top of hers, long, teal fingers fitting between her stark, salt white ones. "The Weaver works on so many layers and levels of the weave that it's impossible to truly comprehend her, but I think she knew I'd need your skills if I were ever to stand a chance of success. Much as I appreciate that recognition, I loathe the idea that you were dragged into this like a wild dog brought to heel."

Arcana chuckled, hoping he didn't catch the breathless edge to it as she stared down at their joined hands. "Fenris, nobody's capable of bringing me to heel. Not Flare, not the Council of Elders, not Burke, not Caelum, not the Weaver and certainly not you. I go where I will, and I do what I think is right. Fighting against Taelon and the warg? Even if it costs me my life, it's right." She bumped her shoulder against his bicep. "I thought we weren't doubting ourselves anymore."

"I'm not."

"Then what *are* you doing?"

He curled his fingers through hers, turned their joined hands over, and pressed a kiss to the centre of her palm. "I am starting to think it is time to follow your example and make my own choices."

"Oh?"

"Yes. For one so long devoted to the word of his queen, it's an unusual feeling." Fenris released her, then reached back down to tap several of the runes in sequence before spreading his hand over the plinth, digging long fingers into the design. "Hmm. Deactivated."

"Permanently?"

"Yes and no." Fenris' brows furrowed as he stared down at the plinth. "The portal network is like a web, with the Weaver at the centre. There are seven master gates inside the Timeless Kingdom, from which spread the rest of the portals in the greater universe. This particular portal has both structural integrity and power crystals but sleeps because the master gate is disconnected." He hesitated. "The Weaver's last instruction was to close all the master gates in order to prevent the spread of the warg. I managed five, and destroyed another as I fell through it."

"Leaving one intact." Arcana ran one hand along the smooth curve of the portal. It was cool to the touch, as though immune to the inherent humidity of the jungle around them. "But it can't be working properly, or Taelon would have the warg everywhere by now."

"Indeed." Fenris straightened, dusting his hands on the hem of his jacket. "Murtagh, from whom Shirimm took the crystals, is our head portal technician and a Guardian who commands much respect. Once the Keeper and the Walker ordered the evacuation of our homeland, I believe Murtagh would have set the final portal to remain open for a certain length of time, and then removed the crystals so that Taelon could not follow him through."

Arcana's jaw dropped. "You can do that?"

"*I* cannot," Fenris corrected, "But Murtagh is older than old. He helped the Weaver design and build the portals, so yes, he could do it. I pray he did not give his life for the crystals Shirimm stole - once this is done, we will need him."

"If Murtagh is as old as you say, he must know his way around a weapon or two. I doubt he'd be an easy target."

Fenris hitched a shoulder noncommittally. "Murtagh is an excellent warrior but all Guardians are and for the first time, we are not united against a common enemy but fractured and fighting amongst ourselves. Victory is never a sure thing." His jaw tightened, that now familiar muscle beginning to twitch. "Taelon has enough portal knowledge that he, like myself, could take the crystals Shirimm has, replace the ones in this gate with them, and force a dirty connection to a different master gate. We *must* recover those crystals."

"We will." When he didn't answer, Arcana slipped her hand into his, twining their fingers back together. "Fenris."

Burning jade eyes sought hers, filled with grief. "I was taught these gates are sacred. How did it come to this?"

"I don't know, but we'll find a way to fix it. Together we are strong," she reminded, squeezing his hand. Fenris searched her face and though the pain in his gaze didn't lessen, after a long moment he squeezed back. Arcana thought over his words and, voice gentle, said; "You want me to destroy this portal, don't you?"

"Yes."

"All right." She looked up into his face, at the agony there and knew if it were to be done, then it would be best done quickly. Arcana raised the hand which had been resting against the portal and let her eyes drift shut as she gathered her magic, threading it through the stone. The portal crystals, though technically dormant, seethed with barely contained energy when she brushed against them. Biting back a shiver as she recalled the awful time flux they'd discovered back on Sorcen, Arcana bound each crystal in a thick layer of magic and, using skills she'd not bothered accessing for years, wove the strands of energy into a binding spell.

Without giving Fenris any further warning, she closed her raised hand into a fist and bore down heavily with her magic. There was a groaning, as of crumbling masonry and then the giant structure disintegrated, enveloping the platform in a cloud of shimmering dust. Power slammed hard into Arcana's chest as the portal crystals dissolved, unleashing their dormant energies upon the binding spell in a manic attempt at freedom. Once more Arcana felt that unseen wind whipping around her, no longer a breeze but a gale that blasted her hair back from her face and threatened to knock her off her feet. She clung to Fenris and absorbed the blow through gritted teeth, pulling tight on the drawstrings of her spell until the energy had nowhere to go but into itself, endlessly turning and consuming and burrowing until, with a pop she felt more than heard, it died out entirely.

"Arcana? Arcana!"

She opened her eyes to find Fenris bent over her, arms tight around her waist as though they'd been dancing and he'd dipped her back with a flourish. "I'm okay," she managed, her voice slightly hoarse.

Fenris let out a sigh, his face twisting in relief, and lowered his forehead to rest against hers. "You frightened me."

"Sorry." Clearing her throat, Arcana addressed the fading breath of half-heard sound that lingered at the edges of her understanding. "You're welcome."

"The Weaver spoke to you?" Fenris' eyes were lined with silver as he helped her to her feet. "What did she say?"

"There were no words… but we did as she wanted us to."

He exhaled long and slow, lashes drifting closed for a fraction of a moment. "That goes a long way toward healing my spirit."

"Good. Now tell me that I didn't create a screaming zombie vortex and you'll be healing *my* spirit."

"What?" He blinked, skated his eyes across the platform, then returned them to Arcana. "No. There is a definite lack of zombies and time fluxes. How did you manage it?"

Arcana shrugged a shoulder. "An old binding spell. Originally intended to hold back or shape water - but I altered it a little and it seemed to do the trick. I don't often need to cast them anymore but once in a while, those skills sure come in handy." She blew out a long breath. "I'm glad those stones were dormant. I'd hate to come into contact with something truly active - it'd blow my socks off."

"Do you realise the full extent of what you just did?" Fenris brushed a thumb across her cheeks, his expression full of wonder. "That energy should have torn you apart, yet you banished it with an altered children's trick and sheer willpower."

"I couldn't very well let the explosion tear the planet apart, now could I?" Feeling her cheeks burn, Arcana cleared her throat and shoved out of the circle of his arms. Turning away from the awe on Fenris' face, she brushed portal dust off her clothes and said; "Just forget it, okay? We've got more important things to worry about. And with that in mind, I have a question."

"Yes?"

"If Taelon hasn't got any active portals, how is he planning to get in and out of the Timeless Kingdom? Let alone manage the network." Arcana frowned. "He also has to get the portal crystals there, one way or another, and all the gates are shut."

Fenris' velvet voice turned grim. "I believe he plans to use the deerken."

"How?" Arcana looked over her shoulder at Caelum, who was watching them with wide eyes and pricked ears. "Surely they'd never agree to help."

"Not willingly." Fenris wrapped an arm around her shoulders, nudging Arcana back down the shallow steps. "Deerken may be able to wander between the layers of time, space and reality at will, but that gift comes with a heavy price. Outside of the Timeless Kingdom, they gradually weaken and fade, their minds fracturing, until they are at last reabsorbed into the weave. It is the reason a deerken never ventures beyond the Timeless Kingdom without a Warden and Guardian as escort." His face hardened. "With Taelon's knowledge, it would be a small matter to keep captured deerken starved and fractured enough to use for his own purposes."

"Won't they fight?" Caelum's body trembled with indignation. "If it was me, I'd dump Taelon's useless ass in the middle of a star and be done with it."

"Not all deerken are built like you, brother." Fenris' smile was sad. "Auron would have fought - and his son, Dendrite, the first of the deerken - but they have both been lost for over a hundred years."

Caelum frowned. "Why? What happened?"

"It is a long story, but…" Fenris ran a hand through his hair, shaking free the portal dust which had turned his dark teal curls beige, and sighed. "I told you back on Sorcen that there was a deerken poaching, and that without kin to stabilise the resulting implosion, the deerken's death tore a hole in the weave."

"Yes, I remember."

"What I did not tell you was that the energy flux grew to such catastrophic proportions that the Weaver found it impossible to repair. The rift continued to widen, swallowing worlds and bending reality, causing our queen untold agony. Eventually her consort, Auron, the Keeper of Life and father to all deerken, travelled to the rift with his eldest son Dendrite and a small team of other deerken, Guardians and Wardens. Their goal was to quell the restless energy so that the Weaver could suture her wounds."

"And?" Arcana asked quietly.

Fenris tensed, his eyes downcast. "Auron was forced to enter the rift in a desperate attempt to calm it, and the Weaver had to mend the tear in reality whilst he was inside. Neither he, nor any of those who accompanied him, ever returned. The weave was healed but without her mate, the Weaver - and her children - fell into a deep melancholy. Taelon begged and begged to follow Auron, swore he'd be able to find him and bring him home. The Weaver told him it was too dangerous." Fenris shrugged. "He went anyway and he, too, disappeared without trace."

"And then resurfaced years later with the warg in tow… batshit crazy and wanting to take Auron's place?"

"Yes." Fenris turned to Caelum, his face sad. "When Auron disappeared, the deerken became infertile. With Dendrite also gone, they lacked their leader, their protector. And with the Weaver bereft, they were adrift without support. The Wardens did their best but the entire species shut down, losing a great deal of their autonomy and, dare I say it aloud, their sanity. They wander lost in an ancient grief, their only defence the Wardens and Guardians who swore to protect them."

"Until Taelon incited those same people to treason." Caelum's ears laid flat against his skull. "I hate that guy more with every passing second."

"Indeed." Fenris bared his teeth in a silent snarl, but his eyes were sad. "I wish I knew what happened. Before he disappeared, Taelon was the most passionate champion of our cause and a man I respected. It is a grave thing for one to change so -" He broke off, whirling towards the now empty dais.

"What is it?" Arcana took two steps forward and stopped as the air at the top of the stairs began to shimmer and distort, as though under the influence of great heat. A soft popping noise broke the silence and a woman appeared, collapsing heavily onto the stone pavers. Standing over her was the translucent form of a deerken, her petite body almost invisible. She was barely as tall as Caelum's shoulder yet her antler rack spread higher and wider, dripping with an array of ethereal blossoms and berries. The creature lowered her head to nudge the woman on the ground but her nose passed straight through a leather-clad shoulder.

"Brianne!" Fenris leapt forward, dropping to his knees on the stone and pulling the woman into his lap. Her mocha complexion was pale and blood ran from a shallow gash on her forehead. Thick black tattoos curled around closed eyes and disappeared into her hairline. "Weaver's grace, what happened?"

Arcana knelt on the woman's opposite side, leaning in to get a closer look at her face. Brianne made no sound, no movement save for the faintest shift of her chest to show she still lived. "Looks like she's taken a fair blow to the head. Who is she?"

"Brianne is a Warden," Fenris explained. He flicked a glance up at the deerken and jerked in surprise. "*Mirokke*?"

The deerken called Mirokke seemed unaware Fenris had even spoken, instead focussing milky white eyes on Caelum. Her fur drifted in an unseen wind, the blossoms on her antlers opening and closing like thousands of tiny mouths. Caelum's hackles rose as he met Mirokke's unblinking stare. "She's blind, isn't she?"

"Yes." Fenris made a sad noise in the base of his throat. "She has been away from the Timeless Kingdom too long and has begun to unravel. How she got Brianne here in such condition is a mystery."

Phase clicked and squeaked and Fenris cut him a glance. "I know. I am sorry for the delay, but we cannot leave her."

"Don't worry about Burke yet. I'm sure the Pariah wants to use her as leverage - otherwise Shirimm would have killed her back on the Run. We have time," Arcana muttered, trailing her hands down Brianne's stocky body, poking and squeezing as she went. "Looks like her arm is broken, and... oh, shit." She peeled back layers of bloody leather and linen until she found a sinister looking wound in Brianne's gut. "She's been shot."

Fenris' nostrils flared as he leant forward to sniff the blood on Arcana's fingers. "I smell poison. We must get her to safety at once." He tucked the unconscious Brianne close to his chest and stood. "Mirokke? Can you hear me?"

Silence followed, and they all stared at Mirokke whilst she swayed dreamily from side to side.

"I feel like she's trying to talk to me... but I can't quite hear." Caelum's ears were pricked forward, his brows furrowed. "There's whispering. So much whispering... A door. Fire."

"Stop!" Fenris shoved against Caelum with his hip, careful not to jar Brianne in the process. When Caelum blinked blearily and looked up at him, he said; "Deerken do not talk like you and I. They do it in a series of images and thoughts passed through the dreambank - but Mirokke's unravelling and her energy is dangerous. If she draws you into the dream-bank now, you may not be able to return and you will take Arcana with you."

Caelum's chest heaved as though he'd been running and he shook his head to clear it. "I can still hear it."

"Block her out," Fenris snapped.

"And then what? She dies? *Alone?*"

Seeing the look on Caelum's face, Fenris sighed. "I am not suggesting exile, merely caution. Without access to the Timeless Kingdom for grounding, Mirokke will continue to fade and eventually die. But you cannot let her take you, Caelum - all it will accomplish is two deaths rather than one."

"I can't just ignore her."

"Stop, both of you." Arcana stepped between them, one hand on Caelum's quivering nose and the other on Fenris' shoulder. She squinted at Mirokke, tracing the barely visible lines of her body. Her proportions were similar to Caelum's and yet strangely alien. Long, stick like legs and tiny cleft hooves rose to a short, pert barrel of a body, which in turn gave way to a slender neck and a delicate, pointed face. "We need to think, not argue. Brianne's injured and Burke's still waiting for us."

Fenris opened his mouth and paused as Brianne stirred, her eyelashes fluttering open. "Fenris?" she wheezed, her breath bubbling in her throat. "Is that you?"

"Yes," he soothed. "You are safe now."

"No, listen. Mirokke..."

Fenris turned so Brianne could see her charge. "She's here."

"We were ambushed." Brianne's face was pasty with effort and she went so far as to push weakly against Fenris' shoulder. "Take her and run, before it's too late."

"I'm not leaving you," Fenris replied, shaking his head. "Save your strength and -"

"*No,*" Brianne panted, gritting her teeth. "Mirokke is..."

"Pregnant," Arcana gasped, squinting her eyes at the doe. "Now that I'm looking, she's very, *very* pregnant."

Fenris' face drained of all colour as, for the first time, he turned his full attention on Mirokke. "Weaver's grace, how?"

"I don't know but it's true," Brianne groaned, struggling against Fenris' hold. "Now go, before-"

"Duck!" Caelum knocked Arcana to the ground as something whizzed overhead. She hit the stone hard, gasping for air as Caelum's bulk slammed into her back, covering her entirely. It only lasted a moment before the deerken was on his hooves again, rushing to where Fenris had Brianne cradled in one arm and the greatsword in the other. "Give her to me," he commanded, bending enough for Fenris to slide the wounded Warden onto his back.

"Here," Phase appeared at Arcana's side, offering a hand to haul her upright.

"Thanks."

A tall man in battle black stepped from the trees, fitting a fresh bolt into the small crossbow he held and firing without appearing to aim. Fenris, greatsword now in both hands, deflected the bolt down into the platform, a wicked metal tip with a glass barrel containing a roiling grey liquid that exploded on impact. Smoke billowed outward, obscuring their attacker from view but Fenris didn't hesitate; he leapt into the cloud and disappeared from sight.

Arcana backed into Caelum on one side, aware of Phase doing the same on the other. The smoke engulfed them in moments, thick and cloyingly sweet, making Arcana's eyes sting and blur. She took deep, measured breaths, absorbing the smoke into her lungs, testing the essence of it with her power. As soon as her magic adapted, her eyes stopped stinging but it was still impossible to see; the soupy air was so thick and grey that if Arcana hadn't felt the ground underfoot or Caelum's flank pressed against her back, she'd have thought she was bodiless, floating forever in murk.

Anxiety fluttered in her gut and a sweet, sticky flavour clung to the inside of her throat. Grabbing instinctively for Caelum's head, she caught the base of a bladed antler and swung herself close. "The smoke is drugged!"

"To incite a fear response," Caelum agreed. "Don't suppose we can use that to our advantage?"

"Not sure, but I know I can do this," Arcana responded, flattening her hands and shoving them palm down towards the ground. The smoke responded at once, sinking until it swirled around Arcana's knees.

Fenris appeared, fighting a pair of figures with tiny, whirling hatchets who wore battle black leathers like the man with the crossbow, hooded jackets pulled low over their faces. Though the pair spun and hacked in unison, their speed and strength terrifying, Fenris fought with overt ease and Arcana realised he'd been speaking, his voice pitched low for his opponents' ears alone. Abruptly one of the attackers shouted angrily, dropped formation with their partner and leapt at Fenris with renewed fury. The other half of the pair hesitated - and Fenris stepped inside the warrior's guard, the greatsword slicing upwards from hip to shoulder in a stroke so mighty it cut the figure in half. The corpse fell away from his blade and he spun to deflect the assault coming his way, batting aside the twin hatchets with the flat of the greatsword's blade. Reversing direction, Fenris slammed the hilt of the weapon into the depths of his opponent's hood and whilst they stumbled back in shock, he flipped the greatsword over and drove it right through the centre of the warrior's chest.

"Stop!" A voice like rough gravel cut through the sudden silence. Fenris straightened, the body of his opponent hanging from the end of the greatsword, and turned in the direction of the voice. It was the man with the crossbow, his weapon shoved hard against the back of Phase's head. "Put it down, Overlord. We both know I can shoot this fool and be gone before you've so much as blinked."

"You think I care for my mercenaries' lives, Daelan?" Fenris replied, his expression impassive and his grip on the greatsword never wavering.

"Of course. You care for every life," Daelan sneered, the insult clear.

"Although, honestly, you'd be better off letting this one go. Barely a whiff of the reahllin gas and he dropped his swords and pissed himself."

"Good help," said Fenris quietly, "Is hard to find." With a swift jerk, he pulled the greatsword out of his opponent and watched dispassionately as the body slumped into the smoke and out of sight. "I thought you were better than this."

"And I thought you were dead." Daelan laughed, a sinister, tinkling chime of a sound, and reached up with a gloved hand to shuck his hood. "Looks like we were both mistaken. Now, brother, sword down."

Fenris raked his burning gaze over the other male and finally lowered his sword point down into the fog. Crossing his arms over the hilt the way Arcana had seen him do so often back on Sorcen, he said; "Brianne is injured. Dare I assume you had something to do with it?"

"She wouldn't be injured if she hadn't run." Daelan smirked, the expression partially hidden behind a waterfall of silver-white hair which hung dead straight almost to his waist. The left side of his face was completely masked by the silver curtain, the right side revealing a blood red eye and a raggedly pointed ear. "You know how I hate it when they run."

"Wipe that grin off your face, traitor," Brianne spat, her chest heaving with effort as she fought to sit upright on Caelum's back. "Fenris won't be bought by your platitudes."

Daelan sighed, his expression one of deep disinterest. "We both know you'll be dead in minutes, little Warden. If I were you, I'd be praying to my gods rather than attempting a lecture."

Brianne growled and made to swing her legs around but Arcana caught hold of her wrist and shook her head. "No. He's trying to goad you."

"I know and I don't care. If the last thing I do is wipe the smile off that slime bucket's face, it'll be worth it."

"Be still, Brianne." Fenris' voice was calm but Brianne stopped and allowed Arcana to drape her more comfortably along the length of Caelum's neck. He watched until the Warden was settled, then turned back to Daelan. "You used the gorlani venom on one of your own, brother. Can you not see what Taelon's insanity has bought upon us?"

"Oh please, the Weaver's been losing her grip since Auron fell." Daelan rolled his red eye, the movement surprisingly elegant in a vicious, pointed face. "If you weren't so starry eyed for her, you'd have seen it yourself. Taelon is offering a solution. A future."

Fenris lifted his chin, his face so cold it seemed inhuman. "I will have no part of a future that involves destroying everything we have ever fought for."

"Somehow I knew you'd say that." Daelan laughed, the musical sound akin to the tinkling of chimes. "You're not alone, either - your father led a rebellion after you disappeared." Fenris startled at that and Daelan pressed his crossbow harder against the back of Phase's head. "Uh uh, Overlord. Stand down, or I shoot this rather intriguing combination of man and couch right now."

Phase rumbled at that but wisely said nothing. Arcana tried to catch Fenris' eye but the Guardian seemed to be deliberately avoiding meeting her gaze. Instead, he waved a casual hand at the fog, which Arcana's magic still kept low to the ground. "I am not sure how concerned I should be if you cannot even control the reahllin gas anymore."

Daelan's top lip pulled back in a sneer. "A bad batch. Mixing conditions aren't always ideal."

"Because you're too busy hunting your own kind?"

"So self-righteous, even now." Daelan shook his head, that chiming laugh raising goose bumps over Arcana's skin. "You know, those of us with vision swore to follow Taelon and so far we've seen nothing but rewards for our sacrifice. Those who followed your father? Well... Rytan didn't look so good when I last saw him."

Arcana watched Fenris' knuckles tighten but he didn't react to the jibe, turning his head as if to look at Brianne - but it was Arcana's gaze those burning eyes locked with. "Not yet," he said quietly.

Daelan laughed again - a sound Arcana was coming to actively hate - likely assuming Fenris spoke to Brianne. But Arcana knew Fenris had seen the thin tendrils of fog slowly weaving their way up Phase's grey legs, camouflaged against his skin in preparation for attack. She'd had some minutes now to work out the composition of the smoke, knew exactly how much would be needed to fill Daelan's lungs and suffocate him. When Arcana didn't immediately release the fog, Caelum shifted his weight, nudging her with his hindquarters. The movement drew Daelan's attention and Arcana raised a brow in his direction. "Something on my face, asshole?"

"I came to kill Brianne," the ex-Guardian replied smoothly. "There's a price on the head of her and those like her, of which your employer's is the largest. I'll make you a deal - assist in his capture and I'll split the reward down the middle."

Arcana's mouth dropped open and a moment later, she laughed.

"Sorry, but I'm not the type to sell out mid contract. I made a deal and I'm sticking to it."

"Huh." Daelan snorted, looking amused, then turned to Fenris. "Well then, it appears we're at an impasse."

Arcana frowned but Fenris bent almost double, thrust a hand into the fog and yanked up a cloaked and hooded figure. "If you want Pierlin to continue breathing, yes. But I am willing to bargain, Daelan. Your comrade's life for Brianne's antidote."

"That's not enough, Fenris," Daelan shook his head and the cloaked Pierlin squeaked in terror. "I need more from you than that."

"Let me guess: you need me alive for your master and you'll spare the lives of my comrades if I come peacefully?" Fenris' gaze moved past Daelan and into the treeline. "There are at least another three of you still hidden in the jungle. Are you ashamed to show me your faces?" He tilted his head, his expression seemingly carved from granite. "I smell Karakk, Breya and Llane - will none of you stand for the comrade whose neck I am about to snap? If memory serves correctly, you took an oath to protect each other, once upon a time."

"Bah, you and your oath! So old fashioned." Daelan picked at his sleeve as though bored - though the hand holding the crossbow did not waver. "Come now, we both know this banter is pointless."

Fenris tightened his grip on the back of Pierlin's neck and the captive ex-Guardian began to make awful choking noises. "Then get to it, Daelan. I should not like to imagine how well Taelon will enjoy hearing that a single Guardian and his mercenaries slaughtered your entire team of cowards."

"Very well." Daelan attempted a sneer, but Arcana saw the flash of nerves on his face. "There is no antidote to the gorlani venom save the one which I carry. Release Pierlin and surrender yourself into my custody and I will make sure Brianne gets her antidote before the longsleep comes to claim her."

Fenris was quiet for a long moment, his eyes roving from Daelan, to the trees, to Brianne and back again. "Very well. We will go with you."

"Are you *serious*?" Arcana hissed through gritted teeth.

Fenris half turned his head in her direction. "Brianne will die if we do not act soon and Daelan is correct - for this poison, he alone has the antidote." His gaze at last shifted to hers, the glamour sliding slowly, gently over Arcana's skin as he added; "Besides, I have some unfinished business to discuss with Taelon."

Arcana crossed both arms over her chest, doing her best to affect the air of a thwarted mercenary. "This is a bad idea, but you're the one paying for it."

"Don't worry, little Terran." Daelan grinned, showing off rows of sharp, pointed teeth. "Fenris won't need you where he's going."

"I won't leave her," Fenris snapped.

"Oh? That was a little too quick, Overlord. I wonder why you'd need this little party of worshippers - particularly a woman who's not even carrying a weapon. Tell me, Fenris, exactly *what* does this unusual looking creature do for you?" He tilted his head to one side, single ruby eye narrowing. "She's pretty enough, I suppose, once you get past that ghastly white skin and those dead eyes. Not a bad figure - but you've never shown much interest in women at the best of times. Still, perhaps Shirimm will be amused if I present her with this Terran's head in a sack."

"Don't be a fool, Daelan. Do you think I tote pretty Terrans about for the fun of it? She and the deerken have a soul merge. Kill one and the other dies - and if you kill either deerken, our deal is off." Fenris raised the still-wheezing Pierlin a little higher, shaking him for emphasis.

Daelan looked over Caelum and then Arcana as though he hadn't noticed them properly before. He turned one shoulder, keeping his eyes on Fenris, and called; "Llane?"

A tall, slender figure in a hooded black cloak swept from the trees, the fabric swishing along the stone as it moved to stand beside Daelan and Phase. "Fenris speaks truly. Take them all," a male voice hissed from inside the hood.

"Shame. Oh well, here." Daelan unhooked several sets of manacles from his belt and tossed them onto the stone. "When you're locked up, Brianne gets her antidote."

Fenris growled deep in his chest. "Give her the antidote first. I will behave."

"He speaks truly," Llane's hissing voice declared. Daelan shrugged, flipped a dial on the end of his crossbow and fired. The bolt buried itself in Brianne's shoulder and she screamed, sagging sideways. Arcana caught the smaller woman before she could topple off Caelum's back and by the time she had her steady, Daelan once again had his crossbow jammed in the back of Phase's neck.

"You're an asshole, you know that?" Arcana snarled, reaching for the projectile.

"I wouldn't, if I were you," Daelan warned, his voice heavy with amusement. "It's a slow release antidote. Pull the bolt out too soon and she won't have had enough."

Arcana looked down at the shaft of the bolt, glass like the one with the gas had been. Inside, she could see a faintly blue liquid turning pink at the base where Brianne's blood seeped inside to mix with the concoction. She glanced up at Fenris and he nodded once. "Leave it in."

"Excellent decision. Now, if you don't mind? I'm on a bit of a schedule." Daelan drew back his hand and thumped the butt of the crossbow into Phase's head, sending the Illithai crumpling into the grey fog at their feet. "Oops."

Fenris' eyes narrowed. "Unnecessary."

"But fun," Daelan grinned, showing off his pointed teeth all over again. "Oh, don't pout, Overlord. You'll end up with wrinkles."

"Laugh while you can," Fenris murmured, sheathing the greatsword with a flourish. "The moment you abandoned your oath and your people, you gave up the right to mercy. Remember that, when I come to claim your life."

"Words, words, words." Daelan waved a dismissive hand. "I held up my end of the deal, Fenris, whether you like the delivery method or not. Now put the manacles on before I run out of patience."

Fenris' eyes narrowed ever so slightly at the corners but he cast a glance at Arcana from under his lashes and nodded. She twitched her fingers and the fog at their feet began to swirl into the trees to dissipate of its own accord. The manacles Daelan had tossed down lay in a slowly widening pool of blood, not far from the hood of one of Fenris' deceased opponents. Without so much as batting an eye, Fenris bent to scoop them up, clapping a set around Phase's wrists even though the Illithai lay unconscious in his own urine.

"Are you sure about this?" Arcana spoke sotto voce as he approached, sidling to block Daelan's view of her face as Fenris placed a set of manacles in her hands.

"Yes. It gets us closer to both Burke and the crystals. Save your magic," he added. "Let them think us fools."

"All right." Arcana's hands shook with fury but she took the manacles and fastened them around Fenris' wrists, wincing when they left smears of dark blood on his teal flesh. She chanced a glance into his face, allowing her voice to become slightly louder so Daelan didn't grow suspicious. "Did you know them?"

The tips of Fenris' fingers brushed her own before he twisted and managed to get the final set of manacles around Arcana's wrists. "I thought I did, once."

"Harsh justice, but I can't say I disapprove," she said in her best mercenary tone. Stepping back, she brandished her bound arms at Daelan. "There. Happy now, asshole? Honestly, the things I do for gold."

"Mercs," Daelan sighed dramatically, spinning the dial on the end of his crossbow once more. "Always the same. Llane, lug the glorified couch over to the rest of them, won't you?"

Llane hissed, a very serpentine sound, then bent to catch Phase under the arms with gloved hands. A moment later, the unconscious Illithai lay by Caelum's front hooves. Llane waved his hands at Arcana and Fenris, motioning them closer together. "Net," he said quietly. "Charged."

Fenris flicked a sharp look up from under his lashes but instead of responding, shoved Arcana closer to Caelum with his body. Llane moved away and Daelan pulled the trigger on his crossbow, a sharp metallic sound filling the air. Arcana flinched instinctively as a thin wire net settled over them, pulling taut enough that she stumbled, slumping against Caelum's hindquarters.

"Hold still, now." Daelan palmed a small teleportation unit, stepped forward and clipped it onto the net. "I've heard limbs can go missing if you struggle mid-port."

"Your care and concern, as always, are of immense comfort," Fenris said, his tone lofty for all the way the net bent him almost double. "Just get on with it, traitor."

Daelan snarled, reaching out to slap the teleporter with his free hand. "I look forward to the party when Taelon's finished with you, Overlord."

Fenris quirked the corner of his lip into an icy smile as the teleporter hummed to life, charging up for the jump. Arcana's skin tingled and she looked up to see Mirokke's body merged partially with her shoulder, the deerken's hindquarters passing through Fenris' hips and her chest buried inside Caelum's ribcage. She turned her head as the teleporter's whine reached fever pitch, her milky gaze locking with Arcana's. A strange energy brushed against her magic, alike and yet not alike the energy she'd sensed upon destroying the portal - and then the teleporter dragged them into jump space, cutting off all sound and thought completely.

CHAPTER
EIGHT

Arcana stumbled and fell, sharp stones digging into her knees. Her
head spun from the jarring energy of the teleporter and she reached
blindly for the comforting weight of Caelum - but he was no longer there.
Blinking fiercely into total darkness, she sank back on her heels to take a
deep, steadying breath. The air reeked of mildew and had the cold, biting
edge of a place that never saw sunlight.

"Caelum?" Arcana flinched, her voice sounding unnaturally loud in
the thick blackness. "Fenris?"

"Over here." Fenris' soft murmur echoed in the chill air. Arcana turned
to see the soft green glow of his eyes not far away. "Are you all right?"

"Yes." Absorbing the energy of the manacles, Arcana unlocked them
and shook her arms free. Briefly massaging the blood back into her wrists,
she turned and crawled towards Fenris, feeling her way over jagged stone
and sludge. After what seemed an eternity Arcana's seeking fingers came
into contact with the thick leather of his boots.

"Where's Caelum?" She asked, feeling her way up his body until she
found his manacles and unlocked them with a swift tap of her fingers.
"Can you see anything?"

"I can see. I would have come to you, but I managed to catch Brianne
as we appeared and I dare not move her." He blew out softly and his
fingers sought Arcana's, squeezing gently. "We're in a small cell, but it
appears the teleporter split us up. Phase and Caelum are not here." Fenris'
eyes tilted and Arcana imagined him pursing his lips in thought. "I am not

sure about Phase but Caelum cannot be far, or he'd have jumped to you by now."

"That makes sense." Arcana rubbed a sticky hand across her forehead and immediately wished she hadn't. "How did Daelan manage to split us up?"

"An energy net can be charged with multiple frequencies, so I suspect the teleporter was programmed to seek those out and separate us accordingly." Fenris sighed, his body shifting against Arcana's leg. "Brianne needs further attention. The antidote is taking effect but I have no way of understanding if she sustained any internal damage during her journey."

"Good point." Arcana shoved her arm into her satchel, brows furrowed as she dug amongst the contents. "Well, best focus on that first, seeing as we can't go looking for the others while she's unstable."

"True," Fenris agreed, but she could hear the curiosity in his voice as he watched her struggle. "What are you doing?"

"We need light. Or I do, anyway." After a few tense moments she drew out a small lantern, setting it on the floor and depressing the switch. Cold blue light flooded their tiny cell, causing shadows to dance erratically across the wall behind them. Fenris squeezed his eyes shut, jaw straining as he turned his face away from the sudden light. He had Brianne cradled in the crook of one arm, the Warden's coffee-coloured skin sheened with an oily sweat and her breathing shallow. Arcana reached back into the satchel and pulled out a rolled up blanket, spreading it onto a drier section of the floor. "Put her down here."

"Thank you." Fenris laid Brianne out on the blanket, bending to check the crossbow bolt still embedded in her shoulder. "The dosage on this is slow."

"Too slow?"

"No, but slow enough to ensure maximum suffering without death." He watched Arcana stash the two pairs of manacles in her satchel and quirked a brow. "Do you normally keep such things in there?"

Arcana couldn't help but give him a crooked grin. "Didn't your mother ever tell you never to question a lady's handbag? Caelum and I have been doing this a while, you know." She rummaged, pulled out a jar of salve. "I've learnt to be prepared."

"Just as well Daelan thought you were a mindless Terran," Fenris observed.

"Pfft. I don't know what he was thinking - I've met a few people who claim dominant Terran genetics and I look nothing like them." Arcana popped the lid on the salve and set it on the blanket.

"Daelan is an arrogant fool," Fenris replied, shrugging. "That, and Terran genes are so heavily diluted they could look like anyone. Every backwater tavern's got a beggar crying out for charity on account of being one hundredth Terran, twice removed."

"Spoken like someone who's seen too many almost-Terrans." Arcana reached over to peel Brianne's blood-soaked tunic away from her stomach. The hole in her abdomen was still bleeding, a steady seepage that covered her dark skin. "Can you see any shrapnel in there?"

Fenris leant closer, probing the wound with gentle fingers. "Daelan has a particular type of crossbow bolt that blossoms on impact. He uses it to administer a variety of substances, of which that particular poison is only one." After a long moment, he shook his head. "I think Brianne managed to remove the bolt intact."

"I'm not sure if I've said this out loud or not yet, but Daelan is a cosmic jerk." Arcana scooped some salve from the jar. "Hold her still."

"She's unconscious. If we haven't woken Brianne poking and prodding at that hole then I doubt your ointment will be an issue," Fenris returned, arranging Brianne's clothes for better access to the wound. "As for Daelan, he has always bordered on vicious. I have never been overly fond of him but I do not choose who the Weaver accepts into our ranks. That is her business alone."

"Clearly the Weaver needs a better vetting system." Arcana braced a steadying hand on Brianne's shoulder and pinned Fenris with a steely gaze. "Now hold her down - I mean it." Taken aback by her manner, Fenris placed one hand on Brianne's chest and the other on her hip. "Thank you." Arcana began packing salve into the wound and moments later Brianne drew in a breath and began to squirm, groaning and flapping her hands weakly.

"Incredible." Fenris tightened his grip, forcing Brianne's body flat against the blanket. "What is in that ointment?"

"I don't know; Lesce gave it to me." Arcana swatted Brianne's hand away so that she could cover the wound with a bandage. "What I do know is that it hurts like a bitch." She studied his face, drawn in the stark light of the lantern, and fought down the desire to smooth at his frown lines with her fingers. "I'm sorry you had to fight those ex-Guardians."

Fenris dipped his head in acknowledgement, his face softening with grief. "So am I."

"You do understand their choices are not your responsibility, right?"

"I suppose." Burning jade eyes caught her own, the glamour sweeping over Arcana's skin with a soft, velvet caress. "But if I do not shoulder this burden, who will?"

"Attempting to carry the weight of the universe will only crush you," Brianne groaned, her eyes fluttering open. "Not that you've listened the thousand other times I've said it, but - let those fools burn in their own fire."

"Brianne." Fenris bent over the other woman, his face creasing in concern. "How are you feeling?"

"The poison's receding," Brianne answered, shifting her weight and wincing. "Why didn't you leave me behind?"

Fenris rolled one shoulder in a shrug. "It was too late."

"Liar." Brianne glanced around the dank cell. "Where's Mirokke?"

"We're not sure, but I'm hoping she's with Caelum - the other deerken." Arcana squinted between the cell bars but the lantern light was too weak to pierce more than a few feet into the hall. "They can't be far."

"Caelum. That's a lovely name." Brianne locked golden eyes on Arcana's face. "And you are?"

"Arcana."

"Hmmmm. Arcana." Brianne's brow twitched. "Doesn't sound Terran."

"It's not."

"More fool Daelan, then." A smile ghosted across the Warden's face, fading as quickly as it appeared. After a long moment, Brianne curled a fist into Fenris' jacket and tugged. "You need to get out of here. Find Mirokke and go."

"No." Fenris captured her hand in both of his. "When we go, we go together."

"You mad idiot!" Brianne's growl turned into a groan. "Ugh. Where've you been the last three months, anyway? We could've used your strength."

"Three months?" Fenris repeated, aghast. "Three *months?*"

Brianne's eyes were hooded as she relaxed against the blanket. "How long has it been for you?"

"Three weeks." Fenris' mouth tightened. "Perhaps four."

"Huh. That would explain why nobody could feel your presence until recently," Brianne mused. "It's widely assumed you died - though your mother refused to believe it."

"That sounds like her." Fenris raised his hands to his face, saw they were bloody, and scrubbed them furiously on his thighs. "Three months. Weaver's grace, no wonder Taelon was so organised."

"Wait... you're saying you *lost* time somehow?" Arcana blinked up at Fenris. "How is that possible?"

The Guardian's jaw twitched, his eyes focussed far off into the middle distance. "I jumped into a destabilised portal. Anything can happen."

"Fenris." Arcana wiped her hand on her pants and reached over to cup his jaw, feathering a gentle thumb over that twitching muscle. "You're alive. That's all that matters."

"Taelon-"

"No," Arcana said firmly, but gently. "Enough. Do *not* give him your power by feeling that guilt. Yes, the lost time is a setback - but you're here now. *We* are here now. Breathe. If not for you, for me."

Fenris' chest inflated at her command, his lips pressed together until they became a thin, hard line. Arcana watched his inner turmoil, played out within those burning eyes, and saw the moment he wrested control from his thoughts. "You are correct, again. I was not making my own choices."

"No, you weren't." Arcana smiled softly. "If it helps, I've had years of practice when it comes to self-flagellation. I know all the signs."

He huffed a laugh at that, nipping at the edge of her palm. "Your comfort, as always, is impeccable."

"I thought so." Arcana's smile spread, and for a long moment they just stared at each other, the glamour curling thick and warm between them.

Then Brianne cleared her throat. "You jumped into a destabilised portal? Are you *insane*?"

Without bothering to break his eye contact with Arcana, Fenris gave his first real smile since they'd left the ship. "Most certainly."

"If you've really missed all that time, you need to listen." Brianne wrapped shaking fingers around Fenris' wrist. "The deerken are scattered throughout the galaxy, accompanied by what remains of our people. Taelon is hunting us and collecting the deerken for his own purposes."

"I know." Fenris spoke gently, his face solemn. "I believe he is using them to access the Timeless Kingdom."

Brianne licked at her lips with a dry tongue. "Probably. Murtagh suspended the portal network after we were all evacuated and took the crystals out of the gate on both sides to make sure there was no way Taelon could track us."

"Good," Fenris nodded his head. "I thought as much."

"Murtagh thought we'd be better off staying put to try and regroup. There were a lot of injuries." Brianne began to shiver, so Arcana shucked off her jacket and laid it over the other woman's chest, earning a tight smile of thanks in response. "As we set up camp, your parents came stepping out of the treeline with Mirokke."

Fenris' face turned thoughtful. "I suppose if anyone's to find a deerken who has been missing for over a century, it would be my mother. Do you know where Mirokke was found?"

"They came across her in the forest one morning, already too far gone to communicate. Vivienne wanted to take her to the Kingdom for grounding but the warg attacked before it could be done and there was no other choice but to care for Mirokke ourselves, as best we could." Brianne closed her eyes briefly. "Over time, more of our brothers and sisters found their way to us, looking for hope and direction. Looking for you."

Fenris loosed a gusty sigh, catching Arcana's hand where it lingered by his leg and twining his fingers through hers. "Did my mother happen to know how Mirokke fell pregnant?"

"No."

"I'm going out on a limb here and guessing that Mirokke was one of the deerken who originally accompanied Auron to the rift and never returned?" Arcana asked. When Fenris nodded, she pursed her lips in thought. "Is it possible they lost time the same way you did?"

Brianne and Fenris exchanged a long, incredulous look. Finally, the Warden nodded. "It's possible."

"Meaning," Arcana theorised, "She could have been pregnant before she went in."

"She wasn't," Brianne negated. "I would have noticed."

"Even if she was newly pregnant?" Arcana pressed. "Conceived just before she left, or not long after?"

"I suppose," the Warden allowed, her brow furrowing. "Mirokke was young and unmated when she left and deerken cannot reproduce until they find their mates - but who knows what truly happened during this last century? Anything is possible."

"Don't I know it," Arcana agreed. "So I guess the only other questions, assuming I'm right, are how did she get out and why was she by herself?"

Fenris shook his head, dark teal curls flopping into his eyes. "Only Mirokke can tell us - and given her current state, we may never find out."

"Agreed." Brianne's face twisted and she turned haunted eyes on Fenris. "Riella... the warg killed her. We were ambushed a week ago."

"I am so sorry, Brianne." Fenris bowed his head, lashes drifting closed. "Riella was an excellent Guardian. May she find peace in the warp and the weft of the weave."

"I loved her, and she me." A shuddering sob wracked the Warden's frame but she swallowed her grief with obvious effort. "One day we will meet again."

"One day," Fenris agreed, brushing hair off Brianne's forehead with his spare hand.

"I'm so tired, Fenris."

"Rest, then. You are safe while I am with you," Fenris promised. Brianne sighed and her eyelids slipped shut, her body relaxing into the uneasy sleep of the heavily wounded.

Arcana tucked her jacket more closely around Brianne's prone body. "Riella was her lover?"

"Yes." Fenris nodded, pushing abruptly to his feet. "They were one of the few who had a settled relationship within the Timeless Kingdom and worked as partners. Brianne is an excellent Warden and one of my oldest friends. Riella was a solid Guardian, always full of light and laughter. She will be missed."

"I wish I could have met her." Arcana stared at Fenris' thinned lips, wondering how many more friends he would have to let go before Taelon's madness was ended - if indeed they could manage to end it. She shivered.

"Are you cold?" Fenris' voice was rough with emotion, his hand trembling as he held it out. "Come here."

Arcana stood, allowing Fenris to draw her to the back of the cell. He put his back to the wall and sank to the floor, tugging her into his lap. She settled her shoulder into the curve of his arm as Fenris tucked the sides of his jacket around both their bodies. He muttered in fey as he worked, soft words to match the soft hands stroking her hair.

"What did you say?" Arcana asked, tilting her head back to look up at him.

Fenris hesitated, his face curiously vulnerable in the shadows. "Do you really want to know?"

"Should I not?"

"I was telling myself off," he admitted, his eyes tracing the lines of her face. "Instead of grieving for Riella or planning our next step, all I can think about is how beautiful you are and how much I enjoy having you pressed against me."

"Oh." Arcana was aware her eyes had gone very wide in the half light. The corner of Fenris' lip twitched and he reached out to tuck her hair behind one ear, trailing his knuckle down the sweep of her jaw. "Why say it in fey?"

Fenris bumped his head gently against hers. "Perhaps because I do not wish to argue about whether your skin looks like polished starlight or not."

"My skin is not like polished starlight," Arcana said automatically, then flushed as he raised a telling brow. "Okay, point taken. I assume anyone saying those sort of things is mocking me."

"That is because you do not see yourself how I see you." Fenris took a deep breath, as though preparing to dive into freezing water, and placed his lips close to her ear. "I think you are exquisite, Arcana. There is not a line, curve, dip or hollow that I do not want to touch. From the swell of your breasts to the curve of your buttocks, the silk of your hair, the shimmer of your skin - by the Weaver but I want to touch you. All of you, everywhere, with my hands and my tongue and..." he trailed off, and even in the soft blue light Arcana could see the colour riding high in his face.

"I see." Arcana swallowed, watching the way his eyes fell to her throat. "I like hearing you mutter in that other language, but perhaps it wouldn't be so awful to understand some of the things you're thinking."

"Are you sure?" Fenris looked mildly surprised - pleased, even.

"I'm sure." Arcana sighed, flattening one hand against the curve of his collarbone. "Burke was right, you know."

"About what?"

"You really do have a glorious chest." She watched through half lidded eyes as he startled, blush darkening further. "You have the perfect blend of lean hips and broad shoulders, just the right amount of muscle... and that scar makes it even better."

"I'm glad you like it." His fingertips trailed over Arcana's chin and down her throat. Fenris' gaze brushed hers, seeking permission before dipping lower, following the burning path of his fingers along the neckline of her low cut tank, tickling across the swell of her breasts.

Arcana's lungs fluttered and she realised she was holding her breath. Watching Fenris' gentle exploration of her curves, she inhaled, the movement pushing her left breast into his palm. He growled low in his throat, fingers curling until he cupped her completely, her less than impressive bosom easily fitting inside the vast expanse of his hand. Arcana dared a look at his face and bit her lip at the intensity in Fenris' gaze, the obvious hunger in his eyes.

"I am reminding myself that we are in a prison cell," he whispered, the glamour a sweet echo to the deep, velvet rumble of his voice. "And that it would be immeasurably foolish to strip you bare upon these slimy cobblestones."

"Is that supposed to be helping?"

"That depends on your definition of the concept." Fenris lowered his head to brush his lips across hers. Arcana stared up at him, safe in the comfort of his glamour, his arms. Here, right here, nothing could reach her - not the past, not the prison cell, nor her twisting, dreadful nightmares. There was only the warmth of his skin, the maddening, incredible feeling of his hands on her body, his lips teasing her own. Arcana's hands crept up to twine in his hair as Fenris leant in further, claiming her mouth in a sweet, soft kiss. His thumb feathered across the swell of her breast, as tentative a touch as a soft summer breeze. She groaned softly and opened for him, delighted when his tongue swept inside her mouth, his other arm locking their bodies tight together. Just when their kiss was bordering on desperate Fenris pulled back, his forehead resting against hers as he laboured for breath. "We have to stop."

"You're right. I wouldn't want you to think I was enjoying myself." Arcana flashed him a wicked grin. "Your ego might swell."

"It is not my ego," said Fenris succinctly, "That is swelling."

"Well I'd advise you to keep any concerning medical issues to yourself," Arcana schooled her face into a calm mask. "I'm not sure I'd be interested in someone with an odd swelling condition."

Fenris growled and nipped at her jaw, nudging her head back for better access to her neck. Arcana squeaked and wriggled as he licked and nibbled determinedly at her neck and shoulder, growling against her skin all the while. He drew back only when Arcana's giggles had dissolved into helpless gasps for breath, and she knew without a mirror that her throat, shoulder and neckline would be reddened by marks from his teeth and lips. Fenris' hair hung forward as he leant over her, glowing eyes casting soft shadows across his face. "This *really* is not going to get us out of this cell."

"About that," Arcana murmured, flicking a glance at Brianne. "I can bust us out as soon as you think it's a good idea."

"I know." Fenris pressed a kiss to her nose and straightened. "I'm worried about Phase and Caelum."

"Me too. It's so quiet down here that I'm sure Caelum's been tranquillised." Arcana sighed and rolled out of Fenris' lap, dusting herself off. She crossed the cell to crouch beside Brianne, the Warden's face still slack with sleep. "I don't want to risk Brianne's life earlier than necessary."

Fenris levered up from the floor and gave himself a quick shake, adjusting the greatsword's harness. "I do not think it will be long before Daelan returns to gloat - not to mention, he did not disarm me, which is something he or Shirimm will seek to rectify."

"You should have cut Daelan's head off while you had the chance." Brianne's voice was croaky and Arcana looked down to find the Warden's eyes open.

Fenris clicked his tongue at her in reprimand. "You should be resting."

"Too sore and too cold," Brianne grumbled, her lips thin. "How long was I out?"

"Perhaps twenty minutes."

"Hmmph." Brianne frowned, lips moving as she sought to order her thoughts. She looked up at Fenris. "You should know that your father was injured when the warg ambushed us. Taelon sensed we were gathering through the blood bond and sent several packs to intervene. Those of us who lived decided it would be safer to separate and run."

"How badly was he wounded?"

"When Riella bought him to us, one eye was a mess and he'd lost a leg. Vivienne managed to stabilise him but they couldn't travel. Rytan was barely conscious when your mother told us to flee with Mirokke. We didn't get far before Daelan showed up with a bunch of ex-Guardians and some warg." Brianne swallowed, her voice cracking. "Riella fought but it was no use."

"That coward will pay, Brianne. I swear it."

The Warden was quiet for a long moment, her eyes rimmed with silver. "Listen to us. They were once our brothers and sisters."

"I know." Fenris growled low in his throat. "I have bloodied my hands and soul already - but there is no other course of action, not when we are being hunted."

Arcana curled her fingers into claws and bared her teeth. "If I could rend Taelon limb from limb with my bare hands, I would."

Fenris stared at her a long moment, his face curiously tender - as though the thought of Arcana ripping limbs off were somehow endearing. "I fear you'd have to join a queue."

"Queue be damned," Arcana seethed. "Anyone who thinks the warg are a viable solution to their personal issues deserves to be put down like the vermin they are."

Brianne snorted a laugh and Fenris opened his mouth to reply but the silence was suddenly filled by the sound of applause.

"Well, well." Shirimm stepped into the lantern's meagre light. Daelan was close beside her, his hands still slapping together in mocking appreciation. "The pet has a voice. Who'd have thought?"

"If that's all it takes to surprise you, Shirimm, you are sorely lacking in imagination." Fenris stepped to Arcana's side, partially blocking Brianne with his body. "I wish I could say it was a pleasure to see you both, but it is not in my nature to lie. Have you come to gloat?"

"Perhaps," Daelan purred, reaching up to tuck his long, silvery locks behind one ear. With his entire face revealed, the ex-Guardian looked distinctly vulpine, with a long nose, pointed chin and pebbly brown skin the texture of overworked leather. His red eyes were focussed squarely on Arcana. "Your ideas are as delightfully simple as I'd expect of a mercenary."

"Better a simple merc than a traitor," Arcana returned evenly.

"Oh my, Fenris, I hope she doesn't have teeth. I shouldn't like to be bitten," Daelan raised a finger to his mouth and winked.

"We always have been different that way," Fenris replied, his face impassive. "What do you want?"

Daelan chuckled. "Come now, did you really think we'd just let you sit around in the cell with that sword strapped to your back, plotting revenge?"

Fenris said nothing, simply stared, arms loose by his sides. Arcana waited until Daelan's smile began to slip and then swaggered into the silence, wrapping her hands around the iron bars of the cell door. "Where's my deerken?"

Shirimm tilted her head, eyes narrowing as she looked Arcana up and down. "Sleeping. Co-operate and you might live to see him again, space mutt."

"Sleeping?" Arcana breathed in the metallic tang of the iron bars, turned her arrogant mercenary glare on Daelan. "You shot him."

As she'd guessed he might, Daelan struck a pose and winked. "Just a tranq, my sweet. We didn't want him wandering off and getting into trouble."

"Stop giving her information," Shirimm snapped, elbowing Daelan in the ribs. "She's playing your dick like a badly tuned instrument."

"My dick?" Daelan turned astonished eyes on Shirimm, rubbing absently at his ribs. "Are you insane? Have you *looked* at this woman?"

Shirimm's eyes gave Arcana a deliberately methodical once over. "Yes, quite. As dead a fish as I thought you liked."

Fenris rumbled a growl, but Arcana merely raised a brow. "Come closer and I'll show you just how dead I am, bitch."

"I think not." Shirimm turned glittering eyes on Fenris. "Sword. Now."

"No."

"You're not in a position to negotiate, *Overlord*." Shirimm hissed, jabbing a long-clawed finger in Fenris' direction. "If it wasn't for

Taelon's insistence on having you alive, I'd have flayed you myself by now."

Brianne's sharp laugh cleft the taut atmosphere. "What hurts more, Shirimm - being denied childish vengeance, or the knowledge that even on opposite sides of this war, Fenris is *still* more important than you are?"

Shirimm's ruddy face darkened with rage and she stepped towards the bars only to have Daelan draw her up short. "They are goading you, my dear, and you are falling for it in spectacular fashion. Enough." He stepped deftly in front of Shirimm, holding out a slim, effeminate hand. "Fenris, I'm going to need your sword now, brother."

"No."

"You know, Taelon wants you alive, but he never stipulated you need be conscious." Daelan yawned, looking supremely bored. "Last warning. Hand the sword over and I leave you in peace, or refuse again and I shoot you with a tranq so heavy duty, you'll have forgotten your mother's name by the time you wake. The choice, as they say, is yours."

"In that case, it seems I have no choice." Fenris drew the greatsword and stepped to Arcana's side, pressing the flat of the blade against the bars of the cell. "Here. Take it with my blessing."

"And walk into range of those hypnotic eyes of yours?" Daelan raised a thin brow. "I'm not that foolish, brother. Poke it through - slowly."

Fenris hefted the sword in his hands, giving the runed blade a considering look. "No."

"Oh, for the Weav- warg's sake," Shirimm snarled, "Just shoot him already."

Daelan swiped the crossbow from his belt and loosed a shot without appearing to aim. Fenris barrelled into Arcana's side and in less than the time it took to blink, he'd shunted them four paces to the left. The crossbow bolt intended for Fenris embedded in the wall behind their heads and stayed there, quivering from the impact and releasing a noxious looking green ooze onto the already slimy bricks.

"Now," Fenris said.

Still cradled in the circle of his arms, Arcana called her magic and the bars of the cell exploded outwards. Daelan and Shirimm threw themselves to the floor as stone and iron rained down, aiming for vital body parts at Arcana's instruction. Shirimm managed to dodge but a sharp piece of iron sheared through Daelan's coat and part of his thigh, eliciting a high-pitched shriek from the ex-Guardian and pinning him to the ground. Fenris set Arcana on her feet and launched forwards but Daelan was quite suddenly gone, leaving his torn and bloody jacket pinned to the floor. Fenris yanked the piece of iron free, spun and threw it into the shadows, following a moment later with teeth bared and sword raised.

Shirimm rolled to her hands and knees, snarling and spitting as she launched across the cracked cobbles towards the vulnerable Brianne. Arcana clenched her fist and the bars of the cell wrenched from the wall, slamming end-first into the floor to create a protective barrier around the prone Warden.

"Bitch!" Shirimm skidded to a halt in front of the impromptu cage, swiping ineffectually at the iron with clawed fingers. When she tuned back to Arcana, her narrow face was incandescent with rage. "What is Fenris to you, little dog? Why defend him?"

"Because I gave my word." Arcana raised her left hand, igniting the brilliant orange runes that spiralled from the back of her hand and up around her wrist. Flare's oath of allegiance captured Shirimm's attention at once, her snake's eyes widening in astonishment.

A forked tongue flicked from between Shirimm's lips, tasting the air as though it were Arcana's flesh. "If you bound yourself to Fenris, you are more of a fool than I would ever credit another person to be."

"Oh?" Arcana raised an eyebrow and did her best to affect a haughty expression, allowing the runes to fade. "What if I bound him to *me* instead?"

"Don't kid yourself." Shirimm snorted dismissively, stalking Arcana across the cell. "Fenris would never put another above his filthy oath to the Weaver."

"Really?" Arcana waved a hand and the iron frame which had once secured the bars to the wall peeled away, popping rivets that flew like bullets into the darkness. Shirimm ducked and dodged each one, allowing herself to be driven away from Brianne's vulnerable body. When the last of the rivets lay quiet and still, Arcana tilted her head at the ex-Guardian and narrowed her eyes. "Is that what Fenris told you, when he threw you out of his bed and his life?"

"I will *kill* you," Shirimm shrieked, her face clouding with rage. "I will kill you and that lying, useless wretch will watch!"

The ex-Guardian leapt, claws held high above her head. Arcana flexed the fingers of both hands and the rivets responded to her call, whizzing out of the darkness with a noise like hornets. They drove into Shirimm's flesh, arresting the other woman in mid-air. She screamed and writhed as the sharp pieces of iron burrowed deeper and deeper inside her body, seeking vital organs. When the screaming reached fever pitch, Arcana flicked a finger and Shirimm was thrown heavily to the floor - where she went suddenly limp and silent.

After a moment to ensure the ex-Guardian was truly no longer moving, Arcana raced across the cell to Brianne, the iron rods peeling open like petals as she approached. "Are you all right?"

Brianne swallowed and managed a nod. "How did you... what are you?"

"I'm a sorceress." Arcana retrieved her jacket from Brianne's torso and dragged it on, tugging the zip up to just under her breasts.

"A sorceress? But there were no spells, no cast time... nothing," Brianne gasped.

"I'll explain later. Right now, we need to move." Arcana bent to slide a hand under Brianne's torso, but the Warden caught her arm in a fierce grip.

"Did you really bind yourself to him?" Brianne turned Arcana's wrist back and forth, staring at the salt-white skin. "To Fenris?"

"No." Arcana ignited the runes again and Brianne leant closer to inspect the ancient Sorcen. "That oath of allegiance is one my brother swore - to me. But Shirimm didn't know that."

Brianne huffed a laugh and released Arcana's hand, allowing herself to be dragged to a sitting position. "Clever."

"Thanks." Arcana smiled. "Can you stand? I'm sorry, but I can't carry you."

"We'll manage." Brianne looped one arm over Arcana's shoulders and scrambled to get her feet beneath her, the movements frightfully weak. "Where's Fenris?"

"I don't know." Arcana spoke through gritted teeth as she dragged Brianne upright. "He and Daelan seem to have disappeared."

Brianne cast feverish eyes over the ruined cell, her mocha complexion pale and sheened with sweat. "He's too smart to be dead, but I'm too weak to sense him. Don't worry - Fenris will track me through our blood bond when he can."

"All right." Arcana shifted Brianne's weight and bent to reclaim the blanket, stuffing it inside her satchel. She snatched the lantern and offered it with a smile. "Can you hold this? Then I can use both arms to help you."

"Gladly." Brianne accepted the lantern and together they began to make their way out of the cell and along the moisture slicked corridor.

The dungeon was packed with small, dank rooms, each one walled in on three sides and finished with metal bars on the last. Suspicious shadows slumped in the corners of a few, but as none moved or made a sound, Arcana assumed with a shudder that death had already come to claim them. Brianne's progress was slow, her breathing heavy and the weight of her body increasing with every step. They came at last to a junction; a darkened corridor to the right and a steep, narrow staircase ascending into the roof.

"I can't go much further," Brianne wheezed.

Arcana frowned. Freedom was most likely at the top of the staircase, but she doubted Brianne's ability to climb them - and even more so, her own ability to drag the Warden up the steep steps without doing either of them an injury. A sparkle flickered at the edge of Arcana's vision and she blinked, twisting past the staircase to peer down the gloomy corridor beyond them. "Did you see that?"

"See what?" Brianne made an effort to lift the lantern, pale blue light zagging crazily over the walls. "I can't see anything."

Arcana squinted into the darkness, but there was no other sign than the peculiar tugging in her heart to say that she'd ever seen anything. Still... "Let's go this way." She turned away from the stairs and began dragging Brianne's flagging body down the gloomy corridor.

The Warden grunted, struggling to keep her legs moving. "Are you sure?"

"No," Arcana admitted. They fell silent, Brianne using all of her energy to stay upright and Arcana devoting her full concentration to keeping her that way.

There were no longer cells beside them but closed, sealed doors. Arcana encouraged Brianne forwards until they came to the final door, where she was sure she had seen the faintest shimmer of movement. The air was so cold their breath rose in clouds, and the metal of the door bit into Arcana's fingers as she shoved against it. Locked. Frowning, Arcana sent her magic into the metal, curling her senses through the mechanism and jiggling until it popped open with a click.

Arcana pushed the door wide and half-dragged Brianne inside. Her first impression was of four spindly legs, bound in pairs; she didn't need to see more to know it was Caelum lying prone on the ground. A hefty chain dangled from the far wall, snaking across the floor to a thick metal collar around his neck. His eyes were closed and his head propped awkwardly against a box, presumably to give whoever had attached the collar better access.

"Caelum?" Arcana struggled further into the room, kicking the door closed behind them. "Can you hear me?"

"Put me down and tend him," Brianne instructed. Arcana settled the

Warden against one wall and went to Caelum's side, lifting his head into her lap. As she did, a shimmering light emerged from the bricks to her left, slowly coalescing into the ghostly form of Mirokke.

"Caelum?" Arcana ran her fingers over his face, feathering down his neck. His pulse was steady and strong but his eyes remained closed, his body limp. "He's definitely been tranqed."

Mirokke's pale form floated closer, the space around her shimmering with flickering lights. She lowered her nose to Caelum's face as though to nudge him, but her flesh passed right through. Brianne drew in a sharp breath. "It's as if she senses Caelum's presence."

"She has to; she led me here." Arcana gestured to the swirling fairy dust glittering in the air. "Those lights are what I saw at the end of the corridor."

"What you're suggesting should be impossible." Brianne's voice was soft with sadness. "Those flickering lights are the beginnings of her death. Mirokke is unravelling and returning to the weave - soon it will be dangerous to be close to her."

"That doesn't seem right; look at her." Arcana pointed. Mirokke stood over Caelum, her spindly legs positioned carefully around his. Her nose was lowered towards his body, her impressive antler rack between his chest and the doorway. "She's protecting him."

Brianne studied the two deerken out of wide eyes. "Fenris said Caelum is bound to you? Like your brother?"

"No, not like my brother." Arcana shook her head. "Caelum and I have a soulmerge; one of us cannot exist without the other. "

"Incredible." Brianne rolled her head sideways to get a better look at Caelum's powerful body. "He is like and yet unlike any deerken I have ever seen. Can you waken him?"

"I'm not sure." Arcana curled her fingers around the heavy collar on Caelum's neck, adding magic to her tugging hands so that the metal rent in two. She set the pieces aside, combing her fingers through his rumpled fur as she tried to project her feelings at him the way she'd done on Corrin's Run. He remained still and silent in her lap. "The tranq's got him too deep."

Brianne leant back and closed her eyes. "Then we wait."

Arcana slithered out from underneath Caelum's head so she could untie his legs. The bindings had been pulled tight enough to leave marks in his fur and she spent a moment massaging each ankle to help restore circulation. "I'll bet this is why they took so long to come to us," she muttered, checking Caelum over to ensure there were no other injuries.

Arcana turned to see Brianne watching her through barely slitted eyelids, the other woman's face sickly pale in the cold lantern light. "Are you all right?"

"No. Daelan's work was thorough."

"The antidote isn't working?" Arcana eyed the crossbow bolt still buried in the Warden's shoulder and belatedly noted the awkward angle of her arm. "Great gods of Sorcen, your arm's broken! Why didn't you remind me?"

Scrambling to the Warden's side, she snatched half of Caelum's collar off the floor and used her magic to straighten it into a splint. Arcana set the arm as best she could, splinting it with the thin steel and binding it in place with strips torn from the sleeve of the Warden's thin jacket. Brianne offered a watery smile, her face tight with pain. "Don't worry yourself too much."

"Fenris will kill me if he thinks I'm neglecting you," Arcana returned equably. She leant back to inspect her handiwork and sighed. "I'm no healer, but it'll do. Now, the antidote - tell me the truth. How are you feeling?"

Chuckling at the command, Brianne said; "The antidote is working but I am ruined inside. The bolt Daelan shot me with was covered in poison but it also opens like a flower made of knives." The Warden flicked her fingers open in emphasis. "We have nothing here to repair that sort of damage. Soon I'll be joining Riella in the longsleep."

"Fenris said we're getting out of here together," Arcana said sternly. "You'd best keep that in mind."

Brianne rolled one shoulder in a shrug. "He doesn't always get what he wants. Speaking of Fenris, it's clear to me your relationship is not that of a merc and an employer."

"It's an easy cover story," Arcana admitted.

"So are you two…"

"I'm not really sure."

"Oh?" Brianne raised an eyebrow. "I saw you reach to comfort him - and he let you. That in itself is no mean feat. The way he speaks to you is also something I've never seen before."

Arcana frowned. "What do you mean?"

"He speaks with warmth. With life. Like a companion or a lover." Brianne shaped a woman's hourglass figure in the air with her hands. "I've known Fenris since he first came to the Timeless Kingdom, and I've never seen him so at ease as he is with you. In a prison cell, no less."

"Really?" Arcana sat back on her heels, considering the difference in

Fenris since she had first met him. "I suppose he's become less formal as time's gone on. He was definitely a little stuffy when we first met."

Brianne barked a short, sharp laugh. "A little? You've thawed Fenris more in four weeks than his mother has in over one and a half centuries. The face he shows to you is one I've never seen - and I've known Fenris since he was a lanky teenager." She paused, appraising Arcana through eyes that glittered with emotion. "Whatever your plans, I beg you not to break his heart."

"What?" Arcana sat back so quickly she almost toppled onto Caelum. "I hadn't thought... It's very early on and I... we..." she took a deep breath. "I would never do that to him."

"I see," Brianne said softly - and Arcana feared that she did, indeed, see. "I was Fenris' mentor when he first became a Warden, you know. Riella liked him, too."

Arcana's heart ached at the raw grief in the Warden's eyes. "I'm sorry for your loss."

"Thank you. We enjoyed more than two centuries of life together, and still it seems so short." Her face tightened. "Too short."

Seeking to distract Brianne, Arcana seized on the first thing that came to mind. "So, what was Fenris like as a boy?"

"Intense. If you think he's serious now, you should have seen him back then. All arms and legs, carrying the weight of the universe on his shoulders." Brianne's face softened in memory. "He had few friends and little interest in making them - unless you count the deerken. Those, Fenris knew by name within a month of arriving at Warden's Hall."

"I'm not sure I could handle a more serious Fenris." Caelum's voice was foggy and thick, but his eyes slid open to reveal the swirling stars within. "He already looks like he's in pain when he smiles."

"Caelum!" Arcana's voice hitched unsteadily and she lifted his head to plant kisses all over his nose. "You worried me. How are you feeling?"

"Can't breathe," Caelum muttered - but he whuffed in her ear and lipped affectionately at her hair. "What did I miss?"

Arcana grinned, rubbing her nose against his. "I blew up a dungeon cell, killed Shirimm and Daelan eloped with Fenris."

"Huh." One ear flickered. "So, not much, then."

"Nope." Arcana laid her cheek against his, her soul settling at the contact. "Not much."

"He... you... You speak," Brianne managed. Arcana twisted to look at the Warden, Caelum's head still propped against her palms. Brianne's eyes were wide in astonishment, her body struggling into a more upright position.

Caelum blinked owlishly. "Have we met?"

"This is Brianne - the Warden who came with Mirokke." Arcana kissed his nose again and then smiled at Brianne. "Yes, Caelum can talk."

"It is an honour to meet you," Brianne said fervently. "You truly are exceptional."

"I get that a lot." Caelum's ears flickered again. "Mirokke is worried about you. Your wounds are getting worse." He turned to squint up at the ethereal doe beside him. "You really don't need to hover like that. I'm fine."

Brianne goggled. "Mirokke is *talking* to you?"

"In a fashion." Caelum waited until Mirokke turned her milky gaze on him and said; "Seriously, I'm going to get up. You might want to move."

Arcana's jaw dropped as Mirokke dipped her ghostly nose to Caelum's and then floated out of the way. "I'm assuming she can hear you as well as speak to you?"

"Yeah. We met in the dreambank while I was unconscious. Mirokke was surprised, too." Caelum heaved himself upright, legs wobbling. "Wow. What did they shoot me with?"

"Tranquilliser," Arcana answered. "Lots of tranquilliser."

"Bastards." Caelum wavered unsteadily for a moment, squeezing his eyes shut. When his body ceased to sway, he cracked an eyelid and focussed on Arcana. "So my bad feeling was an accurate one, then."

"Pretty much." Arcana pushed to her feet, giving him a hasty explanation of all that had happened since they'd been caught in Daelan's energy net.

"Hmmm. Frying pan to fire, as always - but at least we don't need to try and sneak inside anymore." Caelum pinned Brianne with a measuring look. "Don't you guys all have that mystical blood connection?"

"Yes, but I'm too weak to feel much further than the door," Brianne murmured. "We must trust Fenris to find us."

"Mirokke is showing me some strange images... I think Fenris is with one of the other traitors." Caelum blinked rapidly. "Not Daelan."

"There's no way to be sure how accurate she is, particularly in her current condition." Brianne waved a hand towards Mirokke's milky gaze. "Deerken see all layers of the weave and all possibilities for the future simultaneously. The information is difficult to decipher at the best of times, but now? Nothing she says can be trusted."

"Be prepared to eat your words, lady, because *I'm* a deerken and I can't see all layers of the weave; only the here and now," said Caelum tartly. "Blathering on with generalisations like that only narrows your mind to new possibilities. I'm telling you, Mirokke is talking to me and I'm also telling you that she's only seeing one thing. At a time. In a very specific order. Okay?"

Brianne's jaw dropped open. "I... my apologies."

"Forget it. Just do yourself a favour and either ignore what you know, or shut your mouth."

"Caelum!" Arcana thwacked his solid shoulder but the deerken didn't as much as flinch.

"What? I'm cranky and my tongue tastes like rotten berries and I hate it when people get all superior for no reason." Caelum fell silent as Mirokke floated closer. One of his ears flickered. "Mirokke says she's no longer adrift on the weave. Her eyes don't work, but she's seeing through yours, and mine, and Arcana's - even Fenris' - all at once."

Brianne's brow creased, but it was a thoughtful look rather than a skeptical one. "Incredible."

"She also says to tell you..." Caelum wrinkled his nose, staring at something far off. "I am underground? No. I am the ground." He shook his head. "That doesn't make sense."

"You're grounding her," Brianne murmured, her jaw slack. "That... I'm not even going to say impossible any more. I no longer know what impossible is."

"I'm impossible," Caelum replied cheerfully, winking at Arcana. "Anyway, as long as Mirokke stays close to me, she seems to feel better. She says the fawn is getting stronger, too. Look at her," he invited, stepping out of the way.

Arcana gasped. Where before Mirokke had been almost invisible, the doe was now a definite silvery grey. The flickering specks of light had faded and she stood with purpose. Brianne shook her head in astonishment. "The implications of this... Caelum, you could save hundreds of deerken."

"How?"

"For the most part, it looks as though simply standing nearby will do it." Brianne adjusted her position against the wall and grimaced. "I have other ideas... but I'll need Fenris. His mind is clearer than mine."

"Fenris is coming," Caelum announced. On cue, the door swung open and Fenris stepped through, greatsword at the ready. Close on his heels was a tall, hooded figure in black and grey, who pushed the door shut behind them and slid the bolt.

"It's all right." Fenris held out a hand to forestall Arcana. "He's with me."

"Llane?" Brianne queried, her brows drawn.

"Brianne." Llane's hissing tones were filled with regret. He lifted olive skinned hands and pulled back his hood to reveal a serpentine head with dull red eyes. "I'm sorry about Riella's passing."

"Excuse me, but aren't you on *their* side?" Arcana asked, fisting one hand on her hip.

"Llane has been playing both sides." Fenris sheathed the greatsword in one fluid motion, three long strides carrying him to Arcana's side. He framed her face with both hands and bent to press a quick, hard kiss to her lips. "Are you all right? There is blood all over you."

"None of it's mine."

Fenris' nose crinkled. "I can smell that," he chided, sweeping her hair back over one shoulder. "Just because the blood is not your own does not guarantee your welfare."

"Were you worried about me, Guardian?" Arcana teased, poking him in the chest. "*I* wasn't the one who disappeared into the shadows with a crossbow-wielding lunatic."

"Sorry about that." Fenris made a face, sliding his hands across her shoulders and kneading at tight muscles with long, talented fingers. "I pursued the advantage while I had it - but Daelan escaped nonetheless."

"He has been sentenced," Llane hissed. "He will pay."

"Wow. You're a cheerful one." Arcana tipped her head forward, resting her head on Fenris' chest while he continued to turn her muscles to jelly. "I bet you're a constant at all the hardcore parties."

Caelum snorted loudly and Arcana felt Fenris' chest vibrate with the faintest chuckle. His hands moved further down her spine, drawing her closer as he bent his head to her ear. "Stop it."

"Fine. Seriously, though, how do we know he's not going to turn us in?"

Fenris straightened and turned towards Llane, whose olive green complexion - scales, Arcana realised - was a mask of calm. "Llane has sworn he remains loyal to the Weaver and his species are unable to lie. He can also detect when someone else is lying."

"Yet he betrayed us," Brianne said softly, "And watched Riella die."

Llane hissed between serrated teeth, displaying a long, thin white tongue. "Betrayal is a matter of perception. My loyalty is to the Weaver - but I cannot protect her if I am running, or dead." The Guardian paused for effect, his body undulating in what Arcana assumed was some sort of a shrug. "I decided to serve in Taelon's guard until an opportunity presented itself where I may stand for the Weaver openly. I did not take part in the murder of your lover, nor the attack upon yourself - and well you know it - but to attempt to stop it openly would have blown my cover and seen us all killed."

"So you chose to do nothing."

"I chose, painful as it was, to wait." Transparent lids flicked briefly over dull red eyes. "If that earns me your hatred, so be it. I cannot say I wouldn't feel the same - but before you poison your heart, tell me Riella would have made a different choice. Tell me she'd have put her own life above that of our queen's."

Brianne grunted, staring off into a corner. "You walk a fine line this way, Llane."

"Perhaps." Llane inclined his head, then added; "But I am not the only one."

Arcana stepped out of Fenris' embrace, subtly positioning herself in front of Brianne, and crossed her arms. "If you're really on our side, how are you down here without arousing suspicion?"

Llane extended a long finger with too many joints towards Brianne. "I was sent here to tie up a loose end."

"*What?*"

"Peace," Brianne murmured from behind. "That's no real surprise. I'm injured and I will only slow the journey down. Taelon won't try to recruit me - he knew Riella and he knows me. Knows I'll refuse. It's a logical decision." The Warden sighed and shifted; Arcana heard her grunt in pain. "But I don't trust you, Llane. All this talk of crossing and crossing and crossing... where does it end?"

Llane bristled, his wedge shaped head extending towards Arcana on a long, flexible neck. "What would you have me do? Stand alone, while Taelon turns the universe into his personal mud pit?" He jabbed a finger at Brianne's belly. "You tried that already, and you will die for it."

"At least I will die with honour," Brianne returned. "I cannot say the same for you."

"I will gladly sully my honour to save the Weaver's life," Llane snapped, red eyes flashing. "If I had truly turned you'd already be dead and we both know it."

"Enough," Fenris commanded, his voice deep with disapproval. Silence encased the room, sudden and complete. Llane dropped to one knee, his alternate hand fisted on the floor, head bowed. Brianne rolled her eyes but said nothing.

"My apologies, Overlord," Llane hissed. "It was not my intention to disrespect you."

Fenris braced one hand on his hip and scrubbed the other over his face, an uncharacteristically vulnerable gesture which actually caused Llane to flinch. Finally, he flicked a rueful glance at Arcana. "What do you think? Twenty lashes each for bad behaviour?"

"I dunno." Caelum sniffed gingerly at Llane's kneeling form. "I think Llane's got at least thirty in him."

There was a long silence, during which Arcana bit the inside of her cheek and had to stare off into the middle distance to avoid laughing.

"Are you... is he... *joking*?" Brianne demanded at last.

"I do have a sense of humour," Fenris crossed both arms over his chest and raised an eyebrow. Arcana choked back another laugh as Brianne's eyes only widened. "Is that really so difficult to believe?"

Llane looked up from his position of supplication. "I was not aware this was a joking matter," he said, his tone edged with censure.

"It's called breaking the tension," Caelum answered, nudging at Llane with his nose. "If you spend all your time walking around being serious, you'll lose sight of the bigger picture. Now, more importantly, do you have bones or are you all wiggly under that cloak?"

"I have a skeletal structure," Llane answered stiffly - and rose to his feet with such unnatural grace that Arcana immediately doubted the words. The Guardian turned to Fenris. "I would still beg forgiveness, Overlord."

"Given." Fenris answered with an ease that spoke of long practice. "We have lost too many brothers and sisters to fight amongst ourselves."

"Agreed." Llane sighed, a sibilant sound much like the rattling of dead leaves. "We shouldn't linger here. I will be expected to return with Brianne's head soon."

"How soon?" Arcana asked.

Llane stared down the length of his snout until Fenris cleared his throat in warning. "The Pariah is hosting a banquet tonight. I'm to present it to him after the soup course."

"How appetising." Arcana crossed her arms over her chest. "And when is the soup course?"

Llane slid a long, narrow glance at Fenris before answering. "A few hours."

"All right." She tapped a forefinger on her chin. "We need to find our other companion before we go. Do you know where he is?"

The moment Llane's beady red eyes settled once again on Fenris,

Arcana clenched both hands into fists. The remaining half of Caelum's sundered metal collar shot up off the floor, catching Llane around the throat and slamming him into the wall. The Guardian struggled but the metal curled deeper and deeper into the brickwork until Llane's breath wheezed between his teeth.

Arcana stalked through the silence, stopping just out of reach, her black eyes locking with Llane's red ones. "When I ask you a question, you look at me while you answer. Not Fenris; *me*. Understand?"

Llane raised both hands to the collar and tried to work his fingers underneath, but the fit was too snug. His long white tongue snaked out, sampling the air, probing the seamless metal around his neck. Arcana waited silently, listening to the whistling rasp of Llane's breathing as he determined there was truly no way to escape. Red eyes sought hers, then, and he coughed delicately. "I understand. My apologies."

"Apology accepted." Arcana waved a hand and the collar dropped away - only to be replaced an instant later by the shimmering edge of the greatsword.

"I warned you," Fenris growled.

Llane swallowed heavily, holding himself so still he seemed not to breathe. "She is not one of us, my lord."

"*You* don't get to make that decision." Fenris' chest rumbled with the threat of violence and he drew back his lips to bare sharp fangs. "I will say this once, and once only: disrespect Arcana and you disrespect me."

"Yes, Overlord. I am sorry. Again."

Arcana watched Fenris sheath the greatsword and raised her eyebrow. "I can take care of myself, you know."

"I know." Fenris slung an arm around Arcana's shoulders and pressed a kiss to her brow in apology. "But I interceded for a different reason than you think. The Timeless Kingdom is a secular society; Guardians and Wardens are trained to answer only to the Three, or to the Weaver. Whilst Llane did not need to be so rude," he flicked a warning glance at the other Guardian, who coughed politely and backed up a step, "His reticence is long programmed into us as a people. It is my duty to teach him otherwise."

Arcana crossed her arms over her chest. "Sounds like you're just trying to justify a solid bout of male posturing, honestly."

"Actually, I was trying to -" Fenris tilted his head to the side and frowned. "Was it *really* male posturing?"

"Borderline," Caelum declared.

Fenris' grin was slow and broad and had a distinct bedroom edge to it.

"I didn't know I could do that." His voice hummed with velvet undertones and he stepped into Arcana's body, his hands warm and broad across her back. "How about now?"

Arcana rolled her eyes. "Definitely now," she returned, but softened against him, standing on tiptoe to press an answering kiss to Fenris' chin. At the last moment, he ducked his head so their lips brushed instead. "Just don't do it again."

"Why? Will you beat me for it?" Fenris purred, clenching his fists in her jacket until she was pressed tightly against his chest.

"Gods above and below - please don't make me vomit," Caelum pleaded.

Arcana flipped a vulgar gesture over one shoulder, nibbling at Fenris' jaw for good measure. Caelum groaned loudly and Fenris laughed, his chest rumbling beneath Arcana's hand. "I don't think he appreciates affection."

"He's just jealous." Arcana winked and turned, leaning back against Fenris' chest. He wrapped both arms around her waist, folding his body until his chin rested on top of her head and together they studied the shocked faces of both Brianne and Llane. Arcana smiled and said; "So. We have three hours to find the portal crystals and free my friends - the Illithai male who came with us and the female who is already here. What can you tell me, Llane?"

The Guardian cleared his throat, very carefully meeting Arcana's eyes as he replied. "The female Illithai is chained up in the Pariah's Great Hall. The male will be held close by, in preparation for his execution at the hands of the warg following the dessert course."

"And the crystals?"

"In the Pariah's personal safe. I can take you there," Llane added.

Arcana drummed her fingers along the back of Fenris' knuckles. "I say we retrieve the crystals first, then crash the Pariah's party."

"I thought you wanted Burke first?" Fenris murmured, turning his lips into her hair.

"I do, but I think it'll be easier to sneak in and get the crystals before we free them." She looked at Llane. "I'm assuming it's not going to be possible to free them subtly."

Llane undulated his body in response. "That is correct."

"Very well. Crystals first, then the Illithai." Fenris unfolded to his full height. "Caelum, can you carry Brianne?"

"Yes." Caelum paused, both ears flickering. "But Mirokke says it will likely kill her."

Fenris frowned but Brianne waved a hand to cut him off. "Save your breath, Overlord. The sun is setting for me no matter what we do."

"I won't have your death on my conscience," he growled.

"Daelan shot me, not you - the blame is not yours."

"She speaks truly," Llane's hissing voice was filled with sadness.

"You cannot save everyone," Brianne murmured. "All I ask is not to die alone."

Fenris drew in a breath and held it, his face smoothing out into an almost eerie calm. After a long moment, he strode across the room to scoop Brianne into the cradle of his arms. "Then Caelum will carry you, for better or for worse."

The Warden patted his chest. "Thank you." Fenris rumbled a response too soft for Arcana to make out as he arranged Brianne's body face down along the length of Caelum's spine. "I'm not sure how well I can hold on."

"I won't let you fall," Caelum promised. Mirokke's wavering form bumped against his shoulder. "Mirokke says she'll watch over you, too."

"Thank you," Brianne murmured, and closed her eyes on a line of unshed tears.

"We must go carefully," Llane hissed. "If Daelan finds you, there will be trouble."

Fenris nodded. "I lost him somewhere in the lower levels. With any luck, he is still searching for me."

"I thought you were chasing him?" Arcana frowned, her heart lurching uncomfortably. "Please don't tell me Daelan is faster than your super speed."

"No, but he can teleport short distances." Fenris measured a gap between both of his palms. "Not a proper jump, just to places that are in his line of sight. He has honed the skill to a point where he is difficult to catch and even more difficult to evade. I left off our cat and mouse pursuit when it became impossible to tell if I was being led into a trap."

"Great," Arcana muttered. "A teleporting lunatic with a crossbow. Just what we need."

"Frying pan. Fire," Caelum said lightly, swishing his tail back and forth. "If Daelan's so good, why'd he run?"

"He prefers strength in numbers, and leverage," Llane hissed, tugging the cell door open. "Fenris is right - Daelan would have been trying to lure him into a trap."

"So he's a *cowardly* teleporting lunatic with a crossbow. Got it." Arcana nodded, snatching her lantern from where it rested on the floor.

Llane's red eyes glittered in the light and Arcana was almost certain he looked amused. "This way. Please turn off the lantern before we ascend the stairs."

The Guardian pulled up his hood and ducked out into the corridor. Arcana motioned for Caelum to follow, Mirokke gliding along close behind. She and Fenris slipped out last of all, tugging the door closed behind them. "Are we really just going to walk through the place?" Arcana whispered, flicking the lantern off and sliding it back into her satchel. "The deerken will stand out like sore thumbs."

"Llane is simply escorting his prisoners." Fenris shrugged. "Try to look worried."

"I *am* worried. What if we get busted?"

That court-calm mask fractured, revealing an icy rage underneath. "No witnesses. No mercy."

Arcana walked alongside him, watching the steady bob and swish of Llane's hooded cloak up ahead. She chewed her lip for a second then murmured; "And Llane?"

"I believe he's on our side but if I'm wrong, he will likely target me first. Kill him swiftly," Fenris answered. Arcana's heart ached at the haunted light flickering in his eyes, and she reached out to briefly squeeze his fingers. He returned the gesture, offering a tight smile as they arrived at the base of the stairs.

Llane raised a scaly finger to his lips, then pointed up at the sealed trap door. "This way."

The staircase was steep and narrow, forcing them to move single file - bar Mirokke, who floated alongside Caelum, heedless of the fact that half of her body was inside the slick dungeon wall. Llane set the curve of his spine against the trap door and heaved; the solid metal sheet swung open, hydraulic hinges bringing it to a hissing stop inches above the floor. Arcana trailed Caelum's mottled rump into a room made entirely of cream and gold marble, with tall, narrow windows framing the encroaching jungle outside. The grand architecture continued into the halls beyond, where great columns rose to arched ceilings and the marble floors were decorated with plush burgundy carpets.

Llane hooked a booted foot beneath the trap door and hauled it back over the hatch, flipping a nearby rug into place over the top. "Keep your heads down. Let me do the talking, if it needs to be done."

Arcana stared out into the vaulted hall. "Where is everyone?"

"Most of us are stationed above the warg dens." Llane glanced out the window, eyeing the watery sun. "At this time of day, anyone not on essential duty is preparing for the evening banquet. The Pariah demands a high standard of dress and none are excepted from attendance to his meals - for the next hour or so, the palace will be largely deserted."

"Fortunate for us," Fenris murmured.

"Yes, but we may still run into patrols or servants." Llane adjusted his hood and gave them a critical once over. "Try to look like prisoners."

Arcana did as she was told, walking beside Fenris with her eyes downcast, Caelum and Mirokke following behind. Llane led them down echoing corridors and through cavernous rooms, each richly appointed with vivid tapestries, voluminous curtains and tall windows that made the most of the cool afternoon sunlight. As they progressed through the palace's multiple levels, servants in multi-hued robes began to appear, flitting around the edges of the room, bowing and muttering to Llane as he passed by. Though Arcana's breath caught in her throat each time, not a single one spared her or her companions a second glance.

Llane approached a set of tall double doors with a soldier on either side. Both were tall and golden skinned, wearing cream livery and burgundy sashes with long, ornamental spears beside them. Arcana's heart skipped a beat but the two men nodded companionably at Llane, one of them dropping the butt of his spear onto a lever which pulled the doors wide open. Continuing down a long corridor and turning left through an archway, they came to the base of a long, double armed staircase whose embrace framed an elegant fountain. Llane gestured for them to stop, pulling up close to where the water cascaded into the pool.

"We're approaching an area where you may be recognised," he murmured to Fenris. "The Pariah's personal safe is located within his office, which is in the upper reaches of this area of the palace. It's also the wing that houses those of Taelon's guard who have been stationed here. I will try and maintain my cover as long as possible, but if Daelan has raised the alarm we will have to fight."

"I understand. If you wish to remain incognito, you may leave us," Fenris offered.

"If we're seen, I will aid you," Llane replied, nodding to himself. "An investigation will be launched upon your escape. Better to have an easy scapegoat than risk revealing others who lie waiting."

"Or you could blame Fenris' glamour," Arcana said, dropping onto the edge of the fountain.

"I beg your pardon?" Fenris turned in surprise.

She curled her fingers around the cool marble, letting the empty elegance of the palace soak through her skin, and looked up at Fenris from beneath her lashes. "Your glamour. It's pretty much the monster under the bed, isn't it?"

"I hide nothing under anyone's bed, thank you very much."

Brianne choked a reluctant laugh. "What he means to say is: Yes, we whisper nasty stories about Fenris' glamour around late night campfires."

"Thought so." Arcana threw a quick smile in the Warden's direction. "And everybody already knows not to look you in the eye, right?"

"Of course." Fenris looked even more miffed. "I have no wish to control someone against their will."

"*I* know that - but now the tables are turned and these former allies are bad guys." Arcana motioned towards Llane. "We can avoid endangering any under-cover Guardians by letting slip that you used your glamour to control Llane and make him do your evil bidding."

Fenris crossed both arms over his chest. "The only problem with that idea is that Llane cannot lie."

"That'll work in his favour," Arcana said. "If you zap him for a bit, Llane can legitimately say you used your glamour. Everyone will believe him because he only speaks the truth and there will be no need for an investigation."

The two men stared at her in silence, Llane's face thoughtful and Fenris' carefully blank. "I think it will work," Llane said at last, nodding slightly. "Do it."

"No." Fenris' voice was hollow as a death knell.

"You can do this," Arcana told him. "It doesn't have to be much, just a touch."

Fenris' arms tightened, as though he was hugging himself. "My glamour is not a toy."

"No, it's a tool which we can employ to our benefit." Arcana pushed to her feet, laying a gentle hand across the solid muscle of his forearm. "This might save Llane's life."

"You don't know what you are asking."

Arcana fisted a hand in Fenris' jacket and yanked him down until they were nose to nose. His glamour swirled around them as their eyes met, a familiar cloak of feathers and velvet. "Yes," she said softly, "I do."

"Fenris..." Brianne's tone was full of warning, her expression dark.

"Be still, sister. My glamour doesn't work on Arcana," Fenris snapped. A short, pregnant silence fell, and from the corner of her eyes Arcana noted both Brianne and Llane staring at Fenris open-mouthed.

"She's immune?" Brianne said at last.

"Entirely," Arcana answered. "Watch." She rose on tiptoe and poked Fenris firmly between the eyes with an index finger.

He flinched and growled, swatting at her hand. "Do you *mind*?"

"Not at all."

"Would someone care to explain exactly *how* Arcana is immune to the glamour?" Brianne demanded.

Fenris tilted his head, his eyes never leaving Arcana's. "I do not understand why or how Arcana is immune - only that she is."

"Have you tried forcing it on her?"

"*Brianne.*"

"It's important to know the limits," Brianne returned equably. "Well?"

"He tried, against his better judgement," Arcana answered.

"Huh. Interesting," Brianne inspected Arcana as though she were something strange and new. "So you can't enchant her at all?"

"Only the usual way." Fenris' lips curled into a half smile. "Apparently I need more practice."

"Practice makes perfect, or so my instructors used to say," Arcana returned. "Now, can we get back on topic? Nobody's asking you to turn Llane inside out - just make him do some star jumps or something. Then he can truthfully say you controlled him with your glamour."

"*Star jumps?*"

Arcana shrugged and grinned. "Unless you know some suitably embarrassing dance moves."

"Do it." Llane shucked his hood and stepped closer, extending his serpentine neck until he and Fenris were the same height. "I trust you."

Fenris muttered under his breath in fey, scrubbing one hand over his face. His gaze skittered reluctantly over Llane's cheeks and along his snout before finally settling on those brilliant red eyes. The other Guardian twitched and then relaxed, his posture turning curiously fluid. After a long moment Fenris began to walk backwards with slow, deliberate steps. Llane mirrored the motions like a marionette and Arcana watched in fascination as the two of them circumnavigated the fountain. When they returned to the place they started, Fenris blinked and looked away, his chest heaving unsteadily.

"How unsettling." Llane raised one hand to his forehead, several of his translucent eyelids opening and closing in rapid succession. "To move without being in control of my own body... I've never felt such a thing."

"My apologies," Fenris croaked.

"Your apology is unnecessary - I have suffered nothing." Llane clasped

Fenris' arm in a forearm grip and squeezed lightly. "You know I speak the truth, brother."

Unable to stand the self-recrimination she saw in his eyes, Arcana moved to Fenris' side and slipped her arm around his hips. He flinched and then pulled her tightly against him, fingers bunching in her clothes and eyelids squeezing shut. Arcana rested her head against his chest, listening to the thunderous roar of his heart beneath her ear, and waited. After a long moment, Fenris pulled back and looked down with a tentative smile. "Thank you."

"Welcome," she murmured. "You okay?"

"I will be." He took a deep, steadying breath and let it hiss out between his teeth. "We need to keep moving. The longer we stay here, the more we risk discovery."

"Yes." Llane nodded and pulled up his hood. "This way."

The wide stairs cradling the fountain were shallow and easy to climb, cloaked in a thick, burgundy carpet whose edges had been trimmed in gold. Arcana craned her neck as they passed several landings with open doors but there were only vast, empty rooms and more corridors beyond.

"Stop," Caelum whispered.

They halted a few steps down from the next landing, Arcana's heart leaping in her chest. "What's the matter?"

"Mirokke says to wait." Caelum's eyes crossed and he blinked, shaking his head to clear it. Mirokke's milky gaze was focussed on the wall beside them, her head tilted on an angle so that the ripening fruit swayed gently from her antler rack. "There are four guards on the other side of the wall. Near the doorway."

Arcana considered the wall and frowned. "Are they moving?"

"No. They're playing dice - and one of them has a direct line of sight through the archway." Caelum jerked his chin towards Llane. "All in black leathers and some with basic body armour, so I'm guessing they're yours."

"Yes." Llane considered the information, red eyes glimmering within the depths of his hood. "This is the landing for our quarters. If they see us - see Fenris - they will raise the alarm."

"Sounds like we need a distraction, then." Arcana laid her palm against the wall, feeling out the palace. "I could -"

"Wait." Caelum's ears flickered in response to something only he could hear. "Mirokke says she'll do it."

Arcana stared at the ghostly doe, one eyebrow hiked. "Are you sure?"

Mirokke dipped her nose once, then turned and ghosted through the wall. Shouts broke out on the other side, followed quickly by crashing furniture and slamming doors. Caelum's ear flickered again. "*Now.*"

They turned as one, hurrying past the archway. Several dice lay scattered on the floor among overturned chairs and a greasy, half eaten burger with entirely too much pickle. Caelum sneered at the food but before he got a chance to lash out with a hoof, Arcana wrapped a hand around the base of an antler and tugged onward. "Leave it."

"Pickles are a crime!" He hissed, but followed nonetheless.

Oblivious to their exchange, Llane hurried along the next landing and slipped through an archway identical to all the others. He stopped in a round receiving room whose walls were lined with elegant chairs and gestured to a door on the left. "This is the Pariah's study."

Fenris moved to the door and laid his ear against it. After a moment's concentration, he turned the handle and pushed. "Locked."

"Are we surprised?" Arcana stepped to his side and flattened her hand against the door, Fenris' breath tickling the back of her knuckles. She sent her magic into the lock which, at face value, appeared simple - but the more Arcana felt it out, the more she realised it was anything but. She frowned, jiggling the innards of the lock carefully, feeling out where they connected to a system of wiring which was most likely an alarm. If she moved this bolt *here* and pushed that lever *there*, simultaneously spinning these three cogs a quarter turn to the left... the lock clicked and the door swung open. Arcana withdrew her magic and blew out between her teeth. "Okay. Let's go."

The room was as cavernous and majestic as any they'd yet seen. Hexagonal in shape, half of the walls were set with enormous windows whose voluminous curtains were pulled wide to reveal a breath-taking view of the jungle's upper canopy. Minimal but striking furniture was set strategically around the space, most notably a dark wood desk burnished with gold accents and a pair of matching chairs with scarlet velvet upholstery.

"It seems almost criminal for a desk this large to be so empty." Arcana drifted over to the enormous desk and eyed the glossy surface. It was easily big enough to stretch out on, and was set with a crisp white notepad and a gold pen. "Or so unused."

Caelum snorted. "Or for a floor to be this reflective." Indeed, the marble flooring had been polished until Arcana could see her own reflection as clearly as if she looked into a mirror. She watched Caelum make faces at himself and then grimace. "Great Gods of Sorcen, I can see my own undercarriage."

Arcana palmed her face and glanced at Llane from between her fingers. "Where's the safe?"

"This way." Llane crossed to a large tapestry and flipped it aside to reveal a recess in the wall. Arcana moved to join him, bending to peer into the hole just as Mirokke's face floated out of the stone.

"Shit!"

"What is it?" Fenris was there in an instant, catching Arcana as she leapt backwards. "What's wrong?"

Arcana pointed at the deerken slowly emerging from the wall. "Not funny!"

"She's sorry," Caelum said from across the room. "The Guardians are searching the lower levels for her... but it probably means someone will eventually think to check the cells."

"At least she had the sense to lead them away from us." Arcana held her hand out to Mirokke and was surprised to feel the faintest tickle of fur when the deerken snuffled her fingers. "She's more solid than before."

"Her sight isn't back yet, though," Caelum replied, his voice worried. He crossed the room to stand beside Mirokke, Brianne clinging to his back with her eyes squeezed shut. "I hope the loss isn't permanent."

Arcana studied both deerken and noted how similar the markings were in their short fur, how their bodies swept and curved in the same clean lines. "You're so much like her. It's uncanny."

"I *am* a deerken," Caelum reminded her.

"I know, but - never mind. Now is not the time." Arcana sighed, patting Fenris' arm until he set her back on her feet. "What can you tell us about the safe, Llane?"

"Not much. The Pariah always blocks the view with his body."

Arcana narrowed her eyes, considering the recess before her. The long, rectangular hole looked as though it should contain something, only didn't. "Hmmm." She flattened her hands against the marble edge and extended her magic into the wall. After a long moment feeling about, she gave a little magical nudge and the back of the alcove dropped away, revealing a silver lockbox two handspans wide and half as tall.

"Don't touch it." Fenris' breath tickled Arcana's cheek as he leant over her shoulder to peer at the box. "This seems incredibly easy."

"Perhaps the trick was just opening the back of the recess?"

Fenris frowned - an expression she couldn't see but felt in the way his face crinkled where it brushed her own. "I am almost certain the Pariah would have better security than that."

"I assure you that he does, brother," Daelan drawled. Arcana spun to see the ex-Guardian reclining on the Pariah's desk, twirling his crossbow around one finger. "Me, for a start."

"Daelan." Fenris drew the greatsword and leant on the hilt. "Last I saw, you were fleeing to the gardens. Have you become suddenly courageous? You rarely fight alone."

Daelan nodded at the hooded Guardian standing to one side of the alcove. "I have Llane."

"Llane is under my compulsion." Fenris stepped in front of Llane, dragging the tip of the greatsword across the other Guardian's chest. "He cannot help you; he belongs to me now."

"You wouldn't." Daelan flicked a glance at Llane from behind his silvery locks. "Everyone knows you hate using it."

"You know what they say, *brother*. Desperate times call for desperate measures." Fenris took another step forward, dropping the tip of his blade so that it scraped across the marble floor like nails across a blackboard. "The Weaver has been kidnapped. My brothers and sisters have, for the most part, turned against me. The deerken are scattered and Taelon has scented my blood. What would you do in such a situation? Better yet, if it meant your survival, what would you *not* do?"

Daelan sat up, crossing his legs beneath him and regarding his former Overlord through narrowed eyes. Fenris stood with his head up, shoulders back, court-calm mask firmly in place. He snapped his fingers and Llane flowed forwards, halting bare moments from the back of Fenris' hand. Daelan watched the scene with pursed lips. "By all that's holy, Fenris... you *did* do it."

Arcana set her back against the recess, using her magic to ripple the marble inside and pull the lockbox forward. The stone whispered beneath her influence, the softest, barest sound - which Fenris abruptly concealed by dragging the greatsword's tip across the marble floor again, leaving a nasty score in the pristine cream stone. "I told you, did I not, my brother? I took an oath. I will wield whatever weapons I must for the Weaver."

"And the sorceress, too?" Daelan looked over at Arcana and whistled in appreciation. "I must credit you for that particular stroke of genius. The Pariah is looking forward to meeting her - much to Shirimm's disappointment."

"So Shirimm is alive?" Fenris clicked his tongue in annoyance. "I'm surprised you didn't finish what my sorceress started. That would place you by the Pariah's side, would it not?"

"Hah!" Daelan loosed his perfect, chiming laugh. "Has your opinion of me really sunk so low?"

"Yes," Fenris admitted. "It has."

Arcana flexed her fingers and the lockbox inched closer, the cool edges of the metal brushing her fingertips. This time the sound was minimal, easily covered by Daelan's low hiss of anger.

"Shirimm and I share the same rank here, so killing her is of no benefit to me. Your companions, however..." Daelan ceased twirling his crossbow and, without bothering to level or aim, pulled the trigger.

Arcana hadn't so much as blinked when Fenris appeared in front of her, snatching a bolt out of the air that would otherwise have pierced her forehead. With a smooth movement, he snapped the tiny crossbow bolt in half. "That wasn't very polite."

Daelan's answering smile was almost sensual, the glittering light in his eyes filled with the promise of violence. "I see your reflexes are as good as ever. Too bad for you this is the end." He fired the crossbow again - directly into the locking mechanism of the study door. It swung open and six cloaked figures marched in. "Not only are these brothers and sisters with *me*, that bolt will have triggered an alarm palace-wide. Everyone knows you're here now, Overlord. Care to come quietly?"

"You know I won't." Fenris faced the newcomers as they fanned out in front him, resting the greatsword point down on the floor. "Guardians of the Weaver, you have flouted your oaths and spurned your gifts. Repent, or die in the Weaver's name."

"Oh, please." Daelan fired another bolt but Fenris caught it without looking and once again snapped it in two. Two of the hooded Guardians flinched and Daelan's lips twisted into a snarl. "Don't tell me any of you are actually intimidated by this half-feral creature?"

Silence. Fenris stood impassively, his posture casual as he waited. Moving as quietly as she could, Arcana worked her fingers over the lockbox until she found a latch. The lid flipped open as soon as she pushed it aside. Using her body to block the lockbox from view whilst endeavouring to keep the standoff in her own line of sight, Arcana glanced down to see a myriad of jewels, a personal teleportation device with a crack down the centre and three milky blue portal crystals. She half turned her head to see Brianne watching and gave the Warden a subtle nod.

Brianne closed her eyes for a brief moment, the lines of her face changing from pain to relief. Then she struggled upright, clinging to Caelum's neck for support, and cast a cold stare over her former brethren. "Your Overlord calls," Brianne shouted, pointing a trembling finger at Fenris. "Who will answer?"

The room echoed with the rustling and fidgeting of robes as the collected Guardians swung towards Brianne as though noticing her for the first time. While their attention was diverted, Arcana dragged her satchel bag closer and scooped the portal stones inside. She flipped the lid of the lockbox shut and shoved it back into the recess, using her magic to replace the stone panel.

"I answer the Overlord's call," a voice rang out. Arcana swung around in time to see a short, curvy Guardian shuck her hood, revealing hot pink skin and tight white curls from which two gnarled black horns emerged. She shunted her arms down at the shoulders and a short blade shot out of each sleeve. With a graceful whirl, she buried both blades in the back of the hooded Guardian beside her. Using the falling body as leverage, she cartwheeled to Fenris' side. "For the Weaver!"

"Kella," Llane gasped. After a moment's hesitation, he shucked his own hood. "I answer the Overlord's call."

"Traitors!" Daelan shrieked. "Kill them!"

The remaining four Guardians drew their weapons and charged. Fenris ducked a bladed staff and drove the greatsword upwards into his opponent's abdomen; the staff skittered along the floor to thump against Arcana's boots. She swept the weapon up and threw it - clumsily, but true enough that the ex-Guardian advancing on Caelum leant backwards in surprise. Kella stepped deftly in front of the deerken, her short blades a whirlwind of motion. Arcana clenched her fist and the floor buckled, sending sharp shards of marble up through the enemy's legs. Kella slashed her screaming opponent's arms aside and then buried one of her blades deep within the ex-Guardian's hood, silencing them forever.

"Thanks." She nodded at Arcana as she yanked the blade free, kicking the body aside. "I guess that means you're on our side."

"Yeah," Arcana hooked a thumb at Caelum. "I'm with him."

Kella nodded again and dove away, narrowly missing the crossbow bolt which thunked into the floor where she'd been standing. Arcana backed up until she felt the warm bulk of Caelum's shoulder against her spine. "Can you see Daelan? Your eyes are better than mine."

"He's teleporting around the room," Caelum's words were punctuated by a cry and Llane dropped to the ground, a crossbow bolt protruding from his chest. A second bolt slammed into the Pariah's desk, narrowly avoiding Fenris as he parried a heavy spiked club. "It's hard to keep track."

Arcana traced the bolt's trajectory and spotted Daelan clinging to the roof, half hidden in the shadows. She curled her fingers and the decorative moulding fractured, knocking the ex-Guardian free. He teleported away in a cloud of sparks, leaving a heavy section of carved marble to slam into the floor with a shuddering crash. A flicker of light to the left caught Arcana's attention and Daelan reappeared atop the gilt lip of an arched window. She sheared the stone out from under him and the ex-Guardian fell - but not before he sighted down the length of his crossbow and pulled the trigger.

"He got Fenris in the shoulder," Brianne cried. "Hurry!"

"I'm trying." Arcana scanned the room for the tell-tale shower of sparks. She loosed the roof again when Daelan appeared but the ex-Guardian swung himself on top of the falling rock and used it to balance, shooting Kella in the leg before disappearing with a mocking laugh. Fenris bent and swept Kella's feet from under her, sending his ally crashing to the ground as an axe whizzed through the space where her head had been.

Arcana twisted her wrist, undulating the floor until Kella rolled to Llane's side. Clutching her injured leg with one hand, the Guardian threw the edge of her cloak over Llane's twitching body, wrist blade flashing as she prepared to defend him. Daelan reappeared, clinging to a tapestry as he sighted over his crossbow. Arcana called a layer of marble up from the floor, curving it over the two injured Guardians just as he pulled the trigger, the deadly bolt bouncing harmlessly off her impromptu shield.

Daelan snarled and swung towards Arcana but she wrenched a piece of marble from the wall beside him, driving it into the ex-Guardian's shoulder and knocking him off his perch. The crossbow flew across the room as Daelan thumped to the floor, rolling twice before finishing face up against one of the Pariah's velvet chairs. Arcana clenched her fingers and the floor buckled, long tendrils of stone shooting out to bind Daelan firmly in place. The ex-Guardian looked momentarily startled, then laughed and disappeared in yet another shower of sparks.

"Shit," Arcana growled. A faint breeze stirred her hair and she jerked aside but Daelan had already materialised behind her, locking one arm around her body and setting a short, notched blade against her throat.

"Fenris! How much do you value your little pet?"

Across the room, Fenris ducked inside his opponent's heavy, two handed swing and with a twist of his wrist, took the other's head off. He shoved the falling body aside, eyes widening as he took in the scene before him. "I wouldn't do that, if I were you," Fenris cautioned into the sudden silence.

"Quiet," Daelan snapped. "Move and she dies."

Fenris set the greatsword point down against the floor and leant on the hilt, unconcerned by the blood splashed over his face and body or the corpses on the floor at his feet. "As you wish, brother." He reached over his shoulder, tugged out the crossbow bolt lodged there, inspected it briefly, then snapped it in half. "But don't say I did not warn you."

"*Warn* me?" Daelan laughed, pressing the blade harder against Arcana's skin. "One wrong move from you and I teleport us away -" His hold abruptly loosened and Daelan slithered down the length of Arcana's body to fall in a heap at her feet. She turned to see Brianne standing behind her, face pale and body trembling. The crossbow bolt which had been buried in the Warden's shoulder was gone, it's point now deep inside the back of Daelan's head.

"For the Weaver," Brianne managed, and toppled. Arcana caught her, dragging her away from the dark tide of blood that was rapidly turning Daelan's silver hair black.

"No!" Fenris was by their side in an instant, running his fingers over the gushing wound in Brianne's shoulder, pulling at the blood soaked bandage around her middle. "What have you done to yourself?"

"I made sure Daelan paid his debts," she murmured, letting her head drop against his shoulder.

"Arcana had her magic half cast - you should have let her handle it," Fenris snarled, his hands slick with the Warden's blood as he tried to staunch the flow.

"This was my payment to take... and now I go to Riella." Brianne caught Fenris' desperate hands in her own. "Stop it. Fenris, *stop*."

"Let me help you."

"No. There is nothing more to do, brother." Brianne took a deep, rattling breath, her face more serene than Arcana had yet seen it. She reached up with a trembling hand and chucked Fenris' chin, much like an aunt might do with her favoured nephew. "Do not be afraid of the setting sun. I am not."

"Brianne..." Fenris' voice was heavy, pleading.

"Hush. If anyone can stop this madness, it is you. Be brave. Look after Mirokke and find the Weaver." Brianne sought Arcana's gaze and held it a moment, her expression knowing. "Take care of him for me."

"I will," Arcana promised. Brianne nodded, then smiled up at Fenris. She was still smiling as death came to claim her, cajoling the breath from her lungs and crooning a siren song to her heart so that it ceased to beat entirely.

CHAPTER
NINE

"Brianne." Fenris drew the Warden to his chest, a single tear rolling down his cheek. "Weaver guide you, Auron keep you. May you find peace beyond the weave."

Arcana reached out to close Brianne's eyes with gentle fingers. "She's with Riella now."

"That *is* all she wanted." Fenris sighed, fingers twisting in the fabric of Brianne's tunic until the knuckles turned white. "And yet I feel as though I let her down."

"Never," Arcana bristled. "Brianne knew what was coming and she made a choice. Don't lessen that decision with self-pity. Instead, remember who you saved." She waved a hand to banish the curling wall of marble that shielded both Llane and Kella. The two Guardians sat up, blinking blearily, Kella with her hand pressed firmly to Llane's sternum. He held a short crossbow bolt in his long, many-jointed fingers, the end smeared with greenish-yellow ichor.

"Daelan didn't pierce anything vital." Llane wriggled his shoulders in what Arcana assumed was a shrug. "My wounds clot quickly."

"It helps that your blood's more viscous than normal." Kella prised her hand free of the wound and squinted at it. "Looks okay for now."

Llane's eyes fell on Brianne's limp body. "Leave it be, Kel. We've lost a guiding light today."

"What do you - oh, no." Kella crawled to Brianne's side and lowered her head. "Weaver guide you and Auron keep you, sister. I wish there was more we could have done."

"Brianne had no regrets." Caelum stepped close, followed by Mirokke, and the two lowered their noses to huff kisses over Brianne's cheeks. "Mirokke says she was an excellent Warden, kind and honourable."

"She was." Kella nodded, brushing the Warden's hair back off her brow. "Brianne cared for everybody." After a moment, she frowned and looked back at the deerken. "Wait - did you just *speak*?"

Caelum lent forward, his tail switching restlessly, and said; "Boo."

"Weaver's grace!"

"Stop it." Arcana shoved his giant head away. "Now is not the time; Brianne needs us to take care of her as best we can."

"I'm aware of that." Caelum looked up from beneath his lashes. "You should offer absolution."

"What?" Arcana stiffened, shock turning her blood cold. "I'm not sure that would be appropriate."

"Why not?"

Arcana gritted her teeth. "You know why."

"Bah," Caelum gave a loud snort. "Those laws are stupid."

"Be that as it may, Brianne was not from Sorcen," Arcana pointed out, all too aware of their audience. "I don't want to be disrespectful."

"Just like the Council when-"

"Caelum."

"Or that time they -"

"*Caelum*."

Fenris cleared his throat. "May I ask what absolution is?"

Arcana pressed her lips together in a thin line. "The ritual of absolution is the highest burial honour Sorcen offers. It's a cremation ceremony performed by a Class One fire sorcerer at the specific request of the Council. The ritual sets the soul free from the flesh, so that Breogh can guide the wandering spirit home."

"When Arcana ascended, Flare broke a bunch of rules and taught her the ritual - among other things," Caelum interjected. "Mostly to piss the Council off, but she knows it nonetheless."

"I'm not a fire sorcerer." Arcana fought to keep the tension from her voice. "I'm not ordained to perform the ritual. I know it, yes, but I'd be breaking one of Sorcen's most sacred lores by offering it to Brianne."

"What do you mean you're not a fire sorcerer?" Fenris frowned. "I'm sure I've seen you use fire magic."

"You have," said Caelum. "She is."

"I'm not a member of the Fire Tower." Arcana dropped her eyes to the ground. "I don't have the right to perform a spell like that. It'd be high treason."

Caelum snorted. "You're the best sorcerer Sorcen's ever seen and the Council knows it! That whole mess about the rosters was just a bluff to try and bring you under their control."

Arcana narrowed her eyes. "I will remind you that both Flare and Lesce are on that Council."

"Yeah, but he wasn't then, and Lesce was outvoted; you're splitting straws and you know it." Caelum tossed his head impatiently. "Maybe now that Flare's in place, he can shake the hierarchy up a little - but either way, who cares? Nobody will know about the ritual but us."

"That's not the point," Arcana growled. "What you're offering is heresy and I have no wish to sully Brianne's honour with my own particular brand of taint."

Silence fell, and as one they looked to Fenris. He closed his eyes. "First of all, I would say that as all and none, there would be no sorceress more suited to performing this ritual for Brianne than you. The Timeless Kingdom is a place where customs are blended and I care naught for heresy or the hidebound rulings of your stuffed up Council. When it comes to honouring those who are important to us, boundaries can be - and often are - transcended. In fact, *you* were the one who pointed such things out to me not so very long ago." Fenris opened his eyes and his gaze burnt all the way to Arcana's soul. "Secondly, I know Flare, and even as the Fire Elder, I believe he would tell you to follow your heart. Thirdly, and perhaps the most important, you are not tainted. In fact it would honour Brianne - and the rest of us - if you would perform this ritual."

"I'm not a good choice -"

"You are," Fenris said quietly. His eyes reached across the distance between them, the warm velvet slide of his glamour a balm to her jangled nerves. "Please."

Arcana pushed to her feet, shoving trembling hands into her jacket pockets. Her heart was a jackhammer against her ribs, her jaw a hard, unforgiving line. "Fine. Give me a minute to find some fire."

Fenris nodded and Arcana turned away, simultaneously hot and cold as her temper warred with bitter memories. Caelum trailed her to the Pariah's desk, watching as she yanked out a drawer and began flicking through the contents. "You're angry."

"Later," she hissed, shoving aside pens and staplers.

"Now," Caelum insisted. "I don't understand your emotions; I thought you liked Brianne. I only offered to be polite."

"Polite?" Arcana lowered her voice, though she knew whatever she said, Fenris would hear it regardless of volume. "It's not about manners, or whether I liked Brianne, and you know it. This is about asking me for something I'm not qualified for."

"You are."

"I'm *not*. I was rejected from Sorcen's society years ago; it's why we left." Arcana slammed the drawer shut and moved to the next. "Now, not only are you asking me to spit on tradition - which, though I've been ostracised from it, is still the only tradition I know - you're slowly and irrevocably bringing us into *their* world when we don't belong in it."

"I do," Caelum answered.

Arcana froze partway through the second drawer, a ledger forgotten in one hand. Tears pricked unbidden at the corners of her eyes as her heart fractured, the pain swift and deep. "Well," she whispered, letting the ledger slip back into the drawer and closing it quietly. "How lovely for you."

"That isn't what I meant." Caelum's voice sounded strained, and Arcana realised it was likely the first time he'd ever felt the true depths of her loneliness.

"Of course not." The words were empty but she said them anyway, tugging the third drawer open and pulling out a box of rough, thick cut matches. "Go and get Brianne, please."

"Arcana -"

"*Go.*" Acid edged her tone and Caelum went, ears drooping mournfully. Arcana set the box of matches on the Pariah's enormous desk and struck one, dropping it on top of the rest. The outer casing was made of a thin wood which caught immediately, followed quickly by the remaining matches. The little fire leapt high, spreading over the mirrored varnish of the desk in a rolling wave. Arcana held her hands out to the heat, sloughing off the earth magic and absorbing the crackling energy of the flames.

Fenris arrived, carrying Brianne and flanked by the two other Guardians. They stood in fascinated silence while the desk burned, the flames leaping skyward as Arcana stoked it with her magic. She closed her eyes and inhaled, smoke curling into her nostrils and tickling her lungs. Was it really heresy, to offer love and peace to the companions of a fallen warrior? If Flare were here, he wouldn't hesitate, but nothing he ever did was wrong. Her brother's actions were gilt in gold, his reputation beyond tarnish. Arcana swallowed a bitter laugh, opening her eyes to watch flames lick over the marble ceiling. Flare's irreverence for the rules was almost as legendary as his prowess in bed, and he was adored for it - whilst she, Arcana, had always done her best to abide by those laws and had become an object of awe and fear. She clenched one fist, her magic sucking and moulding and pulling until the bonfire went out with an indignant puff, leaving a cooling pile of ashes in the centre of the room. Reacting to the fire's energy, the runes circling her wrist and hand glowed so brightly orange they were almost fluorescent. Flare's oath - an oath of fealty, of love, of trust in Arcana and her decisions. She sighed. Heresy or not, she didn't have it in her heart to deny Brianne this honour.

She looked up at Fenris from beneath her lashes and felt her heart stutter at the intensity in his expression. Swallowing, she managed; "Are you ready?"

His eyes locked with hers, his glamour rose around them and for that single moment, it felt as though they were the only two in the room. "Are you?"

"Yes." Arcana lifted her glowing hand and began to trace a rune on Brianne's forehead, feeling, as she did so, that she were cutting some final, invisible tether to her past. She expected to feel lost, or even ill; instead she felt the first flickering of temper. Who were the Council, to tell her what she should and should not do? Who were those fusty scholars, to say who she was and was not? She completed the rune and set the tips of her index fingers against Brianne's temples. "Breogh, mother above, Maker of souls. Take here this, a beacon of flesh, as guiding light for she who once rested within. See her freed, see her soar and bring her home that she may be Made anew within the palms of your hands." Arcana didn't need the spell but she wove it anyway, twisting the threads of magic into the rune on Brianne's forehead exactly the way Flare had once shown her. The mark began to glow with a pure, white light. "Craddagh, mother below, blessed Unmaker. Take here this, a beacon of flesh, and accept into your cauldron the shadows once housed within. See them eased, see them cleansed and by the grace of your love, raise us from grief into peace and understanding." Arcana pushed more power into her spell and the rune on Brianne's forehead caught fire. White flames licked and curled out over her body but there was no heat, no sound or scent to denote a burning. Arcana looked up at the three Guardians. "It is tradition to lay your hands upon Brianne as she goes, to send your love along with her, if you'd like. The fire won't burn you."

"I will." Kella reached into the flames and after a trembling hesitation,

Llane followed suit. Arcana put her own hand into the fire, raising her eyes to meet Fenris', who had not so much as flinched when the body in his arms caught alight.

"Brianne of the Timeless Kingdom, I hereby grant you the absolution of the flame, in Firius' name. Be freed, sister soul, until we meet again." Arcana drew more and more magic until the entirety of the fire's energy pulsed in her palms - and then she expelled it all in one final rush. The sheer force of the magic and the intense heat of the contained fire disintegrated Brianne's body instantaneously, leaving only shimmering sparks of white light behind. In the empty space where the Warden had been, the three Guardians' hands were interlinked - a final, connecting twist of the absolution spell. Arcana cleared her throat. "Fare you well Brianne, Warden to the deerken and beloved of Riella. May Breogh keep you and may we be drawn closer together in your memory." She traced the symbol for peace in the air; it shimmered white and orange before blinking out. Arcana swallowed and murmured; "Sleep sweetly."

Caelum repeated the phrase from behind her, and after a moment's hesitation, the three mourning Guardians followed suit. Arcana made to retract her hands and found them suddenly covered by Fenris' larger ones, his teal skin a stark contrast to her pale, soot-streaked fingers. "Thank you," he said.

Arcana nodded, finding it suddenly difficult to look at his face, and even more difficult to look at their joined hands. She tried to shove the rising tide of her feelings down, groping instead for words she'd heard from his own mouth. "I hope she finds peace in the warp and the weft of the weave."

Fenris looked as though he would say more, but was interrupted by Kella extending a vibrant pink arm towards Arcana. "I don't know you, but I owe you my life. Thank you - and thank you for the ritual, too. It was perfect. I'm Kella, by the way."

Arcana forced a smile onto her face, tugging her hand free from Fenris' to return Kella's forearm grip. "You're welcome. I'm Arcana."

"Arcana," Kella mused, then flicked a gaze at Fenris. "New Guardian?"

"Not as such." Fenris' lips quirked with the hint of a smile, as though he'd been anticipating the question. "Arcana and I met approximately four weeks ago. She saved my life, too."

"But the deerken..." Kella trailed off and frowned up at Caelum. "He's new."

"Caelum came with Arcana, and Mirokke with Brianne." Fenris paused and Kella waited with the expectant air of one used to her leader's whims.

"We have two other companions to rescue from the Pariah, but after that I am returning to the Timeless Kingdom to find the Weaver and end this madness."

"Madness indeed," Kella agreed. She swept aside her cloak and yanked out the crossbow bolt embedded in her thigh. "Ugh. That's going to slow me down."

"I can cauterise it," Arcana offered quietly. When Kella nodded, she added; "It won't be pleasant."

The Guardian bared her teeth in a feral smile. "It never is."

Arcana found her own lips twisting in response, and as she laid the cleaner of her two hands over Kella's thigh, decided she liked the other woman immensely. She sent her magic into the wound, burning out any foreign material before melting Kella's flesh back together. When Arcana retracted her hand, there was a neat, shiny round scar where the wound had been. "I'm afraid that mark will last."

"Incredible," Kella poked at the scar and then winced. "Bit tender, but better than bleeding all over the place. I like it."

"I like mine, too," Fenris volunteered. There was a short silence, during which Kella blinked up at him in surprise. Eventually Fenris tugged at the hem of his stained t-shirt, revealing the scar which ran from chest to hip.

Kella gave a low, appreciative whistle. "She did that?"

"Arcana healed it," Fenris clarified. "Taelon did it."

Llane hissed, his white tongue flicking between serrated teeth. "You're lucky to be alive."

"If not for Arcana, I wouldn't be." Fenris dropped his shirt back into place and adjusted the greatsword. "I intend to spend my second chance at life teaching Taelon to regret invading our home and stealing our queen."

"You know what they say about old dogs and new tricks, right?" Kella's grin was wicked sharp. "Still, no harm in trying. If you intend to start your education with the Pariah, he instructed Daelan to present you at the feast. He'll be lording it at the head of ridiculously gilt table as we speak."

"Well then," Fenris looked down at Daelan's body, limp in a pool of congealing blood, and curled his lip. "I should hate to disappoint him by being late. Will you accompany us?"

"Of course," Kella's grin was wide. "I've been waiting for a chance to hold the Pariah accountable for his part in this mess."

"Llane?" Fenris glanced up at the other Guardian, who had shucked his hood and was glaring at Daelan's corpse with frightening intensity.

"I will come with you," Llane replied. "Do I have time to eat Daelan first?"

"No! He'll give you indigestion." Kella made a face and poked Llane in the shoulder. "He was ever the greasy sort. Besides, the Pariah demanded his presence at the feast - I think we should take him with us, don't you?"

"That *is* an appealing idea," Llane mused, then shrugged and turned to Fenris. "Very well. We are yours to command, Overlord."

They fell to discussing the layout of the Palace and how the Pariah's banquet would proceed. Arcana drifted away from the trio, unable to shake the aching loneliness that Caelum had ignited with his earlier comments. The bodies on the floor were mostly covered by their cloaks but even so, she couldn't leave them lying there. Once, someone had loved them - and perhaps they still did, somewhere. She set about incinerating each body, forgoing the honour of a proper ceremony but cleaning up the remains nonetheless. When Arcana reached Daelan's side, she stopped. The long, slender planes of his face were sunken, his lips pinched with cruelty even beneath the veil of death. The ex-Guardian's past was a mystery, but it had taken little effort to glean that the Timeless Kingdom was a close knit community who'd worked together for hundreds - perhaps thousands - of years before Taelon had turned them against each other. Arcana's breath shuddered in her lungs, trying to imagine how it would feel if Flare or Lesce woke up one morning and started murdering the people of Sorcen. Her lips twisted and as she examined Daelan's pointy features, she saw Algae's face laid over the top. Both men had turned on their loved ones, had made greedy, selfish decisions that resulted in pain and death and destruction. The similarity was so sharp it hurt, so Arcana turned away and dusted the soot from her hands, watching Caelum from beneath her lashes. The deerken stood with Mirokke, and from the far off look in his eyes and the way his ears flickered, she knew they were deep in silent conversation.

He really *did* belong in this world, and to those people and creatures who inhabited it. The more Mirokke solidified, the more Caelum's similarities to her became obvious. They had the same silver fur, the same mottled markings, the same charcoal ridge down their spines. Arcana sighed. Even their disproportionately tiny cloven hooves were the same, though Caelum didn't float quite so obviously above the floor.

Arcana drifted to the door and, for lack of anything better to do, wrenched Daelan's crossbow bolt free of the locking mechanism. How was it that with every step closer to answers for Caelum, she felt as though her own grip on normality were slipping? Once upon a time, she'd fit in - a home, a life, a future that had been taken for granted. When she'd first bonded with Caelum, Arcana had believed that old life still possible but time spent squirming beneath the scrutiny of countless scholars and being paraded across the countryside like a prize pony had changed that. It was Flare, holding her in the ruins of Algae's townhouse whilst they both wept, who'd encouraged her to forge a new path and be damned what anyone else thought about it.

A new path. Arcana twirled the crossbow bolt between two fingers without really seeing it. Her brother's advice was well meant, but easier said than done. She'd been much too ruined after Algae to advocate properly for herself, so she'd seized Caelum's heritage as a distraction and fled. Arcana's fingers curled around the bolt's wooden shaft and it caught alight, the flames crackling up between her fingers. Caelum had found his answers; or at least, the road which would lead to them, and each step gave him new purpose. But that left Arcana... alone. Naked and vulnerable and alone - bound to Caelum body and spirit, but without a place she truly belonged. The flames died and she opened her fingers to stare down at the ashes, throat aching with unshed tears. There wasn't time for self-pity. No time for grief or pain or the longing for lost dreams. No time to wonder -

"You are hurting," Fenris murmured, his breath tickling her ear. Arcana jumped, sending the ashes of the crossbow bolt flying into the air like so much black and grey confetti. His chest was warm and solid against her shoulders, arms circling hers so he could capture her trembling hand. "I can smell it."

Arcana closed her eyes as the soft satin of his skin whispered across her senses. "It doesn't matter."

"It matters to *me*." He exhaled across her palm, removing the last of the ashes. "Did you burn yourself?"

"No, and I'm not injured anywhere else." Arcana tugged at her hand but Fenris held firm, crowding closer until his hips bumped against her spine and her body fitted neatly into the shelter of his own. "I can fight just fine."

"I am not interested in your combat readiness; I can smell pain and grief. That ritual you did-"

"It was the least I could offer." Arcana sighed, opening her eyes to stare again at the contrast of their two differently coloured hands. "Caelum was right about that."

"And yet it has upset you." Fenris hesitated, and she could picture him forming his thoughts into careful words. "Would it really be so terrible to bring our two worlds closer together?"

"You heard that, huh."

"I did. And I thought, given that we've kissed each other until our lips were red and swollen, that we were already on the way to bringing two worlds closer together." There was no mistaking the edge in his voice, the licking whip of hurt.

Arcana turned her head, catching a glimpse of Llane and Kella out of the corner of her eye. They were carefully poking through the ashes, sorting weaponry and generally attempting not to look like they were eavesdropping. Arcana lowered her voice and, praying Fenris would understand, said; "You and I kissing in the greenhouse seems like an entirely different reality to what we face standing here right now. You're bound to the Weaver and these people are your *family*. They need you; they don't need me."

"What about what I need?" Fenris spun Arcana to face him, pressing her back against the door. "What about what *you* need?"

"I don't know what I need." The admission tore at her throat, her heart. "I've spent the last fifty years trying to help Caelum find where he belongs and now that he's found it, I realise there's nothing left for me."

"Not true." Fenris crowded closer, blocking Arcana's view of the room with his body. "The past cannot be changed but the future is an open book, begging to be written. You can still have the life you want, if you decide to pursue it."

"I don't know what I want." Tears rose unbidden, followed swiftly by that aching loneliness that had been buried for so long. Arcana choked back a sob. "I don't even know who I am - only who I used to be."

"*I* know who you are," Fenris slid a hand beneath her buttocks and lifted, pinning her against the door with his chest. "And I know what I want." His kiss was as searing as the fire had been; perhaps more so. Arcana tasted her tears on his lips and whilst part of her screamed a warning to *run*, she wrapped her legs around his waist. Fenris shoved her harder against the wood, as though he would meld their bodies together to drive away her pain. One hand crushed her against him and the other fisted in her hair, tilting her head to deepen the kiss.

She was lost. Helplessly, hopelessly adrift, with Fenris her only anchor to the world - and it was terrifying. Exhilarating. Arcana sobbed into his kisses, her ankles tightening around his waist, arms looping around his neck until they were crushed so tightly against each other she wondered whose bones would break first. Fenris was ruining her, breaking her apart piece by piece and reforging her into something new - and worse than that was the stark, underlying realisation that she welcomed it. Welcomed him. *Needed* him.

"What have you done to me?" Arcana whispered against his lips. She was shaking, weaker than a newborn in his arms. Fenris shook his head, dark curls caressing her face as he kissed away her tears, his tongue whispering across her cheeks with an intimacy that made them both groan.

"Whatever I have done, you have also done to me." His teeth grazed her jawbone and Fenris growled; "Weaver save us both."

At mention of the Weaver, Arcana stiffened, abruptly remembering where they were and what they were meant to be doing. She made to push Fenris away but he captured her lips again, sweeping his tongue into her mouth and digging his fingers into her buttocks in silent, unyielding demand - as though afraid that if he let go, she might dematerialise entirely. Arcana recalled Brianne's admission that she'd never seen Fenris so warm and open with anyone, and wondered if that crack in his exterior might not also make him vulnerable, as raw as she felt herself. So she kissed him back, relaxing until her curves moulded to his body, marvelling as she did so that the heart she thought was broken beyond repair had such a vast capacity to feel.

They broke apart at last, when neither could breathe and the fire between them had built so high it either needed to be extinguished or acknowledged. Fenris leant his forehead against Arcana's as they both laboured for breath, safe in the cage of the other's arms. His eyes sought hers and the glamour cloaked Arcana in warmth and life, mending her flagging spirit and strengthening her resolve. Sensing - or most likely scenting - the positive change, Fenris squeezed her backside and Arcana unhooked her ankles, sliding down his body to the floor. He slung an arm across her shoulders and turned around, leading the way back out into the middle of the room. Arcana blushed as she realised both Llane and Kella were staring in open-mouthed amazement.

"Wow," Kella said at last. She flicked a look at Llane. "You never kiss *me* like that."

Llane had the grace to look indignant. "You haven't asked me to kiss you in over twenty years."

"Probably because I almost choked on your tongue the last time," Kella retorted. She eyed Arcana speculatively. "I like you. I don't suppose you have a brother?"

Arcana barked a self-conscious laugh. "As a matter of fact, I do."

Kella clapped her hands in girlish glee, crossing the room to grab

Arcana's hands in her own smaller ones. "How does he feel about pink skin?"

"Flare loves everyone. If we live through this, I'll introduce you," Arcana promised.

"Flare," Kella rolled the syllables over her tongue and then squealed in delight. "Oh by the weave, Fenris, can we keep her? She's adorable *and* she has a brother. And a deerken!"

"Arcana's not a pet, Kella." Fenris spoke with the good natured amusement of someone familiar with such behaviour. "She can decide her own future. And in the meantime, we have work to do."

"The Pariah appears to be holding court two levels down from us," Caelum said. His eyes were looking off in the middle distance and Arcana realised with a start that Mirokke was missing. "Large room, lots of people. Whatever alarm Daelan spoke about clearly never went off, because everyone's lounging around drinking and eating. I can see Burke and Phase. They're... oh."

"What is it? What's wrong?" Arcana asked.

"Er, they appear to be... wow. Okay." Caelum blinked rapidly. "Wow."

"*Caelum.*"

"You know how Burke's in heat? They've let her hormones work her into a frenzy, then put her and Phase in the pit together." Caelum rubbed his head on one foreleg. "And they're watching."

Arcana stared, horrified. "Watching while Phase and Burke...?"

"Yeah. I'm getting an education, that's for sure."

"Great gods of Sorcen." Arcana rubbed a hand over her brow. "We need to get down there."

"I'm not sure you want to see this," Caelum negated. "I didn't even know half of it was physically possible."

"Once the Pariah is bored, he will send the warg in to tear them apart," Llane hissed. "We should hurry if you want to retrieve them alive."

"Good point." Kella sauntered over to Daelan and, with a strength astonishing for her small frame, slung the ex-Guardian's body over one shoulder. "Wouldn't want Daelan to be late for his meeting."

"Are you seriously going to take him with us?" Llane's nostrils curled as Kella wandered over to join them. "It's not too late for me to eat him."

Kella narrowed her eyes. "Don't you dare. He's *my* little trophy." To emphasise the point, she patted Daelan's backside in a frighteningly maternal gesture.

Caelum's tail swished back and forth, the only sign of his discomfort. "You don't think that's a little... macabre?"

"Daelan betrayed and murdered people who cared for him, and laughed while he did it. Consider this penance for those crimes." Kella jerked a thumb at the door, signalling the conversation to be over. "The quickest way down is the way we came in."

"Wrong." Arcana dropped to one knee, spreading her palms against the smooth marble flooring and exchanging her fire magic for the cool, solid stone of the palace. She felt curiously giddy, as though some invisible tether had been snapped and there was now only falling or flying. "Two floors straight down, you said?"

"That's right." Caelum flicked an ear. "Mirokke's moving out of the way. Are you sure this is a good idea?"

"Very," Arcana asserted. She looked at Kella and Llane. "Hold on to each other."

"What are you -" Kella broke off with a curse as the floor beneath them shuddered, the marble splitting as though a large fist had thumped against it. Fenris and Caelum crowded close and after a moment the other two Guardians followed suit, each crouching on the floor.

"Here we go." She shoved again with her magic, shearing clean through the marble floor. They fell, contained on a small platform barely three paces across, of which Arcana was the epicentre. She had the quick impression of what may or may not have been some sort of gaming room, then their sheet of marble slammed into the floor - and through it, directly into the Pariah's great hall. Arcana poured magic into her platform of stone, arresting their downward plummet a good five paces from the ground. The room was more than large enough to allow for it, with arched ceilings two stories high and shadowed galleries overlooking the space beneath. A dais stood against the far wall, draped in burgundy carpet and topped by a long, whitewood table. The diners were headed by a man who sat upon a throne of shimmering gold, hazel eyes bright and tousled brown hair badly in need of brushing. The Pariah, for it could be no other, was shirtless beneath a vivid scarlet vest that emphasised muscular biceps and golden skin which had been oiled to a sheen. As debris rained down from the shattered ceiling and the Pariah's guests shrieked and ducked for cover, the warlord simply tilted his chin back and looked up with narrowed eyes.

"Look." Fenris pointed, and Arcana followed the line of his arm to a shallow bowl hollowed into the marble floor. An electrified fence rose around the circumference of the indentation, the pointed sides curving inwards to form a dome that imprisoned the occupants inside. Burke and Phase writhed on the floor, unaware of the commotion created by Arcana's sudden arrival despite the fact that several large pieces of marble had dented the roof of their cage.

Arcana coughed and looked away, her cheeks heating. "Great gods of Sorcen."

"Told you," Caelum snorted.

"Who *dares* interrupt my feast?" The Pariah pushed back his golden chair and climbed on top of it, fisting both hands on his hips. "This is a sacred temple, and you are defiling it!"

Arcana peered over the edge of the platform and blinked down at the gathering. "Did he really just say that?"

"Yeah." Caelum frowned. "Just looks like dinner with a bunch of people in black robes to me - discounting the weird cage, of course."

Kella straightened to her full height and heaved Daelan's body off the platform. The ex-Guardian's limbs flipped and twisted unnaturally as he fell, somersaulting end over end only to slam into the Pariah's dining table, splattering food and wine all over the horrified diners. "We're not interrupting," Kella called, lips twisted into a rictus grin. "Just delivering Daelan to your feast as ordered."

"Cretins!" The Pariah jabbed a furious finger in their direction, seemingly oblivious to Daelan's bloodied hair mingling with his gravy. "If you're going to barge in here and interrupt, the least you can do is identify yourselves!"

Arcana flicked a glance up at Fenris. "He's not from the Timeless Kingdom?"

"That bilge rat? Give us *some* credit." Kella snorted. "No, Taelon dug him up from the Weaver knows where." She turned to Fenris and gestured at the table. "Now would be an excellent time to introduce yourself, my lord."

Fenris unfolded from his crouch and regarded the Pariah down the length of his nose. "My name is Fenris, Overlord of the Three, Guardian to the Weaver and Warden to the deerken; and these are *not* your people." He turned from the Pariah, appraising the rest of gathering. Row after row of black-hooded faces were turned towards him and though Arcana could only see shadows, Fenris' jade eyes paused as though spotting faces he knew. "I have come in the name of your queen," he announced, his voice smooth and cool. "Taelon has usurped her kingdom and laid claim to our home. The lies he has fed you are just that - fabricated tales to justify his own personal quest for power and revenge. You swore an oath to protect the Weaver above all else; to work for peace and harmony, to protect those who cannot protect themselves. Taelon and his warg care not for life, nor do they hold sacred the values we have long treasured." Fenris drew the greatsword and set it point down against the platform, leaning on the hilt. "To break your oaths is not only a stain upon our collective honour, but an offence punishable by death. It is now time to make your choice: stand for your home, or remain in Taelon's service with full understanding of the punishment that will invoke. I have been proud to live and laugh among you - but those who choose Taelon will be sentenced to death for high treason, and I will not hesitate to carry out the sentence at once."

"Shirimm!" The Pariah turned to his right and Shirimm limped out of the shadows, fresh bandages visible beneath her clothing. "Is he really that good?"

"Yes, my lord Pariah." Shirimm spoke through clenched teeth, her eyes glittering with malice as she stared up at Fenris. "If he's here, the others are dead." A murmur ran through the assembled crowd and Shirimm's face hardened. "Taelon desires Fenris above all else because he is the greatest threat to our calling."

"Hmmm." The Pariah drew a dagger from his belt, polishing it on the hem of his vest. When the steel was clean, he looked at Shirimm and shrugged. "Release the warg. *All* of them."

"And Fenris?" Shirimm had the grace to look doubtful. "Taelon specifically requested him alive, my lord."

The Pariah looked up at their floating platform, his average features twisting into an expression of pinched cruelty. "A lot of fuss for an odd looking creature, I must say. Well, Overlord, if you're as good as Shirimm says, the warg will only slow you down. And if you die - well, I suppose I'll have to hold Shirimm personally responsible, since Daelan has already been despatched." The Pariah dropped into his throne and put his booted feet on the table, one at a time. "I rather think I'm going to enjoy this show more than the last one. Best get to it, my dear. His life - and yours - are on the line."

Shirimm had gone pale, but she drew a whip from her belt. Her eyes swept the room of silent watchers, then tracked up past Fenris and at last settled on Arcana. The ex-Guardian cleared her throat, resolution turning to hatred. "Release the warg. Bring Fenris to me and kill the rest."

"You can still walk away, Shirimm," Fenris called, flourishing the greatsword. "It does not have to end like this."

Shirimm closed her eyes a long moment as howls echoed from the shadowed galleries set around the balcony. "Yes, it does."

"So be it." Fenris turned to Arcana. "I'm going to my people, to see who will stand with us."

She nodded. "I'll free Burke and Phase."

"There's a mass teleporter in the courtyard," Kella announced, shunting her arms down at the shoulders to release her twin blades. "Just through those double doors at the front of the hall."

Arcana and Fenris shared a glance, and she offered him a grim smile. "I'll meet you there."

He stepped to the edge of the platform, pausing to lock gazes briefly. "Stay safe - and give no mercy."

"You too," Arcana replied, but Fenris had already leapt from the side of their perch and disappeared. Kella flicked Arcana a salute and followed, Llane on her heels.

"All right." Caelum raised his head, antlers shimmering as they hardened into blades. Warg boiled onto the balconies surrounding the second floor, their howls echoing off the vaulted ceiling. "How are we going to do this?"

"Like only we can. Tell Mirokke to meet us at the teleporter - and stay close to me."

Caelum stepped in, his forelegs braced either side of Arcana's shoulders so that she crouched beneath the protection of his body. "I'm not sure I like that tone."

"You'll live." Arcana set her teeth and called her magic, crumbling their marble perch into thousands of tiny, sharp shards of rock. The projectiles spiralled outwards, slicing into the first lines of warg and toppling them where they stood. Caelum swore loudly, hooves dancing over open air as he plummeted straight down. Arcana wrapped one hand around the base of his left antler as they fell, swinging onto his back as Caelum smashed into the Pariah's dining table, cloven hooves digging deep gouges in the whitewood surface.

"What is *wrong* with you?" He shouted, rearing back on his haunches to extricate his forelegs from the wood. "I could have broken a leg!"

"Don't be ridiculous." Arcana slipped off his back and swept her foot along the table, kicking a half-eaten bowl of soup squarely into the face of an elegantly dressed diner hastily trying to draw his blaster. The man howled and toppled backwards over his chair, broth dripping down the front of his tunic. "You've leapt off higher things before and been fine."

"You've lost your mind," Caelum announced, yanking a hind leg free and using it to kick away a guard in cream livery. "I'm sorry I upset you before. It was an accident. Please don't kill us."

"I'm not going to kill us." Arcana rolled her eyes. "Stop being so dramatic. I'm going to get Burke and Phase - watch my back."

Caelum wrenched his final leg out of the table and lowered his antlers at the approaching tide of warg. "Do me a favour and don't take too long."

"Got it." Arcana turned and sprinted down the table. The air was filled with screams and the sound of weaponry as the warg clashed with whatever force Fenris had managed to accrue, but she dared not look away from her own task to see how heavily the odds were stacked against them. She reached the edge of the dais and leapt off, crashing into the side of the cage surrounding Phase and Burke. "Hey! Are you guys done in there?"

"Arcana?" Burke looked up from the floor, adjusting her gauze wrappings and blinking rapidly. "Where are we? What's going on?"

"You were kidnapped, remember? Just hold on while I-" Arcana cut off as the electric current sang through her body, snapping her teeth together and causing her fingers to clench more tightly around the mesh of the cage. Her body twisted, curling in on itself in a vain attempt to block out the agony arcing through her veins. Then it eased as her magic swept in, welcoming the energy, mirroring and repurposing it for Arcana's own use. Her breath came back in a rush and she dashed tears out of her eyes with the back of one hand. "Just hold on while I get you out of there."

"Did you just *electrocute* yourself?" Burke demanded, scrabbling up the side of the indented floor. "Holy shit, there are warg everywhere. And what are - watch out!"

Something tight wrapped around Arcana's leg and tugged. She lost her grip and fell forward, rapping her chin on the wire mesh of the cage as she slid unceremoniously onto the floor. Her hands scrabbled at the marble and slipped as her body was yanked viciously backwards. Arcana rolled over in time to see Shirimm ready her arm for a third wrench on the whip, the other end of which was wrapped firmly around Arcana's calf.

"Did you think I'd just let you go? We have unfinished business," Shirimm hissed, jerking Arcana forward again. "I'm going to dig your heart out of your chest with my bare hands, and after I capture Fenris, I'm going to make him eat it."

Arcana bared her teeth at the ex-Guardian. "You want my heart? Come and get it - if you can."

"If I can?" Shirimm laughed, reeling Arcana in like a fish. "I'd like to see you try and stop me. It's no wonder Fenris fled, if he surrounds himself with weaklings like you."

"The way I hear it, he left because he couldn't stand the sight of your hateful face."

"*Bitch!*" Shirimm drove her foot into Arcana's ribs, knocking the wind from her lungs. "You know *nothing*. You think you can win him? You can't." She kicked again. "You should thank me, you know; I'm saving you from the same humiliation I endured. He would've left you, right when you thought you had him. But this way..." Shirimm dropped her knee onto Arcana's chest and leant close enough to share breath. "This way you get to die thinking he actually cares."

Arcana looked deep into the other's hate-filled eyes, her breath rasping in her throat. "You're still in love with him, aren't you?"

"What?" Shirimm blinked, and for a fraction of a moment, her awful rage stuttered.

Arcana's hands shot out, grabbing fistfuls of tunic and pulling the ex-Guardian down until they were nose to nose. "Want to know a secret? He never loved you. *Ever*. So this bitter, pathetic revenge you're seeking? The only person it's going to hurt is you."

Shirimm's eyes went wide and her clawed hands wrapped around Arcana's wrists. "You hideous, venomous slug. I'm going to enjoy killing you."

"No," Arcana whispered, "You're not." And she pumped the full voltage of her magic out through her hands, sending wave after wave of vicious electricity into Shirimm's body. The ex-Guardian's mouth opened and then clacked shut, her teeth cracking under the strain. Her eyes went wide and then exploded, spraying membrane and fluid that was quickly consumed by golden lightning as hot as any flame. That same crackling energy tore through Shirimm's every cell and shredded it, levitating her smoking, lifeless husk into the air before dumping it on top of Arcana's chest. As she rolled the woman's body off, staring into blackened, empty eye sockets, her only thought was how she would possibly explain to Fenris what she had done.

"Sweet mother of mercy." Burke's voice was equal parts horror and awe. "I think her brain's leaking out of her nose."

"I'm fine, by the way, thanks for asking." Arcana sat up, shaking her hands and sending sizzling body fluids flying off into the unknown. She set to work unwinding the whip, her slimy fingers slipping over the tight coils. "Your concern is overwhelming."

"Oh please, I knew you'd be fine. Besides, Shirimm was a bitch and she had it coming." Burke waved a dismissive hand and then paused, her attention suddenly turned outwards. "Fenris is here?"

"Of course Fenris is here." Arcana pushed to her feet, kicking the whip aside with a grimace. She limped back to the cage and laid her hand over the locking mechanism. Electricity licked over her palm, frying the system and causing the door to swing open. "If this is the first time you noticed, the heat fever must have been really bad."

"It was." Phase appeared by Burke's side, his chest sheened with sweat and bruises tracking down one side of his face. Long gouges rent his chest and back, shallow and bloody - from Burke's nails. Arcana tried not to look at them, focussing instead on the Illithai's face as he said; "Needed to fix."

"Fix?" Arcana echoed. Phase frowned and chattered rapidly in Illithai.

"He says I was delusional from hormonal overload and there was no other choice but to screw me back to reality if we wanted to stand half a chance of living," Burke translated. She stepped out of the cage and blanched at the battle raging over Arcana's shoulder. "Did they... all watch?"

Arcana wrinkled her nose, a blush riding high on her cheeks. "I'm afraid so. We came as quickly as we could, but you were already busy."

"And you *knew* that?" Burke swatted at Phase's shoulder with one of her four arms.

"No choice." Phase shrugged, looking as equally nonplussed as his mate. After a long moment, a purely masculine grin tugged at the corners of his mouth. "Performing for audience better than death." When Burke made no argument, he looked to Arcana and patted his naked, bleeding chest. "No swords."

"I can fix that." Arcana turned, scanning the fracas until she spotted a group of five warg prowling in their direction. One wore a bandolier with an energy rifle holstered across his shoulder, and the other carried a double bladed warglaive in each hand. Arcana splayed her fingers and electricity arced from her palm, sweeping across the group until they were no more than piles of scorched, twitching fur on the floor. She gestured to the weaponry. "Be my guest."

Burke kicked one of the bodies aside and yanked the energy rifle free, checking the charge before raising an eyebrow at Arcana. "First her, now them? I don't think I've ever seen you so vicious."

"Desperate times," Arcana replied, and got a feral grin from the other woman in return.

"Good." Burke stepped aside so that Phase could claim the pair of glaives. "About time you hardened up. Where now?"

"There's a teleporter out in the courtyard." Arcana pointed to the tall double doors on the other side of the hall. "We need to collect Caelum and meet Fenris there."

"Sounds like a plan." Burke cocked the rifle, aimed over Arcana's shoulder and loosed a blast of icy blue energy. She smiled into the resulting shrieks and said, "Oh, I like *this*."

"Come on." Arcana trailed the circumference of the cage back towards the dais, where Caelum stood firm in the wreckage of the Pariah's dining table. His bladed antlers were a whir of motion, twisting to block weapons and heaving opponents across the room in pieces. A warg leapt in front of Arcana and she raised her hands to intercept it, only to have Phase's enormous glaive slice off the creature's head before she had the chance. Arcana wiped the resulting blood spatter off her cheek with the back of one wrist and grimaced. "You'd think they'd find a new strategy other than the eternally unhinged 'swarm everything.'"

"They're not all crazy, you know," Burke said, kicking the body aside. "There are a stack of warg in Taelon's service who are brutal, efficient and intelligent. I don't remember much from the trip here, but I do remember that."

"Smart warg? Maybe that's how Taelon and the Pariah are controlling them." Arcana set her hands against the edge of the dais and sent a current of electricity surging through the floor. The warg advancing on Caelum howled as one, dropping to the ground in a twitching mess.

Caelum spun in a panic to find the new threat, spotted Arcana and shook his great head, sending a spray of blood and gore flying. "I thought you said you weren't trying to kill us!"

"I'm not," Arcana returned, vaulting onto the dais beside him. The Pariah's expensive whitewood table was no more than splinters, the remains of the meal strewn over the burgundy carpet. Shunting a stained table leg out of her way, Arcana offered her deerken a reassuring smile. "I knew you wouldn't be electrocuted. You float."

Caelum stared, frozen in place bar for the blood dripping steadily from his antler rack. "You *have* lost your mind. I've never seen you like this."

"Of course you have." Arcana stomped her foot on the edge of a plate, caught the cutlery which flung up into the air, charged it with electricity and sent it with surprising accuracy into the back of an ex-Guardian's head. "I use magic all the time."

"Not like this," Caelum denied, following the arc of her throw. "How did you even know that was a bad guy?"

"Because she was sighting over her blaster at Llane." Arcana twisted her hand in Caelum's bloody fur and swung astride his back. "Where's the Pariah?"

"He ran like a rabbit as soon as he realised we weren't going down easy." Caelum jerked his nose towards the Pariah's golden throne, now empty and overturned.

"Coward," Arcana growled. "I'd like to have words with him for what he did to Burke."

"You know, I'm not sure I like this bloodthirsty side of you," Caelum muttered, but he began a slow and purposeful walk to the edge of the dais, picking his way over the still twitching bodies of the electrocuted warg. "Why not just fry the entire room and make this easy on everyone?"

"Because I'd fry the ones on our side as well," Arcana returned evenly.

"That was a witty piece of rhetoric which I'm terrified you found the need to respond to," Caelum declared, hopping down to the floor beside Burke. He looked the Illithai up and down. "You okay?"

"Yes. Now that my hormones aren't trying to kill me," Burke added. She reached out and ruffled Caelum's fur. "Thanks for coming - again. I won't forget."

"Save it for when we get outside." Arcana leant over Caelum's neck as the deerken began picking up speed. Burke laughed and swung onto Phase's back, sighting her rifle over his shoulder with two hands and wrapping the other two around her mate's torso. Though smaller in stature than Caelum, Phase kept easy pace, his four clawed feet sure even through the mess of blood and wine coating the floor of the great hall.

They dove into a sea of warg who slashed and writhed, spit and snarled. Some fought back to back with Taelon's black cloaked Guardians, wielding weapons with skilful ease - but most had fallen prey to their innate bloodlust, ripping and tearing into anyone around them. Fenris and Llane stood shoulder to shoulder a third of the way down the room, their greater height marking them above all others. Several of the Guardians surrounding them wore braided golden cords around their foreheads and fought former comrades with grim determination.

Burke whistled a warning as a blast of blue energy sizzled through the thickest part of the warg, cleaving a gap into which Caelum lowered his antlers and charged. The energy rifle sounded again and again, filling the room with the scent of burning flesh and a repetitive whining thump that sounded strangely like a heartbeat. Caelum's powerful head dipped and swung, his bladed antlers catching the stragglers and either slicing them open or hurling them bodily over the crowd. Arcana aimed concentrated bolts of electricity at warg who seemed most consumed by their frenzy, lessening the pressure on Guardians who fought valiantly in the face of multiple opponents. Fenris shouted something unintelligible over the roar of the battle but his Guardians began to move, converging towards

Arcana, towards the door. Fenris himself became a blur of preternatural speed, marked only by the shining flash of the greatsword as he carved his way through the warg, Kella and Llane close behind.

"Mirokke's outside. She says it's clear out there," Caelum's shout was almost drowned out by the howls and growls and screams that echoed off the ruined ceiling. "We need to get out of here before we're overrun."

"Not much further to the door." Arcana craned her neck to see between his antlers. "Kella's already there and it looks like she's got it open."

"Best thing you've said all day," Caelum grunted, twisting to catch a leaping warg in his antlers. It screamed as the bladed edges cut deep into furred flesh but continued to struggle, pushing forward with snapping jaws. Arcana laid her hand on the warg - a female's - forehead and shoved downwards, turning those snapping jaws away from both herself and the back of Caelum's neck. The creature continued to struggle, her breath hot on Arcana's arm, her body beginning to come apart on the deerken's sword-sharp antlers as she strove to twist and sink her fangs into the closest available flesh.

Clenching her teeth, Arcana dug her fingers into the warg's fur and summoned her magic. The sooner she blasted this creature, the better for all of them. As the electricity surged through her veins, the warg looked up and their gazes locked. A curious dizziness stole over Arcana and the sounds of death dropped away as time slowed to the consistency of thick honey. The feral amber light in the warg's eyes abruptly faded to soft brown, her focus sharpening until it felt she peered directly into Arcana's soul.

"Please," said the warg, her voice cool and crystalline. "Help us. Set us free."

"What?" Arcana clutched desperately at her magic, trying to rein it in but the moment was already gone. Time crashed onwards, seeming to overflow in an effort to make up for those drawn out seconds, and so too did the inevitable tide of electricity. It poured out of Arcana's fingers and into the warg, turning her movements from aggressive to convulsive as the female twitched, arched and died.

Arcana snatched her hand back as Caelum shook his great head, dismembered body parts flinging off into the fracas. Burke's energy rifle whined and thumped and suddenly they were free, surrounded by tall marble pillars and humid jungle air. Arcana slid bonelessly to the ground, racing back to the doorway as their allies came rushing out of it.

"That's everyone," Kella shouted, and together she and Llane laboured to bring the doors together.

"Wait!" Arcana's voice was hoarse and stuck in her throat. The great metal doors - solid gold, she realised as she slapped her palms against them - shut with a boom.

"Are you out of your mind? They're in a feeding frenzy in there." Kella waved a hand at the door. "Our only hope at this point is that they all eat each other."

"I can set the lock, but it will only hold until someone overrides the security code," Llane warned, his scaly fingers tapping at a command console set into the door. "Then we'll have warg all over us." As though in answer to his statement, the massive doors shuddered beneath the weight of many bodies and a wave of metallic howls echoed from the other side. Arcana took a deep breath. Kella was right; now was not the time to investigate further.

"I can seal them in." Arcana waited until Kella and Llane stepped back, then channelled her magic into the two enormous doors before her. The gold sucked in the electric current with eager delight and she wove a quick, simple binding spell to keep it circulating. Arcana stepped back from the door and stared at the bloody handprints she'd left behind. In her mind's eye, the female warg stared back at her, sighing in relief as she fried to death in the grip of that same magic.

Caelum's nose appeared over Arcana's shoulder, his furry chin dripping blood as he snuffled her face. "Are you all right?"

"I don't know." Arcana shook her head. "I killed her."

The deerken lifted his head and studied the bloody prints on the door. "Killed who?"

"There was a warg - that warg who got stuck on your head." Arcana reached up to tap the base of an antler. "She spoke to me."

"I didn't hear anything." Caelum's voice was thoughtful, though not disbelieving. "What did she say?"

"Please," Arcana repeated, ears tickling as she heard the warg's voice again in her mind. "Help us. Set us free."

"Wow." Caelum took a half step back and shivered. "Creepy."

"I know. I tried to stop the magic but it was too late. I zapped her and she died." Arcana wrapped her arms around herself and squeezed. "She looked... grateful."

"Maybe Burke's right and there *is* more to the warg than we thought. Hard to imagine when they're busy trying to eat us." He curled his head to the side, using his neck to tuck Arcana against his chest in the deerken equivalent of a hug. "I know it's weird, but you gave her the peace she clearly needed. The rest, we'll have to think about later, when we have the chance."

"Yeah." Arcana sighed. "I guess you're right."

Caelum's ear flickered and his eyes glazed over. "Mirokke says the teleporter is almost ready and we should hurry down. Also, everyone is staring, so don't freak out when you turn around."

"At the moment, staring is the least of my worries." Arcana lifted her chin to kiss his jaw, paused when she saw blood and gods knew what else matting his fur, and contented herself with a pat instead. "Come on."

The sweeping staircase at the front of the palace would have looked more at home on a temple; wide, shallow marble steps edged by carved balustrades capped in yet more gold. Rather than meet the collective gaze of the gaping Guardians at the bottom, Arcana examined the intricate carvings framing the steps as she descended. They were clearly religious, with kneeling figures offering food, wine and gifts to animalistic gods and goddesses, who were accepting in various postures that made them seem benevolent and generous. The stairs ended in a courtyard surrounded by thick flora, the closest of the trees bearing signs of recent pruning. The teleporter had been bolted to a weathered plinth in the centre of the area, with all manner of clamps and cables snaking away from the glowing pad like some nightmarish medical array.

"That thing looks awful," Arcana made a face at the teleporter as they crossed towards it. "What an affront to the natural peace of this place."

"I'll remind you to let Taelon know when we see him," Caelum replied, earning several snorts of hastily muffled laughter from the bedraggled group of Guardians clustered around the teleporter. Perhaps a dozen, maybe more, all covered in blood and wearing gold braided headbands. They parted to let her through, several leaning on their comrades for support and a few more darting wondering glances at Caelum.

Arcana walked straight up to Fenris, who was frowning down at the teleporter's command console, and laid her hand on his arm. "Where are we going?"

"*We* are going back to the *Sorceress*, to continue our journey," he replied, flashing her a flicker of a smile. "Burke, Phase and the others are going to -"

"Corrin's Run, apparently," Burke groused, jabbing a finger at Fenris. "*He* seems to think it's the best place for this ragtag bunch of losers."

"My people need medical attention." Fenris typed in a string of commands and then prodded at the star map which appeared on the screen. "Corrin's run will be a safe place for them to recuperate."

"And what do you think Taelon's going to do when he realises we've given him the shaft?" Burke made a rude gesture with her upper set of arms to demonstrate.

"The same thing he will do regardless of whether you have fourteen Guardians to assist you in defending the station," Fenris replied calmly. "Taelon will not take kindly to your defiance."

Burke crossed all four arms over her chest and glared at Arcana. "Will you talk some sense into this idiot? Screw it into him if you have to."

Someone choked in the group of Guardians but Arcana ignored the noise, raising an eyebrow at Burke instead. "I'm surprised you can even think about screwing right now, after what happened back in the temple."

"It's the heat fever and you know it." Burke waved a hand in irritated dismissal. "And if you're trying to goad me into a fight to distract me from protecting the people of Corrin's Run, it won't work. I don't care how much I want to lick Fenris all over - these Guardians need to find somewhere else to go."

There was a short silence, during which Fenris was not the only one blinking in embarrassed surprise. Then Phase stepped in, holding up both hands for peace. "No," the Illithai said. "They come."

"They *what*?" Burke's mouth dropped open.

Phase jabbed a finger first at Burke, then himself. "Dead," he said succinctly, then patted Fenris. "Alive." He finished it off with a rapid fire speech in Illitani, to which Fenris nodded agreement.

Burke narrowed her eyes, but sighed. "Fine. We owe you. Get them through before I change my mind." She glared as the assembled Guardians limped their way onto the platform. "I hope you're all willing to work for a living. And *you*," she rounded on Fenris and gave him a simmering once over. "I'll take this out of your hide another time."

"No." Arcana, Fenris and Phase spoke in perfect chorus, then looked at each other and blinked. Phase spoke quickly in Illitani as he ushered Burke onto the teleporter pad, winking at Arcana over one shoulder.

"Oh? Really?" Burke peered back at Arcana in open delight. "Good. Very good."

"Yes," Phase agreed, slinging one arm around Burke's shoulder and waving at Arcana with the other. "Good."

Arcana returned the wave, aware that beside her, Fenris' shoulders were shaking with silent laughter as he flipped the switch and the teleporter hummed to life. Blue light encompassed the group and a moment later they all disappeared, leaving the faint impression of sparkling lights and Burke's three fingered salute imprinted on the back of

Arcana's eyes. She sighed and turned to Fenris. "All right, what did he say?"

"He said that if Burke were to so much as sniff me wrong, you'd electrocute her and he wouldn't bother stepping in to help," Fenris tapped at the panel on the teleporter, his face creased with mirth.

"I would not," Arcana scoffed, and then coloured at his raised brow. "Okay, well, maybe just a little shock - which she more than deserves."

Fenris' grin only widened. "Of course."

"Stop it." Arcana poked him in the ribs, adding just enough electricity for it to tingle. "You're not immune to my wrath either, you know."

"If you fry this machine, it's a long walk back to the ship," Fenris warned, but the bite in his voice was missing, replaced instead by a low, velvet chuckle.

"You know the co-ordinates for the ship off the top of your head?" Arcana leant around his blood-soaked sleeve for a better look, and noticed he was favouring the arm. Her good humour immediately sobered. "How much of this blood is yours?"

"Some. Enough," Fenris conceded. "The warg are frighteningly vicious - I am not always faster."

The teleporter beeped again and he stepped back. Arcana frowned at the admission. "Should I be worried?"

"Only if there's more warg," Fenris replied evenly. "I intend to get us out of here before that becomes a problem."

Arcana ran her eyes down the rest of his body, but it was impossible to tell the full extent of his injuries. "We can't go without Mirokke."

"She's here," Caelum announced. Arcana turned to see the two deerken standing together, Mirokke now so corporeal that her silver-grey coat glittered in the late afternoon sunlight. Caelum's ears flickered and he cut a glance at Mirokke before looking back at the teleporter. "No, I'm not sure how it works."

"She looks much healthier. Do we have any idea how long until-" Arcana cut off as Fenris' body cannoned into hers, stealing the breath from her lungs. His shoulder curled in, shielding her from the worst of the impact as they hit the ground with a hefty thump. An explosion punctuated their fall, followed by a wave of hot air, smoke and debris. Fenris took the worst of the blast, grunting as he rolled them upright. The teleporter - and the altar it had been clamped to - had been reduced to a melted pile of slag.

"Plasma grenade," Fenris muttered, adjusting his grip so that Arcana was cradled against his chest. "The Pariah has not been idle."

"I can walk," Arcana protested, but he was already running, calling to Caelum as he accelerated until the scenery became a greenish blur. Howls went up through the jungle around them and Fenris took a nauseating leap straight upwards, narrowly missing a pair of warg who erupted out the undergrowth. Arcana clenched at his shirt as they ducked and dove through a maze of branches. "Caelum can't jump straight up! What are you doing?"

"Leading them away." Fenris' lips brushed the shell of her ear, his voice unruffled despite the stomach-knotting speed at which they moved. "Caelum will take Mirokke and we'll meet him further on."

"Caelum will jump directly to me the moment you move outside of thirty paces." Arcana leant around his shoulder and fired an arcing bolt of electricity blindly into the forest behind them. There was a boom and a crack, followed by the smell of burning wood - but no howls of pain. "And the warg will follow the scent of blood no matter where we go."

"I know that, but if Caelum can feel your emotions he can certainly track your location and stay within range. Thirty paces is not as small as you think. Apart, we can confuse the warg and perhaps buy enough time to get back to the ship," Fenris replied, calmly dropping into a narrow ravine. He slid down the wall, bracing one leg against the opposite side and plunging Arcana into a darkness that was absolute save for the soft glow of his eyes. "Do you still have that tooth?"

Arcana's hand slid inside the neckline of her jacket, closing around the familiar weight of the tooth at her throat. "Of course."

"Be ready, then." Fenris hit the base of the ravine and began jogging along it, sacrificing speed for silence. They followed the jagged line of dappled sunlight above, and the howls of the warg grew steadily more distant as the creatures were forced to backtrack to pick up their scent. With little else to do but trust and wait, Arcana laid her cheek against Fenris' chest and listened to the steady thump of his heart - which did not so much as falter when he began to ascend the ravine in a series of quick, hair-raising leaps. True to Fenris' prediction, Caelum was waiting at the top of the ravine, Mirokke serene in a shaft of sunlight beside him.

"About time," the deerken said. Arcana rolled out of Fenris' arms and raced to Caelum, throwing both arms around his neck. He nuzzled her hair and looked up at Fenris. "Slowpoke."

"Hah!" Fenris lifted Arcana onto Caelum's back and climbed up behind her. "I was carrying someone, you know."

"I carry her all the time. She's not that heavy." Caelum began picking his way through the undergrowth, picking up speed as he moved away from the ravine. Mirokke, for all her shorter legs and rotund belly, kept easy pace alongside.

"You both realise I'm right here?" Arcana prodded Caelum with one finger and then jabbed her elbow backwards into Fenris. The Guardian's breath caught and she belatedly remembered his injuries. "Are you okay?"

"For now."

Arcana bit her lip, worried at the weariness creeping into his tone. "Sorry I hit you."

"I deserved it." He wrapped one arm around her waist and drew the greatsword with the other. "You are most welcome, however, to make it up to me later."

Caelum's ears pricked up. "Hear that?"

"Yes. They are coming." Fenris adjusted his grip on both Arcana and the greatsword, twisting to look over one shoulder. "I suggested to Arcana that we use one of your mother's teeth to jump out of this situation."

"Good idea." Caelum gathered his legs and leapt nimbly over a fallen tree. "Best get started, then. The warg will be upon us in minutes."

"Minutes," Arcana repeated, releasing her hold on the electricity. It zipped and fizzed inside her veins, a final, protesting surge, then faded away into oblivion. "Here goes nothing." She slipped her magic inside the tooth, merging with the lingering energy that Caelum's mother had left behind. Instead of flickering to life as it usually did, the interior of the tooth became an enormous vault, sucking at Arcana's energy with fierce determination. She obliged, dredging deeper into her reserves in an attempt to fill the cavernous space, mingling her own essence with that of the deerken who had once owned the tooth.

A large crash sounded behind them followed by howls alongside; Caelum began ducking and weaving behind Mirokke in an attempt to shield her from the rapidly approaching warg. Had it been a few minutes already? Arcana's breath came in gasps as she poured more and more magic into the tooth, labouring in vain to fill the interior.

"Arcana? One of them has a blaster cannon," Caelum dodged aside as a sizzling lance of white-hot energy struck the jungle floor. Warg flickered in the shadows alongside and he dodged again as a second bolt slammed into a nearby tree, setting it alight. "Mirokke can't go any faster! Why are we still here?"

"It's not working." Arcana's heart hammered as she thrust her magic into the tooth. Warg crowded in from either side but there were a million tiny stars dancing across her vision, masking their faces from view. She heard the greatsword sing as it sliced the air, the sound punctuated with snarls of rage and yet more of the warg's incessant howling.

"*Arcana!*" Caelum shouted - or was it Fenris? Their voices were a blur, the jungle fading behind the sparkling starlight of complete blindness. She tried to concentrate on her heart beat but it had an echo. Her lungs laboured, no longer two but four. For a long moment she saw only white mist and the odd suggestion of shapes - then a crackling explosion split the air, filling her nose with smoke and the odour of burning flesh. Agony blossomed in her chest, someone screamed and the starlit mist turned red. Arcana's magic wrenched, the sensation so swift and deep her stomach tied in a knot - then there was nothing. Numb, blind and deaf, she drowned in a bottomless pool of energy over which she had no control.

As suddenly as it had started, the feeling vanished and cool air rushed into her lungs. Oppressive black lightened to a pale grey nothingness, as though a thick fog had fallen and obscured all features of the landscape. Arcana became aware of Caelum's soft warmth beneath her and Fenris' firm chest at her back, his breathing heavy in her ear. She began to make out Caelum's shoulders, his antlers. Arcana's own white fingers leapt into focus, curled into claws that had dug hard enough into Fenris' forearms to draw blood. She forced her hands to relax, turning them over to reveal the tooth still sitting intact in her palm.

"What happened?" Her voice was curiously muffled in the strange, grey almost-place, the air thick and still in her lungs.

Caelum cleared his throat twice before attempting an answer. "I don't know. Mirokke? Where are you?"

In response to his call, the fog receded to reveal the doe lying on the shadowy ground in front of them. Blood splattered her silver fur and pumped steadily from a huge, gaping hole in her chest.

"Great Gods of Sorcen." Arcana slid from Caelum's back, her heart flip flopping in her chest. She'd seen this before; knew the injury almost as intimately as she knew herself. Swallowing the horrific understanding fluttering at the edges of her mind, she hurried towards Mirokke. The air was like honey, dragging at her limbs until she moved with dreamlike slowness. "She must have jumped in front of the blaster cannon."

"Mirokke? Can you hear us?" Fenris struggled to Arcana's side and together they fell to their knees beside the deerken, whose dark lashes fanned across silver cheeks. "She's unconscious."

Caelum moved to Mirokke's other side, ears laid flat against his skull. His eyes were wide and deep, deep black, the stars within so few Arcana felt as though she were looking in a mirror. "Where are we?"

Arcana swallowed and shook her head. "I don't know. The tooth didn't work; the energy kept looping back on itself and I couldn't trigger the jump effect."

"Mirokke must have jumped us out." Fenris probed the edges of the wound with gentle fingers. "The laser has cauterised part of the area but this is very serious. Without help, she will die."

"I can't help her - I had to dump my magic to try and bond with the tooth." Arcana stared down at the prone deerken, an awful, twisting feeling wrenching her gut. Every second that passed felt like a lifetime as Mirokke's heart emptied her lifeblood all over her beautiful, soft fur. Arcana had seen this before - and though she knew it was useless, she unzipped her jacket and tore a strip from her top, pressing it to the wound and watching the way Mirokke's blood oozed between her fingers and over the back of her hands. Again. "I'm so sorry."

Mirokke's eyes swept open, the milky white mark of blindness gone. The deerken stared at Arcana from a pair of deep brown eyes, pinning her as effectively as any pair of manacles. Once again her senses dropped away, but this was no soft, dreamy state; it was the painful jolt of two minds slamming into each other. Mirokke's consciousness was fast and efficient, flipping through the vast well of Arcana's memories with terrifying ease. Their minds spun and danced around one another in a curious routine that seemed to both last an eternity and disappear in an instant. Arcana was released with such speed that she fell backwards, clutching at her head in a vain attempt to stop the waves of dizziness.

Fenris caught her as she fell, grunting as his body protested the strain. "Are you all right?"

Still tangled in the memories she'd been forced to relive in rapid succession, Arcana could only watch as Mirokke turned next to Caelum. His body stiffened as the blade of her mind sliced into his, their two noses touching ever so briefly before a long shudder rippled across Mirokke's belly.

"The fawn is coming." Fenris swore, a long string of fey that Arcana knew was foul from the tone of his voice alone. After a long, tortured moment he said: "I do not know what to do. We are ill-equipped to deliver a fawn here - Caelum's energy alone may not be enough to act as an anchor. With injuries like that..." Fenris trailed off as Mirokke swung her head towards him.

"Death is a doorway through which I must pass, Overlord. I do not fear the next stage of my journey, and nor should you. There are things to be done." Mirokke's voice was everything and nothing, a chiming of winds and a rushing of rivers. Behind her, a shining light appeared and began to widen, forming a doorway through which a springtime forest could be seen. The deerken gathered her feet beneath her and, leaning heavily on Caelum for support, struggled upright.

"You... *That's* where you learnt to talk. You lifted it from Caelum's mind," Fenris murmured, his eyes wide in sudden and awful comprehension. "You're going to Sorcen."

"Yes." Mirokke's voice winged by on a thousand invisible wings and Arcana could have sworn her lips curled, ever so briefly, into a smile. "There is a clearing in the forest waiting for me. Two young women will be walking nearby, carrying baskets and searching for berries. They will find me bleeding, and one will run for help. The other will stay to deliver a fawn made of starlight - and everything will change forever."

"If you're Caelum's mother, then that means -" Fenris broke off, looking between Mirokke's rippling belly and the full-grown stag beside her. "Weaver save us."

"This time it is you who must save her, Overlord - and you cannot do it alone." Mirokke turned to Caelum, brushing her cheek against his. "My son. My glorious, perfect fawn - your bond with Arcana is incomplete."

Caelum choked back tears and managed; "Incomplete?"

"Yes. The bond *must* be fulfilled if you are to emerge victorious."

"How?" When Mirokke didn't answer, Caelum stepped closer, rubbing his chest against her shoulder. "Mother, please."

"I do not know," she said finally. "I cannot see it. The journey is one only the two of you can make, across the bridge between souls."

"But we're already connected."

"Not enough." Mirokke's eyes sought Arcana's. "Will you fight for each other, my daughter of starlight?"

"Yes," Arcana whispered, tears streaming down her face. She leant forward to kiss Mirokke's nose. "I will always fight for him."

"Remember that together you are strong," Mirokke said, leaves rustling in her voice as she turned towards the portal. "Remember that the weave is eternal, and we are always together. Remember that I loved you both then, I love you both now, and I will love you both always. Do not let grief crumble your resolve - this is the way it was meant to happen." And then she was gone, the bright gate swallowing her and fading into nothing, leaving behind the faintest rattle of autumn leaves. "Be strong, my children of starlight."

Caelum lowered his head to the ground, eyes squeezed closed. Arcana waded through the strange grey nothing to throw her arms around him and together they cried, their tears mingling and hearts breaking anew. Fenris' strong arms wrapped around them both, and when he spoke, his voice was leaden with equal parts grief and disbelief. "Weaver guide you and Auron keep you, Mirokke. May you find peace beyond the weave."

"She knew from the start." Caelum shuddered with grief. "She ghosted through my memories when we met in the dreambank, and she said nothing."

"If you had known the truth, you would have tried to save her," Fenris answered. "Such a thing may have meant you never existed to stand here, now, in this moment. Mirokke is familiar with the workings of the weave in a way we will never understand. Trust her judgement."

"She left me a message... inside my head. A box. She said it will open in my dreams."

"Then your mother has more to tell you, when the time is right," Fenris murmured.

"*Our* mother," Caelum corrected. "Arcana's and mine. She made us... well, us."

"She certainly did. Even though I still have my biological mother, it was your mother who wrought me into the woman I am today, and I've always felt a kinship with her." Arcana pressed a kiss to Caelum's cheek, her heart squeezing painfully. "At least now I know why the tooth didn't work. The magic was trying to connect us to Mirokke, but she was already here."

"It should work now."

"I don't want to use it," Arcana whispered, her hands trembling.

"Neither do I, but how else will we get out?" Caelum sighed. "You heard her. We must be strong."

"Together," Arcana clarified.

"There's no other way." Caelum rubbed his cheek against hers, his fur wet with tears. "I was trying to tell you that before, when you got upset. Our place is together - wherever that may be."

Arcana swallowed past the lump in her throat. "I'm sorry I was angry."

"No, I understand. I turned your life upside down with my birth, and we never spent the time needed to right it. I was too young to realise back then but I'm not now." Caelum's mouth dropped open in a wry grin. "There's room for both of us in this soulmerge, you know. My mother just said so."

"*Our* mother," Arcana reminded him, and just like that, the tension which had plagued them since their argument in the Pariah's office dissolved.

"I am loathe to interrupt, but we should not linger here." Fenris squeezed them both a final time and stepped back, his injured arm cradled across his chest. "In fact, the sooner we leave, the better."

"Are you all right?" Arcana asked.

"I don't know." Fenris cast her an odd look, then cleared his throat and swore in fey. "Can you not feel it?"

"Feel what?" Arcana twisted to look over her shoulder but there was only the vast, grey fog around them. "I don't feel anything."

"We are between layers of the weave, where time is fickle. The longer we stay here, the quicker things run together, blending past and present and future into one. I feel as though I am seeing you for the first time all over again," Fenris murmured, his expression tender. "Grimy and huffy and vibrating with life."

"I... thanks?" Arcana smiled in spite of herself.

"I suppose it doesn't sound much like a compliment out loud." Fenris shook his head again, took a step towards her and staggered. "Weaver's grace."

"Here." Arcana swung onto Caelum's back and held an arm down to Fenris.

He clutched her tightly and vaulted up behind, pressing his face into the crease of her neck. "Thank you."

"No problem." Arcana called her magic and, heart beating double time, reached out to the tooth in her hand. It responded immediately, fizzing and sparking with the energy which she'd poured in earlier. "Thank the gods. It's working."

"Fenris is slipping," Caelum warned, dancing back and forth in his efforts to keep the Guardian upright.

"Fenris?" Arcana asked sharply. "Hold on."

His arms came around her waist, shaking as he tried to grip and didn't quite manage it. "Weaver save me," Fenris whispered, his voice hoarse. "It *is* you."

"What are you talking about?" Arcana struggled to make out his words, her attention divided between the tooth and the man whose breathing had become suddenly laboured. The air shimmered and twisted and Caelum's muscles bunched beneath them in readiness. "Fenris?"

"Hurry." Fenris' voice, no more than a soft exhalation, danced at the edge of Arcana's hearing. "Before I cannot stop myself."

The grey atmosphere distorted and fizzed, dragging them once again into the blackness of jump space. Arcana felt the scrape of Fenris' teeth against her neck, then everything went *pop* as her magic dragged them through the weave.

CHAPTER
TEN

THE FAMILIAR LINES OF THE *WANDERING SORCERESS* SWAM INTO FOCUS AND Arcana found herself staring into the empty eye sockets of Mirokke's grinning skull. Caelum sank to the floor, a boneless movement that undulated down the length of his spine until his chin rested in the fluffy tufts of his favourite rug. The movement, combined with the weight of Fenris pressing against her spine, sent Arcana tumbling with dreamlike slowness off the deerken's back.

Caelum swung his head in a belated attempt to still their fall and Arcana managed to grasp the low hanging curve of one of his antlers, saving her from a graceless, face-first plop onto the thick shag pile. Fenris' body bore down on hers, his arms loosely clasped around her waist and his head buried in the space where neck and shoulder curved together. She wriggled beneath him, trying to escape but succeeding only in rousing him enough that he groaned, tightened his grip and shoved his face further into her hair.

"Fenris," she complained breathlessly, "You're squashing me."

After a long moment his arms fell away, followed by the rest of his body as Fenris shifted sideways to flop onto the rug. "Sorry."

Arcana twisted to peer into his face, relieved when he opened his eyes and locked them with her own. "Are you all right? You're a little pale."

"I..." he shook his head, matted hair sticking to his skin. "That place. I feel as though I've been turned inside out."

Arcana frowned. "I don't feel any different."

"I am not surprised." His chest rose on a slow, shuddering breath. "Your bond to Caelum will protect you from the strange intricacies of the weave but I have no such armour."

"You said you saw things," Arcana recalled, brow furrowing. "And you tried to bite me."

Fenris winced. "Thankfully I was weak enough not to go through with it, or we'd be far worse off than we are now. The sensations I was experiencing were quite overwhelming." He bit his lip, studying her face, before adding; "Imagine seeing a thousand fractured images layered atop each other, and feeling the emotions that go with them all at once."

"That sounds like a fairly painful journey of self-discovery," Arcana joked, and was gratified to get a twitching of lips in response.

"It was certainly illuminating, but I dare not dwell - there is no telling what was real and what was not." Fenris closed his eyes and took a deep breath. "We need to get airborne before the Pariah tracks us."

"Yeah." Arcana flicked a look over her shoulder at Caelum, who had returned to his resting place on the carpet, his starry eyes locked on his mother's skull.

Fenris laid a gentle hand over hers. "Stay with him. If you give me the engine codes, I can get us into orbit."

"What about your injuries?"

"After," he assured her, leaning forward just enough that their foreheads bumped together. "I promise."

"All right," Arcana murmured. "Pre-programmed sequence thirty two will get us into space. The engine code is charcoal."

"Charcoal," Fenris repeated. "Thank you." He pressed a tender kiss to the hollow at the base of her jaw and rolled to his feet. After a moment's hesitation, he slipped the greatsword's harness off over his head, leant the scabbard against one wall and limped out of the room.

Caelum raised his head into the silence, starry eyes locked on Mirokke's grinning skull. "Hard to believe we were only talking to her minutes ago... but her head's been mounted on the wall for fifty-two years."

"Not to mention, you were inside her belly and standing next to her fully grown at the same time." Arcana stretched herself along the length of Caelum's body, fitting her head into the crook of his neck and wrapping both arms around him. "My brain might explode if I think about this too much."

"Mine already has." Caelum shuddered. "I can't believe I didn't recognise her."

"How would you have known? You never saw your mother," Arcana said gently. "I did, and I didn't recognise her."

"You saw her the once, a long time ago, and she was bleeding," Caelum defended, and then paused. "Oh."

"See?" She reached out to stroke his nose. "You're being too hard on yourself."

He blew out a long, sad sigh. "I suppose so. It's just… you even said how alike we were and she never said a word."

"Mirokke was trying to protect you. That's a mother's job." Arcana continued stroking his fur as the crystal engines whined to life, their spooling shriek rapidly fading into a background hum that was comforting in its normality.

Caelum shifted at the sound, rolling his eyes to look back at Arcana. "I can't stop thinking that our mother got shot because she was with us, then died so that I could be born, and we could bond. We never really knew each other, but she shared our lives through our memories - then went back to the exact time and place to make sure those memories happened." The hackles on the back of his neck rose. "We're responsible for our own existence."

"In a way, I guess we are." She smoothed his ruff back into place with long, firm strokes. "Then in other ways, we're not. My mother - my Sorcen mother - still bore me into the world with no knowledge of the future it held. I was raised to make my own choices, to be my own person. I grew and loved and learnt and I made the decision to intervene that day not because future me designed it, but because I wanted to." Arcana smiled sadly, her fingers lingering at the base of his jaw. "I know it's hard to accept, but this is the way things were meant to happen. Mirokke said that herself."

He cut her a glance from beneath half-mast lids. "I thought you didn't believe in fate."

"I don't - but even you have to acknowledge there's someone with their finger in our personal pot, stirring it every which way."

"Yes," Caelum said sourly. "The Weaver; and through her, us. Or is it because of us now that she had an opportunity to fiddle with the natural order of things back then?"

"We'll never know. My point," Arcana said, holding up a hand when he would have interrupted, "Is that for all the pot stirring, we've still made our own choices for our own reasons. Life's not about what happens to you, Caelum. It's about what you do with what happens to you."

"You're right, I guess. I just wish I'd known. I could've done something," he insisted. "I could've found a way to save Mirokke and spare you the pain of being leashed to me forever."

"Is that how you think I feel? Caelum, you're half of my heart," Arcana chided, stroking one ear with a finger. "I would never trade you, not for a thousand normal lifetimes."

"Not even if it meant children?"

"You're connected to my emotions. You tell me."

Caelum sighed, long and deep. "No. Not even for that."

"Exactly. I know I'm a mess, but it's not because of you." Arcana rolled off his back and crawled around so they were nose to nose. "I'm a mess because I never took the time to learn to be myself. All these years running from my old life instead of embracing the new one - that's the demon I'm carrying. But that's not *your* fault, it's mine."

Caelum stirred enough to lip at her hair. "So we do this together."

"Together," Arcana agreed, kissing the tip of his nose. "Always together."

"Plus Fenris," Caelum added, his voice so casually cheerful that Arcana snorted.

"I suppose it's far too late to pretend he's not under my skin." She smiled softly. "If I'm honest, the admission terrifies me, but yes - together plus Fenris."

"True bravery is understanding fear and finding a way to face it." Caelum flickered an ear as though listening to a voice beyond hearing, and then sighed. "I keep forgetting I'll never hear her whispering to me ever again."

Arcana reached out to capture his fluttering ear, cupping it like a caged butterfly and stroking the soft fur. "In your dreams and memories, you will – and if Fenris is to be believed and all realities exist simultaneously, then somewhere she's always whispering to you."

"I suppose." Caelum rubbed his head on her shoulder and then dropped back onto the rug. "I know I'm covered in blood and gore but I think I want to just stay here awhile."

"You want me to snug you?" Arcana ran her fingers through the fur along his neck, carefully separating matted clumps. "I don't mind."

"I could actually do with some alone time right now. Also, I'm willing to bet Fenris' injuries are worse than he's letting on."

"Me too. It's why I wasn't sure about him wandering off in the first place."

"Then go." Caelum adjusted his position on the rug and closed his eyes. "And tell Fenris if he scratches my ship I'm going to buff it out with his face."

"Hah!" Arcana thumped him affectionately on the shoulder and rolled to her feet, joints protesting the sudden movement. "I suppose that goes for me, too?"

"Of course." His tone was serene but Arcana knew better and looked down at her hands, still stained with Mirokke's blood. After a moment's hesitation she used her elbow to prod the elevator's access plate and then, once inside, the control panel. It was awkward, but it beat having to wipe down the instruments later while Caelum griped about his precious machinery.

She stepped onto the bridge as soon as the elevator door swished open, hesitating when it appeared empty. The deep black of space rolled by the front windscreen, the ship's movement marked by the swish and dip of the stars. A green light blinked steadily above Caelum's console, indicating that the automatic pilot programme had been successfully activated but there was nothing else to say that Fenris had graced the bridge at all, or if he somehow remained. Arcana paused, fingertips lingering on the cool metallic lip of a bulwark as she considered her options. Logic said he may have returned to his room but instinct pulled her forward until she noticed the soft, barely there drip of liquid on steel.

Fenris slouched in her co-pilot's chair, eyes closed and lashes stark against a pale face. Sweat and blood plastered dark teal curls to his skin, echoed by the once white t-shirt beneath his jacket. More blood trickled out the bottom of a shredded sleeve, tracing a curling path over the back of his hand to the end of a finger, where it had no choice but to drip, drip, drip onto the floor.

"Fenris!" His name came out on a rush of air and Arcana dropped to her knees beside the chair, pawing at his jacket in an attempt to reach the man underneath. Though long and lanky, his frame was cloaked in lean muscle that made the Guardian far heavier than he appeared and after a few frustrating attempts to drag him forward, Arcana summoned her magic and sent it burrowing into the armoured fabric. After a moment to allow her senses to recalibrate, she gave a swift tug, tearing through the shoulder of Fenris' jacket and shirt with ease. She dragged the sleeve off to reveal three deep, long gashes running from shoulder to elbow, burgundy blood flowing freely from within.

Arcana reached blindly beneath the chair and pulled out a first aid kit, sitting back on her heels as she flipped open the lid. Lesce's salve waited on top in a shallow metal tin which floated into the air and de-lidded itself at Arcana's magical command. She scooped a generous amount onto her fingers and began packing it into Fenris' wounds, pushing and prodding until the ripped flesh was well and truly plugged with the thick ointment. Arcana wiped her hands on the rag inside the kit and grabbed several sealing strips, tearing the packaging open with trembling fingers. Leaning forward to get a better view, she began taping the edges of the gashes together, forcing herself to be slow and careful. How much blood had he lost, carrying her through the jungle? How quickly did he heal? Why hadn't she thought to check him sooner? Growling curses through clenched her teeth, Arcana finished with the strips and bound Fenris' arm with a bandage, tying it off firmly.

With those wounds attended to, she rose up and set about looking for others; tearing through what remained of the black jacket and then his t-shirt until both were ribbons. Fenris' chest was sticky with blood and sweat but otherwise unmarred. His other arm was also clear, as were his sides. Further exploration revealed the small puncture wound in his shoulder from Daelan's crossbow bolt, which had already clotted. She packed salve into the hole anyway, taping a gauze pad over the top. It was no wonder he'd been vulnerable to the warg; the placement of the shot meant he'd been lucky to be able to use his arm at all.

Arcana hesitated over Fenris' lower half, finally settling for checking over legs and feet while they were still clothed, and breathing a sigh of relief to find everything in one dirty, scuffed piece. She allowed herself a moment to thank whatever gods were listening for that small mercy, then straddled his thighs and reached for a cloth.

Fenris' good arm shot between them like lightning, long fingers circling her wrist in a grip so firm it bordered on bruising. Arcana raised her eyes to find his glowing jade ones staring back at her - and thought perhaps it was the most beautiful thing she'd ever seen.

"That salve," he said succinctly, "Hurts like a bitch." Fenris gingerly raised his other hand, holding up a shredded piece of his clothing. "Were you planning to strip me completely naked?" Ignoring the seductive curl of his lips, Arcana dropped her head onto the solid plane of his chest. Awake. He was alive and awake. Her breath suddenly didn't quite fit in her lungs and she wheezed unsteadily. "Arcana?" Fenris' tone swung from sultry amusement to concern and through the haze of her fight for oxygen, Arcana wondered again how Brianne – how anyone – had ever thought him cold or distant.

"You were... I thought..." Her words came on breathless gasps, the strain of forming a sentence more than she could bear. Arcana's heart thumped loudly in her ears, her blood a roaring tide that threatened to overwhelm her entirely. "I can't..."

Fenris shifted beneath her and then, so fast she didn't register actually moving, Arcana was stretched out alongside him in the pilot's seat, her body tucked into the lean lines of his and her head pillowed on his good shoulder. Fenris stroked her hair in long, rhythmic movements, murmuring and whispering in fey, the cadence of his voice suggesting it was some sort of old rhyme or soothing chant. Slowly, Arcana's breathing settled and her heart returned to normal.

"It takes more than a few warg to kill me," he murmured, his chest rumbling beneath her cheek. "I am made of sterner stuff than you seem to think."

"Really? You forget that I've seen you almost dead already."

His fingers stilled in her hair for a moment, and she felt the soft press of lips on her forehead. "You taste like warg," he complained, resuming his rhythmic stroking. And then; "When I am injured, my body demands food and rest, pushing me into a near catatonic state to speed up the regeneration process. In that, I suppose I am more like the traditional vampire you might have in your imagination. Sleep helps me recover like nothing else." He paused thoughtfully. "Except, perhaps, your sister - but I suppose you'd understand her magic better than I."

"Not really," Arcana murmured, creeping her arm across the width of his chest. "I can't heal so I never had the opportunity to study it."

"You were only allowed to study what you could do?"

"And even that under sufferance." She sighed. "There was a lot of political blustering about having me privy to the inner workings of more than one Tower at a time - as though I'd run around stealing magical secrets and doing... I don't even know what they thought I'd do."

Fenris tilted his head until it rested against her own. "They are a bunch of fools."

"Flare and Lesce are on that Council," she reminded, prodding him firmly in the ribs.

"Were they back then?"

"No. Vino, Blaze and Brook were, but Lesce was still in training and Flare in the military."

His breath blew softly across her cheek. "Then I return to my previous assertion that they were all fools. Hidebound fools." Arcana chuckled, and he added; "How is Caelum?"

"About as well as can be expected." Arcana grimaced against his chest. "We've mourned Mirokke for so long, and somehow it still seems so fresh. I think now that we know her name and her face it will help, but..."

"It will take time." Fenris wound a lock of her hair around his finger and then let it slip free. "This whole scenario is so unusual, I am not sure what to say or do to offer the appropriate comfort."

"You don't need to do anything but be yourself." Arcana sighed, tracing the lines of his abs with one finger. "Caelum will come to us when he's ready, and if he needs something from you, he'll ask."

"You sound certain."

"I am. He's already included you in our number of safe people."

"Oh?" Fenris' voice was somewhere between surprised and impressed. "How many people feature in that number?"

She chewed on her lip a long moment before admitting. "Me, Flare... maybe Lesce, depending on circumstance. And you."

"Hmm. I'll take that as a compliment."

"You should." Arcana rolled partway onto his chest and propped her chin on the back of her hands. "You don't give yourself enough credit, you know. For the first time in my life I don't feel completely at sea and a great deal of that is because of you. Thank you."

"For dragging you into this mess?" Fenris snorted, his face solemn. "I hardly think tossing you from frying pan to fire, as Caelum puts it, is something worth celebrating."

"But without that, we'd never have learnt where Caelum is from. We'd never have rescued Burke, or met Mirokke, or..." she trailed off, blushed, and cleared her throat, "Or gotten to know one another. I'd still be emotionally absent and you'd be dead. For all the things that have gone awry, I'll never regret dragging you from that icy ruin. Not just for Caelum's sake, but for my own."

Fenris' breath hitched, his hands sliding from her hair to her shoulders, where they squeezed gently. "Now it is my turn to be grateful. It seems both our lives are enriched by the addition of the other."

"And Caelum."

"And Caelum," he agreed. "His sass is impossible to forget."

"Welcome to my life," Arcana drawled, then paused to examine the shadows lurking in his eyes. "What else is bothering you?"

"Me?" His eyebrows shot up in surprise. "Whyever would you think -"

"Because I can read you like an open book."

"I keep forgetting." Fenris grimaced, but there was no real disgruntle-ment in it. "Very well. First off, we are going to have to find my parents after all."

"To use the portal." Arcana nodded; she'd been thinking the same thing. "I assume the crystals came from there in the first place?"

"Either that one, or the master gate on the other side. At this stage, it matters little - the gates are joined and I should be able to arrange things to have one set of crystals remotely power both."

"Is that -"

"Dangerous?" The corner of his lip twitched. "No, so long as we're through quickly. It will likely burn out the crystals, however, making this a one way trip."

"I guess that makes sense," Arcana allowed. "In some ways that's a good thing; nobody will be able to follow us through."

Fenris nodded. "My thoughts exactly."

"All right." She considered him a minute, then ventured; "What else?"

"I... that place between the weave... it affected me." Fenris ceased stroking her hair, his face a picture of vulnerability. "I must confess a certain apprehension for what I am about to ask."

Arcana swallowed around the sudden lump in her throat. "Just say it."

"I want to sleep with you." The words came out in a rush, fingers curling as though Fenris wanted to reach for her and dared not. "Not like that, not like what you are thinking. I mean, yes, like what you are think-ing, but no, that's not what I am suggesting. I would never push, and I - Oh, for the love of -" he cut off, cursed, and then took a deep breath. "I just want to sleep beside you, to share your space while you rest. Just once in my life, I want to curl into your heat and breathe your air while the stars wheel past around us."

Arcana replayed the words over in her head and her heart thumped unevenly – but not for the reason she would have assumed. "Just *once* in your life? Are you planning to die?"

"No." Fenris squeezed his eyes closed and this time his hand curled into a fist. "But it is a distinct possibility. Taelon's army is vast and he is, himself, a warrior beyond compare. Look at us," he cracked an eye and ran it the length of their sweaty, bloodied bodies. "Defeating Taelon will take more than this. It may take everything."

"And you'd give it all... just like that?"

"To stop the slaughter and right the balance? In a heartbeat."

Arcana went cold all over. "I won't let that happen."

"There may be no choice."

"Fenris, I did not come this far to only come this far," Arcana snapped. "When I say I won't let that happen, I mean it."

"I do not doubt your resolve, or your skill. But," and he held up a finger to forestall her response, "I have always known the risks. I was prepared to give whatever was necessary when I took my oath as a Guardian and I cannot balk now. It is only… then, I had nothing to lose."

Arcana's heart faltered, her temper fading. "Fenris -"

"Let me finish. Please. As cliché as it sounds, I cannot help but think that I may never get another chance to lie beside you and listen to the rhythm of your heart while you rest. So while I realise I'm being rather forward, I have no wish to return to my room." His chest expanded beneath her. "I want to go with you to yours."

"And sleep."

"And sleep." Amusement flickered briefly in the depths of those jade eyes. "I am injured and my body will demand rest again soon. I cannot promise my dreams will be chaste, but I can promise on my honour that I will behave myself while I'm awake. I would never seek to take what was not freely offered."

"I know that," Arcana said absently. She bit her lip a long moment. "All right."

"What?"

"Yes," Arcana clarified, "I'm saying yes." Fenris blinked rapidly, his body so deathly still that she realised he'd expected her to say no and was now at a loss. She bared her teeth at him and jabbed a forefinger into one pectoral. "But I have one condition: I'm not a stormy port for a lonely warrior the night before he goes marching off to war. In fact, I've not shared a bed with anyone but Caelum for half a century. So if you do this, I expect you to make every conceivable effort to stay alive so you can do it *again*."

Fenris stared wide-eyed, and she watched the fascinating play of emotions on his face while her words sunk in. "Are you inviting me into your bed on a permanent basis?"

"Not if you're a godsdamned corpse," Arcana snapped. "Besides, you might not like my bed. It's very fluffy."

"That wasn't entirely an answer," Fenris growled, his accent thickening as his voice turned husky.

"Maybe because it was a stupid question." Arcana tossed her head, setting her hair flying. Fenris tracked the movement, moistening dry lips with a hesitant tongue. The strange giddiness that had possessed her since their visit to the Pariah's palace rose in a tide. Calling her magic, she dredged the icy core of the ship's cooling systems and traced a line of icicles on his bare chest. "I need to know how serious you are, Guardian.

I've no interest in a fly by night martyr – don't start down this path if you're going to take the easy way out and keel over."

Fenris' breathing became laboured and he watched the slow progress of Arcana's finger across his chest. "I cannot predict the future, but I swear to you I am not courting death intentionally, nor have I any plans to do so. I just..." he trailed off on a gasp as she traced a swirling, curling rune over his left pectoral. Arcana paused and he shivered. "Weaver save me, whatever you are doing, *don't stop.*"

"Stop? I'm just getting started." Arcana dropped the ice magic and sifted through the ship for the sparkling heat of the star drive. She blew warm air over the rune on Fenris' chest, melting the icicles and leaving him panting, wide-eyed. "You were saying?"

"You expect me to form coherent thoughts after *that?*"

"You're damned right I do." She placed her finger point down in the centre of his sternum, dropped the heat and called the water in the irrigation systems. Fenris writhed beneath her as each tiny, melted droplet began the slow journey over his bare skin to pool around Arcana's finger. "Talk."

"After losing Brianne and Mirokke, after visiting that space beyond the weave and-" Fenris' throat bobbed and when he did at last speak, his voice was several octaves lower, rubbing across her raw nerve endings like rich, dark velvet. "I just need to be near you. That's all I'm asking."

"No death?" Arcana dragged her finger downwards, taking the trail of water on a ponderous, wondrous journey along the ridged lines of his abdomen.

"No death," Fenris repeated, his voice hitching unsteadily as she reached the waistband of his pants.

"Good boy." Arcana paused, eyeing the rather fascinating lines that began at his hipbones and travelled beneath his belt. "I don't know what these are, but I rather like them." She traced a fingernail along one of the lines, dragging her little trail of water up and then back down. Fenris swore, his lilting, rolling fey all the more enticing for its foreign sounds. Arcana's mouth twisted sideways into a mischievous grin. "Well, at least I know how to get your attention."

"You've always got my attention," Fenris panted, a faint sheen of sweat glistening on his brow. "But this is definitely the all-consuming kind."

"Hmmm. How far to your parents' location?"

"I'm working on an estimated forty eight hours – perhaps more. Tracking through the blood bond isn't always exact," he replied, lashes fluttering as Arcana lowered her head and idly licked her way along the ridge of his scar. "Fire and brimstone, are you *trying* to test me?"

"I don't know," she admitted. "I've never done anything like this before. I just wondered what you'd taste like."

"Like warg, I would imagine - at least for the moment. Perhaps Caelum is right and you *have* lost your mind," Fenris managed. His heart was thumping so hard Arcana could see the veins throbbing in his neck. "Not that I'm complaining."

"Good."

He swallowed heavily. "What are you thinking?"

"What am I thinking? Honestly, I'm wondering why you're still keeping your hands to yourself." Arcana tilted her head to the ceiling as though searching for answers. "All this talk about beds and a spare forty-eight hours with nothing to do and yet, somehow, we're still *here*."

To Fenris' credit, his jaw only dropped open halfway. Then he scooped her up and they were gone, the bridge no more than a silvery blur. Arcana stared at her bedroom door in surprise, then reached out to poke the access plate with the grimy toe of her boot. He set her down as it swished open and she headed inside, collecting her pyjamas on the way to the bathroom. A glance over one shoulder revealed a now nervous-looking Fenris, one hand braced on the jamb as he toed the line worn in the carpet by the constantly sliding door.

He met her gaze and swallowed. "Are you-"

"Hungry? Famished. There are some snacks in the fridge over there." Arcana waved a lazy hand towards the tiny kitchenette set into one wall. "I'm showering, then it's your turn. Make yourself at home in the mean-time." And she swept into the bathroom and tugged the door closed with a decisive thump.

Alone at last, Arcana loosed a long, slow breath. Conscious of Fenris' enhanced hearing, she flipped on the hot water and made to undress, pausing when she caught sight of her reflection in the mirror. It should have been pale, but the salt white of her skin was splattered with blood and grime and a bruise was already blossoming underneath her chin. Her midnight hair was lank and hung in clumps, sticking to her jacket and tangling down the back of her neck. Arcana grimaced; *that* was a brushing job she wasn't looking forward to. She yanked off both boots and threw them in the corner, then peeled her clothing free with trembling hands, revealing more burgeoning bruises and heretofore unnoticed minor cuts and scratches. She stared at her naked reflection, critiquing average sized breasts and wishing her legs were longer. Great gods of Sorcen, maybe she *had* gone mad. They'd barely escaped the Pariah's installation with their lives, Fenris had admitted to needing more sleep - in an entirely non-sexy way - and she was worried about her bra size? Huffing a self-deprecating laugh, Arcana turned away from the mirror with a shake of her head. She certainly wasn't acting sane; not only had she licked Fenris' chest and enjoyed every second, she'd invited him into her room with all the fore-thought of a leaf blowing on the wind.

Flare would be delighted.

Arcana grinned at the thought as she stepped into the shower, her spirits bolstered at the thought of her charismatic brother. Hot water sluiced over her body and she closed her eyes, turning her face into the spray. Fenris in her bed seemed like lunacy and complete logic all at the same time – after all, he'd claimed to need her as much as she needed him. It was that need which seemed so crazy; the nagging thought that if she sniffed her skin she'd find traces of his evergreen and cinnamon scent embedded within. Snorting, Arcana snatched her loofah and set about scrubbing the blood and grime from her body, and when that was done washed her hair twice to make sure it was clean. There was something spiritually cleansing about a shower. Above and beyond the simple joy of cleanliness, Arcana emerged feeling as though she'd sloughed off an entire layer of baggage. She towelled herself dry and tugged on her pyjamas, humming under her breath as she brushed her teeth. Everything ached and her bruises stood out in sharp relief now there was no mud and grit to hide them, but it was good to feel clean. Indulging in the luxury of some moisturiser she didn't really need, Arcana dumped her towel into the laundry chute, snatched up her brush and wandered into the bedroom feeling far more relaxed than before.

Fenris had perched on one of the stools beside the kitchenette's bench and looked up as she entered, jade eyes wide as they travelled the length of her body and back again. Arcana chanced a glance down at herself. Soft, grey cotton shorts and an oversized tank top in a lurid shade of plum that Flare once accidentally splattered with bleach, leaving a randomised pattern of salmon coloured splotches along the hem and up one side. Together, the ensemble was potentially the least attractive thing she owned, yet Fenris was staring as though her pyjamas were the most incredible thing he'd ever seen.

He caught her raised eyebrow and shot upright, sidling towards the bathroom she'd just vacated. "I made snacks," he gushed, waving both hands at the little bench. "I'll be right back."

"Okay," said Arcana, but the door was already shut and the water running. She snorted under her breath. "Fenris, Overlord of the Timeless Kingdom, Guardian of the Weaver and Warden of the deerken: afraid of a woman in comfy pyjamas."

The sentiment drew a giggle from her lips and she drifted over to the bench where he'd left a plate of warmed pastries and a pot of tea. Arcana poured herself a cup, swiped the plate and took both to the bed, where she plonked down cross-legged and busied herself with eating. After a pastry and a half's worth of delicious distraction, the bathroom door swished open and it was Fenris' turn to emerge in a cloud of steam. He was rubbing at his dark hair with a towel, wearing a pair of soft black cotton pants and nothing else. The bandage over his arm was wet but still in place, the only accent to his broad expanse of leanly muscled chest save for the long, thin scar Arcana was quickly coming to adore.

"Did you save me any?" His tone was almost normal as he dropped the towel in the laundry chute and padded barefoot towards the bed.

"Of course." Arcana nudged the plate with her knee, hoping she didn't sound as breathless as she felt. "Go for it. I need to brush my hair anyway."

Fenris watched as she set her tea aside and picked up the brush. "May I?"

"Brush my hair?" Arcana asked. He nodded. She shrugged and extended the brush towards him. "Sure, if you're game. It's a mess though."

"I think I can handle it." Fenris accepted the brush and slid onto the bed behind her. A moment later Arcana felt the steadying warmth of one hand on her shoulder whilst he began working through the tangled ends of her hair.

"Forget warrioring. I've found your hidden talent," she sighed, tipping her head back as the brush slid through her hair.

"I'm glad to be good at something," Fenris chuckled, pausing to separate a particularly stubborn tangle with his fingers. "I've had almost as much practice brushing hair as I have training with the greatsword."

"Did you go through the obligatory long-haired phase during your rebellious teenage years?"

"No," he chuckled. "I used to brush my mother's hair."

Arcana blinked. "Really?"

"Yes." A small pause, then, "She's blind, so she cannot do it for herself."

"Your mother is *blind*?" Arcana twisted to see his face and after a small nod, Fenris gently turned her away so he could continue brushing. "I feel like you've spoken about her before as though she could see."

"She can see auras, so she can see in her own way - but a hairbrush has no aura and neither does a mirror," Fenris replied. "My mother was raised to be a weapon for the unseelie court. She was ritually blinded as a child to enhance her aura abilities, thereby rendering her other talents more… useful."

"That's barbaric," Arcana gasped.

"Indeed, though the unseelie king didn't see it like that. It was an honour to be chosen, apparently." Fenris snorted. "He just didn't ask my mother if she agreed."

"Is that why she joined the Weaver?"

"Yes and no. Before she met the Weaver, my mother believed she was only good for death and destruction. Now, her aura abilities make her the best Warden there is." There was pride and love in his voice and Arcana smiled. "The Weaver taught my mother to use her powers for things other than killing, and in doing so gained herself a lifelong ally."

"You love her very much."

"I do. For a long time, she and Father were all I had," Fenris admitted. "My mother taught me how to be soft in a hard world, something I am ever thankful for - even if I rarely show that softer side. If I'd followed in my father's footsteps, I'd have hit you over the head and dragged you off by your hair weeks ago."

Arcana laughed. "I'm surprised he didn't do that to your mother."

"Oh, he tried; or so the story goes." Fenris chuckled. "She thought it was rather endearing and decided not to eat him."

"True love," Arcana managed, unsure whether to laugh or not. "Considering we're on our way to meet these people, I'm not sure if I should be worried or not."

"They are strong personalities, but their hearts are true." Fenris set the brush aside and began to braid Arcana's hair with deft fingers. "I have no doubt you can hold your own." Meaning she'd have to, if she wanted their respect. Right. Fenris finished the braid and leant around her for a pastry, tugging Arcana back against his chest while he ate. "These are good."

"Told you I don't just make desserts." Arcana played with the fabric of his pants, suddenly nervous. "Fenris… there's something you should know."

"What is it?" He swallowed noisily and, when she didn't immediately continue, laced pastry-flecked fingers through hers. "You smell worried."

Arcana bit her lip and then turned in his arms, coming up on her knees so they were face to face. "I killed Shirimm. Well, I mean, I thought I'd killed her in the cell, but… I really killed her this time. It… wasn't pleasant."

"Ah. That." Fenris drew a deep breath and gave her a sad smile. "I know."

"You do?"

"I felt her light go out," Fenris tapped his chest. "And I smelt her on you at the teleporter. Also, Burke said you made her brain dribble out of her nose."

Arcana winced. "Maybe."

He raised an eyebrow. "And her eyeballs explode?"

"I electrocuted her," Arcana mumbled, hanging her head. "I'm sorry."

"Sorry? Do not be sorry. Shirimm made her own choices and in the end she got what she deserved. Come now," he reached out to tip up her chin. "She would have killed you if she could. I, for one, am glad she failed."

"Oh." Arcana blinked back sudden tears and made no protest as Fenris gathered her gently in his arms and slid them both under the bed covers. She pillowed her head on his bicep and he fitted his body around her curves, a jigsaw that connected perfectly.

"For the record, your bed is exceptional." Fenris tucked a stray strand of hair behind her ear and leant forward to kiss her nose. "This would be perfect, in fact, if I'd thought to turn out the light."

"Oh, don't worry about that." Arcana reached out with her magic and the room darkened at once. "I've got loads of practice."

Fenris sighed, a deep, rattling sound of contentment. "You are even more beautiful in the dark. Did you know that your skin shimmers like starlight? Of course you do. I've said it before." He traced a finger down the column of her throat, pausing a moment over her pulse. "Shadows and stardust. Perfection."

Arcana blushed, snuggling closer. "I forgot the darkness makes you wax poetic."

"It is my home," Fenris agreed, and by the soft glow of his eyes, Arcana watched his cheeks dimple with a smile. "My mother always said that I was never alone so long as the stars were with me."

"That's beautiful," Arcana yawned, her eyes drifting closed. "As long as you're not so busy staring at the sky that you forget to sleep."

"I don't need to watch the sky," he purred, stroking her hair. "I found something infinitely more interesting."

Arcana opened her mouth to reply but it was altogether too difficult. Fenris must have agreed because his breathing began to even out, matching the rhythm of hers – and before she had a chance to think much on *that* particular phenomenon, Arcana drifted off to sleep in the circle of his arms.

CHAPTER
ELEVEN

I⊤ SEEMED ONLY A MOMENT LATER THAT SHE WOKE WITH A GROAN, NOTICING first and foremost the blinking blue light on the holo console by the bed, followed swiftly by the ache in her muscles, and then last but certainly not least, the weight of a leg thrown across hers. Arcana frowned, watching the blue light blink steadily, trying to remember not only her own name and where she was, but whether or not the person in her bed was actually supposed to be there. She turned her head and came hard up against a long face, soft teal skin, high cheekbones and a pair of steadily burning jade eyes.

"Good morning," Fenris said.

Arcana pulled the pillow over her head. "Go away."

She heard a throaty chuckle and the weight on the bed suddenly eased, leaving her with the confusing feeling that she hadn't actually wanted him to go at all. A few moments passed and then the weight returned, followed by that hypnotic, burning gaze as Fenris poked his head under the pillow.

"I recalled Caelum once complaining about your tendency to wake up gruff," he said, daring so much as to rub his nose against hers. Arcana snarled and tried to bite the offending face, earning herself yet another chuckle. "I have food."

"Food?"

"And fresh tea."

Arcana sat up abruptly, the pillow tumbling forgotten across the rumpled quilt. Her room. Her bed. Her... Fenris? Memory flung open a groggy door in her mind and came stomping in, dropping the events of the previous day like so much heavy luggage. Arcana rubbed both hands over her face and then peeked out between her fingers. "Tell me it's chai."

"Chocolate chai." Fenris held out a steaming cup and a plate of oat cakes that had been slathered liberally with both butter and jam.

"Sweet gods above us, I love you," she breathed, accepting his offerings with ill-disguised delight.

Fenris snorted. "If I'd known it was that easy, I'd have fed you from the beginning."

"Eh?" Arcana frowned around a mouthful of oat cake, replayed her words in her head and then blushed. "Oh." Fenris watched her colour further, his grin so wicked that Arcana made the most obscene gesture she could think of. "Don't get ahead of yourself. I was talking to the chai."

Fenris let out a loud laugh, dropping onto the bed beside her and snatching an oat cake for himself. His deep teal hair was adorably rumpled, with one side stuck in gentle curls to his forehead and the other fluffed up like a dog's hackles. He finished the oat cake in two massive bites and then flopped back on the bed, indicating the flashing blue light. "That came in about half an hour ago."

"It'll be Flare. How long were we out?" Arcana washed her cake down with a sip of delightfully scalding tea, breathing deep of the chocolate tinted scent. "This tea is *so* good."

"I was down seven hours. You managed just over eight." Fenris watched her sipping, his fingers laced behind his head. "You definitely look better this morning."

Arcana patted her sleep mussed hair and humphed. "I doubt that. Only eight hours? That's barely a nap."

"Champion sleeper?"

"Twelve hours or bust." Arcana smiled and set her empty plate on the bedside table with her cup on top. She crawled up beside Fenris, dropping onto her back on the bed, and reached over to slap the flashing blue light on the holovid console. "Let's see what Flare has to say."

"How can you be sure it's Flare?"

"Because he's the only person with the code for my personal receiver," Arcana replied. An encryption code popped up in the air above the bed and she pointed to the swirling flourish in the corner of the panel. "See? That's his signature."

"Page 52, paragraph 13. Black," Fenris read aloud. "What is that?"

"Flare and I encrypt our messages with obscure references to spells," Arcana replied, drumming her fingers on her ribs. "52, 13, black.

Hmmmm. Computer: answer is Braelian's Lesser Firelance, Tuesday edition."

"*Tuesday* edition?"

"Braelian was an odd guy." Arcana winked at him as the console chimed a correct noise and the holovid came to life. "Innovative fire sorcerer, but strange person."

"Hey sis." Flare plopped into his faded green velvet armchair, flame-orange hair in complete disarray. "I hope your day's been better than mine. This godsdamned Elder business is the absolute pits." He took a deep, unsteady breath and yanked the front of his robe open, peeling off outer layers to reveal a broad, muscular chest dusted with a thin layer of curling orange hair. "And I'm bloody hot all the time. Haven't been using enough magic."

Arcana rolled her head sideways on the pillow and gave Fenris a cursory once over. "How come you don't have any chest hair?"

"Genetics," he replied, patting his smooth chest with one hand. "Something to do with the fey blood, I think, because my father's people are quite hairy."

"Huh." Arcana turned her attention back to the holo, watching Flare pour himself a firewhiskey. "His eyes are too sunken. He hasn't been sleeping properly."

"So I've been collating Gravella's research on you – damn but she was clever. Actually, crazy might be a better word. Idiot woman had a whole book full of spells she was working on, all dedicated to either permanently or temporarily expanding the amount of magic a body can contain. If the warg hadn't killed her, that blasted obsession to be the best of the best definitely would have." Flare swirled his glass, watching the dark amber liquid slosh from side to side. "I keep seeing her disappear into that stairwell, Arcana. I dream it, and it wakes me up. I see her face looking back at me when I stare into the mirror. I want to hate her, and I do, but then I can't, because I think I used her as much as she used me." He sighed. "It doesn't help that everyone seems to think we were... you know. Together."

"You *were* together, you daft idiot," Arcana muttered.

"Anyway, in addition to handling Gravella's research I'm also helping to negotiate Sorcen's entry into the Galactic Alliance." Flare grinned suddenly, a vicious baring of teeth that was nevertheless a sparkling example of masculinity. "You'll be pleased to know that after a couple of meetings, the vote was unanimous. Lesce and I are quite the team, when we've a mind to be - although I was disappointed the rest of the Council didn't put up more of a fight." He leant back in his chair, his rose gold chain of office glittering in the light. "Naturally the Alliance wants our souls, but I'm pretty sure I can convince them otherwise."

"Of course you can." Arcana waved a dismissive hand at Flare's pensive face. "Show up half naked and they'll give you *their* souls."

Fenris choked, rolling closer. "Are you always this acidic upon waking?"

"Usually worse," Arcana admitted, patting the arm that was now slung casually across her ribs. "But you fed me, so you get bonus happy points. Now shhh, he's still talking."

"I wish you were here, even if just for my own benefit." Flare slugged the last of his drink and slammed the glass down on a nearby side table covered with similarly empty glasses. "I think I'm going to lose it in this job, sis. All I do is rattle around inside either my head or my office or that blasted council chamber. Everywhere I turn are walls, and they're starting to close in. I need to get out – I need to *do* something." He grimaced and leant forward, bracing both forearms on his knees. "Listen to me, I sound like I've lost the plot already. Hmmmm. What else can I tell you? The cleanup effort is going well here and they've added some other ridiculous honorific to your title after that feat of strength with the Healing Tower. Although, I don't think Lesce was too pleased that you smashed her beloved workplace to bits. It's hard to tell the difference between her happy frown and her grumpy frown."

"True," Arcana murmured, smiling in spite of her worry.

"Well, I'm gonna go and pretend to get some sleep." Flare ran both hands through his hair and tugged at the ends, standing the tousled strands straight up as if he were charged with static electricity. On anyone else, it would have looked ridiculous. On Flare, it made him look edgy and brought out the sharp angles of his cheekbones as he sighed gustily. "Take care of yourself, sis. Oh and lick Fenris for me, will you? I asked last time but it never happened. Go on - tell me if you think he tastes like ginger-bread." Flare winked, and for a moment the familiar twinkle returned to his eyes. "Pictures or it didn't happen. Love ya."

The holovid flicked off and Arcana basked expectantly in the silence that followed. Eventually, his tone filled with indignation, Fenris said; *"Gingerbread?"*

"You're the one who kissed him, not me." Arcana shrugged, biting her lip to contain her smile.

"He kissed *me*," Fenris protested. He tried to sit up but Arcana splayed a hand across his chest and grinned.

"Revenge is going to be sweet, then, isn't it?"

Fenris gave her a guarded look. "What do you mean?"

"I mean, Flare looked pretty down, don't you think?"

"I… yes," Fenris agreed slowly, his brows furrowed. "I still don't see what that has to do with revenge for gingerbread."

"Well, if someone's down, you want to cheer them up, yeah?"

"But -"

"Just follow my lead." Arcana flipped the holocam on and smiled into the lens, well aware that the camera had an excellent view of both herself and Fenris, sleep tousled and curled in each other's arms on the bed. She gave Flare a little wave then turned to Fenris, kissing her way along his tensed jaw before licking a long, slow trail from the hollow beneath his ear to his temple. She looked at the camera and frowned. "Definitely not gingerbread. I think you're losing your touch, brother." Fenris rumbled noncommittally beneath her and as Arcana made to draw away he pounced, dragging her against his body and kissing her fiercely. The embrace was brief, but intense enough to leave her stunned and breathless as Fenris turned to look down the barrel of the camera and growl deep in his chest, flipping Flare an obscene gesture. Arcana burst out laughing and then flicked the holovid off. "That was perfect," she crowed, sitting up to encrypt the holo and send it off through space to her brother's personal receiver. "Flare's going to lose his mind."

"*I'm* going to lose my mind," Fenris growled. Arcana took one look over her shoulder at the predatory leer on his face and squeaked; a moment later she was pinned to the mattress by a very warm, very male body. Fenris' eyes raked across her, taking in every sleep tousled inch he wasn't already sprawled on top of. "I know I promised to behave, but you can't just go around licking people and not expecting a response," he rumbled. "I simply do not have that level of control."

Arcana took a deep breath, the action pressing her breasts against his chest, the thin cotton of her tank the only barrier between them. She looked up at Fenris, making sure she had full eye contact as she brazenly raked her fingers over his hips. "I'm not running."

His answering grin was slow and wicked, and Arcana gasped as he rocked his hips against her. Tiny streaks of lightning crept over her skin, centred around the sudden, delicious tension curling in her core. Fenris lowered his head and captured her lips, a long, teasing kiss that drew a whimper from Arcana as she melted beneath him. He nipped at the corners of her mouth, one hand sliding over her bare leg, across her shorts and underneath the hem of her flimsy tank. "Is this okay?"

"Yes," Arcana whispered, breath catching in her throat. Fenris kissed her again, a languorous melding of lips and tongue, his hand shaking as it crept further up the cage of her ribs.

One fingertip brushed the underside of her breast and he rasped against her lips, "Now?"

"Yes." Arcana gasped into his mouth, arching her back as he cupped her breast, kneading gently.

"And now?" His thumb traced over her nipple, a slow, torturous circle that was answered immediately by a throbbing down lower.

"Yes." Her hips bucked of their own accord and Arcana tightened her grip on the waistband of his cotton pants as he ground against her a second time. "Great gods above, yes."

Fenris' kiss became hungry then, his tongue demanding. Arcana responded eagerly, shifting her legs so that he was better cradled between them and dragging her nails over the lean musculature of his back. The thick length of his erection pressed immediately against her core, hard and hot through the layers of clothing between them. He growled into her mouth, fingers tightening on her breast and sending jolts of pleasure flitting through her bloodstream. Arcana moaned, digging one hand into his hair while the other began to slide south.

Just as her fingertips brushed the base of his spine, the door to her room swished open. "Arcana, have you seen Fenris? I want to ask him about the – oh." Caelum paused, ears flickering uncertainly. "Don't worry, I found him."

"Caelum." Fenris sighed, dropping his forehead onto Arcana's and closing his eyes. "Your timing, as always, is impeccable."

"Okay now *that* time was definitely sarcasm," Caelum declared, "But in my defence, I wasn't expecting to find you here."

"Neither was I." Fenris removed his hand from beneath Arcana's top and rolled sideways, propping himself on one elbow and pulling her against him. "And yet, here we all are."

"Clearly my ability to block you out is working exceptionally well." Caelum looked at Arcana and wrinkled his nose. "Sorry. I shut out last night after Mother - I didn't think you'd be - sorry."

"It's fine." Arcana covered her face with both hands to hide the burning of her cheeks. "Just pretend I'm not here."

Fenris tugged gently at her wrists. "There is no cause to be embarrassed."

"Not at all," Caelum agreed. "I'm the one who walked in without checking for a sock over the door handle or whatever it is you're supposed to do."

"A sock?" Fenris tugged again at Arcana's wrists but she stayed firmly behind her palms.

"Something Flare said once. What would I know? I'm a virgin, and I don't wear socks," Caelum said cheerfully. "Although honestly, when you think about it, we don't have any door handles either."

Arcana groaned, wishing the bed would swallow her, and pressed the heels of her palms harder into her eyes. "CAELUM. WHAT DO YOU WANT?"

"Oh! Well, I wanted to ask Fenris' advice on what happened with that warg. I'm wondering if Taelon's using some sort of magic to control them. Like a binding spell or something," Caelum said, sounding thoughtful. "Also, you left your satchel in my room. I figured Fenris would want to check the portal stones over." A weight dropped onto the bed near Arcana's head, and her nostrils filled with the scent of chocolate and burnt sugar as he nuzzled the back of her hands. "You really don't need to hide from us. We're inside of you."

Fenris spluttered and choked. "*Caelum.*"

"Well, shit. That's not what I meant," the deerken protested. "I meant inside your heart. Part of you - we're part of you. Please, Arcana." There was no mistaking the desperation in his voice. Very, very slowly, Arcana lowered her hands and looked down the length of Caelum's soft nose to his dark eyes, the galaxies within swirling anxiously. "I'm sorry, I really am. I know this is difficult for you."

"Difficult?" Fenris stiffened, leaning over until Arcana's entire field of vision was filled with a distorted view of their joint concern. "Are you all right? Did I hurt you?"

"I'm fine. Really, I'm fine." She waved them off and sat up. "Just... fine."

"Tea," Caelum commanded, and less than an instant later Fenris was offering a fresh cup of chai, worry pinching his brows and making his bedroom hair even more puppyish than before.

"I said I'm fine." Arcana sighed and accepted the tea, sipping gently to restore her equilibrium. "I told Fenris he could share my bed."

"I rather got that impression, considering he's in here and still breathing." Caelum's voice was relieved and amused simultaneously. "Did you tell him about that weird thing with the warg lady?"

"No," Arcana admitted and, realising the deerken had no intention of leaving, launched into a swift retelling of the incident. She looked up at Caelum once she was finished. "I can see why you'd think of a binding spell, but you're talking about something big enough to enslave an entire race. I'm not sure that's even possible."

"Taelon is a Rukkha, the same race as my father. They have no magical abilities to speak of." Fenris shook his head, brow furrowed. "And the warg's mindless craving for death and destruction has been legend long before Taelon sought to weaponise it."

"Well, Taelon's pulling their leashes somehow." Caelum stomped one hoof in frustration. "There's more to this than we're seeing, I know it."

"Agreed." Arcana straightened, fingers tightening around her cup as realisation struck. "And whatever it is, he wants Fenris for it."

The Guardian in question stood and stretched. "Taelon wants to make an example of me. I am the face of the Weaver's defiance - Shirimm said as much."

"No, it's more than that." Arcana stared into the depths of her tea, as though it would reveal what she instinctively knew to be true. "A head on a pike is far more demoralising than parading you around while you're still breathing. He's going to too much trouble to keep you alive."

Fenris paused in the act of rummaging through the fridge. "As discomforting a thought as that is, you have a point." He frowned. "What would Taelon possibly want from me?"

"If you've got no idea, we're not likely to." Arcana took a long drink of her tea and then set the cup aside, dragging over the satchel that Caelum had deposited on her bed. She reached inside and pulled out the first of the pale blue portal stones, turning it over to admire the milky white striations. "These really are lovely."

"Lovely and notoriously fickle." Fenris spoke around a chunk of cheese, drawing a circle in the air with one finger. "The crystals work together to form a circuit. If one is so much as chipped, the entire triad ceases to function. Setting them back into the portals may be a long and fiddly process."

"Could Taelon want you for your knowledge of the portals?"

Fenris jammed the last of the cheese into his mouth and chewed thoughtfully. "It is possible," he conceded at last, "But highly unlikely. I know as much about the portals as Taelon does – perhaps less, given he and Murtagh were once close friends."

"Something's obviously changed since Taelon first surfaced." Caelum tilted his head to the side, eyes narrowing in thought. "Something precipitated by your reappearance, even?"

"Perhaps. When Taelon first invaded the Timeless Kingdom, he sought to kill me." Fenris patted his scarred chest for emphasis. "It was only after we clashed with him on Sorcen that... sweet mercy."

"What?" Arcana set her tea aside as the Guardian dropped onto the edge of the bed. "What is it?"

"You," Fenris whispered, half to himself. "He doesn't want me at all - he wants *you*."

"Me?" Arcana fisted one hand on her hip. "That doesn't make any sense."

"It does," Fenris insisted. "Algae would've sung your praises like a bird in a gilded cage, and the fact that you come with your own deerken is like icing on the cake. Taelon came to Sorcen for me, but struck a bargain with Algae for all of us - a very convenient front for his own plans."

"Okay, let's say you're correct. We escaped Sorcen and traipsed across space to Corrin's Run, but the wanted poster wasn't for me, it was for you," Arcana reminded him.

"Yes, because you are an unknown quantity, solitary and almost impossible to track. But after Sorcen, Taelon knew we were travelling together, and I am a far easier target for him to acquire." Fenris began ticking items off on his fingers as he spoke. "He can find me through the blood bond, through the warg, through his stolen Guardians, through the wanted posters that were likely put in place during the months I was missing, and through cleverly laid traps like Corrin's Run. And if Taelon has me, not only does he have the means to demoralise the resistance but he also has a way to control *you* – and through you, that enormous power of yours. Think what chaos he could cause with your magic at his disposal."

Arcana frowned. "Like I'd do anything Taelon asked me to."

"Not even if my life hung in the balance?"

"Well..." Arcana trailed off. Even before she'd dared to acknowledge a romantic interest in Fenris, she would never have sacrificed his life – they'd demonstrated that well enough on Sorcen. And now? She shivered. "Shit."

"As you say." Fenris bit his lip, looking down at Arcana with a frown. "If Taelon is tracking me to get to you, then I am endangering you simply by being here."

"No. Oh, no." Arcana leant across the bed and thumped him on the arm. "Don't you dare."

"What?"

"I am endangering you. I shall forthwith remove myself from your company and go on this ridiculously suicidal venture all by myself." Arcana set her palms beneath her chin and fluttered her eyelashes. "Don't try and stop me, fair maiden, for my mind is made up. This sacrifice of extreme masculine stupidity is my right as an eternal jerk and I shall hereby abandon you to swan mournfully across the galaxy to my inevitable death alone, save for the giant dick growing out of my forehead."

Fenris' jaw dropped. "I do *not* sound like that." Arcana shoved him hard in the chest and earnt a growl. "Stop that. I am not leaving."

"Bullshit." Arcana shoved him again and Fenris caught her by the wrists, dragging her into his lap.

"I am *not leaving*," He snarled, the muscles standing out in his neck as he flashed fang. "Even if I chose to ignore the fact that the Weaver sent you to me, or that Mirokke told us all to stay together if we wish to succeed, I couldn't leave. I have no wish to leave."

"You said-"

"It was an observation," he snapped, jaw clenched.

"An *observation* that's going to get you thumped." Arcana struggled but Fenris held firm, leaning close enough that their foreheads brushed.

"Before you start throwing punches, I might remind you that neither of us are in good enough shape for this," he hissed, fangs poking out over his lower lip. "And if you really want me to kiss you that badly, just ask."

"I don't," Arcana glared up at him, her breath slicing through her lungs.

Fenris' mouth slid into a feral grin and her rage immediately turned into a very different kind of heat. "Liar," he murmured, crowding her with his body. "Your scent is all around me."

She yanked at her arms, summoning her magic, but Fenris spun and moments later Arcana was pinned to the bed, his hands slamming hers against the mattress and his lips hard and hot against her own. She growled into his mouth and shifted but Fenris bore down, his hips shoving against hers with a lack of mercy that sent shivers of excitement up Arcana's spine as she kissed him back with everything she had.

"Well, now I know how you two wrecked the greenhouse," Caelum said conversationally. "You're as bad as each other."

"Indeed we are." Fenris' breathing was ragged, his teeth snapping together only moments from her throat. "I have never had anyone infuriate me like you do."

"Feeling's mutual. Hungry?" Arcana pressed her flesh against his fangs. "Go on. Do it."

"Can we *not* kill each other?" Caelum said to nobody in particular. "I'd prefer not to clean up guts this early in the morning."

"He can take it," Arcana growled, whilst Fenris simultaneously announced: "She's not made of glass." Then they both pulled back, and he raised an eyebrow, and she snorted a laugh - and just like that, the tension dissolved as though it had never been.

Caelum swished his tail. "So... the plan is to go full postal because you know the other one is strong enough to handle it?"

"That is the definition of having an equal." Fenris loosened his crushing grip and brushed his lips across Arcana's forehead. "If you cannot be yourself – all aspects of yourself – then what is the point?" He cupped her face in his hands and kissed her, gentler though with no less intent than before. "I have never been in a situation where I can think, or feel, or be myself until I met the two of you. I did not know I was capable of the depths of emotion which Arcana draws out of me." Fenris narrowed his eyes, locking that burning jade gaze with her own. "And despite what she seems to think, I'm not about to give it up."

"Good," Arcana snapped, but she saw the twitch of his lips and knew the fire had faded from her face. "You scared me."

"I am sorry. It was not my intention." He tilted her head to one side. "The bruise underneath your chin is truly glorious, by the way."

"You can thank Shirimm and her whip," Arcana muttered.

"I shall do nothing of the sort." His fingers tightened around her jaw and Fenris leant in to trail a line of heartbreakingly tender kisses across her blemished skin.

"This is better than all the books in my Lord Whitehaven collection put together," Caelum announced. "You guys are great!"

Arcana twisted out of Fenris' hold to glare at him across the bed. "I'm going to ignore that comparison to your pithy romance novel fetish and assume you're feeling much better this morning." She examined his sleek fur with a critical eye. "Did you sleep?"

"Some. Mostly I just tried to sort out the entire mess in my head, which is how I ended up in here babbling about warg and crystals. Also, someone bled all over the floor in the bridge and I am *not* cleaning it." Caelum shook his shoulders in emphasis, the artificial light glinting off the velvet whorls on his antlers. "I'm heading down to the greenhouse in a bit but I'd like to refine the ship's course first – for which I need to borrow tall, teal and shirtless here."

Fenris blinked rapidly, one hand splayed over his chest as he mouthed 'tall, teal and shirtless' over again. Arcana snorted a laugh and reached out to scrub the fur between Caelum's ears. "Take him. I might head to the study and record a real message for Flare." She shot a glance at Fenris. "Dinner once you're done?"

"Certainly." He kissed her and rolled away, eyes twinkling. "I shall look forward to it once I've finished scrubbing my offensive leakage off Caelum's floors."

"I *knew* it was you," Caelum grunted, poking the door panel with his nose. "Come on then, before the water goes cold."

Arcana watched them leave, shoulders shaking in silent amusement, then padded into her closet and pulled on an ancient knit jumper. It had long since stretched out of shape and hung listlessly off one shoulder but it was her favourite, and more than warm enough for schlepping about on the ship. She wandered down the hall and into the comforting familiarity of her study, taking a moment to breathe in the scent of books and ink. It reminded her of many things; home, childhood, her mother painstakingly showing Arcana how to make paper and bind it into journals for herself. She smiled and sat at her desk, pulling her current journal out of the drawer and turning it over in her hands. It would've been simple for her mother to magic up a book for her daughter, being a nature sorceress, but she was adamant that a journal be made by the author's own hands - and even now that Arcana could use her own magic to streamline the process, she chose to do most of it exactly how her mother had shown her.

She set the journal on the desk, flipped it open, snatched up her favourite pen and began writing; mindless scribbles and notes that helped ease the kinks in her psyche and bring clarity to her thoughts. When her hand began to cramp from effort, Arcana carefully set the journal aside and returned the pen to the jar from whence it came. Her heart was in those pages; hopes, fears, dreams and often disjointed accounts of her life. And for every illustration, every fractured note she made, her heart beat stronger and her soul felt lightened. More than anything else in her life, it was a sort of magic that could not - and did not need to be - explained.

Which left only the task of recording a message for Flare. Arcana sighed, tapping a few keys on her desk console. Now that she'd poured her thoughts into her journal her head was much clearer, but that didn't change the fact that unlike the message in the bedroom, the one she was recording for her brother now was going to be far less pleasant. She watched pensively as the holovid camera popped down from the ceiling, the sensor automatically directing it at her face. Arcana stared into the machine's soulless eye for a long moment, then tapped the record button and forced a smile.

"Hey you," she said by way of greeting. "I'm not sure I'm ready to talk about all this yet but I don't know when I'll next get a chance to send you something, so here goes." Arcana gave a quick rundown of the events at the Pariah's palace, managing not to stumble over her decision to perform the ritual of absolution. When she was finished, she leant back in her chair and hugged her knees to her chest. "It's been a long journey, but we're heading to the Timeless Kingdom now and things could get messy. Really messy." She took a deep breath and grimaced. "I know you said the negotiations were going well, but... get into the Galactic Alliance as soon as you can. If we can't put a lid on Taelon, the warg will keep spreading and killing - and the safest place will be Alliance space. With any luck this will be a quick in and out style scenario and we'll be drinking firewhiskey and laughing in a week or so. But if not..." Arcana trailed off and sighed. "Remember how much I love you, Flare. Always and forever. Stay safe, brother."

The holovid clicked off and Arcana sat in silence until Fenris appeared in the doorway. He'd pulled on a dark chocolate t-shirt that offset his complexion beautifully and wore an easy, breath-taking smile. "Brooding?"

"Something like that. I don't like the idea that we're being shaken around inside a giant dice cup," Arcana replied. She tapped a finger on the leather cover of her journal. "This helps, but... I don't know. I suppose prior to this I assumed Taelon was like a naughty child throwing a tantrum because he was denied his favourite toy. But now it's clear that he's actually very organised, with an army and commanders and an overall plan that we probably need to thwart, only we don't know what it is."

Fenris crossed the room to perch on the side of the desk, covering Arcana's drumming fingers with his own. "I feel the same way."

"You do?"

He nodded, brushing a thumb over her knuckles. "It's why I am so determined to get back into the Timeless Kingdom. If we can sneak in and cut the head off the snake..."

"Then the body dies and the babies are easier to squash. I suppose that makes sense. But you sent the other Guardians back to Corrin's Run with Burke," Arcana pointed out.

"They were mostly injured, but Taelon will not take Burke's defiance lightly. The extra help may keep her alive. And perhaps, if Taelon's focussing on Corrin's Run, he will be paying less attention to this," Fenris thumped his chest, "And therefore us."

"Making it slightly more likely that we'll succeed?"

The corner of his lip twitched. "Indeed. It is a fool's errand, Arcana. Are you sure -"

"I promised," Arcana shrugged. "And we've had this fight already. Unless you want to explain to your mother why I handed your backside to you rather than letting you rest?"

Fenris tipped back his head and howled with laughter. "No, that simply would not do. Very well, I shall keep my mouth closed on that particular topic. In fact, speaking of my mother, we have about another twenty seven hours to go – unless you want to do something to speed us up."

Arcana pursed her lips in thought, running some calculations in her head. "I can more than halve that time if I overcharge the star drive. But… is that such a good idea?" She brushed a hand over her bruises and gestured at his bandaged arm. "Neither of us is in particularly fabulous shape right now."

"Well…" Fenris worried his lower lip with a fang, then finally admitted; "As I said before, I heal quickly, particularly when rest is involved. The sleep we have managed thus far has done wonders; if I can garner another five or six hours, I'll be back at full strength. It is your injuries which give me pause."

"Oh." A frown pinched Arcana's brow. "Well, unfortunately I heal at the same snail's pace most other people do. That said, my physical injuries are minor, so shouldn't cause us too much trouble."

"What about your magic -"

"Eh," She cut him off with a careless wave of her hand. "I didn't use anywhere near enough to cause a problem."

Fenris' eyes roved her body, mouth tight. "You look thinner than you should be. You certainly felt it."

"Magic takes energy," she reminded him, unable to stop the blush which crept up her neck. "But I promise, what Flare told you on Sorcen was true. As long as I get in a few good meals before we leave the ship, I'll be fine."

"If you say it, I believe you," Fenris said, but his eye carried a glint which told Arcana he'd be making sure she ate until she was fit to burst. "I have no wish to cut short the peaceful time we might steal together, but I cannot shake the feeling that the sooner we move, the better."

She stared down at the desk, where he was still playing with the knuckles on her hand, and considered. "I have to be careful how I handle the star drive, but I can get us there - wherever there is - in a little over thirteen hours."

"Caelum suggested as much."

Arcana clicked her tongue at him. "And here I thought you were just visiting for the pleasant conversation." Fenris chuckled and flicked the side of her palm playfully. "All right, I'll do it – but that means you're cooking."

"Deal." He pushed to his feet and headed for the door. "I'll be waiting."

Arcana returned his smouldering expression with a rude gesture and closed her eyes, savouring the sound of Fenris' laughter as she spread out her magic in search of the star drive.

CHAPTER
TWELVE

Arcana stood at the edge of the airlock and stared out at the frosted landscape, screwing up her nose. The planet itself was beautiful, albeit in a stark kind of way. Short, thinning grasses gathered in clumps across the grey bones of the earth, each jutting boulder and swaying blade limned with ice that glittered like diamonds.

"It had to be wintry, didn't it?" Caelum came to stand beside her, his fur lengthening as a chill wind blew into their faces.

"Yeah. At least it's not snowing." Arcana drew her thick coat closer, walking down the gangplank to look up at the dawn-grey sky. "Looks like a clear day."

"I hope so." Caelum followed her down the ramp and squinted into the rising sun. "According to the surface scan, the planet is covered in deep clefts and valleys - some of them big enough to hide a whole city. The data I checked showed water and plant life, so I'm assuming the lower terrain will be a better climate."

"I hope so," Arcana muttered, shoving both hands in her pockets. "Because this is going to suck otherwise."

"Says the woman who is immune to freezing? I should think it is the rest of us who will find this unpalatable." Fenris appeared at the top of the ramp in a thick, pale grey coat and a navy scarf. He plucked at it uncertainly as he stomped down the ramp to join them, his black armoured trousers once more tucked into sturdy black boots. "I have never worn a scarf before."

Arcana's jaw dropped open. "What, never?"

"What if I get in a fight? Someone might strangle me with it." He frowned at Arcana's neatly arranged scarf, fussed with the loose tails of his own and then threw both hands in the air in disgust.

"Like this," Arcana laughed, tugging the scarf free. "Watch: fold it in half. Over your head - bend, dammit - over your head, and then pull the loose ends through the loop. Now get it in the right place," she settled the knot over the hollow of his throat, "And tuck the ends inside your jacket. Easy. See?"

"Hmmph." Fenris reared his head back in an attempt to get a better view and then shrugged. "If you say so. I suppose I'm less likely to be garrotted this way."

"So dramatic." Arcana ducked under the access ramp and flipped aside a small panel, revealing a console set into the ship's exterior. She keyed in a string of commands, closed the panel and watched as the airlock irised shut. A moment later the shields hummed to life, barely visible around the hull of the vessel.

"It's a shame we never followed up on that cloaking device," Caelum muttered, his long winter coat swaying as he looked back at the ship.

Arcana reached out to tug on the tuft of fur which had grown beneath his chin. "You say that now, but I seem to recall you didn't think it was a worthwhile deal at the time."

"Well, when someone's asking for one of your testicles as payment, it's a lot less appealing," he replied, flicking his tail in irritation. "I just wish we'd gone back afterwards and liberated the parts ourselves."

"Someone wanted one of your testicles?" Fenris asked, his lip curled in distaste.

"For their soup, no less. I don't think so," Caelum snorted, scuffing at a tuft of grass. "That was one of the shadier leads Burke gave us."

"It was a long time ago. I like to think we're smarter now," Arcana said, closing her eyes and breathing deep. Magic swirled through her body, her veins filling with ice and snow. "The solar array wouldn't have worked properly with a cloaking device anyway. As long as there's no earthquakes the ship will be fine until we get back."

"No seismic activity out here," Caelum replied. "I checked already. What magic did you get?"

"Ice," Arcana answered, tugging one hand out of her pocket. She clicked her fingers and a puff of snow shot into the air. "I could have had the earth, but it's cold and I couldn't be bothered fighting."

Fenris watched the conjured flakes fall with a delighted expression, then frowned. "Do you dislike the ice magic?"

"No, it's just harder to control. Air is actually the worst - I try not to use that unless I absolutely have to." She tilted her head as he shuffled his shoulders uncomfortably, trying to settle the greatsword into a better position beneath his coat. "Wouldn't you be better off with the greatsword *over* your jacket? It looks ridiculous sticking out the back of your neck like that."

Fenris grunted, pushing the hilt to one side. "Too unwieldy - I'd want the coat off in a fight."

"A fight?" Arcana looked off into the distance, her brow furrowed. "We got here in record time. Are you still expecting an ambush?"

"Honestly? Yes." Fenris shrugged, offering a sheepish grin. "I'm always expecting an ambush. That way, I am never surprised if it actually happens." He pointed to the edge of the rocky shelf. "We go that way."

Arcana swung onto Caelum's back and winked down at her Guardian. "You were surprised when *I* ambushed you."

"You ambushed me in my own room," Fenris purred, vaulting up behind her and wrapping both arms around her waist. "I didn't think I was in enemy territory and so wasn't prepared."

Arcana leant back against him, savouring the warmth of his breath on her cheek. "More fool you, then."

"Indeed." Warm lips on her ear, followed by the faintest scrape of fang. "Perhaps, were you to try it again, I'd be much better equipped to handle the situation to our mutual satisfaction."

"Do you two *mind*? I just ate," Caelum complained, moving to the edge of the shelf where Fenris had indicated. The embankment below was quite steep and after a moment's ear flickering consideration, he began picking his way down on cautious hooves. For all his best efforts, the incline became so steep that Caelum slid the last few feet on his haunches, arriving at the bottom in a flurry of dust. "That was a little hairier than I anticipated. Everyone all right?"

"I think so," Arcana replied, glad all over again that Fenris' arms were tight around her. As the one with the most precarious seat, he'd have been the first to fall.

"I too am fine," Fenris reassured. "Keep going in this direction."

Caelum trotted obligingly across the stringy grass and entered a grove of withered, wind-tossed trees. The branches streamed out fantastically, the bark a stark white. Arcana reached up as they passed, running her fingers along the slippery surface of a low hanging leaf as large as her palm.

"Are they dead?" She wondered, entranced by the way her own stark white skin blended into the foliage.

"I don't think so." Caelum slowed to a walk, gliding through the maze of tree roots which snaked across the ground. "It doesn't make me any more confident about the hospitality of the place, though. The sort of wind that can permanently change a tree's shape has got to be nasty. "

"The valleys may be different." Fenris pointed towards the bowl of a particularly gnarled trunk - beyond which was only thin air. "We are close now."

Caelum came abreast of the cliff and Arcana gasped. A verdant valley spread out below them, steam rising into the early morning. Watery winter sunlight glittered off both the rocks and the ribbon of a river that peeked out between a shock of jewel-green trees. Arcana followed the line of the river to a grassed area at the far end of the valley, where the portal was clearly visible atop a paved platform.

"Great Gods of Sorcen, it's beautiful," Arcana breathed. "Hard to believe it was recently the scene of a battle."

Fenris peered over her shoulder, his cheek cool as it brushed against hers. "We need to go down. My parents are almost directly below us."

"Guess I need that earth magic after all." Arcana exhaled the icy cold on a cloud of frosted breath and as she inhaled, focussed on the hard packed earth beneath their feet, drawing the quiet strength of the planet into her body. A second later, she waved a hand and the cliffside groaned, rearranging itself so that Caelum stood on a small rounded platform jutting out from the edge. "Ready?"

The deerken widened his stance and tensed. "Ready."

"Here we go, then." Arcana waved her hand again and the platform began to move, sliding down the cliff face with a soft grinding sound. The air warmed rapidly as they dropped lower and by the time the platform made ground level, Arcana had pushed back the hood on her coat and was craning her head to get a better view of the multitude of fruits and blossoms hidden underneath the thick branches. "Incredible. It's like a completely different planet," she murmured, sliding from Caelum's back and stepping down onto the lush grass.

"Fenris?" A soft, querulous voice preceded a willowy figure out of the trees. "Thank the Weaver, it *is* you!"

"Hello, Mother." Fenris jumped to the ground, crossed the space between them with three quick strides and enfolded his mother in a tight embrace. She was a tall woman with impossibly thin limbs and a narrow, pointed face which was beautiful in spite of the vicious scar that slashed right through the place where her eyes should have been. Her skin was a pale, dusty blue and pointed ears poked up on either side of an elegantly wound bun. Tendrils of navy hair curled becomingly around her temples and she wore a long indigo gown whose voluminous skirts trailed along the forest floor behind her.

"Oh my dear, sweet baby. I'm so glad to see you - I was incredibly worried." She leant back to cup Fenris' face in her hands and Arcana could see at once where he'd received his long, flowing limbs and high cheek-bones. The woman was breathtaking and entirely fey, moving with an otherworldly grace that made Arcana jealous even as she shivered. She'd met a few fey in her travels and each and every one of them had possessed that same fluid way of moving which made them seem beautiful and harmless - right up until they bared their fangs and tore your throat out. As though sensing the tone of Arcana's thoughts, Fenris' mother stiffened, her head turned unerringly in their directions. "You are not alone, my son?"

"No, Mother." Fenris turned his mother in their direction but she pulled out of his grip before he could complete the movement, stepping forward with her palms extended.

"Please excuse my lack of manners," she cooed, crossing the grass in their direction. "My name is Vivienne."

"It is an honour to meet you, my lady." Arcana tugged off her gloves and moved to place her hands inside Vivienne's. "I'm Arcana and this is Caelum."

"My lady? No need to be so formal, my dear, not at all. Vivienne is fine - oh my. By all the threads that bind us," Vivienne gasped, her head turning from Arcana to Caelum and back again. "Your auras... they are partially joined. Incredible."

Arcana smiled, her discomfort slipping away in the face of the other woman's open delight. "Caelum and I have a soulmerge."

"It is truly beautiful. But... incomplete?"

Fenris shot Arcana a quick look. "You can see that?"

"Of course. It is like a half-finished garment. Sewn enough to be struc-turally sound but with enough loose threads that it would be barely practical."

Arcana tilted her head, considering. "Interesting terminology."

"Too many centuries with the Weaver," Fenris muttered sourly. "You can tell the older ones by their fabric analogies."

"Oh, piffle. Mayhap we're just not all as jaded as you, hmmm?" Vivienne moved closer to Caelum, again offering her hands palm outward. "Greetings, sweet one."

The deerken pushed his nose into her palm. "It's a pleasure to meet you."

Vivienne leapt backwards, one spindly hand pressed to her mouth to catch the tiny squeak which emerged. "You can *speak*?"

"Yes," Caelum answered, the corner of his mouth tipping into a grin.

"But how is that so? I have never - of course, the soulmerge. What might you be capable of if it were completed, I wonder?" Vivienne inched back towards Caelum, her hands once again extended, and smiled as he huffed into her palms. "Truly incredible."

"Mother, whilst I understand your fascination, may we talk about this inside?" Fenris' face wore a mixture of resignation and amusement. "I don't know about Arcana, but I should like to divest myself of this coat."

"Yes, of course! I'm sorry, I get a little carried away sometimes. Please, follow me." Vivienne tangled spidery fingers in the skirts of her elegant gown and turned away, gliding into the forest.

Fenris held out an arm to Arcana and she linked her elbow through his, raising an eyebrow in silent question. "Trust me," he whispered, his lips tickling the shell of her ear. "She can be difficult to keep track of."

Shrugging, Arcana allowed him to lead her through the forest, Caelum following close behind. The trees were packed tightly together and in the shadow of the cliff face, Vivienne blended into the environment until she was almost impossible to see. The further they progressed, the harder Arcana squinted until eventually she gave up, unsure whether the other woman was even there at all.

"Great Gods of Sorcen," Arcana breathed, her skin covered in a wave of goose bumps. "I hate to say it, but she's very, *very* fey."

"Indeed." Fenris chuckled and patted her hand. "Don't worry, I won't let her eat you."

"Comforting," Arcana muttered. She'd have liked to ask more questions but the trees ended abruptly, revealing a narrow open area at the foot of a sheer cliff. Vivienne stood waiting in a lone shaft of sunlight, beyond which was a boulder that partially concealed the narrow mouth of a cave.

"There you are." Fenris' mother smiled as they approached. "Your father is inside, dear. Follow me."

The cave was shallow and at first glance seemed empty, but a fold in the rear wall hid a short tunnel which opened out onto a much larger cavern - big enough to house a makeshift sleeping pallet, some woven cushions and a small cooker. Light poles had been driven into the rock in three places and provided a cool white glow very similar to the wintry daylight outside.

"Darling, are you awake? Rytan?" Vivienne moved to the sleeping pallet, where a large form hulked beneath a threadbare blanket. She reached down to shake the sleeping man, then emitted a squeak of surprise as the blanket was thrown over her head and she was bundled onto the floor. "*Rytan!*"

"Viv?" Rytan was a full head shorter than his son with a build similar to Taelon's - broad shouldered, short legged and muscles on his muscles. His skin was a dirty shade of khaki and his head of dark olive hair more like a mane than anything else. He wore a thick bandage over one eye, another across his shoulder and a third around the stump of his left leg, which had been severed just above the knee. Balancing precariously on his remaining leg, Rytan twitched the blanket off his wife and winced. "Sorry, love. You startled me."

"Really, Rytan, that foolish fight reflex will get us both killed one day," Vivienne snapped, regaining her feet with quick, irritated movements. "Fortunately for you, we have guests."

"Eh? Where - Fenris!" Rytan's craggy face split into a broad grin, displaying tusk-like fangs on both the bottom and top rows of his teeth. He covered three paces' worth of cave floor in a single hop and snatched his son into a bone cracking hug. "I knew you'd turn up eventually." Rytan leant back to give Fenris a cheerful once over. "You look well."

"I wish I could say the same in return, Father." Fenris crossed both arms and gave his father a critical once over. "What happened to you?"

"Warg happened to me." Rytan reached down beside him for a long stick, which he propped under one arm like a crutch. "Worthless bastards chewed my leg clean off. If I hadn't already lost my eye, I would've seen - bless the Weaver, is that a deerken?"

Fenris ran one hand through his hair, his expression somewhere between resigned and amused. "Yes, Father. This is Caelum, and over there is Arcana." He waved his free hand at the bandaged warrior. "This is my father, Rytan."

Caelum dipped his head. "Pleased to meet you."

"Did that deerken just *talk?*" Rytan squinted at Caelum out of his one eye and then turned to his wife, who was meticulously poking strands of twilit hair back into her bun. "Viv?"

"Soulmerge," Vivienne answered absently.

"Soulmerge! With this creature, I assume?" Rytan stumped forward, pinching Arcana's sleeve between two fingers and lifting her arm into the air. "You're rather lovely under all that black and white, aren't you? Bit fragile looking, though." Rytan leant a little closer, nostrils dilating as he took a deep breath. "Hmmmmmm. I can smell my son all over you, little biscuit. I hope he didn't break any bones when he took you to bed."

"*Father!*"

Rytan jiggled Arcana's arm, eyes glittering with challenge. "Don't take that tone with me, son - you're the one getting down to it with a biscotti. Honestly, I could snap these pretty little limbs with one hand. No offence intended, of course," he added, patting her shoulder in a conciliatory manner. "My son is a strong lad. Anything less than a warrior simply won't do."

"Arcana is a warrior," Fenris' cheeks were dark with embarrassment but the fire in his eyes was real as he drew himself up to his full, considerable height. "She's handed my own carcass to me on multiple occasions. Convincingly."

"Really?" Rytan snorted in disbelief. "What type of warrior are you, then, little biscuit?"

"I'm a sorceress." Arcana gave Rytan a smile that dripped sugar, well aware her tone was anything but sweet. "And for the record, while your son might have finagled his way into my bed, he's got a lot more work to do if he's interested in getting my pants off. Which, incidentally, is none of your business."

Fenris coloured further but his father gave a loud, startled bark of amusement. "Oh ho! Viv, did you hear that? She's got a little bit of fierce in her! Making him work, are you, sweet morsel?"

"Rytan, leave the poor woman alone," Vivienne smacked her husband's hand until he released Arcana and took a wobbly step backwards. "She is our guest and, as she so concisely pointed out, her relationship with Fenris is none of your concern. Not everyone is a barbarian, you know. I'm certain our son has perfectly good reasons for not having made love to her yet."

"Weaver save me." Fenris dropped his head into his palms, the dark blush now creeping down his neck. "Someone remind me why we came here again."

In spite of her irritation, Arcana found laughter bubbling in the back of her throat. She laid a gentle hand on Fenris' arm, noting the way both his parents watched the gesture like hawks, and said; "We came here because it was the next logical step in finding the Weaver. You said so yourself."

"Yes, but I did not expect to be harangued about *this*, of all things,"

Fenris growled, dropping his hands to glare at his mother. "There is more to a relationship than sex, mother. You taught me that."

"Of course, dear, but really - I can see the way your auras yearn towards each other. I would certainly have succumbed by now." Vivienne's scarred brow puckered. "Have your tried taking your clothes off in front of her? Maybe she's not getting the right idea."

"Father. Mother. Please," Fenris begged. "The Weaver is in danger. There are far more important things at hand than the complicated situation between Arcana and myself."

Complicated. Well, that's one way to put it. Arcana's thought thoughts cut off as Rytan appeared in front of her, lips peeled back from his tusks as he snarled into her face. "Is there something wrong with my son, little biscuit? Is he not good enough for you?"

"A moment ago you were insinuating that I wasn't good enough for him," Arcana said, her voice cold. "Now it's the other way around." She twisted one hand into the rough bandages crossing Rytan's chest and, since he was far too burly to bend upon her whim, used the leverage to drag her face close. "Fenris is kind, calm, and strong. He is the epitome of grace, with a canyon-wide sensitive streak he goes to great pains to conceal and a delectable sense of humour. He's a natural leader, an incredible warrior and a man of infinite patience and respect - and he is *mine*, in whatever capacity it is that we have chosen for each other, not because he knows where to jam his cock but because he's the first man I've ever met who doesn't think the way to a woman's heart involves taking his pants off and flapping his erection at her." Arcana bared her teeth, her grip on the bandages tightening until she could feel Rytan's heavy heartbeat beneath her forearm. "Fenris has a job to do and the Weaver - *your* Weaver - sent me to make sure he has the opportunity to do it. It's my duty, my choice and my *honour* to be the one who watches his back and I'll do it no matter what you think."

Silence filled the cavern and after a long, frozen moment, Arcana felt gentle fingers at her waist and allowed Fenris to tug her away from his father. "I'm sorry," he murmured, jade eyes wide. "I did not think he'd behave this way."

"He loves you," Arcana returned and if her voice was a little terse, she couldn't quite bring herself to care. "And I didn't forget the caveman warning."

The corners of his lips tilted ever so slightly, and then those pianist's hands cupped her face and tilted it upward. "You meant those things you said."

"Of course," she replied, her own lips tugging in response. "Surely you could smell it."

"I could." His gaze flickered down to her lips and back again, the glamour sliding over her skin with such seductive warmth that Arcana knew he was longing to kiss her. Instead, Fenris cleared his throat and, without breaking eye contact, said; "Are you satisfied now, Father?"

Rytan grunted. "I'd be better convinced by action over word."

"Oh?" Arcana turned in Fenris' arms, twining her fingers through his. "Were you so busy listening to my words you didn't even notice the action? And here I thought you were a warrior."

"What?" Rytan frowned, then looked down and gawped in surprise. His body was encased entirely in stone from waist to toe. "Weaver's grace!"

"Anything else?" Arcana asked sweetly.

He stared in silence, then looked up at Vivienne, who somehow detected the motion and shrugged. "You brought it on yourself, dear. It would serve you right if the poor woman left you there all night."

Rytan roared with laughter at that, then held his hand out to Arcana. "I like you, biscuit. Good show."

"Thank you." Arcana waved a dismissive hand and the rock receded, taking the tension that had permeated the cave with it. She stepped forward and returned Rytan's forearm grip - gentle in spite of his blustering. "Pleased to meet you. And it's Arcana, not biscuit."

"Arcana," Rytan repeated, his eyes twinkling. He transferred his gaze to his son. "I can see why you like her."

"You don't know the half of it," Fenris murmured, but there was laughter in his tone, and he dropped his head to press a kiss into Arcana's hair.

"In the spirit of goodwill, we've bought you a gift." She flipped the lid on her satchel and drew out the portal crystals, offering them in cupped palms. "I believe these were once in your safekeeping."

Vivienne's face softened as she bustled forward, closing her hands over Arcana's. "The biggest gift you could ever bestow is the return of my son. I feared -" she paused and cleared her throat. "Nothing else matters to a mother but her child's safety."

"He's been worried about you, too," Arcana said softly. With a gentle squeeze of her spindly fingers, the older woman blew past her, throwing her arms around a startled Fenris and burying her face in his neck. Arcana raised her eyes to Rytan and extended the crystals towards him. "Well? Shall we start again?"

Rytan chuckled. Instead of taking the crystals, he gripped both her elbows and leant forward to bump his forehead against hers. "If you guard those stones half as well as you guard my son, they are safest with you." Without another word, he stumped past her in pursuit of his wife.

Caelum edged to her side as she tucked the crystals back into her bag. "These people are nuts," he muttered, his lips tickling her ear. "I can't decide if they love us or hate us."

"They've been through a lot and Fenris is their only child. Don't forget they thought he was dead." Arcana smoothed Caelum's fur as she watched Fenris embracing both his parents, his face etched with relief now that the confrontation had passed.

Vivienne spoke in the same lilting fey her son often used, her soft voice so like a song that Arcana fancied she could listen to it all day and not get bored. The more she spoke the more Fenris' lips curved until, when he at last replied in the same tongue, his face was wreathed in a grin that was so beautiful it hurt Arcana's heart to witness it. Rytan watched them both with a squinty, suspicious expression she assumed was his standard face, throwing in the odd rumbling refrain in his deep, gravelly voice. After a few minutes Vivienne shook her head and began patting Fenris down, her hands moving over his face and shoulders with a practised air.

"Mother," Fenris chuckled and pressed a kiss to Vivienne's forehead. "I assure you I am still in one piece."

"Let me be," Vivienne returned, continuing her inch by inch inspection. "I cannot see you for myself, remember?" Spidery fingers paused at his coat. "Did you not say you were too hot in this?"

"Yes, but I know you're only reminding me so that you can feel over my chest for injuries," Fenris returned, his tone laced with laughter.

"Off," his mother demanded. When he hesitated, her voice took on a sharp edge and she tugged imperiously at his collar. "*Off.*"

With a long suffering sigh, Fenris was convinced to remove his coat, his scarf, the greatsword, a dark grey knit jumper and then, much to Arcana's amusement, the navy t-shirt underneath. "Mother," he grumbled, his clothes piled in a heap on the floor and his cheeks dark with embarrassment as his chest was bared. "I am not stripping everything off for your amusement. I -"

"What is this?" Vivienne gasped, her palms splayed over the raised ridge of Fenris' scar. Long, pale blue fingers found the topmost corner and traced it to the opposite hip, stopping when it disappeared into the waistband of the armoured trousers he wore. "*He* did this."

"Yes."

Vivienne clenched her hands in her son's pants and for a moment, Arcana worried she was going to yank them down to see how far the scar actually went but after a few seconds, she smoothed her way back up the ridges of Fenris' abdomen and across his pectorals, checking for any other injuries she may have missed on the original journey. "It is not like our kind to scar so."

"I'm afraid that's my fault," Arcana murmured. "When I found Fenris, he was dying. I had to seal the wound to stop the bleeding."

Rytan blinked. "With stone?"

"With fire," she answered quietly. "My sister did the rest with her healing magic but the scar is permanent, I'm afraid."

Vivienne let out a little sob and Fenris quickly covered her hands with his own. "Mother," he murmured, tugging her close. "Don't cry. I am alive, and I bear this scar with pride because Arcana gave it to me."

The wail which burst from Vivienne was so otherworldly that Arcana flinched, but the noise was soon muffled as she buried her head in Fenris' chest. The half-naked Guardian wrapped his mother in an even tighter embrace, his face pained as he rubbed her back with soothing hands.

"When we lost contact with you, your mother went crazy," Rytan grunted, poking Fenris in the shoulder to get his attention. "Whatever instinct possessed you to jump into that destabilised portal, hold it tight. I'd never be able to live with her like that on a permanent basis."

"Rytan," Vivienne sniffled, her delicate brow pinching as she leant backward. "You're being unkind."

"I don't think so, Viv - you didn't see you," Rytan returned, shaking his head. "It was terrifying."

"*Really?*" Vivienne's purr took on a sharp edge and her face tightened. Fenris bent to murmur in her ear and the tension immediately eased. "Don't be silly, dear. Will you be staying the night?"

"If it's not too much trouble." Fenris shot a glance at Arcana and she nodded once. "We need to return to the Timeless Kingdom as soon as possible, but there is much to discuss before then."

"Of course it's no trouble." Vivienne slipped out of her son's embrace and clapped her spidery hands in delight. "I'll get started on the stew right away."

"Come on, son." Rytan slapped Fenris on the shoulder and started limping for the door. "We should find something to add to your mother's pot, or it'll be just mushrooms and water - and I'm bloody tired of mushrooms and water."

"What a foolish thing to say," Vivienne huffed. "You don't even eat the stew."

"No, but I eat you, and you eat the stew, and then you taste like mushrooms all the damned time," he growled. "Time for a change."

"Rytan, stop and think a moment," Vivienne shrilled, her hands flapping desperately. "You're in no shape to hunt."

"No, but Fenris is!" Rytan grinned, watching as his son hastily dragged his t-shirt and then his grey jumper back on. Barely had Fenris' head appeared through the neck hole than his father shoved him cheerfully in the direction of the greatsword. "Come on, come on."

"Rytan!"

He threw a broad wink at his wife, uncaring that she couldn't see it. "Don't worry, love. We'll be back soon."

Fenris snatched up the greatsword and slid the scabbard over his head, bending to brush his lips across Arcana's before rushing down the tunnel after the stumping footsteps and off-key humming of his father. She watched him go with amusement, fingers smoothing Caelum's fur for several minutes after they were out of sight. When she turned away she found Vivienne's scarred face turned unerringly in her direction.

"Vivienne?"

"Oh, sorry, my dear. I shouldn't stare, I know, but your aura really is fascinating." Vivienne's smile was brighter than cut jewels. "This all must seem so strange to you."

"Having some old dude with one leg try to kill us, then a blind lady stripping her son almost naked? Nah," Caelum drawled. "That's pretty much a daily occurrence where we come from."

Arcana turned wide eyes on the deerken but Vivienne tittered a laugh. "Rytan may be brutish at times, but his intentions are well meant. In fact, his reaction has warmed my aching heart - before you arrived, my mate wished only to sleep and drink. I feared his mind would never mend."

"I'm not sure it has," Caelum muttered, still watching the tunnel where Rytan and Fenris had disappeared. "He's a lunatic."

"I suppose it must appear that way to you - I know when I first met Rytan, I was often confused by his actions." She smiled briefly, crossing to the small cookery unit and setting a chopping board on the bench. "I wish he was gentler at times, but he is driven by emotions he is not always able to express. His culture, like my own, had its faults." Vivienne's face pinched with sadness as she palmed a knife large enough to be a dagger and began chopping mushrooms. "I tried to make sure Fenris did not inherit that same disconnection."

Arcana watched the blind woman's hands blur with speed, her stomach knotting unintentionally. Unable to look away, she managed; "He didn't. Well, he tries to keep himself aloof, but for some reason that doesn't work with me."

"No," Vivienne sounded amused. "It appears not. However, I feel that is less to do with my parenting and more to do with… other things."

"Other things?" Arcana repeated, raising an eyebrow. Realising the other woman couldn't see the gesture, she elaborated; "What do you mean?"

"Oh, you know." The fey woman paused her gut-wrenching dicing and vaguely waved the knife around. "Things."

A frown puckered Arcana's brow. "You mean because I'm immune to his glamour."

"Not exactly," Vivienne hedged, tapping the flat of the blade against her chin in a contemplative manner. "I mean… well, it's not really my place. It is for Fenris to say."

"You saw something in our auras," Arcana guessed. When the other woman's brow lifted in surprised, she added; "I'm a sorceress. What seems mystical and is easily misunderstood by others stands out to me."

"Ah, yes. I suppose it would." Vivienne returned to her mushrooms, the knife slow and purposeful as she gathered her thoughts. When she spoke, her voice was soft and pensive. "Yes, I saw something in your auras. Many things. Fenris, however, must be the one to explain them."

"He's keeping things from me?"

The knife clattered onto the block and Vivienne whirled to catch Arcana's hands in her own. "No! No, dear. No. He doesn't know what he knows and for this, we must give him time. I realise we're not particularly well acquainted but I ask you to trust me on this - or, failing that, trust what you know of my son's honour."

"All right." Arcana relented with a sigh. "I believe you."

"Excellent." Vivienne smiled, patting the back of Arcana's hand in a maternal gesture. "Now, while I think of it - did a deerken named Mirokke ever find her way to Fenris? I sent her after him with Brianne, a fellow Warden, and I had so hoped…"

"She found us." Caelum's nose drooped and his face shuttered. "She died."

"Oh, no." Vivienne gasped, her hands fluttering to her face. "And what of the fawn?"

"The fawn survived." Arcana swallowed around the lump in her throat and reached out to stroke Caelum's fur. "Mirokke sacrificed herself so that he could live."

"He? Where is he? A fawn so young requires specialised care and -"

"I am he," Caelum interrupted. In halting words, he gave the Warden a quick run-down of what had happened since Mirokke and Brianne appeared at the base of the portal, ending in her death. When he was finished, Vivienne took a step back, her sightless face travelling the length of him and back again.

"The weave is a mysterious, wondrous thing," Vivienne said at last, her voice heavy with awe. "Now I look, I can see the similarities in your aura. Mirokke has given us a miracle."

"It doesn't bother you that he's a good fifty years old?" Arcana asked.

Vivienne chuckled. "I have been a Warden for a very long time, my dear. I'm well versed in the unusual nature of the weave and the odd behaviour of deerken in particular." She cocked her head, a delicate, bird-like motion. "That, and auras never lie."

"Do you..." Caelum hesitated, visibly gathering himself. "Did she ever say who my father was?"

"No. Mirokke was beyond the ability to communicate clearly when we found her," Vivienne sighed, her face sad. "Nevertheless, I'm glad you got to spend time with your mother."

"We didn't know until the very end, and by then it was too late for much of anything," Caelum said, his voice trembling.

"If not for the beauty of the weave, you would never have met her at all," Vivienne said softly, her spindly fingers combing through the fur behind his ear. "See also the gifts, Caelum."

The deerken lowered his head and butted it carefully against the waif-like Warden. "You're right. Thank you."

"Of course." Vivienne smiled. "You are most welcome."

"Here you are, my love, fresh off the blade." Rytan's voice boomed down the tunnel and Arcana winced, covering both ears with her hands. Vivienne turned to meet her husband as he stumped enthusiastically across the floor, Fenris trailing behind him. "Come on, come on, show your mother what we caught!"

"Your aura trembles." Vivienne's brow pinched as she accepted a small mammal from Fenris. "Did your father feed from you?"

Fenris braced as if for a blow. "He said you've been doing it by yourself."

"There was little option; he wouldn't get out of bed." Vivienne snatched her son's wrist and turned it upright, running a thumb over the two neat puncture wounds she revealed. "I knew it! Rytan, for shame - he's not staying overlong and can't afford to lose too much."

Rytan shrugged. "It was Fenris' suggestion, not mine."

Arcana bit her lip, recalling the blood Fenris had lost barely forty-eight hours earlier. She peered up into his face, noting it was frightfully pale. "Do you need to replace what you lost?"

"No." He offered her a weary smile. "A good sleep, and my body will regenerate. Remember?"

Arcana nodded, but Vivienne was not so easily convinced. She waved an angry finger under both male's noses. "You should both know better! I was doing just fine before and I will continue to do just fine once you're gone."

Fenris' face set into a mulish expression. "If you let him drink too much, you'll be too weak yourself - and we all know where that leads, Mother. I won't have it."

"He made me promise to feed off the local animals from now on," Rytan muttered, making the sort of face one might wear when presented with a plate of soggy, boiled cabbages. "Which I'll do, seeing as I'm up and about."

"It's not necessary."

"It is," said Fenris firmly. "You know it is."

Vivienne bared delicate, pointed teeth. "Ooooooh you are making me so frustrated!"

"Only because he's right, Viv," Rytan grumbled. "If something happens, you're our only defence."

Vivienne humphed and set about skinning and cleaning the small mammal on the bench, her knife flicking and flashing with such skill that Arcana wondered exactly what sort of vision her aura abilities allowed. Trained as a weapon, Fenris had said – and whilst Vivienne's familiarity with the knife certainly suggested such, Arcana found it hard to equate the idea with the elegant, willowy dream that Vivienne appeared to be. She cleared her throat. "Do you need a hand with that?"

"No, my dear," Vivienne's voice was gruff. "Let me work off my temper on this poor creature, or I'll be forced to eviscerate someone I care about - which I'd really rather avoid."

"All right." Arcana flicked a glance at Caelum, who after circling the cave several times had dropped to the floor against one wall, head propped on his forelegs. Moving to his side, she shucked her thick coat and folded it neatly by the sleeping pallet, adding her scarf and knit jumper to the pile.

Fenris appeared beside her, dropping the greatsword on top of the pile even as he bent to peer into her face. "You smell worried."

"Perhaps." Arcana examined his pallor and sighed. "You look so pale you're almost as white as I am. Are you sure you didn't give too much?"

"You're worried about me?" When she nodded, his lips twitched into a bemused smile and he tugged her body flush against his. When he spoke, his voice thrummed in his chest, sending frissons of awareness through Arcana's body. "Careful now, you might have me thinking you're becoming emotionally invested."

"Hard for someone without emotions," she teased, meeting his gaze and shivering as the glamour poured hot and velvety over her skin. "The Weaver will hardly thank me for delivering you weak and bloodless, will she?"

"Hmmm." His voice had dropped into the timbre which threatened to steal all Arcana's good sense. "Sleep will fix it."

"So you're going to wander around like this for, what? The next few hours?" She sighed. "It's a shame you can't just bite me and replace what you lost."

Fenris froze, tongue darting out to moisten his lips. "You should not say such things."

"Why not?" Unable to resist the heat seeping from his body to settle in her veins, Arcana tilted her head to one side. "We can't, of course, but there's nothing wrong with thinking about it."

He hissed in a breath, eyes blazing a line down the column of her throat to the pulse point in her neck. "Thinking about it is madness when you know we can't."

Unsure why it was important but unable to let go, Arcana breathed; "But you want to."

"Weaver's grace, I want to." Fenris shuddered and leant in, fangs scraping gently across her skin. "If this is you trying to prove my own resistance again, I fear you've chosen a poor time."

"I can't help it," she admitted, fingers curling in his jumper. "I want you to."

Great gods of Sorcen, but that was the understatement of the century. In spite of the dangers involved, every cell in Arcana's body cried out for Fenris, insisting it needed whatever his bite could give her - what that was, exactly, she didn't know, save it was he and he alone who could provide. She knew she should have been afraid, but the result was entirely the opposite, with heat pooling low in her body and goosebumps raising over her flesh. Her heart seemed to beat in time with his and her thighs clenched in response to every sweeping scrape of his fangs across her skin. Arcana was vaguely aware of Caelum's shout of alarm as Fenris' embrace tightened, one steely arm supporting her weight while the other angled her head better. His tongue traced a circle on her neck, marking, warning, and she buried her hands in his hair, holding on tight -

"Fenris! No!"

Vivienne's voice was followed by a wash of cold, and Arcana staggered as she was abruptly released. She fell against Caelum, whose solid weight kept her mostly upright while she wiped water out of her eyes and gasped for breath. When she could see again, it was Caelum's starry-eyed face in front of hers, his neck twisted back on itself so he could peer at her where she rested against his haunches. "Are you okay?"

"Yeah, I…" Arcana shook her head, sending water everywhere, and then grimaced down at herself. "Gah."

"What happened?" Vivienne's voice preceded her appearance as Caelum drew back a little. The Warden's delicate brows were furrowed, her spindly hands still clenched around the empty bucket she'd no doubt thrown over them. "I felt a surge in Fenris' aura and Caelum started shouting."

"I tried to bite Arcana," Fenris said wearily.

"Well, why shouldn't you?" Rytan stumped closer, squinting at them through his one eye. "She didn't look like she was protesting."

"No… but…" Fenris hesitated, then sagged and told his parents about the last time he'd bitten her, followed by the resulting decision that it would be foolhardy to attempt such a thing again. His eyes were full of guilt as he raked them over Arcana, the glamour whispering across her skin for a fraction of a second before Fenris tore it away. "I've done well so far, but just now…"

"Huh." Rytan stumped closer, leaning in towards Arcana until Fenris snarled a low, clear warning. The Guardian froze, raising an eyebrow at his son before straightening up to a safer distance. "Tell me - How does she smell to you?"

Fenris' chest expanded, his hands clenching into fists. "Chocolate and burnt sugar," he said finally.

"That," said Rytan, "Is not what I meant and you know it."

"I…" Fenris' breath caught in his lungs and quite suddenly he was panting, avoiding Arcana's gaze and muttering under his breath in fey.

She glared. "Universal galactic, please."

"I'm not sure -"

"Fenris."

He squeezed his eyes shut. "When the temptation is upon me, she smells like water after a week in the desert. Air after suffocation. It is almost overwhelming. But after what happened the last time, I dare not. It is as well Mother thought to stop us."

"Viv?" Rytan turned to his mate. "Can you see what's going on?"

"Some," Vivienne admitted as she set the bucket down. "There is a lot of magic in her veins. Too much." The Warden's hands fluttered through the air like butterflies, framing the immediate space around Arcana. "It ripples in the air around you, as though you are pulling from the very essence of the weave."

"And it's in my blood," Arcana said slowly, nodding. She glanced to Fenris to find his eyes open and contemplative. "Which is what we already assumed. I think Fenris' buried powers absorbed it and tried to use it to escape."

Vivienne looked alarmed, and a moment later crossed to lay her hands flat over Fenris' heart, brow furrowing in concentration. "Yes," she said at last. "But the barrier is tied to his life force. Too large an influx of your blood, and thereby your magic, would kill him." She tilted her head to the side, comprehension dawning on her lovely face. "That's why you haven't taken her to bed; you don't know if you can control yourself."

Fenris' expression twisted and he looked at the ceiling, as though searching for some sort of rescue. When it didn't appear, he growled; "Yes. I think I'd bite her, in spite of my best intentions."

Vivienne hissed out a long breath. "You cannot take that risk until you're certain you can restrain the urge."

"That's what we thought, too." Arcana took a step back, her heart constricting. "I don't want to kill him."

Rytan winked and jabbed her with a conspiratorial elbow. "Give it time, I'm sure there'll be a moment."

"Father," Fenris frowned, easing off the wall. "This is not a moment for levity."

"If you say so." Rytan shrugged and gave his son an unrepentant grin. "Besides, who says I was joking, eh?"

Fenris growled and turned to his mother. "Are you sure?"

"Very sure. To drink from her without a way to mitigate the magic in her blood would mean the death of both of you."

The words were like blows and Arcana leant back against Caelum, surprised when Fenris appeared on her other side, his arm sliding around her waist for support. "Then why do I *want* to bite her so badly?"

Vivienne's face twisted into a mysterious little smile and though she had only scar tissue where her eyes should have been, Arcana could have sworn she felt the featherlight touch of the other woman's gaze as she examined their auras. "You know why."

"I don't," Fenris growled, and when Vivienne's smile only turned more ethereal, he spat a fey curse. "Should I stay away from her, then?"

"Oh, no." Vivienne shook her head. "Distance will only make it worse. Stop for a moment and think, dear. You have been fine up until this point; it is only because you let your father bite you that your instincts became so strong. You are low on blood, and your body demands either rest or restitution."

He grunted, fingers tightening around Arcana's waist. "What do you suggest?"

"An immediate infusion of blood to replace what you lost. I know you don't like it, but considering what just happened, it is the safest route." Vivienne sighed, laying a hand on Rytan's arm. "Take him to the forest, my love. Help him find something to eat and clear his head."

Fenris was silent a long moment, and then he turned and looked at Arcana. "Will you be all right?"

"Of course. But I thought you don't like -"

"I don't. Mother, however, is correct." He brushed a gentle kiss to her temple. "I will be back as soon as I can."

"Wait!" Arcana held up a hand and closed her eyes. The water had well and truly soaked through her clothes, settling on her skin and whispering in her veins. Gathering her magic, she waved a finger and drew the moisture from her clothing and then Fenris', opening her eyes in order to direct the floating droplets back into the bucket from whence they came. "Okay. Now go."

"Thank you." This time, his lips brushed against hers, but disappeared before the fire that had claimed them earlier could reignite. Without a glance at either of his parents, Fenris turned and jogged out of the cave.

Vivienne turned to her mate. "Go on. I said to help him, and I meant it. You know he hates this."

"I've only got one leg," Rytan protested, gesturing at his crutches. "You know how fast he is!"

"Then I suggest you hurry, lest the remnants of the warg catch him while he's in a mood," Vivienne said, raising one sweeping eyebrow. "He wouldn't be in this position if you hadn't allowed him to feed you in the first place."

"Warg! Shit, I forgot those bastards are still wandering around." Rytan snatched a double headed axe from the floor near the sleeping palette and disappeared down the tunnel so fast he was only a blur. "Fenris, wait!"

Vivienne chuckled as they left, then turned her head and looked at Arcana, the movement all the more unnerving in her eyeless face. "Boys, hmmm? Are you sure you're all right, dear?"

"Yeah, I'm fine."

"Well, then, the stew is on the cooker and we've naught to do but wait - will you walk with me a little?"

Arcana smiled. "Of course."

"Excellent. I have had so little opportunity to wander since Rytan was injured; it will be a lovely distraction." Vivienne's answering smile was wide as she gestured to the tunnel. "Come, my dear."

Arcana followed her out into the afternoon sunlight, pausing at the cave entrance to allow her eyes to adjust. "Were you serious about the warg?"

"Unfortunately, yes." Vivienne hoisted her skirts and began picking her way through the trees, leaving Arcana and Caelum to follow. "We defeated them for the most part but the remainder retreated into the wilderness. Rytan and I have had a couple of skirmishes since, but a singular warg here and there is nothing compared to the threat of a whole pack, albeit a smaller one. When the easier prey has been exhausted we will see them, I am sure - they have no way off planet and are single minded in their bloodlust."

"No way off planet? Most of the warg we've encountered have been equipped with teleportation devices."

Vivienne shook her head. "Not this pack. They had a single, larger device which teleported in a group at a time. It was destroyed, but at great cost."

"I'm sorry," Arcana murmured.

"So am I, but the cost would have been far greater had we done nothing. This way, some of my people survived, the remaining warg were stranded and we ourselves live to fight and laugh another day. Stay close to me, dear, or I will fade into the shadows," Vivienne added, stepping into a stray ray of sunshine and smiling over her shoulder.

"Sure." Arcana hurried closer, her brow furrowed. "I wonder where Taelon's getting all his teleporters from. They're expensive, to say the least."

"That much I can answer, dear. Before we were forced to separate, one of my fellow Wardens reported that Taelon appropriated the planet Gargalax and left one of his Generals, a woman named Prynna, in charge."

Slender hands clenched to fists in the depths of Vivienne's skirts. "Gargalax is responsible for the vast majority of teleportation devices - and now their sole efforts belong to the warg."

"Prynna." Caelum frowned. "So the Pariah isn't the only General, then."

"No." Vivienne's lips thinned. "If ever the galaxy is to know peace, Taelon and his generals must be impeached."

"And in order for that to happen, we must restore the Weaver's power and protect the Timeless Kingdom, right?" Arcana smiled ruefully and shook her head. "That's what Fenris has been drumming into me these last few weeks, anyway."

"It is true." Vivienne led the way down a small, barely visible pathway and paused before a swift rushing creek. "I shudder to think how few of us are left to fight."

Arcana stared into the gurgling water. "Fenris has the same fear."

"Oh?" Vivienne crouched to fill her hands, sipping carefully before asking; "And you do not?"

Caelum chuckled. "We're used to fighting on our own. Even adding Fenris to our number makes the ship feel half the size."

"I see." Drying her hands on her skirts, Vivienne stared in her sightless way and Arcana fidgeted under the inspection. The other woman tilted her head suddenly. "You can feel me, can't you?"

"I beg your pardon?"

"You can feel it when I brush your aura… like this."

The same, tingly feeling Arcana had noted earlier brushed against her senses and she nodded. "Yes."

"And can you…" Vivienne trailed off with a start as Arcana brushed the leading edge of her magic against the other woman's. "By all the threads that bind us - I felt that, *and* I saw it."

"Your magic is strong," Arcana acknowledged.

Vivienne had one hand pressed to her mouth, the other across her chest. "And yours is… bottomless. The weave come to life. Your aura is a rainbow of incredible, impossible things given form." Again, that tingling wash of energy. "You would best me with ease, were it to come to that."

Rather than address what sounded oddly like relief in the other woman's voice, Arcana said; "What else do you see when you look at my aura?"

"As I said before, my dear: many things. Many, many things. Some of which you would understand and some, without my particular talents, you would not."

"I suppose you see things differently than the rest of us," Arcana acknowledged.

"Indeed I do. This may sound sudden, but may I tell you a story?" Vivienne moved to a large boulder and perched on top, patting the stone beside her in invitation. Sensing the other woman wouldn't speak otherwise, Arcana climbed up beside her. When Caelum had also settled comfortably against the boulder, Vivienne took a deep breath, her face turned out towards the forest as though to pierce the veils of time and space. "Genetics have not been kind to my son. As a boy, he was long and lanky and his body was entirely disproportionate. The Rukkha are a primitive, barbaric people but we lived among them because Rytan was not ready to leave and I had been exiled from the fey courts."

"I thought you were with the Weaver when Fenris was born?"

"Oh yes, I was, but the Timeless Kingdom is a closely guarded secret. I could not have taken my family there without risking the safety of the deerken and the Weaver, so we lived with Rytan's tribe. But as Fenris grew, it became apparent to me that his body, his mind, his soul - they did not match that place. See, the Rukkha believe in two things; sex and fighting, fighting and sex. Strength and physique are prized above all else, and both their males and females are great, hulking brutes." Vivienne waved a delicate hand. "You've seen Taelon. You know what I mean."

"I do," Arcana agreed, neglecting to mention that Rytan, too, had those same physical characteristics.

Vivienne smiled. "As Fenris grew, it became apparent to me that he was as far removed from that sort of personality and body type as it were possible to be. I thought I could protect him from the sharper edges of tribe society and for the most part I did, but there were occasions when my duties as a Warden called me away. On one such occasion, when Fenris was about twelve years old, the other local younglings took it upon themselves to pay a visit to our home."

Arcana's heart skipped a beat at her ominous tone. "Surely Rytan was there to help him?"

"He was out hunting. The Rukkha only live about sixty years and so grow quickly - at twelve years old they are almost completely matured, both physically and mentally. Their coming of age happens by fifteen, when they step fully into society as an adult." Vivienne's lips twisted bitterly. "The fey live hundreds of years and mature much slower. By the grace of his mixed genes, Fenris was still very much a child when those others his age were not."

"What happened?"

"There were four of them. They dragged Fenris from our hovel and dumped him in the centre of the tribal camp, where there is almost permanently a ring of mud and blood and semen, and commenced beating him." Vivienne's face remained calm, but her voice was a writhing current of rage. "When the rest of the tribe noted what was happening, they joined in."

"They *joined in*?" Arcana repeated, trying to picture a tiny Fenris facing an entire village of Taelons. "Tell me he fought back."

"I believe he tried, but he was just a boy. My boy, who I failed to protect. My boy, my beautiful, precious boy, who they would have murdered for being different. For being weak." She straightened her spine, visibly gathering herself, and when Vivienne continued her voice was cool and calm as a glacier. "When I returned to the camp, every single member of the tribe was dead. Fenris lay broken and bloodied in the epicentre of that massacre, completely and utterly unconscious - but alive."

"Rytan caught them and intervened?"

Vivienne shook her head. "No. When I managed to revive Fenris, he told me that while his bones shattered and they laughed, while they stabbed and slapped and punched and spat on him, he knew he was going to die. And something... *other* moved beneath his skin."

"Magic," Arcana breathed. "His fey magic."

"It shouldn't have been; he was too young. We don't normally develop our powers until early adulthood but, as I said before, my son is graced with mixed genes and his situation was extreme. So, yes, in response to his overwhelming terror, his magic surfaced." Her face tightened. "The power was so vast and brutal that it took him over completely, roaring through his shredded veins and using his body like a puppet. He only had to look at his attackers - just *look* at them - and the screaming started. Fear was what they had inflicted, and that was what this dark magic used. It reached into their minds and made them see their own worst fears. Made them *want* those fears, even while they screamed and fought. Then it made them enact those fears." Vivienne paused for breath, her fingers twisting together. "Some killed themselves, with blade or fist or axe or fire. Some leapt from heights, some drowned in water that was a figment of their imaginations. Some rammed their heads into trees, rocks, buildings - anything to get the images out, to stop the voices. Some simply died, their hearts arrested by the mind-numbing terror. And when it was over, and each and every single one was slaughtered, my sweet, precious boy's body gave out beneath the strain of that enormous power and he fell unconscious."

"Great gods of Sorcen," Arcana whispered, tears streaming down her cheeks. "The glamour."

"Glamour is what Fenris calls it, but I fear it is more than that." Vivienne shook her head sadly. "I have never been more grateful to be blind than then, for when Rytan and the other hunters returned and beheld what had been done, all they could do was vomit and shit themselves. My son was horrified, of course, and in true Fenris style, blamed himself entirely."

"And still does, I'll wager."

"Very much so," Vivienne agreed. "I had hoped the glamour would return to whence it came but once woken, the power only grew. Everyone Fenris looked at, he ensnared - and he had no control over what they saw, what they felt, what they did. Only I was safe because, of course, it is impossible to ensnare someone without any eyes." There was a dry sort of humour in her voice at that particular irony. "So I did the only thing I could think of - I tapped into his aura, took hold of that vast well of darkness and leashed it."

"But such a spell…" Arcana's mind boggled at the complexity.

"Yes." Vivienne spread her hands as though to stare at them, but of course that was impossible. "It was far beyond the reach of my natural scope of abilities but I had no choice if I wished to save my son."

"And by using Fenris' very life force, it gave you a larger pool of energy to work with, meaning you could achieve a greater spell than if you'd worked alone," Arcana mused, nodding. "It makes sense, even if he is now magically crippled."

Vivienne startled, then laughed. "Forgive me, I forget you are intimate with the inner workings of magic. Yes, that was my reasoning, too. My own magic is of death, you see, or at least that is its root. In order to twist it into something else, I had to work creatively."

Arcana nodded. "I understand completely."

"Do you… is death a skill of yours?"

"Not the way you mean, but all magic is that of death if wielded correctly." Arcana considered and, seeing no harm in it, said; "My people's magic is largely elemental in nature. Fire, water, earth, nature and healing. Since my bonding to Caelum, I can use all except healing, as well as some other energies… metal, electricity, air and so on. Some of those skills my people have in lesser denominations, some are unique to me." She gave a small smile, even though Vivienne couldn't see it. "I'm certainly alone in my ability to change schools of magic at will but I am by no means all powerful as many assume."

The Warden regarded her silently for some moments, her peculiar energy causing the skin on Arcana's scalp to tingle. "You have seen and caused much death in your time. So have I."

"Sometimes, it's necessary." Arcana shivered, her heart shying away from the thought. She cleared her throat and forced her voice to smooth out. "So what happened to Fenris once he was stabilised? What was the punishment?"

"There was no punishment." Vivienne shook her head, a tendril of midnight escaping her bun to curl around her temple. "The laws of the Rukkha are that strength is celebrated - and how could they argue that Fenris was not the stronger? The tribe - now composed of my small family and three other males - dissolved into the forest and walked away from the village. *We* did not return, but the scars in my sweet boy could not so easily be left behind. They run deep and dark and house not only a fear of that awful power, but of the theft of free will. Nobody knows the theft of free will better than Fenris."

Arcana scrubbed both hands over her face. "Why tell me that story?"

"Because," said Vivienne very quietly, "It is likely he never will - and there may come a moment in the future when this knowledge defines your reactions."

"That sounds almost like a premonition," Arcana murmured, shivering.

"Perhaps, though that has never been a skill of mine." Vivienne scanned Arcana from head to toe, her long, pointed face inscrutable. "You have seen deeper into the true well of Fenris' feelings in these last four weeks than I have in all the long years since that fateful day - and I would be lying if I did not tell you I was jealous. But I am also grateful, sorceress, for whatever it is you have discovered in him. Fenris has walked a long road, and I had begun to worry he would never thaw."

"The same can be said of me, too." Arcana smiled ruefully, reaching out to pat the other woman's long, spidery hand in a comforting gesture. "In that, Fenris and I are alike."

"Oh?" Vivienne considered her for another long moment. "Yes, your aura hints at such. Come, my dear. I have shared with you my son's deepest scars. Perhaps now it is time to speak of yours."

Arcana stared down at the grass, watching the blades dance with each other in the cool afternoon breeze. She had hoped for this exact opportunity not long ago but now that it was here, her words seemed stuck in her throat. "Fenris said that Caelum and I are Timeless," she said at last. "And that the Timeless can't bear children."

"Ah. No, we cannot." Vivienne slid an arm around Arcana's shoulders and squeezed gently. "I take it you didn't know?"

"No. There was no-one to teach us when Caelum and I bonded. We didn't even know what Timeless was until Fenris came along."

Vivienne pressed a maternal kiss to Arcana's forehead. "Sometimes fate can seem unkind. I am sorry, dear."

"So am I." She fell silent, her fingers biting deep into the side of the boulder. Vivienne waited, her impossibly thin arm surprisingly comforting. Finally Arcana said; "But you had Fenris."

"Ah, yes. That I did," Vivienne chuckled. "It was quite an accident, I'm afraid. I was told it was impossible for us to conceive and for all I loved Rytan, I expected him to age and wither as mortal beings do. I went to the Weaver as soon as I realised something was amiss and the Keeper - her mate, Auron - confirmed I was with child. Rytan became a Guardian the same day." Vivienne shrugged. "As far as I am aware, my pregnancy is a unique occurrence."

"So you don't really know how it happened?"

"The usual way, if you must know." Vivienne chuckled again, leaning back far enough that Arcana could see her mischievous smile. "I'm certain you don't need an explanation."

"No," Arcana muttered, shaking her head. "That wasn't entirely what I meant, either."

"I know." Vivienne slumped. "I wish I had more information for you. The best person to ask would be the Keeper of Life - if anyone knows, it would be he. But Auron is lost to us."

"So Fenris tells me." Arcana drew her knees to her chest and propped her chin on top. "I suppose, in the grand scheme of things, my ability to procreate is fairly unimportant."

"Not true. As a woman - and a mother - I feel I can sympathise. But... the rule was made for a reason. I was part of the Timeless Kingdom before it was such a place, and the first of the Guardians were still fertile. Those who bred had to watch their children age and die while they lived on, and it was..." Vivienne trailed off and shook her head sadly. "It was enough that the Weaver changed the conditions of her oath. No parent should have to bury a child."

Arcana stared, aghast. "Why didn't she just make the children Timeless, too?"

"For a start, it was against many of the children's wishes. They wanted lives other than what we had to offer. Second of all, there are certain qualities one needs to possess before they can be made Timeless." Vivienne's mouth thinned to a line. "And no, I do not know what they are, but I have witnessed the tragedy of one who was turned when they should not have been."

"But Fenris-"

"Luck," Vivienne interrupted with a shrug. "Luck that he had the desire and the compatibility to enter our world."

Silence fell and Arcana found she did not have the heart - or the words - to break it. She'd begun to get an inkling of Vivienne's true age, and the mere thought was enough to make her head spin. Caelum, however, rolled to his feet and shook thoroughly, his fur whispering in soft harmony to the babbling stream. "The sun looks like it's getting ready to set. Are the days short here?"

"Yes, and the nights are long, which suits Rytan and I."

"Do you think Fenris will be-" Arcana cut off as a tree branch snapped loudly behind her, preceding a symphony of howling which echoed in the late afternoon air.

"Warg," Fenris gasped, tumbling out of the trees with his father close behind. "Lots of warg."

"Hello, my sweet boy. Did you feed?" Vivienne tilted her head, her sightless face travelling the length of Fenris' body and back again. "Yes, you did. Excellent."

"Mother," Fenris began, his tone exasperated, "Did you hear what I said?"

"Yes, dear, the warg. I heard." Vivienne reached up to pat his cheek. "I was wondering when they would come. Never mind."

"This ain't no skirmish this time, Viv," Rytan growled, leaning heavily on the haft of his axe. "We scented 'em up by the portal. I got the scout, but the blood set the rest off and they're hungry bastards."

"Hmmm, I'm not entirely surprised by that. There's so little food for them here, the poor things." Vivienne nodded, her voice soft. "Well, I suppose it can't be helped. We'll simply have to deal with them."

"Mother, I-" Fenris ran a hand through his hair and took a deep, steadying breath. "There may be as many as fifty of them. We should retreat to the cave as soon as possible or better yet, make a run for Arcana's ship."

"Nonsense. They've been allowed to frolic around for far too long and I for one am not running just because some overgrown puppies are drooling on my doormat." Vivienne slid off the boulder and dusted both hands on her skirts. "Now where are these filthy creatures? I'm hungry."

A short silence fell at that statement, and Arcana blinked from Rytan's concerned expression to Fenris' horrified one.

"Hungry?" Caelum echoed at last. "A pack of nearly fifty slavering warg makes you *hungry*?"

"Yes, of course. Come now, let's not meet them here; we don't want to ruin the stream. I quite like sitting out here in the evening." Vivienne lifted her skirts and began following the line of the water, moving at a right angle from the frenzied howling. "If I recall, there is a little flat area around to the west which should do nicely."

"I'm not sure this is a good idea, Mother," Fenris cautioned. "Maybe you should take father inside."

"Nonsense. They're only warg, darling." Vivienne paused to look over her shoulder, her sightless face gathering shadows and giving her a haunted look. "Besides, I've got you here to keep everyone safe, should it come to that."

"But the Weaver said-"

"The Weaver is *not here*," Vivienne hissed, a sinister edge to her tone. "But I am, and *I am hungry*."

"Leave it, son." Rytan clapped Fenris soundly on the back. "It'll help her recover what she's lost feeding me. We'll pick up the stragglers, if there are any."

Fenris took a deep breath and threw his hands up in defeat. "Very well then. But I'm not explaining this to the Weaver."

Vivienne gave a less than elegant snort, hitched her skirts high enough to reveal bare feet and skinny ankles as spindly as the rest of her body, and stalked off ahead. After shooting his son a disapproving glance, Rytan, using his upside down axe like a crutch, hurried after her.

"Are you really all right?" Arcana murmured as Fenris dropped into step beside her.

He nodded, glowing eyes downcast. "I fed."

Catching the defeated hitch in his voice, Arcana slid her fingers through his and squeezed. "You needed to."

Jade eyes flashed her way, then back to the ground. After a moment, he gently returned the squeeze of her hand and admitted; "I didn't think about how it would affect my desire for you."

"To bite me?"

"And the rest." A self-deprecating smirk crossed his face and was gone just as quickly. "The feelings are linked, as you well know."

Arcana considered the two encounters they'd had involving his teeth - three, really, she supposed - and nodded. "For me, too." She watched his face crease with astonishment and grinned. "Come on now, don't give me that face. You know; you can smell it."

"I do," he acknowledged, "I just never expected to hear you say it. I - this is not helping my resolve regarding your body."

She reached out to squeeze his hand. "We'll work it out."

Caelum, who'd been following silently, chose that moment to shove his great head between theirs. "I hate to interrupt this scintillating, pheromone-laden conversation, but can we discuss, for a moment, the idea of facing down nearly fifty warg on our own?"

Fenris fell silent, his brow furrowing as he listened to the steadily increasing cacophony of howls in the distance. "My count was off. There are less than thirty," he said at last.

"Oh, well, that makes it so much better," Caelum drawled. "And how do you propose we handle *thirty* warg? I'll remind you we don't have any handy Towers around to drop on them this time."

"Arcana crushed hundreds, not thirty." Fenris waved an absent hand, his attention still on the wargs' wild howling. "And we won't be handling them, not really. Mother will."

Caelum's jaw dropped open and he began to speak, but was cut off by Vivienne's cheerful voice announcing; "Here we are!"

They'd stopped in the middle of a grassy clearing surrounded by tumbled rocks on one side and trees on the other. The portal's circular silhouette rose in the distance, a dark shape against the twilit sky. The frenzied howl of the warg echoed all around and Arcana spread her magic into the earth, feeling out the hollows and protrusions in the landscape to get a better idea of their location. Should it come to fleeing, she had no wish to do it in the dark, surrounded by completely unfamiliar terrain.

"Howls are coming from over that ridge," Rytan said, levelling his axe to the west. "Less than a minute, now."

"Excellent." Vivienne turned her face into the chill air and smiled delicately. "Make sure you all stay back."

Fenris glanced around, then pointed at the copse of trees to their left. "There."

"Quick now," Rytan cautioned, already hopping and skipping towards the treeline. "She's on the move."

Arcana hesitated, watching Vivienne glide serenely across the grass as the first of the warg appeared atop the jumbled pile of rocks that marked the ridge. A few moments later he was joined by another, and another - until there was a pack of near-on thirty warg snarling and snapping from across the way. A tall male stepped into the clearing on his hind legs, a tarnished silver chain slung across his chest. He growled something to his pack, the words low enough to be swallowed by distance - but the intent in his tone was more than clear enough. No mercy.

"Arcana?" It was Fenris, his hand insistent at her elbow.

"Your mother -"

"Leave her." When she turned on him in astonishment, Fenris grimaced and explained; "Once she gets started, she'll be unable to tell friend from foe. None of us are safe here."

"Come on!" Rytan shouted. "It's starting!"

Arcana looked up to see blue-tinted clouds forming above Vivienne's head, and felt the crackle of magic in the air. Propelled forward by the ominous, heavy feeling of that energy, she swung up onto Caelum's back and shimmied forward as Fenris vaulted up behind her. "Get Father."

"I'm not an invalid," Rytan grumbled as they stopped long enough for Fenris to drag him up behind them. A moment later, his strong arms sand-wiched Fenris against Arcana's back as Caelum launched forward with startling speed. "Weaver's grace!"

"Hold on," Caelum warned belatedly, muscles bunching as he shot across the grass. "I've already been gouged across the hindquarters recently, and have no wish to repeat it anytime soon."

Arcana twisted in place, studying the rapidly growing cloud hanging over the clearing while the warg milled and snarled along the ridgeline opposite. Vivienne stood between them, alone, with her face upturned to the dusky sky. The energy which surrounded her was both the same and yet vastly different from the one Arcana had brushed up against earlier. This magic had barbed edges and some primal instinct bade her reel her own energy in and sit on it, lest she be forced to defend herself against a woman who was supposedly their ally.

Caelum reached the trees and propped, swinging on his haunches to face back the way they had come. Arcana clutched convulsively at his fur, steadying both Fenris and Rytan behind her. "Should we get down?" She wondered.

"No." Fenris' arms tightened and his voice was grim. "Stay together, in case Mother or the warg come this way."

A surge in the thick, heavy energy Arcana had sensed earlier drew her attention back outward. The warg had begun to lope down the small incline, racing towards their single, frail looking opponent. Vivienne remained still and serene, her lips turned up at the corners in a faint smile that sent shivers down Arcana's spine. The blue-tinted cloud descended, the leading tendrils curling around the warg like long fingers which, in their slavering frenzy, they all ignored. As both Vivienne and her snarling, snapping opponents disappeared, the cloud darkened to shades of midnight and begun to roil. In the space of a heartbeat, the clearing was entirely consumed and a strange silence fell.

The hairs on the back of Arcana's neck rose as a keening howl echoed across the clearing, a sound of incredible terror that cut horrifically and suddenly short. The dark cloud rolled, puckered and lifted, revealing Vivienne standing as Arcana had last seen her - face upturned to the sky. Her expression remained serene but there was a shadowed quality to her face that made the scene somehow off-kilter. The warg who had gathered at her feet were now row upon row of desiccated corpses which turned to dust as the cloud dissipated, the ash-like remains drifting away on the arms of the evening breeze.

"Wow," Caelum said.

"Shhhhh!" Rytan hissed, thumping Caelum in the side with his good leg. "Not yet."

Vivienne turned towards the sound but her movements were jerky, her ethereal grace replaced by a chilling, predatory speed. She seemed to scan the clearing without really seeing anything and Arcana bit her lip as the other woman's head rotated a full three hundred and sixty degrees on her neck before settling back into place. Nobody dared to move or breathe as Vivienne's chest expanded, joints twitching erratically - then she shook out her skirts, tucked a few loose strands of hair back into her bun and smiled.

"Viv?" Rytan's voice was tentative.

"I'm all right, dearest." Vivienne's voice carried easily across the clearing and her sated expression rose more hairs, this time down Arcana's arms. "My, that was refreshing."

"Are you all right?" Fenris murmured into Arcana's ear. "You're shaking."

She swallowed heavily. "I think so. I've never seen anything like that before."

"Many haven't, dear." Vivienne began to glide towards them across the grass and Arcana didn't even bother to question how the unseelie wight had heard her. When the Warden stood before Caelum, she smiled broadly, showing off two rows of delicate, pointed teeth. "Shall we return home for some stew? I'm afraid I'm full, but that's all the more for the rest of you."

"Er," Arcana replied.

Fenris squeezed her waist reassuringly. "Good idea, Mother. A hot meal will do wonders."

"Excellent. Shall we?" Vivienne gathered her skirts, turned in place and swept back the way they had come.

Caelum followed, ears flickered uneasily as they passed the place where the corpses had drifted into dust on the wind. "So, seeing as nobody else is going to ask - what did you do to those warg?"

"Oh, my sweet one. I ate them," Vivienne giggled, the sound so unearthly Arcana was glad she was facing away from them.

"They didn't look like anything I've ever eaten," Caelum muttered.

"Mother eats souls," Fenris elaborated.

"She eats *souls*?" Caelum repeated, propping to a standstill. "Please tell me I didn't just hear that."

"I'm afraid so." Vivienne gave a delicate little nod as she stopped by the mouth of the cave, her lips curled in a secretive smile. "The Weaver rehabilitated me for the most part but from time to time, when the situation calls for it, I have a little relapse."

Arcana twisted to look at Fenris. "Is that what you meant by your mother being the last line of defence?"

"Yes." He slid to the ground and linked his hands to help Rytan dismount, face grim. "It is a last resort because, in her frenzy, she's as likely to eat us as them."

Caelum shuddered. "You mean if we'd been caught in that cloud…"

"I'm afraid so, dear; that's why I'm not really allowed to participate in a proper battle. But don't worry, all's well that ends well." Vivienne reached up to ruffle the fur between Caelum's antlers, her smile doting. "Besides, those nasty creatures got what they deserved. Now come along, we don't want the stew to spoil. If you're leaving in the morning, it pays to make sure you eat and sleep properly tonight." And she disappeared into the cave with Rytan close behind her.

CHAPTER
THIRTEEN

Arcana stared up at the towering portal, a chill trickling down her
spine. She felt like she hadn't slept a wink, though she supposed she must
have. In her time she'd spent many a night curled against Caelum's flank,
but last night was the first she'd ever done so with Fenris by her side. That,
too, was a misnomer - without the threat of bloodlust hanging overhead,
the Guardian had wrapped himself around her like a vine, arms strong,
heartbeat steady and warm breath tickling the back of her neck. It had
been more than pleasant, it had been incredible, and Arcana had spent the
hours dozing fitfully between sharp bouts of wondering how any of it
could possibly be real.

Vivienne had roused them early with gentle hands and a hot breakfast
which, in spite of her restlessness, Arcana hadn't noticed her stirring over
the little stove which had kept the cave temperate all night long. After
some more stew and a quick assurance that the Timeless Kingdom would
be warm enough that she didn't need her thick coat or scarf, the party had
set out for the portal and the next stage in their journey.

Dawn's approach could now be seen on the horizon and the twin
moons were setting, bathing the platform in a weak half-light which
turned everything a pale shade of lavender. Rytan lounged against Caelum
several paces away, keeping guard. Vivienne, almost invisible in the
strange light, stood by Arcana and wrung her hands as Fenris climb the
face of the dormant portal. "Oh, I wish we hadn't sent Murtagh away," she
moaned. "Are you sure you can do this?"

"I can do it, Mother," he replied for the tenth time. "I promise."

Arcana watched as Fenris reached the top of the circle, shifted his weight and then hung on by what appeared to be willpower alone, using both hands to trace the interior of one of the carved runes with his fingertips. "What are you doing?"

"Looking for - hah!" Fenris grunted in satisfaction as part of the portal came away in his hands, revealing a hollow underneath. He tipped his head back to look at Arcana, the jade glow throwing his cheekbones into sharp relief. "May I have the stones?"

"Sure." Arcana reached into her satchel and dug the stones out.

Fenris unrolled his body so that he was suspended from one knee and reached down to pluck them from her outstretched hands. "Thank you."

"Is it a complex process?" Arcana asked, watching as he swung away to fit a crystal neatly into the hollow.

"Not really." Fenris fiddled with the placement until it was just so, then flashed her a grin. "Setting the stones is actually the easy part. If we are to have a problem, it will be with how long the stones can power both gateways."

"You will have to be swift," Vivienne agreed. "That, and have faith in the Weaver."

"She may be unable to assist us, Mother. There is no telling what state Taelon has her in." He slid the cover back into place and crawled along the edge of the portal as though glued to it, feeling out the cradles for the other two stones and setting them just as carefully. "That is as good as things are going to get."

"The Weaver would not leave you without options," Vivienne scolded, lips pursed as Fenris dropped soundlessly to the ground. "You should have more faith in her."

Fenris shot his mother an amused look as he slung the greatsword's harness over his shoulder and settled it into place. "She's not a deity, Mother, she's a woman. An exceptional woman, but, in her words, far from perfect. I cannot rely on her assistance beyond what she has already managed."

"Not a deity?" Vivienne snorted derisively and waved a dismissive hand. "She creates the very fabric of the universe and is the mother of time. How can she be less than a deity? I've met gods and goddesses who pale in comparison."

"Met?" Rytan asked, his tone arch.

Vivienne waved her hand again. "Eaten, met - it is the same."

Caelum choked at that, turning wide eyes on Arcana, who bit her lip to keep from laughing. "You don't have a high opinion of them, by the sounds of it."

"Of course not." Vivienne frowned. "I would hardly have eaten them otherwise, would I?"

Fenris and his father shared wide, boyish grins, then Fenris moved to the portal and placed his hand palm down on the surface of the carved pedestal beside it. The pedestal immediately began to glow with a pale blue light, throwing the circle of runes into stark relief around his splayed fingers. "It has power," he breathed, eyes closing briefly. "What a relief."

"So this is goodbye," Vivienne murmured, hugging her arms to her chest. Arcana's heart caught at the vulnerability on the other woman's face.

"Oh, Mother." Fenris removed his hand from the pedestal and crossed to enfold her in a tight embrace. "It is only for now."

"You could take us with you," the Warden returned, her mouth tightening at the corners.

"We have had this discussion already - Father's in no state. You must let us go." Fenris leant back to press a soft kiss to his mother's forehead. "Trust in the weave."

Rytan stepped up beside his mate and son and threw an arm awkwardly around each of their shoulders. "Viv. Let him go."

"Very well. But you better tear Taelon's heart out," Vivienne whispered, her spindly fingers clenching to fists in Fenris' shirt. "Tear it out with your bare hands."

"I will. I swear it."

"Weaver guide you," Rytan slapped his son solidly on the back, eliciting a wince from the younger Guardian. "Auron keep you."

"And you," Fenris managed, wriggling out of his parent's embrace. He returned to the pedestal and began tapping purposefully at the runes, bringing the gateway to humming life behind them. "Once this is active, we will not have long. Be ready."

"Thank you for having us as your guests," Arcana said, taking Vivienne's hands in hers and squeezing them. "It's been lovely to meet you."

To her surprise, the Warden enfolded her in a fierce hug. "The pleasure and the honour have been mine, dear child."

Fenris tugged Arcana's hand and she let him draw her to the base of the portal, where blue light now swirled uncannily bright within the confines of the stone circle. She eyed the roiling energy with a frown. "Is it meant to look like that? The portals on Sorcen are usually much calmer."

"It is because the stones are powering two gates; they are overloading." He looked to his father. "The stones will likely crack after we go through. If they do not, take them out of the portal and bury them. We cannot risk the crystals falling into Taelon's hands."

Rytan nodded, his face grim. "It will be done."

Vivienne tipped her face up to the portal, jaw set in a way that reminded Arcana instantly of her son. After a long moment, she said something in fey, to which Fenris immediately responded in kind. Nodding, Vivienne turned to Arcana. "Hold on tight to him, sorceress. It is up to you, now."

Fenris made a choking sound in the back of his throat, but Arcana smiled and laid a hand over her heart. "On my word, I will not fail you - or him."

"Thank you."

"Go, Fenris. Before your mother loses it," Rytan growled, wrapping both arms around his mate as though he thought she'd make a dive for them. "We've got your back."

Fenris nodded and tightened his grip on Arcana's hand. "I cannot say what waits on the other side," he murmured.

"One way to find out," Arcana replied, forcing herself to smile. She flipped a quick salute to Rytan and Vivienne, closed her eyes and stepped into the portal, tugging Fenris along behind her. Cool energy slid over her skin, filling her ears with a musical thrumming. She hung suspended, hair floating around her face as though underwater and wild, raw energy crackled through her veins. The feeling faded as quickly as it had come, leaving Arcana blinking into balmy air and bright sunlight. Fenris coalesced beside her, one hand still twined firmly with hers. Caelum appeared an instant afterwards and they jumped away from the portal as a sound much like that of shattering glass rent the air. The blue glow from whence they'd come disappeared and with a small, pathetic groan, the pedestal beside the portal went dark.

"It is done. Weaver save us all," Fenris whispered, his face a mixture of relief and regret as he stared back at the gate. "At least this way, they cannot ignore my orders and follow us."

Caelum twitched an ear. "Would they?"

"Oh yes." Fenris gave a hollow laugh. "I may occupy a higher rank within the court, but they are still my parents. They can - and often do - exactly as they wish."

He was now squeezing Arcana's fingers so tightly she was sure her bones were creaking, and her voice was somewhat strangled as she said; "They'll be all right."

Fenris released her immediately. "Sorry."

"Don't worry about it. For now, we have bigger fish to fry." Arcana looked around her pointedly. The portal sheltered in a small hollow, occupying a far more humble site than the ones outside of the Timeless Kingdom. Beyond the protective cradle of rock, dirt and debris flew through the air in the grip of a gale force wind, obscuring everything else from sight. She took a half step forward, squinting into the dust storm. "It's a wasteland."

"Stop!" Fenris dragged her into the shelter of the hollow, setting his spine against the rock. "Something is moving out there."

Arcana stood silent in the solid cage of his arms, listening to the shriek of the winds and the rhythmic hiss of the storm. "I can't sense anything, but my magic doesn't like it here... the elements feel muddy. Heavy, somehow."

"It may be something to do with the Kingdom itself," Fenris answered, his breath tickling her ear. "I only saw shifting shadows beyond the dust and the clouds - but we should be looking at a forest, not a sandstorm."

Arcana chewed her lip a long moment. "Caelum?"

"I can't tell, either." The deerken shifted uneasily. "But I agree with you. This place feels... wrong."

"Wrong how?"

"I don't know." Caelum shook his great head. "Just wrong."

Fenris released Arcana so that he could inch to the edge of the hollow and peek around the lip of the rock. "It is impossible to know what's beyond the storm. We will simply have to risk it."

"Maybe, maybe not." Arcana propped her fists on her hips, mind churning. "Where are we headed?"

"To the Weaver's tower, which is inside the castle." Fenris drew the greatsword and began to sketch in the dirt with the tip. "Imagine the Kingdom is egg shaped and the castle is the yolk. There is forest here, a lake here, fields here..."

"And we are?"

He dug the sword in above the 'forest'. "Top end of the egg, furthest from the castle."

"Of course." Arcana couldn't help her humourless grin. "All right, first step is to take care of the storm."

Fenris flicked a look at her from beneath his lashes. "You cannot mean to control it, surely? Your magic -"

"I said it feels heavy, not that it was useless." Arcana smiled when he hesitated. "Trust me."

"Very well." Fenris tightened his grip on the greatsword, mouth pressed into a thin line. "Caelum and I will watch your back."

"Thanks." Arcana stepped around the edge of the hollow and into the raging elements. Wind buffeted her body and she staggered sideways, narrowly missing a large, twisting branch that flew past in the arms of the sand. Tiny granules scoured her face and hands, sought to reach the flesh inside her clothing. She closed her eyes and called her magic, allowing the elements to whip around and through her rather than attempting to corral one consciously. She hoped for the sand but was unsurprised when the wild winds began to keen inside her blood, her hair lifting of its own accord and her lungs tickling with a sudden overload, as though she might inflate like a balloon and simply float away.

Drawing the storm's feral strength into her body, Arcana whispered softly to the wildly bucking winds and bid them calm. The air slipped and slid in her grasp like a desperate fish - until the wind abruptly ceased, sand and dirt falling into gentle dunes with a soft hiss while debris thudded around her like so much rain. Arcana exhaled on an eddying zephyr and opened her eyes, spitting sand onto the ground. "I hate air magic."

"Are you all right?" Fenris materialised at her shoulder, examining the side of her face critically. "Your skin is covered in grazes."

"I'll heal. What happened here?" she jerked her chin outwards. The forest before them stood stark and barren, a thousand lifeless trunks poking out of the sandy dirt. Each branch and twig had been scoured paper smooth by the dust storm, the trunks bearing scars from bigger pieces of wreckage the wind had thrown their way. Arcana ran her hand down a low hanging branch and it snapped off in her grasp, echoing like a gunshot in the suddenly still air. "I'm going to guess the forest doesn't normally look like this."

"No." Fenris shook his head sadly. "This forest is normally green and lush - a haven for the deerken."

"Time flux, maybe?" Caelum extended his nose to sniff the branch in Arcana's hand. It disintegrated at his touch and he sneezed violently, covering himself in a thin veil of dusty splinters. "It's as if these trees have been dead for centuries."

Fenris nodded, his gaze focussed off in the distance. "Something is very wrong. We must hurry to the Weaver."

"Hmm." Arcana squinted between the trunks but even in death, the forest was so dense that it was impossible to see very far. "Do either of you see or hear anything that might want to kill us?"

"No. Now that the storm has settled, there is only silence." Fenris turned to face the thickest part of the forest as Caelum murmured an agreement. "We go that way."

Arcana suppressed a shiver and began moving away from the portal, Fenris so close beside her their arms brushed with every step. Clouds of dust rose as they walked but were easily soothed with a brush of air magic, leaving the path clear. The forest was so dense that travelling quickly became a team effort, with Caelum using his antlers to snap and shove brittle undergrowth aside while Fenris and Arcana wove between dead trunks and ducked low hanging branches.

"Stop." Caelum propped in place a few steps ahead, nostrils dilating. Arcana came abreast of him to see a jumbled heap of bones at the base of the next tree, the bleached ivory partially buried beneath a dune. Fenris slithered past her body and then picked his way closer to the tree in question, balancing the greatsword across his knees as he crouched to inspect the remains.

"It's a deerken," he said softly, brushing the swishing, hissing sand aside. "Maybe two."

Arcana watched as Fenris unearthed more bones. "I thought they couldn't be killed without tearing a hole in the weave?"

"Those rules only apply beyond the Timeless Kingdom," he answered, his tone grim. "Here, anything can happen."

"But why kill them?" Caelum's tail swished as he stared down at a grinning skull heartbreakingly similar to Mirokke's. "It doesn't even look like they fought... more that they just laid down and never got up again."

Fenris hesitated, and when he turned to look at Caelum his brow was pinched with sorrow. "There are two possibilities."

"One, they're all pacifists, blah blah blah, Auron's disappeared, blah blah blah, I'm the only deerken with a backbone, boo hoo hoo." Caelum rolled his eyes, his hackles raising. "I refuse to believe an entire race just laid down and accepted death by warg, so what's the second option?"

"Exhaustion." The Guardian ran a hand through his hair, dusting the dark teal curls with a faint layer of grit. "If Taelon was keeping the deerken half starved, then forcing them to travel through the weave, it's likely he used them until there was nothing left to give, then dumped them here to die."

"Three," Arcana added, "They were taken by surprise when larger and more formidable predators appeared very suddenly in their home. I know you're angry, Caelum, but it's not Fenris' fault."

"I know, I know, it's Taelon's." Caelum rolled his eyes back to stare at the undeniably impressive - and deadly - antler rack atop his head, the whirling velvet abruptly replaced by shimmering, vicious blades. "The more I hear about him, the more I'm determined to show him just what a deerken can do."

Fenris reached out to soothe the fur between Caelum's shoulders. "If anyone can save the living and avenge the lost, my brother, it is you."

Caelum delivered a withering, sideways glance. "Shouldn't that be your job, as a Warden?"

"It should be," he agreed, "But you got through to Mirokke when nobody else could - and I do not believe it was because she is your mother. If we come out of this alive, you can make a difference. You can give the deerken a gift we Wardens simply cannot." Fenris paused, face twisted in sadness. "I wager this will not be the last skeleton we see."

"No," Caelum growled, "I'd say not." As one, they looked stared at the bleached, brittle bones. Then, his voice full of quiet determination, Caelum said; "Let's go."

Following in his wake, Arcana and Fenris returned to their slipping, slithering struggle to navigate the unruly terrain. A few minutes on she spied another set of bones, this time a deerken and a humanoid who had fallen together. Further on again, a vaguely bipedal skeleton with too many arms and another two deerken. Arcana shivered, wondering how many more corpses they'd missed in their walk because they were buried beneath the dunes.

"Look over there - a warg." Caelum drifted towards a new jumble of bones approximately ten paces ahead.

Clinging to Fenris in an attempt to prevent twisting her ankle in the soft sand, Arcana struggled to Caelum's side and looked down upon the bones of their enemy. Devoid of flesh the warg were frighteningly human, with femurs and tibias and rib cages and toe bones all laid out in the same manner as her own skeleton was. It was the sharp claws tipping the hands and feet and the lupine skull filled with curved teeth that gave them away - that and the bushy wolf's tail which was marked by a pebbling path of tiny bones descending from the creature's pelvis.

"Looks like a fight took place here," Fenris mused, leaning against a nearby tree trunk. "Two, maybe three warg? And a Guardian."

"A Guardian? How can you tell?" Arcana moved to his side and paused as the edge of a plate spaulder caught her eye, mostly concealed by the dirt. "Oh. I wonder why the armour didn't rust away like everything else?"

"I don't know," Fenris answered softly. His gaze was on the armour but his hand had fluttered up to spread across his chest, where his scar rested. "But I draw some mild comfort from knowing that there was, at least, some sort of resistance."

"You were overwhelmed," Arcana replied, laying one of her own hands atop his and peering into his face. "There was nothing you could have done."

He sighed. "I know, but the knowing doesn't make it any easier."

Caelum backed away from the macabre scene, nose crinkling in distaste, and turned in the direction they'd been travelling. "Is it me, or is the forest beginning to thin?"

"It is thinning," Fenris confirmed. "Soon we will reach Warden's Hall and from there it is only a short trip through the gardens to the back of the castle."

Arcana stared for another few seconds at the Guardian's plate armour, recalling the way Fenris' chestplate had been torn like tinfoil when they first met. As though sensing the train of her thoughts, he tugged her against his body and brushed his lips across her nose before letting go, and together they shadowed Caelum through the silent tomb of the forest.

The trees began thinning in earnest and after a few more minutes' struggling, they arrived at a wide lodge made from rough-hewn stone. The back wall nestled between thick tree trunks but an open space belled out in front in what Arcana presumed was once a grassed courtyard. Fenris held a finger to his lips as they sidled along the building, narrowing his eyes at darkened windows and weathered thatching. When nothing moved in the shadows, they slid around the corner and into the yard - which was now no more than bare dirt and aching, eerie loneliness.

"There hasn't been water here for a long time," Caelum murmured, poking his head into an empty water trough. "It's like the place has been abandoned for so long that even the ghosts have left."

Arcana ducked through the open archway and into the lodge, blinking to adjust her eyes to the sudden gloom. The vast stone hall was empty, furniture long rotted to nothing and doorways gaping like so many toothless mouths. Dust swirled around her feet, tickling her nose with the odour of a place long lost to the embrace of eternity. She looked up to where Fenris was silhouetted in the doorway, his face bleak, and said; "Time flux. It has to be."

"Yes." He entered at last, walking straight to the back of the room to stare at the blank wall with such intensity that Arcana wondered what had once hung there. "As impossible as it would seem, centuries have passed in the space of months."

Caelum poked his nose into a darkened doorway and then yanked it back out again. "Wait - we're not going to get more zombies attacking us, are we? Like that cave back on Sorcen?"

"I hope not." Fenris shrugged and Arcana felt the hairs rise on her arms as she stared into the inky shadows. All at once the silence seemed oppressive, stagnant - and rather than call a breeze to waft through the room and stir whatever memories had been lost here, she staggered back out into the sunlight.

Caelum joined her by a tumbledown wall which had perhaps once been a gatepost, or a short fence. "You all right?"

"Yeah. Just..." Arcana shook her head. "The air seemed to change for a moment. As if it was listening. Waiting."

"Great gods of Sorcen." The charcoal ridge of fur that marched down Caelum's spine rose into a stiff ruff. "Please don't ever say that again. Especially when we're talking about zombies."

"Sorry." Arcana palmed a stone from the wall, brushing away crumbling mortar with her thumb. "I have to say, this wasn't what I was expecting."

"Nor I." Fenris' tone was grim as he loped out to join them. "I came here expecting warg, and blood, and death - but certainly not an echoing tomb. Whatever Taelon has done to entrap the Weaver, it has transformed my home beyond recognition."

"It can be restored." Arcana stepped closer, sliding her arm around his waist. "I'm a firm believer in the idea that it's never too late."

Fenris was silent a long moment, face impassive as he stared at the lodge. Then he shook himself and smiled down at her, locking their eyes so that the glamour feathered over her skin. "You are right, of course. Thank you."

"We should keep moving, then?" Caelum wondered aloud. When Fenris nodded, he ventured; "Maybe there'll be some clues inside the castle."

"Perhaps, though at this point I am most concerned about the Weaver herself." Without sparing another glance for the Warden's Hall, Fenris stepped around the crumbling gate post and set off along a path so overgrown that Arcana didn't realise it was there until she was hurrying along it.

Winding beneath tall, broad and very dead trees, the path took them around the corner of the lodge and hooked a sharp left. Fenris' long legs had already taken him around the bend and Arcana jogged to catch up - and promptly cannoned straight into the back of him, bouncing off those broad shoulders and staggering sideways. A short, crumbling rock wall very similar to that by the Warden's Hall broke her fall, and Fenris caught her before she toppled over it.

His hands may have been firm on her shoulders but his eyes were trained beyond them, jaw twitching. Arcana immediately turned to follow his gaze, taking in what had once been a garden. Instead of flora, withered corpses in plate armour sagged from a series of scarecrow frames, their limbs held in place by lengths of thin, vicious looking chain.

"Great gods of Sorcen," Arcana whispered, covering her mouth in horror.

"I will kill him," Fenris whispered, his voice no more than a tremor of sound in his chest. "I will kill him for what he has done."

"It'd be too kind a punishment," Caelum grunted, appearing on their left. "Do you recognise any of them?"

Fenris shuddered. "No. They are too far gone."

They stared in silence at the bodies. Eventually Arcana said; "Do you want to cut them down?"

"Yes." He drew the greatsword with a flourish, stepping over the short wall to move quickly between the frames. In a matter of moments the dead were all slumped on the ground, their chains in pieces around them. Unlike the skeletons in the forest, these corpses still sported patches of hair and scraps of clothing beneath their plate armour.

Arcana narrowed her eyes at the closest body. "There's no sign of battle damage."

"No." Fenris regarded his handiwork with a grim expression. "They were captured, then hung out here to starve in a garden full of food."

She moved to his side, crouching to inspect what had once been a living being but was now a jumbled mess of rotting parts. "I'd offer them absolution, but there's no fire here. I could bury them, though, if you like?"

When he nodded, she shoved her hands into the dirt, absorbed the energy of the earth, and carefully opened holes beneath each and every body. As they disappeared beneath the surface, Fenris closed his eyes and murmured; "Weaver guide you, Auron keep you. May you find peace beyond the weave."

Repeating the sentiment under her breath, Arcana closed the earth over the fallen Guardians and then got to her feet, dusting her hands on her pants. "That's the best I can do."

"It is enough." With a final look over the newly settled earth, Fenris strode from the garden and continued along the path, his voice carrying back over one shoulder. "Thank you."

"It was my honour." Arcana followed him toward the looming outer wall of the castle, unable to look at the graves a second longer. They stopped in the lee of a tiled patio, the brickwork smooth and the paving stones neatly fitted together. Empty herb boxes framed thick paned windows and a decaying wooden door. Slouched against the door jamb was yet another body.

"Warg." Caelum lowered his head to nose at the remains, this one still bearing patches of fur and fabric. "Someone crushed her skull."

Fenris inched past the warg to kick out the remaining wood in the doorway. That done, he glanced back down at the corpse and said; "There were a few Guardians who favoured war hammers. If not for my people being vastly outnumbered, I would expect to see more such bodies as this one."

"That and the warg are known for eating people - even their own kind," Arcana pointed out.

Fenris nodded slowly. "True. Are you all right, Caelum? Your hackles are raised again."

"I don't know. I just…" The deerken turned from the warg to eye the murky doorway, his nostrils dilating. "I do *not* want to go in there."

Fenris drew the greatsword with a silken hiss and peered into the gloom. "It is a fool who ignores the warning of a deerken, but we have no other choice," he said at last. "We must go in."

Arcana followed him into what had once been a mud room, though the wooden benches had long rotted away. Fenris paused briefly to examine the stone sink and iron coat hooks but when they revealed nothing, he led them out into a short hall. High set windows gave the airy hallway ample light, illuminating the way to room after empty room. Some of the crumbling furnishings Arcana was able to identify - laundries with rusting tubs, bathing chambers with darkened water wells and dry basins - whilst others were mystifyingly empty.

Barely two minutes in, Caelum stopped. "Did you hear that?"

The sound of metal echoing against stone seemed unnaturally loud in the silence, even to Arcana's ears. Fenris frowned in concentration. "The kitchen," he mouthed.

Caelum's ears flickered incessantly as he floated forwards, the sharp blades on his antler rack glittering as he traced the noise to the next open doorway. He paused for a long moment then stepped through, Fenris hard on his heels. After a cursory glance backwards to ensure they weren't being followed, Arcana went after them.

The castle's kitchen was a large, square room with an enormous island bench in the centre. In the middle of the island, rocking slowly from side to side, was a shining silver spoon. A second spoon, identical to the first, lay on the floor in front of the bench. Both were pristine, the silver surfaces sparkling as though freshly polished. Fenris edged forward, sheathing the greatsword in order to scoop the spoon from the floor and turn it over in his hands.

Arcana spread her magic through the room, feeling behind cupboards and under benches, and shook her head. "There's nobody here."

The clatter of silver on stone made her an instant and total liar. As one, they shot around the other side of the large island bench to stare at the spoon rocking back and forth on the floor. "What manner of creature," Fenris muttered, running his thumb over the spoon in his hand, "Drops silverware?"

"I have no idea." Arcana shook her head, the movement echoed by Caelum. While they stared at each other in mystified silence, another tinkle echoed through the kitchen. She turned to see another spoon, a little behind the first. "Whatever it is, it's trying to get our attention."

Caelum lowered his head to sniff at the newest spoon. "I think they're making a trail."

"A trail of cutlery?" Fenris' voice was thick with skepticism. "To *what*? There is nothing here."

"There must be, else why bother?" Arcana followed the line of spoons to one of the chiller units opposite. She placed a hand on the steel door and jerked back in surprise as a shaft of frigid energy shot up her arm. "Shit!"

"What is it?" Fenris was there in an instant. "Are you all right?"

"I'm fine." She considered the chiller unit and then ventured; "But the door is charged with magic."

"A magic fridge?" Caelum shook his great head, snorting a sharp laugh. "Does the Weaver have to lock up her ice cream, or something?"

"No." Fenris frowned. "Perhaps it is a trap."

"Inside the *refrigerator*?" Caelum demanded. "Come on, Taelon's a vampire. He's not expecting us to pop by the kitchen for a snack."

"Okay, enough." Arcana waved them both off with an impatient hand. "You've both got a point, but I'm going to open it either way."

"Are you sure?" Fenris peered worriedly from Arcana to the fridge and back again. "It might be better to leave -" he cut off with a muffled curse as a spoon dropped heavily onto the top of his head.

Arcana caught the silverware as it tumbled free, and said; "I'm opening it. Keep watch."

Before he could argue anew, she curled her fingers around the handle and tugged but the chiller's ancient sealing mechanism groaned in protest and the door remained shut. After muttering something in fey that sounded like a curse, Fenris leant over to add his own strength, yanking the door wide with ease. Arcana ducked under his arm to inspect the interior but instead of the shelves and drawers she'd expected, the chiller's cavity was filled with a large, singular block of ice. Runes covered the surface and from the frigid depths, two striking blue eyes stared out. Each one was the size of a golf ball, with slitted black pupils that dilated at the sudden influx of light. The enormous eyes were set into a white and orange furred face bearing a soft pink nose and absurdly long whiskers Arcana imagined would wave rather comically in the wind.

"It's... a cat?" She stepped towards the frozen creature and stopped as Fenris' arm shot out, dragging her up against his chest. "Do you *mind*?"

"Sorry." He loosened his grip at once. "I'm still worried about a trap."

"It's a frozen cat and some spoons. How could it possibly be a trap?" Arcana pushed at the wall of his chest and slowly, reluctantly, he let her go. "I'm not denying there's magic involved, but I cannot for the life of me believe that this is some sinister scheme of Taelon's.

"But those runes, that creature..." Fenris ran a hand through his hair, staring into giant blue feline eyes that stared rather unnervingly back. "How is it still alive?"

Arcana shrugged. "Magic."

"I suppose that was a foolish question," he mused, raising a hand as if to trace one of the runes and then dropping it. "I have never seen such a thing before."

"Yes you have." Arcana reached out to tap his bicep, where she'd once scrawled similar characters in black eyeliner. "Those runes are ancient Sorcen."

"Okay, whoa, wait." Caelum hustled forward, bending to peer at the runes. "Are you saying that whoever put that odd-looking mammal in there meant for *you* to find it?"

"They must have," she replied simply. "As far as I'm aware, Flare and I are the only active sorcerers who can read the older spells. Don't get me wrong, there are a few doddery scholars with a passing understanding, but nobody's really bothered since all the ancient books were translated into Universal Galactic for the official Tower texts."

Fenris blinked once, very, very slowly. "If I know my magic correctly, then Flare, as a fire sorcerer, could not manage this spell?"

"No, ice is a rarer derivative of water magic. Flare could read the runes, but that's it."

"Meaning that you are the only person in the entire universe to handle this spell - And the Weaver sent you to me." Fenris swallowed heavily. "She knew we would all come here."

Caelum snorted. "You *think*?"

Ignoring the sarcasm, Fenris took a deep breath and gestured to the curling characters etched into the ice. "What does it say?"

Arcana tilted her head to one side, lips moving silently as she translated. "It's a binding spell to keep the ice intact. Frozen in time."

"Okay, I have another question. If there are no active sorcerers who can read the old language, how did the ice get here?" Caelum demanded. When neither of them answered, he groaned, shoulders drooping. "This place is making my bones ache."

"Peace," Arcana soothed, stroking the soft fur on his neck. "The Weaver clearly set this up with us - all three of us - in mind."

Caelum's ears flickered, his eyelids half mast. "You clearly haven't thought about this, have you?"

"What do you mean?"

"Think about Mirokke." When she continued to stare in confusion, Caelum said; "We caused the injury that led to her death, my birth and our bonding because time isn't a straight line, it's a kaleidoscope in the hands of a tap dancing drunkard. We already said that you're the only person who could cast a spell like this; who's to say that you *didn't* cast it?"

Arcana blinked. "Because I haven't."

"Yet," Caelum said softly, his tail swishing back and forth. "You haven't cast it *yet*."

She stared at the ice block in the fridge, goosebumps marching their way up her arms and across her body in a wave. "Great gods of Sorcen, I can't even think about that right now. That's just - Caelum, that'd mean - holy shit."

"Whatever the spell's origins, there's certainly no way Taelon or one of his warg could read it, let alone set it here," Fenris interjected, his voice soothing. "And as we've already covered, the only living soul in the entire universe who can melt that ice is Arcana. I think that means that, for better or worse, you are meant to melt this ice."

"Yeah, I agree." Shaking off her heebie-jeebies, Arcana stalked to the chiller and placed her hands flat on the ice. Magic immediately shot up her arms and she grit her teeth against the chill, feeling around the runes and slowly absorbing the essence of the frozen water. The strange creature inside the ice stared back at her, frozen into unblinking silence. "Here we go; be ready to catch the kitten."

Fenris peered uncertainly at the ginger creature in the ice. "A kitten?"

"I think so. Disproportionately large head, enormous eyes... definitely not an adult. Either way, be ready to get it out."

"All right."

Arcana immediately commanded the ice to melt, wincing as freezing water rushed over her wrists, trickling down the outside of the chiller unit to pool on the floor. She might be immune to freezing, but that didn't mean she still didn't feel the bitter chill seeping into her bones.

"Look!" Caelum exclaimed. The kitten's ears were revealed and immediately began to twitch. "It's working."

"Pull it out as soon as you can." Arcana closed her eyes to better concentrate on the ice block. As each rune of the ancient spell dissolved, the strange chill crept further across her skin, raising a trail of goose bumps as it went. Before long her arms burned with the cold, her shoulders and chest wrapped in an icy fist.

"It's almost free." Fenris' shoulder bumped hers as he reached into the chiller to grasp the kitten. Arcana opened her eyes in time to see the bedraggled little ginger mewing at the Guardian, snuggling into his warm body as he stepped away. Safe and very much alive, thank the gods. She tried to remove her hands from the ice then but it held fast, the freezing effect creeping up her neck and across her face, stealing all rational thought. Ancient Sorcen characters began to dip and dance behind her eyes, and the sigh of settling glaciers filled her ears.

"Arcana?" Caelum's voice rose in alarm but it came from far away. She tried to answer but it was no use; the bitter chill closed over the top of her head, plunging her into a strange world of frosted glass and pale blue light.

Into the silence walked a woman, clad in a full suit of plate armour and carrying a small wooden box. She glanced left and right, hurrying through shadowed halls draped with colourful hangings until she entered what Arcana recognised as the castle's kitchen. Half rolled dough lay abandoned on the bench and a rack of wooden utensils was smashed on the floor. The woman hastened to the chiller unit and tugged it open, placing the box inside. It immediately shifted, sliding on the uneven surface. She pushed it back but the box slid again, toppling out of the chiller. Swearing under her breath, the woman caught the box and turned towards the bench, grabbing a heavy metal serving spoon. She shoved the box inside the chiller and set the heavy spoon on top, exhaling in relief as the arrangement remained in place.

"Are you done?" A wiry man wearing a simple linen tunic and pants raced into the room, a bloodied axe in his hands. "There are warg everywhere."

"I'm done." She closed the door and pulled a small glass globe from a leather pouch at her belt. "I just have to detonate it."

"Well do it," the man urged, his eyes on something beyond Arcana's field of vision. "They'll be here any minute."

"Get back, then. We'd be better off if you had your armour on, you know," the woman answered, setting her spine to the wall and cradling the glass globe in her hands.

"It's too late for that now. All that matters is carrying out the Weaver's instructions," he grunted, swinging the axe. Something yelped, the sound quickly turning into a vicious snarl. "Hurry!"

The woman raised the globe to her lips, blew on it, then threw it on the floor. It smashed in a spectacular display of glittering shards, emitting a light so bright Arcana flinched away, her eyes squeezed shut. When she opened them, she was alone in the pale blue nowhere, surrounded by the sound of rushing water. The cacophony of crashing waves grew until she cried out in protest, whereupon it cut off, leaving her ears ringing in the silence.

Not all roads lead to ruin, child. Follow the soul song. The secret is hidden behind your face, a woman's voice whispered, not so much speaking as forming the words in the warm, safe space inside Arcana's mind. A curious vertigo clutched at her gut and she opened her eyes with a gasp, looking up into the concerned faces of Caelum and Fenris.

"Arcana? Can you hear me?"

The room tilted crazily and she closed her eyes again to block out the dizziness, gulping down great breaths of fresh air. "Cold."

"Caelum?" Fenris' hands felt like brands as he smoothed the hair back from her face. "Should she not be immune to the chill?"

"Her body's absorbing the energy; give it time. Anyone else would've died."

Arcana's eyes shot open again as she realised her frozen fingers were pressed to the naked skin of Fenris' chest, her body ensconced within the circle of his. "Why haven't you got a shirt on?"

The Guardian stared at her for a long moment and then snorted a laugh. "Body heat," he answered. "It was all we could think of."

Arcana blinked blearily, her stomach lurching as the room spun again. She caught the barest glimpse of Caelum behind her, both male bodies curled around hers to make a nest, before she shut her eyes again and leant into Fenris' warmth. The remains of the frozen energy swirled through her body in waves, slowly lessening in frequency until her magic claimed the last frigid drop for itself. Arcana took a deep breath and exhaled a plume of icy snowflakes, opening her eyes to watch them float up into the air before settling onto the stone floor and melting.

"What happened?" Caelum asked, his soft nose snuffling at her hair.

"It was a message," Arcana answered. "I saw a Guardian carrying a box. She put it in the fridge and then took out a small glass ball, which she smashed on the ground. There were warg chasing her."

"A woman? Was she alone?" Fenris asked.

"No, she had a man with her. A Guardian too, though he wasn't wearing armour. Short, with an axe. They were carrying out the Weaver's instructions."

"The Weaver instructed them to put a box in the fridge?" Caelum asked, his tone filled with disbelief.

Arcana shrugged. "Apparently."

"And the kitten?" Fenris asked.

"What kitten?" Arcana raised her head to see a furry orange face peering curiously at her from atop Fenris' shoulder. "Oh. That kitten."

Now freed from the ice, the creature was even more peculiar. Giant, sky-blue eyes peered out of an oversized head, orange and white striped fur covering a slim body with short, stumpy legs and a long, long, *long* tail. Curious, Arcana reached out a hand and the creature hissed and abruptly disappeared. Something solid bounced off her head a moment later and she winced, rubbing at the lump as a spoon tumbled into her lap.

"It seems to only like Fenris." Caelum's voice was full of barely contained laughter. "And spoons."

"Spoons," Arcana repeated, turning the silverware over in her hands. "Of course. In my vision, the Guardian was having trouble getting the box to stay in the chiller. She weighted it down with a large silver spoon. Watch." Arcana drew back her arm and tossed the spoon across the room. It clattered onto the stone benchtop, careening towards the opposite side. The orange kitten appeared in front of it, catching the sliding silverware in two front paws before promptly disappearing again, taking the treasure with it.

"It's... a spoon kitten?" Caelum flickered his ears in confusion, then turned an accusing glare on Fenris. "This place is bizarre."

"So the kitten was in the chiller by accident?" Fenris rolled his eyes as Caelum continued to glare, adding; "I have never seen such a creature before. The Timeless Kingdom is not normally so unusual a place."

"Hmmmph." Caelum lifted his nose to the ceiling. "The evidence says otherwise."

"It could be an accident, I suppose," Arcana mused. "I mean, if the kitten saw the spoon and jumped into the chiller just as the ice spell was activated, it would've been caught in the crossfire." She frowned. "It's a fairly large coincidence, though."

"In my experience, there is no such thing as coincidence," Fenris murmured. He sighed, and Arcana felt the press of his lips in her hair. "I'm glad you are safe." She hummed softly in response, glorying in the feel of his skin and the vast strength of his lean body. Now feeling far warmer than a minute ago, she couldn't help but trace her fingertips along the topmost edge of his scar. Fenris' teeth nipped the curve of her ear and he whispered; "Are you planning to frost me again?"

"Maybe." Arcana tested the idea, sending ice out of the tip of her finger to trace a swirling design on his pectoral, and got a shiver in return. "Better?"

"Not in the slightest," Fenris admitted, his voice husky. "In fact, you are making it incredibly difficult to focus on the task at hand."

Caelum made a sound suspiciously close to gagging. "Get a room already - preferably one without me in it."

Arcana grinned and rolled out of Fenris' lap, dusting both hands on her thighs. "Lest you two think I'm completely distracted..." She moved over to the chiller, where the last of the melted ice had formed a pool in the base of the unit, and plunged her hand into the frigid water. After a quick rummage, Arcana withdrew a sodden wooden box - and the heavy spoon which had held it in place.

"There it is," Fenris approved, nodding. He stood, tugged his shirt and jumper on over his head and strapped the greatsword back into place. "What is inside?"

Arcana set both spoon and box on the kitchen bench. The box was nothing special, a simple thing whose joins were swollen from the water and gave no hint as to what may be waiting inside. She licked her lips and flipped the lid. "It's a piece of stone."

Caelum stared as she drew out the unassuming lump of grey rock and offered it up for inspection. "A chunk of statue, maybe?"

"I've never seen that symbol before." Fenris plucked the stone from her grasp and frowned down at the carving inset on the smooth surface. "It looks like a glyph or a rune."

"I don't recognise it either but your people forfeited their lives to hide it at the Weaver's request, so it must be important," Arcana said.

"Agreed." Fenris nodded, tucking the stone into the leather pouch on his belt. "Perhaps, like so many other things so far, the reason will become clear in time. Are you well enough to keep moving?"

"Yeah, the magic's well and truly settled in now." Arcana turned the heavy spoon over in her hands. "I'm surprised the kitten didn't try to-" she cut off with a yelp as something solid bounced off her head and a spoon clattered onto the bench. The kitten appeared atop Fenris' shoulders, baring her teeth and hissing at Arcana. "What was *that* for?"

"I don't think she likes you," Caelum chuckled. "That, and you're manhandling her spoon."

Arcana reached towards the kitten and snatched her hand back as tiny claws swiped in her direction. When she retreated a half step, the kitten purred and rubbed her cheek against Fenris' neck. "Huh."

"Told you," Caelum chuckled.

"Looks like you've got yourself a new friend," Arcana said, grinning as she slapped both spoons against Fenris' chest. "Better name her."

Fenris, eyes wide, dubiously offered the spoons to the kitten on his shoulder. She mewed in delight, snatched the two pieces of silverware out of his grasp and disappeared. "Her?"

"Her," Arcana and Caelum said in unison. When Fenris muttered under his breath about the peculiarities of deerken and their mistresses, she simply grinned all the more. "Come on, she's a cute little thing and she clearly adores her big, sexy rescuer."

Fenris glared, then sighed and threw both his hands up. "Whatever - she has disappeared, anyway."

"She'll be back," Caelum said, his voice heavy with amusement as he floated towards the door. His ears twitched, his voice now carrying a frown. "Looks like it's getting dark. Why do we always end up exploring the creepy places at sunset?"

"Dark?" Fenris blinked. "It shouldn't be getting dark yet."

"And yet, it is." Arcana stepped into the corridor, waving a hand at the darkened windows above. "More time flux?"

Fenris paused beside her, craning his neck to stare at the gathering shadows. "I have no idea," he replied at last. "Best we find the Weaver quickly."

"Too bad we can't ask the kitten where she is," Caelum said, glancing back over his shoulder at the empty kitchen.

As though summoned, the spoon kitten appeared on top of Fenris' head, kneading her paws into his dark teal curls. "No," He growled, reaching up to grab the kitten by the ruff and looking deep into her enormous blue eyes. "That will not do." The kitten squeaked, disappeared, and rematerialised on his shoulder, where she began washing one tiny paw with an equally dainty pink tongue. Fenris stared helplessly at Arcana, who stifled a laugh behind one hand. "I am stuck with her, aren't I?"

"Looks that way." She bit her lip, then added; "You must have a very impressive cutlery collection."

"Hmmmm." Caelum tilted his head, giving Fenris a dramatic once over. "That or he has a fabulous… personality."

Fenris growled incoherently and stalked off down the hall, leaving Arcana and Caelum sniggering behind their hands. "This really wasn't the place or time," she gasped, leaning on her deerken for support.

Caelum's shoulders shook with badly suppressed mirth. "Definitely not. But his face!"

"Great gods of Sorcen, his face," Arcana gasped, dashing at her eyes with the back of one wrist. "We better catch up though, before he gets jumped by a warg or something."

"Or a zombie." Caelum made a face and they both hurried up the corridor after Fenris.

The Guardian stopped beneath a moulded archway and swung back to face them, the spoon kitten still clinging to his shoulders. Her extraordinarily long tail was wrapped twice around his neck like a scarf, the ginger and white striping bright against Fenris' soft teal skin. He propped one hand on his hip and glared at them, a pose which would have been intimidating but for the kitten, who chose that moment to rumble a loud purr and rub her overlarge head against the Guardian's twitching jaw. His look of surprise was so adorable that Arcana burst out laughing, hastily stuffing her fist in her mouth as the empty castle echoed the sound back at her.

"Sorry," she managed, reaching out blindly to pat him on the chest. "It's just so cute."

"Cute?" Fenris repeated, his tone indignant. "*Cute?*"

"Oh no, you used the C-word," Caelum whispered, and then they were both lost, laughter pouring out of them like sunlight.

Fenris issued a long suffering sigh. "I'm aware that laughter breaks nervous tension and lightens stressful situations, but this is ridiculous."

When the spoon kitten mewled in adorable agreement Arcana just laughed harder, sagging against Caelum all over again. She regained control of herself after what seemed like hours but was likely only a minute, looking up to find Fenris with his arms crossed over his chest and his lips quirked in a reluctant smile. Clearing her throat, she managed; "Sorry."

He raised a single, sculpted brow. "For the inappropriate laughter, potentially giving away our position to enemies, or calling me cute?"

"All of them," Arcana allowed, then bit her lip. "It is cute, though."

Rolling his eyes to the ceiling, Fenris let out another dramatic sigh which was entirely ruined by the widening smile transforming his face. After a long moment, he dragged her into his arms and pressed a kiss to the top of her head. "Forgiven."

"Thanks." Ignoring the hissing, spitting kitten on his shoulder, Arcana stood on tiptoe to brush her lips to his. "Come on, we better get moving before the zombie warg appear."

Both brows went up at that, but Fenris made no further comment when she stepped around him and through the archway. They now stood in a tiled entrance hall, no less magnificent for all its apparent neglect. To her right, twin stained glass windows loomed either side of enormous, formal doors that were thrown open to the elements. The floors were covered in a thick layer of dust, but a mosaic depicting the changing of the seasons could still be seen underneath. Fenris had said they were to ascend, but the grand, formal staircase which dominated most of the back wall seemed like a giant, open mouth complete with lolling tongue. A shiver went down Arcana's spine at the thought of having to climb it and she turned away, trying to imagine how the room must have looked when it was full of life.

"Can you hear water?" Caelum asked suddenly.

"Yes." Fenris hesitated, then pointed around the back of the staircase. "Over there."

Caelum's ears flickered. "From here it almost sounds like singing."

"In my vision I heard rushing water." Arcana followed the curve of the stairs to an elegant, understated archway in a gloomy corner. Fitted with two carved stone doors, it blended into the soft grey bricks of the castle and had a distinctly neglected air about it. Now that she was closer, Arcana could hear the faint, musical sound of rushing water. She ran her hands over the carved surface and tugged the iron handle, but the door was stuck fast. "Where does this go?"

"It is a service stairway to the Weaver's tower. Allow me - this is not a commonly used door." Fenris reached around her to grasp both handles and set his shoulders. The doors groaned, shuddered and then flung wide, drenching them all in a shower of cold water. Arcana took an instinctive step back, the movement echoed by Fenris as his arms came around her waist, helping to pull her aside. The spoon kitten screeched in their ears, a sound of pure rage, and disappeared in a flurry of orange fur.

"What in the world?" Caelum shook himself thoroughly, sending a second wave of cold water flying all over the place. "Is that a *waterfall*?"

"It appears to be." Fenris released Arcana and stepped forward again, wiping sodden hair out of his eyes as he squinted at the torrent of water. "But... why?"

"It's a message." Arcana stepped past him, holding up a hand to shield her face from the spray. Try as she might, the water cascaded down with such force that she was unable to see beyond the lip of the doorway. "After I saw the vision of those Guardians and the box, I heard a voice: 'Not all roads lead to ruin, child. Follow the soul song. The secret is hidden behind your face.'"

Fenris turned to look over his shoulder at the grand staircase, lips pursed. "Not all roads lead to ruin... that implies an incorrect choice will be set with traps."

"Yes, and I think following the soul's song is the only way we can choose the right path." Arcana blinked water off her eyelashes and squinted upwards again. "Caelum even said the water was singing."

"Indeed," he agreed quietly, worrying at his lower lip with a fang. "It is just..."

"Weird?" Caelum offered. "*Impossible?*"

"Hah," Fenris shook his head, running a frustrated hand through sodden hair. "Point taken, my brother."

Arcana reached her hands out, catching the leading edge of the fall on her fingertips. A familiar chill shot up her arms and she pressed her lips into a thin line. "This is the way."

"Whilst I agree, there's no way we can climb that tower," Caelum muttered. "Unless Fenris has some mermaids handy?"

"That won't be necessary - we've already been given the answer to this problem, too. Watch." Arcana raised both arms and called her magic. The spray from the waterfall receded as the torrent slowed to a downpour, then shrank to a shower and finally became little more than a drip. When she dropped her arms and gave them a shake, the tiny ice crystals which had formed across her skin sloughed to the floor with a tinkling sigh. "See?"

"The ice magic. Of course." Fenris stuck his head through the archway and nodded. "No wonder the power was forced upon you; if not for that spell, you might have left without it."

"Exactly." Arcana stepped through the archway and into the tower, where the waterfall had solidified into a glittering stairway of ice. "How far up is it?"

He peered up into the featureless gloom. "Far enough. There are four floors to the base of the Weaver's rooms in the main part of the castle and we are much lower than that."

"Best we get started, then." She set her hand against the frosted interior wall for balance and began to climb the icy stairs. The tower was eerily silent, even the sound of their footsteps muffled. There was no light, but the ice itself let off a soft blue phosphorescence that was enough for even Arcana to see by.

"I feel compelled to point out that we have been sealed inside," Fenris announced.

Arcana looked back and blanched to see the archway had disappeared and the stairs spiralled endlessly down into darkness. "Great. Probably a security measure in case the wrong person gets in."

"Indeed." He met her gaze, lips pressed into a grim line. "It appears the test of our mettle is not over yet."

"That's fine." Arcana took a deep breath and offered a smile. "I can hold the ice like this for as long as it takes us to figure out what comes next."

"That probably means it's a bad idea to point out that the shadows are advancing on us," Caelum said, his eyes on the bottomless pit below. "This puzzle has a time limit."

"Great," Arcana muttered, picking up her pace. She stared at the tower around them, searching for the answer to whatever puzzle they had inadvertently walked into. Ice slicked everything, obscuring the walls and filling the atmosphere with cold air. "There must be an answer. After all, so far we've been given everything we needed to - wait. Fenris, come here."

He was by her side at once, a pillar of heat and strength. "What is it?"

"Look." Arcana brushed a hand over the wall. The ice dissipated under her touch, revealing a decorative moulding lining the bricks at chest height. "Does that seem familiar to you?"

Fenris grunted and dug into his leather pouch, holding up the section of stone they had retrieved from the kitchen. "It matches."

"I'll bet if we find the place where that fits, we find the exit."

"Better start looking, then." Caelum pushed up close behind them, ears flickering uncertainly. "The darkness is gaining and every cell in my body says that being caught up in it would be very, very bad."

Arcana leant over the edge of the stairs. The shadows were now only a few spirals below them, oozing up over the bricks and consuming the frozen staircase with single minded intensity. "Great. No pressure, then."

"Here, take this." Fenris pressed the stone into her free hand and drew the greatsword. "I'll guard the rear."

Arcana swung back up the stairs, keeping her hand firmly on the decorative stone relief. Ice swept away at her touch, forming tiny drifts on the stairs that tinkled and swished as her companions passed by. Half of her attention remained on keeping the tower frozen whilst the other half examined the wall. It was almost impossible to see through the ice to the stone beneath, and she would have liked to go more slowly, but the creeping darkness behind them made that impossible.

"Ouch!" She jerked backwards as a spoon bounced off her head, then looked up to see the spoon kitten perched on the stairs a few spirals above. "What was that for, you little cretin?"

The kitten mewed down at them and then pulled back from the edge of the stairs with a flick of her extraordinarily long tail. A flash of teal and a soft whispering of air was all the warning Arcana got before Fenris' head peered out from the stairs above, the spoon kitten now in his arms. "I think she's trying to tell us something. Quickly, up here."

"She could have found a better way," Arcana muttered, removing her hand from the wall and putting all her effort into hurrying up the narrow staircase. A few agonising flights later, they came upon Fenris and the kitten, who hissed as she approached.

"Look here," Fenris gestured to a section of ice which he had wiped clean. Arcana melted the area at once, revealing a hole in the relief beyond. "Surely this is the spot."

Arcana slid the missing piece of stone into place and breathed a sigh of relief as it matched perfectly. She looked expectantly around the tower but nothing happened, and when she withdrew her hand the piece of relief promptly fell out. It spiralled through the air for several heart stopping moments before Fenris snatched it, his hand moving so fast it was little more than a blur.

"Interesting," the Guardian said, pushing the piece back into the cavity. "It's the correct place, of that much I am certain. What have we missed?"

Arcana chewed on the inside of her cheek, a sinking feeling knotting her stomach. "The piece fits but the relief isn't whole."

Fenris stared at the minute cracks around the edge of the relief and frowned. "How can you possibly be expected to -"

"I can fix it," Arcana cut him off. "With magic. But… I'd have to dump the ice power and absorb the stone's energy instead."

"And leave us standing on melting ice? Nice," Caelum growled. His ears flickered as he looked down at the approaching shadows. "Can anyone else hear that?"

"Yes." Fenris moved to the edge of the stairs and peered over. Even the spoon kitten's oversized ears were pricked, her long, waving whiskers twitching. "I cannot see anything but… It sounds like warg." He looked over his shoulder at Arcana. "We need to hurry."

"All right." She held out her hand for the piece of stone, clenching her fingers around the sharp edges as Fenris placed it in her palm. "When I let go of the ice, it'll melt quickly. Be ready."

Fenris nodded, readjusting the spoon kitten so that she hung around his neck like a scarf. "We will."

Arcana drew a deep breath and turned back to the wall, purging the ice magic from her body with a shove that left her momentarily giddy. The frozen staircase beneath their feet creaked ominously as she set the broken section of relief into the cavity and laid her palm flat over the top, sending her magic into the walls of the tower. With the ice and cold so prevalent, the energy of the stone came slower than she would have liked - but it came, trickling into her veins, hardening her bones.

"Shit!" Caelum's hooves scrabbled and a moment later the staircase below them broke free with a giant crack, tinkling and sloshing down into oblivion.

"Caelum?" Arcana wanted to look but dared not, concentrating instead on commanding the fractured edges of the relief to merge back into the wall from whence it had come. "Tell me you're alive."

"Fenris caught me," he replied, then swore again as a section of stairway above them came free and whooshed downwards. Arcana glimpsed the flick of Caelum's antler rack out of the corner of her eye and heard his grunt of effort, and a moment later both deerken and Guardian were pressed against the wall either side of her.

"That was close," Fenris murmured.

"Yeah." Caelum peered nervously over the edge of their swiftly shrinking perch and sighed. "No pressure, but you really need to hurry up."

"Almost there," Arcana murmured. The final cracks in the relief smoothed away as she spoke, and the symbol beneath her hand began to glow with pale blue light. The wall in front of them shimmered and disappeared, revealing an archway and a shadowy landing beyond. "Done!"

The stairs tipped precariously underfoot and Arcana shoved Caelum backwards through the archway as he began to slide. He lowered his head and she grabbed for the nearest antler, but the stairs chose that moment to give way with a slithering whoosh. Arcana choked on a scream as she fell, reaching desperately for her magic. The energy was sluggish to respond and she knew she'd never make it before the snarling, snapping shadows claimed her for their own - and then her descent halted, the sudden arrest jarring her bones and snapping her teeth together.

"I've got you," Fenris said calmly, his grip tightening on her wrist. He pulled and Arcana shot upwards, tumbling through the archway only moments ahead of the howling darkness. She landed heavily on his chest and they rolled together, ending in a heap with his narrow hips pinning hers to the floor and his arms braced either side of her head. The Guardian looked strangely young with his sodden curls stuck to his forehead, face soft and jade eyes half lidded. He lowered his head, brushing his nose against hers, shifting his body in a way that sped her heart up for an entirely different reason. Then the spoon kitten's face appeared around the curve of Fenris' neck, and the oddly proportioned ginger cat hissed, dropped a spoon onto Arcana's forehead, caught the silverware as it bounced back up - and disappeared.

"Damned cat," she muttered, dropping her head back against the floorboards. "I should have left you to freeze in that giant ice block."

Fenris choked on what might have been a laugh. "Are you all right? Did I hurt you?"

"No." Arcana caught her fingers in his, drew his palm to her lips and kissed it. "That was close. Thanks for the save."

"Welcome," Fenris replied, lips curving with a sinfully wicked smile. The moment hung between them and for a second Arcana thought he might kiss her after all, but the Guardian sighed and rolled away, tugging her to her feet. "We should keep moving."

He was right, but Arcana still wrinkled her nose in annoyance. She covered the action by tugging her clothes back into place and squeezing water out of her hair as best she could. Caelum heaved himself upright beside her, carefully shaking out each of his four long legs and then his body. "Please tell me this is the right place."

"It is." Fenris ran a hand through his wet curls and then shook it, sending a spray of water onto the wall. "I am familiar with this place - the

Weaver's chamber is on the other side of that door." He jerked his chin to a small, unassuming wooden door at the end of the landing.

"As long as we've passed all her tests," Caelum muttered, flicking a look over his shoulder at the tower, now completely cloaked in darkness. "At least the shadows didn't follow us in here."

"Indeed." Fenris studied the door for a long moment then drew the greatsword. "Ready?"

Arcana strode to join him and they shared a long look. When she finally nodded, Fenris flicked the latch and pushed the door wide, stepping through with his sword raised.

The Weaver's chamber was a small, round room with regularly spaced windows through which bright sunlight streamed. Golden dust danced in the rays, settling over disused chairs and a long, narrow bench with a loom at one end. Cobwebs hung from almost every conceivable surface, refracting the light so that they glittered with a rainbow of colour.

"She's not here." Fenris' boots stirred up swirls of dust as he walked to the centre of the room and turned a circle, eyes saucer-wide. "How can that be?"

Arcana studied the cobwebs hanging from the ceiling, her mind in chaos. All their travel and sacrifice had been to come here, only to find the Kingdom in ruins and the tower empty. In fact, if not for the absolute horror on Fenris' face, she might have come to wonder if his story had ever been true at all. No, she told herself - she'd met Taelon. She'd seen the warg. Whatever Fenris had originally believed about their appearance in the icy temple, he'd not lied to her about his purpose. Gathering her thoughts, Arcana took a deep breath and crossed to twine her fingers through his. "Taelon must have taken her out."

"I..." Fenris swallowed heavily, the tip of the greatsword lowering to rest on the floor. "I've never seen her leave. I didn't think it was possible - she is a part of this place as much as it is a part of her. Or she was."

"It would certainly explain the scenery outside if she wasn't here," Caelum said slowly, his eyes on the golden sunlight streaming in through the windows. "And the fact that the Kingdom can't seem to decide if it's night or day or somewhere in between."

Fenris nodded, his expression numb. "I suppose it might cause some rather dramatic time fluxes, but I cannot say for certain. This is beyond the realm of my experience."

"Hmmm." Arcana reached a hand up to a piece of cobweb dangling by her shoulder and paused just short of it. Now that she looked again, it wasn't a cobweb at all but a shred of tapestry, woven in a bright rainbow of colours. She stared around the room, Fenris' words ringing in her ears, and felt her heart stutter. "These are scraps of the weave, aren't they?"

"Yes." Fenris sheathed the greatsword and reached to brush the same dangling piece of tapestry. "I anticipated Taelon might damage the weave in an effort to control her, but this... This would be agony. Like having an arm torn off."

She stared at the colours brushing over his knuckles and swallowed. "May I touch it?"

"Of course."

The silken threads were soft and light in Arcana's fingers and as soon as she touched them, they detached from the ceiling and fell into her hand. She tugged her other hand free of Fenris' grip to examine them, noting the strands were long and strong in spite of their frayed ends. After a moment's hesitation, she sorted them into three groups and began to plait them together. "If the Weaver is gone," she said as she worked, "We'll simply have to find her. Can you track Taelon through your blood bond?"

"In theory." Fenris took a half step back and ran both hands over his face. "The blood bond does not give me an exact location or a distance, only the vague idea that Taelon is in *that* direction." He waved an arm off to one side, brow furrowed. "I could follow that vague notion but he would feel me approaching and it would take little to evade me - as I have been evading him in turn."

"That makes sense." Arcana tied off the end of the plait and examined her work, noting the faint shimmer to the threads and the incredible strength in the length she'd bound together. "Also, considering Taelon has been manipulating the blood bond from the beginning, he's probably not dumb enough to hang out near the Weaver for any great length of time."

"No."

Arcana titled her head to the side. "Is it possible to break the blood bond?"

"Not that I know of - aside from death, of course. Perhaps the Weaver has a way, but if she did, surely she'd have cut Taelon free by now." Long fingers twisted into dark teal curls, grown over the last couple of months into an adorably messy mop that brushed the nape of his neck. "I was so sure she would be here. So *certain* that slipping into the Kingdom would give us a resolution." Fenris loosed a low growl, tugging at his hair in frustration. "That's why it was so easy - Taelon knew what I would do. He planned for me to arrive at this point and know I had been outsmarted. I am a fool."

"Hey." Arcana caught his hand, tugging until he turned to look at her.

"You did what you were trained to do. Taelon is a step ahead, yes, but that doesn't make you a fool." She looped the plaited threads of the weave around his wrist and used her magic to join the ends seamlessly into one another, securing it permanently in place. "You are the Weaver's chosen warrior. She led us here for a reason, Fenris." She bent to kiss his wrist where the impromptu bracelet rested, its deep, jewel tones complementing his pale teal skin as though made for it. "Hope. There is always hope."

Slowly, Fenris' other hand lowered and he closed his fingers over Arcana's. His eyes were on the plaited bracelet, and they were lined with silver that he blinked rapidly to clear. "Hope," he repeated, his voice thick with emotion, "Is a tenuous notion."

"I don't think so - I've lived my whole life on a steady diet of hope," Arcana corrected gently. "It's done me well enough so far." She wrapped her arms around his waist and laid her head against his chest, listening to the steady thumping of his heart. "Together. We'll find her together."

Fenris' arms came around her and a moment later, his head rested atop her own. "How can you be so certain?"

"Apart from hope?" Arcana forced herself to chuckle, her hands slipping under the hem of his jumper to move soothingly over the sculpted muscles of his back. "The Weaver made us work awfully hard to gain access to a room that she's no longer inhabiting. I'm willing to bet she knew Taelon would take her out of here, and was planning for it even as she sent you to close the portals."

"She knew I would fail," he sighed.

"No - she knew you would live," Arcana corrected. "If you'd stayed here, Taelon would've overcome you with sheer numbers alone. Am I right?"

Fenris gave a noncommittal grunt. "Perhaps."

"So sending you to close the portals - which worked, for the most part - also gave you a chance to escape when the time came. And once you were gone, she prepared for your return. Our return, even." Arcana leant back to stare into his face, feeling the soft, tickling glide of feathers over her skin as their gazes locked. "I do not believe for a second that this is only an empty room."

His chest expanded against hers and after a moment, Fenris reached to stroke a hand down her hair, lips tugging into a grudging smile as he unwittingly came away with a handful of water. Shaking it off, he gripped her chin and bent to brush a trembling kiss across her lips. "Thank you."

Arcana melted into his embrace, returning his sweet kiss with one of her own. "Welcome."

"That water's not moving," Caelum said suddenly.

"Huh?" Arcana blinked and turned as the deerken lowered his head to sniff at the floor. The water from her hair sat shimmering on the wood in a curious lump, neither soaking into the cracks nor spreading out. "Well, that's something you don't see every day."

"Of course," Fenris murmured and quite suddenly he was crouched by the water droplets, one hand splayed on the floor for balance as he examined them. "The tower is in suspension."

"Suspension?"

"Yes." He blew gently on the water and watched it wriggle and roll awkwardly across the floor without dissolving. "This room is timeless in every sense of the word - suspended in a single moment."

"I suppose that makes sense given the way the rest of the castle has decayed." Arcana bit her lip, casting a glance around the chamber. "Hard for us to find whatever the Weaver left if time crumbles everything to dust."

"Yes." Fenris pushed upright, his fingers playing with the plaited bracelet Arcana had tied around his wrist. After a moment, he blinked and turned to her. "So far everything has been aimed at you. I'm willing to wager that this part of the test is, too."

"Maybe." Arcana moved to the edge of the room and laid both hands flat against the wall, sending her energy into the stone. The tower reacted instantly, humming beneath her palms with a tone that jarred her senses. "Ack!"

"What is it?" Fenris' face creased in concern.

Arcana winced and rubbed her head. "The wall rejected my magic. Whatever power the Weaver used to suspend the tower gives off a terrible dissonance."

"Oh?" Fenris strode to Arcana's side and brushed a hand over the bricks. "It feels no different than usual, but perhaps the sound means something?"

"I suppose there's only one way to find out." She returned her hands to the wall. Instead of absorbing her energy the stone reflected it back with that same clanging cacophony, but Arcana was prepared this time and held fast. The awful feeling shuddered through her bones as she swept the room with her magic, seeking some sort of clue. Two thirds of the way around the tone changed, becoming lighter and infinitely more pleasant, and the strange discordance ceased. "There."

Caelum's ears pricked with excitement. "You found something?"

"I think so." She crossed the room, splaying both hands across a section of wall that looked like any other, and felt around with her magic again. Unlike the rest of the tower, the energy was soothing - but when she tried to manipulate the stonework, Arcana's magic abruptly winked out.

"Arcana?" Fenris caught her as she sagged, peering into her face. "Are you all right?"

"Yeah, yeah. Just a shock." Straightening, she tapped the wall in question. "I need you to smash this."

He blinked. "Smash it?"

"Yes. It rejects my magic. I can't break it."

Ever so slowly, he turned in place to measure up the masonry, then wrapped one hand over the top of the other and hammered his conjoined fists into the stone. It cracked immediately, spidery lines making their ponderous way out from the centre point until a single piece of stone tumbled into Fenris' outstretched hands. He turned it over in his fingers, then bent to peer into the hole. "There's another wall behind this one."

Arcana could only stare as the Guardian curled long fingers around the edge of the masonry and began to peel it away like so much paper. With his preternatural strength, it took less than a minute to reveal a shallow recess, the shape and size reminiscent of a picture frame. Made from darker masonry than the rest of the tower, it was pockmarked by a series of indentations in the two upper corners.

"What is it?" Caelum asked, tilting his head to one side.

"I'm not sure." Fenris brushed his fingers over one of the indentations. "It looks as though something is meant to fit here."

"But we don't have anything to *put* in there," Arcana grumbled. "So far, it's been a case of find the thing, put the thing, but there's nothing - oh." She exhaled on a rush, jaw dropping for the second time in as many minutes. "We *do* have something to put in it."

Caelum raised his brows in surprise. "We do? What?"

"You," Arcana answered, her heart thumping rapidly in her chest. "Put your antlers in - you know, like you did in the temple where we found Fenris."

"My antlers?" Caelum swung back to the wall, examining the markings. After a long moment he set the points of his antler rack into the topmost of the indentations and leant forward, rolling his neck until the entire sweep of his antlers fit neatly into the hollows. The wall glowed green, a gentle glow that expanded outwards, intensifying until it was blindingly bright. When the light faded, a narrow doorway and a darkened tunnel were revealed.

Arcana crossed to the opening, peering into the narrow corridor beyond. "I guess we go in."

Fenris was quite suddenly in front of her, greatsword in hand. "Allow me to go first. Just in case."

"You still think there'll be traps?"

"Now more than ever." He ducked through the doorway and paused on the other side, brows furrowed slightly. "Nothing... yet."

Caelum's nose crinkled. "Do I smell forest?"

"A forest... in a tower?" Arcana looked from deerken to Guardian and back again. "You're not making me feel better."

"Since when are you worried about weird stuff like that?" Caelum shoved her with his shoulder. "Come on, let's get this done."

CHAPTER
FOURTEEN

Solid pillars of silver-veined stone rose from a matching floor littered with leaves. Thick vines hung in tresses from the roof, whose stone arms supported a network of stained glass in shades of blue and green. Some of the panes were missing, letting in stray rays of sunlight that fell haphazardly across the floor.

"Where are we?" Arcana wondered, her voice hushed.

Caelum's head swung from side to side, his silvery fur dappled in shades of teal by the stained glass windows high above. "It feels like some sort of temple."

"It must be." Dried leaves crunched underfoot as she moved down a broad central walkway with two neat rows of columns either side. "Nobody puts this amount of effort into any old building."

Fenris stood five paces ahead, his teal skin almost glowing in the forest coloured lighting. The air was warm, carrying with it the scent of blossoms and curling ferns - and indeed, Arcana could see several of them sprouting from cracks in the temple walls. "Look," Fenris said, his soft voice sighing through the shadows. "An altar."

Arcana squinted towards the back of the hall. Sunlight fell through a circular hole in the ceiling to illuminate a short dais with an enormous stone chair on top. "Is that a throne?"

"It is," Fenris affirmed. He glanced back at her, jade eyes bright in the half light. "There is also someone sitting on it."

Arcana paused and frowned. "Should we be worried?"

"Not at the moment. It is another skeleton."

"Of course it is." Caelum snorted, kicking at a drift of leaves as he passed by. "Just for something new, I'd like to find someone alive."

"Be careful what you wish for," Arcana muttered, trailing Fenris down the peaceful avenue. The altar was no more than a narrow rectangle of stone, barely large enough to house the enormous throne perched atop it. The skeleton reclined upon a seat large enough to fit both she and Fenris with room to spare. Arcana noted long legs, clawed feet and hands and a long muzzle full of curving fangs. "Another warg?"

"It appears so." Fenris stepped up beside her, head cocked to one side. "Longer legs and thinner shoulders than any we've seen to date, however."

Arcana looked up at the throne, where elaborate leaf and vine carvings wound across the back of the chair. Runes had been chiselled into the stone in a semi-circular design and she imagined they would appear as a crown to whoever sat beneath. "Clearly an important chair. Too bad it's not more ancient Sorcen."

"I cannot read it either," Fenris said.

"You sound surprised."

"Mildly," he agreed. "I am fluent in seventy-three of the more common languages in the known universe, and twelve of the lesser. I can read them all and write in most. So yes, it is somewhat of a surprise to find something I have not at least seen in passing before - aside from your ancient Sorcen, that is."

Arcana blinked, doing a quick mental tally. "You speak eighty-five languages?"

He nodded. "Not counting Universal Galactic."

"You... why?"

Fenris raised an eyebrow. "Languages interest me, and the Timeless Kingdom doesn't get holo reception."

"I literally have nothing to say to that." Arcana shook her head, boggling at the idea of speaking that many different tongues. "Is there anything you *can't* do?"

"Fly," he returned equably, and then winked. "I also have it on good authority that I am a terrible singer."

Caelum snorted a laugh and Arcana reached up to massage her temples. "Okay, the idea of that - I don't need a demonstration," she added, earning a mischievous grin from Fenris. She turned resolutely back to the throne and frowned. "Something about these symbols looks oddly familiar. I just can't think where I've seen their like before."

"If it's warg script, maybe we saw it at a previous ruin," Caelum suggested.

"Maybe. Weird to think of warg being literate, though." Arcana drifted towards the back wall of the temple, looking for alternative exits or hidden alcoves. As she drew closer, she noticed the vines covering the back wall were woven together - not in the wild, haphazard way one might expect of a place left to ruin, but dipping and looping through one another as though part of a fabric. Sprouting tendrils and enormous foliage helped disguise the effect but the more she stared, the more Arcana was certain the vines had been coaxed to grow that way. Up close, each trunk was as thick as her wrist, the individual leaves large enough to shade her face. She brushed her fingers along the pebbly bark and her magic leapt to the forefront, guzzling down the essence of the vines.

"What are you doing?" Caelum asked, appearing around the corner of the dais.

"I'm not sure." Arcana splayed her fingers and the vines began to wriggle and twitch, unravelling their intricate pattern. "These vines don't seem natural - my magic's back to normal though."

"Nothing in this place seems natural." Caelum moved to stand beside Arcana, his velvety antler rack rapidly sprouting miniature leaves that were an exact replica of those dangling from the vines above. Together they watched the giant wall of greenery disentangle itself and sweep aside like a living curtain, revealing the back wall of the temple. The smooth, silver-veined stone had been carved with thousands of tiny faces, each one smaller than the palm of Arcana's hand. Some were humanoid, some bestial and others somewhere in between, wearing a wide range of expressions. Caelum took a half step forwards and then stopped, ears twitching. "I feel as though 'wow' isn't really adequate here. Whoever did this had more free time on their hands than Fenris on his day off."

"I do not get days off," Fenris announced, dropping down off the dais to join them. "That workmanship is incredible. Why allow the vines to cover it over?"

"I don't know, but the vines didn't just grow there. They were woven together on purpose." Arcana fisted both hands on her hips. "What if this is the message? After all, the last clue was: 'The secret is hidden behind your face.'"

"That's a lot of faces," Caelum pointed out. "How do we know which one is keeping secrets?"

"I'm not sure." Arcana reached out with tentative fingers and poked a withered looking alien in the forehead. The stone face frowned in response, lips parting to reveal sharp teeth. One by one the other faces came to life, screwing up their noses and poking out their tongues, glaring and hissing. Arcana jumped back as they began to move, shuffling and slithering across the wall until their order was completely different. With a final, collective pout, they settled and froze.

"Well, that's going to make it difficult to search," Caelum remarked.

"No kidding." Arcana craned her neck to try and get a better view. "Okay, search for something familiar, but nobody touch unless we're certain." It was easier said than done - the faces were innumerable. Though each one seemed different at first, the more Arcana stared at the wall, the more the features appeared to run together, until she had to step back, blinking furiously and rubbing at her eyes.

"I see my mother," said Caelum suddenly.

Arcana followed the line of his quivering nose to see a doe's face set into the wall. "She's a little young, don't you think? That could be any deerken."

"This one looks like Flare." Fenris indicated a male's face, chin lifted and hair rakishly unruly.

"It could be." Arcana frowned. "It's hard to tell without colour and life. I'm not sure."

"There's Lesce!" Caelum reared up on his hind legs, dancing to and fro for balance, eyes swirling in excitement.

"And my father," Fenris added, his voice equally enthusiastic.

Arcana stared at the faces they indicated, screwing up her nose. The resemblances seemed more coincidental than intentional. "I'm not sure I - don't touch!"

Fenris' hand froze mid reach. "It's my mother," he protested. "I'm certain."

"And there's Burke," Caelum's nose inched closer to a woman's boned headplate.

"Stop, both of you!" Arcana snapped, her voice slicing through their eagerness. "It's a trick. A trap."

Fenris blinked at her in surprise. "What are you talking about?"

"The wall." Arcana slapped at his wrist as it rose again. "The faces are blanks, waiting for your imaginations to supply the resemblance. I don't see any of the people you've mentioned - I see the potential for them, but I don't see *them*. There is magic here and it's trying to fool you into making the wrong choice."

"If we get it wrong, so what?" Caelum rolled his shoulders in a shrug, ears fluttering in annoyance. "The wall rearranges and we start again."

"That's the Weaver. I'm sure of it," Fenris murmured, his expression distant. "Her face would certainly be the right choice." He leapt at the wall beside the carvings and scaled it like a ladder, passing beyond Arcana's reach before she'd so much as registered the words.

"No!" She shouted, but too late - the Guardian's hand snaked out and pressed firmly against the face of a woman who could have been anyone. Her stone mouth opened wide, emitting a keening wail which shook the cavernous room. Arcana stumbled sideways as the floor undulated beneath her feet and leaves rained down from the vinework above. Fenris fell heavily to the floor, clutching at a short spear protruding from his hip while several others whizzed by overhead.

Caelum stood transfixed as the faces on the wall began to bulge outwards, his nose inching closer to the carving he believed to belong to his mother. The doe opened stone jaws to reveal neat rows of tiny fangs glistening with venom and stretched towards the soft flesh of his muzzle. Arcana rolled upright and leapt, catching the deerken's antler rack and yanking his head away.

"No! Mother!" Caelum lifted his head and shook, rattling Arcana's bones inside her skin. When she didn't immediately dislodge he set his legs in preparation to smash her against the wall, the great muscles in his neck and shoulders bunching. Arcana tightened her grip on his antlers and swung both legs up to kick at his knee, buckling the foreleg and sending them both crashing to the floor. She landed flat on her back with the deerken's weight on top, his head slamming into her chest and the edges of his antlers narrowly missing her face.

Arcana willed her lungs to work and was denied for what seemed an eternity before at last the air rushed in. "Caelum?"

"I'm here," he answered, voice trembling. "You can let go."

"Are you sure?"

He relaxed against her. "I'll behave. I'm free now."

Arcana loosed her grip and groaned as Caelum rolled onto his stomach. "You're heavy," she complained, turning onto her hands and knees. She raised her head to see Fenris in a sitting position, both hands covering his face and the spear embedded deep in his flesh.

"Sorry." Caelum staggered as he stood, left foreleg tucked awkwardly against his chest. "You lamed me, if that helps."

"No, that doesn't help." Arcana sat back on her heels. "I'm sorry."

"Forget it - Better lame than whatever the wall would've done." Caelum shook his head vigorously, leaves raining from his antlers to fall amongst those already on the floor. "Those teeth... I couldn't help it."

"I know." Arcana eyed the spear sticking out of Fenris' hip and caught her lip between her teeth. "You still with us, Guardian?"

"I'm alive," Fenris said, his voice muffled behind his palms. "Now I know how it feels to be caught in a glamour."

Caelum's ears flickered. "A bit like being shot in the arse?"

"Hip," Fenris corrected, cracking his fingers just enough to eyeball Caelum from between them. "It's definitely in my hip."

"Arse, or I'm a warg's aunt."

"Enough!" Arcana levelled a trembling finger at them both. "Stop. Just stop. If Fenris hadn't been halfway up the wall, those spears would have hit his chest and head."

A short, tense silence.

"I'm fine," Fenris said finally.

"You are *not* fine," Arcana growled, crawling to his side. She dropped to her elbows to examine the entry point, blinking rapidly to clear the tears from her eyes. "You both could've died and then where would we be?"

"Arcana," Fenris' voice was soothing. "We're all alive. The rest will -"

"*Shut up!*"

"Death'd be a reprieve from all this shouting, at least," Caelum muttered. "I'm going to have nightmares about that tiny doe's face."

"We're fortunate Arcana was immune to the spell," Fenris agreed.

She stared at the Guardian in disbelief. "You still got shot!"

"It could be worse. This spear hit home, but the impact broke the compulsion and I was able to dodge the rest." He tipped her chin up with one finger, jade eyes brimming with regret. "I'm sorry I ignored your warning."

"Yeah, yeah, we're all sorry now that we can't walk," she snapped, the effect completely ruined by the way her lower lip trembled.

"The wound to my pride will last far longer than this." Fenris gestured down at the spear. "... But I will need you to pull it out."

"I know. Hold still." Arcana wrapped one hand around the spear, braced the other against his ribs and yanked the projectile free in one swift movement.

Fenris grunted, pressing his hand to the wound to stem the tide of dark blood, his complexion so pale Arcana worried he might faint. When she rummaged in her satchel and drew out Lesce's tin of salve, however, his back stiffened. "Do you really think that's necessary?"

Arcana raised an eyebrow. "This will help stop the bleeding and stave off any infection."

"Yes but -" He cut off with a gasp as she batted his hand away and began packing salve into the wound. "Weaver save me but that hurts."

"Complain to Lesce, not me." Arcana tossed the salve back in the satchel and pulled out a bandage, prodding Fenris onto his knees so that she could try to bind his hip, blushing as her hands passed dangerously close to his groin. "Okay, that's the best I can do for now. As long as the spear wasn't poisoned, that should tide you over until we get back to the ship."

"A night or two's solid rest and all will be well; I heal quickly." Fenris scooped up the spear and sniffed the bloodied tip carefully. "No poison. We have been fortunate."

"Fortunate," Arcana echoed, her gaze travelling between the two males. "Can either of you stand?"

"I think so." Fenris frowned, shifting his weight back and forth on his knees. "Yes. But I will rest while I can."

"You both should. Let me take care of this."

"Very well. Considering you did not fall prey to the spell, it seems the best course of action regardless of our physical state." Fenris' gaze was on the wall, where the myriad of faces stared innocently back. "I would guess that for each incorrect answer, there will be a punishment of increasing intensity."

"Best not to make another mistake, then." Arcana pushed upright and moved back to the wall, examining the faces with care. "None of these are familiar."

"The answer is hidden behind your face," Fenris murmured, drumming restless fingers on one thigh. He took up a perch on the edge of the dais, angling his body to avoid putting too much pressure on his wound. "It sounds simple enough on the surface."

"Yes, but whose face? Yours? Mine? Caelum's?" Arcana gestured in frustration at the wall. "None of these look like us."

Fenris laid the greatsword across his knees, tracing one finger along the runes etched into the blade. "I believe it will be your face. You were given the clue and are the only one who can look at the wall without being trapped in the magic." He paused, frowning at the distorted reflection in the flat of the blade. "I suppose it may also depend on whether the clue is figurative or literal - or both."

"Literal?" Arcana frowned, pressing both hands to her cheeks. "What's behind my face that could possibly be useful here?"

"Teeth. Brain. Eyes..." Fenris ticked the options off on his fingers as he spoke. "Blood, hair, saliva, magic."

"I'm not licking the wall... magic, however, is an interesting thought."
She tapped her chin thoughtfully. "I mean, it's a magic puzzle, right?"

"You're going to mess with an enchanted wall?" Caelum's voice held a
note of alarm and Arcana heard his hooves scrabbling on the stone floor as
he tried to stand on three legs.

"And risk setting off the next round of traps? No," Arcana waved him
down, smiling in reassurance. "There's more to magic than destroying
things - you know that. It can be used to build, to fix and to protect. Or..."
Arcana grinned suddenly. "Or to view things from a different angle."

She stretched out a hand and one of the vines hanging from the roof
reached down to curl around her waist, lifting her up to view the higher
sections of the wall. A female face caught her eye almost immediately. It
was a young woman's face, with wavy, shoulder length hair and an easy
smile. Arcana commanded the vine to steer her closer and as she
approached, the stone eyes swivelled to stare into her own. The tiny stone
woman smiled and Arcana shivered.

"Did you find something?" Caelum stood directly below her, lamed leg
tucked into his chest and face creased in concern. "I'm too scared to look in
case it gets me again."

"I found something." Arcana examined the fall of the carving's hair, the
soft play of freckles across her nose and cheeks, the easy smile wielded so
readily. "It's me. Only it's not me. It's me... from before." She reached out a
trembling finger and touched the stone cheek. The tiny carving laid a
gentle kiss on her fingertip then spun away, turning into the wall and
revealing a tiny recess.

"Well? Did it work?"

"Yes." Arcana cleared her throat, frustrated by the lump in it. "It
worked." She reached inside the hole and withdrew a small leather
bundle. As soon as her hand was clear, the face of Spring returned, winked
and fell still.

The answer is hidden behind your face. Clever, really, for no agent of
Taelon would recognise that woman, or realise that she and Arcana had
once been the same. Arcana signalled the vine to set her on the ground and
flicked a finger to dismiss it, clutching the leather bundle to her chest.

"You are still that person, you know," Fenris said quietly, limping
across the floor to stand before her. "She's not gone, simply evolved."

"And who told you that?"

"Those books Flare pressed upon me revealed your full name as
Arcana Spring Lurien, but it was my own perceptions that have led me to

believe in your evolution." His face softened. "Growth does not mean abandoning the old, but incorporating it into the new."

"I guess so. It's just... it's a lifetime ago now." She held a salt white hand up to the light and turned it back and forth. "And I look completely different."

"You do - I've seen the pictures." Fenris caught her fluttering hand and drew it to his lips, pressing a kiss to Arcana's palm that rippled all the way to her belly. His mouth drew into a wicked grin and he winked. "I like you better this way."

Arcana swallowed as her heart thumped a little harder. "Really?"

There was too much pain in that question; too much longing. Fenris closed his eyes for a brief second, then opened them to cup her face in both hands and stare directly into her face. "You are perfect, Arcana. Never doubt it."

"Oh." Blinking rapidly, she offered him a smile that, unlike the previous one, was real. Shy and small, but real. "Thank you."

His thumbs feathered across her cheekbones even as the glamour feathered across her skin. "You are most welcome."

Drawing a deep, steadying breath, Arcana held out the leather bundle she'd retrieved. "Here," she said. "It's most likely for you."

Fenris accepted the bundle with a subtle nod, picking the knot and flipping the leather open. Inside was a skein of grey thread, two grey and black feathers and a long, curved incisor.

"A tooth," Caelum murmured, sniffing delicately at the serrated edge.

"I'll bet you any money it fits inside that skeleton on the throne." Arcana frowned, plucking the tooth out of the bundle and holding it up to the light. "Looks wargish to me."

"And the rest?" Caelum wondered. They both looked at Fenris.

"Thread... like what is used in the weave." The Guardian frowned, running a finger over the skein. "Only it's blank. Empty."

"Ready to be used?"

"Perhaps. And the feathers - I have never seen their like. They could be for or from anything." He made a frustrated noise in the base of his throat and flipped the leather cover closed. "I grow tired of such cryptic communications. We should start with what we know."

"The tooth." Arcana climbed the steps to where the skeleton reclined atop its oversized throne and peered at the skull waiting there. There were several teeth missing but only one incisor, so she wrapped her hand around the ivory muzzle and pushed the tooth into place. No sooner had she stepped back than a gust of wind swept through the room, stirring the leaves and bringing with it the odour of sulphur.

"Look at the sun," Caelum gasped. Arcana looked up in time to see it sweep across the sky, trailing the moon and a blanket of stars only to return almost instantly, a dizzying cycle of days and nights which passed in moments. Her stomach lurched and she lowered her gaze, gripping Fenris' arm as the bones began to twitch and jerk, inching back together. Muscle bloomed like moss, followed by tendons, organs, a cloak of pale skin and soft grey fur.

"Well, it's definitely a warg," Arcana murmured, the hairs on her arms standing straight.

"In a dress," Caelum added. True to his word, a white linen gown formed, hugging the warg's figure and enhancing feminine curves accentuated by sleek fur and a long, elegant muzzle. The warg sat up slowly, joints clicking and jerking into place. Long, clawed hands sat neatly in her lap and enormous pointed ears rotated forward, their silver fur tipped with black. At last the creature's eyes opened, skewering them with an icy blue gaze.

"You have come at last," she breathed, her soft voice tinged with a gravelly undertone. "I am Iniron, Matriarch of the Warg. Welcome to my home."

"I'm Arcana, and this is Caelum. And Fenris-"

"Overlord to the Weaver," Iniron finished, the corners of her wolfish lips twitching into a smile. "Yes, I know who you are. I've waited an eternity for you, young warrior."

Fenris swept her a half bow. "Then it seems we are in the right place, Matriarch. Forgive me, but you are not like any other warg I've ever met."

"That's because you've never met a warg, Overlord. You have freed many, but met not a one." Iniron blinked owlishly, allowing her words to sink in, and turned pale eyes on Arcana. "Except you, child. I can see it in your face - you have peered beyond the veil."

Arcana shivered, recalling with sudden clarity those soft, dreamy moments at the Pariah's palace. "She asked me to set her free."

"Yes." Iniron's ears flickered in a movement not unlike that which Caelum made when he was thinking. "And did you?"

"I killed her," Arcana whispered, unsure why she was confessing to a warg, of all creatures. "She seemed... relieved."

Iniron inclined her head. "Then you have my thanks. My people were once as I am now, but a dark sickness overcame us." The Matriarch gestured to the sky, still wheeling and turning from night to day above them. "We succumbed quickly and wholly, our minds lost in a sea of bloodlust and our culture buried beneath the bodies. We gained strength and speed but became as beasts." Iniron's clawed hand clenched into a fist capable of crushing skulls - but when she looked at Arcana, her face was gentle. "When you kill a warg, you do not end a life. You free a spirit - and you earn my eternal gratitude."

Feeling all the more confused, Arcana swept the Matriarch a bow of her own. "In all honesty, it was self-defence."

"Much mercy is." Iniron's tongue lolled out in silent laughter. "But I know you are not here to discuss my people." She slid her eyes to Fenris. "Particularly you."

"We are looking for the Weaver."

Iniron inclined her head again - a queen on her throne, regal and graceful. "I know. We have spoken, she and I, on a plane not anywhere near to this one. She told me this day would come. Our fates are more entwined than you might think, Overlord."

Fenris shifted his weight in a rare display of discomfort. "How so? I do not wish to offend, but my primary duty is to free the Weaver."

Once again that silent laugh. "And so it should be - but rescuing the Weaver will not stem the tide of death. The warg are everywhere and their bloodlust will only increase." Iniron sighed and shook her head. "They must be freed from the yoke which binds them."

Fenris went very still. "Do you mean Taelon?"

"The usurper?" The Matriarch snarled, lips drawing back to reveal her sharp teeth. "The beast who walks amongst the warg in my place, believing his own delusions? The creature who snuck to my side, whispering into my addled mind, twisting and turning my thoughts the same way he twisted and turned his knife?" Iniron clutched her chest, and her hands came away coated with blood. "He is a stain upon the honour of life. A disease."

Arcana frowned down at the blood, now flowing freely from a stab wound in the warg's chest. "He killed you."

"He freed me and took my burden as his own. He thought himself the stronger. The better. The fiercer," Iniron spat. One of her eyes fluttered and when it opened again, the pale blue colour was gone, replaced instead by the dull amber with which Arcana was familiar. "But he is no Matriarch, your traitor. None at all."

"Fenris..." Arcana murmured, brushing her fingers to his.

"It's a flux," he replied. "Time is passing incredibly quickly, condensing years into seconds." Fenris squared his shoulders. "Tell me, Matriarch - the Weaver. Surely she left you a message for us?"

"She has left several, Overlord, if you've been paying attention." Iniron grinned, and this time her smile had a vicious edge. "If you're looking for words, however, I can offer you this: do not give in to despair. The cycle must be broken before it can be restored. Blood for blood, life for life. Keep sharp your blade and place your faith in the weave." Iniron's voice faded into a growl and she clutched at the arms of the chair, blood streaming down her chest and across her lap. When she spoke again, her voice came on a gasp. "This is what I have been tasked to remind you."

"More riddles and the back half of the Guardian's oath." Fenris clenched his fists until the knuckles went white. "Is that really what the Weaver sent us here to find?"

Iniron snarled. "Are you really so bloody minded as all that? My entire presence here is a sign, foolish boy. Wake up and start using your brain."

"Talking in circles and piling on insults does not help -"

"Time is against us, Overlord." Iniron's voice dropped and distorted, her words slurred. "There is no more I can give you. I ask only one thing: Set me free, as the Weaver promised you would." Iniron hunched over, her shoulders bulking, frame extending and claws curving. The last of the blue disappeared from her good eye and she drew back her lips in a snarl.

Fenris inclined his head reluctantly. "As you wish, Matriarch."

Iniron howled, the sound a curious mix of grief and rage. She gathered powerful legs beneath her and launched - straight at Arcana. The greatsword sang through the air, a blur of silver that cleft Iniron's head from her neck. The warg's body slammed into Arcana's chest, throwing them both backwards onto the floor, warm blood spurting over her face and neck. The Matriarch's head thumped into the drifting leaves, the amber fading from her eyes in death.

Arcana shoved uselessly at the dead weight, gasping in relief as Caelum swept the body aside with his antlers. "You okay?"

"Yeah. Thanks." She spat blood and fur onto the floor, wiping her face on her sleeve. "Gross."

"We need to leave." Fenris hobbled over and bent to tug Arcana upright. She swayed against him and the Guardian stumbled, steadying them both by setting the tip of the greatsword against the floor like a crutch. He pointed his free hand at Iniron's body, where flesh was melting away to reveal the bones beneath. "Time is still passing too quickly and I can hear warg approaching." As if in response to his warning, howls echoed through the temple. Fenris pushed Arcana down the columned avenue towards the Weaver's tower. "Hurry."

"*Hurry?* Neither of you can walk properly!" Arcana shook off his grip, ushering Caelum ahead of her. The deerken picked up speed, trotting awkwardly on three legs and glancing regularly over his shoulder.

"I know." Fenris bared his teeth and limped alongside. "We will have to make do."

Warg began pouring through the hole in the ceiling, grim punctuation to his words. They hit the floor and barrelled forward in a slavering tide, swarming over the throne and passing Iniron's skeleton as though it never existed. Arcana's heart seized in her chest. They weren't going to make it. "Get Caelum out of here," she shouted, turning to face the approaching threat. "I'll buy us some time."

Magic thrummed in her veins and Arcana raised her arms, calling for the vines. Thick and steady and sure, they dropped from the roof and shot out from the walls, weaving together to form a thick net. The warg hit the other side and bounced back, howling and yelping as she raced after her comrades, catching up as they entered the Weaver's chamber.

Caelum's ears quivered as he looked back through the tunnel. "That net won't hold them long."

"I know." Arcana dumped the nature magic and flattened her hands against the wall, gritting her teeth as the odd dissonance of the suspended tower reacted to her touch. She pushed against the spell, seeking the energy of the stone underneath but the tower resisted, shrieking in her ears until Arcana groaned aloud. And still the warg were howling.

"Smash it!" Caelum yelled. "Break the cycle."

A moment later the tower shuddered; Arcana looked up to see Fenris' arm buried elbow deep in a solid stone block. She gasped as the pressure between her ears abruptly lifted and energy rushed into her veins. Harnessing the magic at once, she tore massive stone blocks from the wall behind her and sent them into the corridor, hastily jamming and fusing each one together until the way was blocked. "It won't be enough."

"Here." Fenris shoved the long wooden bench in front of the barrier, snatching the loom from the end and smashing it on the floor. He bent the metal pieces into sharp spikes and jammed them into the surface of the bench, angled towards the corridor. "That should buy us some time."

Caelum limped over to what had once been the window but, thanks to Arcana's magic, was now a gaping hole in the side of the tower. "Whatever we did to break the suspension has stirred up a flux Kingdom wide."

Fenris hobbled to his side, catching the edge of the tower and leaning out of the hole. "Time is spiralling out from the tower in cycles."

Arcana followed after them and felt her breath catch as she looked outside. Below them, a green field cut abruptly into desert. A pond along the edge of the field was both dry and full in two separate moments, with the sunlight at various stages of day only meters apart. "Will it slow down?"

"It doesn't matter." Fenris blew out softly between his teeth. "The trap is sprung."

"What trap? I don't -" Arcana cut off as a shadow directly below her moved and what she'd assumed to be a bush stood and shook itself out. "Oh. More warg."

Caelum jumped as a loud howl sounded behind them, followed by a dull thud. "They're through the net."

"Indeed." Fenris raised his head to stare up at the flickering sky. Fangs flashed for a moment, a fleeting gesture of pure frustration before he turned to Arcana. "I hate to ask, but do you have another of Mirokke's teeth?"

She nodded, reaching into the neck of her jumper, then blinked and withdrew a hand stained with blood. "It's gone."

"Gone?"

"I know I put it on before we left the ship," she managed. "I never leave without it."

Fenris bent to inspect Arcana's neck, his breath tickling her collarbone. "There is a scratch here and your clothing is torn." He laid gentle fingers against the exposed skin at the base of her throat. "Iniron must have shorn the tooth free when she attacked."

"That's why she went for me and not you." Arcana blinked against a sudden rush of tears. "It was the last one."

"I know." Fenris brushed a thumb over her cheek and it came away wet. "I also know what it meant to you both - but for now we must think and live."

Another thump echoed through the room, and the stone wall behind them began to bulge. Arcana dashed away her tears and began threading her energy through the bricks as she'd done with the Healing Tower on Sorcen, adding her own strength to the masonry. "I've got it for now. Ideas, anyone?"

Caelum lowered his head, squinting down at the landscape below. "What about a portal?"

Fenris shook his head. "They have all been deactivated."

"Is there a chance you could re-activate one?"

"No - but there is another option. A fool's hope." He pointed toward the front gates of the castle, where the top of a portal jutted up above the crumbling masonry. "That portal was not deactivated. One of the stones cracked a few days before Taelon entered the Kingdom and it was scheduled for a new crystal. Iniron said there were messages everywhere, if we knew how to look."

"And?" Arcana grunted as another thud sent a shockwave through her magic and rattled her bones. "I'm kind of busy here; you're going to have to spell it out."

"The Weaver had you repair the relief in the tower, did she not? Perhaps so that we would think to repair the crystal."

"Meaning the portal could be turned back on, and we can escape." Arcana nodded. "It's possible, I guess. I mean, it's certainly better than standing here while a shit tonne of warg break down the wall."

Fenris flicked a glance over his shoulder. "I am surprised it has held this long."

"I told you I had it." Arcana grunted as the brickwork shifted sideways. "Not for long, though. The bricks are literally crumbling."

"We need to get down from here, then." Caelum leant out over the edge of the tower and swished his tail nervously. "For the record, I am *not* jumping."

"Hang on." Arcana raised one arm, dividing her attention between the warg and the new task at hand. The Weaver's chamber began to dissemble around her, bricks lifting and reforming to make a sloping ramp down the side of the tower.

Fenris ushered Caelum onto the first few blocks, both males wobbling unsteadily as they began to descend. The sound of tortured masonry echoed in Arcana's ears and she sank to her knees as the stonework disintegrated and her magic recoiled like a whip. A howling mass of warg bowled into the room, snapping and yowling but she was so dizzy she could only stare them down. Then the world blurred and suddenly Arcana was pressed against the outside of the tower, Fenris' body pinning her in place. "Are you all right?"

She managed a nod, staring as a waterfall of warg howled their way out of the hole in the Weaver's chamber, bodies vaporising as they passed from one time flux to the next.

"Please tell me that won't happen to us," Caelum said, peering over the edge of their ramp.

Fenris leant backwards to follow Caelum's line of sight, keeping one hand on the tower beside Arcana's head for support. "It won't. Those warg belonged to the flux inside the temple and by leaving it have sealed their own fates."

Arcana forced herself to concentrate on breathing, dragging air into her lungs - air that smelled tantalisingly of evergreen and cinnamon - and expelling it out again. When Fenris turned back to her, his jade eyes seemed to take up her entire field of vision, the glamour sliding over her skin with feathers that turned swiftly to midnight's finest velvet. "Fenris -"

His lips sealed hers, swallowing her words as his tongue thrust into her mouth. Arcana melted with a groan, thrusting her hands into his hair and succumbing to the wild, rushing heat that swept over them. Fenris broke away after only a few moments but it was enough to have them both panting. "Sorry."

"Sorry?"

"You frightened me. When I saw those warg bearing down on you, I -" he closed his eyes, forehead resting against hers. "Weaver's grace but I'm a mess."

"You're not a mess." She feathered her fingers down his neck, revelling in the way it made him shiver. "You moved like lightning, and we're all still here. We still have a chance."

"A chance." Fenris sighed heavily, lashes sweeping up and glamour searing her for a glorious moment before he took a reluctant step back. "Yes, you're right. How is your body holding up?"

Arcana grimaced. "I'm tired. The magic is starting to drag."

"I would that we could rest," Fenris murmured, "But I fear that's going to be impossible until we are out of the Kingdom."

"I know. Don't worry, as long as I'm careful, we'll be fine. I'm aching, but it's not serious yet." Gathering her wits, Arcana locked her knees, summoned her magic and began yanking more bricks from the upper section of the tower to complete the ramp. Caelum moved ahead, gingerly testing each block with his good leg while Fenris followed behind, the greatsword's tip clicking on the stone as he leant against it for support.

"We're almost down. Looks like we're going to end up in - great gods of Sorcen," Caelum drew back from the leading edge of the ramp, the fur on his neck standing on end.

Arcana froze. "What is it?"

"Don't look. I don't think Fenris should look, either. I don't want to look. I want to un-look," the deerken replied, his ears flat against his skull.

"We have no choice, Caelum," Arcana murmured, soothing his hackles with long, reassuring strokes. It didn't work. "We need to go that way."

He shuddered, still refusing to move. "Don't say I didn't warn you."

Fenris and Arcana exchanged a glance, then leant over the edge in silent accord. The ramp hung suspended above the garden, where once desiccated Guardians groaned and writhed upon the scaffolding. Faces were puckered and flesh lean but against all the odds they lived - barely.

"What?" Arcana gasped, her heart plummeting. "But... we *buried* them."

"It must be a peculiarity of the flux." Fenris leapt off the side of the stonework, rolling through the dirt and limping swiftly to the closest scaffold. He lifted the greatsword and sliced the Guardian free, catching him in gentle arms. The man wailed incoherently, his eyes beyond the ability to focus.

"Go gently!" Arcana arranged the blocks to take her down into the garden, hurrying to Fenris' side. "He's been tied to that scaffold an awfully long time. In theory, anyway."

"Mercy," the man groaned, scrabbling at Fenris' jumper with clawed hands. "Have... mercy."

Arcana tried to loosen his grip but the Guardian's fingers were like claws, his moaning and begging a continuous litany. She looked up at Fenris. "What do we do?"

"Grant his wish." Fenris stood, yanking the clawed hands free with astonishing ease. As the Guardian fell to the ground with a piteous wail, he drew the greatsword and buried it in the male's heart, a swift, clean stroke straight through the plate armour. "Weaver guide you, brother." Fenris yanked the greatsword free and, with a flick of his wrist, decapitated the now silent Guardian. "Auron keep you. May you find peace beyond the weave."

Arcana's throat closed over but she managed, somehow, to repeat the ritual words as, for a second time, she opened the earth and buried the body. "Do you want to do the rest?"

"Yes."

"Wait... Fenris, wait," a thready voice called.

Arcana turned to see a female Guardian, her shining suit of plate armour a stark contrast to lank hair and cheeks pinched with starvation. "She's the one from my vision."

"Celeste." Fenris hobbled to the woman's side, slicing her bonds and catching her as she fell. "It is all right, sister. You are free now."

"You sentimental idiot." Celeste's face was sallow, her eyes sunken as she glared up at him. "Leave us. We are already dead."

Fenris' jaw tightened. "I will help you if I can. Jorgan was too far gone but if we get you out of the flux-"

"Stop. Stop and listen to me," Celeste snapped. There was enough strength in her voice that Fenris immediately yielded. "The fluxes come and go - this was not the first and it will not be the last. Did you find the message I left for you?"

"Yes. We retrieved the box."

Celeste sighed. "Good."

"You must let us help you," Fenris insisted, his face pinched with grief. "I have lost too many brothers and sisters to simply walk away."

"No. There's no time. The flux is -" Celeste gasped, back arching and lip curling. "The flux is a loop, Fenris. You must get out before the warg come. And they *will* come."

"When?"

"As... we... die..." Celeste's eyes turned milky and her skin began to wither and peel like so much old paint. "Run, Fenris... Live. For the Weaver..."

"Celeste?" Fenris' knuckles whitened around the curve of her plate greaves and he bowed his head. "Weaver guide you, sister. Auron keep you." He lowered Celeste to the ground and struggled upright, lifting the greatsword once more. "May you find peace beyond the weave."

Fenris drove the blade home, once more piercing straight through that silver armour, and this time he leant on the hilt for a moment, silver lining his eyes. Arcana blinked away her own tears, her throat tight. "She didn't deserve this."

"None of them did." Fenris tore the sword free and cleft Celeste's head from her body, watching as it rolled a few feet away to bump against the foot of the nearest scarecrow frame. "It is getting progressively more diffi-cult to kill the people I care about."

Arcana brushed a stray curl back from his forehead. "It should never be easy. Otherwise you'd be just like Taelon."

"On that note, I can hear warg howling in the forest," Caelum said, his ears flickering nervously.

"So can I." Fenris straightened, casting a regretful eye over the Guardians who remained on the scaffolding. "There isn't time to cut them free now. We must go."

"We'll come back," Arcana promised. "And we'll bring fire."

He nodded once and hobbled away, heading around the curve of the castle toward the front gate. Arcana ushered Caelum ahead of her, hearing the howling herself now. The dead forest seemed to be watching, full of unseen eyes and echoing with the promise of death. Caelum and Fenris were slow, staggering over ground that rippled in the grip of the flux, so Arcana took up a position at the rear, calling her magic and flexing her fingers until several of the large stone blocks she'd used to make the ramp floated in the air before her. The howls picked up in intensity as warg boiled out from between the trees, shambling across the open ground with frightening speed. Arcana flung an arm out, hurling her masonry into the pack. The stones bounced and thumped across the ground, crushing warg beneath them and slowing the progress of those who managed to dodge aside.

"Arcana! Come on!" Caelum shouted. She swung around and away, racing after his tail as it disappeared around the curve of the wall.

The castle courtyard opened onto a grand, paved promenade, the entrance of which was marked by two smashed wooden gates. A portal stood tall and proud twenty paces further on and beyond it, the crumbling ruins of a town. Fenris had just reached the shattered gates when a warg leapt from the ruins, claws outstretched. He ducked neatly beneath the creature's body, twisting at an impossible angle to slice the warg in half. Somehow managing to retain his balance, the Guardian completed his spin one legged and continued towards the portal.

"Warg in the town ruins," Caelum panted, swirling eyes focussed off into the distance. "On the left, hiding in the shadow of the second house from the gate."

"All right." Arcana raised her hand and clenched it into a fist. The house in question toppled forward and though she couldn't see the warg, she heard their cut-off yowls as the stone building crushed them flat.

Caelum grunted in satisfaction - or perhaps pain - as he levered his body up onto the wide, circular platform that all portals boasted. "Good shot. Now third from the right, one row back. Push it towards the road."

"Okay." Arcana shoved at the air, her magic mimicking the movement. "Did I get them?"

"Mostly. One straggler coming this way -" Caelum broke off as she flicked a finger, imploding the building in front. "Got him. Though I'm sure there's more out there."

"Let me know when you see them." Arcana took up a place beside Fenris, who was fiddling with the back of the portal's control pedestal. "What do I need to do?"

"I cannot give you specifics - only that one of the crystals is cracked." His voice was muffled from behind the pedestal. "But first I have to flip the breaker, or it will never activate." Fenris straightened up, leaning on the pedestal and looking into her face. The glamour shivered over Arcana's skin and she breathed in deep of his scent, feeling for all the world like he was wrapping her in a warm velvet blanket. Oblivious to the effect he had on her, Fenris continued; "The energy works in a circuit, as I've explained before. If the stone can be repaired, the gate will open."

"In theory." Arcana broke the eye contact and looked up at the portal looming above them. "Let's pray it works."

"I have faith in very little, but in you, I have no doubt," Fenris said softly.

She smiled, then, clean and clear and bright. "Together."

"Together."

"Arcana," Caelum called. "More warg."

"Coming." She spun away, lifting her arms to pull the stones from the short wall bordering the town. The warg snapped and snarled and rolled and leapt - but they all went down, crushed and smashed and impaled by the deadly arsenal of stone. When it was done, she leant on Caelum, chest heaving. "I won't be able to keep this up while I'm working on the portal."

He set his three good legs and lowered his antlers. "Go while there's a lull."

"Yes." Fenris appeared on her other side. "We'll buy you time when the next wave arrives."

"Okay." She stroked a hand down his cheek and backed up against the edge of the portal. "Be ready when I call, both of you."

Fenris watched her out of blazing eyes, his expression curiously intense. "Arcana, I -"

"What's the matter, Overlord?" A deep, booming voice preceded a tall figure out of the ruined town. Taelon's lip curled maliciously as he flipped back his grey-furred hood. "Have your vast talents and overworked knowledge finally failed you?"

"Taelon." Fenris sighed, limping to Caelum's side so that his body blocked Arcana from sight. "I might have known you'd come to gloat."

"Of course." Taelon barked a sharp laugh. "It wasn't a particularly clever trap, but you are nothing if not insufferably predictable."

Predictable? Arcana called her magic, curling her fingers around the curve of the portal. The house behind Taelon fractured apart, shards of sharpened stone scything towards him - and he was gone, reappearing at the edge of the platform.

"Naughty, naughty sorceress." Taelon clicked his tongue in reprimand. "That might've worked if I hadn't been prepared." He raised one arm and Arcana gasped to see a deerken sagging in his grip. The creature's ribs were visible beneath patchy fur and her eyes were closed. Taelon tightened his fingers around the creature's skinny neck and gave a little shake. "They do run out of juice fairly quickly, I'm afraid. Never mind."

"What have you done?" Fenris demanded, his shoulders slack with horror. "Put her down."

"Put her down," Taelon mimicked. Half a moment passed, then he tossed the deerken over his shoulder like a dirty rag. The doe didn't so much as struggle as her body twisted and spun through the air, colliding with the ruins of a portico and dropping down out of sight. "There. As for what I've done - surely even one as blind as you understands how weak and useless a creature the deerken are." Taelon paused, eyeing Caelum with open hunger. "Except, perhaps, for you. I look forward to working out what makes you different from the rest."

Caelum said nothing, only brandished his bladed antlers. Fenris stepped very deliberately in front, raising the greatsword in a two-handed grip. "He is not for you to destroy, brother. Nor were any of the others you've slaughtered in your quest for dominance."

"You actually intend to fight me?" Taelon cocked his head in amusement. "You're held together by bandages and willpower, Fenris. You're no match for me at all - but even less like that."

"We shall see." Fenris lunged, his body a teal blur that made Arcana's eyes water. Taelon seemed not to move at all, but his arm was somehow raised and Fenris' body thumped and cracked as it flew heavily backwards, rolling across the pavement.

"Fenris!" Arcana called her magic, heaving the earth upwards to create a shield in front of his body.

"No," Fenris looked back at her, eyes blazing. "Let me handle this. Do what we came here to do." He dug his hand into the stone shield and dragged himself upright, swaying unsteadily for a moment before setting his feet. "I will not go so easily into the dark."

She swallowed heavily, feeling like her throat was full of blades, then nodded and smoothed the stone shield back into the platform. Taelon immediately began a slow circle but Fenris, rather than turning to follow his movements, simply closed his eyes and waited.

The portal was a smooth, cool weight against her back and after a heart-rending moment of indecision, Arcana spread her magic through the circular frame until she found the crystals lying dormant within. The moment she brushed against the stones they flared to searing life, as though someone had taken all the fury of a star and stuffed it into a sphere the size of her palm. Arcana felt the fracture in the centre stone, a hairline fissure which rendered the energy inside a chaotic maelstrom. It rejected her touch with a jolt that she felt in the depths of her bones.

Taelon stopped his circling and tilted his head to one side, drawing her attention outward. "How did it feel to know I had trapped you, I wonder? After our encounter on Sorcen, I knew you would come here, of course. You'd never have risked more innocent lives by trying to build an army. Not you, the poster boy of altruism." Taelon turned his head and spat on the ground, then grinned. "All I needed was patience - something I've become very good at over the years."

Fenris growled deep in his chest but remained still. "What have you done with the Weaver?"

"I've put her somewhere safe." Taelon's grin turned vindictive. "If you come with me, I'll re-unite you. She has a soft spot where you're concerned."

"Jealous?" Fenris shifted his grip on the greatsword. "Whatever leverage you think you can gain by dragging me before her in chains is a pipe dream. I will see her again, but not on your terms."

"Do you really believe you have a choice? I can smell your blood from here. How many ribs did I break with that last blow? Two? Three?" Taelon trailed off with a sharp laugh. "Don't be a fool, Fenris. I have three warg packs surrounding you, the time flux working in my favour, and weapons in my hand." He swept his wargskin cloak aside and drew forth two short, vicious looking axes. "You've already lost."

"Don't fight him," Caelum muttered. "It's suicide."

"He leaves little choice," Fenris returned, lashes raising as he at last opened his eyes. His face was pale, expression set as he lifted the greatsword and settled into a battle stance. The movement caused a muscle in his jaw to leap and Arcana saw his eyelids flutter involuntarily. In her head, Taelon's words mocked her.

How many ribs did I break with that last blow? Two? Three?

Arcana's breath caught and she knew Fenris would lay down his life, here and now, if it meant Taelon was defeated - not because he wished it, but because he truly felt there was no other way.

No. Gritting her teeth, Arcana began to thread her magic back into the portal, building a net of energy that would not be so easy for the fractured stone to shuck off. It would work; it had to work.

Taelon stepped onto the platform, cloak rippling as he twirled both axes in sweeping, lazy movements. Muscles rippled across his broad chest and shoulders and the pavement creaked beneath his heavy tread. Fenris watched silently, greatsword steady for all his chest heaved with the effort.

"You can't let him do this," Caelum hissed, his voice barely a whisper. A muscle jumped in Fenris' jaw and Arcana bit back her reply. If Fenris could hear them, then Taelon surely could, too. And if Taelon got a whiff of her intentions before she was ready, it would all be over very quickly.

"Yes I can." Arcana forced her tone to remain stiff, all the while praying for the deerken to look deeper. "This is what Fenris does."

"Arcana -" Caelum cut off, his ears flickering. Had he felt it? Had he reached through their connection and felt that her feelings did not match her words? "Very well."

Good. She finished threading her essence through the portal and tightened the net around the fractured portal stone. Wild magic flared through her body but Arcana held firm, inviting the stone to fuse back together. The energy immediately rebelled, striking out with such ferocity that the fracture widened, almost shearing the stone in half. The backlash coursed through her veins like a lightning strike and Caelum stiffened beside her, chest contracting as he suppressed a gasp. Arcana wrestled briefly with both pain and portal stone before her magic lost its tenuous grip and left them both shaking in the aftermath.

Taelon chose that moment to dart forward and Fenris barely parried, staggering backwards on his injured leg before disappearing in a blur of movement. Taelon spun in search of his foe, axe whirling, and for a brief moment both combatants were difficult to see. Then Fenris thumped onto the stone, rolling to an awkward lump at Arcana's feet and leaving a smear of blood on the pavement behind him. She bent to help him but the moment her hands touched his flesh he jerked away, shaking his head in silent warning.

"You cannot win like this, Guardian. Or should I say Overlord? It *is* your title now, after all. The best of the best." Taelon laughed, swinging his axes lazily. "Submit and save yourself further injury. We both know I'm only warming up."

Fenris rolled to his knees and, though his breath rattled in his lungs, gained his feet. "I seem to remember you were faster than this. Perhaps all that warg blood is slowing you down." His lips peeled back in a bloodied grin. "You always did like to overindulge."

Taelon roared in rage and took a step forward but Fenris had disappeared, a whipcrack of motion. Arcana watched him fight, knowing it was a losing battle. Her body was close to collapse; she didn't have the energy to repudiate Taelon and fight off the warg, much less find them another way out of the Timeless Kingdom. Tears streamed down her face at the hopelessness of it all - and all of a sudden, she knew what to do. "Caelum."

"I'm here."

"Get Fenris. We're leaving." Arcana poured her magic into the portal, disregarding subtlety in favour of brute force. The stone was fissured but that didn't mean it was over - because what was she, if not a living conductor? Instead of commanding the crystals to repair, she summoned the vast, depthless well of her energy and tunnelled into the fractured crystal to complete the circuit.

The portal flared instantly to life, the centre filling with blue light which spilled across the platform. Caelum charged, forcing Taelon to leap aside or be skewered on his bladed antlers - but instead of pursuing, those blades faded and he scooped up Fenris, greatsword and all, and turned back towards the portal.

"What are you doing?" Fenris cried, jade eyes wide. "Caelum, no!"

"Hurry," Arcana growled. The energy of the portal burned through her, the fire in her veins unlike anything she'd ever experienced - a furious, unrelenting pain that drove her to her knees and stole the burning air from her lungs. "I can't hold it much longer."

Something yanked her sideways and the cool caress of the gateway swept across her body, stoking the furious maelstrom which scoured her from the inside out and increasing it a hundredfold. Arcana screamed helplessly, feeding the energy even as it shredded her to pieces.

"Let it go, we're through. Arcana, let it go!" Fenris' voice came from far away but she latched onto the sound, releasing her hold on the broken crystal and allowing the portal to collapse behind them. The gateway closed at once but the energy refused to retreat from her body, arching her back until bones shattered and blue fire poured from her eyes, her mouth, her fingertips.

And then it was gone.

Arcana opened her eyes to a strange haze, savouring the cool, blissful silence. The energy of the collapsing portal rushed around her and she could see Fenris and Caelum tumbling end over end towards a rapidly narrowing circle of sunlight. Fenris had something clutched to his chest, a bundle of rags that hung listless and blackened in his arms.

Hello, child.

The voice was everywhere and nowhere, a woman's voice both old and young, emanating from the very space around her. Arcana tried to open her mouth but found it useless, so instead she simply formed the words inside her head. *Hello.*

Do you know who I am?

The Weaver.

Yes.

You were waiting for us - for this.

It was the only way to reach you.

Arcana looked down at her chest and saw a strange cord the thickness of her wrist, extending into the great beyond where Caelum had now disappeared from sight. *Have I died?*

Yes… and no. Your body is ruined, scorched by the portal energy. But so long as your soul remains here, you live - after a fashion.

Why?

It is the only way I can talk to you.

This is how you kept Fenris alive.

Yes, though his body was intact. I tried to reach him but he could not hear me. You, however, are a child of the stars. Of the void. Of the weave. Mine.

Because of the soulmerge with Caelum.

Yes.

What do you want?

To be free, of course, but that is not so simple a task. For now, Fenris cannot fall into Taelon's hands, and neither you nor Caelum are strong enough to defend him.

We figured that part out already.

Stay your anger, child; the journey is not over. I will buy you time and send you where you need to go but the path will be difficult to walk.

Of course it will. Arcana looked down at the cord in her chest, wondering if the Weaver understood sarcasm. *It's a little hard to help you without any direction, though. Or a body.*

Outside of this place, I must remain cryptic to keep Taelon at bay. As for your body, I can return you to it, should you wish - but I advise you to consider your answer carefully. Reality may not be as you assume.

I'll be the judge of that. Arcana wrapped both hands around the cord in her chest and blinked as, all of a sudden, she was crouched on a bed of hot sand, her left foreleg pulsing in agony. Fenris was hunched over a woman on the ground, her skin peeling as though from a heavy burn, closed eyes leaking blood down her cheeks.

"Arcana? Arcana, please." Fenris repeated the word over and over, caressing the woman's face with a trembling hand, smearing the blood across her cheek. He looked over one shoulder and his eyes blazed with an emotion so intense it stole her breath. "Bring her back, Caelum. You can save her."

Caelum? Where was he? Arcana tried to turn, couldn't.

"You know it doesn't work that way; we're dependent on each other. If Arcana goes into the long night, I have no choice but to follow," Caelum said. His voice echoed unusually loud, rumbling through Arcana's own chest and causing her to start in fright.

Immediately she was back in the swirling maelstrom, staring down at the cord in her chest. *I want to go back.*

It will be done, but not immediately. Your body must heal before you can fight.

Arcana felt a thrill of desperate fear. *Taelon will find us.*

No. I have torn a hole in the weave and thrust you into a world far from Taelon, and I have severed Fenris' blood bond.

You severed his blood bond? Why not Taelon's?

I cannot sever Taelon's.

Why?

I do not know. I have tried. This, however, I can do. Taelon cannot track you now.

Nor can we track him.

It was necessary.

Does Fenris know?

He's in too much pain to have noticed. You will have to explain it to him, when you wake.

He's going to be devastated. You're his world.

It is time for that to change. To be successful, he must find another reason to live and fight.

If you're referring to me, you're going to be disappointed. Fenris' oath to you is the most important thing in his life.

Is it? Listen.

"Please, Arcana. Please." Fenris' voice fell around her like rain, coating her in an emotion that made her pause.

Stop that. I won't be manipulated to your whims.

What will you do, then?

She sighed, irritation stirring. *I'm aware you've been pulling our strings from the beginning, and I'm also aware there's little choice now but to do as you ask - but I'm not going to lie down and let you trample my will into the dust. I'm a person, not a tool.*

I see. A negotiation, then. What do you wish?

A few moments in my body. Let me reassure them, at least.

Are you sure? It will be painful and you will have quite literally a few moments. Your body is close to death; I will need to reclaim your spirit for safekeeping while you heal.

I'm sure.

Very well. I need a minute to repair your eyes, and then I will send you. What happens beyond that, we will discuss later.

Sounds more like a threat than anything else. The energy around Arcana rippled, and she could have sworn she felt the Weaver laugh.

Indeed. I hope you are ready, child of the void. After this, there will not be another opportunity.

I'm ready. Arcana curled her fingers around the cord in her chest and waited on the Weaver's whim. She hovered for a long, uncertain moment and then a nauseating shove toppled her forward into her body.

Arcana opened her eyes, gasping for breath. Her lungs burned. Her limbs burned. Her heart burned. Ruined, the Weaver had said - and it felt like it. Still, there was something to be done. She stared up into blinding sunlight, wondering how to get her companions' attention, when a shadow fell across her vision. Fenris.

The Guardian's soft, teal skin was pale. Tears streaked his grimy cheeks and his mouth was pinched with grief. Arcana drank him in, those high cheekbones and the long, dark teal curls that tumbled across his brow. She'd never seen him before. Not like this, her own personal miracle, framed by sun and sweat and blood and *life*.

"Fenris," she whispered, her voice no more than an exhalation. His eyes met her own, the glamour rising around them like a warm blanket.

"Weaver's grace," he murmured, resting his forehead against hers and squeezing his eyes shut. "I thought I'd lost you."

Arcana longed to wrap her arms around him, to twine her fingers in his hair, but her useless body refused to respond. She sought words of comfort but could no longer speak. Desperation sparked and she tilted her head - a minute movement, but enough. Her lips brushed his, the softest, barest connection. Fenris' arms tightened and his eyes flew open, their jade fire filling her vision. Arcana knew without seeing that she was cradled in his lap, safe in the cocoon of his body, wrapped in the velvet cloak of his glamour. *Live*, she willed him. *For me, for us. Live.*

Fenris spoke but his voice was too far away. Exhaustion called - the Weaver called - and Arcana succumbed, allowing unconsciousness to close over her head and block out the world.

CHAPTER
FIFTEEN
FENRIS

He'd been a fool.

Single minded in his focus. Unable – unwilling – to look beyond the boundaries he'd set within his own thoughts. And now...

Fenris looked down at the woman cradled in his arms. So frail. Arcana's clothing was torn and burnt and covered in blood, fused to her body in some places and entirely missing in others, revealing horrific blisters and scorch marks across her skin. Her ebony hair was a matted mess, so badly singed at the ends that it would need cutting before it could be brushed and set right again. She felt like a bird, fragile and feather light, the everburning spirit which drew him like a moth to a flame reduced to no more than a whisper. And still she had spoken. Kissed him, with what might have been her final moments of consciousness. Fenris' fingers shook as he brushed a thumb across her cheek, unable to resist the shimmering lustre of her skin, even cloaked as it was beneath soot and sweat and blood. So pale. The wrong kind of pale, the pale of bone deep wounds and impending oblivion.

He'd been a fool, and Arcana had risked everything to save him. Fenris clenched his teeth hard enough that his jaw ached - along with the myriad other wounds his battered body was already labouring to mend. He should have been a wreck and yet all he could feel was the hollow space in his chest where her smile had once been. Fenris bowed his head, resting it gently against Arcana's hair, savouring the faint whisper of her barely-there breathing in his ears.

He'd been a fool.

"She lives, brother." Caelum's nose whuffed into his hair, tousling those godsdamned curls that never stayed put. "It's not too late. Can you walk?"

Perhaps. Fenris drew a deep breath, savouring the slicing pain of his broken ribs. Three. No, four, but the puncture in his lung felt significantly less than it had earlier. He raised his eyes to the torturous landscape around them, reluctant to look away from Arcana for even a second but knowing it necessary should he wish to stand half a chance of helping her. Sand stretched endlessly in every direction, unbroken save for the odd heaping of rocks at the foot of which the portal – without a gate, without direction, against all odds – had deposited them. If they did not move, they would die where they sat. "Yes, I can walk. Though for how long, I cannot say."

"You and me both." Caelum was still lamed, his foreleg tucked up beneath his belly, and unlike Fenris he did not heal swiftly. His silvery fur had shortened to little more than a second skin in the baking heat, accentuating the broad chest, oversized head and elongated limbs that characterised his species. His antler rack rose in stark salute to the cloudless sky, like so many withering branches beneath the unforgiving sun.

"You're not bleeding." Not a question. Fenris could smell sand, sweat, tears, ash and blood – but none of it belonged to Caelum. No, the deerken's burnt sugar scent was smooth and steady as always, as though the grittier aspects of life held no claim to him.

"No. But you are." Caelum tugged a torn piece of fabric out of the sand with his teeth and shook it out. "Bind your wounds. I can't carry both of you."

Fenris laid Arcana gently in the sand at his feet. Everything - she'd been willing to sacrifice everything so that he would live. He still couldn't quite believe it, and certainly couldn't accept he was worth such a thing, yet it had happened nonetheless. Selfless sacrifice from a woman who'd offered him not just her body, which he craved with an intensity bordering on obsession, but something far more precious. Understanding. Empathy. Affection. Warmth. A balm for his cold, lonely soul. And in return, he had shown her death, and fear, and ruin. Had dragged her across space and time for a quest which had been forced upon her. Arcana had bent to the task without the barest flicker of an eyelash, soothing him when he was too afraid, reaching him when he was too stubborn and giving courage when he was too frightened to think. And inside the Timeless Kingdom, surrounded by horror and yet more death, in a world which was entirely alien, Arcana's primary thoughts had been of *him*. Again, and again, and again.

He'd been a fool.

Fenris accepted the cloth – the remains of Arcana's navy long sleeve – and began tearing it into strips. His own knit jumper and shirt were long gone, as was one leg of his pants, leaving him with the unexpected advantage of being able to locate the worst of his surface wounds with minimal effort. Reducing blood loss was paramount; the less work his body had to do to repair, the swifter the healing process. So he wound strip after strip of fabric around his limbs, tying them in place with a mixture of fingers and fangs. Once he was done, Fenris scooped Arcana back into his arms and forced his body to unfold.

"I can take her," Caelum offered, but he wasn't looking at Fenris – as though he already knew the answer.

"I need to hold her for now." He said it anyway, and received the barest flicker of an ear in silent acknowledgment. "However… several of my ribs are broken. We may have to take turns before this is over."

"That's fine," Caelum said, his star-filled gaze trained on the endless, rolling dunes of the desert. "If Arcana wakes, she can find us water and shelter and perhaps even food."

"If she wakes." Fenris stared down at the enchanting curve of midnight lashes over stardusted cheeks. "If she wakes, I…"

"You'll what? Finally tell her how you feel?" Caelum's voice was as sharp as any blade. "Don't make any promises you don't intend to keep, Guardian."

His heart lurched. "Am I so transparent?"

"Not to Arcana. She's clueless." Finally, the deerken turned to pin him in place with his fathomless gaze. "I promised Flare back on Sorcen that I'd gore you if you got this wrong, you know."

Fenris smelt the truth in that statement and smiled. Such honesty was why he liked Caelum so much. "Shall I string myself up for your convenience?"

"That depends." The voice of a warrior, of an older brother. A tone it was likely Arcana herself rarely, if ever, encountered. "What will you do to ensure she lives?"

"Anything. Everything." Fenris knew, as those words came out, that he meant them. Part of him quailed at the thought, the idea that one single woman could be wound so tightly around his heart that there was room for little else. For the most part, he only wished he'd had a chance to tell her – no, to show her – that there was more. That *he* was more. Clearing his throat, he said; "I only held back for her comfort. I did not wish to force -"

"Oh, quit it. You were scared," Caelum scoffed.

Blessed darkness behind his eyes, a lurching thump in his chest. "Yes."

"And?"

"Arcana believes it is never too late. I plan to take that advice."

"Good." Caelum's nose was soft against his cheek and Fenris opened his eyes in surprise. "Let's go, then," the deerken murmured. "I think I can see some trees in the distance."

Fenris shifted his shoulders, settling the greatsword into a better position. His own sight was suited to the dark – in this blisteringly bright desert, where the sand glittered like cut diamonds, Caelum had the advantage. So he blinked, trying to ignore the raging glare which already threatened to give him a headache, and looked to the deerken for guidance. "Lead on, brother. I am with you."

They walked for what seemed like days, stopping regularly to shift Arcana's weight between them. Blood soaked the bindings on Fenris' wounds and Caelum's leg stiffened until each step was a torture, though neither had the energy to say as much. The sand shifted often, leaving even Caelum floundering chest deep or sliding precariously down a dune as the side of it gave way. Fenris was relieved when he was at last able to distinguish the shape of trees on the horizon. By mute agreement they renewed their efforts, cloaked in the pervasive scents of blood and sweat and desperation. They arrived to discover the oasis was small - no more than a collection of scraggly bushes crowned with a trio of desert palms - but it contained a soak of water that fed a drinking bowl sized pool.

Caelum went down first, dropping to his knees in the sand and sliding Arcana's unconscious body into the shade of a bush. That done, he toppled away from her, flanks heaving and eyes closed. Fenris managed the few steps to the edge of the pool, using cupped hands to sip some of the water before deciding it was clean enough to offer to Caelum in the same way. He made certain they both drank, retaining enough to trickle moisture between Arcana's lips and gently sponge the wicked burns that lashed her body like the scars from a whip. It was a mercy she was unconscious; if the damage outside was half as bad as what he could smell inside, it would be an agony to be awake.

"What did she do?" His voice was croaky, his movements stiff.

Caelum's tail swished once. "I'm not sure. I don't think the stone repair worked - I felt her desperation and despair. She did something else."

"You may be unsure, but you've guessed." Fenris propped Arcana gently against Caelum's flank and sagged down alongside, allowing his lashes to drift closed. A moment. He would just rest a moment. "Share your theory, brother."

"If I had to make a wager, I'd say she bypassed the portal crystal and offered herself as a substitute." Caelum's chest rose and fell in a great sigh, the movement not unlike being in a boat on a gentle sea. "It would certainly explain why she caught fire from the inside out."

Fenris shivered, knowing that particular image would be scorched into the back of his retina as long as he lived. He'd seen many things in his life, both beautiful and terrible, but nothing could compare to the sight of those great gouts of blue flame which had erupted from Arcana's orifices and crawled from her pores. He had burns on his own body to prove how hot it had been, though they were pitiful in comparison to what she had chosen to endure.

He'd been a fool. Fenris forced himself upright enough to draw the greatsword, setting his teeth as the motion wrenched at his broken ribs, and lifted his lashes enough to drink in the sight of Arcana's broken body. She should be melted, no more than a puddle of sizzling bodily fluids. Yet somehow, against all odds, his sorceress had survived. A puzzle - a miracle - that he might never get a chance to comprehend. Watching the subtle rise and fall of her chest, Fenris set the greatsword across his knees and said the first thing that came to mind. "I wonder why the greatsword's harness didn't disintegrate in the fire like the rest of my clothing."

If Caelum thought the statement odd, he gave no sign. "Leather's magically enhanced to buffer against damage, like Arcana's bag. It'll take more than that to destroy it."

"Where is Arcana's bag?" Fenris looked around, realising for the first time that it was gone.

"I don't know; it disappeared while we were inside the portal."

"She won't be pleased about that." Fenris traced the runes etched into the greatsword. "None of this makes sense. I thought her power was limitless."

"It might be, but you already know her body isn't." Caelum snorted, creating a cloud of sand which promptly caused him to sneeze. "Don't you remember getting Arcana drunk on Sorcen so she could bypass her pain reflex and burrow us out of the earth?"

He did - mostly because he remembered the way her eyes had danced in the moonlight, and how the soft warmth of her lips had felt as she'd wrapped her mouth around his finger and bitten it. Fenris sighed, leaning back against Caelum's flank again. "So you're saying her magic didn't give out, her body did?"

"That's what it felt like," Caelum rumbled. "Burning agony and then nothing."

"I cannot reconcile it," he admitted. "She has always absorbed the energies before they overcame her."

"Yeah, but that still takes time and she suffers in the interim." Caelum shifted his weight and stilled when Arcana's head lolled to the side. When she made no movement or sound, he relaxed. "I don't know what sort of power was inside those stones, but it is without doubt the most concentrated, furious thing I've ever felt - and I get it second-hand. Arcana should be incinerated. All I can think is that she managed to shut the magic off before it got that bad."

"Perhaps." Fenris stared up at the broad palm leaves above, wishing for answers to what had become an impossibly lengthy list of questions. Without the stars, he had no way to estimate their positioning in the universe, and his internal compass was unusually silent. "I cannot feel anyone nearby through the blood bond."

"Is that a good or a bad sign?"

"It could go either way at this point. Good, because it means nobody is nearby to track us before we are ready. Bad, because nobody is nearby to rescue us before we die at the hands of the elements." Fenris chuckled, a dry, helpless sound that cut off when it rattled his ribs. "Weaver save us all."

"Somehow," said Caelum softly, "I get the feeling it's going to be up to us."

He had nothing to say to that, so he closed his eyes, laid his head as close to Arcana's as he dared and allowed himself to slide into the uneasy sleep of the incredibly exhausted.

He'd been a fool.

Fenris woke with the words in his mind, on his lips, startling into a sitting position and reaching for the greatsword even as his wounds screamed a protest. He'd barely touched a trembling finger to the leather-wrapped hilt when a stone tipped spear pricked the flesh at his throat. The desert's blazing sun made it impossible to look up at his captors so he cut a glance sidewards, gathering his energy for a blind lunge - and froze. Another spear at Arcana's throat, far enough away that he'd be forced to choose which one of them lived and which one died. Caelum watched through silent eyes, unable to intervene without dislodging Arcana and shoving her into the sharp edge of the spear. Trapped, then.

Someone spoke – female, by the timbre, in a language that was beyond Fenris' comprehension. He frowned. That was now twice in one day his linguistic knowledge had failed him. Unwilling to admit complete defeat, he tried to search out a pattern or sound that was familiar but the strange whistling and trilling was like nothing he'd ever heard before. The language of the spears, however, was perfectly clear. Fenris shifted his body towards Arcana's, using the silhouette of a bush to block the sun from his eyes, and looked up.

Harpies. At least, that was the impression he got before the butt of a spear cracked him heavily across the jaw and Fenris' vision was filled with sparkling lights. Very well. If sight was not to be his source of information, he would use other senses. Fenris squeezed both eyes shut and drew in a deep, steady breath. Females, mostly – five females and two males, if his nose and ears were to be trusted. The females were armed and the males... chains clinked, coming close enough that he risked cracking an eyelid. A male, dirty and wearing a scrap of leather which wished it was a loincloth, crouched in front of him and spoke swiftly. The male had no wings but his arms bore heavy, crater-like scarring down the outside edge where they should have been. Though he looked reasonably young, the patchwork of pale lines and ridges across his body attested to a lifetime of imprisonment. That and the thick metal collar around the male's neck, partially hidden beneath the matted mass of downy feathers that tumbled over his shoulders in place of hair.

The male spoke again, more insistently this time, and Fenris shook his head. "I do not understand what you are saying," he said steadily. It was a fool's chance, to hope they recognised Universal Galactic – but a collective gasp went up from the group and after a long few moments of tweeting and trilling, one of the females sashayed forwards.

"You speak the language of the goddess, slave?" The female tapped a foot – no, a talon. A bird's talon, complete with wickedly sharp claws. Fenris altered the angle of his head slightly and without lifting his gaze, managed to glimpse magnificent grey and tan speckled wings and several strings of beads in shades of turquoise and white.

He frowned. "What makes you think I am a slave?"

The butt of the spear connected with his jaw again and this time, Fenris bit down on a groan. The woman before him waved off her guard, chuckling indulgently. "All males are slaves - and are you not male? Or shall I check?"

Fenris ran his eyes over the two collared males, noting again their grimy skin and lank, matted feather-hair. And their eyes – broken.

"Indeed, I am male." He moistened his lips and tasted blood, mind churning. In his current state, he was no match for these women, no match for even a stiff breeze. Caelum, still silent, was no better off. So he gestured towards Arcana and said; "I speak this language to better serve my mistress."

A claw-tipped hand shot out and Fenris was startled by how small it was as his jaw tilted upward. "Where is your collar?" He could see her face now, the backswept mane of downy feathers that matched the grey and tan mottled wings. Young, pretty in a birdlike way but for the cruel pinch to her mouth. The same turquoise and white beads that hung in strings around her neck had been worked meticulously into her feather-hair at the temples and clacked as she tilted her head to the side. "Answer or die."

"We were attacked by ravenous beasts. My collar was lost in the battle," Fenris replied, debating whether or not to try ensnaring her with his glamour. She was too far away at the moment, her arm extended to full stretch as though he might be contagious; but even if he were successful, it would be immediately obvious to the other harpies that something was amiss. And then he - and more importantly, Arcana - would die. No, better to play along for now. "My mistress is gravely injured." He gestured again towards Arcana's limp body. It was easy not to look the harpy in the eye; he had a lifetime's practice. It was far less easy to imitate the same submissive posture of the other two males. "We travel in search of aid for her."

"Interesting. And what say you of the crime of ensnaring a sacred beast?" The female jerked her chin at Caelum. "For that, the punishment is death."

Meaning, Fenris assumed, that the only reason he was still breathing was their curiosity.

"I'm not ensnared," Caelum announced, lifting his head so that the shadow of his antler rack dappled Arcana's skin. "I follow of my own free will."

"Great horned one." The harpy dropped to her knees, eyes wide with awe. "You speak the language of the goddess."

Caelum blinked, and Fenris could almost see him biting back his pithy retort. Eventually he settled on, "Yes."

"And this woman... this woman who looks so strange... where are her wings? Why do you wander so bloody and weak in the desert?" The harpy's tone was breathless and her eyes were actually brimming with tears as she watched Caelum lipping at Arcana's lank hair. Fenris sank into the familiar court calm he'd spent years cultivating lest he snort in disgust at the hypocrisy.

"Arcana is under my protection," Caelum announced, his ears flickering in emphasis to that statement. Cleary he'd reached the same conclusion as Fenris - if either of them had the power to bargain, it was the deerken. "This male is her... mate."

Mate. Fenris tried not to let his suddenly thundering heart change his expression, though why he was shocked that Caelum had figured out the truth was beyond him. Yes, he was her mate - and he had failed her. The harpy looked as nonplussed as he felt as she said, "If this one is her mating male, then we cannot punish him. Only the Empress has the authority to order the punishment of a mating male." She tilted her head to one side, eyes narrowing. "Although, she is not of Hiraptha... so perhaps in this instance the rules do not apply."

"I know naught of your empress, but if you punish the male without consulting Arcana first, I will be most displeased," Caelum rumbled, the formal diction falling stiffly from his mouth. "She's placed her faith in me and would be very angry to wake and discover her male had been badly treated - and if she is angry, *I* am angry."

The harpy paused at that, blinking owlishly. "I mean no disrespect, oh great and honoured beast."

"Caelum," he supplied.

"Caelum," she echoed reverently. "Very well. If the male agrees to follow our rules, I will speak to the Empress regarding your mistress' healing."

Caelum tilted his head to one side, considering - as though they had a choice. "We are not from here; we came by magic from far away. You will have to explain the rules."

"Of course, honoured Caelum." The harpy stood and walked away, so confident in her own authority she didn't bother to watch her back. That alone sent a chill of warning down Fenris' spine. Sand whispered as the female returned, tossing something heavy onto the ground at his feet. A metal collar with a sturdy loop and a thick chain on one side. The harpy hunkered down and tipped his chin up, her avian eyes glittering like shards of topaz. "Listen and listen closely, slave. I will take your mistress for medical treatment but her safety depends upon your cooperation. Here, a slave's deeds reflect upon his mistress, particularly that of a mating male." The woman's gaze drifted down his body with brazen intensity. "If you so much as breathe wrong, your mistress dies. And once she wakes –

well, we shall see what the Empress makes of you." Her lips curled into a vicious smile. "You're exotic enough to fetch a high price at market."

Fenris stared down at the collar. A slave. A creature without voice, without choice. Without free will. His heart balked at the thought, but… anything, he'd said to Caelum. Anything to save her. So he reached down and snatched up the collar, noting the way it was designed to fuse together once closed so that only someone with the right tool would be able to open it. He felt Caelum stiffen beneath him but there was little choice – they would die if they fought and they would die if they did nothing. Here, now, was their best chance. Arcana's best chance. Fenris fastened the collar around his neck, fighting the urge to flinch as the locking mechanism snicked shut at the nape of his neck. "I understand."

"Good." The harpy rose and twittered at the guard closest, waving a dismissive hand in his direction. Fenris saw the guard shift and closed his eyes, making no move to stop the butt of the spear as it raced toward his head.

He'd been a fool.

Now it was time to make amends.

~ THE END ~

Thanks for reading!

Can't wait for the next instalment?

Keep up to date with all the latest shenanigans at:

www.sliceofsammy.com

ACKNOWLEDGMENTS

To Cam, who reads everything and loves it, even after all these years. You were my first fan and I will never forget that.

To Ellyse, for volunteering despite my warnings otherwise, and being caught up in all the furore that follows that decision.

To Jenni, who has workshopped my work since we shared classes and who asked me out of the blue to be included, even knowing in advance my penchant for waffle.

To Marshy, Orion and Piper, who have put up with my craziness during the conception, creation and completion of this piece - this is the first of many, so buckle up and get ready for the ride! I love you always.

IF YOU LOVED THIS ONE...

Please leave a review!

Reviews really help authors; it directs our books into the right kind of hands, which in turn allows me to keep writing more books for you to enjoy.

So, if you had a blast reading this story, I'd be ever so grateful if you left a review wherever you can.

Thank you!
♥

ALSO BY SAMANTHA STORMFURY

Prince of Storms. Lady of Shadows.

God of Chaos.

Bound in eternal servitude to the Atlantean royal family, dark fairy Liria Atlannon spends her days bending to the whims of her mistress. When Atlantis' youngest Princess announces her betrothal to the great Pharaoh Taos of Egypt, Liria has no choice but to follow her Princess across the sea to a kingdom - and a life - unlike anything she has known before.

As Commander of the Pharoah's honour guard, it is Prince Raiden Horushood's duty to defend his brother at all costs. He's never met a foe he couldn't conquer - until Set the Anarchist, god of war and chaos, attempts to steal the Pharaoh's fiancee from her own welcome banquet. While Raiden rages helplessly in the thrall of Set's magic, Liria, the softly spoken handmaiden who spends most of her time staring at the floor, not only turns Set away but injures him in the process.

With the threat of an unpredictable god hanging overhead, Raiden begs Liria to join the Pharoah's honour guard. Though Liria aches to become part of something greater, self preservation dictates she stay away from the vital, strong, and irritatingly handsome Prince Raiden. For if the warrior angel gets too close, he'll discover that the biggest threat to Merged Egypt is not Set at all – it is Liria Atlannon, damned by the magic which shackles her soul, steals her free will and shapes her actions… until all that remains is a shadow.

Read on for a sneak preview of Chapter One!

HEARTH AND HOME

Liria Atlannon looked around at the cool marble pillars of Princess Ione's quarters and knew she wouldn't miss it for even a moment. There was something to be said for the elegance of gold-shot marble which glowed in the light of the noonday sun, and perhaps even something to be said for the open, breezy architecture and gauzy drapes in Atlantean aqua - but for her, the paradise island of Atlantis had only ever been a prison.

Moving quietly to the edge of the balcony, Liria set delicate hands on the railing and cast her gaze out over the cheery city which glittered in the sun, shimmering marble and deep gold sandstone broken up by swathes of cloth in all the shades of the ocean. Beyond that, the azure sea lapped lazily at a pristine shore of pale sand that sparkled with hints of silver silica. A pair of Atlantean Dreadnaughts bobbed offshore, one with her steel decks unfurled like a silvered ocean lily, and the other curled in tight upon itself in preparation for an underwater journey.

"Beautiful, and yet I don't see that I will miss it."

Liria lowered her head as the Princess Ione came up beside her, lest the other woman see the way her face set into an involuntary grimace. The motion shifted her focus to her fingers, gripping tight to the balcony rail. Her skin had begun to turn the mottled blue-grey of a storm-tossed sky, her emotions slipping their leash and causing the truth of her nature to creep through. Drawing deep of the salt-laden air, Liria forced her face into smooth lines and exerted just enough power to shift her skin back to the blemish-free cream her mistress preferred.

"You won't miss it?" she asked, her voice carefully modulated to be soft and submissive. "Surely Atlantis is in your bones, your highness."

Princess Ione tossed her head. She was beautiful - exquisite, even, with long black hair that hung in perfect curls midway down her back, softly tanned skin and deep, dark blue eyes - yet there was a glitter in her gaze, an edge to her cultured smile that spoke of bitter hunger.

"No," Ione said, her lip curling. "I am meant for greater things than to be the fifth child of the ruling family of Atlantis. I am meant to be a queen."

"And so you will be," Liria answered, bowing slightly from the waist. "Your marriage to the Pharaoh of Egypt will ensure such."

An arranged marriage sounded like the worst kind of torture to Liria, but Princess Ione had been the driving force behind the entire affair. In fact, Liria's eavesdropping around the palace had her safe in the certainty that the King and Queen of Atlantis had only acquiesced to keep Ione happy; no-one had actually expected Pharaoh Taos to accept.

"Yes. Soon, I will be Queen of Egypt," Ione breathed, spreading her arms wide and tipping her head back to stare at the sky. "Soon, I will witness the technological marvel of Egypt's great airships, and view their crystal-topped pyramids with my own eyes. I shall rule over the country which stands at the forefront of science and magic, sip wine with the most powerful of gods and be bathed in the adoring praise of my subjects – while Atlantis will become but a faded memory, a pale imitation to be laughed at and forgotten." The Princess clasped her hands at the base of her throat, gleaming midnight eyes locking on Liria's face. "Are you ready, my shadow, to follow me on this path to greatness?"

It wasn't like she had any other choice, but Liria knew better than to say such things aloud. Instead, she bowed deeply, locking her gaze on the embroidered hem of Ione's gown. "Of course, your highness."

Princess Ione ran her slender fingers across the shimmering surface of Liria's wings, the sensation akin to hot knives slashing her wide open. Her breath caught in her throat, the urge to protest becoming the very thing that ensured her silence as the magical chains which bound her to her mistress snapped into full effect.

"Such flawless mystery in you, Liria. The subtlety of twilight, of hidden, magical things. You are well suited to accompany a jewel such as I." Another caress of Ione's fingers, her movements flicking away the long layers of trailing gauze that served to shield Liria's wings from view. "I wonder if Pharaoh Taos' wings are as magnificent as yours?"

"He's of the blood of Horus, your highness, and thus carries the wings of the falcon - whereas I am but a lowly fairy. I'm sure my wings are as nothing in comparison to the strong, feathered pinions of the angels."

"Hmmm. I suppose we shall see, soon enough." Ione tapped Liria's spine, silent permission for her to straighten. "I've heard the angels can even carry passengers, should the need arise."

So had Liria, but she didn't say as such, lest the Princess ask where she'd come across the knowledge. Instead, she adjusted the many layers of gauze which hung from her shoulders so that they once more protected her wings from casual view and said, "Perhaps, once you are wed, you can convince the Pharaoh to take you flying."

"Oh, yes." Ione clasped her hands to her full breasts, dark blue eyes shining. She blinked a few moments later, a crease forming between her brows. "And you will follow us, my shadow, will you not?"

Liria inclined her head again, glad of the way her hair swung forward to hide her face. "Such is my duty, your highness."

Want to find out what happens next?

Grab your copy here:

https://sliceofsammy.com

LOVE A FREE BOOK?

LEARN TO LET GO... OR BURN.

Dating Noah Acheson has always been gentle, predictable and above all, safe – but when the softly spoken foxkin breaks the rules of their carefully crafted relationship, Deanna cuts him off, retreating to her private sanctuary deep in the Australian bush.

Stinging from Deanna's rejection, Noah returns from a brief stint fighting fires in New South Wales to face an infinitely more vicious fire front in Victoria. Though his broken heart still very much belongs to Deanna Schellponte, he's determined not to chase her – until the wind changes, turning the fires towards pack land, and Deanna is reported missing.

With fire raging all around, Noah races into the bush to find the wolfkin he loves. To survive, Deanna and Noah must confront not only the fury of Mother Nature… but the ghost whose memory tore them apart.

Get your FREE copy here:

https://sliceofsammy.com/contact

OTHER TALES BY SAMANTHA STORMFURY

Sorcery and Stardust

A sweeping science fiction series following the adventures of Arcana, Fenris, Caelum and Flare as they work to save time and space from the bestial warg and their vicious leader.

The Kin Chronicles

A paranormal romance series featuring the Kin, a race of people who can shift into animals and live alongside humanity in an alternate contemporary reality.

The Merged Worlds

A fantasy and paranormal romance series that starts in a time before our written history, when gods roamed the Earth, technology was crazily advanced and humanity shared their space with angels, vampires, fairies and a host of other magical creatures.

A Perfectly Paranormal Anthologies

A collection of paranormal romance anthologies in conjunction with several other wonderful authors.

To find out more about any of these, visit my website:

www.sliceofsammy.com

WANT TO KEEP IN TOUCH?

I love to hear from, and hang out with, like minded people (yes, that's you!) and expand my tribe. Whilst I'm most active in my newsletter, you can also find me in other places from time to time! If you've already joined my mailing list and are still looking for more, then check out the following:

BLOG - www.sliceofsammy.com/blog

INSTAGRAM - @sliceofsammy

Or send me an email at -

samwrites@sliceofsammy.com

I love hearing from readers and authors alike!

See you there ^_^

Love,
  Sammy
  XOXO

ABOUT THE AUTHOR

Hi, I'm Sam!

I've been writing my whole life, scribbling stories on anything close to hand – from the shopping list to napkins to post-it notes.

I grew up reading fantasy of the likes of Anne McCaffrey, Terry Pratchett, and their peers. I'm also a lifelong vampire fan, along with all things spooky. In my late teens I was introduced to paranormal romance and discovered a whole new layer of storytelling with a bit of a spicy edge! Taking what I learnt from all of the above, I devoted myself to creating full-bodied characters, meaty plots, epic adventure, and a little bit of naughty sauce on the side.

I completed a Diploma of Professional Writing and Editing after high school and spent the next several years in my writing cave, working on a novel that is now in a drawer somewhere, followed by a couple of others who shared the same fate. (What can I say? I'm a recovering perfectionist.)

I came close to debuting my novel career in 2009, then ended up pregnant and took some time off to have kids. I debuted for real in 2019 with *Sorcery and Stardust* and won ARRA's Favourite Debut Romance Author for 2019, which was extremely cool!

I write speculative fiction that is a fusion of multiple sub-genres and therefore doesn't fit particularly well into any of them, but after many years and a lot of angst, I'm okay with that. I love all my characters and their stories for different reasons, but have a soft spot for an excellent villain and a tortured protagonist.

I had an attack of the Real Life in the early 2020s which resulted in a long hiatus, followed by a gradual rebuild into the Samantha Stormfury you know today. I learnt that sometimes, there is nothing you can do but hold on, even if it feels like there's nothing left to hold onto - and in doing so, I had a strength I never realised I was capable of.

I believe in unicorns, dragons, and true love. I'm passionate about great writing, interesting characters, chai tea - and, until the stars burn out of the sky, holding on for happily ever afters.